THE NOVELS OF

Muriel Spark

✧ VOLUME 2 ✧

THE NOVELS OF
Muriel Spark
✦ VOLUME 2 ✦

LOITERING
WITH INTENT
✦
THE GIRLS OF
SLENDER MEANS
✦
THE ABBESS OF CREWE
✦
THE BACHELORS
✦
THE BALLAD OF
PECKHAM RYE

HOUGHTON MIFFLIN COMPANY
BOSTON   NEW YORK

Library of Congress Cataloging-in-Publication Data
Spark, Muriel
[Novels. Selections]
The novels of Muriel Spark.
p.   cm.
Contents: v. 1 The prime of Miss Jean Brodie ; The comforters ;
The only problem ; The driver's seat ; Memento mori —
Loitering with intent ; The girls of slender means ; The Abbess of Crewe ;
The bachelors ; The ballad of Peckham Rye.
ISBN 0-395-72670-0 (v. 1). — ISBN 0-395-72671-9 (v. 2)
I. Title.
PR6037. P29A6   1995
823'.914 — dc20   94-44400
CIP

Printed in the United States of America
QUM 10 9 8 7 6 5 4 3 2 1

CONTENTS

Loitering with Intent

ACKNOWLEDGMENT

The quotations from the *Life* of Benvenuto Cellini are gratefully taken from Miss Anne Macdonell's translation in the Everyman edition.

ONE

One day in the middle of the twentieth century I sat in an old graveyard which had not yet been demolished, in the Kensington area of London, when a young policeman stepped off the path and came over to me. He was shy and smiling, he might have been coming over the grass to ask me for a game of tennis. He only wanted to know what I was doing but plainly he didn't like to ask. I told him I was writing a poem, and offered him a sandwich which he refused as he had just had his dinner himself. He stopped to talk awhile, then he said good-bye, the graves must be very old, and that he wished me good luck and that it was nice to speak to somebody.

This was the last day of a whole chunk of my life but I didn't know that at the time. I sat on the stone slab of some Victorian grave writing my poem as long as the sun lasted. I lived nearby in a bed-sitting-room with a gas fire and a gas ring operated by pre-decimal pennies and shillings in the slot, whichever you preferred or had. My morale was high. I needed a job, but that, which should have been a depressing factor when viewed in cold blood, in fact simply was not. Neither was the swinishness of my landlord, a Mr Alexander, short of stature. I was reluctant to go home lest he should waylay me. I owed him no rent but he kept insisting that I should take a larger and more expensive room in his house, seeing that I had overcrowded the small single room with my books, my papers, my boxes and bags, my food stores and the evidence of constant visitors who stayed to tea or came late.

So far I had stood up to the landlord's claim that I was virtually living a double-room life for single-room pay. At the same time I was fascinated by his swinishness. Tall Mrs Alexander always kept in the background so far as the renting of rooms was concerned, determined not to be confused with a landlady. Her hair was always glossy black, new from the hairdresser, her nails polished red. She stepped in and out of the house with a polite nod like another, but more superior, tenant. I fairly drank her in with my mind while smiling politely back. I had nothing whatsoever against these Alexanders except in the matter of their wanting me to take on a higher-priced room. If he had thrown me out I would still have had nothing much against them, I would mainly have been fascinated. In a sense I felt that the swine Alexander was quite excellent as such, surpassingly handpicked. And although I wanted to avoid him on my return to my lodging I knew very well I had something to gain from a confrontation, should it happen. In fact, I was aware of a *demon* inside me that rejoiced in seeing people as they were, and not only that, but more than ever as they were, and more, and more.

At the time I had a number of marvellous friends, full of good and evil. I was close on penniless but my spirits were all the more high because I had recently escaped from the Autobiographical Association (non-profit-making) where I was thought rather mad, if not evil. I will tell you about the Autobiographical Association.

Ten months before the day when I sat writing my poem on the worn-out graves of the dead in Kensington and had a conversation with the shy policeman, 'Dear Fleur,' came the letter.

'Dear Fleur.' Fleur was the name hazardously bestowed at birth, as always in these cases before they know what you are going to turn out like. Not that I looked too bad, it was only that Fleur wasn't the right name, and yet it was mine as are the names of those melancholy Joys, those timid Victors, the inglorious Glorias and materialistic Angelas one is bound to meet in the course of a long life of change and infiltration; and I once met a Lancelot who, I assure you, had nothing to do with chivalry.

However all that may be, 'Dear Fleur,' went the letter. 'I think I've found a job for you! . . .' The letter went on, very boring. It was a well-wishing friend and I have forgotten what she looked like. Why did I keep these letters? Why? They are all neatly bundled up in thin folders, tied with pink tape, 1949, 1950, 1951 and on and on. I was trained to be a secretary; maybe I felt that letters ought to be filed, and I'm sure I thought they would be interesting one day. In fact, they aren't very interesting in themselves. For example about this time, just before the turn of the half-century, a bookshop wrote to ask for their money or they would 'take further steps'. I owed money to bookshops in those days; some were more lenient than others. I remember at the time thinking the letter about the further steps quite funny and worth keeping. Perhaps I wrote and told them that I was quite terrified of their steps approaching further, nearer, nearer; perhaps I didn't actually write this but only considered doing so. Apparently I paid them in the end for the final receipt is there, £5.8.9. I always desired books; nearly all of my bills were for books. I possessed one very rare book which I traded for part of my bill with another bookshop, for I wasn't a bibliophile of any kind; rare books didn't interest me for their rarity, but for their content. I borrowed frequently from the public library, but often I would go into a bookshop and in my longing to possess, let us say, the Collected Poems of Arthur Clough and a new Collected Chaucer, I would get into conversation with the bookseller and run up a bill.

'Dear Fleur, I think I've found a job for you!'

I wrote off to the address in Northumberland setting forth my merits as a secretary. Within a week I got on a bus to go and be interviewed by my new employer at the Berkeley Hotel. It was six in the evening. I had allowed for the rush hour and arrived early. He was earlier still, and when I went to the desk to ask for him he rose from a nearby chair and came over to me.

He was slight, nearly tall, with white hair, a thin face with high cheekbones which were pink-flushed, although otherwise his face was pale. His right shoulder seemed to protrude further than the left as if fixed in the position for shaking hands, so that his general look was very slightly askew. He had an air which said, I am distinguished. Name, Sir Quentin Oliver.

We sat at a table drinking dry sherry. He said, 'Fleur Talbot – are you half French?'

'No. Fleur was just a name my mother fancied.'

'Ah, interesting ... Well now, yes, let me explain about the undertaking.'

The wages he offered were of 1936 vintage, and this was 1949, modern times. But I pushed up the starting price a little, and took the job for its promise of a totally new experience.

'Fleur Talbot ... ' he had said, sitting there in the Berkeley. 'Any connection with the Talbots of Talbot Grange? The Honourable Martin Talbot, know who I mean?'

I said, 'No.'

'No relation to them. Of course there are the Talbots of Findlay's Refineries. Those sugar people. She's a great friend of mine. Lovely creature. Too good for him if you ask my opinion.'

Sir Quentin Oliver's London flat was in Hallam Street near Portland Place. There I went to my job from nine in the morning till five-thirty in the afternoon, passing the B.B.C. edifice where I always hoped to get a job but never succeeded.

At Hallam Street every morning the door would be opened by Mrs Tims, the housekeeper. The first morning Sir Quentin introduced her to me as 'Beryl, Mrs Tims,' which she in a top-people's accent corrected to Mrs Beryl Tims, and while I stood waiting with my coat on, they had an altercation over this, he maintaining politely that before her divorce she had been Mrs Thomas Tims and now she was, to be precise, Beryl, Mrs Tims, but in no circumstances was Mrs Beryl Tims accepted usage. Mrs Tims then announced she could produce her National Insurance card, her ration book and her identity card to prove that her name was Mrs Beryl Tims. Sir Quentin held that the clerks employed in the ministries which issued these documents were ill-informed. Later, he said, he would show her what he meant under correct forms of address in one of his reference books. After that, he turned to me.

'I hope you're not argumentative,' he said. 'An argumentative woman is like water coming through the roof; it says so in the Holy Scriptures, either Proverbs or Ecclesiastes, I forget which. I hope you don't talk too much.'

'I talk very little,' I said, which was true, although I listened a lot because I had a novel, my first, in larva. I took off my coat and handed it somewhat snootily to the refined Mrs Tims, who took it away roughly and stalked off hammering the parquet floor with her heels. As she went she looked contemptuously at the coat which was a cheap type known then as 'Utility.' Utility was at the time the People's garment, recognizable by the label with its motif of overlapping quarter-moons. Many of the rich, who could afford to spend clothing coupons on non-Utility at Dorville, Jacqmar or Savile Row, still chose to buy Utility, bestowing upon it, I noticed, the inevitable phrase, 'perfectly all right'. I have always been on the listen-in for those sort of phrases.

But perfectly all right was not what Beryl Tims thought of my coat. I followed Sir Quentin into the library. 'Come into my parlour, said the spider to the fly,' said Sir Quentin. I acknowledged his witticism with a smug smile which I felt was part of my job.

In the interview at the Berkeley he had told me the work was to be of a '... literary nature. We are a group. A group, I may add, of some distinction. Your function will be highly interesting, although of course on you will depend the efficiency and typewriting – how I hate that word stenography, so American – and of course the stationery cupboard is dreadfully untidy at the moment and will need seeing to. You will have your work cut out, Miss Talbot.'

I had asked at the end of the interview if I could get some pay at the end of the first week as I couldn't hold out for a whole month. He went aloof, a little hurt. Perhaps he suspected that I wanted to put the job on a week's trial; this was partly true but my need for speedy pay was equally true. He had said, 'Oh well, yes, of course if it's a case of *hardship*,' as one might say a case of sea-sickness. In the meantime I had wondered why he had called the interview at a London hotel instead of at the flat where I was to work.

Now that I was actually in the flat he answered that question himself. 'It isn't everybody, Miss Talbot, whom I invite to enter my home.' I replied agreeably that we all felt like that and I cast my eyes round the room; I couldn't see the books, they were all behind glass. But Sir Quentin was not satisfied with my 'We all feel like that'; it put us on an equal footing. He set about making plain that I had missed the point. 'What I mean,' he said, 'is that here we have formed a very special circle, for a very delicate purpose. The work is top secret. I want you to remember that. I interviewed six young ladies, and I have chosen you, Miss Talbot, I want you to remember that.' By this time he was seated at his very splendid desk, leaning back in his chair, eyes half-closed, with his hands held before him at chest level, the finger-tips of each hand touching the other. I sat at the opposite side of the desk.

He waved towards a large antique cabinet. 'In there,' he said, 'are secrets.'

I wasn't alarmed, for although he was plainly some sort of crank and it struck me, of course, that he might be up to no good, there was nothing in his voice or manner that I felt as an immediate personal menace. But I was on the alert, in fact excited. The novel I was writing, my first, *Warrender Chase*, was really filling my whole life at that time. I was finding it extraordinary how, throughout all the period I had been working on the novel, right from Chapter One, characters and situations, images and phrases that I absolutely needed for the book simply appeared as if from nowhere into my range of perception. I was a magnet for experiences that I needed. Not that I reproduced them photographically and literally. I didn't for a moment think of portraying Sir Quentin as he was. What gave me great happiness was his gift to me of the finger-tips of his hands touching each other, and, nestling among the words, as he waved towards his cabinet, 'In there are secrets,' the pulsating notion of how much he wanted to impress, how greatly he desired to believe in himself. And I might have left the job then and there, and never seen or thought of him again, but carried away with me these two items and more. I felt like the walnut cabinet itself towards which he was waving. In here are secrets, said my mind. At the same time I gave him my attention.

After all these years I've got used to this process of artistic apprehension in the normal course of the day, but it was fairly new to me then. Mrs Tims had also excited me in the same way. An awful woman. But to me, beautifully awful. I must say that in September of 1949 I had no idea at all if I could bring off *Warrender Chase*. But whether I was capable of finishing the whole book or not, the excitement was the same.

Sir Quentin went on to tell me what the job was about. Mrs Tims brought in the post.

Sir Quentin ignored her but he said to me, 'I never deal with my correspondence until after breakfast. It's too upsetting.' (You must know that in those days the mail arrived at eight in the morning and people who didn't go out to work read their letters with their breakfast, and those who did, read them on the bus.) 'Too upsetting.' In the meantime Mrs Tims went to the window and said, 'They're dead.' She was referring to a bowl of roses which had shed their petals on the table. She gathered up the petals and stuck them into the rose bowl, then lifted the rose bowl to carry it away. As she did so she looked at me and caught me watching her. I continued to watch the spot where she had been, as if in glaze-eyed abstraction, and perhaps, thus, I succeeded in fooling her that I hadn't been consciously watching her at all, only looking at the spot where she stood, my thoughts on something else; perhaps I didn't fool her, one never knows about those things. She continued to grumble about the dead roses till she left the room, looking all the more like the wife of a man I knew; Mrs Tims even walked like her.

I turned my attention to Sir Quentin, who waited for his house-keeper's exit with his eyes half-shut, and his hands in an attitude almost of prayer, his elbows on the arm-rests of his chair, his finger-tips touching.

'Human nature,' said Sir Quentin, 'is a quite extraordinary thing, I find it quite extraordinary. You know the old adage, Truth is stranger than Fiction?'

I said yes.

It was a dry sunny day of September 1949. I remember looking towards the window where intermittent sunlight fingered the muslin curtains. My ears have a good memory. If I recall certain encounters of the past at all, or am reminded perhaps by old letters that they happened, back come flooding the aural images first and the visual second. So I remember Sir Quentin's way of speech, his words precisely and his intonation as he said to me, 'Miss Talbot, are you interested in what I am saying?'

'Oh yes. Yes, I agree that truth is stranger than fiction.'

I had thought his eyes were too shut-in on his thoughts to notice my head turning towards the window. I know that I had looked away to register within myself some instinctive thoughts.

'I have a number of friends,' he said, and waited for this to sink in. Dutifully now, I kept my eyes on his words.

'Very important friends, V.I.P.s. We form an association. Do you know anything about the British laws of libel? My dear Miss Talbot, these laws are very narrow and very severe. One may not, for instance, impugn a lady's honour, not that one would wish to were she in fact a lady, and as for stating the actual truth about one's life which naturally involves living people, well, it is quite impossible. Do you know what we have done, we who have lived extraordinary – and I mean extra-ordinary – lives? Do you know what we have done about placing the facts on record for posterity?'

I said no.

'We have formed an Autobiographical Association. We have all started to write our memoirs, the truth, the whole truth and nothing but the truth. And we are lodging them for seventy years in a safe place until all the living people mentioned therein shall be living no longer.'

He pointed to the handsome cabinet faintly lit by the sun filtering through the gathered muslin curtains. I longed to be outside walking in the park and chewing over Sir Quentin's character in my mind before even finding out any more about him.

'Documents of that sort should go into a bank vault,' I said.

'Good,' said Sir Quentin in a bored way. 'You are quite right. That is possibly the ultimate destination of our biographical reminiscences. But that is looking ahead. Now I have to tell you that my friends are largely unaccustomed to literary composition; I, who have a natural bent in that field, have taken on the direction of the endeavour. They are, of course, men and women of great distinction living full, very full, lives. One way and another these days of change and postwar. One can't expect. Well, the thing is I'm helping them to write their memoirs which they haven't time to do. We have friendly meetings, gatherings, get-togethers and so on. When we are better organized we shall meet at my property in Northumberland.'

Those were his words and I enjoyed them. I thought them over as I walked home through the park. They had already become part of my memoirs.

At first I supposed Sir Quentin was making a fortune out of the memoir business. The Association, as he called it, then comprised ten people. He gave me a bulky list of the members' names with supporting biographical information so selective as to tell me, in fact, more about Sir Quentin than the people he described. I remember quite clearly my wonder and my joy at:

Major-General Sir George C. Beverley, Bt., C.B.E., D.S.O., formerly in that 'crack' regiment of the Blues and now a successful, a very successful businessman in the City and on the Continent. General Sir George is a cousin of that fascinating, that infinitely fascinating hostess, Lady Bernice 'Bucks' Gilbert, widow of the former chargé d'affaires in San Salvador, Sir Alfred Gilbert, K.C.M.G., C.B.E. (1919) whose portrait, executed by that famous, that illustrious, portrait painter Sir Ames Baldwin, K.B.E., hangs in the magnificent North Dining Room of Landers Place, Bedford-shire, one of the family properties of Sir Alfred's mother, the late incomparable Comtesse Marie-Louise Torri-Gil, friend of H.M. King Zog of Albania and of Mrs Wilks who as a debutante in St Petersburg was a friend of Sir Q., the present writer, and daughter of a Captain of the Horse at the Court of the late Czar before her marriage to a British Officer, Lieutenant Wilks.

I thought it a kind of poem, and all in a moment I saw Sir Quentin, a good thirty-five years my senior as he was, in the light of a solemn infant intently constructing his wooden toy castle with its moats and turrets; and again, I thought of this piece of art, the presentation of Major-General Sir George C. Beverley and all his etceteras, under the aspect of an infinitesimal particle of crystal, say sulphur, enlarged sixty times and photographed in colour so that it looked like an elaborate butterfly or an exotic sea flower. From this first entry alone on Sir Quentin's list, I thought of numerous artistic analogies to his operations and I realized, all in that moment, how much religious energy he had put into it.

'You should study that list,' Sir Quentin said.

The telephone rang and the door of the study was thrown open, both at the same time. Sir Quentin lifted the receiver and said 'Hallo' while his eyes turned to the door in alarm. In tottered a tall, thin and extremely aged woman with a glittering appearance, largely con-veyed by her many strings of pearls on a black dress and her bright silver hair; her eyes were deeply sunk in their sockets and rather wild. Sir Quentin was meantime agitating into the phone: 'Oh, Clotilde, my dear, what a pleasure – just one moment, Clotilde, I have a disturbance ... ' The old woman advanced, her face cracked with make-up, with a scarlet gash of a smile. 'Who's this girl?' she said, meaning me.

Quentin had placed his hand over the receiver. 'Please,' he said in an anguished hush, fluttering his other hand, 'I am talking on the telephone to the Baronne Clotilde du Loiret.

The old woman shrieked. I suppose she was laughing but it was difficult to tell. 'I know who she is. You think I'm ga-ga, don't you?' She turned to me. 'He thinks I'm ga-ga,' she said. I noticed her fingernails, overgrown, so that they curled over the tips like talons; they were painted dark red. 'I'm not ga-ga,' she said.

'Mummy!' said old Sir Quentin.

'What a snob he is,' screamed the mother.

Beryl Tims turned up just then and grimly promoted the old lady's withdrawal; Beryl glared at me as she left. Sir Quentin resumed his conversation on the phone with many apologies.

His snobbery was immense. But there was a sense in which he was far too democratic for the likes of me. He sincerely believed that talent, although not equally distributed by nature, could be later conferred by a title or acquired by inherited rank. As for the memoirs they could be written, invented, by any number of ghost writers. I suspect he really believed that the Wedgwood cup from which he daintily sipped his tea derived its value from the fact that the social system had recognized the Wedgwood family, not from the china that they had exerted themselves to make.

By the end of the first week I had been let into the secrets of the locked cabinet in Sir Quentin's study. It held ten unfinished manuscripts, the products of the members of the Autobiographical Association.

'These works when completed,' said Sir Quentin, 'will be both valuable to the historian of the future and will set the Thames on fire. You should easily be able to rectify any lack or lapse in form, syntax, style, characterization, invention, local colour, description, dialogue, construction and other trivialities. You are to typewrite these documents under conditions of extreme secrecy, and if you succeed in giving satisfaction you may later sit in at some of our sessions and take notes.'

His aged Mummy came and went from his study whenever she could slip away from Beryl Tims. I looked forward to her interruptions as she came waving her red talons and croaking that Sir Quentin was a snob.

At first I suspected strongly that Sir Quentin himself was a social fake. But as it turned out he was all he claimed to be by way of having been to Eton and Trinity College, Cambridge; he was a member of three clubs of which I only recall White's and the Bath, he was moreover a baronet and his refreshing Mummy was the daughter of an earl. I was right but only in part, when I accounted to myself for his snobbery, that he had decided to make a profitable profession out of these facts themselves. And indeed it crossed my mind during that first week how easily he could turn his locked-up secrets to blackmail. It was much later that I found that this was precisely what he was doing; only it wasn't money he was interested in.

Going home at six o'clock in the golden dusk of that lovely autumn, I would walk to Oxford Street, take a bus to Speakers' Corner at Hyde Park, then cross the park to Queen's Gate. I was fascinated by the strangeness of the job. I made no notes at all, but most nights I would work on my novel and the ideas of the day would reassemble themselves to form those two female characters which I created in *Warrender Chase*, Charlotte and Prudence. Not that Charlotte was entirely based on Beryl Tims, not by a long way. Nor was my ancient Prudence anything like a replica of Sir Quentin's Mummy. The process by which I created my characters was instinctive, the sum of my whole experience of others and of my own potential self; and so it always has been. Sometimes I don't actually meet a character I have created in a novel until some time after the novel has been written and published. And as for my character Warrender Chase himself, I already had him outlined and fixed, long before I saw Sir Quentin.

Now that I come to write this section of my autobiography I remember vividly, in those days when I was writing *Warrender Chase*, without any great hope of ever getting it published, but with only the excited compulsion to write it, how I walked home across the park one evening, thinking hard about my novel and Beryl Tims as a type, and I stopped in the middle of the pathway. People passed me, both ways, going home from their daily work, like myself. Whatever I had been specifically thinking about the typology of Mrs Tims went completely out of my mind. People passed me as I stood. Young men with dark suits and girls wearing hats and tailored-looking coats. The thought came to me in a most articulate way: 'How wonderful it feels to be an artist and a woman in the twentieth century.' That I was a woman and living in the twentieth century were plain facts. That I was an artist was a conviction so strong that I never thought of doubting it then or since; and so, as I stood on the pathway in Hyde Park in that September of 1949, there were as good as three facts converging quite miraculously upon myself and I went on my way rejoicing.

I often thought of Beryl Tims, a type of woman whom I had come to identify in my mind as the English Rose. Not that they resembled English roses, far from it; but they were English roses, I felt, in their own minds. The type sickened me and I was fascinated, such being the capacity of my imagination and my need to know the utmost. Her simpering when alone with me, her acquisitive greed, already fed my poetic vigilance to the extent that I simpered somewhat myself to egg her on and I think I even exercised my own greed for her reactions by provoking them. She had admired a brooch I wore; it was my best, a painted miniature on ivory, oval, set in a copper alloy. It was an eighteenth-century brooch. The painting was the head of a young girl with her hair rustically free. Beryl Tims admired it where it sat on my lapel, for I was wearing a matching coat and skirt which was right in those days. I hated Beryl Tims as I sat having my morning coffee with her in the kitchen and she simpered about my lovely brooch. I hated her so much I took it off and gave it to her really to absolve my own hatred. But the glint in her eyes, the gasp of her big thick-lipped mouth, rewarded me. 'Do you mean it?' she cried.

'Yes, of course.'

'Don't you like it?'

'Yes, I do.'

'Then why are you giving it away?' she said with the nasty suspiciousness of one who perhaps had always been treated badly. She pinned the brooch on her dress. I thought that perhaps Mr Tims had given her a rough time. I said, 'You can have it, have it with pleasure,' and meant it. I took my coffee cup to the sink and rinsed it under the tap. Beryl Tims followed me with hers. 'I get lipstick on the rim of my cup,' she said. 'Men don't like to see lipstick on the rim of your cup and your glass, isn't that so? And yet they like you to wear lipstick. I always get admired for the colour of my lipstick. It's called English Rose.'

She really was very like my lover's awful wife. Next thing she said, 'Men like to see a bit of jewellery on a girl.'

It was always a question of what men liked when we were alone together. The second week of my job she asked me if I was going to get married.

'No, I write poetry. I want to write. Marriage would interfere.' I said this in a natural way and without previous calculation, but it probably sounded lofty for she looked at me in a shocked sort of way and said, 'But you could get married and have children, surely, and write poetry after the children had gone to bed.' I smiled at this. I was not a pretty girl but I knew that I had a smile that transformed my face and, one way and another, I had made Beryl Tims furious.

That shocked look of hers reminded me very strongly of the look on the face of my lover's wife, Dottie, on another occasion. I must say that Dottie was a better educated woman than Beryl Tims, but the look was the same. She had confronted me with my affair with her husband, which I thought tiresome of her. I replied, 'Yes, Dottie, I love him. I love him off and on, when he doesn't interfere with my poetry and so forth. In fact I've started a novel which requires a lot of poetic concentration because, you see, I conceive everything poetically. So perhaps it will be more off than on with Leslie.'

Dottie was relieved that she wasn't in danger of losing her man, at the same time as she was horrified by what she called my unnatural attitude, which in fact was quite natural to me.

'Your head rules your heart,' she said in her horror. I told her this was a stupid way of putting things. She knew this was true but in moments of crisis she fell back on banalities. She was a moralist and accused me then of spiritual pride. 'Pride goes before a fall,' said Dottie. In fact if I had pride it was vocational in nature; I couldn't help it, and I've never found it necessarily precedes falls. Dottie was a large woman with a sweet young face, plump breasts and hips, thick ankles. She was a Catholic, greatly addicted to the cult of the Virgin Mary about whose favours she fooled herself quite a bit, constantly betraying her quite good mind by simpering about Our Lady.

However, having said her say, Dottie left it at that. I saw a bottle of scent in her bathroom called 'English Rose,' and this both repelled me and gave me happy comfort as confirming a character forming in my own mind. I learned a lot in my life from Dottie, by her teaching me some precepts which I could usefully reject. She learned nothing of use from me.

But Beryl Tims was the better English Rose and the more frightful. And just then, I saw her more frequently than I did Dottie. But I didn't see Beryl Tims fully in action until some weeks later, at an informal gathering of the Autobiographical Association whose members' memoirs I had been typing and putting into recognizable English sentences. Up to then I had seen how Beryl treated Sir Quentin, always with a provocative tone which failed to provoke in the way that she wished; Beryl could not see why, but then she was stupid.

'Men like you to stand up to them,' she said to me, 'but Sir Quentin sometimes takes me up wrongly. And I've got his mother to watch over, haven't I?' She positively battled with Sir Quentin; obviously she was trying to arouse him sexually, to no avail. Only a high rank or a string of titles could bring an orgiastic quiver to his face and body. But he kept Beryl Tims in a state of hope. Also, I had watchfully noted Beryl with the ancient Lady Edwina, Sir Quentin's Mummy. Beryl was her prison warder and companion.

TWO

The memoirs written by the members of the Autobiographical Association, although none had got beyond the first chapter, already had a number of factors in common. One of them was nostalgia, another was paranoia, a third was a transparent craving on the part of the authors to appear likeable. I think they probably lived out their lives on the principle that what they were, and did, and wanted, should above all look pretty. Typing out and making sense out of these compositions was an agony to my spirit until I hit on the method of making them expertly worse; and everyone concerned was delighted with the result.

A meeting of the ten members of the Association was called for three in the afternoon of Tuesday, October 4th, five weeks after I had started the job. So far I hadn't met any of them, for their last monthly meeting had been held on a Saturday.

That morning Beryl Tims made a scene when Sir Quentin said, 'Mrs Tims, I want you to keep Mummy under control this afternoon.'

'Under control,' said Beryl. 'You might well say under control. How can I keep her ladyship under control and serve tea at the same time? How can I check her fluxive precipitations?' This last phrase I had taught Beryl myself to while away a dull moment when she had been complaining of the old lady's having wet the floor. I had only half expected my version to catch on.

'She should be in a home,' Beryl said to Sir Quentin, 'She needs a private nurse,' and so she wailed on. Sir Quentin looked troubled but impressed. 'Fluxive precipitations,' he said, with his eyes abstractly on the side wall, as if he were tasting a wine new to his experience, but which he was prepared to go more than half way towards approving.

Now, by this time I had become rather fond of Lady Edwina, I think largely because she had taken an extraordinary liking to me.

But also I enjoyed her dramatic entrances and her amazing statements. I could see she was more in charge of her senses than she let appear to her son or to Beryl, for sometimes when I had been alone with her in the flat she had rambled on in a quite natural tone of voice. And for some reason on these occasions alone with me she would sometimes totter off to the lavatory in time. So that I presumed her incontinence and wild behaviour with Sir Quentin and Beryl was due to her either fearing or loathing both of them, and that in any case they got on her nerves.

'I can't take responsibility for your mother this afternoon, not me,' Beryl stated through her English Rose lips, that morning before the meeting.

'Oh, dear,' said Sir Quentin. 'Oh, dear.'

In swayed Lady Edwina herself to add to the confusion. 'Think I'm ga-ga, don't you? Fleur, my dear, do you think I'm ga-ga?'

'Of course not,' I said.

'They want to hush me up but I'm damned if they will hush me up,' she said.

'Mummy!' said Sir Quentin.

'They want to give me sleeping pills to keep me quiet this afternoon. That's funny. Because I'm not going to take any sleeping pills. This is my flat, isn't it? I can do what I like in my own flat, can't I? I can receive or not receive according to my likes, is that not so?'

I assumed that the old woman was rich. She had rattled on to me one day how her son wanted her to do something to avoid death duties, hand over her property to him, but she hadn't much property and anyway she was damned if she was going to be Queen Lear. And I hadn't responded much to this line of talk, preferring to switch her over to a quite lucid and interesting speculation as to the possible nature and characteristics of the defunct Queen Lear herself. There was really nothing wrong with Lady Edwina except that her son and Beryl Tims got her down. As to her bizarre appearance, I liked it. I liked to see her shaking, withered hand with its talons pointing accusingly, I liked the four greenish teeth through which she hissed and cackled. She cheered up my job with her wild eyes and her pre-war tea-gowns of black lace or draped, patterned silk always hung with glittering beads. Now, as she stood confronting Mrs Tims and Sir Quentin with her rights I wondered about the history of it all.

This must have been going on for years. Beryl Tims was looking in a frigid sort of way at the carpet beneath Lady Edwina's feet, no doubt waiting for another fluxive precipitation. Quentin sat with his head thrown back, his eyes shut and his hands touching at the finger-tips as in precious prayer.

I said, 'Lady Edwina, if you'd like to take a rest this afternoon then afterwards you could come home to supper with me.'

She accepted the bribe with alacrity. They all accepted the bribe, with a gabble and clack: Take her in a taxi, I'll be delighted to pay, we can book a taxi for six, no it's not necessary to book, I'm delighted to accept, my dear Miss Talbot, what an excellent, what a very original idea. The taxi will . . . We can come and fetch you home, Mummy, in a taxi. My dear Miss Talbot, how grateful we are. Now, Mummy, after lunch you will go and rest in your room.

Lady Edwina wavered out of the study to call up her hairdresser on the telephone, for she had a young apprentice girl who always came at her bidding to do her hair. I remember how Sir Quentin and Beryl Tims went on about being so very grateful; it didn't occur to them that I might actually want to spend an evening with my new and ravaged friend, an embarrassment to them but not to me. I thought of what there was for supper: tinned herring roes on toast with instant coffee and milk, a perfect supper for Lady Edwina at her age and for me at mine. The tins of roes and the coffee were part of a small hoard I kept of precious rarities. Food was tightly rationed in those days.

By half-past two she had gone to bed for her rest, having first looked in to tell me she had decided to wear her dove grey with the beaded top if only to spite Mrs Tims, who had advised her to put on an old skirt and jumper that would go better with my bed-sitter. I told her she was quite right, and to wrap up warm.

'I have my chinchilla,' she said. 'Tims has got her eyes on my chinchilla but I've left it to the Cochin Mission to be sold for the poor. That will give Tims something to think about when I die. If she survives me. Ha! But you never know.'

Only six out of the ten members called to the meeting could come.

It was a busy afternoon. I sat at my typewriter in a corner of the study while in straggled the six.

I had probably expected too much of them. For years I had been working up to my novel *Warrender Chase* and had become accustomed to first fixing a fictional presence in my mind's eye, then adding a history to it. In the case of Sir Quentin's guests the histories had been presented before the physical characters had appeared. As they trooped in, I could immediately sense an abject depression about them. Not only had I read Sir Quentin's fabulous lists of Who was Who among them, but I had also read the first chapters of their pathetic memoirs, and through typing them out and emphatically touching them up I think I had begun to consider them inventions of my own, based on the original inventions of Sir Quentin. Now these people whose qualities he had built up to be distinguished, even to the last rarity, came into the study that calm and sunny October afternoon with evident trepidation.

Sir Quentin dashed and flitted around the room arranging them in chairs and clucking, and occasionally introducing me to them. 'Sir Eric – my new and I might say very reliable secretary Miss Talbot, no relation it appears to the distinguished branch of that family to which your dear wife belongs.'

Sir Eric was a small, timid man. He shook hands all round in a furtive way. I supposed rightly that he was the Sir Eric Findlay, K.B.E., a sugar-refining merchant whose memoirs, like the others, had not yet got farther than Chapter One: Nursery Days. The main character was Nanny. I had livened it up by putting Nanny and the butler on the nursery rocking-horse together during the parents' absence, while little Eric was locked in the pantry to clean the silver.

Sir Quentin's method at this early stage was to send round advance copies of the complete set of typed and improved chapters to each of the ten members so that each of the six members present, and the four absent, had already seen their own and others' typescripts. Sir Quentin had at first considered my additions to be rather extravagant, don't you think, my dear Miss Talbot, a bit too-*too*? After a good night's sleep he had evidently seen some merit in my arrangement, having worked out some of the possibilities to his own advantage for the future; he had said next morning, 'Well, Miss Talbot, let's try your versions out on them. After all, we are living in modern times.' I had gathered, even then, that he had plans for inducing me to write more compromising stuff into these memoirs, but I had no intention of writing anything beyond what cheered up the boring parts of the job for the time being and what could feed my imagination for my novel *Warrender Chase*. So that his purposes were quite different from mine, yet at the same time they coincided so far as he had his futile plans as to how he could use me, and I was working at top pace for him: photocopy machines were not current in those days.

At the meeting I gave close attention to the six members without ever actually studying them with my eyes. I always preferred what I saw out of the corners of my eyes, so to speak. Besides little Sir Eric Findlay, the people present were Lady Bernice Gilbert, nicknamed Bucks, the Baronne Clotilde du Loiret, a Mrs Wilks, a Miss Maisie Young, and an unfrocked priest called Father Egbert Delaney whose memoirs obsessively made the point that he had lost his frock through a loss of faith, not morals.

Now Lady Bernice Gilbert swam in and at first dominated the party. 'Bucks!' said Sir Quentin, embracing her. 'Quentin,' she declared hoarsely. She was about forty, much dressed up in new clothes which people who could afford it were buying a lot of, since clothes had come off the ration only a few months ago. Bucks was got up in an outfit called the New Look, a pill-box hat with an eye-veil, a leg-of-mutton-sleeved coat and long swinging skirt, all in black. She took a chair close to me, her physical presence very scented. She was the last person I would have attached to her first chapter. Her story, unlike some of the others, was by no means illiterate in so far as she knew how to string sentences together. The story opened with herself, alone in a church, at the age of twenty.

However, I was called, at that moment, to shake hands with Miss Maisie Young, a tall, attractive girl of about thirty who walked with a stick, one of her legs being encased in a contraption which looked as if it was part of her life, and not a passing affair of an accident. I took considerably to Maisie Young; indeed I wondered what she was doing in this already babbling chorus; and still more I was amazed that she belonged to the opening of the memoirs attached to her name, this being an unintelligible treatise on the Cosmos and how Being is Becoming.

'Maisie, my dear Maisie, can I put you here? Are you comfortable? My dear Clotilde! My very dear Father Egbert, are you all comfortable? Let me take your wrap, Clotilde. Mrs Tims – where is Mrs Tims? – Miss Talbot, perhaps you would be so kind, so very kind as to take la Baronne Clotilde's ... '

The Baronne Clotilde, whose ermine cape I took to the door and passed over to the bubbling Mrs Tims outside, had set her memoirs in a charming French château near Dijon where, however, everything conspired to do down the eighteen-year-old Baronne. While I had the time to think at all, I was momentarily puzzled by the fact that in the autobiography Clotilde had been eighteen in 1936 whereas now in 1949 she was well into her fifties. But on to Father Egbert, who wore a Prince of Wales check jacket and grey flannel trousers; his face resembled a snowman's with small black pebbles for eyes, nose and mouth; his autobiography had begun, 'It is with some trepidation that I take up my pen.' Now he was shaking hands with Mrs Wilks, a stout, merry-faced lady in her mid-fifties, clad in pale purple with numerous veil-like scarves, and painted up considerably. Since she had been brought up at the court of the Czar of Russia her memoirs should have been interesting, but so far she had written only a very dull account about the extreme nastiness of her three sisters and the discomforts of the royal palace, where all four girls had to share a bedroom.

All of these people's writings, with the exception of Bernice Gilbert's, were more or less illiterate. I now waited, as they first chattered and exclaimed, to hear what they thought of my improvements.

Mrs Tims came into the study on some busy mission and told me in passing that Lady Edwina was sleeping peacefully.

It was to me a glorious meeting. The first twenty minutes were taken up with introductions and exclamations of all sorts; Father Egbert and Sir Eric, who apparently knew the four missing members, spent some time discussing them. Then Sir Quentin said, 'Ladies and Gentlemen, may I have your attention please,' and everybody stopped talking except Maisie Young who decided to finish what she was saying to me about the universe. She sat with her crippled leg in its irons stuck out in front of her, which did indeed give her a sort of right to hold forth longer than anybody else. Her handbag had a soft strap handle; I noticed that she held this handle threaded through her fingers like a horse-rein; I wasn't surprised to learn, later on, that Maisie's paralysed leg was the result of a riding accident.

The rest of the room was hushed and Maisie's voice went on, qualmless and strong, to assert, 'There are some universal phenomena

about which it is not for us mortals to enquire.' I took very little notice
of this silly proposition as such, although the actual words sound on in
my mind. She had been talking quite a lot of nonsense, largely to the
effect that autobiographies ought to start with the ultimates of the
Great Beyond and not fritter away their time on the actual particulars
of life. I was thoroughly against her ideas; however, I had taken a
liking to Maisie herself, and I particularly liked the way in which she
went on, in the room which had been called to silence, insisting that
there were things in life not to be enquired into, at the same time as
she had opened her own autobiography with precisely these enquir-
ies. Contradictions in human character are one of its most consistent
notes and so I felt Maisie had a substantial character. Since the story
of my own life is just as much constituted of the secrets of my craft as it
is of other events, I might as well remark here that to make a character
ring true it needs must be in some way contradictory, somewhere a
paradox. And I'd already seen that where the self-portraits of Sir
Quentin's ten testifiers were going all wrong, where they sounded
stiff and false, occurred at points where they strained themselves into
a constancy and steadiness that they evidently wished to possess but
didn't. And I had thrown in my own bits of invented patchwork to
cheer things up rather than make each character coherent in itself.

Sir Quentin, who was always polite to his customers, sat smiling
while Maisie finished her emphatic say: 'There are some universal
phenomena about which it is not for us mortals to enquire.'

Beryl Tims then charged in on some practical but unnecessary
mission. It seemed that as she was being overlooked as a woman she
was determined to behave as a man. Naturally she succeeded in
drawing everyone's attention to herself, with her clatter and thumping, I forget what about.

When she had gone Sir Quentin made to resume his introductory
speech but he had to lay it aside. Sir Eric Findlay spoke. He had
obviously summoned up courage to do so.

'I say, Quentin,' he said, 'my memoirs have been tampered with.'

'Oh dear,' said Sir Quentin. 'I hope they're none the worse for it. I
can arrange to delete any offensive item.'

'I didn't say offensive,' said Sir Eric, looking nervously around the
room. 'Indeed, you have made some very interesting changes.
Indeed, I wondered how you guessed that the butler locked me in the

pantry to clean the silver, which he did indeed. Indeed he did. But Nanny on the rocking-horse, well, Nanny was a very religious woman. On my rocking-horse with our butler, indeed, you know. It isn't the sort of thing Nanny would have done.'

'Are you sure?' said Sir Quentin, pointing a coy finger at him. 'How can you be sure if you were locked in the pantry at the time? In your revised memoir you found out about their prank from a footman. But if in reality ... '

'My rocking-horse was not at all a sizeable one,' said Sir Eric Findlay, K.B.E., 'and Nanny, though not plump, would hardly fit on it with the butler who was, though thin, quite strong.'

'If I might voice an opinion,' said Mrs Wilks, 'I thought Sir Eric's piece very readable. It would be a pity to sacrifice the evil nanny and the dastardly butler having their rock on the small Sir Eric's horse, and I like particularly the stark realism of the smell of brilliantine on the footman's hair as he bends to tell the small Sir Eric-that-was of his discovery. It explains so much the Sir Eric-that-is. Psychology is a wonderful thing. It is in fact all.'

'My nanny was not actually evil,' murmured Sir Eric. 'In fact – '

'Oh, she was utterly evil,' Mrs Wilks said.

'I quite agree,' said Sir Quentin. 'She was plainly a sinister person.'

Lady Bernice 'Bucks' Gilbert said in her bronchial voice, 'I suggest you leave your memoir as Quentin has prepared it, Eric. One has to be objective about such things. I think it vastly superior to the opening chapter of my memoirs.'

'I will sleep on it,' said Eric mildly.

'And your memoir, Bucks?' Sir Quentin said anxiously. 'Don't you care for it to date?'

'I do and I don't, Quentin. There's something missing.'

'That can be remedied, my dear Bucks. What is missing?'

'A *je ne sais quoi*, Quentin.'

'But,' said the Baronne Clotilde du Loiret, 'you know, Bucks, I thought your piece was very much you. My dear, the atmosphere as the curtain rises as it were. As the curtain rises on you in the empty church. In the empty church with the fragrance of incense and you praying to the Madonna in your hour of need. I was carried away, Bucks. I mean it. Then comes Father Delaney and lays his hands on your shoulder – '

'I wasn't there. It wasn't I.' This was Father Egbert Delaney speaking up. 'There is a mistake here that needs rectifying.' He looked at Sir Quentin and then at me with his round pebbly eyes and his pudgy hands clasped together. He looked from me back to Sir Quentin. 'I must say in all verity that I am not the Father Delaney described in Lady Bernice's opening scene. Indeed I was a seminarian at the Beda in Rome at the time she refers to.'

'My dear Father,' said Sir Quentin, 'we need not be too literal. There is such a thing as the economy of art. However, if you object to being named – '

'It was with some trepidation that I took up my pen,' Father Delaney declared, and then he looked with horror at the women, including myself, and with terror at the men.

'I didn't actually name the priest,' said Bucks. 'I never said that all this exchange took place in the church, I only – '

'Oh but it has an effect of great *tendresse*,' said Mrs Wilks. 'My memoir is nothing like as touching, would that it were. My memoir – '

But Lady Edwina just then came tottering into the room. 'Mummy!' said Sir Quentin.

I jumped up and pulled forward a chair for her. Everyone was jumping up to do something for her. Sir Quentin fluttered his hands, begged her to go and rest and demanded, 'Where is Mrs Tims?' He obviously expected his mother to make a scene, and so did I. However, Lady Edwina didn't make it. She took over the meeting as if it were a drawing-room tea party, holding up the proceedings with the blackmail of her very great age and of her newly revealed charm. I was greatly impressed by the performance. She knew some of them by name, enquired of their families so solicitously that it hardly mattered that most of them were long since dead, and when Mrs Tims entered with the tea and soda buns on a tray, exclaimed, 'Ah, Tims! What delightful things have you brought us?' Beryl Tims was amazed to see her sitting there, wide awake, with her powdered face and her black satin tea dress freshly spoiled at the neck and shoulders with a slight face-powder overflow. Mrs Tims was furious but she put on her English Rose simper and placed the tray with solicitude on the table beside old Edwina, who was at that moment enquiring of the unfrocked Father, 'Are you the Rector of Wandsworth in civilian clothing?'

'Lady Edwina, your rest-hour,' wheedled Mrs Tims. 'Come along, now. Come with me.'

'Dear no, oh dear no,' said Father Egbert, sitting up and putting to rights his Prince of Wales jacket. 'I don't belong to a religious hierarchy of any persuasion!'

'Funny, I smell a clergyman off you,' said Edwina.

'Mummy!' said Sir Quentin.

'Come now,' said Mrs Tims, 'this is a serious meeting, a business meeting that Sir Quentin – '

'How do you take your tea?' said Lady Edwina to Maisie Young. 'Weak? Strong?'

'Middling please,' said Miss Young, and looked at me sideways from under her soft felt hat as if to gain courage.

'Mummy!' said Quentin.

'Whatever have you done to your leg?' said Lady Edwina to Maisie Young.

'An accident,' replied Miss Young, softly.

'Lady Edwina! What a thing to ask . . . ' said Mrs Tims.

'Take your hand off my arm, Tims,' said Edwina.

After she had poured tea, and asked the Baronne Clotilde how she had managed to preserve her ermine cape without the smell of camphor, and I had helped Sir Quentin to pass the teacups, Edwina said, 'Well, I must take my nap.' She gave Beryl Tims' hand a shove-away and allowed Sir Eric to help her to her feet. When she had gone, followed by Mrs Tims, everyone exclaimed, How charming, How wonderful for her age, What a grand old lady. They were going on like this in between bites of their soda buns and accompanied by a little orchestra of teaspoons on china, when Lady Edwina opened the door again and put her head round it. 'I enjoyed the service very much, I always hate hymn-singing,' she said, and retreated.

Beryl Tims minced in and collected the tea things, muttering to me as she passed, 'She's gone back to bed. Calling me Tims like that, what a cheek.'

I sat at my typist's desk in the corner and made notes while they talked about their memoirs till six o'clock, half an hour past my time to go home.

'When I come to my war experiences,' said Sir Eric, 'that will be the time, the climax.'

'It was during the war that I lost my faith,' declared Father Egbert. 'For me, too, it was a moment of climax. I wrestled with my God, the whole of one entire night.'

Mrs Wilks remarked that it was not every woman who had witnessed the gross indelicacies of the Russian revolution and survived, as she had. 'It gives one a quite different sense of humour,' she explained, without explaining anything.

I had been taking notes, there at my corner table. I recall that the Baronne Clotilde turned to me before she left and said, 'Have you got everything that is germane?'

Maisie Young, leaning on her stick and with a hand still twined round her bag-strap as if it were a horse-rein, said to me, 'Where can I find the book Father Egbert Delaney has been telling me about? It's an autobiography.'

She had been conversing privately with the priest, apart from the hubbub. I turned to Father Delaney, my pencil poised on my notebook, for enlightenment. 'The *Apologia pro Vita Sua*,' he said, 'by John Henry Newman.'

'Where can I get it?' said Miss Young.

I promised to get her a copy from the public library.

'If one is writing an autobiography one should model oneself on the best, shouldn't one?' she said.

I assured her that the *Apologia* was among the best.

Father Egbert murmured to himself, but for us two to hear, 'Alas.'

It was a quarter past six before they had left. I went to fetch Lady Edwina to take her home to have supper with me.

'She's fast asleep,' Beryl Tims said. 'And in any case she broke her promise to us, why should you be bothered with her?' Sir Quentin stood listening. Beryl Tims appealed to him. 'Why should we pay for a taxi and all the bother? She interrupted the meeting, after all.'

'Oh, but everybody was delighted,' I said.

Sir Quentin said, 'But speaking personally I had a *mauvais quart d'heure*; one never knows with my poor mother what she may say or do. I decline responsibility. A *mauvais quart d'heure* – '

'Let her sleep on,' said Beryl Tims.

As I left Sir Quentin said to me, 'We have a gentleman's agreement, you and I, that none of the Association's proceedings will ever be discussed or revealed, don't we? They are highly confidential.'

Not being a gentleman by any stretch of the sense, I cheerfully
agreed; I have always been impressed by Jesuitical casuistry. But
at the time I was thinking only of the meeting itself; it filled me with
joy.

It was after seven when I got home. My landlord, Mr Alexander,
lumbered downstairs to meet me as I let myself into the hall. 'An
elderly party's waiting for you. I let her into your room as she needed
to sit down. I let her use the bathroom as she needed to go. She wet the
bathroom floor.'

There, in my room, I found Lady Edwina, wrapped in her long
chinchilla cape; she sat in my wicker armchair between the orange
box which contained my food supply and a bookcase. She was
beaming with pride. 'I got away,' she said. 'I foiled them completely.
There wasn't a taxi anywhere but I got a lift from an American. Your
books – what a lot there are. Have you read them all?'

I wanted to telephone to Sir Quentin to tell him where his mother
was. There was a phone in my room connected to a switchboard in the
basement. I got no reply, which was not unusual, and I rattled to gain
attention. The red-faced house-boy, underpaid and bad-tempered,
who lived with his wife and children down in those regions, burst into
the room shouting at me to stop rattling the phone. Apparently the
switchboard was in process of repair and a man was working overtime
on it. 'The board's asunder,' bellowed the boy. I liked the phrase and
picked it out for myself from the wreckage of the moment, as was my
wont.

'Lady Edwina,' I said, 'will they know where you are? I can't get
through on the phone.'

'They will never know I'm out,' she said. 'As far as they're
concerned I've gone to bed with a sleeping pill, but I dropped the pill
down the lavatory pan. Call me Edwina, which I don't permit, mind
you, of Beryl Tims.'

I got out cups and saucers and plates and set about making an
evening of it. I propped the old lady's feet on three volumes of the
complete Oxford English Dictionary. She looked regal, she looked
comfortable; she had no difficulty with her bladder and only asked to
be taken to the lavatory once; she cackled with delight over her

herring roes comparing them to caviar 'which is the same thing only a different species of fish'.

'Your studio is so like Paris,' she said. 'Artists I have known . . . ' she mused. 'Artists and writers, they have become successful, of course. And you, too . . . '

Now I hastened to assure her that this wasn't likely. It rather frightened me to think of myself in a successful light, it detracted in my mind from the quality of my already voluminous writings from amongst which eight poems only had been published in little reviews.

I looked out an unpublished poem by which I set great store even though it had been rejected eight times, returning to roost in my own stamped and addressed envelope among my punctual morning letters, over a period of a year. It was perhaps because of its outcast fate that I felt an attachment to it. The old lady's hands clutched her chinchilla with her long red fingernails dug into the silver-grey pelt. The poem was entitled *Metamorphosis*.

> This is the pain that sea anemones bear
> in the fear of aberration but wilfully
> aspiring to respire in another,
> more difficult way, and turning
> flower into animal interminably.

As I was reading this first verse my boy-friend Leslie let himself in the door with the spare key I had given him. He was tall and stoopy with a lock of blond hair falling over one eye and a fresh young face. I was proud of him.

'How are you?' said Edwina when I introduced him. She had told me that since she was forgetful of names and faces she always greeted people with 'How are you?' in case she had met them before.

'I'm fine, thanks,' said Leslie without returning the question. Very often he irritated me in the extreme by small wants of courtesy. He was very much absorbed with numerous private anxieties which he was too self-centred to overcome now, when I was presenting him with this splendid apparition, Edwina, an ancient, wrinkled, painted spirit wrapped in luxurious furs.

Edwina enquired kindly, as he took off his coat and sat on the divan bed, 'What is your profession, Sir?'

'I'm a critic,' said Leslie.

I was suddenly disenchanted with Leslie. It was a feeling that came over me ever more frequently, leading to quarrels in the end. Leslie just sat there and let himself be interviewed, unable to forget himself and his own concerns, with his young face and good health contrasting with Edwina's dotty shrewdness, her scarlet nails, her bright avid eyes. I saw in the pocket of Leslie's coat the top of a bottle which he had evidently brought along for the two of us. I pulled it out; smuggled Algerian wine.

'You're a music critic?' Edwina asked Leslie.

'No, a literary critic.' He turned to me, 'As a matter of fact, that poem you were reading – what was that line, "aspiring and respiring" . . . ?'

I put down the bottle and took up my poem.

'They think I've got a screw loose,' said Edwina. 'But I haven't got a screw loose. Ha!'

'A very bad line,' said Leslie.

I read it out: 'Aspiring to respire in another . . . ' It seemed to me Leslie was right but I said, 'What's wrong with it?'

'Is that a bottle of something?' Edwina said.

Leslie said, 'Too feeble. Bad-sounding.'

I said, 'Edwina, it's Algerian wine. I would love you to have some but I think it would be bad for you.'

'Let me open it,' said Leslie, finding the corkscrew in a proprietary way. He was ambivalent about my writings, in that he often liked what I wrote but disliked my thoughts of being a published writer. This caused me to reject most of his criticism. As for his being a literary critic, that was not an untrue claim for he reviewed books for a periodical called *Time and Tide* and for other little reviews, although for his daily job he was a lawyer's clerk.

Leslie uncorked the bottle while Edwina assured him she was equal to a sip of Algerian wine.

There was a knock on my door. It was the irate house-boy with Mr Alexander, my landlord, at his back.

'Someone is ringing on Mr Alexander's private number, 'tis a great inconvenience,' said the boy. Mr Alexander himself said, 'The house phone's out of order. I can let you take this call in our sitting-room as your friend says it's urgent. But please tell your friends not to intrude further.' He went on like this as I followed him to his sitting-room where his wife with her bubble-cut black hair sat stretching her long legs.

It was Sir Quentin on the phone. 'Mummy is not here,' he said, 'We – '

'She's here with me. I'll bring her home.'

'Oh, we've been so anxious, my dear Miss Talbot. We had great difficulty getting hold of you. Mrs Tims – '

'Please don't ring this number again,' I said. 'The people object.' I hung up and started to apologize to the Alexanders: 'You see, there's an elderly lady . . . ' They were looking at me with icy dislike as if my very voice was an offence. I got back to my own room quickly, where I found Leslie and Edwina drinking happily together. Edwina's charm was beginning to work on Leslie. He was reading her my poem and attacking it line by line.

He agreed to take Edwina home. He went out to phone someone and to find a taxi which he brought back to the door.

'I'll go straight home afterwards,' he said to me as she toddled out on his arm. 'Got to have an early night.'

'Me too,' I said. 'I've got a lot to think about.'

Edwina said, 'He's jealous of you, Fleur,' although what she meant I was not sure.

Before she was put in the taxi she said, 'Is that a real Degas you have in your room?'

'School of,' I said.

Leslie laughed, very delighted. I saw them off and went back to my room. I remember looking at my painting of two women with red pompoms in their brown hard hats, driving a carriage; and I wondered how it could be thought a Degas. It was an English painting signed J. Hayllar 1863.

I had started to clear up and get ready for bed, on the whole deeply satisfied with my day, when I heard a woman singing 'Auld Lang Syne' down in the street below my window. Now this was the signal that a very few of my friends used so that I could let them in at night without incurring the complaints of the implacable management and staff. I opened the window and looked out. I was astonished to see the large bulk of Leslie's wife Dottie in the lamplight, for it was already getting on for midnight and she had never so far called on me so late, if only for the reason that she might find her husband there. I imagined some emergency had brought her. 'What's the matter, Dottie?' I said. 'Leslie's not here.'

'I know. He phoned me that he's taking an old woman friend of yours home and then he has to go to some literary party in Soho that he can't get out of. Fleur, I want to see you.'

I heard a window open above my head. I didn't look up. I knew it was one of the Alexanders about to make a fuss. I merely said, 'I'll let you in, Dottie.' The upstairs window closed. I went down and let Dottie in, her sweet face swaddled in scarves, smelling of her English Rose scent.

I poured some Algerian wine. She began to cry. 'Leslie,' she said, 'is using us both as a cover. He has someone else.'

'Who is it?' I said.

'I don't know. But it's a young poet, a man, I know for sure,' said Dottie. 'The love that dares not speak its name.'

'A homosexual affair,' I said, daring to speak its name somewhat to Dottie's added distress.

'Aren't you surprised?' she said.

'Not much.' I was wondering how he found the time for us all.

'I was flabbergasted,' Dottie said, 'and hurt. So deeply wounded. You don't know what I'm suffering. I'm starting a novena to Our Blessed Lady of Fatima. I didn't suffer so much when I knew you were his mistress, Fleur, because – '

I interrupted her to cavil at the word 'mistress' which I pointed out had quite different connotations from those proper to my independent liaison with poor Leslie.

'Why do you say "Poor Leslie," why "poor"?'

'Because obviously he's in difficulties with his life. Can't cope.'

'Well, he calls you his mistress. It's his word.'

'It's an affectation. Poor Leslie.'

'What am I to do?' she said.

'You could leave him. You could stay with him.'

'I can't decide. I'm suffering. I'm only human.'

I had known that sooner or later she would say she was only human. I sensed that in a short while she would come round to accusing me of not being human. Suddenly I had an idea.

'You could write your autobiography,' I said. 'You could join the

Autobiographical Association where the members write their true life stories and have them put away for seventy years so that no living person will be offended. You might find it a relief.'

It was after two in the morning before I got to bed. I remember how the doings of my day appeared again before me, rich with inexplicable life. I fell asleep with a strange sense of sadness and promise meeting and holding hands.

THREE

While I recount what happened to me and what I did in 1949, it strikes me how much easier it is with characters in a novel than in real life. In a novel the author invents characters and arranges them in convenient order. Now that I come to write biographically I have to tell of whatever actually happened and whoever naturally turns up. The story of a life is a very informal party; there are no rules of precedence and hospitality, no invitations.

In a discourse on drama it was observed by someone famous that action is not merely fisticuffs, meaning of course that the dialogue and the sense are action, too. Similarly, the action of my life-story in 1949 included the work I was doing when I put my best brains into my *Warrneder Chase* most nights and most of Saturdays. My *Warrender Chase* was action just as much as when I was arguing with Dottie over Leslie, persuading her not to get him with child, as she came round the next night to tell me she was determined to do. My *Warrender Chase*, shoved quickly out of sight when my visitors arrived, or lest the daily woman should clean it up when I left home in the morning for my job, took up the sweetest part of my mind and the rarest part of my imagination; it was like being in love and better. All day long when I was busy with the affairs of the Autobiographical Association, I had my unfinished novel personified almost as a secret companion and accomplice following me like a shadow wherever I went, whatever I did. I took no notes, except in my mind.

Now the story of *Warrender Chase* was in reality already formed, and by no means influenced by the affairs of the Autobiographical Association. But the interesting thing was, it seemed rather the reverse to me at the time. At the time; but thinking it over now, how could that have been? And yet, it was so. In my febrile state of creativity I saw before my eyes how Sir Quentin was revealing himself chapter by chapter to be a type and consummation of

Warrender Chase, my character. I could see that the members of the Autobiographical Association were about to become his victims, psychological Jack the Ripper as he was.

My Warrender Chase was of course already dead by the end of my first chapter, where the family, his nephew Roland and his mother Prudence are waiting for the eminent ambassador-poet and moralist to arrive, and where the car accident in which the great man Warrender dies is announced. You remember, perhaps, that, before his death is actually established, at the point where Roland's wife, Marjorie, finds that his face is unrecognizable, she says, 'Oh, he'll have to have operations, like wearing a mask for the rest of his life!' I intended this to come out as one of those inane helpless things people say at moments of hysteria and shock. But it does transpire that he dies and it does in fact transpire that the mask is off, not on, for the rest of his life. His life, that is, in the pages of my novel, after Prudence, against the wishes of the rest of the family, confides Warrender's letters and other documents to the American scholar, Proudie. In my novel the documents were already in Proudie's hands when I began to see the trend of Sir Quentin's mind.

As you know I had already suspected that Sir Quentin was engaged in some form of racket, with maybe an eye to blackmail. At the same time I didn't see where the blackmail came in. He was not losing money on the project; on the other hand he was apparently quite rich and the potential victims of the Association were more marked in character by their once-elevated social position than for that out-standing wealth which tempts the crude blackmailer. Some of them had actually fallen on hard times.

I noticed by the correspondence that the four members who had not shown up at the meeting were already trying to wriggle out of it, and I too had decided that as soon as my vague uneasiness and my suspicions about Sir Quentin's motives should crystallize into any-thing concrete I would simply leave.

The four retreating members were a pharmaceutical chemist in Bath who pleaded pressure of business, and the much-cherished and widely-connected Major-General Sir George Beverley who wrote in to say his memory was sadly failing, he couldn't alas, recall anything of the past at all; there was also a retired headmistress from Somerset who wrote first to explain that her activities at the Tennis Club unfortunately precluded her giving time to her memoirs as she had hoped, and then, when further coaxed by Sir Quentin, gave a further excuse that her arthritis prevented her from the constant use of her typewriter or from taking up her pen. The fourth member to withdraw was that friend of mine who had got me the interview for the job. Now that I was established in the job I supposed she thought better of revealing her life-story to Sir Quentin since it would go through my hands. She wrote and told him that her biography was so interesting that she was going to write it with a view to publication; she also wrote to me on the same lines, begging me to sneak out the preliminary pages she had already given to Sir Quentin and post them back to her. Which I did. And Sir Quentin, I think, knew I had done this, for although he looked for my friend Mary's three pages and failed to find them in their place, he didn't ask me if I had done anything with them. I was quite ready to tell him I'd sent them back, but he merely looked at me with a smile and said, 'Ah, well – interesting, were they not?'

'I don't know,' I said. 'I never read them.' Which was true.

After some further cajoling letters from Sir Quentin to the four defectors, and ever more determined and, in a way, frightened replies from them, they got out of it. The chemist in Bath actually went so far as to get his solicitor to write to Sir Quentin firmly withdrawing from the Association. I sensed hysteria in the action of going to a solicitor when in fact the mere ignoring of Sir Quentin's letters would have had the same effect.

Well, what I found common to the members of Sir Quentin's remaining group was their weakness of character. To my mind this is no more to be despised than is physical weakness. We are not all born heroes and athletes. At the same time it is elementary wisdom always to fear weaknesses, including one's own; the reactions of the weak, when touched off, can be horrible and sudden. All of which is to say that I thought Sir Quentin was up to something quite dangerous in his evident attempt to get that group of weak people under his dominion for some purpose I couldn't yet make out. However, I confided all this to Dottie before I brought her into the Autobiographical Association. I warned her not on any account to give herself away but to get some amusement if she could out of the proceedings. For I wanted some joy to enliven and transfigure those meetings and those writings, the solemn intensity of which was so vastly out of proportion to the subject-matter. However sinister the theme of my *Warrender Chase* which was then uppermost in my mind, no one can say it isn't a spirited novel. But I think that ordinary readers would be astonished to know what troubles fell on my head because of the sinister side, and that is part of this story of mine; and that's what I think makes it worth the telling.

Dottie immediately set about making friends at the Autobiographical Association. She easily entered into the spirit of nostalgia; she felt herself persecuted and she had a great longing to be loved. I was alarmed at her sincerity and inability to detach herself from the situations of the others. I warned her, I kept on warning her that I suspected Sir Quentin was up to no good. Dottie said, 'Have you planted me in that group for your own ends?'

'Yes. And I thought it might amuse you. Don't get dragged into it. Those people are infantile, and every day becoming more so.'

'I shall pray for you,' said Dottie, 'to Our Lady of Fatima.'

'*Your* Lady of Fatima,' I said. Because, although I was a believer, I felt very strongly that Dottie's concept of religion was of necessity different from mine, in the same way that, years later when she made dramatic announcements that she had lost her faith, I was rather relieved since I had always uneasily felt that if her faith was true then mine was false.

But now in my room after returning with me after a meeting at Sir Quentin's, Dottie said, 'You planted me. I'll pray for you.'

'Pray for the members of the Autobiographical Association,' I said.

I don't know why I thought of Dottie as my friend but I did. I believe she thought the same way about me although she didn't really like me. In those days, among the people I mixed with, one had friends almost by predestination. There they were, like your winter coat and your meagre luggage. You didn't think of discarding them just because you didn't altogether like them. Life on the intellectual fringe in 1949 was a universe by itself. It was something like life in Eastern Europe to-day.

We were sitting talking over the meeting. It was already late November. I had argued with Dottie all the way home, on the bus and standing with her in a queue at a food shop which ran out of stock of whatever it was Dottie had her eye on while the queue was still forming, and we the tenth; and anyway, it was closing time so that the brown-aproned grocer shut his doors with a click of the bolt and we plodded away.

The Autobiographical Association had taken her mind off Leslie. Neither of us had seen him for over three weeks. I had decided to finish with him as a lover, which was easy for me although I missed his face and his talk. Dottie was infuriated by my indifference, she desired so much that I should be in love with Leslie and not have him, and she felt I was cheapening her goods.

That afternoon was the third time I had attended a meeting of Quentin's autobiographers since I had been at the job. So far Dottie had produced no biographical writing of her own for the others to see. She had in fact written a long confessional piece about Leslie and his young poet and her consequent sufferings. I had torn it up, violently warning her against making any such true revelation. 'Why?' said Dottie.

I couldn't tell her why. I didn't know why. I said I would be able to explain when I had written a few more chapters of my novel *Warrender Chase*.

'What has that got to do with it?' Dottie reasonably said.

'It's the only way I can come to a conclusion about what's going on at Sir Quentin's. I have to work it out through my own creativity. You have to follow my instinct, Dottie. I warned you not to give yourself away.'

'But I like those people and Beryl Tims is so sweet. Sir Quentin's odd, but he's very reassuring, isn't he? Like a priest I once knew as a girl when I was at school with the nuns. And I'm sorry for him with that dreadful old mother. He has real goodness ... '

I sat with Dottie in my room trying to muddle my way into clarity. Whereas Dottie, with perfect clarity, was arguing a case for her own complete involvement, and I sensed trouble, either for her or from her.

'If you feel as you do,' Dottie said, 'you should leave the job.'

'But I'm involved. I have to know what's going on. I sense a racket.'

'But you don't want me to be involved,' she said.

'No, it's dangerous. I wouldn't, myself, dream of getting involved with – '

'First you say you're involved. Next you say you wouldn't dream of getting involved. The truth is,' said Dottie, 'that you resent me getting on so well with everybody, Sir Quentin and the members and Beryl.'

She did get on well with everybody. That afternoon all of the remaining members had turned up, including Dottie, seven in all.

Mrs Tims had immediately cornered Dottie to enquire in low tones, there in the entrance hall, if she had heard from her husband. Dottie murmured something with a soulful look. I was busy with the arrival of Maisie Young, sportily managing with her bad leg, and nervous Father Egbert Delaney, but I had heard Beryl Tims exclaim from time to time in the course of Dottie's confidences, phrases such as, 'The swine!', 'It's an abomination. They ought to be put on an island.' I tried to get Dottie out of this but she was in no mind to follow me into the study until she had finished her chat with Beryl Tims. I had to abandon the two English Roses and be about my business.

During the past seven weeks the members who had remained faithful to the Association had seen some alarming changes made to their biographies. There was a certain day, late in October, when Sir Quentin told me, 'I think your amusing elaborations of our friends' histories have so far been perfectly adequate, Miss Talbot, but the time has come for me to take over. I see that I must. It's a moral question.'

I didn't object, but I had always found that people who said, 'It's a moral question' in that precise, pursed way that Sir Quentin said it were out to justify themselves, and were generally up to no good. 'You see,' said Sir Quentin, 'they are being very frank, most of them, very frank indeed, but they have no sense of guilt. In my opinion ... '

I had stopped listening. It was only a job. In many ways I was glad to be rid of the task of applying my inventiveness to livening up these dreary biographies. With the exception of Maisie Young who was still producing a quantity of material about the Beyond and the Oneness of life, they had started drafting out their first amorous adventures, egged on by Sir Quentin. I wouldn't have called them frank, as Sir Quentin rather too often did. All that had been achieved so far was Mrs Wilks having had her blouse ripped open by a soldier before her escape from Russia in 1917; Baronne Clotilde had been caught in bed with her music tutor in the charming French château near Dijon; Father Egbert Delaney, he who had taken up his pen with some trepidation, had continued with the same trepidation for many pages to delineate the experience of impure thoughts the first time he had heard a confession; Lady Bernice 'Bucks' Gilbert had effected a flashback to her teens, devoting a long chapter to her lesbian adventure with the captain of the hockey team, to which many descriptions of sunsets in the Cotswold hills lent atmosphere. With timid Sir Eric, it was a prep-school affair with another boy, the only interesting part of this adventure being that, while doing whatever he had unspecifically done with the other boy, young Eric's mind had dwelt all the time on an actress who had come to stay with his parents the last half-term.

Sir Quentin called these offerings 'frank', with a most definite emphasis, and it bored me. 'It's time for me to take over. It's a moral question,' he said.

'I wish you hadn't torn up my piece,' Dottie said as she sat with me in my room that late November evening. 'It made me feel awful having nothing to offer.'

'You seemed to have offered the whole story to Beryl Tims,' I said.

'One had to confide in someone. She's a real friend. I think it's a scandal the way she has to run around after that revolting old woman.'

In the past few weeks a nurse had been employed to take care of Lady Edwina. This nurse was a quiet woman, much despised by Beryl Tims. Certainly, Edwina was now no burden on Mrs Tims and the old lady was wilder and funnier than ever. I really loved her. At the latest meeting of the Autobiographical Association, which I was now chewing over with Dottie, Edwina had made her appearance with the tea, dressed in pale grey velvet with long and many strings of pearls. Her rouged wrinkles and smudgy mascara were wonderful to behold. She had behaved with expressive graciousness and was continent: only when it was time to withdraw and the nurse tiptoed bashfully into the room to fetch her, Edwina had given vent to one of her long cackles followed by, 'Well, my dears, he's got you where he wants you, hasn't he? Ha! Trust my son Quentin.' The bony index finger of her right hand pointed to Maisie Young. 'Except you. He hasn't started on you, yet.' Maisie's eyes were hypnotized by the long red fingernail pointed at her.

'Mummy!' said Quentin.

I had looked over to Dottie. She was murmuring with Beryl Tims, nodding wisely, very sympathetically.

I didn't reply to Dottie when, sitting sulkily that night in my room, she continued to emphasize how sorry she felt for Beryl Tims and how strongly she felt that Edwina should be sent to a home. It seemed to me Dottie was trying to provoke me. I could see Dottie was tired. For some reason I seldom remember feeling tired, myself, in those days; I suppose I must have felt exhausted at times for I got through an amazing variety and number of things in the course of every day; but I simply can't recall any occasion of weariness such as I could see in Dottie at that moment.

I made tea and I offered to read her a bit of my *Warrender Chase*. I did this for my own sake as much as to entertain, and, in a way, flatter her; for my own sake, though, because I intended to write some more pages of the book after Dottie went home, and this reading it over was a sort of preparation.

Now I had come to the bit where Warrender's nephew Roland and his wife Marjorie have decided to start going over Warrender's papers in preparation for Proudie, since Prudence, Warrender's ancient mother, has appointed the scholar Proudie to deal with them. This is three weeks after the quiet country funeral for the family, which I described in detail. Dottie had already heard the funeral bit which she said was 'far too cold', but that hadn't bothered me; in fact I felt her criticism was a rather good sign. 'You haven't brought home the tragedy of Warrender's death,' Dottie had said. Which hadn't bothered me, either. Anyway, this was the new chapter which is written from Roland's point of view. Which was that his uncle, Warrender Chase, had been a great man tragically cut off in his prime; it has been abundantly acknowledged, it is a public commonplace. He has successfully established his importance.

The family, secretly enjoying their stricken status, are counting on Roland and Marjorie to do their job conscientiously, to go through his papers with Proudie and eventually produce a *Life and Letters* or a memorial of some sort for Warrender Chase; whatever they do, even if it takes years, can't help but be interesting. The task naturally saddens Roland, who leafs through the dead man's papers. Warrender Chase, so vital a few weeks ago, and now so absolutely gone. Roland is sad, a bit unnerved. Why then has Marjorie, hitherto a rather neurotic and droopy woman of thirty, begun to perk up? Her new bloom and spirits have been increasingly noticeable day by day since the funeral. Proudie is very well aware of Marjorie's new happiness.

The above is of course a rough reminder. But when I read it to Dottie that evening in my bed-sitting-room I could see she wasn't liking it. I will quote the actual bit she finally objected to:

> 'Marjorie,' said Roland, 'is there anything the matter with you?'
> 'No, nothing at all.'
> 'That's what I thought,' he said.
> 'You seem to accuse me,' she said, 'of being all right.'
> 'Well, I do, in a way. Warrender's death doesn't seem to have affected you.'
> 'It's affected her beautifully,' said Proudie.

(I changed 'beautifully' to 'very well' before sending the book to the publisher. I had probably been reading too much Henry James at that time, and 'beautifully' was much too much.)

It was at this point Dottie said, 'I don't know what you're getting at. Is Warrender Chase a hero or is he not?'

'He is,' I said.

'Then Marjorie is evil.'

'How can you say that? Marjorie is fiction, she doesn't exist.'

'Marjorie is a personification of evil.'

'What is a personification?' I said. 'Marjorie is only words.'

'Readers like to know where they stand,' Dottie said, 'And in this novel they don't. Marjorie seems to be dancing on Warrender's grave.'

Dottie was no fool. I knew I wasn't helping the reader to know whose side they were supposed to be on. I simply felt compelled to go on with my story without indicating what the reader should think. At the same time Dottie had given me the idea for that scene, towards the end of the book, where Marjorie dances on Warrender's grave.

'You know,' Dottie said, 'there's something a bit harsh about you, Fleur. You're not really womanly, are you?'

I was really annoyed by this. To show her I was a woman I tore up the pages of my novel and stuffed them into the wastepaper basket, burst out crying and threw her out, roughly and noisily, so that Mr Alexander looked over the banisters and complained. 'Get out,' I yelled at Dottie. 'You and your husband between you have ruined my literary work.'

After that I went to bed. Flooded with peace, I fell asleep.

Next morning, after I had fished my torn pages of *Warrender Chase* out of the wastepaper basket and glued them together again, I went off to work, stopping on the way at the Kensington Public Library to get a copy of John Henry Newman's *Apologia*, which I had long promised Maisie Young. She could quite well have procured it for herself during all those weeks, disabled though she was, but she belonged to that category of society, by no means always the least educated, who are always asking how they can get hold of a book; they know very well that one buys shoes from a shoeshop and groceries from the grocer's, but to find and enter a bookshop is not somehow within the range of their imagination.

However, I felt kindly towards Maisie and I thought the sublime pages of Newman's autobiography would tether her mind to the sweet world of living people, in a spiritual context though it was. Maisie needed tethering.

I found the book on the library shelves and, while I was there in that section, I lit on another book I hadn't seen for years. It was the autobiography of Benvenuto Cellini. It was like meeting an old friend. I borrowed both books and went on my way rejoicing.

FOUR

I began to take Edwina out for Sunday afternoons towards the end of November. It solved the problem of what to do with her when the nurse wasn't on duty and Mrs Tims was off to the country with Sir Quentin. It suited me quite well because in the first place I liked her and secondly she fitted in so easily with my life. If the weather was fine I would fetch her in a taxi and then set her up in her folding wheel-chair for a walk along the edges of Hampstead Heath with a friend of mine, my dear Solly Mendelsohn, and afterwards we would go to a tea-shop or to his flat for tea. Solly was a journalist on a newspaper, always on night duty, so that I rarely saw him except in daylight hours.

There was nothing one couldn't discuss in front of Edwina; she was delighted with all we did and said, which was just as well, because Solly in his hours of confiding relaxation liked to curse and swear about certain aspects of life, although he had the sweetest of natures, the most generous possible heart. At first, in deference to the very aged Lady Edwina, Solly was cautious but he soon sized her up. 'You're a sport, Edwina,' he said.

Solly had a limp which he had won during the war; our progress was slow and we stopped in our tracks frequently, when the need to rest from our push-chair efforts somehow neatly combined with a point in our conversation that needed the emphasis of a physical pause, as when I told him that Dottie continued to complain about my *Warrender Chase* and consequently I was sorry I had ever started reading it to her.

'You want your brains examined,' said Solly, limping along. He was a man of huge bulk with a great Semitic head, a sculptor's joy. He stopped to say, 'You want your head examined to take notice of that silly bitch.' Then he took his part of Edwina's pram-handle, and off we trundled again.

I said, 'Dottie's sort of the general reader in my mind.'

'Fuck the general reader,' Solly said, 'because in fact the general reader doesn't exist.'

'That's what I say,' Edwina yelled. 'Just fuck the general reader. No such person.'

I liked to be lucid. So long as Dottie took in what I wrote I didn't care whether she disapproved or not. She would pronounce all the English Rose verdicts, and we often had rows, but of course she was a friend and always came back to hear more. I had been reading my book to Edwina and to Solly as well. 'I remember,' said Edwina in her cackling voice, 'how I laughed and laughed over that scene of the memorial service for Warrender Chase that the Worshipful Company of Fishmongers put on for him.'

Several people turned round to look at Edwina as she spoke with her high cry. People often turned round to stare at her painted wizened face, her green teeth, the raised, blood-red fingernail accompanied by her shrieking voice, the whole wrapped up to the neck in luxurious fur. Edwina was over ninety and might die any time, as she did about six years later. My dear, dear Solly lived into the seventies of this century, when I was far away. He started during his last illness to send me some of the books from his library that he knew I would especially like.

One of these books, which took me back over the years to wintry Hampstead Heath, was a rare edition of John Henry Newman's *Apologia pro Vita Sua* and another was a green-and-gold-bound edition, in Italian, of my beloved Benvenuto Cellini's *La Vita*.

Questa mia Vita travagliata io scrivo . . .

I remember Solly at his sweetest during those walks at Hampstead, with our Edwina always ready to support the general drama of our lives, crowing like a Greek chorus as we discussed this and that. I had not yet finished *Warrender Chase*, but Solly had found for me a somewhat run-down publisher with headquarters in a warehouse at Wapping who on the strength of the first two chapters was prepared to contract for it, on a down payment to me of ten pounds. I recall discussing the contract with Solly on one of our walks. It was a dry, windy day. We stopped while Solly scrutinized the one-page document. It fluttered in his hand. He gave it back to me. 'Tell him to wipe his arse with it,' said Solly. 'Don't sign.' 'Yes, oh yes, oh yes,' screamed Edwina. 'Just tell that publisher to wipe his arse with that contract.'

I wasn't at all attracted to obscenities, but the combination of circumstances, something about the Heath, the weather, the wheel-chair, and also Solly and Edwina themselves in their own essence, made all this sound to me very poetic, it made me very happy. We wheeled Edwina into a tea-shop where she poured tea and conversed in a most polite and grand manner.

This, about the middle of December 1949. I had sat up many nights working on *Warrender Chase* and already had a theme for another novel at the back of my mind. I was longing to have enough money to be able to leave my job, but until I could get enough money from a publisher there was no possibility of that.

And here comes a further point. My job at Sir Quentin's held my curiosity. What went on there could very well have continued to influence my *Warrender Chase* but it didn't. Rather, it was not until I had finished writing the book in January 1950 that I got some light on what Sir Quentin was up to.

It was the end of January 1950 that I began to notice a deterioration in all the members of the Association.

I had been down with 'flu and away from work for two weeks. Just after the New Year Dottie had fallen ill with 'flu and I had spent most of my evenings with her in her flat, feeling fatalistically that I would catch her 'flu. I'm not sure that I didn't want to. During those first weeks of January when I went to Dottie's every night with the bits of shopping and things that she needed, Leslie often came round. He was no longer living with Dottie, having moved in with his poet. But something about the 'flu made Dottie very much more relaxed. She was less of the English Rose. She refrained from telling Leslie that she was praying for him. It is true she had some relics of her childhood, a teddy-bear, some dolls and a gollywog in bed with her, all lying along Leslie's side of the bed. She had always draped these toys on top of her bed, along the counterpane. I knew that they had got on Leslie's nerves but now that she was ill I suppose he felt indulgent, for he sometimes brought her flowers. There were no recriminations between us and we merrily skated on thick ice, while I privately wondered what I had ever seen in Leslie, he seemed so to have lost his good looks, at least in a virile sense. However, we were happy. Dottie even managed to laugh at some of my stories about Sir Quentin although at heart she was taking that Autobiographical Association very seriously.

Now that it was my turn to be ill I lay in bed all day with my high temperature, writing and writing my *Warrender Chase*. This 'flu was a wonderful opportunity to get the book finished. I worked till my hand was tired and until Dottie showed up at six in the evening with a vacuum flask of soup or some rashers of bacon which she fried on my gas ring, cutting them up kindly into little bits for me to swallow for my health's sake. She had got thinner from her own 'flu and wisps of hair fell down from its handsome upward twist so that she looked less English Rose for the time being. She had been to Sir Quentin's to give a helping hand in my absence.

'Dottie,' I said, 'you simply mustn't take that man seriously.'

'Beryl Tims is in love with him,' she said.

'Oh, God,' I said.

I had just that day been writing the chapter in my *Warrender Chase* where the letters of my character Charlotte prove that she was so far gone in love with him that she was willing to pervert her own sound instincts, or rather forget that she had those instincts, in order to win Warrender's approval and retain a little of his attention. My character Charlotte, my fictional English Rose, was later considered to be one of my more shocking portrayals. What did I care? I conceived her in those feverish days and nights of my bout of 'flu which touched on pleurisy, and I never regretted the creation of Charlotte. I wasn't writing poetry and prose so that the reader would think me a nice person, but in order that my sets of words should convey ideas of truth and wonder, as indeed they did to myself as I was composing them. I see no reason to keep silent about my enjoyment of the sound of my own voice as I work. I am sparing no relevant facts.

Now I treated the story of Warrender Chase with a light and heartless hand, as is my way when I have to give a perfectly serious account of things. No matter what is described it seems to me a sort of hypocrisy for a writer to pretend to be undergoing tragic experiences when obviously one is sitting in relative comfort with a pen and paper or before a typewriter. I enjoyed myself with Warrender's mother, Prudence, and her sepulchral sayings: and I made her hand over the documents to the American scholar, Proudie, whom she thought so comical. I did it scene by scene: Marjorie's obvious release from some terrible anxiety after Warrender's death and the consequent disapproval of her husband, Roland, with his little round face and his adoration of his dead uncle; then came the discovery of those letters and those notes left by Warrender Chase, pieced together throughout the book, which finally show with certainty what I had prepared the reader slowly to suspect. Warrender Chase was privately a sado-puritan who for a kind of hobby had gathered together a group of people specially selected for their weakness and folly, and in whom he carefully planted and nourished a sense of terrible and unreal guilt. As I wrote in the book, 'Warrender's private prayer-meetings were of course known about, but only to the extent that they were considered too delicate a matter to be publicly discussed. Warrender had cultivated such a lofty myth of himself that nobody could pry into his life for fear of appearing vulgar.' Well, he was supposed to be a mystic, known to be a pillar of the High Church of England; he made speeches at the universities, wrote letters to *The Times*. God knows where I got Warrender Chase from; he was based on no one that I knew.

I know only that the night I started writing *Warrender Chase* I had been alone at a table in a restaurant near Kensington High Street Underground eating my supper. I rarely ate out alone, but I must have found myself in funds that day. I was going about my proper business, eating my supper while listening-in to the conversation at the next table. One of them said, 'There we were all gathered in the living-room, waiting for him.'

It was all I needed. That was the start of *Warrender Chase*, the first chapter. All the rest sprang from the phrase.

But I invented for my Warrender a war record, a distinguished one, in Burma, and managed to make it really credible even although I filled in the war bit with a very few strokes, knowing, in fact, so little about the war in Burma. It astonished me later to find how the readers found Warrender's war record so convincing and full when I had said so little – one real war veteran of Burma wrote to say how realistic he found it – but since then I've come to learn for myself how little one needs, in the art of writing, to convey the lot, and how a lot of words, on the other hand, can convey so little.

I never described, in my book, what Warrender's motives were. I simply showed the effect of his words, his hints. The real dichotomy in his character was in his public, formal High Churchism, and his private sectarian style. In the prayer-meetings he was a Biblical fundamentalist, to the effect, for instance, that he induced one of his sect to give up his good job in the War Office (as the Ministry of Defence was then called), to sell all his goods to feed the poor, and finally to die on a park bench one smoggy November night. This was greatly to Warrender's satisfaction. But he himself, I made quite clear, understood Christianity in a far more evolved and practical light. 'Induced' is perhaps not the word. He goaded with the Word of God and terrorized. I showed how four women among his prayer-set were his greatest victims, for he was a deep woman-hater. One woman committed suicide, unable to stand the impressions of her own guilt that he made upon her and convinced that she had no friends; two others went mad, and this included his housekeeper Charlotte, that English Rose who was enthralled by him. His nephew's wife, Marjorie, was on the point of mental crash when the car crash killed Warrender. All these years since, the critics have been asking whether Warrender was in love with his nephew. How do I know? Warrender Chase never existed, he is only some hundreds of words, some punctuation, sentences, paragraphs, marks on the page. If I had conceived Warrender Chase's motives as a psychological study I would have said so. But I didn't go in for motives, I never have.

I covered the pages, propping them on the underside of a tray, to finish *Warrender Chase* on my sick-bed that winter, even when my 'flu had turned bronchial and touched on pleurisy. I was too hoarse to read it to Dottie when she came to see me. But when she spoke of Sir Quentin and said, 'Beryl Tims is in love with him,' I sat up in my fever and said, 'My God!' The idea that anyone could be in love with Quentin Oliver was beyond me.

FIVE

I noticed the deterioration in the members of the Autobiographical Association precisely at the end of January 1950, a week after I had finished the book. I felt low from my 'flu but cheerful that my work was finished and behind me. I had no great hopes of success with *Warrender Chase* but already I had plans for a better book. Solly had found me another publisher to replace the one whose contract he had so despised. This publisher, an elderly man, was called Revisson Doe. He had a round, bald head of the shiny type I always wanted to stroke if I sat behind it in church or at the theatre. He said he thought *Warrender Chase* 'quite evil, especially in its moments of levity', and that 'the young these days are spiritually sick', but he supposed his firm could carry it at a loss in the hope of better books to come. He gave me what he said was the usual form of contract, on a printed sheet, and it wasn't such a bad contract nor was it a good one. Only, I found later by personal espionage that his firm, Park and Revisson Doe, had a printing press on which they produced 'the usual form of contract' to suit whatever they could get away with for each individual author. But Revisson Doe commended himself to me by his entertaining reminiscences of his youth, when he was an office-boy on a literary weekly and had been sent out to Holborn Underground to meet W. B. Yeats: 'A figure in a dark cape. I said, "Are you the poet Mr Yeats?" He stopped, raised his hand high and said, "I yám."'

But these matters were of the past and I had said a temporary good-bye to Revisson Doe on signature of the contract. *Warrender Chase* was to be published some time in June, and I only had to wait for the proofs. At the end of January when I went back to my work at Sir Quentin's I had almost obliterated the book from my thoughts.

The proofs came in March, and when I came face to face with my *Warrender Chase* again I was so far estranged from it that I couldn't bring myself to look through the proofs for typographical errors.

Instead I went with Solly one afternoon to St John's Wood to see our friends Theo and Audrey, a married couple who had both published their first novels and who consequently enjoyed a little more respect, in that very hierarchical literary world, than did my unpublished friends whom I used to meet at poetry readings at the Ethical Church Hall. Theo and Audrey had agreed to read my proofs for me. I exhorted them to make no changes but only to look for spelling errors.

I handed over my proofs.

These were kind people. 'You look haunted,' said Theo. 'What's the matter with you?'

'She is haunted,' said Solly.

'I am haunted,' I said, but I wouldn't explain any further. Solly said, 'Her job's getting her down', and left it at that.

Audrey made me up a package of buns and sandwiches left over from tea, to take home.

Since the end of January and for the past two months I had come to feel that the members of Sir Quentin's group resembled more and more the bombed-out buildings that still messed up the London street-scene. These ruins were getting worse, month by month, and so were the Autobiographical people.

Dottie couldn't see it.

Sir Eric Findlay said to me, 'Do you *really* think Mrs Wilks is in her right mind?'

I thought it safest to say, 'What is a right mind?' He looked frightened. We were alone having coffee after lunch in the ladies' sitting-room of the Bath Club which, because of a fire in its original premises, was housed within another club, I think the Conservative.

'What is a right mind? Well, you have a right mind, Fleur, and everyone knows it. The point is that the Hallam Street set are saying ... Don't you think it's time we all had it out with each other? One big row would be better than the way we're going on.'

I said that I didn't care for the idea of one big row.

Sir Eric waved his hand in mild greeting to a middle-aged couple who had just come in and who sat down on a sofa at the other end of the room. Other people presently joined them. Sir Eric waved and nodded across the room in his timid way as if making a side-gesture to some sweet discourse with me about the London Philharmonic, the Cheltenham Gold Cup or even my own charms, instead of this depressing conversation about what was wrong with the Autobiographical Association. I longed for the power of the Evil Eye so that I could cast it on Eric Findlay in revenge for his taking me out to lunch and then assaulting me with his kinky complaints.

'One big row,' he said, his timid little eyes glinting. 'Mrs Wilks is not in her right mind but you, Fleur, are in your right mind,' he said, as if there was some question that I wasn't.

I felt some panic which, however, I knew I could control. I felt I should sit on quietly as one would in the sudden presence of a dangerous beast. The atmosphere of my *Warrender Chase* came back to me, but grotesquely, without its even-tempered tone. When I first started writing people used to say my novels were exaggerated. They never were exaggerated, merely aspects of realism. Sir Eric Findlay was real, sitting there on the sofa by my side complaining how Mrs Wilks had failed to appreciate the latest part of his autobiography, his war record, and thus was out of her mind. All Mrs Wilks could think of, he said, was the foolish incident in his schooldays with another boy while thinking of an actress. 'Mrs Wilks harps on it,' said Eric.

'You shouldn't have revealed it. Those autobiographies are dangerous,' I said.

'Well, a lot of them were your doing, Fleur,' he said.

'Not the dangerous passages. Only the funny parts.'

'Sir Quentin insists,' he said, 'on complete frankness. Are you leaving that sugar?' He pointed to a tiny lump of sugar on the saucer of my coffee-cup. I said I didn't want it. He put it in his pocket in a small envelope he kept for the purpose. 'They say it will be off the ration in three months,' he said in an excited whisper.

Dottie said to me that evening, 'I quite see Eric's point of view. Mrs Wilks has an obsession about sex. I don't believe she was raped by a Russian soldier before she escaped. It's wishful thinking.'

'It makes no difference to me what any of you did,' I said. 'I just can't stand all the gossip, the canvassing, the lobbying, amongst the awful members.'

'Sir Quentin insists on complete frankness and I think we should all be frank with each other,' Dottie said.

I looked at her, I know, as if she were a complete stranger.

Maisie Young had found out where I lived. She had come to my room one Saturday afternoon, only some days before I met Sir Eric Findlay at his club for lunch. She had come complaining too, as it turned out, although she at first protested she didn't want to come in, she only wanted to leave me a book and she had kept the taxi waiting. We sent the taxi away.

'Oh,' said Maisie, 'what a delightful little wee room, so compact.' She herself came out of the best half of a house in Portman Square and enjoyed the rent of the other half. I think Maisie was rather stunned at the spacelessness of this room where I lived all of my present life, she was amazed that anyone could have space for intelligent ideas when they lived with a gas ring for cooking, a bed for sitting and sleeping on, an orange box for food stores and plates, a table for eating and writing on, a wash basin for washing at, two chairs for sitting on or (as on the present occasion) hanging washing on, a corner cupboard for clothes, walls to hold shelves of books and a floor on which one stepped over more books, set in piles. All this Maisie, clutching her bag like a horse's rein, took in with a dazed look-round as if she had been thrown from her horse yet again. I believe it was out of sheer kindness that she kept on saying, 'Compact, compact, it's really ... it's really ... I didn't know they had this sort of thing.'

I bundled the washing off one of the chairs and settled Maisie into it with two volumes of the *Encyclopaedia Britannica* and the complete Chaucer piled up for a footstool whereon to rest her poor caged leg, as I always did for Edwina and for Solly Mendelsohn when they came to see me. She took this very kindly. I sat on the bed and smiled.

'I mean, I didn't know they had this sort of thing in Kensington,' said Maisie. 'I mean in Kensington – nowadays. Is this where you bring Lady Edwina?'

I said yes, sometimes. I set about making tea, so much to the renewed astonishment of Maisie in Wonderland that I felt bound to assure her that I often had quite a lot of visitors, five, six, even more, at a time.

'How do you keep so clean, yourself?' said Maisie, looking at me with new eyes.

'There's a bathroom on every landing. A bath is fourpence a time.'

'Is that all?'

'It's too much,' I said, and explained how the proprietors made a fortune out of the penny gas meters in the bathrooms and the shilling meters in the rooms, since they got a refund when the meter-man came to collect, which refunded loot was not shared among the clients.

'I suppose,' said Maisie, 'they have to make some sort of a profit.' I could see whose side she was on and although she then looked round the room enquiringly I didn't enlighten her as to the rent, lest she should exclaim over its dirt-cheapness.

'What a lot of books – have you read them all?' she said.

Still, I liked her very much. She was merely ignorant about penniless realities, as indeed she was about most realities, but she wasn't pretentious. Maisie settled down with her tea and biscuit and started saying what she had come to say.

'Father Egbert Delaney,' said this handsome girl, 'believes that Satan is a woman. He told me as much and I think he ought to be made to resign. It's an insult to women.'

'It does seem so,' I said. 'Why don't you tell him?'

'I think you, as secretary, Fleur, should take it up with him and report the matter to Sir Quentin.'

'But if I tell him Satan is a man he'll think it an insult to men.'

She said, 'Personally, I don't believe in Satan.'

'Well, that's all right then,' I said.

'What's all right then?'

'If Satan doesn't exist, why bother if it's man or woman we're talking about?'

'It's Father Delaney we're talking about. Do you know what I think?'

I said, what did she think?

'Father Delaney is Satan. Satan himself. You should report the whole thing to Sir Quentin. Sir Quentin insists on complete frankness. It's time we had a showdown.'

I still liked Maisie Young, she had an air of freedom that she wasn't herself aware of, and she reminded me as she sat there in my room of my character Marjorie in *Warrender Chase*. But I didn't dwell on this at the time; I was thinking of her phrase, 'Sir Quentin insists on complete frankness.' It stuck in my mind so that, a few days later when I sat with Eric Findlay in his club and he twice spoke that very phrase, I was convinced that Sir Quentin Oliver had started orchestrating his band of fools. At the moment, sitting with Maisie in my room I was simply irritated by her 'Sir Quentin insists,' I said, 'Complete frankness is always a mistake among friends.'

'I know what you mean,' said Maisie. 'You make out you're happy to see me but really you don't like me coming here. I'm only a cripple and a bore to you.'

I was appalled; for the moment that she had turned my generality on to herself she indeed became a very great bore, not merely for the present hour, but stretching into the future; this apprehension of Maisie in the future affected me with a clutching void in my stomach. All in a moment she had seemed to lose that air of a freedom that she would probably never be aware existed.

I said, 'Oh, Maisie, I had no such thing in mind. I spoke generally. Frankness is usually a euphemism for rudeness.'

'People should be frank,' said the wretched girl. 'I know I'm a cripple and a bore.'

I longed for the telephone to ring but it didn't, or someone else to come in, but just at that moment nobody did. I murmured something to the effect that a physical disability often proved to be an attraction. She replied sharply that she'd rather not discuss her sex-life. So much for my frankness.

Now Maisie lifted up the book she had brought me. It was the copy of John Henry Newman's *Apologia pro Vita Sua* that I had borrowed from the public library for her. 'Sir Quentin has lent me a copy of his own,' said Maisie. She was looking at me without really noticing my presence. For a moment I felt like a grey figment, the 'I' of a novel whose physical description the author had decided not to set forth. I was still, of course, weak from my 'flu. She flicked through the pages of the *Apologia* and found a bit she wanted to read aloud to me. It was the passage, early in the book, where Newman describes his religious feelings as a boy. He felt he was elected to eternal glory. He said the actual belief gradually faded away but that it had an influence on the opinions of his early youth:

... viz. in isolating me from the
objects which surrounded me, in
confirming me in my mistrust of the
reality of material phenomena, and
making me rest in the thought of
two and two only supreme and
luminously self-evident beings,
myself and my Creator . . . .

Maisie finished reading. She said, 'I think that is very, very beautiful and so true.'

Now I got angry. I was impatient with the force of having spent the past three and a half years studying Newman, his sermons, his essays, his life, his theology, and I had done it for no reward, and at the sacrifice of pleasures and happiness which would never come my way again, while Maisie up to the time of her accident had been spending her time at deb dances, riding in the parks of such country-houses as had been restored by the government to their owners after the war, and, since her accident, plotting out with her friends her totally undisciplined theories of the Cosmos. The sacrifice of pleasures is of course itself a pleasure, but I didn't feel up to such pure reasoning at the time; Maisie's reading me this well-known passage of Newman and telling me it was beautiful and true irritated me greatly. I said, 'Newman is describing a passing phase.'

'Oh, no,' said Maisie, 'it goes through and through his book. Two and two only supreme and luminously self-evident beings, my Creator and myself.'

Suddenly I knew there was a sense in which she was right and the whole Newman idea which up to now I had thought enchanting took on a different aspect. I had always up to now had a particular liking for this passage, feeling a fierce conviction of its power and general application as a human ideal. But as Maisie uttered the words I felt a revulsion against an awful madness I then discerned in it. '... My mistrust of material phenomena ... two and two only supreme and luminously self-evident beings, my Creator and myself.' I was glad of my strong hips and sound cage of ribs to save me from flying apart, so explosive were my thoughts. But I heard myself saying, coldly, 'It's quite a neurotic view of life. It's a poetic vision only. Newman was a nineteenth century romantic.'

'Do you know,' she said, 'there are still people alive who remember Cardinal Newman. He was considered to be an angel.'

'I think it awful,' I said, 'to contemplate a world in which there are only two luminous and self-evident beings, your creator and yourself. You shouldn't read Newman in that way.'

'It's a beautiful thought, a very beautiful – '

'I'm sorry I ever told you to read the *Apologia*. It's a beautiful piece of poetic paranoia.' This was over-simple, a distortion; but I needed the rhetoric to combat the girl's ideas.

'Father Egbert Delaney mentioned it to me first,' she said. 'I don't know how that evil fellow can possibly appreciate the book. But it's true you also pressed us all to read it as an example of an autobiography.'

'For my part Father Egbert Delaney is a self-evident and luminous being,' I said. 'So are you, so is my lousy landlord and the same goes for everyone I know. You can't live with an I-and-thou relationship to God and doubt the reality of the rest of life.'

'Have you told Sir Quentin your views?' Maisie said. 'Because,' she said, 'Sir Quentin insists on complete frankness. He has told us we are all to study the *Apologia* as an example of autobiographical writing.'

By this time I had calmed down and I was thinking how much unpaid overtime I had saved myself by failing to remind them of Proust and his fictional autobiography. I wanted to get rid of Maisie and forget the Autobiographical Association for the week-end at least. Those people and their Sir Quentin were sheets of paper on which I could write short stories, poems, anything I cared. Orgulous and impatient I told Maisie while looking at my watch that I had to make a phone call – 'Goodness, the time!' – I moved with these words to the telephone and put through a call to Dottie's number. She wasn't in. I put down the receiver and said to Maisie, 'I'm afraid I've missed my friend.'

She was looking straight ahead as if struck by catalepsy, and oblivious of my phoning and fussing. I thought she had been taken badly, but then she spoke in a trance-like way that made me suspect that it was all put on. 'Father Egbert Delaney is Satan personified. You'll believe me when I tell you what he said about you, Fleur.'

I was instantly agog. 'What – did – he – say – about – me?'

She went into another dream-like state. I knew I was being foolish to press her for more, but I was dying to know.

At last she spoke: 'Your Father Egbert Delaney whom you're so anxious to protect says that you are trying to persuade Lady Edwina to change her will in your favour. He says Beryl Tims is convinced of it. In fact, many of the others are convinced of it.'

I laughed, but the laughter was artificial, which I hoped didn't show.

'Father Egbert Delaney,' she said, 'says, why else should you bother to take the awful old crone out for walks and spend so much time with her?'

I prayed for someone to phone me or look in to see me. That my prayer appeared to be answered within a very short time is no proof of its efficacy; it was six o'clock, a time when any of my friends might ring me up or stop to see me on their way somewhere. Maisie was saying, 'It's a question that's bound to arise, isn't it? Of course I think Egbert Delaney is thoroughly evil. I'm on your side in this, Fleur, and I don't think you need, really, explain why you give so much attention to that disgusting woman.'

'I need not even explain why I give so much attention to you,' I said. 'I daresay you'll die before me but I don't expect you to leave me anything in your will.'

'Oh, Fleur, that's harsh, that's brutal of you. How can you speak like that? How can you think of me dying! And I'm on your side, on your side, and I only told you for your own – '

A knock at the door. It opened, and to my surprise Leslie's poet, who was so literally called Gray Mauser that he wrote under the pseudonym of Leander, put his timid head round the door. Gray had only been to see me once before. I said, 'Oh, Gray, I'm so glad to see you. Come in!'

He looked very much encouraged by my welcome. In came the self-evident and luminous little mess. He was small, slight and wispy, about twenty, with arms and legs not quite uncoordinated enough to qualify him for any sort of medical treatment, and yet definitely he was not put together right. I couldn't have been happier to see him.

'I only just wondered if perhaps by chance Leslie was here,' said Gray.

'Oh, I daresay he'll be along in a moment,' I said. I introduced him

to Maisie and quickly said she would no doubt be grateful if Gray
nipped out to get her a taxi.

He lolloped off to do so immediately, glad to be of help. I followed
with Maisie, helping her with her stick and the straps of her handbag
twined round her fingers. She was probably upset but I didn't care to
verify it one way or another. I got her into the taxi at the door and went
back in, shivering with the cold, followed by Leslie's poet.

That evening we went off to a pub known for its literary clients
where we drank light ale and ate Cornish pasties; in mine, I counted
two small diced cubes of steak, Gray found but one among the small
bits of potato nestling inside the tough envelope of pastry. And this I
find most curious: looking back on it, the idea of that Cornish pasty,
day old as it was, is to me revolting but at the time it was delicious; and
so I ask, what did I see in that lard-laden Cornish pasty? – in much the
same way as I might wonder, now, whatever was the attraction of a
man like Leslie?

I sat with Gray at a lone table of the pub. There were one or two
well-known poets at the bar at whom we glanced from our respectful
distance, for they were far beyond our sphere. I think the poets at the
bar on that occasion were Dylan Thomas and Roy Campbell, or it
could have been Louis MacNeice and someone else; it made no
difference for the point was we felt that the atmosphere was as good as
the Cornish pasties and beer, and we could talk. Gray told me about
his many troubles. Leslie had gone to Ireland with Dottie three days
ago, had promised to be back last night but hadn't turned up. He had
left Gray a consolation present of a grey silk tie with blue spots which
Gray was wearing and which he seemed both proud of and saddened
by. I had very little to say to Gray Mauser but I remember that sitting
with him in the pub that night took the edge off my rage against
Maisie Young. I cheered him up by saying that I didn't really think
Leslie was a lady's man. We decided that men were generally more
sentimental than women, but women generally more dependable.
Then he took some sheets of crumpled paper out of his pocket and
read me a poem about the sickle moon, which he explained was a
sexual symbol.

I had never thought highly of Gray, there was so little to think
anything of. But just that evening, after we parted and I was on my
way home in the Tube, I thought how sane he was compared with

Maisie and the Autobiographical Association in general. When I got out at High Street Kensington it was raining and cold, and I went on my way rejoicing.

So that, a few days later when I had to sit in his club listening to Eric Findlay's complaints, I was somewhat prepared; I was able to control my panic.

SIX

When Dottie came back from Ireland the following weekend, a week later than expected, Leslie again deserted her for Gray. 'I wouldn't mind so much,' Dottie said, when she came to see me, 'but to be abandoned in favour of that little rat is more than I can stand. If he was at least an attractive boy, or bright, intelligent ... But he's so pathetic, that Gray Mauser!'

I pointed out to Dottie that Leslie had by no means moved from herself to Gray. 'It was I whom he left,' I said.

'I didn't mind sharing with you,' Dottie said. I thought this odd. I laughed. Dottie, in turn, thought it odd that I should find the situation amusing.

'Of course,' said the English Rose, 'you're hard and I'm soft. Leslie brings me his work to type, and like a fool I do it. He's writing a novel.' She had taken out her knitting.

I enquired eagerly about the novel. She said she couldn't tell me anything except the title, *Two Ways*. I speculated to myself merrily about the variety of themes the title might fit. 'Leslie will no doubt let you see it, himself, when it's finished,' Dottie said. 'It's very good, very deep.'

'Is it autobiographical?' I enquired.

'Oh, yes, basically,' Dottie said with some pride, as if this was a prime requisite of a good, deep novel. 'Of course he's changed the names. But it's a very frank novel, which is all that matters in the world of to-day. Sir Quentin, for instance, always insists on complete frankness.'

I didn't want to upset Dottie or I would have have laid down my conviction that complete frankness is not a quality that favours art. Then she said, sadly, that no one was ever completely frank, it was an illusion. I said I agreed, and this made her uneasy.

But in any case I was weary of the sound of Sir Quentin's name and all the twanging of harps around his throne.

I told her about my visit from Maisie. I told her about my lunch with Eric Findlay. I realized after a while that Dottie was unusually silent. None the less I went on. I added the detail (which was true) that, while sitting on the low sofa at Eric Findlay's club, side by side with him, he had crossed his legs in such a way that the sole of his shoe was almost in my face; I said that it was unconsciously at least a desire to insult. I told Dottie that I thought Newman's *Apologia* was the wrong book to have introduced into the group, treating as it did of a special case, Newman's self-defence against Charles Kingsley's accusations of insincerity; I said the autobiographies were taking on a paranoiac turn as a consequence of following the *Apologia*. I said a far better model would be the *Life* of Cellini, robust and full-blooded as it was. A touch of normality, I said. Dottie knitted on.

She knitted on. It was a red wool scarf; she frequently came to the end of the row, turning her knitting again and again. I told her that Sir Quentin was conforming more and more to the character of my Warrender Chase; it was amazing, I could have invented him, I could have invented all of them – the lot. I said Edwina was the only real person out of the whole collection. Dottie stopped her knitting for a moment at this and looked at me. She said nothing, then she went on knitting.

And I went on talking without once inviting a response. Her silence didn't seem immediately to matter; indeed I felt that I was making a strong impression. I told her that the whole Autobiographical set were in my opinion becoming unhinged to the satisfaction of Sir Quentin, and I concluded by recounting something that Father Egbert Delaney had muttered to me at a meeting, it was a deprecatory phrase about 'Mrs Wilks' tits'; this, I informed Dottie, was an offence to me, even more than to Mrs Wilks. Vulgarity, I explained, I could take from Solly Mendelsohn or, if he had been alive to-day, the sixteenth century Benvenuto Cellini, because these were big sane men, but I wasn't going to let that Creeping Jesus of a *défroqué* get thrills out of insulting my ear.

'It's getting late,' Dottie said. She put away her knitting in that awful black bag, said good-night, and left.

When she was gone, struck by her silence, I gave it a new interpretation. I gave her time to get home and phoned her.

'Was there anything the matter, Dottie?'

'Look,' she said, 'I think you're unhinged. You're suffering from delusions. There's nothing the matter with us. We're a perfectly normal group. I think there's something the matter with you. Beryl Tims – well, I'll let her speak for herself. Your *Warrender Chase* is a thoroughly sick novel. Theo and Audrey Clairmont think it's sick, it worried them terribly, correcting the proofs. Leslie says it's mad.'

I pulled myself together sufficiently to think of a retort suitable to the occasion, since it was the attack on my *Warrender Chase* that really annoyed me; I didn't care about the rest.

'If you have any influence with Leslie in the matter of his novel,' I drawled in the calmness of my suppressed hysteria, 'you might get him to eliminate that dreadful recurrent phrase of his, "With regard to ... ". He uses it all the time in his reviews.'

I could hear Dottie crying. I meant to tell her more about Leslie's prose, its frightful tautology. He never reached the point until it was undetectably lost in a web of multisyllabic words and images trowelled on like cement.

She said, 'You didn't say this when you were sleeping with him.'

'I didn't sleep with him for his prose-style.'

'I think,' said Dottie, 'you're out of your element in our world.'

So ended one of my million, as it seemed, rows with Dottie.

'Oh, Fleur!' said Lady Bernice 'Bucks' Gilbert in her hoarse drawl, 'Would you mind handing round the sandwiches? You could also help with the coats; my little maid has only one pair of hands. See if anyone needs a drink ... ' She had pressed me to come to her cocktail party, and here I was in her flat in Curzon Street in my blue velvet dress among a crowd of chatterers. I now saw why she had pressed the invitation so hard. Half-heartedly I lifted the plate of cheese biscuits and put it under the nose of a solid-looking young man standing by me.

He took a biscuit and said, 'Fleur, it's you.'

It was Wally McConnachie, an old friend of mine from war-time who worked in the Foreign Office. Wally had been in Canada. We lolled against the wallpaper and talked while Bucks glared at me in a somewhat ugly way. When she had glared enough and I had got back my smile with Wally's talk and a drink, I roped in Wally to take people's coats at the door and to help me in pushing the sandwiches, which were filled with black-market delicacies and of which Wally and I ate our share. This infuriated Bucks the more.

'I'm sure,' she said, as she passed me by, 'that Sir Quentin would want you to help. He hasn't arrived yet.'

I said that Sir Quentin insisted on perfect frankness and to be quite frank I was helping, and the sandwiches were a great success.

Presently Sir Quentin arrived and one by one the members of the Autobiographical Association filtered in amongst the other guests. The room was packed. I saw Dottie talking earnestly to Maisie while looking over at me. Empty glasses stood all over the grand piano on which was a large photograph of Bucks's late and hyper-bemedalled husband. My hostess caught my arm and silently pointed to the glasses.

Wally and I collected them, dumped them in the kitchen and made our get-away. We dined at Prunier's with its tranquillizing aquarium-decor, while we described the lives we had been leading since last we had met. The fish swam and darted in their element, while we talked and looked into each other's eyes a lot over our wine. We went on to Quaglino's whose decor then was picture frames without any pictures on the dark walls, and we danced till four in the morning.

Wally told me numerous amusing stories in the course of the evening. They were very weightless stories but for that very reason I felt restored. For instance he told me about a girl he had met who had an uncanny habit of sneezing if she drank inferior wine, and as a consequence of this talent got a job with a wine-merchandising firm as a taster. He told me about another girl whose mother, to overcome her daughter's strong objections to marrying some man on the grounds that he had chronic bad breath, said, 'Well, you can't have *everything*.' Such blithe anecdotes put me in a frame of mind to see myself once more in a carefree light. I told a number of funny stories to Wally about Sir Quentin's set at Hallam Street, and I gave him an outline of what my life was like on the grubby edge of the literary world. Wally, who was racking his brains as to where he had heard of old Quentin Oliver 'somewhere or other', and was extremely entertained by my stories, at the same time advised me strongly to get another job. 'I should get out of all that if I were you, Fleur. You'd be happier.'

I said, yes, possibly. In fact, it came to me during that evening of high spirits that I preferred to stay in the job; I preferred to be interested as I was than happy as I might be. I wasn't sure that I so much wanted to be happy, but I knew I had to follow my nature. However, I didn't say this to Wally. It wouldn't have done.

I promised Wally that he should meet the fabulous Edwina.

I stayed in bed next morning; about eleven o'clock, when I woke, I telephoned to Hallam Street to say I wasn't coming in.

Beryl Tims answered the phone.

'Have you got a medical certificate?' she said.

'Go to hell.'

'Pardon?'

'I'm not ill,' I said. 'I was out dancing all night, that's all.'

'Hold on while I get Sir Quentin.'

'I can't,' I said. 'There's somebody at my door.'

This was true; I hung up and went to find at the door the red-faced house-boy with a bunch of amber-coloured roses and behind him the daily cleaner, whose unwanted services were thrown in with the rent, in her pink dress and white apron. It was a colourful ensemble. I stared at them for a moment, then I sent the maid away while the house-boy told me that I'd had a visitor the night before – 'That awful nice lady that's married to your gentleman friend. I let her in here to wait, and she waited the best part of an hour. 'Twas after ten she left.' I gathered this was Dottie.

I got rid of the boy and counted the roses, which were from Wally. Fourteen. This pleased me. I always liked getting roses, but the usual dozen seemed always so shop-ordered. Fourteen had been really thought of.

In the late afternoon, at about six, when I was thinking of getting up and doing a bit of my new novel, the Baronne Clotilde du Loiret rang me up. 'Sir Quentin,' she said, 'is worried about you, Fleur. Are you indisposed? Sir Quentin thought there might be something I could do. If you have any problem, you know, Sir Quentin insists on complete frankness.'

'I'm taking a day off. How good of Sir Quentin to be so concerned.'

'But just at this moment, Fleur, as I say, the affairs of the Association are falling to bits, aren't they? I mean, Bucks Gilbert is a bit much, isn't she? Of course, she hasn't a penny. I mean, we all had a very frank discussion this afternoon. I've just left them. Then Quentin introduced a sort of prayer-meeting, my dear, it was most embarrassing. What could one do? I quite see that I for one have a private life and when I say private life I'm sure you know what I mean. But I do object to being prayed over. Do you know, I'm terrified of Quentin. He knows too much. And Maisie Young – '

'Why don't you give it up?' I said.

'What? Our Autobiographical Association? Well, I can't explain, but I do believe in Quentin. I'm sure you do too, Fleur.'

'Oh, yes. I almost feel I invented him.'

'Fleur, do you think there's something, I mean something special, between him and Beryl Tims? I mean, they're very thick with each other. And you know, this afternoon at the prayer part, that awful Mummy of Quentin's came in and started making that sort of insinuation. Of course she's ga-ga, but one wonders. She says she's fond of you, Fleur, and I think Quentin is rather worried about that too. And I mean, is it true you've written a novel about us, Fleur?'

I have the impression that I was tuning into voices without really hearing them as one does when moving from programme to programme on a wireless set. I know there was a lot of activity at Hallam Street. Eric Findlay and Dottie ganged up against Mrs Wilks, arriving at Hallam Street together one morning when Sir Quentin was out at the local Food office trying vainly to get extra tea and sugar rations on behalf of the Association. I remember plainly on that occasion Dottie asking me irrelevantly if I had heard from my publishers. I said I had received a printed acknowledgment of the proofs and now I was waiting for publication. Dottie said, 'Oh!'

Another day came Mrs Wilks in her pastel hues, and her veils, and a wet purple umbrella which she refused to give up to Beryl Tims. She had lost her fat, merry look. I had noticed the last time I saw her that she was losing weight, but now it was quite obvious she had either been very ill or was on a diet. Her painted-up face was shrivelled, making her nose too long; her eyes were big and inexactly focused. She demanded that I change her name in the records from Mrs Wilks to Miss Davids, explaining that she had to be *incognito* from now on since the Trotskyites were posting agents all over the world to find and assassinate her. I remember that Sir Quentin came in while she was raving thus, and sent me out on an errand. When I came back Mrs Wilks was gone and Sir Quentin was leaning back in his chair, eyes half-closed, with that one shoulder of his slightly in advance of the other and his hands clasped before him as if in prayer. I was about to ask what had been the matter with Mrs Wilks when he said, 'Mrs Wilks has been fasting too strictly.' Whereupon he turned to something else. He was very much on the defensive about his little flock. One day, about this time, I made some scornful remark to Sir Quentin about Father Egbert Delaney who had been remonstrating with me on the telephone about Edwina's presence at the meetings. Sir

Quentin replied loftily, 'One of his ancestors fought in the battle of Bosworth Field.'

My job at Sir Quentin's, now that he had taken the actual autobiographies out of my hands, was taken up largely with Sir Quentin's other, quite normal, private and business affairs. He seemed to dictate unnecessary letters to old friends, some of which I suspect he never sent, since he would often put them aside to sign and post himself. I felt sure he now wanted to establish the idea of his normality in my mind. He apparently had business interests in South Africa, for he wrote about them. His villa at Grasse was greatly on his mind, it having been occupied by the Germans during the war; he was anxious only to find out by which Germans. 'Members of the High Command and the Old Guard I have no doubt.' He had an interest in a paint manufacturers who were compiling a history of the firm, *One Hundred Prosperous Years*; I helped with the dreary proofs. I doubted if he needed me at all, except that I was useful in coping with the members when they took to dropping in or telephoning as they now did more and more phrenetically.

It was about this time that he said to me, 'What have you got against the *Apologia*?'

I forget how I answered him precisely. I wasn't at any event about to be drawn into a discussion of that exquisite work or any other with Sir Quentin. All I wanted to know was what he was up to. And besides, I had been thinking about autobiographies in general. From the personal reminiscences of the members I had perceived that anecdotes and memoirs are only valuable if they are extremely unusual in themselves, or if they attach to an interesting end-product. The boyhood experiences of Newman or of Michelangelo would be interesting however trivial, but who cared – who should care – about Eric Findlay's memories of his butler and nanny, he being what Sir Eric Findlay was? It was precisely because I'd found all their biographies so very dull to start with that I'd given them so light-hearted a turn, almost as if the events they described had happened to me, not to them. At least I did them the honour of treating their output as life-stories not as case-histories for psychoanalysis, as they more or less were; I had set them on to writing fictions about themselves.

Now these autobiographies were out of my hands; but I didn't care; they were dreary, one and all.

I was sure that nothing had happened in their lives and equally sure that Sir Quentin was pumping something artificial into their real lives instead of on paper. Presented fictionally, one could have done something authentic with that poor material. But the inducing them to express themselves in life resulted in falsity.

What is truth? I could have realized these people with my fun and games with their life-stories, while Sir Quentin was destroying them with his needling after frankness. When people say that nothing happens in their lives I believe them. But you must understand that everything happens to an artist; time is always redeemed, nothing is lost and wonders never cease.

It wasn't until later that I found he was handing out to all of them, including Dottie, small yellow pills called Dexedrine which he told them would enable them to endure the purifying fasts he inflicted. The pills were no part of my *Warrender Chase*; Sir Quentin thought of them himself, doubting his power to enthral unaided.

Now, on that same day as he asked me this question about the *Apologia* Sir Quentin switched over to the problem of his mother. 'Mummy,' he said, 'is a problem.'

I busied myself placing a sheet of carbon paper between a sheet of writing paper and one of copy paper.

'Mummy,' he said, 'has always been a problem. And I want to tell you, Miss Talbot, that you would do well to ignore any promises Mummy might have effected in your regard as to an eventual legacy. She is probably senile. Mrs Tims and I –'

'The noun "promise" is not generally followed by the verb "effected",' I put in wildly, trying to keep calm. I had seen while he was speaking that he pressed the bell for Mrs Tims. As the door-bell rang at that moment she didn't immediately appear, but Sir Quentin smiled at my little divergence and went on, 'I know you have been very good to Mummy, taking her out on Sundays and I'm sure that if you have been out of pocket we can find ways and means of reimbursement. There is no question but that if you care to continue some little arrangement can be made. It is only that, for the future – '

'For the future I'm well provided for, thank you,' I slammed in. 'And for the past, present and future, I don't take payment for friendship.'

'You have matrimonial prospects?' he said.

I went berserk. I said, 'I have written a novel that's going to be a success. It's to be published in June.' I don't know why I said this, except that I was beside myself with rage. In reality I had no hopes of success of any kind for my *Warrender Chase*. The new novel I was working on – my second, my *All Souls' Day* – occupied my best brains now, my sweetest hopes. I thought that *Warrender Chase* might do respectably well as an introduction to my second book. I didn't know then, as I know now, that it's always the book I am working on that takes precedence in my esteem.

However, I was in no mood for the delicacies of my own opinions at that moment when out I spat the words, 'I have written a novel ... '

'Now my dear Miss Talbot, let us be perfectly frank. Don't you think you've had delusions of grandeur?'

I perceived four things simultaneously: Beryl Tims came hammering with her heels, and, opening the door, simpered that Lady Bernice was waiting; Sir Quentin opened the deep right-hand drawer of his desk with a smile; and, still at the same time, I was rehearing his words, 'Don't you think you've had delusions of grandeur?' which all in a mental moment I noticed was a use of the past tense – why didn't he say, 'You're having delusions ... '? – and finally as the fourth element in this total set of impressions I recognized that his words 'Don't you think you've had delusions of grandeur?' were the very words of my Warrender Chase; in his letter to my fictional English Rose, Charlotte, when he advises her how to question Marjorie, he actually writes, 'Put it to her like this: "Don't you think you've had delusions of grandeur?" And then when my ancient Prudence is trying to recall to my scholar Proudie what happened about the Greek girl at the prayer meeting who later committed suicide, I make my Prudence say, 'Oh, Warrender was aware she was in a very bad way. Only a few days before he had said to her, "Don't you think you've had delusions of grandeur?"'

I noticed these four things together, still fuming as I was. I think my fury put me in a state of heightened perception, for standing up to go I caught a glimpse into the drawer Sir Quentin had opened. In a flash he had shut it again. Now, in the drawer I had seen a bundle of galley proofs, and by the light of reason I should have assumed they were those from the Settlebury Paint Company, founded 1850, their

Centenary book. I only had a distant and quick glimpse of the folded proofs in the drawer. I wasn't near enough to identify the typeface or the spacing or any of the words. Why then did it go through me that those were the proofs of my *Warrender Chase*? The thought went through me but I let it go, remembering about the paint people. Sir Quentin's two sets of proofs were about equal to one set of my novel.

It all happened very quickly. I stood, furious with Sir Quentin, ready to walk out. Beryl Tims hovered for instructions and Sir Quentin, when he had shut the drawer, said, 'Sit down, Mrs Tims. Miss Talbot, be seated a moment.' I refused to be seated. I said, 'I'm leaving.' I noticed that Beryl Tims was wearing the brooch I had given her; she fingered it and said, 'Shall I tell Lady Bernice – '

'Mrs Tims,' said Sir Quentin, 'let me inform you that you are in the presence of an authoress.'

'Pardon?'

'An authoress of a best-selling novel.'

'Lady Bernice seems to be very upset. She must see you, Sir Quentin. I said – '

By this time I had gathered my things and had left the room. Out bounded Sir Quentin after me. 'My dear Miss Talbot, you mustn't, you simply mustn't leave. I spoke for the best. Mummy would be devastated. Mrs Tims – I ask you – Miss Talbot has taken offence.'

I said good-night and went off, too enraged to say more. But as I left I saw Lady Bernice standing in the doorway of the drawing-room with a really distraught look on her face, not at all her dominant self; she was dressed-up as usual but the glimpse I got as I passed her by impressed on me the picture of fashionable clothes all awry and make-up daubed and smeared about her eyes. It was the last time I ever saw her. I heard Sir Quentin say, 'Why, Bucks, whatever . . . ' just as I left, and I was far too wrapped up in my own grievances to dwell on that last look which imprinted itself on my mind so that I can see it now.

I was anxious to get home and was still amazed at my stupidity in making that large prophecy for my *Warrender Chase*, and I wondered where the words had come from, ' . . . a novel that's going to be a success'. I had placed myself at the man's mercy by saying this; not that I regarded success as a disgrace, but that I wasn't thinking of *Warrender Chase* in that light just then, and also, I had known for a long time that success could not be my profession in life, nor failure a

calling for that matter. These were by-products. Why, then, I was
asking myself all the way home, had I fallen into Sir Quentin's trap?
For that was how I saw it. He had been able, then, to bring out those
very words of Warrender Chase, 'Don't you think you've had
delusions of grandeur?'

I had put away my copy of *Warrender Chase*. It was my manuscript
copy, written on foolscap pages, from which I had typed the copy that
went to the publishers. I hadn't taken a carbon copy of the typescript,
not seeing any point in wasting paper. But I had made a parcel of my
manuscript, marked it on the outside, 'Warrender Chase by Fleur
Talbot' and put it on the floor of my clothes cupboard.

When I got home, to make sure I wasn't mistaken about Sir
Quentin's use of Warrender's actual words, I decided to get the book
out and look up the two passages. I was in a flutter, feeling partly that I
had in fact some delusions of grandeur or of persecution or some
other sympton of paranoia. I couldn't have felt more paranoiac when
I discovered that my copy of *Warrender Chase* was not in the
cupboard where it should have been. The package, about the dimen-
sions of a London telephone directory, was not there.

I started to search my room. I began by absurdly turning things
over, the new pages of my current work *All Souls' Day* included. No
sign of *Warrender Chase*. I sat down and thought. Nothing came of
my frantic thinking. I got up and started to tidy the room very
carefully, very meticulously, shifting every piece of furniture, every
book. I did it all rather slowly, moving everything first into the middle
of the room, then moving everything back, piece by piece, book by
book; pencils, typewriter, food stores, everything. This activity was
pure superstition for it was obvious at a few glances that the package
was not in the room, but so minute was my search I might have been
looking for a lost diamond. I found many lost things, old letters, half-
a-crown, old poems and stories but no *Warrender Chase*. I opened
every other package that I had pushed into an old suitcase: nothing.

I poured some whisky into a tumbler, in a very careful and stunned
manner, added some water from the tap, and sat sipping it. The
cleaning woman must have thrown it out. But how? It had been left in
the cupboard. She had worked in the place for years, she never
opened people's cupboards or drawers, never took anything. Besides,
I had always asked her to be careful about my papers and packages

and she always had been careful, not even dusting the table my work was lying on lest she should disarrange it. She grumbled so much about the mess in my room, she hardly flicked a duster anywhere. I started going over in my mind who had been in my room since last I had seen *Warrender Chase* in the cupboard. Wallly had been briefly but only to pick me up to go out somewhere one evening. I thought, could the Alexanders have come rummaging? That was absurd. Leslie? Dottie? I passed them all over, forgetting completely for the moment that Dottie had in fact been in my room during my absence that first evening I went dancing at Quaglino's with Wally. But I didn't think of this till later. At the time I sat and wondered if I were going mad, if *Warrender Chase* existed or had I imagined the book.

I took up the phone to ring Wally. The switchboard was off; I saw it was already nearly midnight.

But the very act of thinking about Wally put me to rights; it didn't matter so very much after all what had happened to my manuscript. The typescript and the proofs were safely with the publishers. I could get back my typescript from Revisson Doe.

I went to bed, and to take my mind off my troubles I started to flick the pages of my beloved Cellini. The charm worked, as I read the snatches of his adventures of art and of Renaissance virility, his love for the goblets and the statues he made out of materials he adored, his imprisonments, his escapes, his dealings with his fellow goldsmiths and sculptors, his homicides and brawls, and again his delight in every aspect of his craft. Every page I turned was, to me, as it still is, sheer magic:

> ...Sure, therefore, that I could trust them, I gave my attention to the furnace, which I had filled up with pigs of copper and pieces of bronze, laid one on top of the other, according to the rules of the craft – that is, not pressing closely one on the other, but arranged so that the flames could make their way freely about them; for in this manner the metal is more quickly affected by the heat and liquefied. Then in great excitement I ordered them to light the furnace. They piled on the pine logs; and between the unctuous pine resin and the well-contrived draught of the furnace, the fire burned so splendidly that I had to feed it now on one side and now on the other. The effort was almost intolerable, yet I forced myself to keep it up.

On top of all this the shop took fire, and we feared lest the roof should fall upon us. Then, too ...

I flicked over the pages, back and forth, reflecting how Cellini had enjoyed a long love affair with his art, how Cellini was comically contradictory in his actions, how boastful he was about his work.

... When I reached Piacenza, I met Duke Pier Luigi in the street, who stared me up and down, and recognized me. He had been the sole cause of all the wrong I had suffered in the castle of St Angelo; and now I fumed at the sight of him. But not knowing any way of avoiding him, I made up my mind to go and pay him a visit. I arrived at the palace just as the table was being cleared. With him were some men of the house of Landi, those who were afterwards his murderers. When I came in, he received me with the utmost effusiveness; and among other pleasant things which fell from his lips was his declaration to those who were present that I was the greatest man in all the world in my profession ...

And so, forgetting my troubles, I flicked back to the opening page, the opening paragraph of this magnificent autobiography:

All men, whatever be their condition, who have done anything of merit, or which verily has a semblance of merit, if so be they are men of truth and good repute, should write the tale of their life with their own hand.

One day, I thought, I'll write the tale of my life. But first I have to live.

... In truth it seems to me I have greater content of mind and health of body than at any time in the past. Some pleasant happenings I recall, and, again, some unspeakable misfortunes which, when I remember, strike terror into me and wonder that I have, indeed, come to this age of fifty-eight, from which, by God's grace, I am now going on my way rejoicing.

The other day, while I was working on this account of that small part of my life and all that happened in the middle of the twentieth

century, those months of 1949–50, I read this last-quoted passage and
went back in my thoughts to the spring of 1950 when I lay reading it in
bed in my room in Kensington. I was reflecting that one could take
endless enchanting poems out of this book simply by flicking over the
pages, back and forth, and extracting for oneself a page here, a
paragraph there, and while I was playing with this idea it came to me
with all apparent irrelevance that Dottie, who knew very well how my
possessions were disposed in my room, had certainly taken my
package that night the house-boy had let her in to wait for me.

It was after two in the morning. I jumped out of bed and put on my
clothes. While dressing I remembered those proofs in Sir Quentin's
desk and my curious passing notion that they were mine. Out I
plunged into the cold night and trudged round to Dottie's. I don't
know if it was raining, I noticed rain very little in those days. But I
was cold, standing under her window singing 'Auld Lang Syne'. I
was afraid of waking the neighbourhood but I was fairly enraged; I
sang in as low a voice as I felt would penetrate Dottie's bedroom
window, but persistently. A light went on in someone else's window,
the sash went up and a head looked out. 'Stop your bloody row at this
time of night.' I moved out of the light of the street-lamp and as I did
so I saw the curtain in Dottie's room pulled aside. By the street-light
I saw a head, not Dottie's, peering through the pane. It became
apparent as I kept watch from the pavement that it was a man's head.
I assumed it was Leslie. Dottie's outraged neighbour had withdrawn
and slammed down the sash, and as the light went out in his window
I saw more clearly, but only for a brief flash, that the head in Dottie's
room was not Leslie's; it was a square face with a hairless head, and
elderly; it seemed to me to be the face of Revisson Doe, my
publisher.

I made quickly for home, convincing myself I had been mistaken.
It is true I had *Warrender Chase* on my mind; it was altogether
possible, considering the loss of my manuscript, that I had it on my
brain.

Now Dottie, English Rose as she was, had always demonstrated
herself to be a very pious, old-fashioned Catholic. I was convinced
she had taken my *Warrender Chase*, but I still wasn't sure if she had
done it as a half-joke or in one of her fits of righteousness; she was
perfectly capable of burning a book she considered evil but I felt she

would hardly go so far with my foolscap sheets. All my experience of
Dottie was that she was basically harmless and, so far as she herself
was conscious of sincerity, sincere. I wondered, too, if she had taken
the novel to show to someone – some Carmelite divine to ask his no
doubt adverse opinion of it, or Leslie, to curry favour with him by
showing him the last part which he had never seen. I wondered
everything. What I wondered most after I got home was who could be
spending the night with Dottie. It wasn't her father, for I had met
him. I thought perhaps it could be an elderly uncle. But back I came
always to that glimpse I had got of the square face and bald head of
Revisson Doe.

But it seemed impossible both that Dottie had a lover and that
Revisson Doe could, at his age, be one.

I sat up all that night bothering myself over these two apparent
impossibilities. On the part of Dottie I saw lying on the table the
evidence of a little folded card she had once left me, and which had
turned up in the course of my search for my package. It was typical of
Dottie. She had paid two shillings and sixpence to enrol me in
something with this card. 'Guild of Our Lady of Ransom' it was
headed, going on to explain 'for the Conversion of England. Jesus
convert England. Under the Heavenly Patronage of *Our Lady, St
Gregory and the Blessed English Martyrs.*' I sat and looked at this,
drinking in Dottie's piety. 'Motto,' it announced on the inside; 'For
God, Our Lady, and the Catholic Faith.' This was followed by
'Obligations. 1. To say the Daily Prayer for the Intentions of the
Guild. 2. To work for the objects of the Guild. 3. To subscribe at least
Two Shillings and Sixpence a year to the Ransom Fund. Fleur
Talbot (in Dottie's handwriting) is hereby enrolled a Red Cross
Ransomer. Partial Indulgences. 1. *Seven Years and Seven Quaran-
tines.* 2. *One Hundred Days.*'

And so it went on, with its bureaucratic Indulgences, its Souls in
Purgatory and all the rest of Dottie's usual claptrap.

I too was a Catholic believer but not that sort, not that sort at all.
And if it was true, as Dottie always said, that I was taking terrible risks
with my immortal soul, I would have been incapable of caution on
those grounds. I had an art to practise and a life to live, and faith
abounding; and I simply didn't have the time or the mentality for
guilds and indulgences, fasts and feasts and observances. I've never

held it right to create more difficulties in matters of religion than already exist.

I say this, because it struck me as strange that a man's head which was not Leslie's should appear at Dottie's bedroom window at two-thirty in the night. Again, as I pondered, I caught in my mind's eye the head of Revisson Doe. I had only seen him a few times. Could it be possible? I began to feel I had perhaps misjudged his age. I had thought him about sixty. In fact, I was sure he was about sixty. The impossible, as I thought on and on, became possible. I hadn't got an impression of a sexually active man, but then I hadn't really looked at him from that point of view. The possibility existed, except, of course, that Dottie would die rather than be unfaithful to a living husband; she would consider it a mortal sin, she would sink straight to hell if she were run over in the street unabsolved. I knew Dottie's way of thinking. It was impossible. And yet, as the birds of Kensington began to chirp in the early spring dawn outside my window, Dottie's infidelity piped up its entire possibility.

I thought it possible she had made a point of meeting Revisson Doe with a view to getting Leslie's novel published. It was possible she was immolating herself on the altar of Leslie's book. She was a pretty woman and it was possible that Revisson Doe, sixty or seventy as he might be, should go to bed with her. It was all unlikely but it was all quite possible. I concluded my due process of induction with the thought that it was not very unlikely, and really quite probable; and I was left with the fact I still didn't know for certain if Dottie had taken my *Warrender Chase*, and, if so, why. It was five in the morning. I set my alarm for eight and went to bed.

EIGHT

I got a letter by the first post in a Park and Revisson Doe Co. Ltd envelope, which I opened bleary-eyed.

> Dear Fleur (if I may),
>
> A small problem has cropped up with regard to your novel *Warrender Chase*.
>
> I think we should talk this over face to face before proceeding further, as the details are too complicated to explain by letter.
>
> Please ring me at your earliest opportunity to make an appointment for us to meet, to think out this delicate matter.
>
> Always,
>
> Revisson

This letter appalled me. It is typical of a state of anxiety that it seems to attract ever more disaster. It was a quarter to nine. Park and Revisson Doe didn't start business till ten. I decided to ring at half-past ten. I read the letter over and over again, each time with greater foreboding. What was wrong with my *Warrender Chase*? I took the letter sentence by sentence; each one looked worse than the other. After half an hour I decided I had to talk to somebody. I had no intention of returning to the Hallam Street carnival. Even before the letter arrived I had made up my mind only to wander in later in the day, collect some things that I had left behind, say good-bye to Edwina and look for another job.

I made an appointment with Revisson Doe for three-thirty that day. I tried to pump him on the phone, whether there was 'something wrong' with my *Warrender Chase* but he wouldn't be drawn into any discussion. He sounded edgy, rather unfriendly. He addressed me as Miss Talbot, forgetting about Fleur if he might. I didn't know then, as I know now, that the traditional paranoia of authors is as nothing compared to the inalienable schizophrenia of publishers.

Revisson Doe on the phone was plainly nervous about something, I supposed about the loss of money my book was likely to incur, I supposed he wanted to revise the terms of the contract, I supposed he might want me to change something vital in the novel and I decided throughout all this supposing that I would refuse to make any changes in the book. I wondered, then, if Theo and Audrey had expressed their adverse opinions on the book to my publisher when they had sent back the proofs. I had written a note to thank them for the proof-reading and had been inclined not to believe Dottie when she had reported with such ferocity what Theo and Audrey, always so good to me, had said. But that morning, sleepless, and with a terrible yesterday behind me, I was fairly at my wits' end. I rang up the Clairmont house; their maid answered and I asked for either Theo or Audrey. The maid came back to say they were both busy in their studios.

I went back to bed and by the afternoon felt ready for my interview with Revisson Doe. I was so far refreshed that I was able to rather look forward to the meeting, anxious to have another look at him from the point of view of his possibly being Dottie's or anyone else's bed-fellow. I just had time on the way to stop at Kensington Public Library to look up his age in *Who's Who*. Born 1884. He had been married twice, one son, two daughters. I got on the bus calculating that he was sixty-six. It seemed older to me in those days than it does now. When I saw Revisson Doe there in his office, I was sure that his was the head I had seen at Dottie's window. I took the chair he waved me into, wondering if Dottie had told the old goat that it was probably I who had been singing 'Auld Lang Syne' at two in the morning. At the same time I thought, whatever Dottie saw in him it was not sex-appeal.

'Now,' he said, 'I want you to know that we value your work highly.' I noticed the 'we' and felt uneasy. At the time when he had been considering *Warrender Chase* he had dithered between 'I' and 'we' quite a lot. To express his enthusiasm and keenness for the book as a new young piece of writing he had used 'I' both in his letters and conversations; to signify the risk of a loss on the deal he had always put it down to 'we'. Now we were back at 'we' again.

'We understand you're working on a new novel?'

I said yes, it was to be entitled *All Souls' Day*.

He said it didn't sound a very selling title. 'Of course,' he said, 'we can change the title.'

I said that was to be the title.

'Oh, well, we have an option on it. We can discuss the title later. We were debating whether it wouldn't perhaps be preferable to leave *Warrender Chase* aside for the time being. You see, a first novel is after all a pure experiment, isn't it? Whereas we were going to suggest if you would let us see the opening chapters of the second novel, your *All Fools' Day* – '

'*All Souls' Day*,' I said.

'*All Souls' Day*, yes, oh, quite.' He seemed to be amused at this, and I took advantage of his little laugh to ask him what was wrong with *Warrender Chase*.

'We can't publish it,' he said.

'Why not?'

'Fortunately for us we've discovered in time that it bears the fault of most first novels, alas, it is too close to real life. Why, look, you know, these characters of yours are lifted clean from that Autobiographical Association you work for. We have, really we have, looked into the matter and we have a number of testimonies to the likeness. And now your employer, Sir Quentin Oliver, is threatening to sue. He sent to us for a set of the proofs and naturally we gave him a set. You make them out to be sinister, you make them out to be feeble, hypnotized creatures and you make Sir Quentin out to be an evil manipulator and hater of women. He drives one woman to drink and another – '

'My novel was started before I met Sir Quentin Oliver. The man must be mad.'

'He's threatening to sue if we publish. Sir Quentin Oliver is a man of substance. We can't afford to risk a libel suit. The very idea . . . ' He put his hand over his eyes for a moment. Then he said, 'It's out of the question. But we do value your potentialities as a writer very highly, Miss Talbot – Fleur, if I may – and if we could offer you some guidance with your second novel from our fund of experience, it may be possible to switch the contract – '

'I don't need your guidance.'

'You would be the first author I've known who could not, between ourselves, do with a little editorial help. You must remember,' said he, for all the world as if I were incapable of disgust, 'that an author is a publisher's raw material.'

I said I would have to consult my advisers and got up to leave. 'We are very unhappy about this, most unhappy,' he said. I never saw him again.

It wasn't till after I got home that I realized he had my only copy of the typescript of *Warrender Chase*. I didn't want to ask for it back until I had consulted Solly Mendelsohn, lest I should jeopardize the contract; I half hoped that Solly would suggest some way in which they could be induced to change their minds; but at the same time I knew I couldn't deal any more with Park and Revisson Doe. The shock and disappointment had been too sudden for me to plunge into the final reality of taking the physical book away from them. But I did, when I got home, ring up Revisson Doe. I got his secretary. He was engaged, could she help me? I said I would be obliged if she could send me a spare set of proofs as I had mislaid my original manuscript and I wanted to look through my *Warrender Chase*. 'Hold on, please,' she said politely and went off the line, I presumed for further instructions, for some minutes. She came back and said, 'I'm so sorry, but the type has been distributed.'

Ignorant as I was then to printers' jargon I said, 'Distributed to whom?'

'Distributed – broken up. We are not printing the book, Miss Talbot.'

'And what happened to the proofs?'

'Oh, those have been destroyed, naturally.'

'Thank you.'

I was able to get Solly on the phone at his office the next night. He told me to meet him at a pub in Fleet Street, and came down from his office for a quick conference.

'It's not them sue you for libel,' Solly mused, 'it's you sue them for saying your book's libellous. That's if they put it in writing. But it would cost you a fortune. Better get your typescript back and tell them to wipe their arse with the contract. Don't give them your next novel. Don't worry. We'll get another publisher. But get the typescript back. It's yours by rights. By legal rights. You're a bloody fool not to have kept a copy.'

'Well, I had the original manuscript. How could I know that Dottie, or whoever it was, would steal it?'

'I would say,' said Solly, 'that it was Dottie, all right. She's been acting like a fool over your novel. However, it's a good sign when people act like fools over a piece of work, a good sign.'

I couldn't see how it was a good sign. I got home just before ten. I made plans to retrieve my typescript from the publisher the next day and also to make it my business to get back my manuscript from Dottie. The possibility that all copies of my *Warrender Chase* had been destroyed was one I couldn't face clearly that night, but it hung around me nightmarishly – the possibility that nowhere, nowhere in the world, did my *Warrender Chase* exist any more.

Then the telephone rang. It was Lady Edwina's nurse.

'I've been trying to get you all afternoon,' she said. 'Lady Edwina's asking for you. We've had a terrible time all day. Mrs Tims and Sir Quentin were called out early this morning because his poor friend Lady Bernice Gilbert passed away. Then they came back and asked for you. Then they went out again. Lady Edwina's been laughing her head off. Hysterics. She's just dropping off now. I gave her a dose. But she wants to see you as soon – '

'What did Lady Bernice die of?'

'I'm afraid,' said the nurse with a quivering voice, 'she took her own life.'

NINE

There and then the determination took me that, whatever Sir Quentin was up to, for myself, I was not any sort of a victim; I was simply not constituted for the role. The news of Bernice Gilbert's suicide horrified but toughened me.

I went along to Hallam Street next morning. I felt sure, now, that not only was Sir Quentin exerting his influence to suppress my *Warrender Chase* but he was using, stealing, my myth. Without a mythology, a novel is nothing. The true novelist, one who understands the work as a continuous poem, is a myth-maker, and the wonder of the art resides in the endless different ways of telling a story, and the methods are mythological by nature.

I was sure, and it turned out that I was right, that Dottie had obtained for Sir Quentin a set of the proofs of *Warrender Chase* to read. I had been too free with that novel, I should never have made it known to Dottie in the first place. Never since have I shown my work to my friends or read it aloud to them before it has been published. However, it was our general custom at that time to read our work to each other, or send it to be read, and to discuss our work with each other; that was literary life as I then knew it.

At the flat in Hallam Street Mrs Tims was dabbing the corners of her eyes with a white handkerchief. 'Where were you yesterday? Just when we needed you,' she said. 'Sir Quentin was most distressed.'

'Where is he?'

She was startled by my tone. 'He had to go out. The inquest is this afternoon. The poor – '

But I had gone into his study, shutting the door with a firm, sharp click. I went straight to the drawer where I had seen the proofs. The drawer was empty except for a set of keys. The other drawers were locked.

I went next to Edwina's room. She was sitting up in bed with her breakfast tray. The nurse was in Edwina's bathroom which led off from the bedroom, washing something. She put her head round the door.

Edwina was in a rational state, for her. She said, 'Suicide. Just like the woman in your novel.'

'I know.'

I sat on the edge of her bed and telephoned to Park and Revisson Doe to ask them to send me the typescript of my *Warrender Chase*.

'Hold on, please.' The girl was away for some long minutes during which I told Edwina that my book wasn't going to be published.

'Oh yes it is,' said Edwina, 'I shall see to it. My friend – ' The secretary had come back on the phone. 'I'm afraid the copy we had has been destroyed. Mr Doe put it on his desk for you to take, and you didn't take it away. He thought you didn't want it.'

'I didn't see it on his desk. I'm sure it wasn't there.'

'Well, Mr Doe says he had it out for you. He says he threw it out. We haven't room to store manuscripts, Miss Talbot. Mr Doe says we take no responsibility for the manuscripts. It is stated in the contract.'

'Tell Mr Doe I'll see my lawyer.'

'That's right,' said Edwina, when I had hung up, 'tell them you'll see your lawyer.'

'I haven't got a lawyer. And it would be no use.'

'But you've given them something to think about,' Edwina said. She had buttered a piece of crisp toast from her breakfast tray, and handed it to me. I munched it, thinking how I could go about writing *Warrender Chase* all over again. But I knew I couldn't. Something spontaneous had gone for ever if it were true that all the copies were destroyed including the proofs Sir Quentin had got hold of. I didn't tell Edwina that Sir Quentin had been the cause of my losing my publisher; on the whole, the old lady bore very well the fact that she had spawned a rotter; it wouldn't have done to rub it in. I thought of Edwina's courageous facing of facts again, later on, when she sat in her wheel-chair in her pearls and black satin, quiet but fully alive, at Sir Quentin's funeral.

It did me good to sit on Edwina's bed that morning, eating the toast that she continued to butter and jam for me, with those ancient star-spangled banners, her long bejewelled hands, fluttering among the small porcelain dishes.

Beryl Tims came in once 'to see if everything was all right'. The nurse, a kindly soul called Miss Fisher, came out of the bathroom to assure her on this point. Edwina glared at Beryl Tims. I went on munching.

'I think,' said Miss Fisher, 'a fresh pot of tea might be called for and an extra cup.'

'Oh, Fleur can come to the kitchen and have her morning coffee with me.'

'Nurse said tea,' said Edwina. 'We want it brought in here.'

'Fleur has her work to do. We wouldn't want to keep Fleur back from her work, would we?' said the English Rose. 'And you know that Miss Fisher didn't get her afternoon-off yesterday. We're hoping Fleur will hold the fort this afternoon, aren't we? I shall be at the inquest with Sir Quentin this afternoon. So you and Fleur can have your tea together, can't you?'

Not a word of this was addressed to me, but I had a plan in mind which made this opportunity of spending some hours in the flat with no one except Edwina an exciting prospect. When Miss Fisher said, 'Oh, I wouldn't dream of leaving Lady Edwina at a time like this,' I quickly put in that I'd be delighted to make afternoon tea and generally look after Lady Edwina.

'Miss Fisher needs a rest,' said Beryl Tims.

'I quite agree with Mrs Tims,' I said, and probably it was the first and only time I ever said such a thing.

So it was agreed. Miss Fisher with a bowl of washing followed Mrs Tims out of the room. I got on the phone, now, to Solly Mendelsohn.

I didn't like phoning Solly during the day, for he slept most of the morning after his long night-duty. I always supposed, too, that he had some other private life, a woman we never met but who occupied his spare time; it wasn't the sort of thing one would want to find out and there was always something about Solly into which no real friend of his could intrude. But at least I knew he wouldn't have the phone off the hook in case of a call from the news-room at his paper, and in the emergency of the occasion I chanced it. He answered, half-asleep. But when he heard my urgent voice making of him a few brief requests, Solly agreed to do exactly what I asked without further explanations.

*

Solly arrived at a quarter to four at Hallam Street, big, bulky and unshaven, wrapped in scarves. He looked very much like a burglar with his big, brown travelling bag. Edwina was sitting up in her chair in the drawing-room.

Sir Quentin had not returned to the flat; he was to meet Beryl Tims at the Coroner's Inquest on Bernice Gilbert's suicide while of unsound mind. But as soon as Beryl Tims had left I had made a good snoop around Sir Quentin's study. The proofs of *Warrender Chase* were nowhere to be found. But the keys in the unlocked drawer of his desk opened the cabinet wherein, as Sir Quentin always said, 'were secrets'.

One after the other of the drawers contained the files, Sir Quentin's notes of the members of the Autobiographical Association. Mrs Wilks was there, the Baronne Clotilde du Loiret, Miss Maisie Young, Father Egbert Delaney, Sir Eric Findlay and the late Bernice 'Bucks' Gilbert, widow of the former chargé d'affaires in San Salvador, Sir Alfred Gilbert . . . These were the files I was interested in. There was a file marked 'Beryl, Mrs Tims,' which I ignored. I had decided to take these files as hostages for my *Warrender Chase* which I was perfectly sure Sir Quentin had arranged with Dottie to steal from my room.

But as I had waited for Solly's arrival I had also flicked through one of the memoirs, for I was curious to see what had been added under Sir Quentin's management since he had taken them out of my hands. And I had time enough to see, as I turned over one file after another, that, although nothing had been added in the form of memoirs, sheets of notes, some typed, some in Sir Quentin's hand had been inserted, familiar passages; they were lifted more or less directly from my *Warrender Chase*.

I closed the cabinet again with its secrets when Solly rang the door bell. Edwina, dressed in her full regalia, exclaimed her joy to see him. I sat him down beside her, rather bewildered as he was, and I explained to them both: 'I'm going to take away the memoirs of the Autobiographical Association to work on at home. Those biographies do need a literary touch.'

Solly seemed to begin to understand. Edwina uncannily seemed to perceive something that even I did not, for she said, 'What a splendid idea! That will save more of these tragedies. Poor Bucks Gilbert!'

I told Solly, then, that Lady Bernice had committed suicide, and that the inquest was proceeding at that moment. And I took his bag, leaving him with Edwina.

I put the files in Solly's bag. It was an exhilarating affair. I thought how easy it was to steal, and I thought of Sir Quentin stealing my book, not only the physical copies, but the very words, phrases, ideas. Even from the brief look I had taken I could see he had even stolen a letter I had invented, written from my Warrender Chase to my character Marjorie. The bag was heavy. I lugged it into the hall and put it by the front door.

When I got back to the drawing-room, Solly had lit a pretty silver spirit-stove under the kettle which Edwina liked to use for her afternoon tea. It was a bit early for tea-time but Edwina was always 'weary for tea' as she put it. There were some buttered scones, some biscuits, which Solly had already started to help himself to. Edwina said, 'Where are the files? Have you put them in that bag?'

I said I had. I said Sir Quentin would not miss them right away, no doubt, but he would realize I was really in better condition working on them at home.

'Take them away, darling,' shrieked Edwina. Then she came out with, 'You'll never get your novel back if you don't do something about it.'

Solly then said to me, 'Haven't you managed to find a copy?'

'No,' I said, 'the whole book's disappeared.'

'I knew it,' said Edwina. 'Somehow I knew it. They think I don't know what's going on in this house because I'm asleep most of the time. But I'm not asleep.'

She went on to list the names of the publishers she knew personally whom she could get to publish my book should she but crook her little finger. Some of them, it is true, had been dead half a century. But we let that go and made ourselves very optimistic over our tea.

Sir Quentin and Mrs Tims came in rather earlier than I had expected, before Solly left.

'To whom,' said Sir Quentin as he came into the room, 'does that bag in the hall belong?'

'It's mine,' said Solly, getting up.

'Baron von Mendelsohn,' I said, 'is only passing through. May I introduce, Sir Quentin Oliver – the Baron von – '

'Oh, please, please, dear Baron, do sit down . . . '. Sir Quentin in his usual orgasm over a title fussed round unshaven Solly, begging him to sit down, to stay, not to leave.

But Solly, solid and unshaken by his new-found title, said polite good-byes all round and limped off, staggering a little at the door under the unexpected weight of the bag.

'Suicide while of unsound mind,' said Sir Quentin when he came back into the room. 'An overdose of sleeping pills knocked back by a pint of whisky. I really must see that something more seemly goes on the death certificate.'

'Tell them,' yelled Edwina, 'to wipe their arse with the death certificate.'

'Mummy!'

I left shortly afterwards, and took an expensive taxi home to catch up with Solly.

TEN

It is not to be supposed that the stamp and feeling of a novel can be conveyed by an intellectual summary. My references to the book have been scrappy: I couldn't reproduce my *Warrender Chase* in a few words; and anyhow, an attempt to save, or not to save, anyone the trouble of reading it would be simply beside the point.

But I can certainly meet my essential purpose, which is to tell how Sir Quentin Oliver tried to arrange for the destruction of *Warrender Chase* as a novel at the same time as he appropriated the spirit of my legend for his own use. I can show how he actually plagiarized my text. And so I am writing about the cause of an effect.

I remember as a young child being obliged to write out in my copy-book, Necessity is the Mother of Invention. The sample had already been effected in beautiful copperplate on the first line, and to improve our handwriting it was our task to copy out this maxim on the lines below, which I duly did, all unaware that I was not merely acquiring an improved calligraphy but imbibing at the same time a subliminal lesson in social ethics. Another maxim was All is not Gold that Glisters, and another was Honesty is the Best Policy, and I also recall Discretion is the Better Part of Valour. And I have to testify that these precepts, which I was too flighty-minded to actually ponder at the time, but around which I dutifully curled my cursive Ps and my Vs, have turned out to my astonishment to be absolutely true. They may lack the grandeur of the Ten Commandments but they are more to the point.

Necessity, therefore, being the mother of invention, it was not surprising that the first thing I did after Solly had left me with the heavy bag of troubles I had taken from Hallam Street was to ring up a number of friends and alert them that I was now looking for another job.

When these seeds had been sown I heaved the bag of biographies into the bottom of my clothes cupboard for the time being. I started to lay plans for the retrievement of my stolen manuscript of *Warrender Chase*. I was tempted to ring up Dottie and confront her with the theft. Discretion is the better part of valour; with difficulty I restrained myself. I felt she wasn't quite the same Dottie with whom I had been basically friendly with an occasional blazing row. Something had happened to change her; almost certainly Sir Quentin's influence. I had torn up her biography; I hoped she had taken my advice and refused to take further part in memoir-writing for Sir Quentin.

I began to brood on the outrages perpetrated upon me and my novel by Dottie, Sir Quentin, Revisson Doe; I tried to imagine the justifications they could have variously produced: that I was mad, the book was mad, it was evil, it was libellous, it ought to be suppressed. There came to my mind a phrase of John Henry Newman's in his journals: '. . . the thousand whisperings against me . . .' No sooner had I thought of this than I decided to put an end to my brooding. Finish. Cut it out.

In the meantime, as often happens when I brood, a plan of action had been forming in my mind. I didn't think Dottie would be so far gone under Sir Quentin's hypnotic influence as to have destroyed my book, but I wasn't prepared to take the risk of alarming her to the extent that she might have time to do so. I determined somehow or other to retrieve my *Warrender Chase* by stealth. For which I would need to get the key of Dottie's flat and I would need to get her out of her flat for some hours without fear of her returning. Furthermore I would have to be sure that Leslie wouldn't burst in on me while I was searching the flat. I felt quite excited. It was like writing the pages of a novel, and I consciously kept these plans fixed in another part of my brain to transform into the last chapters of *All Souls' Day*, as I eventually did in my own shadowy way. People often ask me where I get ideas for my novels; I can only say that my life is like that, it turns into some other experience of fiction, recognizable only to myself. And part of my indignation at having been accused of libelling the Autobiographical Association in my *Warrender Chase* was this, that even if I had invented the characters after, not before, I had gone to work at Sir Quentin's, even if I had been moved to portray those poor people in fictional form, they would not have been recognizable, even to themselves – even in that case, there would have been no question of libel. Such as I am, I'm an artist, not a reporter.

To return to my plan. I needed an accomplice, maybe two. I needed the sort of accomplices who were either completely faithful to the idea that what I was doing was legitimate, or else were not entirely aware of what my plan consisted of.

I wondered, first, if I could somehow wheedle the key to the flat out of Leslie. I could have done so, I think. I'm sure my sexual attraction for Leslie alone would have been strong enough to have brought off some design of that kind. It would have taken time, it would have taken an effort on my part. It was the effort that finally put me right off the idea. Not that I couldn't imagine, in the situation I could have arranged, finding Leslie quite possible to go to bed with, for he really had a great deal of masculine charm. I could see that I could ask him to come round with a book that I needed, as in past times I used so often to do; I could say I needed some help with a passage in Newman, as I did so often in the past when I needed a reference book for those long, devoted, underpaid but often well-appreciated articles I wrote for church newspapers and literary magazines, so making myself into a wayside authority on Newman that I always got Newman books to write about. But the fact that I couldn't just ask Leslie for a loan of the key – that I couldn't trust him merely with my story, and engage him on my side – put me quite off the idea. Absolutely I would have had to go to bed with him again, work up to the old intimacy, before I could confide, or half-confide, my predicament. Nothing doing, I thought. Even though it would have been the natural thing to let him stay the night if I were going to spend an evening with him, nothing doing. I let his handsome young face recede from my thoughts, far handsomer than Wally McConnachie's. Wally's face was big-boned and Wally was built on the heavy side, not quite squat but nothing like so lithe as Leslie. However, Wally's face took shape in my mind's eye as Leslie's receded. I was growing rather fond of Wally.

Now another reflection took hold of me: It is strange how one knows one's friends more clearly as one sees them imaginatively in various situations. The moment I thought of Wally – how it should be if I were to tell him about my *Warrender Chase*, how Dottie (whom he didn't know) had said it was mad, how Theo and Audrey Clairmont (whom he knew) had behaved so oddly, how my publisher had cancelled the contract on an unverified suspicion of libel – if I should tell Wally all this story, and the story of Sir Quentin's plagiarizing my novel, and the story of Dottie's probably stealing my novel, and how I had stolen the biographies – it seemed unfeasible that I should tell Wally all that. One item, perhaps, but not the lot. I ruled Wally out because I knew instinctively how he would react. I could imagine my saying, 'And Wally, you know, Bernice Gilbert's suicide is so like the suicide of a character in my novel.' And Wally would say, 'Look, Fleur, this is all a bit fantastic, you know. Poor Bucks Gilbert has always been a bit, well . . .' And all the time would be working at the back of his mind a word to himself, in relation to his own life, his job, his place in society, a word of caution: Don't get mixed up in this, Wally. He would say to himself, These authors, these bohemians. He would say to me, 'I'd let it rest, Fleur, I really would. I daresay your manuscript will turn up.'

Or suppose I said (as I thought it possible I might), 'Wally, please will you take my friend Dottie to the theatre? I'll arrange it. I want to go and search her flat for my novel.' Then Wally would probably say, 'I wouldn't take that risk if I were you, Fleur dear,' meaning, I don't want to take the risk of implicating myself . . . a scandal . . .

I can never know how it would have gone in reality. But in reality I didn't apply to Wally for help. Wally was a love, and I wanted to keep him for the fun that we had and might have together. It involved keeping him in that compartment of life in which it had pleased God to place him, set apart from my present most mysterious, slightly hallucinatory concerns.

Wally rang me just as I had come to this point in my reflections. He had 'just got away,' was I doing anything? 'Just got away' was one of Wally's frequent phrases, it might have been from his office, from a party; I never asked him, but I've noticed throughout my life that Foreign Office people are generally wont to put in their appearance with the words, I've just got away; one dares not ask from where, it might be Top Secret. Anyway, I said no, I wasn't doing anything, no, I hadn't dined, I had barely touched my tea. It was agreed between us that it was a brilliant idea for me to be ready in half an hour, he would pick me up and we would go to eat in Soho. Wasn't it awful, he said before he hung up, about Bucks Gilbert?

I said it was ghastly.

Before I left I locked the door of my clothes cupboard and took the key.

Wally spoke of Bucks Gilbert at dinner.

'Had you seen her since her party?'

'Only once, very briefly, the same day that she died. She came to Hallam Street. She looked a bit upset.'

'What about?' said Wally.

'Oh, I don't know, I don't know at all.'

'I feel rather guilty,' said Wally. 'I suppose everyone does when a friend takes their life. One feels one could have done more. One could have done something if only one had known.'

'Well, you didn't know.'

'I could have known. She rang me up and left a message. It was a few days after the party. A fellow in the office took the message, I was to ring her back. He said she sounded awfully frantic. That rather put me off, I'm afraid. I wasn't really up to coping. Bucks was a clinging sort of woman, you know, she used to cling. I wasn't up to it.'

'Maybe someone was getting her down.'

'That's what I've been wondering – what makes you say that?'

'An intuition. I'm a novelist, you know.'

'Well, you may be right,' he said. 'Because she rang up some other friends in those days after the party. Three people that I know of. Naturally, they're shattered. In each case they either didn't ring back or made an excuse.'

'Were they people who were at the party?' I said.

He thought for a moment. 'Yes,' he said then, 'they were. Why d'you ask that?'

'Maybe she was putting them to the test, to see if she really had any friends. Maybe that's why she gave the party. Someone could have put her up to it, to undermine her, convincing her she had no real friends.'

'Oh, God, Fleur, I say, now you really are romancing. Oh, God, I hope it isn't true. I only went to the party, because, well, one does look in on a cocktail party. If one can get away. Oh, God, surely she wasn't putting me to a test.'

I was sorry for Wally. I regretted having spoken my thoughts. I was thinking of the Greek girl who committed suicide in my *Warrender Chase*. But I said that, obviously, Bernice Gilbert had some private mental anxiety. 'Nobody can help such people, nobody,' I said. 'The verdict was suicide while of unsound mind, Wally,' I said. 'Like most suicides. One can't do a thing about them, Wally.'

'I wondered, in fact,' Wally went on, 'how she was able to lay on such a sumptuous reception, it really was rather grand, wasn't it? She wasn't a bit well-off, you know. Half of the stuff must have come off the black market. There must have been three hundred people, you remember more were arriving when we left.' Then Wally immediately pulled himself together, and smiled at me. He leant over the table and took my hand. 'We mustn't get morbid. Let's snap out of it,' he said. 'After all, it was at poor Bucks' party that we got together, wasn't it?'

'Yes, that's true.'

'So I can't regret having gone.'

I told Wally I was leaving my job, looking for another.

'That calls for a drink. Will you come back to Ebury Street for a drink?'

I said I wasn't really up to a late night. I meant all night.

'Well, we can go to the Gargoyle. What about the Gargoyle?'

I hesitated. Then I said yes, but first I'd have to go home and get something. Wally agreed, making so little matter of it that I supposed he thought it was my monthly period. In reality I wanted to look in at my room to see that the bag of biographies in my hanging-cupboard was still there. It would have been easy for Dottie to coax her way into my room. She had already got into the good favour of the house-boy by giving him holy pictures of the Little Flower. I knew Sir Quentin would soon discover the loss of the biographies.

Wally waited in the taxi while I dashed indoors.

My room was as usual. Nothing had been touched. The biographies were still there. I felt foolish for my nerviness. I locked the cupboard again and was leaving the room when the house-boy appeared before me. Yes, indeed Dottie had been round to see me.

'Did she wait in my room?'

'No, Miss. Yourself told me the last time the lady was here to wait for you that nobody was to be let in your room again.'

'Oh, thanks very much, Harry. I forgot I'd told you. It was quite right of you. Thanks very much.' I gave him two shillings to ease the affront, which amazed him. As I ran out to the taxi, I thought again how nervy I was becoming. After the loss of my *Warrender Chase* I had told not only Harry, but the maid and the landlord, very firmly that no one should be allowed into my room while I wasn't there. I decided to suppress my nerves and take courage.

We went to the Gargoyle. I had a crème de menthe, Wally a whisky. There were three groups of people, none of whom we knew, and one wispy young man all alone in a shadowy corner with a drink in front of him. I looked at him again; it was Gray Mauser.

'The boy in the corner,' I said to Wally, 'is called Gray Mauser.' This cheered Wally immensely.

'He writes under the name of Leander. He's a poet.' As I spoke Gray looked over to me and I gave him a little wave.

'Would you like him to join us?' said Wally.

'Yes, I would.'

Gray set in immediately to make eyes at Wally, and he flicked his weak little wrists around, and wriggled somewhat. Wally took this in good part.

'My friend,' Gray said, 'has gone to Ireland for three weeks.' He sat so that he was three-quarters facing Wally with the same amount of his back to me. Wally shifted quietly so that Gray had to face us both. 'He gave me this tie, my friend. Do you like it?'

'Very effective,' said Wally, and went on talking affably, so arranging things that Gray was forced to give a little attention to me. Gray was totally unaware of these manoeuvres, for he was genuinely well-meaning but at the same time overwhelmingly taken with Wally.

But when I got Gray's attention I took advantage of the moment to say right out, 'Gray, I wonder if Leslie took the key of Dottie's flat to Ireland with him?'

'No darling,' said Gray. 'It's on our dressing-table at this moment, right where he left it. Why?'

So I explained to them both how I needed to borrow that key, as a secret, because I wanted to go to Dottie's flat to leave a surprise for her. I explained to Wally that Gray's friend was an old friend of mine whose wife, Dottie, was also a friend of mine. By the time we had finished our drinks, and Wally and I had made simultaneous 'Let's-go' signs to each other, Gray had promised to lend me the key and keep it ever such a secret. I was to pick up the key the following afternoon.

*

I fell asleep that night while I was still trying to think of people I could induce to take Dottie to the theatre. I thought of Solly. He had two nights off a week. My dear Solly, he was always so good, I didn't want to become a weight on him. He probably wanted his two nights to himself. Besides he was a poet, and a real one. Then I remembered something that made me exclude Solly, anyway. Dottie disliked him. She would hardly be persuaded to go to the theatre with Solly. I remembered on the two occasions she had met Solly she had asked me afterwards what I saw in him. I thought this strange because everybody else I knew, including Leslie, loved Solly. She had said she thought Solly attractive but vulgar. Solly had not given her the slightest provocation for thinking so. He always kept his invectives and profanities for his nearest and trusted friends and had said nothing Dottie could take exception to. I said he was the least vulgar-spirited of men. 'Oh,' said Dottie, 'I don't mean spiritual vulgarity.' 'What other sort of vulgarity can there be?' I said, which was perhaps arguable. But Dottie had left it at that, since she evidently felt I might win the argument, if by word only.

So I dropped off to sleep musing on the fact that Solly wasn't at all vulgar in the same sense that Dottie was. Dottie, the English Rose.

I woke next morning knowing exactly what to do. I had twice decided not to return to Hallam Street, and now for the second time I was obliged to go back.

I wanted to get to Edwina. It was unlikely that I should get through to her on the telephone. Always, when I phoned her in my private time, Beryl Tims or Sir Quentin would make some excuse, usually that she was sleeping or not very well. If she herself wanted to get in touch with me at week-ends it was easy. She had a phone at her bedside, or sometimes the nurse would convey a message.

Now I wanted to see Edwina. I had a good excuse, too, for calling at Hallam Street, for I could then hand in a proper letter of resignation and collect my pay, my health card with the stamps that papered its folding walls as in a doll's house, and other bureaucratic evidence of my reality, like my pay-as-you-earn tax paper, all of which I had intended to arrange by post, before I woke up with my certainty that I had to see Edwina.

It was a rainy morning, rather cold, and a Saturday.

'Sir Quentin has left for his property in Northumberland,' Beryl Tims announced when I arrived about ten o'clock. Sir Quentin always referred to people's houses in the country or abroad as their property. 'He left by car at eight-thirty,' she added, pompously.

'Where did he get the petrol?' I said sharply. Petrol was still rationed; it would not be off the ration till later in the month, the twenty-sixth to be precise; I remember the date because I had promised Wally to go down for the week-end of the twenty-seventh and twenty-eighth to his cottage at Marlow in his car, to celebrate the end of petrol-rationing. But the petrol-rationing laws still in force were very strict; some prominent people had gone to prison for transgressing them. So my question 'Where did he get the petrol?' was a nasty little question, containing a menace of that citizens' righteousness which was quite rife in those days amongst ill-natured or grievance-burdened people. Beryl Tims was flustered. 'I'm sure, I'm quite positive,' said she, 'that Sir Quentin has Supplementary. He would have to do, I mean, wouldn't he, for his poor mother?'

'Oh, has he taken Lady Edwina?'

'No, she's having her breakfast.'

'Then he shouldn't be using her petrol coupons, should he?' I said. 'We'll have to look into this,' I went on in a voice which fairly took even myself aback. 'Is his journey really necessary? We'll see.' I walked past Beryl to the study door. The door, the stable-door, was locked.

'Sir Quentin,' said the English Rose – she was wearing a shocking-pink twin set she had got for Easter – 'has left instructions that you are not, definitely, to enter the study. Sir Quentin, I believe, has written you a letter of dismissal. He has appointed a certain new lady assistant to commence on Monday.'

'Well, I'll see Lady Edwina,' I said, starting down the corridor that led to her room.

Beryl followed me. 'Sir Quentin told me that if you phoned or called I was to ask you to return immediately the work that you took home with you. It should not have left this house.'

I got to Edwina's door. Beryl clutched my arm. 'You may,' said Beryl, 'see Lady Edwina. You may even,' she said, 'take her out tomorrow so that Nurse Fisher can get away. Lady Edwina's fluxive precipitations have augmented in frequency, and it is only because of the doctor's orders that she's to be spared distress and excitement that you are to be permitted the privilege of seeing her on the condition that she knows nothing of any dispute between yourself and Sir –'

The nurse opened the door just then. 'Oh, good morning, Fleur,' she said, while Edwina squealed from her bed, 'Come and have some tea and toast. Tims – a fresh pot, please, and another cup.'

'It's a quarter past ten,' said Beryl.

'A fresh pot of tea, and step on the gas,' yelled Edwina.

'I'll come and get it,' said Miss Fisher.

When I sat on Edwina's bed she buttered a piece of toast for me and said softly, with many a wild grimace, 'He's got a new secretary.'

'Is it Dottie?'

'Yes, of course. Ha-ha. He got Tims to burn some proofs of a book. She flushed the ashes down the lavatory. What a mess, all black.'

I put my head close to hers and mouthed some words very clearly and carefully. I said, 'Listen, Edwina, I want you to take this in. I want to have Dottie out of the way for three hours tomorrow afternoon. I will say I can't possibly manage to take you out tomorrow. If Miss Fisher offers to give up her afternoon-off, you are to refuse the offer. You are to demand Dottie. Make a fuss till you get Dottie to come. Be sure to keep her with you for at least three hours.'

The old woman's eyes gleamed, her mouth made a great O, her head nodded in time to the rhythm of my phrases. She was taking it in.

'While Dottie is with you, take ill. Make her ring up the doctor. If he's out make her get another doctor. Wet your knickers twenty times. At all costs, get Dottie to stay with you and keep her with you.'

She nodded.

'Three hours.'

'Three hours,' said Edwina.

I rang the bell of Dottie's flat when I went there the next day with a shopping bag in my hand, at two in the afternoon, just in case someone should be there. No answer. I let myself in with the key. I locked myself in.

'Accused was familiar with the flat,' I thought to myself as I went straight into the bathroom in a state of suspicious dread to look for signs of black paper-ash in the lavatory pan. I found no signs. I went into the bedroom, took off my coat and put it on the bed with my shopping bag. I had brought with me in the bag a small present, wrapped in pink tissue paper, a hand-embroidered silk handkerchief-case which I had never used, and which befitted an English Rose more than it did the likes of me. I intended to produce it as an alibi should I be caught in the flat.

I made for Dottie's desk in her bedroom. There was a page in her typewriter; Dottie was evidently making a fair copy of a much-corrected typescript in an open folder on the desk. I would have liked to linger over it, for it was plainly Leslie's novel; I glanced quickly at the cover of the folder to verify this and passed quickly to my main objective. *Warrender Chase* was nowhere on the desk. Nor was it in the drawers, in one of which, however, I came across a letter dated three weeks back, headed Park and Revisson Doe. It began 'Dear Dottie (if I may) ...' I didn't stop to read on but a superstitious impulse caused me to drag my coat and shopping bag off the bed lest they should be contaminated. I left my things on the floor and continued my search of the bedroom. In the cupboards, on top of the cupboards, under the pillows, the mattress. Under the bed was a suitcase. I dragged it out. It was full of Dottie's summer clothes. No *Warrender Chase* anywhere. There remained the sitting-room, a spare bedroom which had also been Leslie's study, the kitchen and the linen cupboard in the bathroom. I disposed of the linen cupboard; nothing there. I felt that the probabilities were in favour of Leslie's study so I left it to the last. I started to ransack the sitting-room, lifting the cushions off the sofa and chairs and putting them back, searching behind the curtains and under piles of magazines. Nearly an hour had passed, and with the familiarity of the objects I touched and under which I peered came the doubt whether Dottie – exasperating but familiar old Dottie – had taken the manuscript at all.

I had finished with the sitting-room; everything was in place. I went out to the little hall to go into Leslie's workroom, the door of which was wide open showing the masses of untidy papers and shelves of books that I knew from old times. I think I even got as far as to look round the room. But as I had passed through the hall I had seen underneath the coats which were hanging on two pegs by the door Dottie's black bag with her knitting, the red scarf, protruding. I turned back to it. The notion came to me that I should examine this; no doubt Dottie had brought her knitting with her the night she had waited in my room and – But already my fingers had found a package the size of a London telephone directory, wedged at the bottom of the ghastly black bag. Out I whisked that package in a flash, and in another flash had opened it. My *Warrender Chase*, my novel, my Warrender, Warrender Chase; my foolscap pages with the first chapters I had once torn up and then stuck together; my *Warrender Chase, mine*. I hugged it. I kissed it. I went to Dottie's bedroom and put it in my own shopping bag. I snatched from Dottie's desk an unopened ream of typing paper. This I wedged at the bottom of Dottie's bag, and carefully arranged the knitting on top of it. I put on my coat, took my shopping bag on my arm, looked carefully round the flat to see if everything was in place. I straightened the covers on the revolting bed, let myself out of the flat and went on my way rejoicing.

I have never known an artist who at some time in his life has not come into conflict with pure evil, realized as it may have been under the form of disease, injustice, fear, oppression or any other ill element that can afflict living creatures. The reverse doesn't hold: that is to say, it isn't only the artist who suffers, or who perceives evil. But I think it true that no artist has lived who has not experienced and then recognized something at first too incredibly evil to seem real, then so undoubtedly real as to be undoubtedly true. I was dying to look into the Pandora's box of Sir Quentin's biographies. But I had first to set about making typed copies of my *Warrender Chase*, it was imperative; for I was determined not to let the work out of my sight until I had spare copies to send to a publisher: I started this business as soon as I got home that Sunday afternoon. I recall that I stopped to ring Solly.

'I got my manuscript back,' I told him. 'All the proofs and the typescripts were destroyed.' I then described my raid on Dottie's flat.

I gave him a full account. He was very solemn. He let loose a number of ill wishes upon the heads of Revisson Doe, Dottie and Sir Quentin Oliver. Then he said he would get me a new publisher if it was the last thing he did. Solly had always believed in the value of *Warrender Chase*. For myself, I felt towards it only that it was mine, my own, mine, and I still felt my novel *All Souls' Day*, which I had started, was far superior.

'Let me know when you've got the novel ready for a publisher,' Solly said.

So I went on typing *Warrender Chase*. I had very few corrections to make, it was simple slog work. I stopped again to ring Hallam Street to enquire how Edwina was.

'She has had a bad day,' said Mrs Tims. 'I can't stop now, good-bye.' And she put down the phone. I had a whisky and soda and ate a poached egg, then I continued my labours. At midnight I was still typing. Every now and then I had to wash my hands because the two carbon sheets – I had determined to make three typed sets of the novel in all – were constantly blackening them. At midnight more or less, Dottie started singing 'Auld Lang Syne' outside my window. I thought her voice unusually high.

I was greatly tempted to throw a jug of water over her head. But I was even more greatly avid to see her. I wanted to know about her afternoon with Edwina. I wanted to know about her affair with Revisson Doe, and what she would say about her new job with Sir Quentin. I was also keen to find out if she had discovered that I had retrieved my *Warrender Chase*.

I let her in.

'I came last night,' she said. 'But you were out.' There was a tone of reproach as she said it, which made me laugh.

'What is there to laugh about?' said Dottie as she took off her coat and sat down in my wicker arm-chair. The manuscript of *Warrender Chase* was visible on the writing-table and the pages I had typed were face downwards on the other side of the typewriter. I had no intention of hiding the book, but she didn't notice it at the moment.

'I had a terrible time with that repulsive old woman,' said Dottie.

'Oh, well, you'll have to get used to it,' I said. 'Edwina's part of the job, in a sense.'

I saw that Dottie was excited and distressed. She was trembling. I felt rather sorry for her.

'I haven't come to discuss the job,' said Dottie. 'I came last night. I came to tell you that Sir Quentin wants those biographies back. I have to work on them. Hand them over, please.'

'Have you come here in the middle of the night to fetch them? Don't you see I'm busy?'

'Give me a drink,' said Dottie. 'I've come for some typing paper. I'm typing Leslie's novel and I've run out of typing paper. I could have sworn I had a new packet of paper, but I can't find it. I must have left it in the shop. I wanted to get on with Leslie's novel because he's coming back from Ireland tomorrow night. He was to be away three weeks, but you know what he is. I won't have time to buy paper tomorrow because I'm starting my job tomorrow morning. And Park and Revisson Doe are probably going to publish Leslie's book.'

I handed her a whisky and water. I said, 'Are you sure you should be drinking? Are you ill?'

She didn't reply. Her eyes were on my *Warrender Chase*.

'What's that?' said Dottie.

'I'm making a few copies of my novel. The old copies got tattered.'

'What novel?'

'The same old *Warrender Chase*.'

'Where did you get it?' said Dottie.

'Dottie,' I said, 'you must be mad. What do you mean, where did I get it?'

'How many handwritten copies of the original did you make?' Dottie said.

'Oh, dear,' I said. 'Don't be boring. Tell me about your affair with Revisson Doe.'

She spilt her whisky as she put the glass down on the floor.

'You don't understand,' she said, 'that sometimes a woman has to make a sacrifice for a man. You're hard. You're evil. Why don't you see a priest?'

Now, seeing a priest is all very well if you have something on your conscience. But there are very few predicaments in a writer's life where it would be the slightest use explaining the ins and outs to a priest. A priest is the person to see if you fear for your immortal soul, but not if you are menaced by someone else's. I told Dottie, 'I would as soon see a priest about you or, for instance, Sir Quentin, as I would go to consult a doctor about your lungs and his kidneys. Why don't you see a priest yourself?'

'I will when it's all over,' said Dottie. 'Leslie needs a publisher.'

She was shaking very badly.

I said, 'You should see a doctor.'

She threw the rest of her whisky all over my typed pages. I got a cloth and blotted them as best I could.

I said, 'Sir Quentin Oliver urged you to take on that old man, didn't he?'

'Sir Quentin,' she said, 'is a genius and a born leader. Now give me those biographies and I'll go.'

'You'll go,' I said, 'but the biographies are staying with me until I've had time to study them. A lot of my *Warrender Chase* has been transferred to those biographies. When I've extracted what's mine I'll hand over the rest.'

'What a fiend you are,' Dottie said.

I don't know what prompted me then to ask, 'Are you taking pills?'

'What pills?' said Dottie.

'Drugs.'

'Only for my weight-reducing,' said Dottie.

'From a doctor?'

'No, I get them from a friend.'

I put together half a ream of typing paper and gave it to Dottie. I told her she was a fool.

She said, 'You're furious because I've taken your job.'

I said that was fair enough, everything she had done was fair enough, because I had once taken her husband. But she was a fool to have any more to do with the Autobiographical Association.

'Who took me there in the first place?' said Dottie.

'I did, I'm sorry to say. But I tore up your biography as soon as I realized there was something wrong.'

Dottie said, 'I enjoy sleeping with Revisson Doe.'

'Get out, I've got work to do. It's late.'

'Have you got a cup of cocoa?'

I made her a cup of cocoa. I gave her the embroidered silk handkerchief-case that I hadn't left at her flat.

'Why don't you give up the idea of being an author?' said the English Rose. 'Everything used to be all right between us and Leslie was your friend too. But that mad novel of yours – Sir Quentin says –'

'Out,' I breathed, so as not to wake the house. This time she went.

ELEVEN

It was not many hours before Dottie discovered that the handwritten copy of my *Warrender Chase* she had seen that night in my room was in fact the one she had stolen; she found the ream of typing paper in her bag under her knitting. She rang me up the next afternoon.

'How did you get into my flat?' she said.

I had already returned the key to Gray Mauser. I didn't answer her question, I didn't even ask how my novel got into her flat. I hung up.

An hour later she rang again. 'Listen, Fleur, Sir Quentin is anxious to have a chat with you.'

'Where are you speaking from?'

'I'm at home. I don't think I can manage the job.'

'You've fallen out with Sir Quentin.'

'Well, not exactly, but – '

'He's furious because you didn't destroy my manuscript.'

'Well, it deserves to be destroyed.'

That evening I finished typing *Warrender Chase*. I had been typing steadily all day; my shoulders ached and I lay on my bed reading it through for typing errors. I could see its defects as a novel but they weren't the sort of defects that could be removed without removing the entire essence. It's often like that with a novel or a story. One sees a fault or a blemish, perhaps in the portrayal of a character, but cosmetic treatment won't serve; change the setting of a scene and the balance of the whole work is adversely affected. So I left my *Warrender Chase* as it was.

Solly looked in for a drink before he went to his night-work and took away two typed copies of my book, one to send to a publisher and the other to keep in the safe at the office. He said, 'You could sue them all, you could give them in charge.'

'Would it do my book any good?' I said.

'No,' said Solly, 'it would only make false publicity. Your novel has to stand on its merits, especially a first novel.'

'What should I do with the biographies?'

'Destroy the bits he's lifted from your novel and give him back the rest.'

I told Solly that was what I intended to do. But first I was interested to see what use Sir Quentin had put my work to. 'I think he's putting my *Warrender Chase* into practice. He's trying to live out my story. I haven't had time to look at the files properly, but that's what I think.'

'You can't control his actions,' said Solly. 'Don't let these people get on your nerves. Just give him back what's his and let him put it away for seventy years. Who cares? You'll get another job, you'll write another book and forget them.'

When I lugged out the bag full of the Autobiographical Association files later that night, and opened it, I began to feel hysterical. The very touch of them seemed to be radio-active with harm. I shuffled through the folders till I came to Lady Bernice 'Bucks' Gilbert,

Then the phone rang. What instinct urged me at first not to answer it? It was only eight-twenty-five. It rang. It persisted. The house-boy must have known I was in. Possibly he thought I had just gone out to the lavatory and would presently be back in the room. On rang the piercing one-tone signal from the household exchange downstairs. I answered it. I heard the boy say, 'Here she is for you.' A click, and, 'Oh Fleur,' said Mrs Tims, 'I'm so glad I caught you in. Something has occurred. It's to do with Lady Edwina, she wants to see you.'

'Is she ill?'

'I wouldn't say she was well. It's a delicate matter. Can you come at once? Sir Quentin will of course pay for the taxi.'

'Put me through to Lady Edwina,' I said.

'Oh, I can't do that.'

'Why not?'

'She's not in a state.'

I asked then, to speak to Miss Fisher.

'Nurse Fisher's gone to her sister's.'

'Have you called the doctor?'

'Well,' said Beryl Tims, 'we were debating ... '

'Don't debate. Send for the doctor,' I said.

'But she wants you, Fleur.'

'Pass me Sir Quentin.'

'I doubt he would have anything to say to you, Fleur. Sir Quentin is very offended.'

'He owes me my pay and a lot of explanations,' I said.

There was a pause while the English Rose evidently covered the receiver to speak to Sir Quentin, for eventually he came on the phone.

'You would do me a great favour,' he said, 'if you would come and see Mummy. It is quite urgent. Whatever has gone wrong between us, I assure you, Miss Talbot, I don't want to come between you and Mummy.'

'I want to speak to her.'

'Alas, that is not possible.'

In the end I went, having first bundled the autobiographies back into my clothes cupboard and locked it. Anyone who has read *Warrender Chase* will know what happened to those autobiographies during my absence. In fact, the possibility was already half in my mind that I was falling into the same trap as Marjorie in my novel when she was called away from Warrender's papers on the pretext that the ancient Prudence needed her. But the very fact that it was half in my mind almost, to the other half of my mind, precluded the possibility that my suspicions could be valid. It seemed quite unlikely that my own novel could be entering into my life to such an extent. I very often err by taking the side of rationality in my distrust of suspicions.

I reached Hallam Street within half an hour.

'Miss Talbot,' said Sir Quentin, 'would you step into my study for a moment? Mummy has fortunately, most fortunately, dropped off to sleep. It would be such a pity to disturb her after all this, after all this ...'

'Well, that's all right, then,' I said. 'I don't need to stay.'

But he had me by the arm and was propelling me into the study. 'Take off your coat, please do, Miss Talbot,' said Sir Quentin. 'There are just one or two small items we have to discuss.'

'If you mean the files of your Association,' I said, 'I'll discuss them when I've studied them better. So far as I can see you've plagiarized my novel *Warrender Chase*. I assure you that I'll sue.'

'Ah, your novel, your novel, I don't know anything about that. I don't wonder you've been unable to give your full attention to your job here with us when you've been scribbling novels at the same time. Delusions of grandeur.'

From the other end of the house came a crash and a shriek. 'Fleur! Is that you, Fleur? Leave me alone, Tims you bitch. I want to see Fleur. I know she's here. I know that Fleur's in the house.'

Sir Quentin continued, 'It is I who shall sue.'

I sat still, as if agreeing to ignore Edwina's noise.

'The question arises,' I said, 'why Bernice Gilbert took her life.'

'It is I who shall – '

But I had leapt up and got out into the passage where Edwina was trying to rid herself of Beryl Tims's restraint.

'Fleur, how wonderful to see you, what a surprise,' croaked Edwina. 'Come along to my room.'

I shoved Beryl Tims out of the way and followed Edwina. From the other end of the passage came Sir Quentin's frail cry, 'Mummy!'

Before I left Hallam Street that night I got my pay and my employment cards. I also got an envelope from Edwina which she cunningly drew out of her pillowcase and crammed into my coat-pocket, shrieking the while; so that Beryl Tims, who had gone into Edwina's bathroom to get some water for Edwina to take with her sleeping pill, wasn't aware of our transaction.

I promised Edwina I would drop in and see her very soon. There was always some reason why I couldn't break with Hallam Street once and for all. This put me in mind of those scenes in *Warrender Chase* where my character, the scholar Proudie, repeatedly comes across letters from Marjorie to Warrender making excuses for not being able to come to see him in the country, and yet obviously she has continued to do so right up to the time of Warrender's death in the car crash. When Proudie asks Marjorie why she went back to the house continually, Marjorie says, 'I wanted to break. But the Greek girl was helpless there. And Prudence, I had to see Prudence.'

I thought of this as I sat in the taxi going home. I remembered the opening scene of my novel, how the group of people are waiting for Warrender to join them. He is late. He doesn't come. He has been killed in a car crash.

My thoughts went like this: Warrender Chase was killed in a car crash while everyone is assembled, waiting for him. Quentin Oliver's destiny, if he wants to enact Warrender Chase, would be the same. It was a frightening thought but at the same time external to me, as if I were watching a play I had no power to stop. It then came to me again, there in the taxi, what a wonderful thing it was to be a woman and an artist in the twentieth century. It was almost as if Sir Quentin was unreal and I had merely invented him, Warrender Chase being a man, a real man on whom I had partly based Sir Quentin. It is true that I felt tight-strung, but I remember those sensations very clearly.

That Sir Quentin was real became obvious when I got back to my room. Nothing seemed amiss, it is true. I got the key of the cupboard out of my bag and opened it. Solly's hold-all was in its place. I opened it and gazed into its emptiness, hypnotized by my predicted loss and the extent of my own folly in not having followed my instinct. The mouth of the bag gaped at me, ha-ha. It had been a professional job. There was no sign of a tampering with the lock of my door, no scratches of a bungling amateur on the cupboard. I had to wait till the morning to confirm with the house-boy that nobody to his knowledge had been to see me. No callers in the house at all? He replied with a lot of thunder, from which there flashed like sheet-lightning in my mind the simple fact that I knew already: a professional thief had been employed to come to the house, straight to the spot where I kept the biographies. The lay-out was known to Dottie, and plainly it was she who, unwittingly perhaps, had provided the information. That night, I looked for my *Warrender Chase* in a suitcase under the bed where I now kept it. In my anxious state I had forgotten that I had abstracted the original manuscript before I had gone out; I had put this under my pillow. So that in the suitcase I found only the spare copy of the new transcript, the two others of which I had given to Solly. But where, where, were my foolscap manuscript pages? I searched my room for an hour and it wasn't till I got into bed that I felt them under my pillow.

This brought to mind the envelope Edwina had thrust into my coat-pocket. I jumped out of bed, quite refreshed and strengthened by this exciting recollection; I'm one of those people who can quickly recover from physical exhaustion if they are in the least stimulated mentally. The blank and crumpled envelope contained some handwritten pages evidently torn out of a diary. They had been torn roughly, so that some of the words at the beginning of each line were partly missing and equally at the end of the lines on the reverse sides. It seemed to me that the handwriting was Sir Quentin's and as I read the first page it was plain that the diary entries were his.

This is the document, which I've kept ever since in memory of marvellous Edwina:

26th April, 1950.

I have gained the confidence
Miss Talbot's friend, Dorothy
ottie', Mrs Carpenter, with
whose husband, Leslie, Miss Talbot
ad an affair.
'Dottie' has obtained for
the printed proofs of a novel
titled 'Warrender Chase' as an
xample of a morbid literary production which in her ('Dottie's')
pinion should be suppressed.
I have read this production
Miss Talbot's inflamed and in-
ne imagination. That such an one
hould have entered my ken!!
The book is an attempted *roman
à clef* if ever there was one!
Query: Is Miss T. a mind-reader?
a medium?
?Evil

I turned over the page:

28th April, 1950.

'Dottie' informed me that tw
Authors, Theodore Clairmont an
his wife Audrey (N.B. not list

in 'Who's Who') have read the
so-called novel. They vehementl
disapprove of that same. I was
informed that the piece of wri
already in printers' proof, is
be published by Messrs Park,
Revisson Doe, a minor but recogni
establishment.

I have consequently made a
rendez-vous with a director of
firm, Mr Revisson Doe himself.
(N.B. Nothing in 'Burke's', 'Haydn',
etc. etc. Undistinguished entry in
'Who's Who'.)

Next page:

1st May, 1950.

As a result of my visit to the
emises of Park, Revisson Doe,
is afternoon, when I saw Mr
evisson Doe himself in his office
stressed the seriousness of the
bellous aspect of the novel so-
alled by Miss Fleur Talbot *vis*
vis my Autobiographical Asscn.
He promptly agreed to withdraw
the novel from publication. (The
hreat of libel is never-failing
ith these people.) I judged Mr
e to be a sound business man but
f no family antecedents to speak
f.

He mentioned that 'Dottie' had
shown him some chapters of a novel
hich her husband is writing, quite
a *tour de force* in which his past

elations with a young ambitious
emale were to those 'in the know'
idently an account of his doings
ith the redoubtable Fleur Talbot!!

He remarked that 'Dottie'
was 'a very pretty girl'. He
remarked that he used this phrase
'as man to man', which I appreciated. I commented that I would do
my best to further his interest i
'Dottie' at which we enjoyed som
innocent laughter. I expressed m
gratitude for his co-operation and
assured him of mine.

Before I left Mr Doe offered
to 'confirm in writing' his undertaking to scrap the contract for
the said 'Warrender Chase'. I beg
him not to make any written record
of our *tête à tête*, assuring him tha
on my part any written record would
be merely a note assigned to a loc
drawer for seventy years. I proffered
this information true to my princi
of complete frankness.

2nd May, 1950.

Pleasurable sensations: Early this
orning, walking in the Park I observ-
d a striped cat among the shrubbery,
orming as it were a pattern with the
pale light and the shadows of the wet
eaves. How nature is at one! I was
ellbound, rapt within a magic ring,
assive, receptive, all unknowing.
I thought in that moment 'twere sweet
to die. My dearest, I would that we

could die together. Had I not my
Mission which I, and I alone, am subtly
     illed to fulfil. But who are your
riends? Where are they?
          Be not discomfited. I etc. etc.

Above letter to Bucks?

Yes, I have done it. And delivered
it! But

Now what infuriated me more than anything in these scraps of
Quentin Oliver's diary was this last entry, 2nd May. It was straight
out of *Warrender Chase*, where I make my character Proudie find the
absurd letter to the Greek girl who thought it far from absurd.

When I had got over my fury at this raid on my *Warrender Chase* I
put the diary papers back into their envelope and stuffed it down at
the bottom of my handbag, determined never to part with it. To
whatever use I might put the knowledge it conveyed, I felt relieved to
know with precision what I had obscurely suspected. Also, I was
highly amused at the thought of Sir Quentin's discovery of the
missing leaves of his diary. I was sure he would imagine I had hired a
professional burglar. This amused me greatly and I fell asleep
rejoicing.

Next morning I had an interview for a job at the B.B.C., which I
didn't get. I sat at a long board-room table with many men and
women to ask me questions. But I didn't have the required experience
and, said the most elderly of the men, did I realize that the six pounds
a week that I was asking was three hundred pounds a year? I said I
thought it was three hundred and twelve. Anyway, I didn't get the
job. I certainly wasn't looking my best. A little later on in my life,
when my fortunes had changed and I was writing for the B.B.C., my
new friends on the production side fell upon the official file in which
that interview was duly recorded and we all made merry of it.

I typed out a fair copy of those leaves of Sir Quentin's diary and
took them along at tea-time to Hallam Street.

Undoubtedly he was a lunatic. I felt sure that was what Edwina had intended to convey by giving me those torn-out sheets.

'Lady Edwina is asleep,' said Beryl Tims. 'But you needn't bother to come and see her any more. There's nothing in it for you. We've discovered that she has no money at all, not to leave to anybody. She bought an annuity and when she dies the money dies with her. She's very, very, cunning, that's the word. Sir Quentin has only just found out. Her fortune's all a myth.'

I had known this for a long time, for one Sunday when I was wheeling Edwina out with Solly she told me, 'I married for money.'

'I consider that very immoral of you, Edwina,' said Solly.

'I don't see why. My husband married me for money. We were a devoted couple. We had several things in common. One was expensive tastes and the other was no money.'

She had then rambled on about Quentin 'coming as a surprise' and 'his own father, of course' had provided for him and a little for Edwina. So that we were fairly in the air as to Quentin's parentage, and we left Edwina's story at that, all charming as it was and unspoiled by explanations.

'Not a penny,' the English Rose was saying, 'beyond her annuity, which just covers her own keep and the nurse.'

Miss Fisher came out of the kitchen just then. 'Good afternoon, Fleur. Lady Edwina will be delighted to see you. She's getting up for tea.'

I said I'd come in as soon as I'd seen Sir Quentin.

Mrs Tims said, 'You want Sir Quentin? Well –'

I opened the study door and found him at his desk, staring into space.

'Is your new secretary here?' I said.

'Why, Miss Talbot. I – She had to go home early.' He waved me to a chair.

'Read this,' I said, putting the typed pages of his diary in front of him. I continued standing.

He looked at the first page and said, 'Where did you get this?'

'From your diary. I have the pages.'

'How did you get at my diary?'

'I have professional help. The originals are locked in a bank vault. Maybe for seventy years, maybe not.'

He got up and started walking round the room, putting things straight. He stopped and looked at the other pages I had typed. He gave a laugh. 'Why, that diary is a little joke of mine. There's nothing serious in it.'

I said, 'You will have to see a psychiatrist. That's number one. Second, you must wind up the Autobiographical Association. If you don't do both by the end of the month I shall make a fuss.'

'Ah, but the members themselves will have something to say about that.'

I left him and went to see Edwina where she was propped up for tea in the drawing-room, wrapped in an Indian shawl. Sir Quentin came in with a leather-bound book in his hand, his diary. He was followed by Beryl Tims.

'Mummy,' he said, 'I want you to know that your friend Miss Fleur Talbot is not our friend. She belongs to the underworld. She has arranged for a professional thief to enter this house and abstract some pages from my private diary. On her own admission. Miss Fisher, have you missed anything? Is Lady Edwina's jewellery intact?'

Edwina stood up and wet the floor.

'Miss Talbot, I must ask you to leave this house.'

'No harm in asking,' said Edwina. 'I pay the rent. Your home is in the country, Quentin.'

Miss Fisher came mopping up round Edwina who finally agreed to be taken back to her room to be tidied up. I waited for her return, helping myself to a sandwich, while Sir Quentin simply stared at me and Beryl Tims moved the plate of sandwiches out of my reach.

The door-bell rang and Beryl Tims went to answer it. 'You are a fiend,' said Sir Quentin. 'Your enthusiasm for John Henry Cardinal Newman was pure hypocrisy. Did he not form under his influence a circle of devoted spiritual followers? Am I not entitled to do the same?'

'But you know,' I said, 'you're off your head. You had this desire to take possession of people before I came along and reminded you of the existence of Newman. You've read my novel, but only recently. You must see a psychiatrist and break up the Association.'

I could hear voices in the hall. I went out to say good-bye to Edwina and on the way I saw that the two new visitors were the Baronne Clotilde and Father Delaney, both looking extremely haggard yet not pitiable. These two were always arrogant, insolent in their folly.

In Edwina's room, where the nurse was rummaging in her ward-robe for another wonderful dress, I said, 'I've told him to see a mental doctor and disband his troupe.'

'Quite right,' said Edwina. 'When am I going to meet your friend Wally?'

'I'll arrange it soon.'

'Wally and Solly,' she cackled with delight. 'Don't you think that's a nice couple of names, Nurse?'

'Very nice. Like on the stage.' Then Miss Fisher said to me, 'I'm concerned about the Dexedrine.'

I didn't locate the word Dexedrine precisely. I thought she meant some medicine for Edwina. I said, 'Would you like me to take a prescription – ?'

'Oh, no. It's the Dexedrine that Sir Quentin gives to his friends. Didn't he give you some?'

'Not me.'

'He does the others. It can be dangerous if the dose is high.'

'They are all of age. I can't feel sorry for them. They can surely look after themselves.'

'Well yes, and no,' said the good nurse.

Edwina was impatient to get into her purple dress. 'They're all on a fast. Except himself and Tims. And we like our food too, don't we, Nurse?'

'Dexedrine,' the nurse explained, 'is an appetite-suppressor. But it affects the brain.'

'Watching their figures,' yelled Edwina. 'They'll go off their heads.'

'Presumably they all have friends,' I said. 'I suppose they have friends and relations who will notice if they fall ill.'

'It still fits,' said Edwina, patting her dress.

'There's nothing you can prove,' said Miss Fisher, 'but I know. Those poor people – '

'They are not infants,' I said.

I was thinking of my novel, *Warrender Chase*; now I had no publisher, thanks to Quentin Oliver. I was impatient for his bunch of self-indulgent fools – I thought of Maisie Young with so many possibilities in her life, ready to sacrifice them all in the name of a mad spiritual leader; and the Baronne Clotilde du Loiret, so stunned by privilege that she didn't know how to discern and reject a maniac.

I went home to get ready for a dinner date with Wally. But I didn't say a word to him about Hallam Street. Instead I told him about the B.B.C.; and arising from this – I forgot by what route – he told me about getting demobilized from the army, how he and his friends all went along to an army centre which was a group of huts, and there they chose their demob clothes. Wally described in detail the range and styles of demob suits. He himself had taken a tweed coat and flannel trousers. 'Perfectly all right,' said Wally in his casual and comfortable way.

It was good to be reminded that there were other things in life besides *Warrender Chase* and the Autobiographical Association. But part of my mind was really elsewhere. I was longing to get home and read Newman. I wanted to see what these people could possibly be making of him. I was interested in that.

But Wally came home with me for a good-night drink. He loved my book-laden room.

'There's a drunk in the street singing "Auld Lang Syne",' said Wally. 'She seems to be happy, doesn't she?'

I let her sing on.

In the morning before I was up, Dottie was at my door. She had the nerve to bring her black bag with her knitting, now a dark green sweater.

'I came round last night. Your light was on.'

'I know.'

'Was Leslie here?'

'Go to hell.'

'Listen,' said Dottie, 'I've got to tell you. Sir Quentin has ordered us all to go to his house in Northumberland. He says we're being persecuted here in London, and he's going to make his house into a sort of monastery.'

'Like Newman at Littlemore?'

'Exactly. You must admit there's something in Sir Quentin's aims.'

I couldn't see any resemblance between Newman and his band of Oxford Anglo-Catholics in their austere retreat at Littlemore, and Sir

Quentin with his bunch of cranks. It is true that Newman suffered some real religious and political persecution for his views, and that he also suffered from a sense of persecution not always coinciding with a cause. Nothing else of Newman's matched the Hallam Street set.

I said to Dottie, 'One would think that Quentin Oliver had heard of only two books. One is Newman's *Apologia* and the other is my *Warrender Chase*. He's obsessed.'

'He believes you're a witch, an evil spirit who's been sent to bring ideas into his life. It's his mission to turn evil to good. I think there's a lot in what he says,' Dottie said.

'Well, you can put the kettle on,' I said, 'for I haven't had my breakfast.'

She filled the kettle and put it on the gas ring.

'They're going to Northumberland, all except me.'

'You have to stay and keep Revisson Doe happy, of course,' I said.

'Was Leslie here last night?'

'My business,' I said.

'My husband,' said Dottie. 'He's mine.'

'Why don't you rent him out by the hour?'

'I wish I could go to Northumberland,' Dottie said. 'Sir Quentin phoned urgently to everyone. They're all going. Maisie rang me. She's going. Father Delaney – '

'It's the best news I've heard for a long time,' I said. 'What about Edwina?'

'Oh, they're not taking her. She'll stay in London with the nurse. You might as well know, if you don't know already, that she won't have anything to leave when she dies.'

I said, and I don't know why I said it (but I was thinking of my character, old Prudence, who inherited my Warrender's estate), 'She might outlive her son and inherit the lot.'

'You and your *Warrender Chase*,' observed Dottie, making the tea.

'Are you taking Dexedrine?' I said.

'No, I've stopped. My doctor made me stop. That's why I can't go to Northumberland, in fact Sir Quentin wouldn't have me.'

'Is Beryl Tims going with them?'

'Of course. She acts as High Priestess at the functions. They're leaving right away. I don't know what to do.'

'Forget them,' I said.

'It's easy for you to forget.'

'No it isn't. One day I'll write about all this.'

I thought of Cellini: 'All men, whatever be their condition . . . should write the tale of their life with their own hand.'

'You've already written it,' Dottie said, clanking down her teacup. 'You know your *Warrender Chase* is all about us. You foresaw it all.'

'Don't be ridiculous.'

When she had packed up her knitting and gone I turned up the passage I wanted in Newman's lovely Apologia:

> . . . I recognized what I had to do, though I shrank from both the task and the exposure which it would entail. I must, I said, give the true key to my whole life; I must show what I am that it may be seen what I am not, and that the phantom may be extinguished which gibbers instead of me. I wish to be known as a living man, and not as a scarecrow which is dressed up in my clothes . . .

And I set it on the table against my Benvenuto Cellini:

> . . . All men, whatever be their condition, who have done anything of merit, or which verily has a semblance of merit, if so be they are men of truth and good repute, should write the tale of their life with their own hand.

I looked from one to another, admiring both. I thought that, one day, when the months between the autumn of 1949 and the summer of 1950 should become long ago and I should have achieved something which 'verily has a semblance of merit,' I would set it forth. I was in a state of acute happiness at Dottie's news. I needed a job and my novel needed a publisher. But in the departure of the Autobiographical Association I felt I had escaped from it. Although in reality I wasn't yet rid of Sir Quentin and his little sect, they were morally outside of myself, they were objectified. I would write about them one day. In fact, under one form or another, whether I have liked it or not, I have written about them ever since, the straws from which I have made my bricks.

TWELVE

It was right in the middle of the twentieth century, the last day of June 1950, warm and sunny, a Friday, that I mark as a changing-point in my life. That goes back to the day I took my sandwiches to the old disused Kensington graveyard to write a poem with my lunch, when the young policeman sauntered over to see what I was up to. He was a clean-cut man, as on war memorials. I asked him: suppose I had been committing a crime sitting there on the gravestone, what crime would it be? 'Well, it could be desecrating and violating,' he said, 'it could be obstructing and hindering without due regard, it could be loitering with intent.' I offered him a sandwich but he refused; he had just had his dinner himself. 'The graves must be very old,' said the policeman. He wished me the best of luck and went on his way. I forget what poem I was writing at the time, but it was probably an exercise in a fixed form, such as a rondeau, triolet or villanelle; also, I was practising Alexandrines for narrative verse about that time, so it might have been one of those; I always found the practice of metre and form for their own sake very absorbing and often, all at once, inspiring. I was waiting till my landlord, Mr Alexander, should be out of the way with his fussing over my overcrowded room.

I couldn't afford to take a larger room, I could hardly afford to pay the rent for my small room. I had found some work, reading manuscripts and proof-reading for the publisher in Wapping, I did some reviewing of poetry and stories. I was also well ahead with my second novel, *All Souls' Day*, and had already planned my third, *The English Rose*. *Warrender Chase* was still unpublished in spite of Solly's efforts and in fact I had given up hope of its being published; all my hopes were on *All Souls' Day*. But my savings were running low and I knew I would have to start selling my books. I was seriously looking for a full-time job.

But that day in the middle of the twentieth century I felt more than ever how good it was to be a woman and an artist there and then. I had been depressed most of the past six weeks, but now it all suddenly passed, as depressions do.

My week-end at Wally's cottage at Marlow on the day after petrol-rationing was lifted, the twenty-seventh of May, had been not quite a disaster, but certainly a mess.

It had started off very well when I took Wally to Hallam Street to breakfast with Edwina before we set off. Sir Quentin had already fled to Northumberland and Edwina was alone with Miss Fisher and a new daily help. Edwina had decked herself out in egg-shell blue trimmed with swansdown that moulted considerably over our break-fast; the colour-scheme was repeated on her eyelids. She must have started preparations for the breakfast some hours before. Her hands were heavily laden with rings and tipped with the brightest varnish.

'Are you Fleur's boy-friend?' she yelled at Wally.

'Yes.'

'She's too good for you.'

'Yes, I know,' said Wally in that genial way of his.

We sat at a small lacy table set in the window of her own small sitting-room. She was alert, happy to have her flat to herself, and she enchanted Wally by her anecdotes about the late Arthur Balfour. When I asked her if Beryl Tims intended to remain in Northumber-land, she said, 'Beryl who?' I didn't see Edwina again until the following week when I wheeled her, all in heavy black with her strings of pearls, into her son Quentin's funeral service.

Wally was greatly taken with Edwina, as he told me on the way to Marlow. 'I'm in love with your Edwina,' he said. At Marlow Wally was upset to find that the woman who came to clean up had not been near the place. I think what annoyed him most was my seeing the evidence of a previous week-end for two. I really didn't mind because the situation itself was a lively one; I do dearly love a turn of events. But I couldn't help wondering who the other girl had been and, observing the mouse-nibbled, greenish crusts of the last breakfast toast on the floor, the black-rimmed green milk in the jug, the two coffee cups and saucers on the draining board, caked with hardened coffee, dry and old, I calculated the age of this evidence; how many week-ends ago, and what had I been doing with Wally the weekdays in between? As Wally stood and swore, I dumped my week-end case in the bedroom with a myopic airiness. The bed was very much crumpled for two, and, as if by a competent stage-manager, Wally's blue cotton pyjama-top hung on the bed-post while the trousers lay, neat and unfolded, on the top of the chest of drawers. A near-empty bottle of whisky and two glasses, one lipstick-stained, were decidedly overdone from the point of view of scenic production, but they were there. We cleared up the place and went out for lunch.

Towards evening I was taken with an attack of nervousness, for no apparent reason, about my almost-forgotten *Warrender Chase*. I was wondering if I had handled that opening scene as well as I might. I had typed and retyped the novel so many times I almost knew it by heart.

'You know, Fleur,' said Wally. 'Sometimes when I'm with you, a very odd thing happens – you're suddenly *not there*. It's creepy. Very often, even when I don't say anything, I feel somehow you're somewhere else.'

I laughed, because I knew he was right. I said, 'I've been thinking about my first novel, *Warrender Chase*, it's preying on my mind.'

'Oh, don't let it do that. I've had ideas for novels myself, but I really haven't the time.'

'Do you think you could write a novel?'

'Oh, if one had the time I daresay one could write as good a novel as the next chap.'

He went out to call at his cleaning woman's house to find out what was the matter with her. He had got over his earlier embarrassment but the week-end already seemed to me to have gone flat. Perhaps we had both been looking forward to it too much. It is as true as any of the copy-book maxims, that love is by nature unforeseen. And I was now so far away in my thoughts that I could only note in his absence that I had a soft spot for Wally, anyway.

We had brought some food with us. I began to set the table for supper and I lit two candles, but I was so abstracted that I can't remember now anything but a general impression of his cottage, or anything about what we had to eat. I think there was a gramophone and that I put on a record.

My mind was unaccountably on *Warrender Chase*, the opening scene where Warrender's mother Prudence, his nephew Roland and Charlotte the frightful housekeeper are waiting for Warrender's arrival in the drawing-room of Warrender's house in the country.

Roland has been playing with one of the South American Indian masks that Warrender collects. Charlotte takes it away from him: 'Your uncle doesn't like it if anyone touches his odds and ends.' Marjorie, Roland's wife, has just answered the telephone in the hall, dashed out and driven off. Prudence keeps saying, 'Where did Marjorie go?' and 'Roland, go and see what's happened to Marjorie. Take the bicycle.' Roland is talking about the adding machines he's selling on a commission basis. Charlotte says she isn't interested in adders. Then she says, all right, adding machines. She says, things are getting to a point where they have nothing to add because Warrender is short of money with too many people to support. Prudence points out that the machines also subtract. She says Warrender has been pronouncing words in a new way. They all discuss the new way. 'Dense' instead of 'dance', 'inter*es*ting,' 'lawst' for 'lost'. Charlotte breaks in with the observation that 'Mr Proudie speaks like that.' 'Proudie's diction is not all that's to be desired of a scholar,' says Prudence. 'However, we may assume that Warrender has been seeing a lot of Proudie. I'm anxious about Marjorie, running off wildly after that telephone call. And Warrender should be here by now. Where has he got to?'

Then I made my character Charlotte go to the window. 'I can hear his car coming.' Roland says, 'No, I'm sure it's Marjorie's car. Warrender's car goes *tum*-te-te-tum. Marjorie's goes tum, tum, *tum*-te-te like this one.'

Prudence says, 'Roland, stop playing with that mask, just to oblige me. Warrender paid a lot for it. I know it's a fake, and so is Warrender, but – ' Marjorie comes into the room. 'What's the matter, Marjorie?' 'Oh, she's ill, give her a drink, water, something.' 'Marjorie, what happened? That phone call. Are you hurt?' At last Marjorie says, 'Warrender is hurt. The car crashed. He's terribly hurt. The police rang here. I went to the hospital. I couldn't identify him at first. His face, Warrender's face . . . ' She passes her hand over her own face and says, 'I think his face is quite demolished.' Roland here goes out to telephone the hospital. Charlotte: 'Is he dead?' Marjorie: 'No, he's still unconscious I'm afraid.' Now Charlotte, the English Rose, seizes on those words 'unconscious, I'm afraid.' 'What do you mean, you're afraid? Do you want him to die?'

Roland comes back: 'He's dead.'

Wally's car pulled up and he came in smiling. 'Mrs Richards had an op. Good thing I called round. She can't work for a few weeks yet. She's awfully reliable, I knew something had happened. Nothing serious, anyway, she didn't show me the op. The men always do.'

I said, 'Did I tell you the Autobiographical Association has moved to Northumberland to Sir Quentin's house?'

'Oh, forget them, Fleur. It was a lousy job. Not your thing at all from the sound of it. Edwina's well out of it too. Awful for her, having a crackpot for a son. Maybe she's too old to care.'

Now I decided to force *Warrender Chase* out of my mind. To do so I began to tell Wally about my new novel, *All Souls' Day*. I think he was fairly interested. After supper we went down to the pub for a drink. We walked home by the river and so to bed. It was simply no good. Anxious not to be abstracted and 'not there' with Wally, my mind was now only too deliberately concentrated on the actuality of the occasion. I found myself very vigilant of every detail in Wally's lovemaking. I was noticing, I was *counting*. I was single-mindedly conscious. In desperation I tried thinking of General de Gaulle, which made matters worse, far, far, worse.

'I'm afraid I've had too much beer,' said poor Wally.

Next morning we went out on the river for an hour. After lunch we tidied up the cottage and set off early for London. Wally dropped me at my house just after five in the afternoon.

Dottie again, at midnight. I put on my dressing-gown and let her in. 'Sir Quentin's been killed in a car accident. A head-on collision last night,' she said.

'What about the other car? Anyone hurt?'

'Oh, they were killed too,' said Dottie with the impatience that denoted she was dealing with an imbecile who couldn't distinguish the kernel from the nutshell.

'How many in the other car?'

'Two, I think, but the point is – '

'Thank God he's dead,' I said.

'So that it proves your *Warrender Chase* to be valid.'

'Nothing to do with my *Warrender Chase*. Quite a different situation. The man was pure evil.'

'They were all waiting for him to join them,' Dottie said. I got rid of Dottie.

The theme of *Warrender Chase* was indeed valid. Such events as I'd portrayed, even in a different way from the reality, could happen. My *Warrender Chase* was valid, and I decided that my Chapter One, which had haunted me at Wally's cottage, could very well stand as it was.

At ten the next morning I rang Miss Fisher at Hallam Street. Edwina, she said, had taken the news very bravely. The doctor had been to see her. Everything was all right, and Edwina was keeping very quiet.

After the funeral Beryl Tims caught up with me and said, in Edwina's hearing, 'You'll have to work out something with Lady Edwina. Sir Quentin's property reverts to her and I have no settlement.'

'Edwina,' I said, 'Mrs Tims is here to present her condolences.'

'I noticed her,' said Edwina.

I wheeled her away, upright as she was, in her glittering black. What shocked me was that Beryl Tims had used almost the very words of my Charlotte, at Warrender's funeral.

From the day of the funeral to the day at the end of June when I sat in the graveyard writing my poem, Dottie kept me abundantly informed about the members of the disbanded Association.

'We were wondering,' Dottie said, 'what had happened to the biographies. They never got a chance to read them.'

'Edwina destroyed them.'

'Had she a right to do that?'

'I suppose so.'

'She wasn't by any chance influenced by you?'

'No, she just told me she'd got Miss Fisher to destroy the papers. Nothing of any interest, and she hadn't the space to hoard them.'

'Poor Beryl Tims. He promised to make a settlement on her. Do you know that Eric Findlay has gone back to his wife?'

'I didn't know he'd left her.'

'Well, Fleur, he left her for you. It was in his autobiography. You had an affair with him, Fleur. I saw it written down in black and white. Sir Quentin showed it to me.'

'Was it written in his own hand?'

'No, well of course, Sir Quentin took it down verbally. He wrote it for Eric.'

'Well, it wasn't true. He invented it.'

'It's just possible,' said Dottie, 'that it wasn't true. On the other hand – '

'Get out.'

So it went on. Maisie Young had a nervous breakdown and got over it, all in those few weeks between the funeral and my special day in the graveyard. Clotilde du Loiret had gone to stay at a convent in France to find her soul, which she felt she had lost. Dottie was seeing a lot of Father Delaney who enjoyed taking her to wrestling matches and who was still consuming Dexedrine. Mrs Wilks had gone back to her family, but visited Sir Quentin's grave every day, where she conversed with him. When I asked Dottie if anyone visited Bucks Gilbert's grave, she said, 'Oh, well, suicide's a mortal sin. She shouldn't have had a Christian burial.'

I saw Edwina frequently all that month of June. And Wally, too; he wanted to take me back to Marlow for a better week-end. But I had to work all my week-ends at my reviewing and my new novel, knowing that soon I would have to take a full-time job.

The day after I met the policeman at the Kensington graveyard was Saturday the first of July. Now began my new life. I got a letter from the great and glorious Triad Press, an old establishment which specialized in publishing books of good quality. It was a simple letter:

Dear Miss Talbot,

We would be grateful if you would make an appointment to visit us here, at your earliest convenience.

Yours Sincerely,
Cynthia Somerville
The Triad Press.

Now Edwina had rambled about the Somervilles of Triad, whose great-uncle she had known. She had thought I might get a job there. Solly, it now came to mind, had also said to me, 'You might get a job at Triad.' It occurred to me that either Edwina or Solly had recommended me for a job. I checked with both of them the next afternoon.

We didn't take Edwina out for a walk that Sunday. I think it rained.
We had tea at Hallam Street. Edwina had now added to her staff a
handsome, sturdy manservant, a widower called Rudder, who had
been a butler in a grand house before the war and a sergeant-major in
the army. He managed the rations so well that Edwina was able to
offer us teas on a grand scale.

'No, I haven't said anything to Triad,' said Solly, turning over the
letter as if it held some secret code. Nor did Edwina seem to know
anything about it.

'Maybe it's about that book of yours, Miss Fleur,' said Rudder,
who was quite one of the family. Indeed, according to Dottie, he was
getting 'very thick' with Miss Fisher and both of them were quite
milking Edwina; that was according to Dottie, but I didn't see that it
mattered since Edwina was so well suited by them both. Rudder now
had the letter in his hand. 'It looks to me like they want your book.
You see, they say grateful. Now, if you go after a position it's never the
employer that's grateful, it's you that's grateful. You see, here,
they've written "We would be grateful if you would make – "'

'My God,' said Solly, 'I sent them *Warrender Chase* four, five
weeks ago. I forgot.'

'I hope they're grateful enough,' Edwina croaked.

For the rest of the tea Solly described the Triad trio. Two brothers
and a sister. They did everything in unison.

'But you'd better not build up your hopes,' Solly said. 'It could be
only about a job. They might have heard from someone you're
looking for a job and there might just be a vacancy.'

'Well, even that would be something,' I said.

It wasn't about a job. It was about *Warrender Chase*.

The famous trio were sitting side by side at a desk. They were
Leopold, Cynthia and Claude Somerville themselves, arbiters of
taste and of *belles-lettres*. I think they shared a soul. Their mournful
grey-green eyes were identical, their long oval faces very similar.
Leopold, the youngest, in his early thirties, gave a little jump in his
chair when he had something to say which excited him. Cynthia sat
perfectly still with her hands clasped before her. She wore a grey-
green dress which picked up the colour of the six Somerville eyes; her

sleeves were wide, with a medieval look. Claude was the eldest, with greying hair; it fell to Claude to discuss the business side which he did with such an air of apologetic and timid regret as to make it positively cruel to question or discuss the terms of the contract which I rejoiced to notice he had ready on the desk before him.

Their long desk was sheer and shiny, no blotting pads, no pen-stands, no In and Out trays. Only my *Warrender Chase* lying in front of Cynthia, a file which contained readers' reports in front of Leopold and the contract in front of Claude. They were ready for their portrait to be painted. They had everything except a *Brandenburg Concerto* in the background. But I'm sure they didn't arrange themselves as consciously as appeared. There was indeed a certain amount of stage-production about the Triad, but as I came to learn throughout the years, their joint and public face was sheer instinct, even genius.

They rose to greet me and sat down again, Leopold with an extra little jump.

'We would be happy to publish your novel,' said Cynthia. The siblings smiled in unison, not a wide smile but a kindly one.

It would have been difficult for me to realize at that moment that Cynthia was in fact having an affair with a fruit-loader at Covent Garden, Leopold was chasing a bandleader and Claude was already married to a rich American widow with four children of her own and two of his. To me it seemed the Triad had come into being out of nothing and, when I should depart, to nothing they would return.

Leopold, patting the file of readers' reports, assured me that these were so mixed as to be stimulating from a publisher's point of view. He jumped in his chair and said, 'Some readers hated it but some readers loved it.' 'So we think it will have a small cult-following,' said Cynthia. 'It will not be a commercial venture, of course,' added Claude. 'The general consensus,' said Leopold, 'is that although the evil of Warrender is a shade over-accentuated, you have a universal theme.' (Jump.)

I said I thought it possible that there were people like Warrender Chase in real life.

The three assented to this in unison. I felt sure that among the readers who had hated the book were Theo and Audrey Clairmont who sometimes read for the Triad Press; and years later I found that the very excess of their attempts to suppress *Warrender Chase* had finally persuaded the Triad in its favour.

I wanted to take the contract away to study it, a reasonable desire. But it would have been beyond me, beyond anyone I knew, to stab gentle, tentative Claude with so profound a knife-wound. I signed it on the spot, only checking first to see if there was an option clause. Claude noticed my glance. 'The option is on terms to be agreed,' he murmured, as if with breathless hope that I wouldn't change my mind. And he added, 'We consider that wording to be the most tactful.' He stressed the word 'tactful', with the result that tact was temporarily cancelled from the contract-signing scene.

But in fact it was a good contract. The advance on royalties was an unheard-of hundred pounds, which I needed. I addressed Cynthia as I told them about my forthcoming *All Souls' Day* and the novel I had planned to follow it, *The English Rose*. She looked at me with her grey-green eyes, Claude sighed with wonder and Leopold jumped twice. So began my long career as a novelist with the Triad Press.

I spun out the money till November when *Warrender Chase* was to be published. A bad month for publishing, but first novels of uncertain futures had to give precedence to certainties. I had corrected the proofs of the book, feeling altogether bored with it. I had nearly finished my *All Souls' Day* which I loved with all my heart in those months.

I think it was in September that Wally took me on a visit to Cambridge. We went to Grantchester, the home of Rupert Brooke. 'Stands the Church clock at ten to three?' The church clock *stood* at ten to three. By order of the management. I had a sudden revulsion against the clock, Grantchester, Rupert Brooke and the ethos of honey still for tea, and I said so at length to Wally. He was not altogether insensitive. He said, 'I hope you don't include me in the whole shooting-match.'

Wally eventually married an English Rose who knew all about *placement* and protocol and was admired by everybody including the children's nanny. In time Wally became an ambassador with a swimming pool which was always surrounded by notable people and their consorts to whom Wally would descend from time to time: 'I've just got away.'

The Triad Press had printed a thousand copies of *Warrender Chase*, reckoning to sell five hundred. 'But we can count on some nice reviews,' said Cynthia on the telephone. They sent a photographer to my room to take my picture for the back of the jacket.

In late October Leslie's novel, *Two Ways*, appeared. It had a portrait of a hard-hearted woman conflicting with a poor Cockney boy for the affections of our hero. My main objection to it was the diction. Leslie was so hard pressed for ways in which to express an idiom that he had fallen back on phonetic spelling, always a literary defect in my opinion. '''Ow can yer do this ter me, guv'ner?' pleads Leslie's young Cockney. When all he had to say (since the reader already knows he's a Cockney) is, 'You can't do this.' Which is far more authentic to the ear than all the '''ows,' 'yers' and 'ters.'

Anyway, Leslie's book got two reviews which Dottie brought round to display to me. They were rather feeble, but better than nothing.

Nothing is what happened to *Warrender Chase* for the first two weeks after it was published. I was saddened by this silence, but not very deeply, for I had half forgotten the book, so much did I prize my new work.

I went over to Solly one Thursday afternoon. He had promised to lend me some money to pay my rent, for I was waiting to be paid for some reviews and articles. In fact I also owed money to a dentist whose receptionist was beginning to lose patience; I had refused to answer the telephone all day, convinced as I was that the persistent calls were from her. The house-boy was quite offended when I told him on the switchboard to say I was out to everybody. He said he didn't like telling lies. I told him that Not at Home wasn't a lie. He agreed, technically, but he sounded sulky.

Solly was sitting among his usual mess of newspapers and journals. I said, 'I don't like having to borrow. But I'll pay you back soon.'

'You should worry,' said Solly. He was smiling in the midst of the papers spread out on his desk and on the chair. There were several weeklies. I saw the *Evening Standard*, too, and then I saw my photograph. Reviews of *Warrender Chase* had appeared all over the place, all quite favourable, all very large. Solly said he had advance information from the Sunday papers that the same thing was going to happen there. The *Evening Standard* picture had the caption, 'Fleur Talbot in the book-lined study of her town house'. It was all a long time ago.

I recall that Theo Clairmont was one of the Sunday reviewers. He said it was undoubtedly an important book, but the author would probably never be able to write another. The prophecy didn't come to pass, for *All Souls' Day* gave as much pleasure as *Warrender Chase*, and after that, *The English Rose* and others, some more, some less.

Another thing I recall, that day when I went over to Solly to borrow the money for my rent: on my return there was Mr Alexander at the door to greet me with a great welcome and a copy of the *Evening Standard* in his hand. He asked me in to have a drink with his wife. I said, another time. The house-boy was also very agitated, not knowing what to do with the phone messages and yet mesmerized by my picture in the paper. He was not quite convinced that I wasn't involved in some wrong-doing.

And I remember Leslie paid me a visit that evening. He congratulated me on my piece of luck. He said, 'Of course, a popular success . . .' and didn't finish the sentence. He said, 'Well, I'll always be your friend,' as if I were out on bail.

The telephone messages had been mounting up. I had a bunch of them from the house-boy, and yet another bunch by nine o'clock that night. I took them to bed with me, feeling somewhat bewildered. I looked them over one by one. Some of the people I was to ring back were Miss Maisie Young, Mrs Beryl Tims, Miss Cynthia Somerville of the Triad Press, Mr Gray Mauser, the features editor of *Good Housekeeping*, the literary editor of the *Evening News*, Mr Tim Sutcliffe of the Third Programme, B.B.C., Mr Revisson Doe; and there were many others including Dottie.

I rang Dottie back. She accused me of having plotted and planned it all. 'You knew what you were doing,' she said. I agreed I had been loitering with intent and said I was leaving for Paris in the morning.

In fact, I took refuge with Edwina in Hallam Street for a few weeks till the fuss died down. I had work to do. Success is a subject like any other subject, and I knew too little about it, just then, to be able to discuss it and answer questions about it. In those weeks the Triad sold the American rights, the paperback rights, the film rights, and most of the foreign rights of *Warrender Chase*. Good-bye, my poverty. Good-bye, my youth.

It was a long time ago. I've been writing ever since with great care. I always hope the readers of my novels are of good quality. I wouldn't like to think of anyone cheap reading my books.

Edwina died at the age of ninety-eight. Her manservant Rudder had married Miss Fisher and they inherited her fortune.

Maisie Young opened a vegetarian restaurant which has flourished under the management of Beryl Tims.

Father Egbert Delaney was arrested in the park for exposing himself and then sent to a rehabilitation centre. Dottie, who is my chief informant on all these people, lost track of him after that.

Sir Eric Findlay died on good terms with his family, having lived long enough to earn the reputation of an eccentric rather than a nut.

The Baronne Clotilde du Loiret also died some time in the sixties, in California, where she had joined a highly-organized religious sect. According to Dottie she died in the arms of her spiritual leader, an oriental mystic.

I have no idea whatsoever what happened to Mrs Wilks.

But it is Solly Mendelsohn I mourn for. Solly, clumping and limping over Hampstead Heath with his large night-pale face. Oh Solly, my friend, my friend.

Dottie has been divorced and married so many times I forget what her name is now. I live in Paris; and Dottie's present husband who is a journalist brought her to Paris a few years ago. She has problems with her children. She has the ugliest grandchild I have ever seen but she loves it. Dottie, under stress, stands under my window late at night singing 'Auld Lang Syne' a ditty that the French fail to relish at one twenty-five in the morning.

The other day when I had looked in on Dottie, in her little flat, and had a row with her on the subject of my wriggling out of real life, unlike herself, I came out into the court-yard exasperated as usual. Some small boys were playing football, and the ball came flying straight towards me. I kicked it with a chance grace, which, if I had studied the affair and tried hard, I never could have done. Away into the air it went, and landed in the small boy's waiting hands. The boy grinned. And so, having entered the fullness of my years, from there by the grace of God I go on my way rejoicing.

The Girls of
Slender Means

For Alan Maclean

ONE

Long ago in 1945 all the nice people in England were poor, allowing for exceptions. The streets of the cities were lined with buildings in bad repair or in no repair at all, bomb-sites piled with stony rubble, houses like giant teeth in which decay had been drilled out, leaving only the cavity. Some bomb-ripped buildings looked like the ruins of ancient castles until, at a closer view, the wallpapers of various quite normal rooms would be visible, room above room, exposed, as on a stage, with one wall missing; sometimes a lavatory chain would dangle over nothing from a fourth- or fifth-floor ceiling; most of all the staircases survived, like a new art-form, leading up and up to an unspecified destination that made unusual demands on the mind's eye. All the nice people were poor; at least, that was a general axiom, the best of the rich being poor in spirit.

There was absolutely no point in feeling depressed about the scene, it would have been like feeling depressed about the Grand Canyon or some event of the earth outside everybody's scope. People continued to exchange assurances of depressed feelings about the weather or the news, or the Albert Memorial which had not been hit, not even shaken, by any bomb from first to last.

The May of Teck Club stood obliquely opposite the site of the Memorial, in one of a row of tall houses which had endured, but barely; some bombs had dropped nearby, and in a few back gardens, leaving the buildings cracked on the outside and shakily hinged within, but habitable for the time being. The shattered windows had been replaced with new glass rattling in loose frames. More recently, the bituminous black-out paint had been removed from landing and bathroom windows. Windows were important in that year of final reckoning; they told at a glance whether a house was inhabited or not; and in the course of the past years they had accumulated much meaning, having been the main danger-zone between domestic life and the war going on outside: everyone had said, when the sirens sounded, 'Mind the windows. Keep away from the windows. Watch out for the glass.'

The May of Teck Club had been three times window-shattered since 1940, but never directly hit. There the windows of the upper bedrooms overlooked the dip and rise of treetops in Kensington Gardens across the street, with the Albert Memorial to be seen by means of a slight craning and twist of the neck. These upper bedrooms looked down on the opposite pavement on the park side of the street, and on the tiny people who moved along in neat-looking singles and couples, pushing little prams loaded with pin-head babies and provisions, or carrying little dots of shopping bags. Everyone carried a shopping bag in case they should be lucky enough to pass a shop that had a sudden stock of something off the rations.

From the lower-floor dormitories the people in the street looked larger, and the paths of the park were visible. All the nice people were poor, and few were nicer, as nice people come, than these girls at Kensington who glanced out of the windows in the early mornings to see what the day looked like, or gazed out on the green summer evenings, as if reflecting on the months ahead, on love and the relations of love. Their eyes gave out an eager-spirited light that resembled near-genius, but was youth merely. The first of the Rules of Constitution, drawn up at some remote and innocent Edwardian date, still applied more or less to them:

> The May of Teck Club exists for the Pecuniary Convenience and Social Protection of Ladies of Slender Means below the age of Thirty Years, who are obliged to reside apart from their Families in order to follow an Occupation in London.

As they realized themselves in varying degrees, few people alive at the time were more delightful, more ingenious, more movingly lovely, and, as it might happen, more savage, than the girls of slender means.

'I've got something to tell you,' said Jane Wright, the woman columnist.

At the other end of the telephone, the voice of Dorothy Markham, owner of the flourishing model agency, said, 'Darling, where have you been?' She spoke, by habit since her débutante days, with the utmost enthusiasm of tone.

'I've got something to tell you. Do you remember Nicholas Farringdon? Remember he used to come to the old May of Teck just after the war, he was an anarchist and poet sort of thing. A tall man with–'

'The one that got on to the roof to sleep out with Selina?'

'Yes, Nicholas Farringdon.'

'Oh rather. Has he turned up?'

'No, he's been martyred.'

'What-ed?'

'Martyred in Haiti. Killed. Remember he became a Brother–'

'But I've just been to Tahiti, it's marvellous, everyone's marvellous. Where did you hear it?'

'Haiti. There's a news paragraph just come over Reuters. I'm sure it's the same Nicholas Farringdon because it says a missionary, former poet. I nearly died. I knew him well, you know, in those days. I expect they'll hush it all up, about those days, if they want to make a martyr story.'

'How did it happen, is it gruesome?'

'Oh, I don't know, there's only a paragraph.'

'You'll have to find out more through your grapevine. I'm shattered. I've got heaps to tell you.'

The Committee of Management wishes to express surprise at the Members' protest regarding the wallpaper chosen for the drawing room. The Committee wishes to point out that Members' residential fees do not meet the running expenses of the Club. The Committee regrets that the spirit of the May of Teck foundation has apparently so far deteriorated that such a protest has been made. The Committee refers Members to the terms of the Club's Foundation.

Joanna Childe was a daughter of a country rector. She had a good intelligence and strong obscure emotions. She was training to be a teacher of elocution and, while attending a school of drama, already had pupils of her own. Joanna Childe had been drawn to this profession by her good voice and love of poetry which she loved rather as it might be assumed a cat loves birds; poetry, especially the declamatory sort, excited and possessed her; she would pounce on the stuff, play with it quivering in her mind, and when she had got it by heart, she spoke it forth with devouring relish. Mostly, she indulged the habit while giving elocution lessons at the club where she was highly thought of for it. The vibrations of Joanna's elocution voice from her room or from the recreation room where she frequently rehearsed, were felt to add tone and style to the establishment when boy-friends called. Her taste in poetry became the accepted taste of the club. She had a deep feeling for certain passages in the authorized version of the Bible, besides the Book of Common Prayer, Shakespeare and Gerard Manley Hopkins, and had newly discovered Dylan Thomas. She was not moved by the poetry of Eliot and Auden, except for the latter's lyric:

> Lay your sleeping head, my love,
> Human on my faithless arm;

Joanna Childe was large, with light shiny hair, blue eyes and deep-pink cheeks. When she read the notice signed by Lady Julia Markham, chairwoman of the committee, she stood with the other young women round the green baize board and was given to murmur:

'He rageth, and again he rageth, because he knows his time is short.'

It was not known to many that this was a reference to the Devil, but it caused amusement. She had not intended it so. It was not usual for Joanna to quote anything for its aptitude, and at conversational pitch.

Joanna, who was now of age, would henceforth vote conservative in the elections, which at that time in the May of Teck Club was associated with a desirable order of life that none of the members was old enough to remember from direct experience. In principle they all approved of what the committee's notice stood for. And so Joanna was alarmed by the amused reaction to her quotation, the hearty laugh of understanding that those days were over when the members of anything whatsoever might not raise their voices against the drawing-room wallpaper. Principles regardless, everyone knew that the notice was plain damned funny. Lady Julia must be feeling pretty desperate.

'He rageth and again he rageth, because he knows his time is short.'

Little dark Judy Redwood who was a shorthand typist in the Ministry of Labour said, 'I've got a feeling that as members we're legally entitled to a say in the administration. I must ask Geoffrey.' This was the man Judy was engaged to. He was still in the forces, but had qualified as a solicitor before being called up. His sister, Anne Baberton, who stood with the notice-board group, said, 'Geoffrey would be the last person I would consult.' Anne Baberton said this to indicate that she knew Geoffrey better than Judy knew him; she said it to indicate affectionate scorn; she said it because it was the obvious thing for a nicely brought-up sister to say, since she was proud of him; and besides all this, there was an element of irritation in her words, 'Geoffrey would be the last person I would consult', for she knew there was no point in members taking up this question of the drawing-room wall-paper.

Anne trod out her cigarette-end contemptuously on the floor of the large entrance hall with its pink and grey Victorian tiles. This was pointed to by a thin middle-aged woman, one of the few older, if not exactly the earliest members. She said, 'One is not permitted to put cigarette-ends on the floor.' The words did not appear to impress themselves on the ears of the group, more than the ticking of the grandfather clock behind them. But Anne said, 'Isn't one permitted to spit on the floor, even?' 'One certainly isn't,' said the spinster. 'Oh, I thought one was,' said Anne.

The May of Teck Club was founded by Queen Mary before her marriage to King George the Fifth, when she was Princess May of Teck. On an afternoon between the engagement and the marriage, the Princess had been induced to come to London and declare officially open the May of Teck Club which had been endowed by various gentle forces of wealth.

None of the original Ladies remained in the club. But three subsequent members had been permitted to stay on past the stipulated age-limit of thirty, and were now in their fifties, and had resided at the May of Teck Club since before the First World War at which time, they said, all members had been obliged to dress for dinner.

Nobody knew why these three women had not been asked to leave when they had reached the age of thirty. Even the warden and committee did not know why the three remained. It was now too late to turn them out with decency. It was too late even to mention to them the subject of their continuing residence. Successive committees before 1939 had decided that the three older residents might, in any case, be expected to have a good influence on the younger ones.

During the war the matter had been left in abeyance, since the club was half empty; in any case members' fees were needed, and bombs were then obliterating so much and so many in the near vicinity that it was an open question whether indeed the three spinsters would remain upright with the house to the end. By 1945 they had seen much coming of new girls and going of old, and were generally liked by the current batch, being subject to insults when they interfered in anything, and intimate confidences when they kept aloof. The confidences seldom represented the whole truth, particularly those revealed by the young women who occupied the top floor. The three spinsters were, through the ages, known and addressed as Collie (Miss Coleman), Greggie (Miss Macgregor) and Jarvie (Miss Jarman). It was Greggie who had said to Anne by the notice-board:

'One isn't permitted to put cigarette-ends on the floor.'

'Isn't one permitted to spit on the floor, even?'

'No, one isn't.'

'Oh, I thought one was.'

Greggie affected an indulgent sigh and pushed her way through the crowd of younger members. She went to the open door, set in a wide porch, to look out at the summer evening like a shopkeeper waiting for custom. Greggie always behaved as if she owned the club.

The gong was about to sound quite soon. Anne kicked her cigarette-stub into a dark corner.

Greggie called over her shoulder, 'Anne, here comes your boy-friend.'

'On time, for once,' said Anne, with the same pretence of scorn that she had adopted when referring to her brother Geoffrey: 'Geoffrey would be the last person I would consult.' She moved, with her casual hips, towards the door.

A square-built high-coloured young man in the uniform of an

English captain came smiling in. Anne stood regarding him as if he was the last person in the world she would consult.

'Good evening,' he said to Greggie as a well-brought-up man would naturally say to a woman of Greggie's years standing in the doorway. He made a vague nasal noise of recognition to Anne, which if properly pronounced would have been 'Hallo'. She said nothing at all by way of greeting. They were nearly engaged to be married.

'Like to come in and see the drawing-room wallpaper?' Anne said then.

'No, let's get cracking.'

Anne went to get her coat off the banister where she had slung it. He was saying to Greggie, 'Lovely evening, isn't it?'

Anne returned with her coat slung over her shoulder. 'Bye, Greggie,' she said. 'Good-bye,' said the soldier. Anne took his arm.

'Have a nice time,' said Greggie.

The dinner-gong sounded and there was a scuffle of feet departing from the notice-board and a scamper of feet from the floors above.

On a summer night during the previous week the whole club, forty-odd women, with any young men who might happen to have called that evening, had gone like swift migrants into the dark cool air of the park, crossing its wide acres as the crow flies in the direction of Buckingham Palace, there to express themselves along with the rest of London on the victory in the war with Germany. They clung to each other in twos and threes, fearful of being trampled. When separated, they clung to, and were clung to by, the nearest person. They became members of a wave of the sea, they surged and sang until, at every half-hour interval, a light flooded the tiny distant balcony of the Palace and four small straight digits appeared upon it: the King, the Queen, and the two Princesses. The royal family raised their right arms, their hands fluttered as in a slight breeze, they were three candles in uniform and one in the recognizable fur-trimmed folds of the civilian queen in war-time. The huge organic murmur of the crowd, different from anything like the voice of animate matter but rather more a cataract or a geological disturbance, spread through the parks and along the Mall. Only the St John's Ambulance men, watchful beside their vans, had any identity left. The royal family

waved, turned to go, lingered and waved again, and finally disappeared. Many strange arms were twined round strange bodies. Many
liaisons, some permanent, were formed in the night, and numerous
infants of experimental variety, delightful in hue of skin and racial
structure, were born to the world in the due cycle of nine months
after. The bells pealed. Greggie observed that it was something
between a wedding and a funeral on a world scale.

The next day everyone began to consider where they personally
stood in the new order of things.

Many citizens felt the urge, which some began to indulge, to insult
each other, in order to prove something or to test their ground.

The government reminded the public that it was still at war.
Officially this was undeniable, but except to those whose relations lay
in the Far-Eastern prisons of war, or were stuck in Burma, that war
was generally felt to be a remote affair.

A few shorthand typists at the May of Teck Club started to apply
for safer jobs – that is to say, in private concerns, not connected with
the war like the temporary Ministries where many of them had been
employed.

Their brothers and men friends in the forces, not yet demobilized,
by a long way, were talking of vivid enterprises for the exploitation of
peace, such as buying a lorry and building up from it a transport
business.

'I've got something to tell you,' said Jane.

'Just a minute till I shut the door. The kids are making a row,' Anne
said. And presently, when she returned to the telephone, she said,
'Yes, carry on.'

'Do you remember Nicholas Farringdon?'

'I seem to remember the name.'

'Remember I brought him to the May of Teck in 1945, he used to
come often for supper. He got mixed up with Selina.'

'Oh, Nicholas. The one who got up on the roof? What a long time
ago that was. Have you seen him?'

'I've just seen a news item that's come over Reuters. He's been
killed in a local rising in Haiti.'

'Really? How awful! What was he doing there?'

'Well, he became a missionary or something.'

'No!'

'Yes. It's terribly tragic. I knew him well.'

'Ghastly. It brings everything back. Have you told Selina?'

'Well, I haven't been able to get her. You know what Selina's like these days, she won't answer the phone personally, you have to go through thousands of secretaries or whatever they are.'

'You could get a good story for your paper out of it, Jane,' Anne said.

'I know that. I'm just waiting to get more details. Of course it's all those years ago since I knew him, but it would be an interesting story.'

Two men – poets by virtue of the fact that the composition of poetry was the only consistent thing they had so far done – beloved of two May of Teck girls and, at the moment, of nobody else, sat in their corduroy trousers in a café in Bayswater with their silent listening admirers and talked about the new future as they flicked the page-proofs of an absent friend's novel. A copy of *Peace News* lay on the table between them. One of the men said to the other:

And now what will become of us without Barbarians? Those people were some sort of a solution.

And the other smiled, bored-like, but conscious that very few in all the great metropolis and its tributary provinces were as yet privy to the source of these lines. This other who smiled was Nicholas Farringdon, not yet known or as yet at all likely to be.

'Who wrote that?' said Jane Wright, a fat girl who worked for a publisher and who was considered to be brainy but somewhat below standard, socially, at the May of Teck.

Neither man replied.

'Who wrote that?' Jane said again.

The poet nearest her said, through his thick spectacles, 'An Alexandrian poet.'

'A new poet?'

'No, but fairly new to this country.'

'What's his name?'

He did not reply. The young men had started talking again. They talked about the decline and fall of the anarchist movement on the island of their birth in terms of the personalities concerned. They were bored with educating the girls for this evening.

TWO

Joanna Childe was giving elocution lessons to Miss Harper, the cook, in the recreation room. When she was not giving lessons she was usually practising for her next examination. The house frequently echoed with Joanna's rhetoric. She got six shillings an hour from her pupils, five shillings if they were May of Teck members. Nobody knew what her arrangements were with Miss Harper, for at that time all who kept keys of food-cupboards made special arrangements with all others. Joanna's method was to read each stanza herself first and make her pupil repeat it.

Everyone in the drawing-room could hear the loud lesson in progress beating out the stresses and throbs of *The Wreck of the Deutschland*.

> The frown of his face
> Before me, the hurtle of hell
> Behind, where, where was a, where was a place?

The club was proud of Joanna Childe, not only because she chucked up her head and recited poetry, but because she was so well built, fair and healthy looking, the poetic essence of tall, fair rectors' daughters who never used a scrap of make-up, who had served tirelessly day and night in parish welfare organizations since leaving school early in the war, who before that had been Head Girl and who never wept that anyone knew or could imagine, being stoical by nature.

What had happened to Joanna was that she had fallen in love with a curate on leaving school. It had come to nothing. Joanna had decided that this was to be the only love of her life.

She had been brought up to hear, and later to recite,

> ... Love is not love
> Which alters when it alteration finds,
> Or bends with the remover to remove:

All her ideas of honour and love came from the poets. She was vaguely acquainted with distinctions and sub-distinctions of human and divine love, and their various attributes, but this was picked up from rectory conversations when theologically-minded clerics came to stay; it was in a different category of instruction from ordinary household beliefs such as the axiom, 'People are holier who live in the country', and the notion that a nice girl should only fall in love once in her life.

It seemed to Joanna that her longing for the curate must have been unworthy of the name of love, had she allowed a similar longing, which she began to feel, for the company of a succeeding curate, more suitable and even handsomer, to come to anything. Once you admit that you can change the object of a strongly-felt affection, you undermine the whole structure of love and marriage, the whole philosophy of Shakespeare's sonnet: this had been the approved, though unspoken, opinion of the rectory and its mental acres of upper air. Joanna pressed down her feelings for the second curate and worked them off in tennis and the war effort. She had not encouraged the second curate at all but brooded silently upon him until the Sunday she saw him standing in the pulpit and announce his sermon upon the text:

> ... if thy right eye offend thee, pluck it out, and cast it from thee: for it is profitable for thee that one of thy members should perish, and not that thy whole body should be cast into hell.
> And if thy right hand offend thee, cut it off, and cast it from thee: for it is profitable for thee that one of thy members should perish, and not that thy whole body should be cast into hell.

It was the evening service. Many young girls from the district had come, some of them in their service uniforms. One particular Wren looked up at the curate, her pink cheeks touched by the stained-glass evening light; her hair curled lightly upwards on her Wren hat. Joanna could hardly imagine a more handsome man than this second curate. He was newly ordained, and was shortly going into the Air

Force. It was spring, full of preparations and guesses, for the second front was to be established against the enemy, some said in North Africa, some said Scandinavia, the Baltic, France. Meantime, Joanna listened attentively to the young man in the pulpit, she listened obsessively. He was dark and tall, his eyes were deep under his straight black brows, he had a chiselled look. His wide mouth suggested to Joanna generosity and humour, that type of generosity and humour special to the bishop sprouting within him. He was very athletic. He had made it as clear that he wanted Joanna as the former curate had not. Like the rector's eldest daughter that she was, Joanna sat in her pew without seeming to listen in any particular way to this attractive fellow. She did not turn her face towards him as the pretty Wren was doing. The right eye and the right hand, he was saying, means that which we hold most precious. What the scripture meant, he said, was that if anything we hold most dear should prove an offence – as you know, he said, the Greek word here was σκάνδαλον, frequently occurring in Scripture in the connotation of scandal, offence, stumbling-block, as when St Paul said.... The rustics who predominated in the congregation looked on with their round moveless eyes. Joanna decided to pluck out her right eye, cut off her right hand, this looming offence to the first love, this stumbling-block, the adorable man in the pulpit.

'For it is profitable for thee that one of thy members should perish, and not that thy whole body should be cast into hell,' rang the preacher's voice. 'Hell of course,' he said, 'is a negative concept. Let us put it more positively. More positively, the text should read, "It is better to enter maimed into the Kingdom of Heaven than not to enter at all."' He hoped to publish this sermon one day in a Collected Sermons, for he was as yet inexperienced in many respects, although he later learned some reality as an Air Force chaplain.

Joanna, then, had decided to enter maimed into the Kingdom of Heaven. By no means did she look maimed. She got a job in London and settled at the May of Teck Club. She took up elocution in her spare time. Then, towards the end of the war, she began to study and make a full-time occupation of it. The sensation of poetry replaced the sensation of the curate and she took on pupils at six shillings an hour pending her diploma.

The wanton troopers riding by
Have shot my fawn, and it will die.

Nobody at the May of Teck Club knew her precise history, but it was generally assumed to be something emotionally heroic. She was compared to Ingrid Bergman, and did not take part in the argument between members and staff about the food, whether it contained too many fattening properties, even allowing for the necessities of war-time rationing.

THREE

Love and money were the vital themes in all the bedrooms and dormitories. Love came first, and subsidiary to it was money for the upkeep of looks and the purchase of clothing coupons at the official black-market price of eight coupons for a pound.

The house was a spacious Victorian one, and very little had been done to change its interior since the days when it was a private residence. It resembled in its plan most of the women's hostels, noted for cheapness and tone, which had flourished since the emancipation of women had called for them. No one at the May of Teck Club referred to it as a hostel, except in moments of low personal morale such as was experienced by the youngest members only on being given the brush-off by a boy-friend.

The basement of the house was occupied by kitchens, the laundry, the furnace and fuel-stores.

The ground floor contained staff offices, the dining-room, the recreation room and, newly papered in a mud-like shade of brown, the drawing-room. This resented wall-paper had unfortunately been found at the back of a cupboard in huge quantities, otherwise the walls would have remained grey and stricken like everyone else's.

Boy-friends were allowed to dine as guests at a cost of two-and-sixpence. It was also permitted to entertain in the recreation room, on the terrace which led out from it, and in the drawing-room whose mud-brown walls appeared so penitential in tone at that time – for the members were not to know that within a few years many of them would be lining the walls of their own homes with paper of a similar colour, it then having become smart.

Above this, on the first floor, where, in the former days of private wealth, an enormous ballroom had existed, an enormous dormitory now existed. This was curtained off into numerous cubicles. Here lived the very youngest members, girls between the ages of eighteen and twenty who had not long moved out of the cubicles of school dormitories throughout the English countryside, and who understood dormitory life from start to finish. The girls on this floor were not yet experienced in discussing men. Everything turned on whether the man in question was a good dancer and had a sense of humour. The Air Force was mostly favoured, and a D.F.C. was an asset. A Battle of Britain record aged a man in the eyes of the first-floor dormitory, in the year 1945. Dunkirk, too, was largely something that their fathers had done. It was the air heroes of the Normandy landing who were popular, lounging among the cushions in the drawing-room. They gave full entertainment value:

'Do you know the story of the two cats that went to Wimbledon? – Well, one cat persuaded another to go to Wimbledon to watch the tennis. After a few sets one cat said to the other, "I must say, I'm bloody bored. I honestly can't see why you're so interested in this game of tennis." And the other cat replied, "Well, my father's in the racquet!"'

'No!' shrieked the girls, and duly doubled up.

'But that's not the end of the story. There was a colonel sitting behind these two cats. He was watching the tennis because the war was on and so there wasn't anything for him to do. Well, this colonel had his dog with him. So when the cats started talking to each other the dog turned to the colonel and said, "Do you hear those two cats in front of us?" "No, shut up," said the colonel, "I'm concentrating on the game." "All right," said the dog – very happy this dog, you know – "I only thought you might be interested in a couple of cats that can talk."'

'Really,' said the voice of the dormitory later on, a twittering outburst, 'what a wizard sense of humour!' They were like birds waking up instead of girls going to bed, since 'Really, what a wizard sense of humour' would be the approximate collective euphony of the birds in the park five hours later, if anyone was listening.

On the floor above the dormitory were the rooms of the staff and the shared bedrooms of those who could afford shared bedrooms rather than a cubicle. Those who shared, four or two to a room, tended to be young women in transit, or temporary members looking for flats and bed-sitting rooms. Here, on the second floor, two of the elder spinsters, Collie and Jarvie, shared a room as they had done for eight years, since they were saving money now for their old age.

But on the floor above that, there seemed to have congregated, by instinctive consent, most of the celibates, the old maids of settled character and various ages, those who had decided on a spinster's life, and those who would one day do so but had not yet discerned the fact for themselves.

This third-floor landing had contained five large bedrooms, now partitioned by builders into ten small ones. The occupants ranged from prim and pretty young virgins who would never become fully-wakened women, to bossy ones in their late twenties who were too wide-awake ever to surrender to any man. Greggie, the third of the elder spinsters, had her room on this floor. She was the least prim and the kindest of the women there.

On this floor was the room of a mad girl, Pauline Fox, who was wont to dress carefully on certain evenings in the long dresses which were swiftly and temporarily reverted to in the years immediately following the war. She also wore long white gloves, and her hair was long, curling over her shoulders. On these evenings she said she was going to dine with the famous actor, Jack Buchanan. No one disbelieved her outright, and her madness was undetected.

Here, too, was Joanna Childe's room from which she could be heard practising her elocution at times when the recreation room was occupied.

> All the flowers of the spring
> Meet to perfume our burying;

At the top of the house, on the fourth floor, the most attractive, sophisticated and lively girls had their rooms. They were filled with deeper and deeper social longings of various kinds, as peace-time crept over everyone. Five girls occupied the five top rooms. Three of them had lovers in addition to men-friends with whom they did not sleep but whom they cultivated with a view to mar-riage. Of the remaining two, one was almost engaged to be married, and the other was Jane Wright, fat but intellectually glamorous by virtue of the fact that she worked for a publisher. She was on the look-out for a husband, meanwhile being mixed up with young intellectuals.

Nothing but the roof-tops lay above this floor, now inaccessible by the trap-door in the bathroom ceiling – a mere useless square since it had been bricked up long ago before the war after a girl had been attacked by a burglar or a lover who had entered by it – attacked or merely confronted unexpectedly, or found in bed with him as some said; as the case might be, he left behind him a legend of many screams in the night and the skylight had been henceforth closed to the public. Workmen who, from time to time, were called in to do something up above the house had to approach the roof from the attic of a neighbouring hotel. Greggie claimed to know all about the story, she knew everything about the club. Indeed it was Greggie who, inspired by a shaft of remembrance, had directed the warden to the hoard of mud-coloured wall-paper in the cupboard which now defiled the walls of the drawing-room and leered in the sunlight at everyone. The top-floor girls had often thought it might be a good idea to sunbathe on the flat portion of the roof and had climbed up on chairs to see about the opening of the trap-door. But it would not budge, and Greggie had once more told them why. Greggie produced a better version of the story every time.

'If there was a fire, we'd be stuck,' said Selina Redwood who was exceedingly beautiful.

'You've obviously been taking no notice of the emergency instructions,' Greggie said. This was true. Selina was seldom in to dinner and so she had never heard them. Four times a year the emergency instructions were read out by the warden after dinner, on which nights no guests were allowed. The top floor was served for emergency purposes by a back staircase leading down two flights to the perfectly sound fire-escape, and by the fire-equipment which lay around everywhere in the club. On these evenings of no guests the members were also reminded about putting things down lavatories, and the difficulties of plumbing systems in old houses, and of obtaining plumbers these days. They were reminded that they were expected to put everything back in place after a dance had been held in the club. Why some members unfortunately just went off to night clubs with their men-friends and left everything to others, said the warden, she simply did not know.

Selina had missed all this, never having been in to dinner on the warden's nights. From her window she could see, level with the top floor of the house, and set back behind the chimney pots, the portion of flat roof, shared by the club with the hotel next door, which would have been ideal for sunbathing. There was no access to any part of the roof from the bedroom windows, but one day she noticed that it was accessible from the lavatory window, a narrow slit made narrower by the fact that the wall in which it was set had been sub-divided at some point in the house's history when the wash-rooms had been put in. One had to climb upon the lavatory seat to see the roof. Selina measured the window. The aperture was seven inches wide by fourteen inches long. It opened casement-wise.

'I believe I could get through the lavatory window,' she said to Anne Baberton who occupied the room opposite hers.

'Why do you want to get through the lavatory window?' said Anne.

'It leads out to the roof. There's only a short jump from the window.'

Selina was extremely slim. The question of weight and measurement was very important on the top floor. The ability or otherwise to wriggle sideways through the lavatory window would be one of those tests that only went to prove the club's food policy to be unnecessarily fattening.

'Suicidal,' said Jane Wright who was miserable about her fatness and spent much of her time in eager dread of the next meal, and in making resolutions what to eat of it and what to leave, and in making counter-resolutions in view of the fact that her work at the publishers' was essentially mental, which meant that her brain had to be fed more than most people's.

Among the five top-floor members only Selina Redwood and Anne Baberton could manage to wriggle through the lavatory window, and Anne only managed it naked, having made her body slippery with margarine. After the first attempt, when she had twisted her ankle on the downward leap and grazed her skin on the return clamber, Anne said she would in future use her soap ration to facilitate the exit. Soap was as tightly rationed as margarine but more precious, for margarine was fattening, anyway. Face cream was too expensive to waste on the window venture.

Jane Wright could not see why Anne was so concerned about her one inch and a half on the hips more than Selina's, since Anne was already slender and already fixed up for marriage. She stood on the lavatory seat and threw out Anne's faded green dressing-gown for her to drape round her slippery body and asked what it was like out there.

The two other girls on the floor were away for the week-end on this occasion.

Anne and Selina were peeping over the edge of the flat roof at a point where Jane could not see them. They returned to report that they had looked down on the back garden where Greggie was holding her conducted tour of the premises for the benefit of two new members. She had been showing them the spot where the bomb had fallen and failed to go off, and had been removed by a bomb-squad, during which operation everyone had been obliged to leave the house. Greggie had also been showing them the spot where, in her opinion, an unexploded bomb still lay.

The girls got themselves back into the house.

'Greggie and her sensations': Jane felt she could scream. She added, 'Cheese pie for supper tonight, guess how many calories?'

The answer, when they looked up the chart, was roughly 350 calories. 'Followed by stewed cherries,' said Jane, '94 calories normal helping unless sweetened by saccharine, in which case 64 calories. We've had over a thousand calories today already. It's always the same on Sundays. The bread-and-butter pudding alone was –'

'I didn't eat the bread-and-butter pudding,' said Anne. 'Bread-and-butter pudding is suicidal.'

'I only eat a little bit of everything,' Selina said. 'I feel starved all the time, actually.'

'Well, I'm doing brain-work,' said Jane.

Anne was walking about the landing sponging off all the margarine. She said, 'I've had to use up soap and margarine as well.'

'I can't lend you any soap this month,' Selina said. Selina had a regular supply of soap from an American Army officer who got it from a source of many desirable things, called the P.X. But she was accumulating a hoard of it, and had stopped lending.

Anne said, 'I don't want your bloody soap. Just don't ask for the taffeta, that's all.'

By this she meant a Schiaparelli taffeta evening dress which had been given to her by a fabulously rich aunt, after one wearing. This marvellous dress, which caused a stir wherever it went, was shared by all the top floor on special occasions, excluding Jane whom it did not fit. For lending it out Anne got various returns, such as free clothing coupons or a half-used piece of soap.

Jane went back to her brain-work and shut the door with a definite click. She was rather tyrannous about her brain-work, and made a fuss about other people's wirelesses on the landing, and about the petty-mindedness of these haggling bouts that took place with Anne when the taffeta dress was wanted to support the rising wave of long-dress parties.

'You can't wear it to the Milroy. It's been twice to the Milroy ... it's been to Quaglino's, Selina wore it to Quags, it's getting known all over London.'

'But it looks altogether different on me, Anne. You can have a whole sheet of sweet-coupons.'

'I don't want your bloody sweet-coupons. I give all mine to my grandmother.'

Then Jane would put out her head. 'Stop being so petty-minded and stop screeching. I'm doing brain-work.'

Jane had one smart thing in her wardrobe, a black coat and skirt made out of her father's evening clothes. Very few dinner jackets in England remained in their original form after the war. But this looted outfit of Jane's was too large for anyone to borrow; she was thankful for that, at least. The exact nature of her brain-work was a mystery to the club because, when asked about it, she reeled off fast an explanation of extreme and alien detail about costing, printers, lists, manuscripts, galleys and contracts.

'Well, Jane, you ought to get paid for all that extra work you do.'

'The world of books is essentially disinterested,' Jane said. She always referred to the publishing business as 'The world of books'. She was always hard up, so presumably ill paid. It was because she had to be careful of her shillings for the meter which controlled the gas-fire in her room that she was unable, so she said, to go on a diet during the winter, since one had to keep warm as well as feed one's brain.

Jane received from the club, on account of her brain-work and job in publishing, a certain amount of respect which was socially offset by the arrival in the front hall, every week or so, of a pale, thin foreigner, decidedly in his thirties, with dandruff on his dark overcoat, who would ask in the office for Miss Jane Wright, always adding, 'I wish to see her privately, please.' Word also spread round from the office that many of Jane's incoming telephone calls were from this man.

'Is that the May of Teck Club?'

'Yes.'

'May I speak to Miss Wright privately, please?'

At one of these moments the secretary on duty said to him, 'All the members' calls are private. We don't listen in.'

'Good. I would know if you did, I wait for the click before I speak. Kindly remember.'

Jane had to apologize to the office for him. 'He's a foreigner. It's in connexion with the world of books. It isn't my fault.'

But another and more presentable man from the world of books had lately put in an appearance for Jane. She had brought him into the drawing-room and introduced him to Selina, Anne, and the mad girl Pauline Fox who dressed up for Jack Buchanan on her lunatic evenings.

This man, Nicholas Farringdon, had been rather charming, though shy. 'He's thoughtful,' Jane said. 'We think him brilliant but he's still feeling his way in the world of books.'

'Is he something in publishing?'

'Not at the moment. He's still feeling his way. He's writing something.'

Jane's brain-work was of three kinds. First, and secretly, she wrote poetry of a strictly non-rational order, in which occurred, in about the proportion of cherries in a cherry-cake, certain words that she described as 'of a smouldering nature', such as loins and lovers, the root, the rose, the seawrack and the shroud. Secondly, also secretly, she wrote letters of a friendly tone but with a business intention, under the auspices of the pale foreigner. Thirdly, and more openly, she sometimes did a little work in her room which overlapped from her day's duties at the small publisher's office.

She was the only assistant at Huy Throvis-Mew Ltd. Huy Throvis-Mew was the owner of the firm, and Mrs Huy Throvis-Mew was down as a director on the letter heading. Huy Throvis-Mew's private name was George Johnson, or at least it had been so for some years, although a few very old friends called him Con and older friends called him Arthur or Jimmie. However, he was George in Jane's time, and she would do anything for George, her white-bearded employer. She parcelled up the books, took them to the post or delivered them, answered the telephone, made tea, minded the baby when George's wife, Tilly, wanted to go and queue for fish, entered the takings into ledgers, entered two different versions of the petty cash and office expenses into two sets of books, and generally did a small publisher's business. After a year George allowed her to do some of the detective work on new authors, which he was convinced was essential to the publishing trade, and to find out their financial circumstances and psychologically weak points so that he could deal with them to a publisher's best advantage.

Like the habit of changing his name after a number of years, which he had done only in the hope that his luck would turn with it, this practice of George's was fairly innocent, in that he never really succeeded in discovering the whole truth about an author, or in profiting by his investigations at all. Still, it was his system, and its plot-formation gave him a zest for each day's work. Formerly George had done these basic investigations himself, but lately he had begun to think he might have more luck by leaving the new author to Jane. A consignment of books, on their way to George, had recently been seized at the port of Harwich and ordered to be burnt by the local magistrates on the grounds of obscenity, and George was feeling unlucky at this particular time.

Besides, it saved him all the expense and nervous exhaustion involved in the vigilant lunching with unpredictable writers, and feeling his way with them as to whether their paranoia exceeded his. It was better altogether to let them talk to Jane in a café, or bed, or wherever she went with them. It was nerve-racking enough to George to wait for her report. He fancied that many times in the past year she had saved him from paying out more ready money for a book than necessary – as when she had reported a dire need for ready cash, or when she had told George exactly what part of the manuscript he should find fault with – it was usually the part in which the author took a special pride – in order to achieve the minimum resistance, if not the total collapse, of the author.

George had obtained a succession of three young wives on account of his continuous eloquence to them on the subject of the world of books, which they felt was an elevating one – he had deserted the other two, not they him – and he had not yet been declared bankrupt although he had undergone in the course of the years various tangled forms of business reconstruction which were probably too much for the nerves of his creditors to face legally, since none ever did.

George took a keen interest in Jane's training in the handling of a writer of books. Unlike his fireside eloquence to his wife Tilly, his advice to Jane in the office was furtive, for he half believed, in the twilight portion of his mind, that authors were sly enough to make themselves invisible and be always floating under the chairs of publishers' offices.

'You see, Jane,' said George, 'these tactics of mine are an essential part of the profession. All the publishers do it. The big firms do it too, they do it automatically. The big fellows can afford to do it automatically, they can't afford to acknowledge all the facts like me, too much face to lose. I've had to work out every move for myself and get everything clear in my mind where authors are concerned. In publishing, one is dealing with a temperamental raw material.'

He went over to the corner curtain which concealed a coat-rail, and pulled aside the curtain. He peered within, then closed the curtain again and continued, 'Always think of authors as your raw material, Jane, if you're going to stay in the world of books.' Jane took this for fact. She had now been given Nicholas Farringdon to work on. George had said he was a terrible risk. Jane judged his age to be just over thirty. He was known only as a poet of small talent and an anarchist of dubious loyalty to that cause; but even these details were not at first known to Jane. He had brought to George a worn-out-looking sheaf of typewritten pages, untidily stacked in a brown folder. The whole was entitled *The Sabbath Notebooks*.

Nicholas Farringdon differed in some noticeable respects from the other writers she had come across. He differed, unnoticeably so far, in that he knew he was being worked on. But meantime she observed he was more arrogant and more impatient than other authors of the intellectual class. She noticed he was more attractive.

She had achieved some success with the very intellectual author of *The Symbolism of Louisa May Alcott*, which George was now selling very well and fast in certain quarters, since it had a big lesbian theme. She had achieved some success with Rudi Bittesch, the Rumanian who called on her frequently at the club.

But Nicholas had produced a more upsetting effect than usual on George, who was moreover torn between his attraction to a book he could not understand and his fear of its failure. George handed him over to Jane for treatment and meanwhile complained nightly to Tilly that he was in the hands of a writer, lazy, irresponsible, insufferable and cunning.

Inspired by a brain-wave, Jane's first approach to a writer had been, 'What is your raison d'être?' It had worked marvellously. She tried it on Nicholas Farringdon when he called to the office about his manuscript one day when George was 'at a meeting', which was to say, hiding in the back office. 'What is your raison d'être, Mr Farringdon?'

He frowned at her in an abstract sort of way, as if she were a speaking machine that had gone wrong.

Inspired by another brain-wave Jane invited him to dine at the May of Teck Club. He accepted with a special modesty, plainly from concern for his book. It had been rejected by ten publishers already, as had most of the books that came to George.

His visit put Jane up in the estimation of the club. She had not expected him to react so eagerly to everything. Sipping black Nescafé in the drawing-room with Jane, Selina, dark little Judy Redwood and Anne, he had looked round with a faint, contented smile. Jane had chosen her companions for the evening with the instinct of an experimental procuress which, when she perceived the extent of its success, she partly regretted and partly congratulated herself on, since she had not been sure from various reports whether Nicholas preferred men, and now she concluded that he at least liked both sexes. Selina's long unsurpassable legs arranged themselves diagonally from the deep chair where she lolled in the distinct attitude of being the only woman present who could afford to loll. There was something about Selina's lolling which gave her a queenly eminence. She visibly appraised Nicholas, while he continued to glance here and there at the several groups of chattering girls in other parts of the room. The terrace doors stood wide open to the cool night and presently from the recreation room there came, by way of the terrace, the sound of Joanna in the process of an elocution lesson.

> I thought of Chatterton, the marvellous Boy,
> The sleepless Soul that perished in his pride;
> Of Him who walked in glory and in joy

Following his plough, along the mountain-side;
By our own spirits are we deified:
We Poets in our youth begin in gladness;
But thereof come in the end despondency and madness.

'I wish she would stick to *The Wreck of the Deutschland*,' Judy Redwood said. 'She's marvellous with Hopkins.'

Joanna's voice was saying, 'Remember the stress on Chatterton and the slight pause to follow.'

Joanna's pupil recited:

I thought of Chatterton, the marvellous Boy,

The excitement over the slit window went on for the rest of the afternoon. Jane's brain-work proceeded against the background echoes of voices from the large wash-room where the làvatories were. The two other occupants of the top floor had returned, having been to their homes in the country for the week-end: Dorothy Markham, the impoverished niece of Lady Julia Markham who was chairwoman of the club's management committee, and Nancy Riddle, one of the club's many clergymen's daughters. Nancy was trying to overcome her Midlands accent, and took lessons in elocution from Joanna with this end in view.

Jane, at her brain-work, heard from the direction of the wash-room the success of Dorothy Markham's climb through the window. Dorothy's hips were thirty-six and a half inches; her bust measurement was only thirty-one, a fact which did not dismay her, as she intended to marry one of three young men out of her extensive acquaintance who happened to find themselves drawn to boyish figures, and although she did not know about such things as precisely as did her aunt, Dorothy knew well enough that her hipless and breastless shape would always attract the sort of young man who felt at home with it. Dorothy could emit, at any hour of the day or night, a waterfall of débutante chatter, which rightly gave the impression that on any occasion between talking, eating and sleeping, she did not think, except in terms of these phrase-ripples of hers: 'Filthy lunch.' 'The most gorgeous wedding.' 'He actually raped her, she was amazed.' 'Ghastly film.' 'I'm desperately well, thanks, how are you?'

Her voice from the wash-room distracted Jane: 'Oh hell, I'm black with soot, I'm absolutely filthington.' She opened Jane's door without knocking and put in her head. 'Got any soapyjo?' It was some months before she was to put her head round Jane's door and announce, 'Filthy luck. I'm preggers. Come to the wedding.'

Jane said, on being asked for the use of her soap, 'Can you lend me fifteen shillings till next Friday?' It was her final resort for getting rid of people when she was doing brain-work.

Evidently, from the sound of things, Nancy Riddle was stuck in the window. Nancy was getting hysterical. Finally, Nancy was released and calmed, as was betokened by the gradual replacement of Midlands vowels with standard English ones issuing from the wash-room.

Jane continued with her work, describing her effort to herself as pressing on regardless. All the club, infected by the Air Force idiom current amongst the dormitory virgins, used this phrase continually.

She had put aside Nicholas's manuscript for the time being, as it was a sticky proposition; she had not yet, in fact, grasped the theme of the book, as was necessary before deciding on a significant passage to cast doubt upon, although she had already thought of the comment she would recommend George to make: 'Don't you think this part is a bit derivative?' Jane had thought of it in a brain-wave.

She had put the book aside. She was at work, now, on some serious spare-time work for which she was paid. This came into the department of her life that had to do with Rudi Bittesch whom she hated, at this stage in her life, for his unattractive appearance. He was too old for her, besides everything else. When in a depressed state of mind, she found it useful to remember that she was only twenty-two, for the fact cheered her up. She looked down Rudi's list of famous authors and their respective addresses to see who still remained to be done. She took a sheet of writing paper and wrote her great-aunt's address in the country, followed by the date. She then wrote:

Dear Mr Hemingway,
    I am addressing this letter to you care of your publisher in the confidence that it will be sent on to you.

This was an advisable preliminary, Rudi said, because sometimes publishers were instructed to open authors' letters and throw them

away if not of sufficient business importance, but this approach, if it
got into the publishers' hands, 'might touch their heart'. The rest of
the letter was entirely Jane's province. She paused to await a small
brain-wave, and after a moment continued:

> I am sure you receive many admiring letters, and have hesitated
> to add yet another to your post-bag. But since my release from
> prison, where I have been for the past two years and four months, I
> have felt more and more that I want you to know how much your
> novels meant to me during that time. I had few visitors. My allotted
> weekly hours of leisure were spent in the Library. It was unheated
> alas, but I did not notice the cold as I read on. Nothing I read gave
> me so much courage to face the future and to build a new future on
> my release as *For Whom The Bell Tolls*. The novel gave me back my
> faith in life.
>
> I just want you to know this, and to say 'Thank you'.
>
> > Yours sincerely
> > (Miss) J. Wright.
>
> PS. This is not a begging letter. I assure you I would return any
> money that was sent to me.

If this succeeded in reaching him it might bring a hand-written
reply. The prison letter and the asylum letter were more liable to
bring replies in the author's own hand than any other type of letter,
but one had to choose an author 'with heart', as Rudi said. Authors
without heart seldom replied at all, and if they did it was a type-
written letter. For a type-written letter signed by the author, Rudi
paid two shillings if the autograph was scarce, but if the author's
signature was available everywhere, and the letter a mere formal
acknowledgement, Rudi paid nothing. For a letter in the author's
own handwriting Rudi paid five shillings for the first page and a
shilling thereafter. Jane's ingenuity was therefore awakened to the
feat of composing the sort of letters which would best move the
recipient to reply in total holograph.

Rudi paid for the writing paper and the postage. He told her he only
wanted the letters 'for sentimental purpose of my collection'. She had
seen his collection. But she assumed that he was collecting them with
an eye to their increasing value year by year.

'If I write myself it does not ring true; I do not get interesting replies. By the way, my English is not like the English of an English girl.'

She would have made her own collection if only she had not needed the ready money, and could afford to save up the letters for the future.

'Never ask for money in your letters,' Rudi had warned her. 'Do not mention the subject of money. It makes criminal offence under false pretences.' However, she had the brain-wave of adding her postscript, to make sure.

Jane had worried, at first, lest she should be found out and get into some sort of trouble. Rudi reassured her. 'You say you only make a joke. It is not criminal. Who would check up on you, by the way? Do you think Bernard Shaw is going to write and make questions about you from the old aunt? Bernard Shaw is a Name.'

Bernard Shaw had in fact proved disappointing. He had sent a type-written postcard:

Thank you for your letter in praise of my writings. As you say they have consoled you in your misfortunes, I shall not attempt to gild the lily by my personal comments. As you say you desire no money I shall not press upon you my holograph signature which has some cash value. G.B.S.

The initials, too, had been typed.

Jane learned by experience. Her illegitimate-child letter brought a sympathetic reply from Daphne du Maurier, for which Rudi paid his price. With some authors a scholarly question about the underlying meaning worked best. One day, on a brain-wave, she wrote to Henry James at the Athenaeum Club.

'That was foolish of you because James is dead, by the way,' Rudi said.

'Do you want a letter from an author called Nicholas Farringdon?' she said.

'No, I have known Nicholas Farringdon, he's no good, he is not likely to be a Name ever. What has he written?'

'A book called *The Sabbath Notebooks*.'

'Is it religious?'

'Well, he calls it political philosophy. It's just a lot of notes and thoughts.'

'It smells religious. He will finish up as a reactionary Catholic, to obey the Pope. Already I have predicted this before the war.'

'He's jolly good-looking.'

She hated Rudi. He was not at all attractive. She addressed and stamped her letter to Ernest Hemingway and ticked off his name on the list, writing the date beside it. The girls' voices had disappeared from the wash-room. Anne's wireless was singing:

> There were angels dining at the Ritz
> And a nightingale sang in Berkeley Square.

It was twenty minutes past six. There was time for one more letter before supper. Jane looked down the list.

Dear Mr Maugham,
    I am addressing this letter to you at your club. . . .

Jane paused for thought. She ate a square of chocolate to keep her brain going till supper-time. The prison letter might not appeal to Maugham. Rudi had said he was cynical about human nature. On a brain-wave she recalled that he had been a doctor. It might be an idea to make up a sanatorium letter. . . . She had been ill for two years and four months with tuberculosis. After all, this disease was not attributable to human nature, there was nothing in it to be cynical about. She regretted having eaten the chocolate, and put the rest of the bar right at the back of a shelf in her cupboard where it was difficult to reach, as if hiding it from a child. The rightness of this action and the wrongness of her having eaten any at all were confirmed by Selina's voice from Anne's room. Anne had turned off the wireless and they had been talking. Selina would probably be stretched out on Anne's bed in her languid manner. This became certain as Selina began to repeat, slowly and solemnly, the Two Sentences.

The Two Sentences were a simple morning and evening exercise prescribed by the Chief Instructress of the Poise Course which Selina had recently taken, by correspondence, in twelve lessons for five guineas. The Poise Course believed strongly in auto-suggestion and had advised, for the maintenance of poise in the working woman, a repetition of the following two sentences twice a day:

Poise is perfect balance, an equanimity of body and mind, complete composure whatever the social scene. Elegant dress, immaculate grooming, and perfect deportment all contribute to the attainment of self-confidence.

Even Dorothy Markham stopped her chatter for a few seconds every morning at eight-thirty and evening at six-thirty, in respect for Selina's Sentences. All the top floor was respectful. It had cost five guineas. The two floors below were indifferent. But the dormitories crept up on the landings to listen, they could hardly believe their ears, and saved up each word with savage joy to make their boy-friends in the Air Force laugh like a drain, which was how laughter was described in those circles. At the same time, the dormitory girls were envious of Selina, knowing in their hearts they would never quite be in the Selina class where looks were concerned.

The Sentences were finished by the time Jane had shoved her remaining piece of chocolate well out of sight and range. She returned to the letter. She had T.B. She gave a frail cough and looked round the room. It contained a wash-basin, a bed, a chest-of-drawers, a cupboard, a table and lamp, a wicker chair, a hard chair, a bookcase, a gas-fire and a meter-box with a slot to measure the gas, shilling by shilling. Jane felt she might easily be in a room in a sanatorium.

'One last time,' said Joanna's voice from the floor below. She was now rehearsing Nancy Riddle, who was at this moment managing her standard English vowels very well.

'And again,' said Joanna. 'We've just got time before supper. I'll read the first stanza, then you follow on.'

> At the top of the house the apples are laid in rows,
> And the skylight lets the moonlight in, and those
> Apples are deep-sea apples of green. There goes
> A cloud on the moon in the autumn night.

FOUR

It was July 1945, three weeks before the general election.

> They are lying in rows there, under the gloomy beams;
> On the sagging floor; they gather the silver streams
> Out of the moon, those moonlit apples of dreams
> And quiet is the steep stair under.

'I wish she would stick to *The Wreck of the Deutschland*.'
'Do you? I rather like *Moonlit Apples*.'
We come now to Nicholas Farringdon in his thirty-third year. He was said to be an anarchist. No one at the May of Teck Club took this seriously as he looked quite normal; that is to say, he looked slightly dissipated, like the disappointing son of a good English family that he was. That each of his brothers – two accountants and one dentist – said of him from the time he left Cambridge in the mid 1930s, 'Nicholas is a bit of a misfit, I'm afraid,' would not have surprised anyone.

Jane Wright applied for information about him to Rudi Bittesch who had known Nicholas throughout the 1930s. 'You don't bother with him. He is a mess by the way,' Rudi said. 'I know him well, he is a good friend of mine.' From Rudi she gathered that before the war he had been always undecided whether to live in England or France, and whether he preferred men or women, since he alternated between passionate intervals with both. Also, he could never make up his mind between suicide and an equally drastic course of action known as Father D'Arcy. Rudi explained that the latter was a Jesuit philosopher who had the monopoly for converting the English intellectuals. Nicholas was a pacifist up to the outbreak of war, Rudi said, then he joined the Army. Rudi said, 'I have met him one day in Piccadilly wearing his uniform, and he said to me the war has brought him peace. Next thing he is psycho-analysed out of the Army, a wangle, and he is working for the Intelligence. The anarchists have given him up but he calls himself an anarchist, by the way.'

Far from putting Jane against Nicholas Farringdon, the scraps of his history that came to her by way of Rudi gave him an irresistible heroism in her mind, and, through her, in the eyes of the top-floor girls.

'He must be a genius,' said Nancy Riddle.

Nicholas had a habit of saying 'When I'm famous ...' when referring to the remote future, with the same cheerful irony that went into the preface of the bus conductor on the No. 73 route to his comments on the law of the land: 'When I come to power ...'

Jane showed Rudi *The Sabbath Notebooks*, so entitled because Nicholas had used as an epigraph the text 'The Sabbath was made for Man, not Man for the Sabbath'.

'George must be out of his mind to publish this,' Rudi said when he brought it back to Jane. They sat in the recreation room at the other end of which, cornerwise by the open French window, a girl was practising scales on the piano with as much style as she could decently apply to the scales. The music-box tinkle was far enough away, and sufficiently dispersed by the Sunday morning sounds from the terrace, not to intrude too strongly on Rudi's voice, as he read out, in his foreign English, small passages from Nicholas's book in order to prove something to Jane. He did this as a cloth merchant, perhaps wishing to persuade a customer to buy his best quality of goods, might first produce samples of inferior stuff, feel it, invite comment, shrug, and toss it away. Jane was convinced that Rudi was right in his judgement of what he was reading, but she was really more fascinated by what small glimpses of Nicholas Farringdon's personality she got from Rudi's passing remarks. Nicholas was the only presentable intellectual she had met.

'It is not bad, not good,' said Rudi, putting his head this way, that way, as he said it. 'It is mediocrity. I recall he composed this in 1938 when he had a freckled bed-mate of the female sex; she was an anarchist and pacifist. Listen, by the way ...' He read out:

X is writing a history of anarchism. Anarchism properly has no history in the sense that X intends – i.e. in the sense of continuity and development. It is a spontaneous movement of people in particular times and circumstances. A history of anarchism would not be in the nature of political history, it would be analogous to a history of the heart-beat. One may make new discoveries about it, one may compare its reactions under varying conditons, but there is nothing new of itself.

Jane was thinking of the freckled girl-friend whom Nicholas had slept with at the time, and she almost fancied they had taken *The Sabbath Notebooks* to bed together. 'What happened to his girl-friend?' Jane said. 'There is nothing wrong with this,' Rudi said, referring to what he had just read, 'but it is not so magnificent a great truth that he should like a great man place it on the page, by the way, in a paragraph alone. He makes *pensées* as he is too lazy to write the essay. Listen . . .'

Jane said, 'What happened to the girl?'

'She went to prison for pacifism maybe, I don't know. If I would be George I would not touch this book. Listen . . .'

Every communist has a fascist frown; every fascist has a communist smile.

'Ha!' said Rudi.

'I thought that was a very profound bit,' Jane said, as it was the only bit she could remember.

'That is why he writes it in, he counts that the bloody book has got to have a public, so he puts in some little bit of aphorism, very clever, that a girl like you likes to hear, by the way. It means nothing, this, where is the meaning?' Most of Rudi's last words were louder-sounding than he had intended, as the girl at the piano had paused for rest.

'There's no need to get excited,' said Jane loudly.

The girl at the piano started a new set of rippling tinkles.

'We move to the drawing-room,' said Rudi.

'No, everyone's in the drawing-room this morning,' Jane said. 'There's not a quiet corner in the drawing-room.' She did not particularly want to display Rudi to the rest of the club.

Up and down the scales went the girl at the piano. From a window above, Joanna, fitting in an elocution lesson with Miss Harper, the cook, in the half-hour before the Sunday joint was ready to go in the oven, said, 'Listen':

> Ah! Sun-flower! weary of time,
> Who countest the steps of the Sun;
> Seeking after that sweet golden clime,
> Where the traveller's journey is done;

'Now try it,' said Joanna. 'Very slowly on the third line. Think of a sweet golden clime as you say it.'

> Ah! Sun-flower! . . .

The dormitory girls who had spilled out of the drawing-room on to the terrace chattered like a parliament of fowls. The little notes of the scales followed one another obediently. 'Listen,' said Rudi:

> Everyone should be persuaded to remember how far, and with what a pathetic thump, the world has fallen from grace, that it needs must appoint politicians for its keepers, that its emotions, whether of consolation at breakfast-time or fear in the evening. . . .

Rudi said, 'You notice his words, that he says the world has fallen from grace? This is the reason that he is no anarchist, by the way. They chuck him out when he talks like a son of the Pope. This man is a mess that he calls himself an anarchist; the anarchists do not make all that talk of original sin, so forth; they permit only anti-social tendencies, unethical conduct, so forth. Nick Farringdon is a diversionist, by the way.'

'Do you call him Nick?' Jane said.

'Sometimes in the pubs, The Wheatsheaf and The Gargoyle, so on, he was Nick in those days. Except there was a barrow-boy called him Mr Farringdon. Nicholas said to him, "Look, I wasn't christened Mister," but was no good; the barrow-boy was his friend, by the way.'

'Once more,' said Joanna's voice.

Ah! Sun-flower! weary of time,

'Listen,' said Rudi:

Nevertheless, let our moment or opportunity be stated. We do
not need a government. We do not need a House of Commons.
Parliament should dissolve forever. We could manage very well in
our movement towards a complete anarchist society, with our great
but powerless institutions: we could manage with the monarchy as
an example of the dignity inherent in the free giving and receiving
of precedence and favour without power; the churches for the
spiritual needs of the people; the House of Lords for purposes of
debate and recommendation; and the universities for consultation.
We do not need institutions with power. The practical affairs of
society could be dealt with locally by the Town, Borough, and
Village Councils. International affairs could be conducted by
variable representatives in a non-professional capacity. We do not
need professional politicians with an eye to power. The grocer, the
doctor, the cook, should serve their country for a term as men serve
on a jury. We can be ruled by the corporate will of men's hearts
alone. It is Power that is defunct, not as we are taught, the
powerless institutions.

'I ask you a question,' Rudi said. 'It is a simple question. He wants
monarchy, he wants anarchism. What does he want? These two are
enemies in all of history. Simple answer is, he is a mess.'

'How old was the barrow-boy?' Jane said.

'And again,' said Joanna's voice from the upper window.

Dorothy Markham had joined the girls on the sunny terrace. She
was telling a hunting story. '. . . the only one time I've been thrown, it
shook me to the core. What a brute!'

'Where did you land?'

'Where do you think?'

The girl at the piano stopped and folded her scale-sheet with
seemly concentration.

'I go,' said Rudi, looking at his watch. 'I have an appointment to
meet a contact for a drink.' He rose and once more, before he handed
over the book, flicked through the type-written pages. He said, sadly,

'Nicholas is a friend of mine, but I regret to say he's a non-contributive thinker, by the way. Come here, listen to this:'

There is a kind of truth in the popular idea of an anarchist as a wild man with a home-made bomb in his pocket. In modern times this bomb, fabricated in the back workshops of the imagination, can only take one effective form: Ridicule.

Jane said, ' "Only take" isn't grammatical, it should be "take only". I'll have to change that, Rudi.'

So much for the portrait of the martyr as a young man as it was suggested to Jane on a Sunday morning between armistice and armistice, in the days of everyone's poverty, in 1945. Jane, who lived to distort it in many elaborate forms, at the time merely felt she was in touch with something reckless, intellectual, and Bohemian by being in touch with Nicholas. Rudi's contemptuous attitude bounded back upon himself in her estimation. She felt she knew too much about Rudi to respect him; and was presently astonished to find that there was indeed a sort of friendship between himself and Nicholas, lingering on from the past.

Meantime, Nicholas touched lightly on the imagination of the girls of slender means, and they on his. He had not yet slept on the roof with Selina on the hot summer nights – he gaining access from the American-occupied attic of the hotel next door, and she through the slit window – and he had not yet witnessed that action of savagery so extreme that it forced him involuntarily to make an entirely unaccustomed gesture, the signing of the cross upon himself. At this time Nicholas still worked for one of those left-hand departments of the Foreign Office, the doings of which the right-hand did not know. It came under Intelligence. After the Normandy landing he had been sent on several missions to France. Now there was very little left for his department to do except wind-up. Winding-up was arduous, it involved the shuffling of papers and people from office to office; particularly it involved considerable shuffling between the British and American Intelligence pockets in London. He had a bleak furnished room at Fulham. He was bored.

*

'I've got something to tell you, Rudi,' said Jane.

'Hold on please, I have a customer.'

'I'll ring you back later, then, I'm in a hurry. I only wanted to tell you that Nicholas Farringdon's dead. Remember that book of his he never published – he gave you the manuscript. Well, it might be worth something now, and I thought –'

'Nick's dead? Hold on please, Jane. I have a customer waiting here to buy a book. Hold on.'

'I'll ring you later.'

Nicholas came, then, to dine at the club.

> I thought of Chatterton, the marvellous Boy,
> The sleepless Soul that perished in his Pride;

'Who is that?'

'It's Joanna Childe, she teaches elocution, you must meet her.'

The twittering movements at other points in the room, Joanna's singular voice, the beautiful aspects of poverty and charm amongst these girls in the brown-papered drawing-room, Selina, furled like a long soft sash, in her chair, came to Nicholas in a gratuitous flow. Months of boredom had subdued him to intoxication by an experience which, at another time, might itself have bored him.

Some days later he took Jane to a party to meet the people she longed to meet, young male poets in corduroy trousers and young female poets with waist-length hair, or at least females who typed the poetry and slept with the poets, it was nearly the same thing. Nicholas took her to supper at Bertorelli's; then he took her to a poetry reading at a hired meeting-house in the Fulham Road; then he took her on to a party with some of the people he had collected from the reading. One of the poets who was well thought of had acquired a job at Associated News in Fleet Street, in honour of which he had purchased a pair of luxurious pigskin gloves; he displayed these proudly. There was an air of a resistance movement against the world at this poetry meeting. Poets seemed to understand each other with a secret instinct, almost a kind of pre-arrangement, and it was plain that the poet with the gloves would never show off these poetic gloves so frankly, or expect to be understood so well in relation to them, at his new job in Fleet Street or anywhere else, as here.

Some were men demobilized from the non-combatant corps. Some had been unfit for service for obvious reasons – a nervous twitch of the facial muscles, bad eyesight, or a limp. Others were still in battle dress. Nicholas had been out of the Army since the month after Dunkirk, from which he had escaped with a wound in the thumb; his release from the army had followed a mild nervous disorder in the month after Dunkirk.

Nicholas stood noticeably aloof at the poets' gathering, but although he greeted his friends with a decided reserve, it was evident that he wanted Jane to savour her full joy of it. In fact, he wanted her to invite him again to the May of Teck Club, as dawned on her later in the evening.

The poets read their poems, two each, and were applauded. Some of these poets were to fail and fade into a no-man's-land of Soho public houses in a few years' time, and become the familiar messes of literary life. Some, with many talents, faltered, in time, from lack of stamina, gave up and took a job in advertising or publishing, detesting literary people above all. Others succeeded and became paradoxes; they did not always continue to write poetry, or even poetry exclusively.

One of these young poets, Ernest Claymore, later became a mystical stockbroker of the 1960s, spending his week-days urgently in the City, three week-ends each month at his country cottage – an establishment of fourteen rooms, where he ignored his wife and, alone in his study, wrote Thought – and one week-end a month in retreat at a monastery. In the 1960s Ernest Claymore read a book a week in bed before sleep, and sometimes addressed a letter to the press about a book review: 'Sir, Maybe I'm dim. I have read your review of ...'; he was to publish three short books of philosophy which everyone could easily understand indeed; at the moment in question, the summer of 1945, he was a dark-eyed young poet at the poetry recital, and had just finished reading, with husky force, his second contri-bution:

I in my troubled night of the dove clove brightly my
Path from the tomb of love incessantly to redress my
Articulate womb, that new and necessary rose, exposing my ...

He belonged to the Cosmic school of poets. Jane, perceiving that he was orthosexual by definition of his manner and appearance, was uncertain whether to cultivate him for future acquaintance or whether to hang on to Nicholas. She managed to do both, since Nicholas brought along this dark husky poet, this stockbroker to be, to the party which followed, and there Jane was able to make a future assignment with him before Nicholas drew her aside to inquire further into the mysterious life of the May of Teck Club.

'It's just a girls' hostel,' she said, 'that's all it boils down to.'

Beer was served in jam-jars, which was an affectation of the highest order, since jam-jars were at that time in shorter supply than glasses and mugs. The house where the party was held was in Hampstead. There was a stifling crowd. The hosts, Nicholas said, were communist intellectuals. He led her up to a bedroom where they sat on the edge of an unmade bed and looked, with philosophical exhaustion on Nicholas's side, and on hers the enthusiasm of the neophyte Bohemian, at the bare boards of the floor. The people of the house, said Nicholas, were undeniably communist intellectuals, as one could see from the variety of dyspepsia remedies on the bathroom shelf. He said he would point them out to her on the way downstairs when they rejoined the party. By no means, said Nicholas, did the hosts expect to meet their guests at this party. 'Tell me about Selina,' said Nicholas.

Jane's dark hair was piled on top of her head. She had a large face. The only attractive thing about her was her youth and those mental areas of inexperience she was not yet conscious of. She had forgotten for the time being that her job was to reduce Nicholas's literary morale as far as possible, and was treacherously behaving as if he were the genius that, before the week was out, he claimed to be in the letter he got her to forge for him in Charles Morgan's name. Nicholas had decided to do everything nice for Jane, except sleep with her, in the interests of two projects: the publication of his book and his infiltration of the May of Teck Club in general and Selina in particular. 'Tell me more about Selina.' Jane did not then, or at any time, realize that he had received from his first visit to the May of Teck Club a poetic image that teased his mind and pestered him for details as he now pestered Jane. She knew nothing of his boredom and social discontent. She did not see the May of Teck Club as a microcosmic ideal society; far from it. The beautiful heedless poverty of a Golden

Age did not come into the shilling meter life which any sane girl
would regard only as a temporary one until better opportunities
occurred.

> A damsel with a dulcimer
> In a vision once I saw:
> It was an Abyssinian maid,

The voice had wafted with the night breeze into the drawing-room.
Nicholas said, now, 'Tell me about the elocution teacher.'

'Oh, Joanna – you must meet her.'

'Tell me about the borrowing and lending of clothes.'

Jane pondered as to what she could barter for this information
which he seemed to want. The party downstairs was going on without
them. The bare boards under her feet and the patchy walls seemed to
hold out no promise of becoming memorable by tomorrow. She said,
'We've got to discuss your book some time. George and I've got a list
of queries.'

Nicholas lolled on the unmade bed and casually thought he would
probably have to plan some defence measures with George. His jam-
jar was empty. He said, 'Tell me more about Selina. What does she do
apart from being secretary to a pansy?'

Jane was not sure how drunk she was, and could not bring herself to
stand up, this being the test. She said, 'Come to lunch on Sunday.'
Sunday lunch for a guest was two-and-sixpence extra; she felt she
might be taken to more of these parties by Nicholas, among the inner
circle of the poets of today; but she supposed he wanted to take Selina
out, and that was that; she thought he would probably want to sleep
with Selina, and as Selina had slept with two men already, Jane did
not envisage any obstacle. It made her sad to think, as she did, that the
whole rigmarole of his interest in the May of Teck Club, and the point
of their sitting in this bleak room, was his desire to sleep with Selina.
She said, 'What bits would you say were the most important?'

'What bits?'

'Your book,' she said. '*The Sabbath Notebooks*. George is looking
for a genius. It must be you.'

'It's all important.' He formed the plan immediately of forging a
letter from someone crudely famous to say it was a work of genius.

Not that he believed it to be so one way or the other, the idea of such an unspecific attribute as genius not being one on which his mind was accustomed to waste its time. However, he knew a useful word when he saw it, and, perceiving the trend of Jane's question, made his plan. He said, 'Tell me again that delightful thing Selina repeats about poise.'

'Poise is perfect balance, an equanimity of body and mind, complete composure whatever the social scene. Elegant dress, immaculate . . . Oh, Christ,' she said, 'I'm tired of picking crumbs of meat out of the shepherd's pie, picking with a fork to get the little bits of meat separated from the little bits of potato. You don't know what it's like trying to eat enough to live on and at the same time avoid fats and carbohydrates.'

Nicholas kissed her tenderly. He felt there might be a sweetness in Jane, after all, for nothing reveals a secret sweetness so much as a personal point of misery bursting out of a phlegmatic creature.

Jane said, 'I've got to feed my brain.'

He said he would try to get her a pair of nylon stockings from the American with whom he worked. Her legs were bare and dark-haired. There and then he gave her six clothing coupons out of his coupon book. He said she could have his next week's egg. She said, 'You need your egg for your brain.'

'I have breakfast at the American canteen,' he said. 'We have eggs there, and orange juice.'

She said she would take his egg. The egg-ration was one a week at this time, it was the beginning of the hardest period of food-rationing, since the liberated countries had now to be supplied. Nicholas had a gas-ring in his bed-sitting room on which he cooked his supper when he was at home and remembered about supper. He said, 'You can have all my tea, I drink coffee. I get it from the Americans.'

She said she would be glad of his tea. The tea-ration was two ounces one week and three ounces the next, alternately. Tea was useful for bartering purposes. She felt she would really have to take the author's side, where Nicholas was concerned, and somehow hoodwink George. Nicholas was a true artist and had some feelings. George was only a publisher. She would have to put Nicholas wise to George's fault-finding technique of business.

'Let's go down,' Nicholas said.

The door opened and Rudi Bittesch stood watching them for a moment. Rudi was always sober.

'Rudi!' said Jane with unusual enthusiasm. She was glad to be seen to know somebody in this milieu who had not been introduced by Nicholas. It was a way of showing that she belonged to it.

'Well, well,' Rudi said. 'How are you doing these days, Nick, by the way?'

Nicholas said he was on loan to the Americans.

Rudi laughed like a cynical uncle and said, himself he too could have worked for the Americans if he had wanted to sell out.

'Sell out what?' Nicholas said.

'My integrity to work only for peace,' said Rudi. 'By the way, come and join the party and forget it.'

On the way down he said to Nicholas, 'You're publishing a book with Throvis-Mew? I hear this news by Jane.'

Jane said quickly, in case Rudi should reveal that he had already seen the book, 'It's a sort of anarchist book.'

Rudi said to Nicholas, 'You still like anarchism, by the way?'

'But not anarchists by and large, by the way,' Nicholas said.

'How has he died, by the way?' said Rudi.

'He was martyred, they say,' said Jane.

'In Haiti? How is this?'

'I don't know much, except what I get from the news sources. Reuters says a local rising. Associated News has a bit that's just come in ... I was thinking of that manuscript *The Sabbath Notebooks*.'

'I have it still. If he is famous by his death, I find it. How has he died ...?'

'I can't hear you, it's a rotten line ...

'I say I can't hear, Rudi ...'

'How has he died ... By what means?'

'It will be worth a lot of money, Rudi.'

'I find it. This line is bad by the way, can you hear me? How has he died ...?'

'... a hut ...'

'I can't hear ...'

'... in a valley ...'

'Speak loud.'

'. . . in a clump of palms . . . deserted . . . it was market day, everyone had gone to market.'

'I find it. There is maybe a market for this Sabbath book. They make a cult of him, by the way?'

'He was trying to interfere with their superstitions, they said. They're getting rid of a lot of Catholic priests.'

'I can't hear a word. I ring you tonight, Jane. We meet later.'

Selina came into the drawing-room wearing a high hoop-brimmed blue hat and shoes with high block wedges; these fashions from France, it was said, were symbols of the Resistance. It was late on Sunday morning. She had been for a seemly walk along the pathways of Kensington Gardens with Greggie.

Selina took off her hat and laid it on the sofa beside her. She said, 'I've got a guest for lunch, Felix.' Felix was Colonel G. Felix Dobell who was head of a branch of the American Intelligence Service which occupied the top floor of the hotel next door to the club. He had been among a number of men invited to one of the club's dances, and there had selected Selina for himself.

Jane said, 'I'm having Nicholas Farringdon for lunch.'

'But he was here during the week.'

'Well, he's coming again. I went to a party with him.'

'Good,' said Selina. 'I like him.'

Jane said, 'Nicholas works with the American Intelligence. He probably knows your Colonel.'

It was found that the men had not met. They shared a table for four with the two girls, who waited on them, fetching the food from the hatch. Sunday lunch was the best meal of the week. Whenever one of the girls rose to fetch and carry, Felix Dobell half-rose in his chair, then sat down again, for courtesy. Nicholas lolled like an Englishman possessed of *droits de seigneur* while the two girls served him.

The warden, a tall grey-skinned woman habitually dressed in grey, made a brief announcement that 'the Conservative M.P. was coming to give a pre-election discussion' on the following Tuesday.

Nicholas smiled widely so that his long dark face became even more good-looking. He seemed to like the idea of *giving* a discussion, and said so to the Colonel who amiably agreed with him. The Colonel seemed to be in love with the entire club, Selina being the centre and practical focus of his feelings in this respect. This was a common effect of the May of Teck Club on its male visitors, and Nicholas was enamoured of the entity in only one exceptional way, that it stirred his poetic sense to a point of exasperation, for at the same time he discerned with irony the process of his own thoughts, how he was imposing upon this society an image incomprehensible to itself.

The grey warden's conversational voice could be heard addressing grey-haired Greggie who sat with her at table, 'You see, Greggie, I can't be everywhere in the club at once.'

Jane said to her companions, 'That's the one fact that makes life bearable for us.'

'That is a very original idea,' said the American Colonel, but he was referring to something that Nicholas had said before Jane had spoken, when they were discussing the political outlook of the May of Teck Club. Nicholas had offered: 'They should be told not to vote at all, I mean persuaded not to vote at all. We could do without the government. We could manage with the monarchy, the House of Lords, the . . .'

Jane looked bored, as she had several times read this bit in the manuscript, and she rather wanted to discuss personalities, which always provided her with more real pleasure than any impersonal talk, however light and fantastic, although she did not yet admit this fact in her aspiring brain. It was not till Jane had reached the apex of her career as a reporter and interviewer for the largest of women's journals that she found her right role in life, while still incorrectly subscribing to a belief that she was capable of thought – indeed, was demonstrating a capacity for it. But now she sat at table with Nicholas and longed for him to stop talking to the Colonel about the happy possibilities inherent in the delivery of political speeches to the May of Teck girls, and the different ways in which they might be corrupted. Jane felt guilty about her boredom. Selina laughed with poise when Nicholas said, next, 'We could do without a central government. It's bad for us, and what's worse, it's bad for the politicians . . .' but that he was as serious about this as it was possible for his self-mocking mind to be about anything, seemed to be apparent to the Colonel, who amazingly assured Nicholas, 'My wife Gareth also is a member of the Guild of Ethical Guardians in our town. She's a hard worker.'

Nicholas, reminding himself that poise was perfect balance, accepted this statement as a rational response. 'Who are the Ethical Guardians?' said Nicholas.

'They stand for the ideal of purity in the home. They keep a special guard on reading material. Many homes in our town will not accept literature unstamped by the Guardians' crest of honour.'

Nicholas now saw that the Colonel had understood him to hold ideals, and had connected them with the ideals of his wife Gareth, these being the only other ideals he could immediately lay hands on. It was the only explanation. Jane wanted to put everything straight. She said, 'Nicholas is an anarchist.'

'Ah no, Jane,' said the Colonel. 'That's being a bit hard on your author-friend.'

Selina had already begun to realize that Nicholas held unorthodox views about things to the point where they might be regarded as crackpot to the sort of people she was used to. She felt his unusualness was a weakness, and this weakness in an attractive man held desirability for her. There were two other men of her acquaintance who were vulnerable in some way. She was not perversely interested in this fact, so far as she felt no urge to hurt them; if she did so, it was by accident. What she liked about these men was that neither of them wished to possess her entirely. She slept with them happily because of this. She had another man-friend, a businessman of thirty-five, still in the Army, very wealthy, not weak. He was altogether possessive; Selina thought she might marry him eventually. In the meantime she looked at Nicholas as he conversed in this mad sequence with the Colonel, and thought she could use him.

They sat in the drawing-room and planned the afternoon which had developed into a prospective outing for four in the Colonel's car. By this time he had demanded to be called Felix.

He was about thirty-two. He was one of Selina's weak men. His weakness was an overwhelming fear of his wife, so that he took great pains not to be taken unawares in bed with Selina on their country week-ends, even although his wife was in California. As he locked the door of the bedroom Felix would say, very worried, 'I wouldn't like to hurt Gareth,' or some such thing. The first time he did this Selina looked through the bathroom door, tall and beautiful with wide eyes, she looked at Felix to see what was the matter with him. He was still anxious and tried the door again. On the late Sunday mornings, when the bed was already uncomfortable with breakfast crumbs, he would sometimes fall into a muse and be far away. He might then say, 'I hope there's no way Gareth could come by knowledge of this hideout.' And so he was one of those who did not want to possess Selina entirely; and being beautiful and liable to provoke possessiveness, she found this all right provided the man was attractive to sleep with and be out with, and was a good dancer. Felix was blond with an appearance of reserved nobility which he must have inherited. He seldom said anything very humorous, but was willing to be gay. On this Sunday afternoon in the May of Teck Club he proposed to drive to Richmond, which was a long way by car from Knightsbridge in those days when petrol was so scarce that nobody went driving for pleasure except in an American's car, in the vague mistaken notion that their vehicles were supplied by 'American' oil, and so were not subject to the conscience of British austerity or the reproachful question about the necessity of the journey displayed at all places of public transport.

Jane, observing Selina's long glance of perfect balance and equanimity resting upon Nicholas, immediately foresaw that she would be disposed in the front seat with Felix while Selina stepped, with her arch-footed poise, into the back, where Nicholas would join her; and she foresaw that this arrangement would come about with effortless elegance. She had no objection to Felix, but she could not hope to win him for herself, having nothing to offer a man like Felix. She felt she had a certain something, though small, to offer Nicholas, this being her literary and brain-work side which Selina lacked. It was in fact a misunderstanding of Nicholas – she vaguely thought of him as a more attractive Rudi Bittesch – to imagine he would receive more pleasure and reassurance from a literary girl than simply a girl. It was the girl in Jane that had moved him to kiss her at the party; she might have gone further with Nicholas without her literary leanings. This was a mistake she continued to make in her relations with men, inferring from her own preference for men of books and literature their preference for women of the same business. And it never really occurred to her that literary men, if they like women at all, do not want literary women but girls.

But Jane was presently proved right in her prediction about the seating arrangements in the car; and it was her repeated accuracy of intuition in such particulars as these which gave her confidence in her later career as a prophetic gossip-columnist.

Meantime the brown-lined drawing-room began to chirp into life as the girls came in from the dining-room bearing trays of coffee cups. The three spinsters, Greggie, Collie, and Jarvie, were introduced to the guests, as was their accustomed right. They sat in hard chairs and poured coffee for the young loungers. Collie and Jarvie were known to be in the process of a religious quarrel, but they made an effort to conceal their differences for the occasion. Jarvie, however, was agitated by the fact that her coffee cup had been filled too full by Collie. She laid the cup and swimming saucer on a table a little way behind her, and ignored it significantly. She was dressed to go out, with gloves, bag, and hat. She was presently going to take her Sunday-school class. The gloves were made of a stout green-brown suède. Jarvie smoothed them out on her lap, then fluttered her fingers over the cuffs, turning them back. They revealed the utility stamp, two half-moons facing the same way, which was the mark of price-controlled clothes and which, on dresses, where the mark was merely stamped on a tape sewn on the inside, everyone removed. Jarvie surveyed her gloves' irremovable utility mark with her head at a slight angle, as if considering some question connected with it. She then smoothed out the gloves again and jerkily adjusted her spectacles. Jane felt in a great panic to get married. Nicholas, on hearing that Jarvie was about to go to teach a Sunday-school class, was solicitous to inquire about it.

'I think we had better drop the subject of religion,' Jarvie said, as if in conclusion of an argument long in progress. Collie said, 'I thought we *had* dropped it. What a lovely day for Richmond!'

Selina slouched elegantly in her chair, untouched by the threat of becoming a spinster, as she would never be that sort of spinster, anyway. Jane recalled the beginning of the religious quarrel over-heard on all floors, since it had taken place in the echoing wash-room on the second landing. Collie had at first accused Jarvie of failing to clean the sink after using it to wash up her dishes of stuff, which she surreptitiously cooked on her gas-ring where only kettles were lawfully permitted. Then, ashamed of her outburst, Collie had more loudly accused Jarvie of putting spiritual obstacles in her path 'just when you know I'm growing in grace'. Jarvie had then said something scornful about the Baptists as opposed to the true spirit of the Gospels. This religious row, with elaborations, had now lasted more than two weeks but the women were doing their best to conceal it. Collie now said to Jarvie, 'Are you going to waste your coffee with the milk in it?' This was a moral rebuke, for milk was on the ration. Jarvie turned, smoothed, patted and pulled straight the gloves on her lap and breathed in and out. Jane wanted to tear off her clothes and run naked into the street, screaming. Collie looked with disapproval at Jane's bare fat knees.

Greggie, who had very little patience with the two other elder members, had been winning her way with Felix, and had enquired what went on 'up there, next door', meaning in the hotel, the top floor of which the American Intelligence was using, the lower floors being strangely empty and forgotten by the requisitioners.

'Ah, you'd be surprised, ma'am,' Felix said.

Greggie said she must show the men round the garden before they set off for Richmond. The fact that Greggie did practically all the gardening detracted from its comfort for the rest of the girls. Only the youngest and happiest girls could feel justified in using it to sit about in, as it was so much Greggie's toiled-at garden. Only the youngest and happiest could walk on the grass with comfort; they were not greatly given to scruples and consideration for others, by virtue of their unblighted spirits.

Nicholas had noticed a handsome bright-cheeked fair-haired girl standing, drinking her coffee fairly quickly. She left the room with graceful speed when she had drunk her coffee.

Jane said, 'That's Joanna Childe who does elocution.'

Later, in the garden, while Greggie was conducting her tour, they heard Joanna's voice. Greggie was displaying her various particular items, rare plants reared from stolen cuttings, these being the only objects that Greggie would ever think of stealing. She boasted, like a true gardening woman, of her thefts and methods of acquiring snips of other people's rare plants. The sound of Joanna's afternoon pupil lilted down from her room.

Nicholas said, 'The voice is coming from up there, now. Last time, it came from the ground floor.'

'She uses her own room at week-ends when the recreation room is used a lot. We're very proud of Joanna.'

Joanna's voice followed her pupil's.

Greggie said, 'This hollow shouldn't be there. It's where the bomb dropped. It just missed the house.'

'Were you in the house at the time?' said Felix.

'I was,' said Greggie, 'I was in bed. Next moment I was on the floor. All the windows were broken. And it's my suspicion there was a second bomb that didn't go off. I'm almost sure I saw it drop as I picked myself up off the floor. But the disposal squad found only the one bomb and removed it. Anyway, if there's a second it must have died a natural death by now. I'm talking about the year 1942.'

Felix said, with his curious irrelevancy, 'My wife Gareth talks of coming over here with UNRRA. I wonder if she could put up at your club in transit for a week or two? I have to be back and forth, myself. She would be lonely in London.'

'It would have been lying underneath the hydrangeas on the right if I was correct,' Greggie said.

> The sea of faith
> Was once, too, at the full, and round earth's shore
> Lay like the folds of a bright girdle furled.
> But now I only hear
> Its melancholy, long, withdrawing roar,
> Retreating, to the breath
> Of the night-wind, down the vast edges drear
> And naked shingles of the world.

'We'd better be on our way to Richmond,' Felix said.

'We're awfully proud of Joanna,' said Greggie.

'A fine reader.'

'No, she recites from memory. But her pupils read, of course. It's elocution.'

Selina gracefully knocked some garden mud off her wedge shoes on the stone step, and the party moved inside.

The girls went to get ready. The men disappeared in the dark little downstairs cloakroom.

'That is a fine poem,' said Felix, for Joanna's voices were here, too, and the lesson had moved to *Kubla Khan*.

Nicholas almost said, 'She is orgiastical in her feeling for poetry. I can hear it in her voice,' but refrained in case the Colonel should say 'Really?' and he should go on to say, 'Poetry takes the place of sex for her, I think.'

'Really? She looked sexually fine to me.'

Which conversation did not take place, and Nicholas kept it for his notebooks.

They waited in the hall till the girls came down. Nicholas read the notice-board, advertising second-hand clothes for sale, or in exchange for clothing coupons. Felix stood back, a refrainer from such intrusions on the girls' private business, but tolerant of the other man's curiosity. He said, 'Here they come.'

The number and variety of muted noises-off were considerable. Laughter went on behind the folded doors of the first-floor dormitory. Someone was shovelling coal in the cellar, having left open the green baize door which led to those quarters. The telephone desk within the office rang distantly shrill with boy-friends, and various corresponding buzzes on the landings summoned the girls to talk. The sun broke through as the forecast had promised.

> Weave a circle round him thrice,
> And close your eyes with holy dread,
> For he on honey-dew hath fed,
> And drunk the milk of Paradise.

SIX

'Dear Dylan Thomas,' wrote Jane.

Downstairs, Nancy Riddle, who had finished her elocution lesson, was attempting to discuss with Joanna Childe the common eventualities arising from being a clergyman's daughter.

'My father's always in a filthy temper on Sundays. Is yours?'

'No, he's rather too occupied.'

'Father goes on about the Prayer Book. I must say, I agree with him there. It's out of date.'

'Oh, I think the Prayer Book's wonderful,' said Joanna. She had the Book of Common Prayer practically by heart, including the Psalms – especially the Psalms – which her father repeated daily at Matins and Evensong in the frequently empty church. In former years at the rectory Joanna had attended these services every day, and had made the responses from her pew, as it might be on 'Day 13', when her father would stand in his lofty meekness, robed in white over black, to read:

Let God arise, and let his enemies be scattered:

whereupon without waiting for pause Joanna would respond:

let them also that hate him flee before him.

The father continued:

Like as the smoke vanisheth, so shalt thou drive them away:

And Joanna came in swiftly:

and like as wax melteth at the fire, so let the ungodly perish at the presence of God.

And so on had circled the Psalms, from Day 1 to Day 31 of the months, morning and evening, in peace and war; and often the first curate, and then the second curate, took over the office, uttering as it seemed to the empty pews, but by faith to the congregations of the angels, the Englishly rendered intentions of the sweet singer of Israel.

Joanna lit the gas-ring in her room in the May of Teck Club and put on the kettle. She said to Nancy Riddle:

'The Prayer Book is wonderful. There was a new version got up in 1928, but Parliament put it out. Just as well, as it happened.'

'What's the Prayer Book got to do with them?'

'It's within their jurisdiction funnily enough.'

'I believe in divorce,' Nancy said.

'What's that got to do with the Prayer Book?'

'Well, it's all connected with the C. of E. and all the arguing.'

Joanna mixed some powdered milk carefully with water from the tap and poured the mixture upon two cups of tea. She passed a cup to Nancy and offered saccharine tablets from a small tin box. Nancy took one tablet, dropped it in her tea, and stirred it. She had recently got involved with a married man who talked of leaving his wife.

Joanna said, 'My father had to buy a new cloak to wear over his cassock at funerals, he always catches cold at funerals. That means no spare coupons for me this year.'

Nancy said, 'Does he wear a cloak? He must be High. My father wears an overcoat; he's Low to Middle, of course.'

All through the first three weeks of July Nicholas wooed Selina and at the same time cultivated Jane and others of the May of Teck Club.

The sounds and sights impinging on him from the hall of the club intensified themselves, whenever he called, into one sensation, as if with a will of their own. He thought of the lines:

> Let us roll all our strength, and all
> Our sweetness up into one ball;

And I would like, he thought, to teach Joanna that poem or rather demonstrate it; and he made spasmodic notes of all this on the back pages of his *Sabbath* manuscript.

Jane told him everything that went on in the club. 'Tell me more,' he said. She told him things, in her clever way of intuition, which fitted his ideal of the place. In fact, it was not an unjust notion, that it was a miniature expression of a free society, that it was a community held together by the graceful attributes of a common poverty. He observed that at no point did poverty arrest the vitality of its members but rather nourished it. Poverty differs vastly from want, he thought.

'Hallo, Pauline?'

'Yes?'

'It's Jane.'

'Yes?'

'I've got something to tell you. What's the matter?'

'I was resting.'

'Sleeping?'

'No, resting. I've just got back from the psychiatrist, he makes me rest after every session. I've got to lie down.'

'I thought you were finished with the psychiatrist. Are you not very well again?'

'This is a new one. Mummy found him, he's marvellous.'

'Well, I just wanted to tell you something, can you listen? Do you remember Nicholas Farringdon?'

'No, I don't think so. Who's he?'

'Nicholas ... remember that last time on the roof at the May of Teck ... Haiti, in a hut ... among some palms, it was market day, everyone had gone to the market centre. Are you listening?'

We are in the summer of 1945 when he was not only enamoured of the May of Teck Club as an aesthetic and ethical conception of it, lovely frozen image that it was, but he presently slept with Selina on the roof.

> The mountains look on Marathon
> And Marathon looks on the sea;
> And musing there an hour alone,
> I dream'd that Greece might still be free;

> For standing on the Persians' grave,
> I could not deem myself a slave.

Joanna needs to know more life, thought Nicholas, as he loitered in the hall on one specific evening, but if she knew life she would not be proclaiming these words so sexually and matriarchally as if in the ecstatic act of suckling a divine child.

At the top of the house the apples are laid in rows.

She continued to recite as he loitered in the hall. No one was about. Everyone was gathered somewhere else, in the drawing-room or in the bedrooms, sitting round wireless sets, tuning in to some special programme. Then one wireless, and another, roared forth louder by far than usual from the upper floors; others tuned in to the chorus, justified in the din by the voice of Winston Churchill. Joanna ceased. The wirelesses spoke forth their simultaneous Sinaitic predictions of what fate would befall the freedom-loving electorate should it vote for Labour in the forthcoming elections. The wirelesses suddenly started to reason humbly:

We shall have Civil Servants . . .

The wirelesses changed their tones, they roared:

No longer civil . . .

Then they were sad and slow:

No longer . . .
. . . *servants.*

Nicholas imagined Joanna standing by her bed, put out of business as it were, but listening, drawing it into her bloodstream. As in a dream of his own that depicted a dream of hers, he thought of Joanna in this immovable attitude, given up to the cadences of the wireless as if it did not matter what was producing them, the politician or herself. She was a proclaiming statue in his mind.

A girl in a long evening dress slid in the doorway, furtively. Her hair fell round her shoulders in a brown curl. Through the bemused mind of the loitering, listening man went the fact of a girl slipping furtively into the hall; she had a meaning, even if she had no meaningful intention.

She was Pauline Fox. She was returning from a taxi-ride round the park at the price of eight shillings. She had got into the taxi and told the driver to drive round, round anywhere, just drive. On such occasions the taxi-drivers suspected at first that she was driving out to pick up a man, then as the taxi circled the park and threepences ticked up on the meter, the drivers suspected she was mad, or even, perhaps, one of those foreign royalties still exiled in London: and they concluded one or the other when she ordered them back to the door to which she had summoned them by carefully pre-arranged booking. It was dinner with Jack Buchanan which Pauline held as an immovable idea to be established as fact at the May of Teck Club. In the day-time she worked in an office and was normal. It was dinner with Jack Buchanan that prevented her from dining with any other man, and caused her to wait in the hall for half an hour after the other members had gone to the dining-room, and to return surreptitiously half an hour later when nobody, or few, were about.

At times, when Pauline had been seen returning within so short a time, she behaved quite convincingly.

'Goodness, back already, Pauline! I thought you'd gone out to dinner with —'

'Oh! Don't talk to me. We've had a row.' Pauline, with one hand holding a handkerchief to her eye, and the other lifting the hem of her dress, would run sobbing up the stairs to her room.

'She must have had a row with Jack Buchanan again. Funny she never brings Jack Buchanan here.'

'Do you believe it?'

'What?'

'That she goes out with Jack Buchanan?'

'Well, I've wondered.'

Pauline looked furtive, and Nicholas cheerfully said to her, 'Where have *you* been?'

She came and gazed into his face and said, 'I've been to dinner with Jack Buchanan.'

'You've missed Churchill's speech.'

'I know.'

'Did Jack Buchanan get rid of you the moment you had finished your dinner?'

'Yes. He did. We had a row.'

She shook back her shining hair. For this evening, she had managed to borrow the Schiaparelli dress. It was made of taffeta, with small side panniers stuck out with cleverly curved pads over the hips. It was coloured dark blue, green, orange and white in a floral pattern as from the Pacific Islands.

He said, 'I don't think I've ever seen such a gorgeous dress.'

'Schiaparelli,' she said.

He said, 'Is it the one you swap amongst yourselves?'

'Who told you that?'

'You look beautiful,' he replied.

She picked up the rustling skirt and floated away up the staircase. Oh, girls of slender means!

The election speech having come to an end, everybody's wireless was turned off for a space, as if in reverence to what had just passed through the air.

He approached the office door which stood open. The office was still empty. The warden came up behind him, having deserted her post for the duration of the speech.

'I'm still waiting for Miss Redwood.'

'I'll ring her again. No doubt she's been listening to the speech.'

Selina came down presently. Poise is perfect balance, an equanimity of body and mind. Down the staircase she floated, as it were even more realistically than had the sad communer with the spirit of Jack Buchanan a few moments ago floated up it. It might have been the same girl, floating upwards in a Schiaparelli rustle of silk with a shining hood of hair, and floating downwards in a slim skirt with a white-spotted blue blouse, her hair now piled high. The normal noises of the house began to throb again. 'Good-evening,' said Nicholas.

> And all my days are trances,
>   And all my nightly dreams
>   Are where thy dark eye glances,

> And where thy footstep gleams –
> In what ethereal dances,
> By what eternal streams!

'Now repeat,' said Joanna's voice.

'Come on then,' said Selina, stepping ahead of him into the evening light like a racer into the paddock, with a high disregard of all surrounding noises.

SEVEN

'Have you got a shilling for the meter?' said Jane.

'Poise is perfect balance, an equanimity of body and mind, complete composure whatever the social scene. Elegant dress, immaculate grooming, and perfect deportment all contribute to the attainment of self-confidence.'

'Have you got a shilling for two sixpences?'

'No. Anne's got a key that opens the meters, though.'

'Anne, are you in? What about a loan of the key?'

'If we all start using it too often we'll be found out.'

'Only this once. I've got brain-work to do.'

Now sleeps the crimson petal, now the white;

Selina sat, not yet dressed, on the edge of Nicholas's bed. She had a way of glancing sideways beneath her lashes that gave her command of a situation which might otherwise place her in a weakness.

She said, 'How can you bear to live here?'

He said, 'It does till one finds a flat.'

In fact he was quite content with his austere bed-sitting room. With the reckless ambition of a visionary, he pushed his passion for Selina into a desire that she, too, should accept and exploit the outlines of poverty in her life. He loved her as he loved his native country. He wanted Selina to be an ideal society personified amongst her bones, he wanted her beautiful limbs to obey her mind and heart like intelligent men and women, and for these to possess the same grace and beauty as her body. Whereas Selina's desires were comparatively humble, she only wanted, at that particular moment, a packet of hair-grips which had just then disappeared from the shops for a few weeks.

It was not the first instance of a man taking a girl to bed with the aim of converting her soul, but he, in great exasperation, felt that it was, and poignantly, in bed, willed and willed the awakening of her social conscience. After which, he sighed softly into his pillow with a limp sense of achievement, and presently rose to find, with more exasperation than ever, that he had not in the least conveyed his vision of perfection to the girl. She sat on the bed and glanced around beneath her lashes. He was experienced in girls sitting on his bed, but not in girls as cool as Selina about their beauty, and such beauty as hers. It was incredible to him that she should not share with him an understanding of the lovely attributes of dispossession and poverty, her body was so austere and economically furnished.

She said, 'I don't know how you can live in this place, it's like a cell. Do you cook on that thing?' She meant the gas grill.

He said, while it dawned upon him that his love affair with Selina remained a love affair on his side only, 'Yes, of course. Would you like some bacon and egg?'

'Yes,' she said, and started to dress.

He took hope again, and brought out his rations. She was accustomed to men who got food from the black market.

'After the twenty-second of this month,' said Nicholas, 'we are to get two and a half ounces of tea – two ounces one week and three ounces the next.'

'How much do we get now?'

'Two ounces every week. Two ounces of butter; margarine, four ounces.'

She was amused. She laughed for a long time. She said, 'You sound so funny.'

'Christ, so I do!' he said.

'Have you used all your clothing coupons?'

'No, I've got thirty-four left.'

He turned the bacon in the pan. Then, on a sudden thought, he said, 'Would you like some clothing coupons?'

'Oh yes, please.'

He gave her twenty, ate some bacon with her, and took her home in a taxi.

He said, 'I've arranged about the roof.'

She said, 'Well, see and arrange about the weather.'

'We can go to the pictures if it's raining,' he said.

He had arranged to have access to the roof through the top floor of the hotel next door, occupied as it was by American Intelligence, which organization he served in another part of London. Colonel Dobell, who, up to ten days ago, would have opposed this move, now energetically supported it. The reason for this was that his wife Gareth was preparing to join him in London and he was anxious to situate Selina in another context, as he put it.

In the north of California, up a long drive, Mrs G. Felix Dobell had not only resided, but held meetings of the Guardians of Ethics. Now she was coming to London, for she said that a sixth sense told her Felix was in need of her presence there.

Now sleeps the crimson petal, now the white;

Nicholas greatly desired to make love to Selina on the roof, it needs must be on the roof. He arranged everything as precisely as a practised incendiary.

The flat roof of the club, accessible only by the slit window on the top floor, was joined to a similar flat roof of the neighbouring hotel by a small gutter. The hotel had been requisitioned and its rooms converted into offices for the use of the American Intelligence. Like many other requisitioned premises in London, it had been over-crowded with personnel during the war in Europe, and now was practically unoccupied. Only the top floor of this hotel, where uniformed men worked mysteriously day and night, and the ground floor, which was guarded day and night by two American servicemen, and served by night- and day-porters who worked the lift, were in use. Nobody could enter this house without a pass. Nicholas obtained a pass quite easily, and he also by means of a few words and a glance obtained the ambivalent permission of Colonel Dobell, whose wife was already on her journey, to move into a large attic office which was being used as a typing pool. Nicholas was given a courtesy desk there. This attic had a hatch door leading to the flat roof.

*

The weeks had passed, and since in the May of Teck Club they were weeks of youth in the ethos of war, they were capable of accommodating quick happenings and reversals, rapid formations of intimate friendships, and a range of lost and discovered loves that in later life and in peace would take years to happen, grow, and fade. The May of Teck girls were nothing if not economical. Nicholas, who was past his youth, was shocked at heart by their week-by-week emotions.

'I thought you said she was in love with the boy.'

'So she was.'

'Well, wasn't it only last week he died? You said he died of dysentery in Burma.'

'Yes I know. But she met this naval type on Monday, she's madly in love with him.'

'She can't be in love with him,' said Nicholas.

'Well, they've got a lot in common she says.'

'A lot in common? It's only Wednesday now.'

> Like one, that on a lonesome road
> Doth walk in fear and dread,
> And having once turned round, walks on,
> And turns no more his head;
> Because he knows a frightful fiend
> Doth close behind him tread.

'Joanna's marvellous at that one, I love it.'

'Poor Joanna.'

'Why do you say poor Joanna?'

'Well, she never gets any fun, no men-friends.'

'She's terribly attractive.'

'Frightfully attractive. Why doesn't someone do something about Joanna?'

Jane said, 'Look here, Nicholas, there's something you ought to know about Huy Throvis-Mew as a firm and George himself as a publisher.'

They were sitting in the offices of Throvis-Mew, high above Red Lion Square; but George was out.

'He's a crook,' said Nicholas.

'Well, that would be putting it a bit strongly,' she said.

'He's a crook with subtleties.'

'It's not quite that, either. It's a psychological thing about George. He's got to get the better of an author.'

'I know that,' Nicholas said. 'I had a long emotional letter from him making a lot of complaints about my book.'

'He wants to break down your confidence, you see, and then present you with a rotten contract to sign. He finds out the author's weak spot. He always attacks the bit the author likes best. He –'

'I know that,' said Nicholas.

'I'm only telling you because I like you,' Jane said. 'In fact, it's part of my job to find out the author's weak spot, and report to George. But I like you, and I'm telling you all this because –'

'You and George,' said Nicholas, 'draw me a tiny bit closer to understanding the Sphinx's inscrutable smile. And I'll tell you another fact.'

Beyond the grimy window rain fell from a darkening sky on the bomb-sites of Red Lion Square. Jane had looked out in an abstract pose before making her revelation to Nicholas. She now actually noticed the scene, it made her eyes feel miserable and her whole life appeared steeped in equivalent misery. She was disappointed in life, once more.

'I'll tell you another fact,' said Nicholas. 'I'm a crook too. What are you crying for?'

'I'm crying for myself,' said Jane. 'I'm going to look for another job.'

'Will you write a letter for me?'

'What sort of a letter?'

'A crook-letter. From Charles Morgan to myself. Dear Mr Farringdon, When first I received your manuscript I was tempted to place it aside for my secretary to return to you with some polite excuse. But as happy chance would have it, before passing your work to my secretary, I flicked over the pages and my eyes lit on . . .'

'Lit on what?' said Jane.

'I'll leave that to you. Only choose one of the most concise and brilliant passages when you come to write the letter. That will be difficult, I admit, since all are equally brilliant. But choose the piece you like best. Charles Morgan is to say he read that one piece, and then the whole, avidly, from start to finish. He is to say it's a work of genius. He congratulates me on a work of genius, you realize. Then I show the letter to George.'

Jane's life began to sprout once more, green with possibility. She recalled that she was only twenty-three, and smiled.

'Then I show the letter to George,' Nicholas said, 'and I tell him he can keep his contract and –'

George arrived. He looked busily at them both. Simultaneously, he took off his hat, looked at his watch, and said to Jane, 'What's the news?'

Nicholas said, 'Ribbentrop is captured.'

George sighed.

'No news,' said Jane. 'Nobody's rung at all. No letters, nobody's been, nobody's rung us up. Don't worry.'

George went into his inner office. He came out again immediately.

'Did you get my letter?' he said to Nicholas.

'No,' said Nicholas, 'which letter?'

'I wrote, let me see, the day before yesterday, I think. I wrote –'

'Oh, that letter,' said Nicholas. 'Yes, I believe I did receive a letter.'

George went away into his inner office.

Nicholas said to Jane, in a good, loud voice, that he was going for a stroll in the park now that the rain had stopped, and that it was lovely having nothing to do but dream beautiful dreams all the day long.

'Yours very sincerely and admiringly, Charles Morgan,' wrote Jane. She opened the door of her room and shouted, 'Turn down the wireless a bit, I've got to do some brain-work before supper.'

On the whole, they were proud of Jane's brain-work and her connexion with the world of books. They turned down all the wirelesses on the landing.

She read over the first draft of the letter, then very carefully began again, making an authentic-looking letter in a small but mature hand such as Charles Morgan might use. She had no idea what Charles Morgan's handwriting looked like; and had no reason to find out, since George would certainly not know either, and was not to be allowed to retain the document. She had an address at Holland Park which Nicholas had supplied. She wrote this at the top of her writing paper, hoping that it looked all right, and assuring herself that it did since many nice people did not attempt to have their letter-heads printed in war-time and thus make unnecessary demands on the nation's labour.

She had finished by the time the supper-bell rang. She folded the letter with meticulous neatness, having before her eyes the pencil-line features of Charles Morgan's photograph. Jane calculated that this letter by Charles Morgan which she had just written was worth at least fifty pounds to Nicholas. George would be in a terrible state of conflict when he saw it. Poor Tilly, George's wife, had told her that when George was persecuted by an author, he went on and on about it for hours.

Nicholas was coming to the club after supper to spend the evening, having at last persuaded Joanna to give a special recital of *The Wreck of the Deutschland*. It was to be recorded on a tape-machine that Nicholas had borrowed from the news-room of a Government office.

Jane joined the throng in its descent to supper. Only Selina loitered above, finishing off her evening's disciplinary recitation:

... Elegant dress, immaculate grooming, and perfect deport-ment all contribute to the attainment of self-confidence.

The warden's car stopped piercingly outside as the girls reached the lower floor. The warden drove a car as she would have driven a man had she possessed one. She strode, grey, into her office and shortly afterwards joined them in the dining-room, banging on the water-jug with her fork for silence, as she always did when about to make an announcement. She announced that an American visitor, Mrs G. Felix Dobell, would address the club on Friday evening on the subject, 'Western Woman: her Mission'. Mrs Dobell was a leading member of the Guardians of Ethics and had recently come to join her husband who was serving with the United States Intelligence Service stationed in London.

After supper Jane was struck by a sense of her treachery to the establishment of Throvis-Mew, and to George with whom she was paid to conspire in the way of business. She was fond of old George, and began to reflect on his kindly qualities. Without the slightest intention of withdrawing from her conspiracy with Nicholas, she gazed at the letter she had written and wondered what to do about her feelings. She decided to telephone to his wife, Tilly, and have a friendly chat about something.

Tilly was delighted. She was a tiny redhead of lively intelligence and small information, whom George kept well apart from the world of books, being experienced in wives. To Tilly, this was a great deprivation, and she loved nothing better than to keep in touch, through Jane, with the book business and to hear Jane say, 'Well, Tilly, it's a question of one's raison d'être.' George tolerated this friendship, feeling that it established himself with Jane. He relied on Jane. She understood his ways.

Jane was usually bored by Tilly, who, although she had not exactly been a cabaret dancer, imposed on the world of books, whenever she was given the chance, a high leg-kicker's spirit which played on Jane's nerves, since she herself was newly awed by the gravity of literature in general. She felt Tilly was altogether too frivolous about the publishing and writing scene, and moreover failed to realize this fact. But her heart in its treachery now swelled with an access of warmth for Tilly. She telephoned and invited her to supper on Friday. Jane had already calculated that, if Tilly should be a complete bore, they would be able to fill in an hour with Mrs G. Felix Dobell's lecture. The club was fairly eager to see Mrs Dobell, having already seen a certain amount of her husband as Selina's escort, rumoured to be her lover. 'There's a talk on Friday by an American woman on the Western Woman's Mission, but we won't listen to that, it would be a bore,' Jane said, contradicting her resolution in her effusive anxiety to sacrifice anything, anything to George's wife, now that she had betrayed and was about to deceive George.

Tilly said, 'I always love the May of Teck. It's like being back at school.' Tilly always said that, it was infuriating.

Nicholas arrived early with his tape-recorder, and sat in the recreation room with Joanna, waiting for the audience to drift in from supper. She looked to Nicholas very splendid and Nordic, as from a great saga.

'Have you lived here long?' said Nicholas sleepily, while he admired her big bones. He was sleepy because he had spent most of the previous night on the roof with Selina.

'About a year. I daresay I'll die here,' she said with the conventional contempt of all members for the club.

He said, 'You'll get married.'

'No, no.' She spoke soothingly, as to a child who had just been prevented from spooning jam into the stew.

A long shriek of corporate laughter came from the floor immediately above them. They looked at the ceiling and realized that the dormitory girls were as usual exchanging those R.A.F. anecdotes which needed an audience hilariously drunken, either with alcohol or extreme youth, to give them point.

Greggie had appeared, and cast her eyes up to the laughter as she came towards Joanna and Nicholas. She said, 'The sooner that dormitory crowd gets married and gets out of the club, the better. I've never known such a rowdy dormitory crowd in all my years in the club. Not a farthing's worth of intelligence between them.'

Collie arrived and sat down next to Nicholas. Greggie said, 'I was saying about the dormitory girls up there: they ought to get married and get out.'

This was also, in reality, Collie's view. But she always opposed Greggie on principle and, moreover, in company she felt that a contradiction made conversation. 'Why should they get married? Let them enjoy themselves while they're young.'

'They need marriage to enjoy themselves properly,' Nicholas said, 'for sexual reasons.'

Joanna blushed. Nicholas added, 'Heaps of sex. Every night for a month, then every other night for two months, then three times a week for a year. After that, once a week.' He was adjusting the tape-recorder, and his words were like air.

'If you're trying to shock us, young man, we're unshockable,' said Greggie, with a delighted glance round the four walls which were not accustomed to this type of talk, for, after all, it was the public recreation room.

'I'm shockable,' said Joanna. She was studying Nicholas with an apologetic look.

Collie did not know what attitude she should take up. Her fingers opened the clasp of her bag and snapped it shut again; then they played a silent tip-tap on its worn bulging leather sides. Then she said, 'He isn't trying to shock us. He's very realistic. If one is growing in grace – I would go so far as to say when one *has* grown in grace – one can take realism, sex and so forth in one's stride.'

Nicholas beamed lovingly at this.

Collie gave a little half-cough, half-laugh, much encouraged in the success of her frankness. She felt modern, and continued excitedly. 'It's a question of what you never have you never miss, of course.'

Greggie put on puzzled air, as if she genuinely did not know what Collie was talking about. After thirty years' hostile fellowship with Collie, of course she did quite well understand that Collie had a habit of skipping several stages in the logical sequence of her thoughts, and would utter apparently disconnected statements, especially when confused by an unfamiliar subject or the presence of a man.

'Whatever do you mean?' said Greggie. '*What* is a question of what you never have you never miss?'

'Sex, of course,' Collie said, her voice unusually loud with the effort of the topic. 'We were discussing sex and getting married. I say, of course, there's a lot to be said for marriage, but if you never have it you never miss it.'

Joanna looked at the two excited women with meek compassion. To Nicholas she looked stronger than ever in her meekness, as she regarded Greggie and Collie at their rivalry to be uninhibited.

'What do you mean, Collie?' Greggie said.

'You're quite wrong there, Collie. One does miss sex. The body has a life of its own. We do miss what we haven't had, you and I. Biologically. Ask Sigmund Freud. It is revealed in dreams. The absent touch of the warm limbs at night, the absent –'

'Just a minute,' said Nicholas, holding up his hand for silence, in the pretence that he was tuning-in to his empty tape-machine. He could see that the two women would go to any lengths, now they had got started.

'Open the door, please.' From behind the door came the warden's voice and the rattle of the coffee tray. Before Nicholas could leap up to open it for her she had pushed into the room with some clever manoeuvring of hand and foot like a business-like parlourmaid.

'The Beatific Vision does not appear to *me* to be an adequate compensation for what we miss,' Greggie said conclusively, getting in a private thrust at Collie's religiosity.

While coffee was being served and the girls began to fill the room,

Jane entered, fresh from her telephone conversation with Tilly, and, feeling somewhat absolved by it, she handed over to Nicholas her brain-work letter from Charles Morgan. While reading it, he was handed a cup of coffee. In the process of taking the cup he splashed some coffee on the letter.

'Oh, you've ruined it!' Jane said. 'I'll have to do it all over again.'

'It looks more authentic than ever,' Nicholas said. 'Naturally, if I've received a letter from Charles Morgan telling me I'm a genius, I am going to spend a lot of time reading it over and over, in the course of which the letter must begin to look a bit worn. Now, are you sure George will be impressed by Morgan's name?'

'Very,' said Jane.

'Do you mean you're very sure or that George will be very impressed?'

'I mean both.'

'It would put me off, if I were George.'

The recital of *The Wreck of the Deutschland* started presently. Joanna stood with her book ready.

'Not a hush from anybody,' said the warden, meaning, 'Not a sound.' – 'Not a hush,' she said, 'because this instrument of Mr Farringdon's apparently registers the drop of a pin.'

One of the dormitory girls, who sat mending a ladder in a stocking, carefully caused her needle to fall on the parquet floor, then bent and picked it up again. Another dormitory girl who had noticed the action snorted a suppressed laugh. Otherwise there was silence but for the quiet purr of the machine waiting for Joanna.

> Thou mastering me
> God! giver of breath and bread;
> World's strand, sway of the sea;
> Lord of living and dead;
> Thou hast bound bones and veins in me, fastened me flesh,
> And after it almost unmade. . .

EIGHT

A scream of panic from the top floor penetrated the house as Jane returned to the club on Friday afternoon, the 27th of July. She had left the office early to meet Tilly at the club. She did not feel that the scream of panic meant anything special. Jane climbed the last flight of stairs. There was another more piercing scream, accompanied by excited voices. Screams of panic in the club might relate to a laddered stocking or a side-splitting joke.

When she reached the top landing, she saw that the commotion came from the wash-room. There, Anne and Selina, with two of the dormitory girls, were attempting to extricate from the little slit window another girl who had evidently been attempting to climb out and had got stuck. She was struggling and kicking without success, exhorted by various instructions from the other girls. Against their earnest advice, she screamed aloud from time to time. She had taken off her clothes for the attempt and her body was covered with a greasy substance; Jane immediately hoped it had not been taken from her own supply of cold cream which stood in a jar on her dressing-table.

'Who is it?' Jane said, with a close inspective look at the girl's unidentifiable kicking legs and wriggling bottom which were her only visible portions.

Selina brought a towel which she attempted to fasten round the girl's waist with a safety-pin. Anne kept imploring the girl not to scream, and one of the others went to the top of the stairs to look over the banister in the hope that nobody in authority was being unduly attracted upward.

'Who is it?' Jane said.

Anne said, 'I'm afraid it's Tilly.'

'Tilly!'

'She was waiting downstairs and we brought her up here for a lark. She said it was like being back at school, here at the club, so Selina showed her the window. She's just half an inch too large, though. Can't you get her to shut up?'

Jane spoke softly to Tilly. 'Every time you scream,' she said, 'it makes you swell up more. Keep quiet, and we'll work you out with wet soap.'

Tilly went quiet. They worked on her for ten minutes, but she remained stuck by the hips. Tilly was weeping. 'Get George,' she said at last, 'get him on the phone.'

Nobody wanted to fetch George. He would have to come upstairs. Doctors were the only males who climbed the stairs, and even then they were accompanied by one of the staff.

Jane said, 'Well, I'll get somebody.' She was thinking of Nicholas. He had access to the roof from the Intelligence Headquarters; a hefty push from the roof-side of the window might be successful in releasing Tilly. Nicholas had intended to come to the club after supper to hear the lecture and observe, in a jealous complex of curiosity, the wife of Selina's former lover. Felix himself was to be present.

Jane decided to telephone and beg Nicholas to come immediately and help with Tilly. He could then have supper at the club, his second supper, Jane reflected, that week. He might now be home from work, he usually returned to his room at about six o'clock.

'What's the time?' said Jane.

Tilly was weeping, with a sound that threatened a further outburst of screams.

'Just on six,' said Anne.

Selina looked at her watch to see if this was so, then walked towards her room.

'Don't leave her, I'm getting help,' Jane said. Selina opened the door of her room, but Anne stood gripping Tilly's ankles. As Jane reached the next landing she heard Selina's voice.

'Poise is perfect balance, an equanimity ...'

Jane laughed foolishly to herself and descended to the telephone boxes as the clock in the hall struck six o'clock.

It struck six o'clock on that evening of July 27th. Nicholas had just returned to his room. When he heard of Tilly's predicament he promised eagerly to go straight to the Intelligence Headquarters, and on to the roof.

'It's no joke,' Jane said.

'I'm not saying it's a joke.'

'You sound cheerful about it. Hurry up. Tilly's crying her eyes out.'

'As well she might, seeing Labour have got in.'

'Oh, hurry up. We'll all be in trouble if –'

He had rung off.

At that hour Greggie came in from the garden to hang about the hall, awaiting the arrival of Mrs Dobell who was to speak after supper. Greggie would take her into the warden's sitting-room, there to drink dry sherry till the supper-bell went. Greggie hoped also to induce Mrs Dobell to be escorted round the garden before supper.

A distant anguished scream descended the staircase.

'Really,' Greggie said to Jane, who was emerging from the telephone box, 'this club has gone right down. What are visitors to think? Who's screaming up there on the top floor? It sounds exactly as it must have been when this house was in private hands. You girls behave exactly like servant girls in the old days when the master and mistress were absent. Romping and yelling.'

> Make me thy lyre, even as the forest is:
> What if my leaves are falling like its own!
> The tumult of thy mighty harmonies

'George, I want George,' Tilly wailed thinly from far above. Then someone on the top floor thoughtfully turned on the wireless to all-drowning pitch:

> There were angels dining at the Ritz
> And a nightingale sang in Berkeley Square.

And Tilly could be heard no more. Greggie looked out of the open front door and returned. She looked at her watch. 'Six-fifteen,' she said. 'She should be here at six-fifteen. Tell them to turn down the wireless up there. It looks so vulgar, so bad . . .'

'You mean it sounds so vulgar, so bad.' Jane was keeping an eye out for the taxi which she hoped would bring Nicholas, at any moment, to the functional hotel next door.

'Once again,' said Joanna's voice clearly from the third floor to her pupil. 'The last three stanzas again, please.'

> Drive my dead thoughts over the universe
> Like withered leaves to quicken a new birth!

Jane was suddenly overcome by a deep envy of Joanna, the source of which she could not locate exactly at that hour of her youth. The feeling was connected with an inner knowledge of Joanna's disinterestedness, her ability, a gift, to forget herself and her personality. Jane felt suddenly miserable, as one who has been cast out of Eden before realizing that it had in fact been Eden. She recalled two ideas about Joanna that she had gathered from various observations made by Nicholas: that Joanna's enthusiasm for poetry was limited to one kind, and that Joanna was the slightest bit melancholy on the religious side; these thoughts failed to comfort Jane.

Nicholas arrived in a taxi and disappeared in the hotel entrance. As Jane started to run upstairs another taxi drew up. Greggie said, 'Here's Mrs Dobell. It's twenty-two minutes past six.'

Jane bumped into several of the girls who were spilling in lively groups out of the dormitories. She thrust her way through their midst, anxious to reach Tilly and tell her that help was near.

'Jane-ee!' said a girl. 'Don't be so bloody rude, you nearly pushed me over the banister to my death.'

But Jane was thumping upward.

> Now sleeps the crimson petal, now the white;

Jane arrived at the top floor to find Anne and Selina frantically clothing Tilly's lower half to make her look decent. They had got as far as the stockings. Anne was holding a leg while Selina, long-fingered, smoothed the stocking over it.

'Nicholas has come. Is he out on the roof yet?'

Tilly moaned, 'Oh, I'm dying. I can't stand it any more. Fetch *George*, I want George.'

'Here's Nicholas,' said Selina, tall enough to see him emerging from the low doorway of the hotel attic, as he had lately done on the calm summer nights. He stumbled over a rug which had been bundled beside the door. It was one of the rugs they had brought out to lie on. He recovered his balance, started walking quickly over towards them, then fell flat on his face. A clock struck the half-hour. Jane heard herself say in a loud voice, 'It's half past six.' Suddenly, Tilly was sitting on the bathroom floor beside her. Anne, too, was on the floor crumpled with her arm over her eyes as if trying to hide her presence. Selina lay stunned against the door. She opened her mouth to scream, and probably did scream, but it was then that the rumbling began to assert itself from the garden below, mounting swiftly to a mighty crash. The house trembled again, and the girls who had tried to sit up were thrown flat. The floor was covered with bits of glass, and Jane's blood flowed from somewhere in a trickle, while some sort of time passed silently by. Sensations of voices, shouts, mounting footsteps and falling plaster brought the girls back to various degrees of responsiveness. Jane saw, in an unfocused way, the giant face of Nicholas peering through the open slit of the little window. He was exhorting them to get up quick.

'There's been an explosion in the garden.'

'Greggie's bomb,' Jane said, grinning at Tilly. 'Greggie was right,' she said. This was a hilarious statement, but Tilly did not laugh, she closed her eyes and lay back. Tilly was only half-dressed and looked very funny indeed. Jane then laughed loudly at Nicholas, but he too had no sense of humour.

Down the street the main body of the club had congregated, having been in one of the public rooms on the ground floor at the time of the explosion, or else lingering in the dormitories. There, the explosion had been heard more than it was felt. Two ambulances had arrived and a third was approaching. Some of the more dazed among the people were being treated for shock in the hall of the neighbouring hotel.

Greggie was attempting to assure Mrs Felix Dobell that she had foreseen and forewarned the occurrence. Mrs Dobell, a handsome matron of noticeable height, stood out on the edge of the pavement, taking little notice of Greggie. She was looking at the building with a surveyor's eye, and was possessed of that calm which arises from a misunderstanding of the occasion's true nature, for although she was shaken by the explosion, Mrs Dobell assumed that belated bombs went off every day in Britain, and, content to find herself intact, and slightly pleased to have shared a war experience, was now curious as to what routine would be adopted in the emergency. She said, 'When do you calculate the dust will settle?'

Greggie said, yet once more, 'I knew that live bomb was in that garden. I knew it. I was always saying that bomb was there. The bomb-disposal squad missed it, they missed it.'

Some faces appeared at an upper bedroom. The window opened. A girl started to shout, but had to withdraw her head; she was choking with the dust that was still surrounding the house in clouds.

It was difficult to discern the smoke, when it began to show, amongst the dust. A gas-main had, in fact, been ruptured by the explosion and a fire started to crawl along the basement from the furnaces. It started to crawl and then it flared. A roomful of flame suddenly roared in the ground-floor offices, lapping against the large window-panes, feeling for the woodwork, while Greggie continued to shrill at Mrs Dobell above the clamour of the girls, the street-crowd, the ambulances, and the fire-engines. 'It was ten chances to one we might have been in the garden when the bomb went off. I was going to take you round the garden before supper. We would have been buried, dead, killed. It was ten to one, Mrs Dobell.'

Mrs Dobell said, as one newly enlightened, 'This is a terrible incident.' And being more shaken than she appeared to be, she added, 'This is a time that calls for the exercise of discretion, the woman's prerogative.' This saying was part of the lecture she had intended to give after supper. She looked round in the crowd for her husband. The warden, whose more acute shock-effects had preceded Mrs Dobell's by a week, was being carried off through the crowd on a stretcher.

'Felix!' yelled Mrs Dobell. He was coming out of the hotel adjoining the club, with his olive-greenish khaki uniform dusky with soot and streaked as with black oil. He had been investigating the back premises of the club. He said: 'The brickwork of the walls looks unsteady. The top half of the fire-escape has collapsed. There are some girls trapped up there. The firemen are directing them up to the top floor; they'll have to be brought through the skylight on to the roof.'

'Who?' said Lady Julia.

'Jane Wright speaking. I rang you last week to see if you could find out some more about –'

'Oh yes. Well, I'm afraid there's very little information from the F.O. They never comment officially, you know. From what I can gather, the man was making a complete nuisance of himself, preaching against the local superstitions. He had several warnings and apparently he got what he asked for. How did you come to know him?'

'He was friendly with some of the girls at the May of Teck Club when he was a civilian, I mean before he joined this Order. He was there on the night of the tragedy, in fact, and –'

'It probably turned his brain. Something must have affected his brain, anyhow, because from what I gather unofficially he was a complete . . .'

The skylight, although it had been bricked up by someone's hysterical order, at that time in the past when a man had penetrated the attic-floor of the club to visit a girl, was not beyond being unbricked by the firemen. It was all a question of time.

Time was not a large or present fact to those girls of the May of Teck Club, thirteen of them, who, with Tilly Throvis-Mew, remained in the upper storeys of the building when, following the explosion in the garden, fire broke out in the house. A large portion of the perfectly safe fire-escape which had featured in so many safety-instruction regulations, so many times read out to the members at so many supper-times, now lay in zigzag fragments among the earthy mounds and upturned roots of the garden.

Time, which was an immediate onward-rushing enemy to the onlookers in the street and the firemen on the roof, was only a small far-forgotten event to the girls; for they were stunned not only by the force of the explosion, but, when they recovered and looked round, still more by the sudden dislocation of all familiar appearances. A chunk of the back wall of the house gaped to the sky. There, in 1945, they were as far removed from the small fact of time as weightless occupants of a space-rocket. Jane got up, ran to her room, and with animal instinct snatched and gobbled a block of chocolate which remained on her table. The sweet stuff assisted her recovery. She turned to the wash-rooms where Tilly, Anne, and Selina were slowly rising to their feet. There were shouts from the direction of the roof. An unrecognized face looked in the slit window, and a large hand wrenched the loose frame away from it.

But the fire had already started to spread up the main staircase, preceded by heraldic puffs of smoke, the flames sidling up the banisters.

The girls who had been in their rooms on the second and third floors at the time of the explosion had been less shaken than those at the top of the house, since there some serious defect in the masonry had been caused indirectly by a bombardment early in the war. The girls on the second and third floors were cut and bruised, but were stunned by the sound of the blast rather than the house-shaking effects of it.

Some of the second-floor dormitory girls had been quick and alert enough to slip down the staircase and out into the street, in the interval between the explosion of the bomb and the start of the fire. The remaining ten, when they variously attempted to escape by that route, met the fire and retreated upward.

Joanna and Nancy Riddle, having finished their elocution lessons, had been standing at the door of Joanna's room when the bomb went off, and so had escaped the glass from the window. Joanna's hand was cut, however, by the glass from a tiny travelling clock which she had been winding at the time. It was Joanna who, when the members shrieked at the sight of the fire, gave the last shriek, then shouted: 'The fire-escape!' Pauline Fox fled behind her, and the others followed along the second-floor corridors and up the narrow back staircase to the third-floor passage-way where the fire-escape window had always stood. This was now a platform open to the summer evening sky, for here the wall had fallen away and the fire-escape with it. Plaster tumbled from the bricks as the ten women crowded to the spot that had once been the fire-escape landing. They were still looking in a bewildered way for the fire-escape stairway. Voices of firemen shouted at them from the garden. Voices came from the direction of the flat roof above, and then one voice clearly through a megaphone ordered them back, lest the piece of floor they stood on should collapse.

The voice said, 'Proceed to the top floor.'

'Jack will wonder what's happened to me,' said Pauline Fox. She was first up the back stairs to the wash-rooms where Anne, Selina, Jane, and Tilly were now on their feet, having steadied themselves on learning of the fire. Selina was taking off her skirt.

Above their heads, set in a sloping ceiling, was the large square outline of the old, bricked-in skylight. Men's voices, the scrabble of ladders and loud thumps of bricks being tested, came down from this large square. The men were evidently trying to find a means of opening the skylight to release the girls, who meanwhile stared up at the square mark in the ceiling. Tilly said, 'Won't it open?' Nobody answered, because the girls of the club knew the answer. Everyone in the club had heard the legend of the man who had got in by the skylight and, some said, been found in bed with a girl.

Now Selina stood on the lavatory seat and jumped up to the slit window. She slid through it to the roof with an easy diagonal movement. There were now thirteen women in the wash-room. They stood in the alert, silent attitude of jungle-danger, listening for further instruction from the megaphone on the roof outside.

Anne Baberton followed Selina through the slit window, with difficulty, because she was flustered. But a man's two hands came up to the window to receive her. Tilly Throvis-Mew began to sob. Pauline Fox ripped off her dress and then her underclothes until she was altogether naked. She had an undernourished body; there would have been no difficulty for her in getting through the slit window fully clothed, but she went naked as a fish.

Only Tilly sobbed heavily, but the rest of the girls were trembling. The noises from the sloping roof ceased as the firemen jumped down from investigating the skylight on to the flat roof area; footsteps beat and shuffled there, beyond the slit window, where throughout the summer Selina had lain with Nicholas, wrapped in rugs, under the Plough, which constituted the only view in Greater London that remained altogether intact.

Within the wash-room the eleven remaining women heard a fireman's voice addressing them through the window, against the simultaneous blare of megaphone instructions to the firemen. The man at the window said, 'Stay where you are. Don't panic. We're sending for tools to uncover the brickwork over the skylight. We won't be long. It's a question of time. We are doing everything we can to get you out. Remain where you are. Don't panic. It's just a question of time.'

The question of time opened now as a large thing in the lives of the eleven listeners.

Twenty-eight minutes had passed since the bomb had exploded in the garden. Felix Dobell joined Nicholas Farringdon on the flat roof after the fire started. They assisted the three slim girls through the window. Anne and naked Pauline Fox had been huddled into the two blankets of variable purpose, and hustled through the roof-hatch of the neighbouring hotel, the back windows of which had been smashed by the blast. Nicholas was as fleetingly impressed as was possible in the emergency, by the fact that Selina allowed the other girls to take the blankets. She lingered, shivering a little, but with an appealing grace, like a wounded roe deer, in her white petticoat and bare feet. Nicholas thought she was lingering for his sake, since Felix had disappeared with the two other girls to help them down to the first-aid ambulances. He left Selina standing thoughtfully on the hotel side of the roof, and returned to the slit window of the club to see for himself if any of the remaining girls were slim enough to escape by that way. It had been said by the firemen that the building might collapse within the next twenty minutes.

As he approached the slit window Selina slipped past him and, clutching the sill, heaved herself up again.

'Come down, what are you doing?' Nicholas said. He tried to grasp her ankles, but she was quick and, crouching for a small second on the narrow sill, she dipped her head and sidled through the window into the wash-room.

Nicholas immediately supposed she had done this in an attempt to rescue one of the girls, or assist their escape through the window.

'Come back out here, Selina,' he shouted, heaving himself up to see through the slit. 'It's dangerous. You can't help anybody.'

Selina was pushing her way through the standing group. They moved to give way without resistance. They were silent, except for

Tilly, who now sobbed convulsively without tears, her eyes, like the other eyes, wide and fixed on Nicholas with the importance of fear.

Nicholas said, 'The men are coming to open the skylight. They'll be here in a moment. Are there any others of you who would be able to get through the window here? I'll give them a hand. Hurry up, the sooner the better.'

Joanna held a tape-measure in her hand. At some time in the interval between the firemen's discovery that the skylight was firmly sealed and this moment, Joanna had rummaged in one of these top bedrooms to find this tape-measure, with which she had measured the hips of the other ten trapped with herself, even the most helpless, to see what were their possibilities of escape by the seven-inch window slit. It was known all through the club that thirty-six and a quarter inches was the maximum for hips that could squeeze themselves through it, but as the exit had to be effected sideways with a manoeuvring of shoulders, much depended on the size of the bones, and on the texture of the individual flesh and muscles, whether flexible enough to compress easily or whether too firm. The latter had been Tilly's case. But apart from her, none of the women now left on the top floor was slim in anything like the proportions of Selina, Anne, and Pauline Fox. Some were plump. Jane was fat. Dorothy Markham, who had previously been able to slither in and out of the window to sunbathe, was now two months pregnant; her stomach was taut with an immovable extra inch. Joanna's efforts to measure them had been like a scientific ritual in a hopeless case, it had been a something done, it provided a slightly calming distraction.

Nicholas said, 'They won't be long. The men are coming now.' He was hanging on to the ledge of the window with his toes dug into the brickwork of the wall. He was looking towards the edge of the flat roof where the fire ladders were set. A file of firemen were now mounting the ladders with pick-axes, and heavy drills were being hauled up.

Nicholas looked back into the wash-room.

'They're coming now. Where did Selina go?'

No one answered.

He said, 'That girl over there – can't she manage to come through the window?'

He meant Tilly. Jane said, 'She's tried once. She got stuck. The fire's crackling like mad down there. The house is going to collapse any minute.'

In the sloping roof above the girls' heads the picks started to clack furiously at the brick-work, not in regular rhythm as in normal workmanship, but with the desperate hack-work of impending danger. It would not be long, now, before the whistles would blow and the voice from the megaphone would order the firemen to abandon the building to its collapse.

Nicholas had let go his hold to observe the situation from the outside. Tilly appeared at the slit window, now, in a second attempt to get out. He recognized her face as that of the girl who had been stuck there at the moment before the explosion, and whom he had been summoned to release. He shouted at her to get back lest she should stick again, and jeopardize her more probable rescue through the skylight. But she was frantic with determination, she yelled to urge herself on. It was a successful performance after all. Nicholas pulled her clear, breaking one of her hip-bones in the process. She fainted on the flat roof after he had set her down.

He pulled himself up to the window once more. The girls huddled, trembling and silent, round Joanna. They were looking up at the skylight. Some large thing cracked slowly on a lower floor of the house and smoke now started to curl in the upper air of the wash-rooms. Nicholas then saw, through the door of the wash-room, Selina approaching along the smoky passage. She was carrying something fairly long and limp and evidently light in weight, enfolding it carefully in her arms. He thought it was a body. She pushed her way through the girls coughing delicately from the first waves of smoke that had reached her in the passage. The others stared, shivering only with their prolonged apprehension, for they had no curiosity about what she had been rescuing or what she was carrying. She climbed up on the lavatory seat and slid through the window, skilfully and quickly pulling her object behind her. Nicholas held up his hand to catch her. When she landed on the roof-top she said, 'Is it safe out here?' and at the same time was inspecting the condition of her salvaged item. Poise is perfect balance. It was the Schiaparelli dress. The coat-hanger dangled from the dress like a headless neck and shoulders.

'Is it safe out here?' said Selina.

'Nowhere's safe,' said Nicholas.

Later, reflecting on this lightning scene, he could not trust his memory as to whether he then involuntarily signed himself with the cross. It seemed to him, in recollection, that he did. At all events, Felix Dobell, who had appeared on the roof again, looked at him curiously at the time, and later said that Nicholas had crossed himself in superstitious relief that Selina was safe.

She ran to the hotel hatch. Felix Dobell had taken up Tilly in his arms, for although she had recovered consciousness she was too injured to walk. He bore her to the roof-hatch, following Selina with her dress; it was now turned inside-out for safe-keeping.

From the slit window came a new sound, faint, because of the continuous tumble of hose-water, the creak of smouldering wood and plaster in the lower part of the house, and, above, the clamour and falling bricks of the rescue work on the skylight. This new sound rose and fell with a broken hum between the sounds of desperate choking cough. It was Joanna, mechanically reciting the evening psalter of Day 27, responses and answers.

The voice through the megaphone shouted, 'Tell them to stand clear of the skylight in there. We'll have it free any minute now. It might collapse inwards. Tell those girls to stand clear of the skylight.'

Nicholas climbed up to the window. They had heard the instructions and were already crowding into the lavatory by the slit window, ignoring the man's face that kept appearing in it. As if hypnotized, they surrounded Joanna, and she herself stood as one hypnotized into the strange utterances of Day 27 in the Anglican order, held to be applicable to all sorts and conditions of human life in the world at that particular moment, when in London homing workers plodded across the park, observing with curiosity the fire-engines in the distance, when Rudi Bittesch was sitting in his flat at St John's Wood trying, without success, to telephone to Jane at the club to speak to her privately, the Labour Government was new-born, and elsewhere on the face of the globe people slept, queued for liberation-rations, beat the tom-toms, took shelter from the bombers, or went for a ride on a dodgem at the fun-fair.

Nicholas shouted, 'Keep well away from the skylight. Come right in close to the window.'

The girls crowded into the lavatory space. Jane and Joanna, being the largest, stood up on the lavatory seat to make room for the others.

Nicholas saw that every face was streaming with perspiration. Joanna's skin, now close to his eyes, seemed to him to have become suddenly covered with large freckles as if fear had acted on it like the sun; in fact it was true that the pale freckles on her face, which normally were almost invisible, stared out in bright gold spots by contrast with her skin, which was now bloodless with fear. The versicles and responses came from her lips and tongue through the din of demolition.

> Yea, the Lord hath done great things for us
>   already: whereof, we rejoice.
> Turn our captivity, O Lord: as the rivers in the south.
> They that sow in tears: shall reap in joy.

Why, and with what intention, was she moved to indulge in this? She remembered the words, and she had the long habit of recitation. But why, in this predicament and as if to an audience? She wore a dark green wool jersey and a grey skirt. The other girls, automatically listening to Joanna's voice as they had always done, were possibly less frantic and trembled less, because of it, but they turned their ears more fearfully and attentively to the meaning of the skylight noises than they did to the actual meaning of her words for Day 27.

> Except the Lord build the house: their labour is but lost that build
>   it.
> Except the Lord keep the city: the watchman waketh but in vain.
> It is but lost labour that ye haste to rise up early, and so late take
>   rest, and eat the bread of carefulness: for so he giveth his beloved
>   sleep.
> Lo, children . . .

Any Day's liturgy would have been equally mesmeric. But the words for the right day was Joanna's habit. The skylight thudded open with a shower of powdery plaster and some lop-sided bricks. While the white dust was still falling the firemen's ladder descended. First up was Dorothy Markham, the chattering débutante whose bright life, for the past forty-three minutes, had gone into a bewildering darkness like illuminations at a seaside town when the electricity system breaks down. She looked haggard and curiously like her aunt, Lady Julia, the chairman of the club's committee who was at that moment innocently tying up refugee parcels at Bath. Lady Julia's hair was white, and so now was the hair of her niece Dorothy, covered as it was by falling plaster-dust, as she clambered up the fire-ladder to the sloping tiles and was assisted to the safe flat roof-top. At her heels came Nancy Riddle, the daughter of the Low-Church Midlands clergyman, whose accents of speech had been in process of improvement by Joanna's lessons. Her elocution days were over now, she would always speak with a Midlands accent. Her hips looked more dangerously wide than they had ever noticeably been, as she swung up the ladder behind Dorothy. Three girls then attempted to follow at once; they had been occupants of a four-bed dormitory on the third floor, and were all newly released from the Forces; all three had the hefty, built-up appearance that five years in the Army was apt to give to a woman. While they were sorting themselves out, Jane grasped the ladder and got away. The three ex-warriors then followed.

Joanna had jumped down from the lavatory seat. She was now circling round, vaguely wobbling, like a top near the end of its spin. Her eyes shifted from the skylight to the window in a puzzled way. Her lips and tongue continued to recite compulsively the litany of the Day, but her voice had weakened and she stopped to cough. The air was still full of powdered plaster and smoke. There were three girls left beside herself. Joanna groped for the ladder and missed. She then stopped to pick up the tape-measure which was lying on the floor. She groped for it as if she were partially blind, still intoning:

So that they who go by say not so much as, The Lord prosper you: we wish you good luck in the Name of the Lord.

Out of the deep have I called ...

The other three took the ladder, one of them, a surprisingly slender girl called Pippa, whose non-apparent bones had evidently been too large to have allowed her escape through the window, shouted back, 'Hurry up, Joanna.'

'Joanna, the ladder!'

And Nicholas shouted from the window, 'Joanna, get up the ladder.'

She regained her senses and pressed behind the last two girls, a brown-skinned heavily-sinewed swimmer and a voluptuous Greek exile of noble birth, both of whom were crying with relief. Joanna promptly started to clamber after them, grasping in her hand a rung that the last girl's foot had just left. At that moment, the house trembled and the ladder and wash-room with it. The fire was extinguished, but the gutted house had been finally thrown by the violence of the work on the skylight. A whistle sounded as Joanna was half-way up. A voice from the megaphone ordered the men to jump clear. The house went down as the last fireman waited at the skylight for Joanna to emerge. As the sloping roof began to cave in, he leapt clear, landing badly and painfully on the flat roof-top. The house sank into its centre, a high heap of rubble, and Joanna went with it.

NINE

The tape-recording had been erased for economy reasons, so that the tape could be used again. That is how things were in 1945. Nicholas was angry in excess of the occasion. He had wanted to play back Joanna's voice to her father who had come up to London after her funeral to fill in forms as to the effects of the dead. Nicholas had written to him, partly with an urge to impart his last impressions of Joanna, partly from curiosity, partly, too, from a desire to stage a dramatic play-back of Joanna doing *The Wreck of the Deutschland*. He had mentioned the tape-recording in his letter.

But it was gone. It must have been wiped out by someone at his office.

> Thou hast bound bones and veins in me, fastened me flesh,
> And after it almost unmade, what with dread,
> Thy doing: and dost thou touch me afresh?

Nicholas said to the rector, 'It's infuriating. She was at her best in *The Wreck of the Deutschland*. I'm terribly sorry.'

Joanna's father sat, pink-faced and white-haired. He said, 'Oh, please don't worry.'

'I wish you could have heard it.'

As if to console Nicholas in his loss, the rector murmured with a nostalgic smile:

> It was the schooner *Hesperus*
> That sailed the wintry sea,

'No, no, the *Deutschland*. *The Wreck of the Deutschland*.'

'Oh, the *Deutschland*.' With a gesture characteristic of the English aquiline nose, his seemed to smell the air for enlightenment.

Nicholas was moved by this to a last effort to regain the lost recording. It was a Sunday, but he managed to get one of his colleagues on the telephone at home.

'Do you happen to know if anyone removed a tape from that box I borrowed from the office? Like a fool I left it in my room at the office. Someone's removed an important tape. Something private.'

'No, I don't think ... just a minute ... yes, in fact, they've wiped out the stuff. It was poetry. Sorry, but the economy regulations, you know.... What do you think of the news? Takes your breath away, doesn't it?'

Nicholas said to Joanna's father, 'Yes, it really has been wiped out.'

'Never mind. I remember Joanna as she was in the rectory. Joanna was a great help in the parish. Her coming to London was a mistake, poor girl.'

Nicholas refilled the man's glass with whisky and started to add water. The clergyman signed irritably with his hand to convey the moment when the drink was to his taste. He had the mannerisms of a widower of long years, or of one unaccustomed to being in the company of critical women. Nicholas perceived that the man had never seen the reality of his daughter. Nicholas was consoled for the blighting of his show; the man might not have recognized Joanna in the *Deutschland*.

> The frown of his face
> Before me, the hurtle of hell
> Behind, where, where was a, where was a place?

'I dislike London. I never come up unless I've got to,' the clergyman said, 'for convocation or something like that. If only Joanna could have settled down at the rectory.... She was restless, poor girl.' He gulped his whisky like a gargle, tossing back his head.

Nicholas said, 'She was reciting some sort of office just before she went down. The other girls were with her, they were listening in a way. Some psalms.'

'Really? No one else has mentioned it.' The old man looked embarrassed. He swirled his drink and swallowed it down, as if Nicholas might be going on to tell him that his daughter had gone over to Rome at the last, or somehow died in bad taste.

Nicholas said violently, 'Joanna had religious strength.'

'I know that, my boy,' said the father, surprisingly.

'She had a sense of Hell. She told a friend of hers that she was afraid of Hell.'

'Really? I didn't know that. I've never heard her speak morbidly. It must have been the influence of London. I never come here, myself, unless I've got to. I had a curacy once, in Balham, in my young days. But since then I've had country parishes. I prefer country parishes. One finds better, more devout, and indeed in some cases, quite holy souls in the country parishes.'

Nicholas was reminded of an American acquaintance of his, a psycho-analyst who had written to say he intended to practise in England after the war, 'away from all these neurotics and this hustling scene of anxiety'.

'Christianity is all in the country parishes these days,' said this shepherd of the best prime mutton. He put down his glass as if to seal his decision on the matter, his grief for the loss of Joanna turning back, at every sequence, on her departure from the rectory.

He said, 'I must go and see the spot where she died.'

Nicholas had already promised to take him to the demolished house in Kensington Road. The father had reminded Nicholas of this several times as if afraid he might inattentively leave London with this duty unfulfilled.

'I'll walk along with you.'

'Well, if it's not out of your way I'll be much obliged. What do you make of this new bomb? Do you think it's only propaganda stuff?'

'I don't know, sir,' said Nicholas.

'It leaves one breathless with horror. They'll have to make an armistice if it's true.' He looked around him as they walked towards Kensington. 'These bomb-sites look tragic. I never come up if I can help it, you know.'

Nicholas said, presently, 'Have you seen any of the girls who were trapped in the house with Joanna, or any of the other members of the club?'

The rector said, 'Yes, quite a few. Lady Julia was kind enough to have a few to tea to meet me yesterday afternoon. Of course, those poor girls have been through an ordeal, even the onlookers among

them. Lady Julia suggested we didn't discuss the actual incident. You
know, I think that was wise.'

'Yes. Do you recall the girls' names at all?'

'There was Lady Julia's niece, Dorothy, and a Miss Baberton who
escaped, I believe, through a window. Several others.'

'A Miss Redwood? Selina Redwood?'

'Well, you know, I'm rather bad at names.'

'A very tall, very slender girl, very beautiful. I want to find her.
Dark hair.'

'They were all charming, my dear boy. All young people are
charming. Joanna was, to me, the most charming of all, but there I'm
partial.'

'She was charming,' said Nicholas, and held his peace.

But the man had sensed his pursuit with the ease of the pastoral
expert on home ground, and he inquired solicitously, 'Has this young
girl disappeared?'

'Well, I haven't been able to trace her. I've been trying for the past
nine days.'

'How odd. She couldn't have lost her memory, I suppose? Wandering the streets...?'

'I think she would have been found in that case. She's very
conspicuous.'

'What does her family report?'

'Her family are in Canada.'

'Perhaps she's gone away to forget. It would be understandable.
Was she one of the girls who were trapped?'

'Yes. She got out through a window.'

'Well, I don't think she was at Lady Julia's from your description.
You could telephone and ask.'

'I have telephoned, in fact. She hasn't heard anything of Selina and
neither have any of the other girls. But I was hoping they might be
mistaken. You know how it is.'

'Selina ...' said the rector.

'Yes, that's her name.'

'Just a moment. There was a mention of a Selina. One of the girls, a
fair girl, very young, was complaining that Selina had gone off with
her only ball dress. Would that be the girl?'

'That's the girl.'

'Not very nice of her to pinch another girl's dress, especially when they've all lost their wardrobes in the fire.'

'It was a Schiaparelli dress.'

The rector did not intrude on this enigma. They came to the site of the May of Teck Club. It looked now like one of the familiar ruins of the neighbourhood, as if it had been shattered years ago by a bomb-attack, or months ago by a guided missile. The paving stones of the porch lay crookedly leading nowhere. The pillars lay like Roman remains. A side wall at the back of the house stood raggedly at half its former height. Greggie's garden was a heap of masonry with a few flowers and rare plants sprouting from it. The pink and white tiles of the hall lay in various aspects of long neglect, and from a lower part of the ragged side wall a piece of brown drawing-room wall-paper furled more raggedly.

Joanna's father stood holding his wide black hat.

At the top of the house the apples are laid in rows,

The rector said to Nicholas. 'There's really nothing to see.'

'Like my tape-recording,' said Nicholas.

'Yes, it's all gone, all elsewhere.'

Rudi Bittesch lifted and flicked through a pile of notebooks that lay on Nicholas's table. He said, 'Is this the manuscript of your book by the way?'

He would not have taken this liberty in the normal course, but Nicholas was under a present obligation to him. Rudi had discovered the whereabouts of Selina.

'You can have it,' said Nicholas, meaning the manuscript. He said, not foreseeing the death he was to die, 'You can keep it. It might be valuable one day when I'm famous.'

Rudi smiled. All the same, he tucked the books under his arm and said, 'Coming along?'

On the way to pick up Jane to go and see the fun at the Palace, Nicholas said, 'Anyway, I've decided not to publish the book. The typescripts are destroyed.'

'I have this bloody big lot of books to carry, and now you tell me this. What value to me if you don't publish?'

'Keep them, you never know.'

Rudi had a caution about these things. He kept *The Sabbath Notebooks*, eventually to reap his reward.

'Would you like a letter from Charles Morgan to me saying I'm a genius?' Nicholas said.

'You're bloody cheerful about something or other.'

'I know,' said Nicholas. 'Would you like to have the letter, though?'

'What letter?'

'Here it is.' Nicholas brought Jane's letter from his inside pocket, crumpled like a treasured photograph.

Rudi glanced at it. 'Jane's work,' he said, and handed it back. 'Why are you so cheerful? Did you see Selina?'

'Yes.'

'What did she say?'

'She screamed. She couldn't stop screaming. It's a nervous reaction.'

'The sight of you must have brought all back to her. I advised you to keep away.'

'She couldn't stop screaming.'

'You frightened her.'

'Yes.'

'I said keep away. She's no good, by the way, with a crooner in Clarges Street. You see him?'

'Yes, he's a perfectly nice chap. They're married.'

'So they say. You want to find a girl with character. Forget her.'

'Oh, well. Anyway, he was very apologetic about her screaming, and I was very apologetic, of course. It made her scream more. I think she'd have preferred to see a fight.'

'You don't love her that much, to fight a crooner.'

'He was quite a decent crooner.'

'You heard him croon?'

'No, of course, that's a point.'

Jane was restored to her normal state of unhappiness and hope, and was now established in a furnished room in Kensington Church Street. She was ready to join them.

Rudi said, 'You don't scream when you see Nicholas?'

'No,' she said, 'but if he goes on refusing to let George publish his book I will scream. George is putting the blame on me. I told him about the letter from Charles Morgan.'

'You should fear him,' Rudi said. 'He makes ladies scream by the way. Selina got a fright from him today.'

'I got a fright from her last time.'

'Have you found her then?' said Jane.

'Yes, but she's suffering from shock. I must have brought all the horrors back to her mind.'

'It was hell,' Jane said.

'I know.'

'Why is he in love with Selina by the way?' Rudi said. 'Why doesn't he find a woman of character or a French girl?'

'This is a toll call,' Jane said, rapidly.

'I know. Who's speaking?' said Nancy, the daughter of the Midlands clergyman, now married to another Midlands clergyman.

'It's Jane. Look, I've just got another question to ask you, quickly, about Nicholas Farringdon. Do you think his conversion had anything to do with the fire? I've got to finish this big article about him.'

'Well, I always like to think it was Joanna's example. Joanna was very High Church.'

'But he wasn't in love with Joanna, he was in love with Selina. After the fire he looked for her all over the place.'

'Well, he couldn't have been converted by Selina. Not converted.'

'He's got a note in his manuscript that a vision of evil may be as effective to conversion as a vision of good.'

'I don't understand these fanatics. There's the pips, Jane. I think he was in love with us all, poor fellow.'

The public swelled on V.J. night of August as riotously as on the victory night of May. The little figures appeared duly on the balcony every half-hour, waved for a space and disappeared.

Jane, Nicholas and Rudi were suddenly in difficulties, being pressed by the crowd from all sides. 'Keep your elbows out if possible,' Jane and Nicholas said to each other, almost simultaneously; but this was useless advice. A seaman, pressing on Jane, kissed her passionately on the mouth; nothing whatsoever could be done about it. She was at the mercy of his wet beery mouth until the crowd gave way, and then the three pressed a path to a slightly healthier spot, with access to the park.

Here, another seaman, observed only by Nicholas, slid a knife silently between the ribs of a woman who was with him. The lights went up on the balcony, and a hush anticipated the Royal appearance. The stabbed woman did not scream, but sagged immediately. Someone else screamed through the hush, a woman, many yards away, some other victim. Or perhaps that screamer had only had her toes trodden upon. The crowd began to roar again. All their eyes were at this moment fixed on the Palace balcony, where the royal family had appeared in due order. Rudi and Jane were busy yelling their cheers.

Nicholas tried unsuccessfully to move his arm above the crowd to draw attention to the wounded woman. He had been shouting that a woman had been stabbed. The seaman was shouting accusations at his limp woman, who was still kept upright by the crowd. These private demonstrations faded in the general pandemonium. Nicholas was borne away in a surge that pressed from the Mall. When the balcony darkened, he was again able to make a small clearing through the crowd, followed by Jane and Rudi towards the open park. On the way, Nicholas was forced to a standstill and found himself close by the knifer. There was no sign of the wounded woman. Nicholas, waiting to move, took the Charles Morgan letter from his pocket and thrust it down the seaman's blouse, and then was borne onwards. He did this for no apparent reason and to no effect, except that it was a gesture. That is the way things were at that time.

They walked back through the clear air of the park, stepping round the couples who lay locked together in their path. The park was filled with singing. Nicholas and his companions sang too. They ran into a fight between British and American servicemen. Two men lay unconscious at the side of the path, being tended by their friends. The crowds cheered in the distance behind them. A formation of aircraft buzzed across the night sky. It was a glorious victory.

Jane mumbled, 'Well, I wouldn't have missed it, really.' She had halted to pin up her straggling hair, and had a hair-pin in her mouth as she said it. Nicholas marvelled at her stamina, recalling her in this image years later in the country of his death – how she stood, sturdy and bare-legged on the dark grass, occupied with her hair – as if this was an image of all the May of Teck establishment in its meek, unselfconscious attitudes of poverty, long ago in 1945.

The Abbess of Crewe

Come let us mock at the great
That had such burdens on the mind
And toiled so hard and late
To leave some monument behind,
Nor thought of the levelling wind . . .

Mock mockers after that
That would not lift a hand maybe
To help good, wise or great
To bar that foul storm out, for we
Traffic in mockery.

From W. B. Yeats,
'Nineteen Hundred and Nineteen'

ONE

'What is wrong, Sister Winifrede,' says the Abbess, clear and loud to the receptive air, 'with the traditional keyhole method?'

Sister Winifrede says, in her whine of bewilderment, that voice of the very stupid, the mind where no dawn breaks, 'But, Lady Abbess, we discussed right from the start –'

'Silence!' says the Abbess. 'We observe silence, now, and meditate.' She looks at the tall poplars of the avenue where they walk, as if the trees are listening. The poplars cast their shadows in the autumn afternoon's end, and the shadows lie in regular still file across the pathway like a congregation of prostrate nuns of the Old Order. The Abbess of Crewe, soaring in her slender height, a very Lombardy poplar herself, moving by Sister Winifrede's side, turns her pale eyes to the gravel walk where their four black shoes tread, tread and tread, two at a time, till they come to the end of this corridor of meditation lined by the secret police of poplars.

Out in the clear, on the open lawn, two men in dark police uniform pass them, with two Alsatian dogs pulling at their short leads. The men look straight ahead as the nuns go by with equal disregard.

After a while, out there on the open lawn, the Abbess speaks again. Her face is a white-skinned English skull, beautiful in the frame of her white nun's coif. She is forty-two in her own age with fourteen generations of pale and ruling ancestors of England, and ten before them of France, carved also into the bones of her wonderful head. 'Sister Winifrede,' she now says, 'whatever is spoken in the avenue of meditation goes on the record. You've been told several times. Won't you ever learn?'

Sister Winifrede stops walking and tries to think. She strokes her black habit and clutches the rosary beads that hang from her girdle. Strangely, she is as tall as the Abbess, but never will she be a steeple or a tower, but a British matron in spite of her coif and her vows, and that great carnal chastity which fills her passing days. She stops walking, there on the lawn; Winifrede, land of the midnight sun, looks at the Abbess, and presently that little sun, the disc of light and its aurora, appears in her brain like a miracle. 'You mean, Lady Abbess,' she says, 'that you've even bugged the poplars?'

'The trees of course are bugged,' says the Abbess. 'How else can we operate now that the scandal rages outside the walls? And now that you know this you do not know it so to speak. We have our security to consider, and I'm the only arbiter of what it consists of, witness the Rule of St Benedict. I'm your conscience and your authority. You perform my will and finish.'

'But we're something rather more than merely Benedictines, though, aren't we?' says Sister Winifrede in dark naïvety. 'The Jesuits –'

'Sister Winifrede,' says the Abbess in her tone of lofty calm, 'there's a scandal going on, and you're in it up to the neck whether you like it or not. The Ancient Rule obtains when I say it does. The Jesuits are for Jesuitry when I say it is so.'

A bell rings from the chapel ahead. It is six o'clock of the sweet autumnal evening. 'In we go to Vespers whether you like it or whether you don't.'

'But I love the Office of Vespers. I love all the Hours of the Divine Office,' Winifrede says in her blurting voice, indignant as any common Christian's, a singsong lament of total misunderstanding.

The ladies walk, stately and tall, but the Abbess like a tower of ivory, Winifrede like a handsome hostess or businessman's wife and a fair week-end tennis player, given the chance.

'The chapel has not been bugged,' remarks the Lady Abbess as they walk. 'And the confessionals, never. Strange as it may seem, I thought well to omit any arrangement for the confessionals, at least, so far.'

The Lady Abbess is robed in white, Winifrede in black. The other black-habited sisters file into the chapel behind them, and the Office of Vespers begins.

The Abbess stands in her high place in the choir, white among the black. Twice a day she changes her habit. What a piece of work is her convent, how distant its newness from all the orthodoxies of the past, how far removed in its antiquities from those of the present! 'It's the only way,' she once said, this Alexandra, the noble Lady Abbess, 'to find an answer always ready to hand for any adverse criticism whatsoever.'

As for the Jesuits, there is no Order of women Jesuits. There is nothing at all on paper to reveal the mighty pact between the Abbey of Crewe and the Jesuit hierarchy, the overriding and most profitable pact. What Jesuits knew of it but the few?

As for the Benedictines, so closely does the Abbess follow and insist upon the ancient and rigid Rule that the Benedictines proper have watched with amazement, too ladylike, both monks and nuns, to protest how the Lady Abbess ignores the latest reforms, rules her house as if the Vatican Council had never been; and yet have marvelled that such a great and so Benedictine a lady should have brought her strictly enclosed establishment to the point of an international newspaper scandal. How did it start off without so much as a hint of that old cause, sexual impropriety, but merely from the little misplacement, or at most the theft, of Sister Felicity's silver thimble? How will it all end?

'In these days,' the Abbess had said to her closest nuns, 'we must form new monastic combines. The ages of the Father and of the Son are past. We have entered the age of the Holy Ghost. The wind bloweth where it listeth and it listeth most certainly on the Abbey of Crewe. I am a Benedictine with the Benedictines, a Jesuit with the Jesuits. I was elected Abbess and I stay the Abbess and I move as the Spirit moves me.'

Stretching out like the sea, the voices chant the Gregorian rhythm of the Vespers. Behind the Abbess, the stained-glass window darkens with a shadow, and the outline of a man climbing up to the window from the outside forms against the blue and the yellow of the glass. What does it matter, another reporter trying to find his way into the convent or another photographer as it might be? By now the scandal occupies the whole of the outside world, and the people of the press, after all, have to make a living. Anyway, he will not get into the chapel. The nuns continue their solemn chant while a faint grumble of voices outside the window faintly penetrates the chapel for a few moments. The police dogs start to bark, one picking up from the other in a loud litany of their own. Presently their noises stop and evidently the guards have appeared to investigate the intruder. The shadow behind the window disappears hastily.

These nuns sing loudly their versicles and responses, their antiphons:

> Tremble, O earth, at the presence of the Lord; at the presence of
>   the God of Jacob
> Who turned the rock into pools of water: and the strong hills into
>   fountains of water.
> Not to us, O Lord, not to us, but to thy name, give glory: because
>   of thy mercy and thy faithfulness.

But the Abbess is known to prefer the Latin. It is said that she sometimes sings the Latin version at the same time as the congregation chants the new reformed English. Her high place is too far from the choir for the nuns to hear her voice except when she sings a solo part. This evening at Vespers her lips move with the others but discernibly at variance. The Lady Abbess, it is assumed, prays her canticles in Latin tonight.

She sits apart, facing the nuns, white before the altar. Stretching before her footstool are the green marble slabs, the grey slabs of the sisters buried there. Hildegarde lies there; Ignatia lies there; who will be next?

The Abbess moves her lips in song. In reality she is chanting English, not Latin; she is singing her own canticle, not the vespers for Sunday. She looks at the file of tombs and, thinking of who knows which occupant, past or to come, she softly chants:

> Thy beauty shall no more be found,
> Nor, in thy marble vault, shall sound
> My echoing song; then worms shall try
> That long-preserved virginity . . .

The cloud of nuns lift their white faces to record before the angels the final antiphon:

> But our God is in heaven:
> he has done all that he wished.

'Amen,' responds the Abbess, clear as light.

Outside in the grounds the dogs prowl and the guards patrol silently. The Abbess leads the way from the chapel to the house in the blue dusk. The nuns, high nuns, low nuns, choir nuns, novices and nobodies, fifty in all, follow two by two in hierarchical order, the Prioress and the Novice Mistress at the heels of the Abbess and at the end of the faceless line the meek novices.

'Walburga,' says the Abbess, half-turning towards the Prioress who walks behind her right arm; 'Mildred,' she says, turning to the Novice Mistress on her left, 'go and rest now because I have to see you both together between the Offices of Matins and Lauds.'

Matins is sung at midnight. The Office of Lauds, which few convents now continue to celebrate at three in the morning, is none the less observed at the Abbey of Crewe at that old traditional time. Between Matins and Lauds falls the favourite time for the Abbess to confer with her nearest nuns. Walburga and Mildred murmur their assent to the late-night appointment, bowing low to the lofty Abbess, tall spire that she is.

The congregation is at supper. Again the dogs are howling outside. The seven o'clock news is on throughout the kingdom and if only the ordinary nuns had a wireless or a television set they would be hearing the latest developments in the Crewe Abbey scandal. As it is, these nuns who have never left the Abbey of Crewe since the day they entered it are silent with their fish pie at the refectory table while a senior nun stands at the corner lectern reading aloud to them. Her voice is nasal, with a haughty twang of the hunting country stock from which she and her high-coloured complexion have at one time disengaged themselves. She stands stockily, remote from the words as she half-intones them. She is reading from the great and ancient Rule of St Benedict, enumerating the instruments of good works:

To fear the day of judgement.
To be in dread of hell.
To yearn for eternal life with all the longing of our soul
To keep the possibility of death every day before our eyes.
To keep a continual watch on what we are doing with our life.
In every place to know for certain that God is looking at us.

When evil thoughts come into our head, to dash them at once on
    Christ, and open them up to our spiritual father.
To keep our mouth from bad and low talk.
Not to be fond of talking.
Not to say what is idle or causes laughter.
Not to be fond of frequent or boisterous laughter.
To listen willingly to holy reading.

The forks make tiny clinks on the plates moving bits of fish pie into
the mouths of the community at the table. The reader toils on . . .

Not to gratify the desires of the flesh.
To hate our own will.
To obey the commands of the Abbess in everything, even though
she herself should unfortunately act otherwise, remembering the
Lord's command: 'Practise and observe what they tell you, but not
what they do.' – Gospel of St Matthew, 23.

At the table the low nuns, high nuns and novices alike raise water to
their lips and so does the reader. She replaces her glass . . .

Where there has been a quarrel, to make peace before sunset.

Quietly, the reader closes the book on the lectern and opens another
that is set by its side. She continues her incantations:

A frequency is the number of times a periodic phenomenon
repeats itself in unit time.
For electromagnetic waves the frequency is expressed in cycles
per second or, for the higher frequencies, in kilocycles per second
or megacycles per second.
A frequency deviation is the difference between the maximum
instantaneous frequency and the constant carrier frequency of a
frequency-modulated radio transmission.
Systems of recording sound come in the form of variations of
magnetization along a continuous tape of, or coated with, or
impregnated with, ferro-magnetic material.
In recording, the tape is drawn at constant speed through the

airgap of an electromagnet energized by the audio-frequency current derived from a microphone.

Here endeth the reading. Deo gratias.

'Amen,' responds the refectory of nuns.

'Sisters, be sober, be vigilant, for the Devil goes about as a raging lion, seeking whom he may devour.'

'Amen.'

The Abbess of Crewe's parlour glows with bright ornaments and brightest of all is a two-foot statue of the Infant of Prague. The Infant is adorned with its traditional robes, the episcopal crown and vestments embedded with such large and so many rich and gleaming jewels it would seem they could not possibly be real. However, they are real.

The Sisters, Mildred the Novice Mistress and Walburga the Prioress, sit with the Abbess. It is one o'clock in the morning. Lauds will be sung at three, when the congregation arises from sleep, as in the very old days, to observe the three-hourly ritual.

'Of course it's out of date,' the Abbess had said to her two senior nuns when she began to reform the Abbey with the winsome approval of the late Abbess Hildegarde. 'It is absurd in modern times that the nuns should have to get up twice in the middle of the night to sing the Matins and the Lauds. But modern times come into a historical context, and as far as I'm concerned history doesn't work. Here, in the Abbey of Crewe, we have discarded history. We have entered the sphere, dear Sisters, of mythology. My nuns love it. Who doesn't yearn to be part of a myth at whatever the price in comfort? The monastic system is in revolt throughout the rest of the world, thanks to historical development. Here, within the ambience of mythology, we have consummate satisfaction, we have peace.'

More than two years have passed since this state of peace was proclaimed. The Abbess sits in her silk-covered chair, now, between Matins and Lauds, having freshly changed her white robes. Before her sit the two black senior sisters while she speaks of what she has just seen on the television, tonight's news, and of that Sister Felicity we have all heard about, who has lately fled the Abbey of Crewe to join her Jesuit lover and to tell her familiar story to the entranced world.

'Felicity,' says the Abbess to her two faithful nuns, 'has now publicly announced her conviction that we have eavesdropping devices planted throughout our property. She's demanding a commission of inquiry by Scotland Yard.'

'She was on the television again tonight?' says Mildred.

'Yes, with her insufferable charisma. She said she forgives us all, every one, but still she considers as a matter of principle that there should be a police inquiry.'

'But she has no proof,' says Walburga the Prioress.

'Someone leaked the story to the evening papers,' says the Abbess, 'and they immediately got Felicity on the television.'

'Who could have leaked it?' says Walburga, her hands folded on her lap, immovable.

'Her lax and leaky Jesuit, I dare say,' the Abbess says, the skin of her face gleaming like a pearl, and her fresh, white robes falling about her to the floor. 'That Thomas,' says the Abbess, 'who tumbles Felicity.'

'Well, someone leaked it to Thomas,' says Mildred, 'and that could only be one of the three of us here, or Sister Winifrede. I suggest it must be Winifrede, the benighted clot, who's been talking.'

'Undoubtedly,' says Walburga, 'but why?'

'"Why?" is a fastidious question at any time,' says the Abbess. 'When applied to any action of Winifrede's the word "why" is the inscrutable ingredient of a brown stew. I have plans for Winifrede.'

'She was certainly instructed in the doctrine and official version that our electronic arrangements are merely laboratorial equipment for the training of our novices and nuns to meet the challenge of modern times,' Sister Mildred says.

'The late Abbess Hildegarde, may she rest in peace,' says Walburga, 'was out of her mind to admit Winifrede as a postulant, far less admit her to the veil.'

But the living Abbess of Crewe is saying, 'Be that as it may, Winifrede is in it up to the neck, and the scandal stops at Winifrede.'

'Amen,' say the two black nuns. The Abbess reaches out to the Infant of Prague and touches with the tip of her finger a ruby embedded in its vestments. After a space she speaks: 'The motorway from London to Crewe is jammed with reporters, according to the news. The A51 is a solid mass of vehicles. In the midst of the strikes and the oil crises.'

'I hope the police are in force at the gates,' Mildred says.

'The police are in force,' the Abbess says. 'I was firm with the Home Office.'

'There are long articles in this week's *Time* and *Newsweek*,' Walburga says. 'They give four pages apiece to Britain's national scandal of the nuns. They print Felicity's picture.'

'What are they saying?' says the Abbess.

'*Time* compares our public to Nero who fiddled while Rome burned. *Newsweek* recalls that it was a similar attitude of British frivolity and neglect of her national interests that led to the American Declaration of Independence. They make much of the affair of Sister Felicity's thimble at the time of your election, Lady Abbess.'

'I would have been elected Abbess in any case,' says the Abbess. 'Felicity had no chance.'

'The Americans have quite gathered that point,' Walburga says. 'They appear to be amused and rather shocked, of course, by the all-pervading bitchiness in this country.'

'I dare say,' says the Abbess. 'This is a sad hour for England in these, the days of her decline. All this public uproar over a silver thimble, mounting as it has over the months. Such a scandal could never arise in the United States of America. They have a sense of proportion and they understand Human Nature over there; it's the secret of their success. A realistic race, even if they do eat asparagus the wrong way. However, I have a letter from Rome, dear Sister Walburga, dear Sister Mildred. It's from the Congregation of Religious. We have to take it seriously.'

'We do,' says Walburga.

'We have to do something about it,' says the Abbess, 'because the Cardinal himself has written, not the Cardinal's secretary. They're putting out feelers. There are questions, and they are leading questions.'

'Are they worried about the press and publicity?' says Walburga, her fingers moving in her lap.

'Yes, they want an explanation. But I,' says the Abbess of Crewe, 'am not worried about the publicity. It has come to the point where the more we get the better.'

Mildred's mind seems to have wandered. She says with a sudden breakage in her calm, 'Oh, we could be excommunicated! I know we'll be excommunicated!'

The Abbess continues evenly, 'The more scandal there is from this point on the better. We are truly moving in a mythological context. We are the actors; the press and the public are the chorus. Every columnist has his own version of the same old story, as it were Aeschylus, Sophocles or Euripides, only of course, let me tell you, of a far inferior dramatic style. I read classics for a year at Lady Margaret Hall before switching to Eng. Lit. However that may be – Walburga, Mildred, my Sisters – the facts of the matter are with us no longer, but we have returned to God who gave them. We can't be excommunicated without the facts. As for the legal aspect, no judge in the kingdom would admit the case, let Felicity tell it like it was as she may. You cannot bring a charge against Agamemnon or subpoena Clytemnestra, can you?'

Walburga stares at the Abbess, as if at a new person. 'You can,' she says, 'if you are an actor in the drama yourself.' She shivers. 'I feel a cold draught,' she says. 'Is there a window open?'

'No,' says the Abbess.

'How shall you reply to Rome?' Mildred says, her voice soft with fear.

'On the question of the news reports I shall suggest we are the victims of popular demonology,' says the Abbess. 'Which we are. But they raise a second question on which I'm uncertain.'

'Sister Felicity and her Jesuit!' says Walburga.

'No, of course not. Why should they trouble themselves about a salacious nun and a Jesuit? I must say a Jesuit, or any priest for that matter, would be the last man I would myself elect to be laid by. A man who undresses, maybe; but one who unfrocks, no.'

'That type of priest usually prefers young students,' Walburga observes. 'I don't know what Thomas sees in Felicity.'

'Thomas wears civilian clothes, so he wouldn't unfrock for Felicity,' observes Mildred.

'What I have to decide,' says the Abbess, 'is how to answer the second question in the letter from Rome. It is put very cautiously. They seem quite suspicious. They want to know how we reconcile our adherence to the strict enclosed Rule with the course in electronics which we have introduced into our daily curriculum in place of book-binding and hand-weaving. They want to know why we cannot relax the ancient Rule in conformity with the new reforms current in the other convents, since we have adopted such a very modern course of instruction as electronics. Or, conversely, they want to know why we teach electronics when we have been so adamant in adhering to the old observances. They seem to be suggesting, if you read between the lines, that the convent is bugged. They use the word "scandals" a great deal.'

'It's a snare,' says Walburga. 'That letter is a snare. They want you to fall into a snare. May we see the letter Lady Abbess?'

'No,' says the Abbess. 'So that, when questioned, you will not make any blunder and will be able to testify that you haven't seen it. I'll show you my answer, so that you can say you have seen it. The more truths and confusions the better.'

'Are we to be questioned?' says Mildred, folding her arms at her throat, across the white coif.

'Who knows?' says the Abbess. 'In the meantime, Sisters, do you have any suggestions to offer as to how I can convincingly reconcile our activities in my reply?'

The nuns sit in silence for a moment. Walburga looks at Mildred, but Mildred is staring at the carpet.

'What is wrong with the carpet, Mildred?' says the Abbess.

Mildred looks up. 'Nothing, Lady Abbess,' she says.

'It's a beautiful carpet, Lady Abbess,' says Walburga, looking down at the rich green expanse beneath her feet.

The Abbess puts her white head to the side to admire her carpet, too. She intones with an evident secret happiness:

> No white nor red was ever seen
> So amorous as this lovely green.

Walburga shivers a little. Mildred watches the Abbess's lips as if waiting for another little quotation.

'How shall I reply to Rome?' says the Abbess.

'I would like to sleep on it,' says Walburga.

'I, too,' says Mildred.

The Abbess looks at the carpet:

> Annihilating all that's made
> To a green thought in a green shade.

'I,' says the Abbess, then, 'would prefer not to sleep on it. Where is Sister Gertrude at this hour?'

'In the Congo,' Walburga says.

'Then get her on the green line.'

'We have no green line to the Congo,' Walburga says. 'She travels day and night by rail and river. She should have arrived at a capital some hours ago. It's difficult to keep track of her whereabouts.'

'If she has arrived at a capital we should hear from her tonight,' the Abbess says. 'That was the arrangement. The sooner we perfect the green line system the better. We should have in our laboratory a green line to everywhere; it would be convenient to consult Gertrude. I don't know why she goes rushing around, spending her time on ecumenical ephemera. It has all been done before. The Arians, the Albigensians, the Jansenists of Port Royal, the English recusants, the Covenanters. So many schisms, annihilations and reconciliations. Finally the lion lies down with the lamb and Gertrude sees that they remain lying down. Meantime Sister Gertrude, believe me, is a philosopher at heart. There is a touch of Hegel, her compatriot, there. Philosophers, when they cease philosophizing and take up action, are dangerous.'

'Then why ask her advice?' says Walburga.

'Because we are in danger. Dangerous people understand well how to avoid it.'

'She's in a very wild area just now, reconciling the witch doctors' rituals with a specially adapted rite of the Mass,' Mildred says, 'and moving the old missionaries out of that zone into another zone where they are sure to be opposed, probably massacred. However, this will be an appropriate reason for reinstating the orthodox Mass in the first zone, thus modifying the witch doctors' bone-throwing practices. At least, that's how I see it.'

'I can't keep up with Gertrude,' says the Abbess. 'How she is so popular I really don't know. But even by her build one can foresee her stone statue in every village square: Blessed Mother Gertrude.'

'Gertrude should have been a man,' says Walburga. 'With her moustache, you can see that.'

'Bursting with male hormones,' the Abbess says as she rises from her silk seat the better to adjust the gleaming robes of the Infant of

Prague. 'And now,' says the Abbess, 'we wait here for Gertrude to call us. Why can't she be where we can call her?'

The telephone in the adjoining room rings so suddenly that surely, if it is Gertrude, she must have sensed her sisters' want from the other field of the earth. Mildred treads softly over the green carpet to the adjoining room and answers the phone. It is Gertrude.

'Amazing,' says Walburga. 'Dear Gertrude has an uncanny knowledge of what is needed where and when.'

The Abbess moves in her fresh white robes to the next room, followed by Walburga. Electronics control-room as it is, here, too, everything gleams. The Abbess sits at a long steel desk and takes the telephone.

'Gertrude,' says the Abbess, 'the Abbess of Crewe has been discussing you with her Sisters Walburga and Mildred. We don't know what to make of you. How should we think?'

'I'm not a philosopher,' says Gertrude's deep voice, philosophically.

'Dear Gertrude, are you well?'

'Yes,' says Gertrude.

'You sound like bronchitis,' says the Abbess.

'Well, I'm not bronchitis.'

'Gertrude,' says the Abbess, 'Sister Gertrude has charmed all the kingdom with her dangerous exploits, while the Abbess of Crewe continues to perform her part in the drama of *The Abbess of Crewe*. The world is having fun and waiting for the catharsis. Is this my destiny?'

'It's your calling,' says Gertrude, philosophically.

'Gertrude, my excellent nun, my learned Hun, we have a problem and we don't know what to do with it.'

'A problem you solve,' says Gertrude.

'Gertrude,' wheedles the Abbess, 'we're in trouble with Rome. The Congregation of Religious has started to probe. They have written delicately to inquire how we reconcile our adherence to the Ancient Rule, which as you know they find suspect, with the laboratory and the courses we are giving the nuns in modern electronics, which, as you know, they find suspect.'

'That isn't a problem,' says Gertrude. 'It's a paradox.'

'Have you time for a very short seminar, Gertrude, on how one treats of a paradox?'

'A paradox you live with,' says Gertrude, and hangs up.

The Abbess leads the way from this room of many shining square boxes, many lights and levers, many activating knobs, press-buttons and slide-buttons and devices fearfully and wonderfully beyond the reach of a humane vocabulary. She leads the way back to the Infant of Prague, decked as it is with the glistening fruits of the nuns' dowries. The Abbess sits at her little desk with the Sisters Walburga and Mildred silently composed beside her. She takes the grand writing-paper of the Abbey of Crewe and places it before her. She takes her pen from its gleaming holder and writes:

'Your Very Reverend Eminence,

Your Eminence does me the honour to address me, and I humbly thank Your Eminence.

I have the honour to reply to Your Eminence, to submit that his sources of information are poisoned, his wells are impure. From there arise the rumours concerning my House, and I beg to write no more on that subject.

Your Eminence does me the honour to inquire of our activities, how we confront what Your Eminence does us the honour to call the problem of reconciling our activities in the field of technological surveillance with the principles of the traditional life and devotions to which we adhere.

I have the honour to reply to Your Eminence. I will humbly divide Your Eminence's question into two parts. That we practise the activities described by Your Eminence I agree; that they present a problem I deny, and I will take the liberty to explain my distinction, and I hold:

That Religion is founded on principles of Paradox.

That Paradox is to be accepted and presents no Problem.

That electronic surveillance (even if a convent were one day to practise it) does not differ from any other type of watchfulness, the which is a necessity of a Religious Community; we are told in the Scriptures "to watch and to pray", which is itself a paradox since the two activities cannot effectively be practised together except in the paradoxical sense.'

'You may see what I have written so far,' says the Abbess to her nuns. 'How does it strike you? Will it succeed in getting them muddled up for a while?'

The black bodies lean over her, the white coifs meet above the pages of the letter.

'I see a difficulty,' says Walburga. 'They could object that telephone-tapping and bugging are not simply an extension of listening to hearsay and inviting confidences, the steaming open of letters and the regulation search of the novices' closets. They might well say that we have entered a state where a difference of degree implies a difference in kind.'

'I thought of that,' says the Abbess. 'But the fact that we have thought of it rather tends to exclude than presume that they in Rome will think of it. Their minds are set to liquidate the convent, not to maintain a courtly correspondence with us.' The Abbess lifts her pen and continues:

'Finally, Your Eminence, I take upon myself the honour to indicate to Your Eminence the fine flower and consummation of our holy and paradoxical establishment, our beloved and renowned Sister Gertrude whom we have sent out from our midst to labour for the ecumenical Faith. By river, by helicopter, by jet and by camel, Sister Gertrude covers the crust of the earth, followed as she is by photographers and reporters. Paradoxically it was our enclosed community who sent her out.'

'Gertrude,' says Mildred, 'would be furious at that. She went off by herself.'

'Gertrude must put up with it. She fits the rhetoric of the occasion,' says the Abbess. She bends once more over her work. But the bell for Lauds chimes from the chapel. It is three in the morning. Faithful to the Rule, the Abbess immediately puts down her pen. One white swan, two black, they file from the room and down to the waiting hall. The whole congregation is assembled in steady composure. One by one they take their cloaks and follow the Abbess to the chapel, so softly ill-lit for Lauds. The nuns in their choirs chant and reply, with wakeful voices at three in the morning:

O Lord, our Lord, how wonderful
is thy name in all the earth:
　　Thou who hast proclaimed thy
　　glory upon the heavens.
Out of the mouths of babes and
sucklings thou hast prepared praise
to confuse thy adversaries:
　　to silence the enemy and the revengeful.

The Abbess from her high seat looks with a kind of wonder at her shadowy chapel of nuns, she listens with a fine joy to the keen plainchant, as if upon a certain newly created world. She contemplates and sees it is good. Her lips move with the Latin of the psalm. She stands before her high chair as one exalted by what she sees and thinks, as it might be she is contemplating the full existence of the Abbess of Crewe.

　　　　Et fecisti eum paulo minorem Angelis:
　　　　　Gloria et honore coronasti eum.

Soon she is whispering the melodious responses in other words of her great liking:

　　　　Every farthing of the cost,
　　　　All the dreaded cards foretell,
　　　　Shall be paid, but from this night
　　　　Not a whisper, not a thought,
　　　　Not a kiss nor look be lost.

TWO

In the summer before the autumn, as God is in his heaven, Sister Felicity's thimble is lying in its place in her sewing-box.

The Abbess Hildegarde is newly dead, and laid under her slab in the chapel.

The Abbey of Crewe is left without a head, but the election of the new Abbess is to take place in twenty-three days' time. After Matins, at twenty minutes past midnight, the nuns go to their cells to sleep briefly and deeply until their awakening for Lauds at three. But Felicity jumps from her window on to the haycart pulled up below and runs to meet her Jesuit.

Tall Alexandra, at this time Sub-Prioress and soon to be elected Abbess of Crewe, remains in the chapel, kneeling to pray at Hildegarde's tomb. She whispers:

> Sleep on, my love, in thy cold bed
> Never to be disquieted.
> My last goodnight! Thou wilt not wake
> Till I thy fate shall overtake:
> Till age, or grief, or sickness must
> Marry my body to that dust
> It so much loves, and fill the room
> My heart keeps empty in thy tomb.

She wears the same black habit as the two sisters who wait for her at the door of the chapel.

She joins them, and with their cloaks flying in the night air they return to the great sleeping house. Up and down the dark cloisters they pace, Alexandra, Walburga and Mildred.

'What are we here for?' says Alexandra. 'What are we doing here?'

'It's our destiny,' Mildred says.

'You will be elected Abbess, Alexandra,' says Walburga.

'And Felicity?'

'Her destiny is the Jesuit,' says Mildred.

'She has a following among the younger nuns,' Walburga says.

'It's a result of her nauseating propaganda,' says lofty Alexandra. 'She's always talking about love and freedom as if these were attributes peculiar to herself. Whereas, in reality, Felicity cannot love. How can she truly love? She's too timid to hate well, let alone love. It takes courage to practise love. And what does she know of freedom? Felicity has never been in bondage, bustling in, as she does, late for Mass, bleary-eyed for Prime, straggling vaguely through the Divine Office. One who has never observed a strict ordering of the heart can never exercise freedom.'

'She keeps her work-box tidy,' Mildred says. 'She's very particular about her work-box.'

'Felicity's sewing-box is the precise measure of her love and her freedom,' says Alexandra, so soon to be Abbess of Crewe. 'Her sewing-box is her alpha and her omega, not to mention her tiny epsilon, her iota and her omicron. For all her talk, and her mooney Jesuit and her pious eyelashes, it all adds up to Felicity's little sewing-box, the norm she departs from, the north of her compass. She would ruin the Abbey if she were elected. How strong is her following?'

'About as strong as she is weak. When it comes to the vote she'll lose,' Mildred says.

Walburga says sharply, 'This morning the polls put her at forty-two per cent according to my intelligence reports.'

'It's quite alarming,' says Alexandra, 'seeing that to be the Abbess of Crewe is my destiny.' She has stopped walking and the two nuns have stopped with her. She stands facing them, drawing their careful attention to herself, lighthouse that she is. 'Unless I fulfil my destiny my mother's labour pains were pointless and what am I doing here?'

'This morning the novices were talking about Felicity,' Mildred says. 'She was seen from their window wandering in the park between Lauds and Prime. They think she had a rendez-vous.'

'Oh, well, the novices have no vote.'

'They reflect the opinions of the younger nuns.'

'Have you got a record of all this talk?'

'It's on tape,' says Mildred.

Walburga says, 'We must do something about it.' Walburga's face has a grey-green tinge; it is long and smooth. An Abbess needs must be over forty years, but Walburga, who has just turned forty, has no ambition but that Alexandra shall be elected and she remain the Prioress.

Walburga is strong; on taking her final vows she brought to the community an endowment of a piece of London, this being a section of Park Lane with its view of Rotten Row, besides an adjoining mews of great value. Her strength resides in her virginity of heart combined with the long education of her youth that took her across many an English quad by night, across many a campus of Europe and so to bed. A wealthy woman, more than most, she has always maintained, is likely to remain virgin at heart. Her past lovers had been the most learned available; however ungainly, it was invariably the professors, the more profound scholars, who attracted her. And she always felt learned herself, thereafter, by a kind of osmosis.

Mildred, too, has brought a fortune to the Abbey. Her portion includes a sizeable block of Chicago slums in addition to the four big flats in the Boulevard St Germain. Mildred is thirty-six and would be too young to be a candidate for election, even if she were disposed to be Abbess. But her hopes, like Walburga's, rest on Alexandra. This Mildred has been in the convent since her late schooldays; it may be she is a nourisher of dreams so unrealizable in their magnitude that she prefers to keep them in mind and remain physically an inferior rather than take on any real fact of ambition that would defeat her. She has meekly served and risen to be Novice Mistress, so exemplary a nun with her blue eyes, her pretty face and nervous flutter of timidity that Thomas the Jesuit would at first have preferred to take her rather than Felicity. He had tried, following her from confession, waiting for her under the poplars.

'What did you confess?' he asked Mildred. 'What did you say to that young priest? What are your sins?';

'It's between myself and God. It is a secret.'

'And the priest? What did you tell that young confessor of your secrets?'

'All my heart. It's necessary.'

He was jealous but he lost. Whatever Mildred's deeply concealed dreams might be, they ran far ahead of the Jesuit, far beyond him. He began at last to hate Mildred and took up with Felicity.

Alexandra, who brought to the community no dowry but her noble birth and shrewd spirit, is to be Abbess now that Hildegarde lies buried in the chapel. And the wonder is that she bothers, or even her favourite nuns are concerned, now, a few weeks before the election, that Felicity causes a slight stir amongst the forty nuns who are eligible to vote. Felicity has new and wild ideas and is becoming popular.

Under the late Abbess Hildegarde this quaint convent, quasi-Benedictine, quasi-Jesuit, has already discarded its quasi-natures. It is a mutation and an established fact. The Lady Abbess Hildegarde, enamoured of Alexandra as she was, came close to expelling Felicity from the Abbey in the days before she died. Alexandra alone possesses the authority and the means to rule. When it comes to the vote it needs must be Alexandra.

They pace the dark cloisters in such an evident happiness of shared anxiety that they seem not to recognize the pleasure at all.

Walburga says, 'We must do something. Felicity could create a crisis of leadership in the Abbey.'

'A crisis of leadership,' Mildred says, as one who enjoys both the phrase and the anguish of the idea. 'The community must be kept under the Rule, which is to say, Alexandra.'

Alexandra says, 'Keep watch on the popularity chart. Sisters, I am consumed by the Divine Discontent. We are made a little lower than the angels. This weighs upon me, because I am a true believer.'

'I too,' says Walburga. 'My faith remains firm.'

'And mine,' Mildred says. 'There was a time I greatly desired not to believe, but I found myself at last unable not to believe.'

Walburga says, 'And Felicity, your enemy, Ma'am? How is Felicity's faith. Does she really believe one damn thing about the Catholic faith?'

'She claims a special enlightenment,' says Alexandra the Abbess-to-be. 'Felicity wants everyone to be liberated by her vision and to acknowledge it. She wants a stamped receipt from Almighty God for every word she spends, every action, as if she can later deduct it from her income-tax returns. Felicity will never see the point of faith unless it visibly benefits mankind.'

'She is so bent on helping lame dogs over stiles,' Walburga says. 'Then they can't get back over again to limp home.'

'So it is with the Jesuit. Felicity is helping Thomas, she would say. I'm sure of it,' Mildred says. 'That was clear from the way he offered to help me.'

The Sisters walk hand in hand and they laugh, now, together in the dark night of the Abbey cloisters. Alexandra, between the two, skips as she walks and laughs at the idea that one of them might need help of the Jesuit.

The night-watch nun crosses the courtyard to ring the bell for Lauds. The three nuns enter the house. In the great hall a pillar seems to stir. It is Winifrede come to join them, with her round face in the moonlight, herself a zone of near-darkness knowing only that she has a serviceable place in the Abbey's hierarchy.

'Winifrede, *Benedicite*,' Alexandra says.

'*Deo Gratias*, Alexandra.'

'After Lauds we meet in the parlour,' Alexandra says.

'I've got news,' says Winifrede.

'Later, in the parlour,' says Walburga. And Mildred says, 'Not here, Winifrede!'

But Winifrede proceeds like beer from an unstoppered barrel. 'Felicity is lurking somewhere in the avenue. She was with Thomas the Jesuit. I have them on tape and on video-tape from the closed-circuit.'

Alexandra says, loud and clear, 'I don't know what rubbish you are talking.' And motions with her eyes to the four walls. Mildred whispers low to Winifrede, 'Nothing must be said in the hall. How many times have we told you?'

'Ah,' breathes Winifrede, aghast at her mistake. 'I forgot you've just bugged the hall.'

So swiftly to her forehead in despair goes the hand of Mildred, so swivelled to heaven are Walburga's eyes in the exasperation of the swifter mind with the slow. But Alexandra is calm. 'Order will come out of chaos,' she says, 'as it always has done. Sisters, be still, be sober.'

Walburga the Prioress turns to her: 'Alexandra, you are calm, so calm . . .'

'There is a proverb: Beware the ire of the calm,' says Alexandra.

Quietly the congregation of nuns descends the great staircase and is assembled. Walburga the Prioress now leads, Alexandra follows, and all the community after them, to sing the Hour.

It is the Hour of None, three in the afternoon, when Sister Felicity slips sleepily into the chapel. She is a tiny nun, small as a schoolgirl, not at all like what one would have imagined from all the talk about her. Her complexion looks as if her hair, sprouting under her veil, would be reddish. Nobody knows where Felicity has been all day and half the night, for she was not present at Matins at midnight nor Lauds at three in the morning, nor at breakfast at five, Prime at six, Terce at nine; nor was she present in the refectory at eleven for lunch, which comprised barley broth and a perfectly nourishing and tasty, although uncommon, dish of something unnamed on toast, that something being in fact a cat-food by the name of Mew, bought cheaply and in bulk. Felicity was not there to partake of it, nor was she in the chapel singing the Hour of Sext at noon. Nor between these occasions was she anywhere in the convent, not in her cell nor in the sewing-room embroidering the purses, the vestments and the altar-cloths; nor was she in the electronics laboratory which was set up by the great nuns Alexandra, Walburga and Mildred under the late Abbess Hildegarde's very nose and carefully unregarding eyes. Felicity has been absent since after Vespers the previous day, and now she slips into her stall in the chapel at None, yawning at three in the afternoon.

Walburga, the Prioress, temporarily head of the convent, turns her head very slightly as Felicity takes her place, and turns away again. The community vibrates like an evanescent shadow that quickly fades out of sight, and continues fervently to sing. Puny Felicity, who knows the psalter by heart, takes up the chant but not her Office book:

> They have spoken to me with a lying tongue and have compassed
> me about with words of hatred:
> And have fought against me without cause.
> Instead of making me a return of love, they slandered me:
> but I gave myself to prayer.
> And they repaid evil for good:
> and hatred for my love.

The high throne of the Abbess is empty. Felicity's eyes, pink-rimmed with sleeplessness, turn towards it as she chants, thinking, maybe, of the dead, aloof Abbess Hildegarde who lately sat propped in that place, or maybe how well she could occupy it herself, little as she is, a life-force of new ideas, a quivering streak of light set in that gloomy chair. The late Hildegarde tolerated Felicity only because she considered her to be a common little thing, and it befitted a Christian to tolerate.

'She constitutes a reliable something for us to practise benevolence upon,' the late Hildegarde formerly said of Felicity, confiding this to Alexandra, Walburga and Mildred one summer afternoon between the Hours of Sext and None.

Felicity now looks away from the vacant throne and, intoning her responses, peers at Alexandra where she stands mightily in her stall. Alexandra's lips move with the incantation:

> As I went down the water side,
> None but my foe to be my guide,
> None but my foe . . .

Felicity, putting the finishing touches on an altar-cloth, is sewing a phrase into the inside corner. She is doing it in the tiniest and neatest possible satin-stitch, white upon white, having traced the words with her fine pencil: '*Opus Anglicanum*'. Her little frail fingers move securely and her silver thimble flashes.

The other sewing nuns are grouped around her, each busy with embroidery but none so clever at her work as Felicity.

'You know, Sisters,' Felicity says, 'our embroidery room is becoming known as a hotbed of sedition.'

The other nuns, eighteen in all, murmur solemnly. Felicity does not permit laughter. It is written in the Rule that laughter is unseemly. 'What are the tools of Good Works?' says the Rule, and the answers include, 'Not to say what is idle or causes laughter.' Of all the clauses of the Rule this is the one that Felicity decrees to be the least outmoded, the most adapted to the urgency of our times.

'Love,' says Felicity softly, plying her little fingers to her satin-stitch, 'is lacking in our Community. We are full of posperity. We prosper. We are materialistic. May God have mercy on our late Lady Abbess Hildegarde.'

'Amen,' say the other eighteen, and the sun of high summer dances on their thimbles through the window panes.

'Sometimes,' Felicity says, 'I think we should tend more towards the teachings of St Francis of Assisi, who understood total dispossession and love.'

One of her nuns, a certain Sister Bathildis, answers, her eyes still bent on her beautiful embroidery, 'But Sister Alexandra doesn't care for St Francis of Assisi.'

'Alexandra,' says Felicity, 'has actually said, "To hell with St Francis of Assisi. I prefer Sextus Propertius who belongs also to Assisi, a contemporary of Jesus and a spiritual forerunner of Hamlet, Werther, Rousseau and Kierkegaard." According to Alexandra these fellows are far more interesting neurotics than St Francis. Have you ever heard of such names or such a doctrine?'

'Never,' murmur the nuns in unison, laying their work on their laps the easier to cross themselves.

'Love,' says Felicity as they all take up their work again, 'and love-making are very liberating experiences, very. If I were the Abbess of Crewe, we should have a love-Abbey. I would destroy that ungodly electronics laboratory and install a love-nest right in the heart of this Abbey, right in the heart of England.' Her busy little fingers fly with the tiny needle in and out of the stuff she is sewing.

'What do you make of that?' says Alexandra, switching off the closed-circuit television where she and her two trusted nuns have just witnessed the scene in the sewing-room, recorded on video and sound tape.

'It's the same old song,' Walburga says. 'It goes on all the time. More and more nuns are taking up embroidery of their own free will, and fewer and fewer remain with us. Since the Abbess died there is no more authority in the convent.'

'All that will be changed now,' Alexandra says, 'after the election.'

'It could be changed now,' Mildred says. 'Walburga is Prioress and has the authority.'

Walburga says, 'I thought better than to confront Felicity with her escapade last night and half of the day. I thought better of it, and I think better of preventing the nuns from joining the sewing-room faction. It might provoke Felicity to lead a rebellion.'

'Oh, do you think the deserters can have discovered that the convent is bugged?' says Mildred.

'Not on your life,' says Alexandra. 'The laboratory nuns are far too stupid to do anything but wire wires and screw screws. They have no idea at all what their work adds up to.'

They are sitting at the bare metal table in the private control room which was set up in the room adjoining the late Abbess's parlour shortly before her death. The parlour itself remains as it was when Hildegarde died although within a few weeks it will be changed to suit Alexandra's taste. For certainly Alexandra is to be Abbess of Crewe. And as surely, at this moment, the matter has been thrown into doubt by Sister Felicity's glamorous campaign.

'She is bored,' says the destined Abbess. 'That is the trouble. She provides an unwholesome distraction for the nuns for a while, and after a while they will find her as boring as she actually is.'

'Gertrude,' says Alexandra into the green telephone. 'Gertrude, my dear, are you not returning to your convent for the election?'

'Impossible,' says Gertrude, who has been called on the new green line at the capital city nearest to that uncharted spot in the Andes where she has lately posted herself. 'I'm at a very delicate point in my negotiations between the cannibal tribe and that vegetarian sect on the other side of the mountain.'

'But, Gertrude, we're having a lot of trouble with Felicity. The life of the Abbey of Crewe is at stake, Gertrude.'

'The salvation of souls comes first,' says Gertrude's husky voice. 'The cannibals are to be converted to the faith with dietary concessions and the excessive zeal of the vegetarian heretics suppressed.'

'What puzzles me so much, Gertrude, my love, is how the cannibals will fare on the Day of Judgment,' Alexandra says cosily. 'Remember, Gertrude, that friendly little verse of our childhood:

> It's a very odd thing –
> As odd as can be –
> That whatever Miss T. eats
> Turns into Miss T. . . . .

And it seems to me, Gertrude, that you are going to have a problem with those cannibals on the Latter Day when the trumpet shall sound. It's a question of which man shall rise in the Resurrection, for certainly those that are eaten have long since become the consumers from generation to generation. It is a problem, Gertrude, my most clever angel, that vexes my noon's repose and I do urge you to leave well alone in that field. You should come back at once to Crewe and help us in our time of need.'

Something crackles on the line. 'Gertrude, are you there?' says Alexandra.

Something crackles, then Gertrude's voice responds, 'Sorry, I missed all that. I was tying my shoelace.'

'You should be here, Gertrude. The nuns are beginning to murmur that you're avoiding us. Felicity is saying that if she's elected Abbess of Crewe she wants an open audit of all the dowries and she advocates indiscreet sex. Above all, she has proclaimed a rebellion in the house and it's immoral.'

'What is her rebellion against?' Gertrude inquires.

'My tyranny,' says Alexandra. 'What do you think?'

'Is the rebellion likely to succeed?' says Gertrude.

'Not if we can help it. But she has a chance. Her following increases every hour.'

'If she has a chance of success then the rebellion isn't immoral. A rebellion against a tyrant is only immoral when it hasn't got a chance.'

'That sounds very cynical, Gertrude. Positively Machiavellian. Don't you think it a little daring to commit yourself so far?'

'It is the doctrine of St Thomas Aquinas.'

'Can you be here for the election, Gertrude? We need to consult you.'

'Consult Machiavelli,' says Gertrude. 'A great master, but don't quote me as saying so; the name is inexpedient.'

'Gertrude,' says Alexandra. 'Do bear in mind that

> Tiny and cheerful,
> And neat as can be,
> Whatever Miss T. eats
> Turns into Miss T.'

But Gertrude has hung up.

'Will she come home?' says Walburga when Alexandra turns from the telephone.

'I doubt it,' says Alexandra. 'She is having a great success with the cannibals and has administered the Kiss of Peace according to the photograph in today's *Daily Mirror*. Meanwhile the vegetarian tribes have guaranteed to annihilate the cannibals, should they display any desire to roast her.'

'She will be in trouble with Rome,' says Mildred, 'if she absents herself from the Abbey much longer. A mission takes so long and no longer according to the vows of this Abbey.'

'Gertrude fears neither Pope nor man,' says Alexandra. 'Call Sister Winifrede on the walkie-talkie. Tell Winifrede to come to the Abbess's parlour.' She leads the way into the parlour which is still furnished in the style of the late Hildegarde, who had a passion for autumn tints. The carpet is figured with fallen leaves and the wallpaper is a faded glow of browns and golds. The three nuns recline in the greenish-brown plush chairs while Winifrede is summoned and presently appears before them, newly startled out of a snooze.

Alexandra, so soon to be clothed in white, fetches from her black pocket a bunch of keys. 'Winifrede,' she says, indicating one of the keys, 'this is the key to the private library. Open it up and bring me Machiavelli's *Art of War*.' Alexandra then selects another key. 'And while you are about it go to my cell and open my locked cupboard. In it you will find my jar of *pâté*, some fine little biscuits and a bottle of my *Le Corton*, 1959. Prepare a tray for four and bring it here with the book.'

'Alexandra,' whines Winifrede, 'why not get one of the kitchen nuns to prepare the tray?'

'On no account,' says Alexandra. 'Do it yourself. You'll get your share.'

'The kitchen nuns are so ugly,' says Mildred.

'And such common little beasts,' says Walburga.

'Very true,' says Winifrede agreeably and departs on her errands.

'Winifrede is useful,' says Alexandra.

'We can always make use of Winifrede,' says Mildred.

'Highly dependable,' says Walburga. 'She'll come in useful when we really come to grips with Felicity.'

'That, of course, is for you two nuns to decide,' Alexandra says. 'As a highly obvious candidate for the Abbey of Crewe, plainly I can take no personal part in whatever you have in mind.'

'Really, I have nothing in mind,' Mildred says.

'Nor I,' says Walburga. 'Not as yet.'

'It will come to you,' says Alexandra. 'I see no reason why I shouldn't start now arranging for this room to be newly done over. A green theme, I think. I'm attached to green. An idea of how to proceed against Felicity will occur to you quite soon, I imagine, tomorrow or the day after, between the hours of Matins and Lauds, or Lauds and Prime, or Prime and Terce, or, maybe, between Terce and Sext, Sext and None, None and Vespers, or between Vespers and Compline.' Winifrede returns, tall and handsome as a transvested butler, bearing a tray laden with their private snack for four. She sets it on a table and, fishing into her pocket, produces a book and Alexandra's keys which she hands over.

They are seated at the table, and the wine is poured. 'Shall I say grace?' says fair-faced, round-eyed Winifrede, although the others have already started to scoop daintily at the *pâté* with their pearl-handled knives. 'Oh, it isn't necessary,' says Alexandra, spreading the *pâté* on her fine wafer, 'there's nothing wrong with *my* food.'

Winifrede, with her eyes like two capital Os, leans forward and confides, 'I've seen the print of that telephoto of Felicity with Thomas this morning.'

'I, too,' says Walburga. 'I don't understand these fresh-air fiends when the traditional linen cupboard is so much better heated and equipped.'

Alexandra says, 'I glanced at the negative. Since when my spirit is impure. It does not become them. Only the beautiful should make love when they are likely to be photographed.'

'The double monasteries of the olden days were so discreet and so well ordered,' Mildred says, wistfully.

'I intend to reinstate the system,' says Alexandra. 'If I am the Abbess of Crewe for a few years I shall see to it that each nun has her own private chaplain, as in the days of my ancestor St Gilbert, Rector of Sempringham. The nuns will have each her Jesuit. The lay brothers, who will take the place of domestic nuns as in the eleventh century, will be Cistercians, which is to say, bound to silence. Now, if you please, Walburga, let's consult *The Art of War* because time is passing and the sands are running out.'

Alexandra gracefully pushes back her plate and leans in her chair, one elbow resting on the back of it and her long body arranged the better to finger through the pages of the book placed on the table before her. The white coifs meet in a tent of concentration above the book where Alexandra's fingers trace the passages to be well noted.

'It is written,' says Alexandra with her lovely index finger on the margin as she reads:

> After you have consulted many about what you ought to do, confer with very few concerning what you are actually resolved to do.

The bell rings for Matins, and Alexandra closes the book. Walburga leads the way while Alexandra counsels them, 'Sisters, be vigilant, be sober. This is a monastery under threat, and we must pray to Almighty God for our strength.'

'We can't do more,' says Mildred.

'To do less would be cheap,' Walburga says.

'We are corrupt by our nature in the Fall of Man,' Alexandra says. 'It was well exclaimed by St Augustine, "O happy fault to merit such a Redeemer! *O felix culpa!*"'

'Amen,' respond the three companions.

They start to descend the stairs. 'O happy flaw!' says Alexandra.

Felicity is already waiting with her assembled supporters and the anonymous files of dark-shaped nuns when the three descend, graceful with Walburga in the lead, each one of them so nobly made and well put together. One by one they take their capes and file across the midnight path to their chapel.

Felicity slips aside, waiting with her cloak folded in the dark air until the community has entered the chapel. Then, while the voices start to sound in the ebb and flow of the plainchant, she makes her way back across the grass to the house quickly as a water bird skimming a pond. Felicity is up the great staircase, she is in the Abbess's parlour and switches on the light. Her little face looks at the remains of the little feast; she spits at it like an exasperated beggar-gipsy, and she breathes a cat's hiss to see such luxury spent. But soon she is about her business, through the door, and is occupied with the apparatus of the green telephone.

At the end of a long ring someone answers.

'Gertrude!' she says. 'Can that really be you?'

'I was just about to leave,' Gertrude says. 'The helicopter is waiting.'

'Gertrude, you're doing such marvellous work. We hear –'

'Is that all you want to say?' Gertrude says.

'Gertrude, this convent is a hotbed of corruption and hypocrisy. I want to change everything and a lot of the nuns agree with me. We want to break free. We want justice.'

'Sister, be still, be sober,' Gertrude says. 'Justice may be done but on no account should it be seen to be done. It's always a fatal undertaking. You'll bring down the whole community in ruins.'

'Oh, Gertrude, we believe in love in freedom and freedom in love.'

'That can be arranged,' Gertrude says.

'But I have a man in my life now, Gertrude. What can a poor nun do with a man?'

'Invariably, a man you feed both ends,' Gertrude says. 'You have to learn to cook and to do the other.'

The telephone then roars like a wild beast.

'What's going on, Gertrude?'

'The helicopter,' Gertrude says, and hangs up.

'Read it aloud to them,' Alexandra says. Once more it is lunch time. 'Let it never be said that we concealed our intentions. Our nuns are too bemused to take it in and those who are for Felicity have gone morbid with their sentimental Jesusism. Let it be read aloud. If they have ears to hear, let them hear.' The kitchen nuns float with their trays along the aisles between the refectory tables, dispensing sieved nettles and mashed potatoes.

Winifrede stands at the lectern. She starts to read, announcing Ecclesiasticus, chapter 34, verse 1:

> Fools are cheated by vain hopes, buoyed up with the fancies of a dream. Wouldst thou heed such lying visions? Better clutch at

shadows, or chase the wind. Nought thou seest in a dream but symbols; man is but face to face with his own image. As well may foul thing cleanse, as false thing give thee a true warning. Out upon the folly of them, pretended divination, and cheating omen, and wizard's dream! Heart of woman in her pangs is not more fanciful. Unless it be some manifestation the most High has sent thee, pay no heed to any such; trust in dreams has crazed the wits of many, and brought them to their ruin. Believe rather the law's promises, that cannot miss their fulfilment, the wisdom that trusty counsellors shall make clear to thee.

Winifrede stops to turn the pages to the next place marked with a book-marker elaborately embroidered from the sewing-room. Her eyes remotely sweep the length of the room, where the kitchen nuns are bearing jugs up the aisles, pouring water which has been heated for encouragement into the nuns' beakers. The forks move to the faces and the mouths open to receive the food. These are all the nuns in the convent, with the exception of kitchen nuns and the novices who do not count and the senior nuns who do. A less edifying crowd of human life it would be difficult to find; either they have become so or they always were so; at any rate, they are in fact a very poor lot, all the more since they do not think so for a moment. Up pop the forks, open go the mouths, in slide the nettles and the potato mash. They raise to their frightful little lips the steaming beakers of water and they sip as if fancying they are partaking of the warm sap of human experience, ripe for Felicity's liberation. Anyway, the good Winifrede reads on, announcing Ecclesiastes, chapter 9, verse 11. 'Sisters, hear again,' she says, 'the wise confessions of Solomon':

Then my thought took a fresh turn; man's art does not avail, here beneath the sun, to win the race for the swift, or the battle for the strong, a livelihood for wisdom, riches for great learning, or for the craftsman thanks; chance and the moment rule all.

The kitchen staff is gliding alongside the tables now, removing the empty plates and replacing them with saucers of wholesome and filling sponge pudding which many more deserving cases than the nuns would be glad of. Winifrede sips from her own glass of water, which is cold, puts it down and bends her eyes to the next book marked with its elaborate markers, passage by passage, which she exchanges with the good book on her lectern. She dutifully removes a slip of paper from the inside cover and almost intelligent-looking in this company reads it aloud in her ever-keening voice: 'Further words of wisdom from one of our Faith':

> If you suspect any person in your army of giving the enemy intelligence of your designs, you cannot do better than avail yourself of his treachery, by seeming to trust him with some secret resolution which you intend to execute, whilst you carefully conceal your real design; by which, perhaps, you may discover the traitor, and lead the enemy into an error that may possibly end in their destruction . . .
>
> In order to penetrate into the secret designs, and discover the condition of an enemy, some have sent ambassadors to them with skilful and experienced officers in their train, dressed like the rest of their attendants . . .
>
> As to private discords amongst your soldiers, the only remedy is to expose them to some danger, for in such cases fear generally unites them . . .

'Here endeth the reading,' Winifrede says, looking stupidly round the still more stupid assembly into whose ears the words have come and from which they have gone. The meal over, the nuns' hands are folded.

'Amen,' they say.

'Sisters, be vigilant, be sober.'

'Amen.'

Alexandra sits in the downstairs parlour where visitors are generally received. She has laid aside the copy of *The Discourses* of Machiavelli which she has been reading while awaiting the arrival of her two clergymen friends; these are now ushered in, accompanied by Mildred and Walburga.

Splendid Alexandra rises and stands, quiet and still, while they approach. It is Walburga, on account of being the Prioress, who asks the company to be seated.

'Father Jesuits,' says Walburga, 'our Sister Alexandra will speak.'

It is summer outside, and some of the old-fashioned petticoat roses that climb the walls of the Abbey look into the window at the scene, where Alexandra sits, one arm resting on the table, her head pensively inclining towards it. The self-controlled English sun makes leafy shadows fall on this polished table and across the floor. A bee importunes at the window-pane. The parlour is cool and fresh. A working nun can be seen outside labouring along with two pails, one of them probably unnecessary; and all things keep time with the season.

Walburga sits apart, smiling a little for sociability, with her eye on the door wherein soon enters the tray of afternoon tea, so premeditated in every delicious particular as to make the nun who bears it, leaves it, and goes away less noteworthy than ever.

The two men accept the cups of tea, the plates and the little lace-edged napkins from the sewing-room which Mildred takes over to them. They choose from among the cress sandwiches, the golden shortbread and the pastel-coloured *petit fours*. Both men are grey-haired, of about the same middle age as the three nuns. Alexandra refuses tea with a mannerly inclination of her body from the waist. These Jesuits are her friends. Father Baudouin is big and over-heavy with a face full of high blood-pressure; his companion, Father Maximilian, is more handsome, classic-featured and grave. They watch Alexandra attentively as her words fall in with the silvery acoustics of the tea-spoons.

'Fathers, there are vast populations in the world which are dying or doomed to die through famine, under-nourishment and disease; people continue to make war, and will not stop, but rather prefer to send their young children into battle to be maimed or to die; political fanatics terrorize indiscriminately; tyrannous states are overthrown and replaced by worse tyrannies; the human race is possessed of a universal dementia; and it is at such a moment as this, Fathers, that your brother-Jesuit Thomas has taken to screwing our Sister Felicity by night under the poplars, so that her mind is given over to nothing else but to induce our nuns to follow her example in the name of freedom. They thought they had liberty till Felicity told them they had not. And now she aspires to bear the crozier of the Abbess of Crewe. Fathers, I suggest you discuss this scandal and what you propose to do about it with my two Sisters, because it is beyond me and beneath me.' Alexandra rises and goes to the door, moving like a Maharajah aloft on his elephant. The Jesuits seem distressed.

'Sister Alexandra,' says the larger Jesuit, Baudouin, as he opens the door for her, 'you know there's very little we can do about Thomas. Alexandra –'

'Then do that very little,' she says in the voice of one whose longanimity foreshortens like shadows cast by the poplars amid the blaze of noon.

Fathers Baudouin and Maximilian will sit late into the night conferring with Mildred and Walburga.

'Mildred,' says handsome Maximilian, 'I know you can be counted on to be tough with the nuns.'

That Mildred the Novice Mistress is reliably tough with the lesser nuns is her only reason for being so closely in Alexandra's confidence. Her mind sometimes wavers with little gusts of timidity when she is in the small environment of her equals. She shivers now as Maximilian addresses her with a smile of confidence.

Baudouin looks from Mildred's heart-shaped white face to Walburga's strong dark face, two portraits in matching white frames. 'Sisters,' Baudouin says, 'Felicity ought not to be the Abbess of Crewe.'

'It must be Alexandra,' Walburga says.

'It shall be Alexandra,' says Mildred.

'Then we have to discuss an assault strategy in dealing with Felicity,' says Baudouin.

'We could deal with Felicity very well,' Walburga says, 'if you would deal with Thomas.'

'The two factors are one,' Maximilian says, smiling wistfully at Mildred.

The bell rings for Vespers. Walburga, looking straight ahead, says, 'We shall have to miss Vespers.'

'We'll miss all the Hours until we've got a plan,' Mildred says decisively.

'And Alexandra?' says Baudouin. 'Won't Alexandra return to join us? We should consult Alexandra.'

'Certainly not, Fathers,' Walburga says. 'She will not join us and we may not consult her. It would be dishonourable –'

'Seeing she is likely to be Abbess,' says Mildred.

'Seeing she will be Abbess,' Walburga says.

'Well, it seems to me that you girls are doing plenty of campaigning,' Baudouin says, looking round the room uncomfortably, as if some fresh air were missing.

Maximilian says, 'Baudouin!' and the nuns look down, offended, at their empty hands in their lap.

After a space, Mildred says, 'We may not canvass for votes. It is against the Rule.'

'I see, I see,' says large Baudouin, patiently.

They talk until Vespers are over and the black shape comes in to remove the tea tray. Still they talk on, and Mildred calls for supper. The priests are shown to the visitors' cloakroom and Mildred retires with Walburga to the upstairs lavatories where they exchange a few words of happiness. The plans are going well and are going forward.

The four gather again, conspiring over a good supper with wine. The bell rings for Compline, and they talk on.

Upstairs and far away in the control room the recorders, activated by their voices, continue to whirl. So very much elsewhere in the establishment do the walls have ears that neither Mildred nor Walburga are now conscious of them as they were when the mechanisms were first installed. It is like being told, and all the time knowing, that the Eyes of God are upon us; it means everything and therefore nothing. The two nuns speak as freely as the Jesuits who suspect no eavesdropping device more innocuous than God to be making a chronicle of their present privacy.

The plainchant of Compline floats sweetly over from the chapel where Alexandra stands in her stall nearly opposite Felicity. Walburga's place is empty, Mildred's place is empty. In the Abbess's chair, not quite an emptiness as yet, but the absence of Hildegarde.

The voices ripple like a brook:

> Hear, O God, my supplication:
> be attentive to my prayers.
> From the ends of the earth I cry to thee:
> when my heart fails me.

Thou wilt set me high upon a rock, thou wilt
    give me rest:
thou art my fortress, a tower of strength against
    the face of the enemy.

And Alexandra's eyes grieve, her lips recite:

For I am homesick after mine own kind
And ordinary people touch me not.
                         And I am homesick
After my own kind . . .

Winifrede, taking over Mildred's duty, is chanting in true tones the
short lesson to Felicity's clear responses:

Sisters: Be sober and vigilant:
for thy enemy the devil, as a raging lion, goeth about seeking
    whom he may devour. Him do thou resist . . .

'Aye, I am wistful for my kin of the spirit'; softly flows the English
verse beloved of Alexandra:

Well then, so call they, the swirlers out of the mist of my soul,
They that come mewards, bearing old magic.

But for all that, I am homesick after mine own kind . . .

THREE

Felicity's work-box is known as Felicity's only because she brought it to the convent as part of her dowry. It is no mean box, being set on fine tapered legs with castors, standing two and a half feet high. The box is inlaid with mother-of-pearl and inside it has three tiers neatly set out with needles, scissors, cottons and silks in perfect compartments. Beneath all these is a false bottom lined with red watered silk, for love-letters. Many a time has Alexandra stood gazing at this box with that certain wonder of the aristocrat at the treasured toys of the bourgeoisie. 'I fail to see what mitigation soever can be offered for that box,' she remarked one day, in Felicity's hearing, to the late Abbess Hildegarde who happened to be inspecting the sewing-room. Hildegarde made no immediate reply, but once outside the room she said, 'It is in poison-bad taste, but we are obliged by our vows to accept mortifications. And, after all, everything is hidden here. Nobody but ourselves can see what is beautiful and what is not.'

Hildegarde's dark eyes, now closed in death, gazed at Alexandra. 'Even our beauty,' she said, 'may not be thought of.'

'What should we care,' said Alexandra, 'about our beauty, since we are beautiful, you and I, whether we care or not?'

Meanwhile Felicity, aggrieved, regarded her work-box and opened it to see that all was in order. So she does every morning and by custom, now, she once more strokes the elaborate shining top after the Hour of Prime while the ordinary nuns, grown despicable by profession, file in to the sewing-room and take their places.

Felicity opens the box. She surveys the neat compartments, the reels and the skeins, the needles and the little hooks. Suddenly she gives a short scream and with her tiny bad-tempered face looking round the room at everybody she says, 'Who has touched my work-box?'

There is no answer. The nuns have come all unprepared for a burst of anger. The day of the election is not far off. The nuns have come in full expectance of Felicity's revelations about the meaningful life of love as it should be lived on the verge of the long walk lined with poplars.

Felicity now speaks with a low and strained voice. 'My box is disarranged. My thimble is missing.' Slowly she lifts the top layer and surveys the second. 'It has been touched,' she says. She raises the lowest recess and looks inside. She decides, then, to empty the work-box the better to examine the contents of its secret compartment.

'Sisters,' she says, 'I think my letters have been discovered.'

It is like wind rushing over a lake with a shudder of birds and reeds. Felicity counts the letters. 'They are all here,' she says, 'but they have been looked at. My thimble is lost. I can't find it.'

Everyone looks for Felicity's thimble. Nobody finds it. The bell goes for the Hour of Terce. The first part of the morning has been a sheer waste of sensation and the nuns file out to their prayers, displaying, in their discontent, a trace of individualism at long last.

How gentle is Alexandra when she hears of Felicity's distress! 'Be gentle with her,' she tells the senior nuns. 'Plainly she is undergoing a nervous crisis. A thimble after all – a thimble. I wouldn't be surprised if she has not herself, in a moment of unconscious desire to pitch all her obsessive needlework to hell and run away with her lover, mislaid the ridiculous thimble. Be gentle. It is beautiful to be gentle with those who suffer. There is no beauty in the world so great as beauty of action. It stands, contained in its own moment, from everlasting to everlasting.'

Winifrede, cloudily recognizing the very truth of Alexandra's words, is yet uncertain what reason Alexandra might have for uttering them at this moment. Walburga and Mildred stand silently in the contemplative hush while Alexandra leaves them to continue their contemplations. For certainly Alexandra means what she says, not wishing her spirit to lose serenity before God nor her destiny to be the Abbess of Crewe. Very soon the whole community has been informed of these thoughts of the noble Alexandra and marvel a little that, with the election so close at hand, she exhorts gentleness towards her militant rival.

Felicity's rage all the next day shakes her little body to shrieking point. There is a plot, there is a plot, against me, is the main theme of all she says to her sewing companions between the Hours of Lauds and Prime, Prime and Terce, Terce and Sext. In the afternoon, she takes to her bed, while her bewildered friends hunt the thimble and are well overheard in the control room in all their various exchanges and conjectures.

Towards evening Walburga reports to Alexandra, 'Her supporters are wavering. The nasty little bitch can't stand our gentleness.'

'You know, Walburga,' Alexandra muses, 'from this moment on, you may not report such things to me. Everything now is in your hands and those of Sister Mildred; you are together with Fathers Baudouin and Maximilian, and you are with the aid of Winifrede. I must remain in the region of unknowing. Proceed but don't tell me. I refuse to be told, such knowledge would not become me; I am to be the Abbess of Crewe, not a programmed computer.'

Felicity lies on her hard bed and at the midnight bell she rises for Matins. My God, there is a moving light in the sewing-room window! Felicity slips out of the file of black-cloaked nuns who make their hushed progress to the chapel. Alexandra leads. Walburga and Mildred are absent. There is a light in the sewing-room, moving as if someone is holding an electric torch.

The nuns are assembled in the chapel but Felicity stands on the lawn, gazing upward, and eventually she creeps back to the house and up the stairs.

So it is that she comes upon the two young men rifling her work-box. They have found the secret compartment. One of the young men holds in his hand Felicity's love-letters. Screaming, Felicity retreats, locks the door with the intruders inside, runs to the telephone and calls the police.

In the control room, Mildred and Walburga are tuned in to the dim-lit closed-circuit television. 'Come quickly,' says Walburga to Mildred, 'follow me to the chapel. We must be seen at Matins.' Mildred trembles. Walburga walks firmly.

The bell clangs at the gate, but the nuns chant steadily. The police sirens sound in the drive, their car having been admitted by Felicity, but the Sisters continue the night's devotions:

He turned rivers into a desert:
   and springs of water into parched ground,
A fruitful land into a salt waste:
   because of the wickedness of those who
      dwelt therein.
He turned a desert into a pool of water:
   and an arid land into springs of water.
And there he settled the hungry:
   and they founded a city to dwell in.

Alexandra hears the clamour outside.

   Sisters, be sober, be vigilant, for the devil as a raging lion . . .

The nuns file up to bed, anxiously whispering. Their heads bend meekly but their eyes have slid to right and to left where in the great hall the policemen stand with the two young men, dressed roughly, who have been caught in the convent. Felicity's voice comes in spasmodic gasps. She is recounting her story while her closest friend Bathildis holds her shaking body. Down upon them bear Walburga and Alexandra, swishing their habits with authority. Mildred motions the nuns upward and upward to their cells out of sight, far out of sight. Alexandra can be heard: 'Come into the parlour, sirs. Sister Felicity, be still, be sober.'

'Pull yourself together, Felicity,' Walburga says.

As the last nun reaches the last flight of stairs Winifrede in her handsome stupor comes out of the dark cupboard in the sewing-room and descends.

And, as it comes to pass, these men are discovered to be young Jesuit novices. In the parlour, they admit as much, and the police take notes.

'Officer,' says Walburga. 'I think this is merely a case of high spirits.'

'Some kind of a lark,' Alexandra says with an exalted and careless air. 'We have no charge to bring against them. We don't want a scandal.'

'Leave it to us,' says Walburga. 'We shall speak to their Jesuit superiors. No doubt they will be expelled from their Order.'

Sister Felicity screams, 'I bring a charge. They were here last night and they stole my thimble.'

'Well, Sister . . .' says the officer in charge, and gives a little grunt.

'It was a theft,' says Felicity.

The officer says, 'A thimble, ma'am, isn't much of a crime. Maybe you just mislaid it.' And he looks wistfully into the mother-of-pearl face of Alexandra, hoping for her support. These policemen, three of them, are very uneasy.

Young Bathildis says, 'It isn't only her thimble. They wanted some documents belonging to Sister Felicity.'

'In this convent we have no private property,' Walburga says. 'I am the Prioress, officer. So far as I'm concerned the incident is closed, and we're sorry you've been troubled.'

Felicity weeps loudly and is led from the room by Bathildis, who says vulgarly, 'It was a put-up job.'

In this way the incident is closed, and the two Jesuit novices cautioned, and the police implored by lovely Alexandra to respect the holiness of the nuns' cloistered lives by refraining from making a scandal. Respectfully the policemen withdraw, standing by with due reverence while Walburga, Alexandra and Mildred lead the way from the parlour.

Outside the door stands Winifrede. 'What a bungle!' she says.

'Nonsense,' says Walburga quickly. 'Our good friends, these officers here, have bungled nothing. They understand perfectly.'

'Young people these days, Sisters . . .' says the elder policeman.

They put the two young Jesuits in a police car to take them back to their seminary. As quietly as they can possibly go, they go.

Only a small piece appears in one of the daily papers, and then only in the first edition. Even so, Alexandra's cousins, Walburga's sisters and Mildred's considerable family connections, without the slightest prompting, and not even troubling to question the fact, weigh in with quiet ferocity to protect their injured family nuns. First on the telephone and then, softly, mildly, in the seclusion of a men's club and the demure drawing-room of a great house these staunch families privately and potently object to the little newspaper story which is entitled 'Jesuit Novices on the Spree'. A Catholic spokesman is fabricated from the clouds of nowhere to be quoted by all to the effect that the story is a gross exaggeration, that it is ungallant, that it bears the heavy mark of religious prejudice and that really these sweet nuns should not be maligned. These nuns, it is pointed out, after all do not have the right of reply, and this claim, never demonstrated, is the most effective of all arguments. Anyway, the story fades into almost nothing; it is only a newspaper clipping lying on Alexandra's little desk. 'Jesuit Novices on the Spree', and a few merry paragraphs of how two student Jesuits gate-crashed the enclosed Abbey of Crewe and stole a nun's thimble. 'They did it for a bet,' explained Father Baudouin, assistant head of the Jesuit College. Denying that the police were involved, Father Baudouin stated that the incident was closed.

'Why in hell,' demands Alexandra, in the presence of Winifrede, Walburga and Mildred, 'did they take her thimble?'

'They broke in twice,' Winifrede says in her monotone of lament. 'The night before they were caught and the night they were caught. They came first to survey the scene and test the facility of entry, and they took the thimble as a proof they'd done so. Fathers Baudouin and Maximilian were satisfied and therefore they came next night for the love-letters. It was –'

'Winifrede, let's hear no more,' Walburga says. 'Alexandra is to be innocent of the details. No specific items, please.'

'Well,' says obstinate Winifrede, 'she was just asking why the hell –'

'Alexandra has said no such thing,' Walburga menaces. 'She said nothing of the kind,' Mildred agrees.

Alexandra sits at her little desk and smiles.

'Alexandra, I heard it with my own ears. You were inquiring as to the thimble.'

'If you believe your own ears more than you believe us, Winifrede,' says Alexandra, 'then perhaps it is time for us to part. It may be you have lost your religious vocation, and we shall all quite understand if you decide to return to the world quietly, before the election.'

Dawn breaks for a moment through the terribly bad weather of Winifrede's understanding. She says, 'Sister Alexandra, you asked me for no explanation whatsoever, and I have furnished none.'

'Excellent,' says Alexandra. 'I love you so dearly, Winifrede, that I could eat you were it not for the fact that I can't bear suet pudding. Would you mind going away now and start giving all the nuns a piece of your mind. They are whispering and carrying on about the episode. Put Felicity under a three days' silence. Give her a new thimble and ten yards of poplin to hem.'

'Felicity is in the orchard with Thomas,' states Winifrede.

'Alexandra has a bad cold and her hearing is affected,' Walburga observes, looking at her pretty fingernails.

'Clear off,' says Mildred, which Winifrede does, and faithfully, meanwhile, the little cylindrical ears in the walls transmit the encounter; the tape-recorder receives it in the control room where spools, spools and spools twirl obediently for hours and many hours.

When Winifrede has gone, the three Sisters sit for a moment in silence, Alexandra regarding the press cutting, Walburga and Mildred regarding Alexandra.

'Felicity is in the orchard with Thomas,' Alexandra says, 'and she hopes to be Abbess of Crewe.'

'We have no video connection with the orchard,' says Mildred, 'not as yet.'

'Gertrude,' says Alexandra on the green telephone, 'we have news that you've crossed the Himalayas and are preaching birth-control. The Bishops are demanding an explanation. We'll be in trouble with Rome, Gertrude, my dear, and it's very embarrassing with the election so near.'

'I was only preaching to the birds like St Francis,' Gertrude says.

'Gertrude, where are you speaking from?'

'It's unpronounceable and they're changing the name of the town tomorrow to something equally unpronounceable.'

'We've had our difficulties here at Crewe,' says Alexandra. 'You had better come home, Gertrude, and assist with the election.'

'One may not canvass the election of an Abbess,' Gertrude says in her deepest voice. 'Each vote is a matter of conscience. Winifrede is to vote for me by proxy.'

'A couple of Jesuit novices broke into the convent during Compline and Felicity is going round the house saying they were looking for evidence against her. They took her thimble. She's behaving in a most menopausal way, and she claims there's a plot against her to prevent her being elected Abbess. Of course, it's a lot of nonsense. Why don't you come home, Gertrude, and make a speech about it?'

'I wasn't there at the time,' Gertrude says. 'I was here.'

'Have you got bronchitis, Gertrude?'

'No,' says Gertrude, 'you'd better make a speech yourself. Be careful not to canvass for votes.'

'Gertrude, my love, how do I go about appealing to these nuns' higher instincts? Felicity has disrupted their minds.'

'Appeal to their lower instincts,' Gertrude says, 'within the walls of the convent. It's only when exhorting the strangers outside that one appeals to the higher. I hear a bell at your end, Alexandra. I hear a lovable bell.'

'It's the bell for Terce,' Alexandra says. 'Are you not homesick, Gertrude, after your own kind?'

But Gertrude has rung off.

The nuns are assembled in the great chapter hall and the Prioress Walburga addresses them. The nuns are arranged in semicircles according to their degree, with the older nuns at the back, the lesser and more despised in the middle rows and the novices in the front. Walburga stands on a dais at a table facing them, with the most senior nuns on either side of her. These comprise Felicity, Winifrede, Mildred and Alexandra.

'Sisters, be still, be sober,' says Walburga.

The nuns are fidgeting, however, in a way that has never happened before. The faces glance and the eyes dart as if they were at the theatre waiting for the curtain to go up, having paid for their tickets. Outside the rain pelts down on the green, on the gravel, on the spreading leaves; and inside the nuns rustle as if a small tempest were swelling up amongst them.

'Be sober, be vigilant,' says Walburga the Prioress, 'for I have asked Sister Alexandra to speak to you on the subject of our recent disturbances.'

Alexandra rises and bows to Walburga. She stands like a lightning-conductor, elegant in her black robes, so soon to be more radiant in white. 'Sisters, be still. I have first a message from our esteemed

Sister Gertrude. Sister Gertrude is at present settling a dispute between two sects who reside beyond the Himalayas. The dispute is on a point of doctrine which apparently has arisen from a mere spelling mistake in English. True to her bold custom, Sister Gertrude has refused to furnish Rome with the tiresome details of the squabble and bloodshed in that area and she is settling it herself out of court. In the midst of these pressing affairs Sister Gertrude has found time to think of our recent trifling upset here at cosy Crewe, and she begs us to appeal to your higher instincts and wider vision, which is what I am about to do.'

The nuns are already sobered and made vigilant by the invocation of famous Gertrude, but Felicity on the dais causes a nervous distraction by bringing out from some big pocket under her black scapular a little embroidery frame. Felicity's fingers busy themselves with some extra flourish while Alexandra, having swept her eyes upon this frail exhibition, proceeds.

'Sisters,' she says, 'let me do as Sister Gertrude wishes; let me appeal to your higher instincts. We had the extraordinary experience, last week, of an intrusion into our midst, at midnight, of two young ruffians. It's natural that you should be distressed, and we know that you have been induced to gossip amongst yourselves about the incident, stories of which have been circulated outside the convent walls.'

Felicity's fingers fly to and fro; her eyes are downcast with pale, devout lashes, and she holds her sewing well up to meet them.

'Now,' says Alexandra, 'I am not here before you to speak of the ephemera of every day or of things that are of no account, material things that will pass and will become, as the poet says,

> The love-tales wrought with silken thread
> By dreaming ladies upon cloth
> That has made fat the murderous moth . . .

I call rather to the attention of your higher instincts the enduring tradition of one belonging to my own ancestral lineage, Marguerite Marie Alacoque of the seventeenth century, my illustrious aunt, founder of the great Abbeys of the Sacré Cœur. Let me remind you now of your good fortune, for in those days, you must know, the nuns were rigidly divided in two parts, the *sœurs nobles* and the *sœurs bourgeoises*. Apart from this distinction between the nobility and the bourgeoisie, there was of course a third section of the convent comprising the lay sisters who hardly count. Indeed, well into this century the Abbey schools of the Continent were divided; the *filles nobles* were taught by nuns of noble lineage while *sœurs bourgeoises* taught the daughters of the *vils métiers*, which is to say the tradesmen.'

Winifrede's eyes, like the wheels of a toy motorcar, have been staring eagerly from her healthy fair face; her father is the rich and capable proprietor and president of a porcelain factory, and has a knighthood.

Walburga's pretty hands are folded on the table before her and she looks down at them as Alexandra's voice comes sounding its articulate sweet numbers. Walburga's long face is dark grey against the white frame of her coif; she brought that great property to the convent from her devout Brazilian mother; her father, now dead, was of a military family.

Mildred's blue eyes move to survey the novices, how they are comporting themselves, but the heart-shape of her face is a motionless outline as if painted on to her coif.

Alexandra stands like the masthead of an ancient ship. Felicity's violent fingers attack the piece of stuff with her accurate and everpiercing needle; she had sometimes amused the late Abbess Hildegarde with her timid venom for although her descent was actually as noble as Alexandra's she demonstrated no trace at all of it. 'Some interesting sort of genetic mutation,' Hildegarde had said, 'seeing that with so fine a lineage she is, you know, a common little thing. But Felicity, after all, is something for us to practise benevolence upon.' The rain pelts harder, pattering at the window against Alexandra's clear voice as Felicity stabs and stabs again, as it might be to draw blood. Alexandra is saying:

'You must consider, Sisters, that very soon we shall have an election to appoint our new Abbess of Crewe, each one of us who is sufficiently senior and qualified to vote will do so according to her own conscience, nor may she conspire or exchange opinions upon the subject. Sisters, be vigilant, be sober. You will recall your good fortune, daughters as the majority of you are of dentists, doctors, lawyers, stockbrokers, businessmen and all the Toms, Dicks and

Harrys of the realm; you will recognize your good fortune that with the advance of the century this Congregation no longer requires you to present as postulants the *épreuves*, that is to say, the proofs of your nobility for four generations of armigerious forebears on both sides, or else of ten generations of arms-bearers in the male line only. Today the bourgeois mix indifferently with the noble. No longer do we have in our Abbey the separate entrances, the separate dormitories, the separate refectories and staircases for the *sœurs nobles* and the *sœurs bourgeoises*; no longer is the chapel divided by the screens which separated the ladies from the bourgeoisie, the bourgeoisie from the baser orders. We are left now only with our higher instincts to guide us in the matter of how our Order and our Abbey proceeds. Are we to decline into a community of the total bourgeois or are we to retain the characteristics of a society of ladies? Let me recall at this point that in 1873 the Sisters of the Sacred Heart made a pilgrimage to Paray le Monial to the shrine of my ancestral aunt, headed by the Duke of Norfolk in his socks. Sisters, be vigilant. In the message conveyed to me by our celebrated Sister Gertrude, and under obedience to our Prioress Walburga, I am exhorted to appeal to your higher instincts, so that I put before you the following distinctions upon which to ponder well:

'In this Abbey a Lady places her love-letters in the casket provided for them in the main hall, to provide light entertainment for the community during the hour of recreation; but a Bourgeoise keeps her love-letters in a sewing-box.

A Lady has style; but a Bourgeoise does things under the poplars and in the orchard.

A Lady is cheerful and accommodating when dealing with the perpetrators of a third-rate burglary; but a Bourgeoise calls the police.

A Lady recognizes in the scientific methods of surveillance, such as electronics, a valuable and discreet auxiliary to her natural capacity for inquisitiveness; but a Bourgeoise regards such innovations in the light of demonology and considers it more refined to sit and sew.

A Lady may or may not commit the Cardinal Sins; but a Bourgeoise dabbles in low crimes and safe demeanours.

A Lady bears with fortitude that *Agenbite of Inwit,* celebrated in the treatise of that name in Anglo-Saxon by my ancestor Michel of Northgate in the year 1340; but a Bourgeoise suffers from the miserable common guilty conscience.

A Lady may secretly believe in nothing; but a Bourgeoise invariably proclaims her belief, and believes in the wrong things.

A Lady does not recognize the existence of a scandal which touches upon her own House; but a Bourgeoise broadcasts it *urbi et orbi*, which is to say, all over the place.

A Lady is free; but a Bourgeoise is never free from the desire for freedom.'

Alexandra pauses to smile like an angel of some unearthly intelligent substance upon the community. Felicity has put down her sewing and is looking out of the window as if angry that the rain has stopped. The other Sisters on the dais are looking at Alexandra who now says, 'Sisters, be sober, be vigilant. I don't speak of morals, but of ethics. Our topics are not those of sanctity and holiness, which rest with God; it is a question of whether you are ladies or not, and that is something *we* decide. It was well said in my youth that the question "Is she a lady?" needs no answer, since, with a lady, the question need not arise. Indeed, it is a sad thought that necessity should force us to speak the word in the Abbey of Crewe.'

Felicity leaves the table and walks firmly to the door where, as the nuns file out, she stands in apprehensive fury looking out specially for her supporters. Anxious to be ladies, even the sewing nuns keep their embarrassed eyes fixed on the ground as they tread forward to their supper of rice and meat-balls, these being made up out of a tinned food for dogs which contains some very wholesome ingredients, quite good enough for them.

When they are gone, and Felicity with them, Mildred says, 'You struck the right note, Alexandra. Novices and nuns alike, they're snobs to the core.'

'Alexandra, you did well,' says Walburga. 'I think Felicity's hold on the defecting nuns will be finished after that.'

'More defective than defecting,' says Alexandra. 'Winifrede, my dear, since you are a lady of higher instincts you may go and put some white wine on ice.' Winifrede, puzzled but very pleased, departs.

Whereupon they join hands, the three black-draped nuns, Walburga, Alexandra and Mildred. They dance in a ring, light-footed; they skip round one way then turn the other way.

Walburga then says, 'Listen!' She turns her ear to the window. 'Someone's whistled,' she says. A second faint whistle comes across the lawn from the distant trees. The three go to the window to watch in the last light of evening small Felicity running along the pathways, keeping well in to the rhododendrons until she disappears into the trees.

'The ground is sopping wet,' says Alexandra.

'They'll arrange something standing up,' Mildred says.

'Or upside down,' says Walburga.

'Not Felicity,' says Alexandra. 'In the words of Alexander Pope:

> Virtue she finds too painful an endeavour,
> Content to dwell in decencies for ever.'

FOUR

The deaf and elderly Abbot of Ynce, who is driven over to the Abbey once a week to hear nuns' confessions, assisted by the good Jesuit fathers Maximilian and Baudouin, has been brought to the Abbey; in company with the two Jesuits he has witnessed the voting ceremony, he has proclaimed Alexandra Abbess of Crewe before the assembled community. The old Abbot has presented the new Abbess with her crozier, has celebrated a solemn Mass, and, helped back into the car, has departed deeply asleep in the recesses of the back seat. Throughout the solemn election Felicity was in bed with influenza. She received from her friend Bathildis the news of Alexandra's landslide victory; her reaction was immediately to stick the thermometer in her mouth; this performance was watched with interest on the closed-circuit television by Alexandra, Mildred and Walburga.

But that is all over now, it is over and past. The leaves are falling and the swallows depart. Felicity has long since risen from her sick bed, has packed her suitcases, has tenderly swathed her sewing-box in sacking, and with these effects has left the convent. She has settled with her Jesuit, Thomas, in London, in a small flat in Earl's Court, and already she has made some extraordinary disclosures.

'If only,' says Walburga, 'the police had brought a charge against those stupid little seminarians who broke into the convent, then she couldn't make public statements while it was under investigation.'

'The law doesn't enter into it,' says the Abbess, now dressed in her splendid white. 'The bothersome people are the press and the bishops. Plainly, the police don't want to interfere in a matter concerning a Catholic establishment; it would be an embarrassment.'

Mildred says, 'It was like this. The two young Jesuits, who have now been expelled from the Order, hearing that there was a nun who —'

'That was Felicity,' says the Abbess.

'It was Felicity,' Walburga says.

'Yes. A nun who was practising sexual rites, or let us even say obsequies, in the convent grounds and preaching her joyless practices within the convent ... Well, they hear of this nun, and they break into the convent on the chance that Felicity, and maybe one of her friends –'

'Let's say Bathildis,' Walburga says, considering well, with her mind all ears.

'Yes, of course, Felicity and Bathildis, that they might have a romp with those boys.'

'In fact,' says the Abbess, 'they do have a romp.'

'And the students take away the thimble –'

'As a keepsake?' says the Abbess.

'Could it be a sexual symbol?' ventures Mildred.

'I don't see that scenario,' says the Abbess. 'Why would Felicity then make a fuss about the missing thimble the next morning?'

'Well,' says Walburga, 'she would want to draw attention to her sordid little adventure. They like to boast about these things.'

'And why, if I may think aloud,' says the Lady Abbess, 'would she call the police the next night when they come again?'

'They could be blackmailing her,' Walburga says.

'I don't think that will catch on,' says the Abbess. 'I really don't. Those boys – what are their dreadful names?'

'Gregory and Ambrose,' says Mildred.

'I might have known it,' says the Abbess for no apparent reason. They sit in the Abbess's parlour and she touches the Infant of Prague, so besmeared with rich glamour as are its robes.

'According to this week's story in *The Sunday People* they have now named Maximilian, but not yet Baudouin, as having given them the order to move,' Walburga says.

'"According to *The Sunday People*" is of no account. What is to be the story according to us?' says the Abbess.

'Try this one for size,' says Mildred. 'The boys, Gregory and Ambrose –'

'Those names,' says the Abbess, 'they've put me off this scenario already.'

'All right, the two Jesuit novices – they break into the convent the first night to find a couple of nuns, any nuns –'

'Not in my Abbey,' says the Abbess. 'My nuns are above suspicion. All but Felicity and Bathildis who have been expelled. Felicity, indeed, is excommunicated. I won't have it said that my nuns are so notoriously available that a couple of Jesuit youths could conceivably enter these gates with profane intent.'

'They got in by the orchard gate,' says Mildred thoughtlessly, 'that Walburga left open for Father Baudouin.'

'That is a joke,' says the Abbess, pointing to the Infant of Prague wherein resides the parlour's main transmitter.

'Don't worry,' says Walburga, smiling towards the Infant of Prague with her wide smile in her long, tight-skinned face. 'Nobody knows we are bugged except ourselves and Winifrede never quite takes in the whole picture. Don't worry.'

'I worry about Felicity,' says Mildred. 'She might guess.'

Walburga says, 'All she knows is that our electronics laboratory and the labourers therein serve the purpose of setting up contacts with the new missions founded throughout the world by Gertrude. Beyond the green lines to Gertrude, she knows nothing. Don't worry.'

'It is useless to tell me not to worry,' the Abbess says, 'since I never do. Anxiety is for the bourgeoisie and for great artists in those hours when they are neither asleep nor practising their art. An aristocratic soul feels no anxiety nor, I think, do the famine-stricken of the world as they endure the impotent extremities of starvation. I don't know why it is, but I ponder on starvation and the starving. Sisters, let me tell you a secret. I would rather sink fleshless to my death into the dry soil of some African or Indian plain, dead of hunger with the rest of the dying skeletons than go, as I hear Felicity is now doing, to a psychiatrist for an anxiety-cure.'

'She's seeing a psychiatrist?' says Walburga.

'Poor soul, she lost her little silver thimble,' says the Abbess. 'However, she herself announced on the television that she is undergoing psychiatric treatment for a state of anxiety arising from her excommunication for living with Thomas in sin.'

'What can a psychiatrist do?' says Mildred. 'She cannot be more excommunicated than excommunicated, or less.'

'She has to become resigned to the idea,' the Abbess says. 'According to Felicity, that is her justification for employing a psychiatrist. There was more clap-trap, but I switched it off.'

The bell rings for Vespers. Smiling, the Abbess rises and leads the way.

'It's difficult,' says Mildred as she passes through the door after Walburga, 'not to feel anxious with these stories about us circulating in the world.'

The Abbess stops a moment. 'Courage!' she says. 'To the practitioner of courage there is no anxiety that will not melt away under the effect of grace, however that may be obtained. You recite the Psalms of the Hours, and so do I, frequently giving over, also, to English poetry, my passion. Sisters, be still; to each her own source of grace.'

Felicity's stall is empty and so is Winifrede's. It is the Vespers of the last autumn Sunday of peace within the Abbey walls. By Wednesday of next week, the police will be protecting the place, patrolling by day and prowling by night with their dogs, seeing that the press, the photographers and the television crews have started to go about like a raging lion seeking whom they may devour.

'Sisters, be sober, be vigilant.'

'Amen.'

Outside in the grounds there is nothing but whispering trees on this last Sunday of October and of peace.

> Fortunate is the man who is kind and leads:
>   who conducts his affairs with justice.
> He shall never be moved:
>   the just shall be in everlasting remembrance.
> He shall not fear sad news:
>   his heart is firm, trusting in the Lord.

The pure cold air of the chapel ebbs, it flows and ebbs, with the Gregorian music, the true voices of the community, trained in daily practice by the Choir Mistress for these moments in their profession. All the community is present except Felicity and Winifrede. The Abbess in her freshly changed robe stands before her high seat while the antiphon rises and falls.

> Blessed are the peacemakers, blessed are the clean of heart:
>   for they shall see God.

Still as an obelisk before them stands Alexandra, to survey what she has made, and the Abbess Hildegarde before her, to find it good and bravely to prophesy. Her lips move as in a film dubbed into a strange language:

When will you ever, Peace, wild wooddove, shy wings shut,
Your round me roaming end, and under be my boughs?
When, when, Peace, will you, Peace? – I'll not play hypocrite

To my own heart: I yield you do come sometimes; but
That piecemeal peace is poor peace. What pure peace allows
Alarms of wars, the daunting wars, the death of it?

In the hall, at the foot of the staircase, Mildred says, 'Where is Winifrede?'

The Abbess does not reply until they have reached her parlour and are seated.

'Winifrede has been to the ladies' lavatory on the ground floor at Selfridge's and she has not yet returned.'

Walburga says, 'Where will it all end?'

'How on earth,' says Mildred, 'can those two young men pick up their money in the ladies' room?'

'I expect they will send some girl in to pick it up. Anyway, those were Winifrede's instructions,' says Alexandra.

'The more people who know about it the less I like it,' Walburga says.

'The more money they demand the less I like it,' says the Abbess. 'Actually, I heard about these demands for the first time this morning. It makes me wonder what on earth Baudouin and Maximilian were thinking of to send those boys into the Abbey in the first place.'

'We wanted Felicity's love-letters,' Mildred says.

'We needed her love-letters,' says Walburga.

'If I had known that was all you needed I could have arranged the job internally,' says the Abbess. 'We have the photo-copy machines after all.'

'Felicity was very watchful at that time,' Mildred says. 'We had to have you elected Abbess, Alexandra.'

'I would have been elected anyway,' says the Abbess. 'But, Sisters, I am with you.'

'If they hadn't taken her thimble the first time they broke in, Felicity would never have suspected a thing,' Walburga says.

Mildred says, 'They were out of their minds, touching that damned thimble. They only took it to show Maximilian how easy it was to break in.'

'Such a fuss,' says the Abbess, as she has said before and will say again, with her lyrical and indifferent air, 'over a little silver thimble.'

'Oh, well, we know very little about it,' says Mildred. 'I personally know nothing about it.'

'I haven't the slightest idea what it's all about,' says Walburga. 'I only know that if Baudouin and Maximilian can't continue to find money, then they are in it up to the neck.'

'Winifrede, too, is in it up to the neck,' says the Abbess, as she has said before and will say again.

The telephone rings from the central switchboard. Frowning and tight-skinned, Walburga goes to answer it while Mildred watches with her fair, unseasonably summer-blue eyes. Walburga places her hand over the mouthpiece and says, 'The *Daily Express* wants to know if you can make a statement, Lady Abbess, concerning Felicity's psychiatric treatment.'

'Tell them,' says the Abbess, 'that we have no knowledge of Felicity's activities since she left the convent. Her stall in the chapel is empty and it awaits her return.'

Walburga repeats this slowly to the nun who operates the switchboard, and whose voice quivers as she replies, 'I will give them that message, Sister Walburga.'

'Would you really take her back?' Mildred says. But the telephone rings again. Peace is over.

Walburga answers impatiently and again transmits the message. 'They are very persistent. The reporter wants to know your views on Felicity's defection.'

'Pass me the telephone,' says the Abbess. Then she speaks to the operator. 'Sister, be vigilant, be sober. Get your pencil and pad ready, so that I may dictate a message. It goes as follows:

'The Abbess of Crewe cannot say more than that she would welcome the return of Sister Felicity to the Abbey. As for Sister

Felicity's recent escapade, the Abbess is entirely comprehending, and indeed would apply the fine words of John Milton to Sister Felicity's high-spirited action. These words are: "I cannot praise a fugitive and cloistered virtue, unexercised and unbreathed, that never sallies out and sees her adversary, but slinks out of the race ..." – Repeat that to the reporter, if you please, and if there are any more telephone calls from outside please say we've retired for the night.'

'What will they make of that?' Mildred says. 'It sounds awfully charming.'

'They'll make some sort of a garble,' says the Abbess. 'Garble is what we need, now, Sisters. We are leaving the sphere of history and are about to enter that of mythology. Mythology is nothing more than history garbled; likewise history is mythology garbled and it is nothing more in all the history of man. Who are we to alter the nature of things? So far as we are concerned, my dear Sisters, to look for the truth of the matter will be like looking for the lost limbs, toes and fingernails of a body blown to pieces in an air crash.'

'The English Catholic bishops will be furious at your citing Milton,' says Walburga.

'It's the Roman Cardinals who matter,' says the Abbess, 'and I doubt they have ever heard of him.'

The door opens and Winifrede, tired from her journey, unbending in her carriage, enters and makes a deep curtsey.

'Winifrede, my dear,' says the Abbess.

'I have just changed back into my habit, Lady Abbess,' Winifrede says.

'How did it go?'

'It went well,' says Winifrede. 'I saw the woman immediately.'

'You left the shopping-bag on the wash-basin and went into the lavatory?'

'Yes. It went just like that. I knelt and watched from the space under the door. It was a woman wearing a red coat and blue trousers and she carried a copy of *The Tablet*. She started washing her hands at the basin. Then she picked up the bag and went away. I came out of the lavatory immediately, washed my hands and dried them. Nobody noticed a thing.'

'How many women were in the ladies' room?'

'There were five and one attendant. But our transaction was accomplished very quickly.'

'What was the woman in the red coat like? Describe her.'

'Well,' says Winifrede, 'she looked rather masculine. Heavy-faced. I think she was wearing a black wig.'

'Masculine?'

'Her face. Also, rather bony hands. Big wrists. I didn't see her for long.'

'Do you know what I think?' says the Abbess.

'You think it wasn't a woman at all,' Walburga says.

'One of those student Jesuits dressed as a woman,' Mildred says.

'Winifrede, is that possible?' the Abbess says.

'You know,' says Winifrede, 'it's quite possible. Very possible.'

'If so, then I think Baudouin and Maximilian are dangerously stupid,' says the Abbess. 'It is typical of the Jesuit mentality to complicate a simple process. Why choose a ladies' lavatory?'

'It's an easy place for a shopping-bag to change hands,' Walburga says. 'Baudouin is no fool.'

'You should get Baudouin out of your system, Walburga,' says the Abbess.

Winifrede begins to finger her rosary beads very nervously. 'What is the matter, Winifrede,' says the Abbess.

'The ladies' toilet at Selfridge's was my idea,' she laments. 'I thought it was a good idea. It's an easy place to make a meeting.'

'I don't deny,' says the Abbess, 'that by some chance your idea has been successful. The throw of the dice is bound to turn sometimes in your favour. But you are wrong to imagine that any idea of yours is good in itself.'

'Anyway,' says Walburga, 'the young brutes have got the money and that will keep them quiet.'

'For a while,' says the Abbess of Crewe.

'Oh, have I got to do it again?' Winifrede says in her little wailing voice.

'Possibly,' says the Abbess. 'Meantime go and rest before Compline. After Compline we shall all meet here for refreshments and some entertaining scenarios. Think up your best scenarios, Sisters.'

'What are scenarios?' says Winifrede.

'They are an art-form,' says the Abbess of Crewe, 'based on facts. A good scenario is a garble. A bad one is a bungle. They need not be plausible, only hypnotic, like all good art.'

FIVE

'Gertrude,' says the Abbess into the green telephone, 'have you seen the papers?'

'Yes,' says Gertrude.

'You mean that the news has reached Reykjavik?'

'Czechoslovakia has won the World Title.'

'I mean the news about us, Gertrude, dear.'

'Yes, I saw a bit about you. What was the point of your bugging the convent?'

'How should I know?' says the Abbess. 'I know nothing about anything. I am occupied with the administration of the Abbey, our music, our rites and traditions, and our electronics projects for contacts with our mission fields. Apart from these affairs I only know what I am told appears in the newspapers which I don't read myself. My dear Gertrude, why don't you come home, or at least be nearer to hand, in France, in Belgium, in Holland, somewhere on the Continent, if not in Britain? I'm seriously thinking of dismantling the green line, Gertrude.'

'Not a bad idea,' Gertrude says. 'There's very little you can do about controlling the missions from Crewe, anyway.'

'If you were nearer to hand, Gertrude, say Austria or Italy even –'

'Too near the Vatican,' says Gertrude.

'We need a European mission,' says the Abbess.

'But I don't like Europe,' says Gertrude. 'It's too near to Rome.'

'Ah yes,' says the Abbess. 'Our own dear Rome. But, Gertrude, I'm having trouble from Rome, and I think you might help us. They will be sending a commission sooner or later to look into things here at Crewe, don't you think? So much publicity. How can I cope if you keep away?'

'Eavesdropping,' says Gertrude, 'is immoral.'

'Have you got a cold in the chest, Gertrude?'

'You ought not to have listened in to the nuns' conversations. You shouldn't have opened their letters and you ought not to have read them. You should have invested their dowries in the convent and you ought to have stopped your Jesuit friends from breaking into the Abbey.'

'Gertrude,' says the Abbess, 'I know that Felicity had a pile of love-letters.'

'You should have told her to destroy them. You ought to have warned her. You should have let the nuns who wanted to vote for her do so. You ought to have –'

'Gertrude, my devout logician, it is a question upon which I ponder greatly within the umbrageous garden of my thoughts, where you get your "should nots" and your "ought tos" from. They don't arise from the moral systems of the cannibal tribes of the Andes, nor the factions of the deep Congo, nor from the hills of Asia, do they? It seems to me, Gertrude, my love, that your shoulds and your shouldn'ts have been established rather nearer home, let us say the continent of Europe, if you will forgive the expression.'

'The Pope,' says Gertrude, 'should broaden his ecumenical views and he ought to stand by the Second Vatican Council. He should throw the dogmas out of the window there at the Holy See and he ought to let the other religions in by the door and unite.'

The Abbess, at her end of the green line, relaxes in the control room, glancing at the white cold light which plays on the masses of green ferns she has recently placed about the room, beautifying it and concealing the apparatus.

'Gertrude,' she says. 'I have concluded that there's some gap in your logic. And at the same time I am wondering what to do about Walburga, Mildred and Winifrede.'

'Why, what have they done?'

'My dear, it seems it is they who have bugged the Abbey and arranged a burglary.'

'Then send them away.'

'But Mildred and Walburga are two of the finest nuns I have ever had the privilege to know.'

'This is Reykjavik,' Gertrude says. 'Not Fleet Street. Why don't you go on television? You would have a wonderful presence, Lady Abbess.'

'Do you think so, Gertrude? Do you know, I feel very confident in that respect. But I don't care for publicity. I'm in love with English poetry, and even my devotions take that form, as is perfectly valid in my view. Gertrude, I will give an interview on the television if need be, and I will quote some poetry. Which poet do you think most suitable? Gertrude, are you listening? Shall I express your views about the Holy See on the television?'

Gertrude's voice goes faint as she replies, 'No, they're only for home consumption. Give them to the nuns. I'm afraid there's a snowstorm blowing up. Too much interference on the line . . .'

The Abbess skips happily, all by herself in the control room, when she has put down the green receiver. The she folds her white habit about her and goes into her parlour which has been decorated to her own style. Mildred and Walburga stand up as she enters, and she looks neither at one nor the other, but stands without moving, and they with her, like Stonehenge. In a while the Abbess takes her chair, with her buckled shoes set lightly on the new green carpet. Mildred and Walburga take their places.

'Gertrude,' says the Abbess, 'is on her way to the hinterland, far into the sparse wastes of Iceland where she hopes to introduce daily devotions and central heating into the igloos. We had better get tenders from the central-heating firms and arrange a contract quickly, for I fear that something about the scheme may go wrong, such as the breakdown of Eskimo family life. What is all that yelping outside?'

'Police dogs,' says Mildred. 'The reporters are still at the gate.'

'Keep the nuns well removed from the gates,' says the Abbess. 'Do you know, if things become really bad I shall myself make a statement on television. Have you received any further intelligence?'

'Felicity has made up a list of Abbey crimes,' says Walburga. 'She complains they are crimes under English law, not ecclesiastical crimes, and she has complained on the television that the legal authorities are doing nothing about them.'

'The courts would of course prefer the affair to be settled by Rome,' says the Abbess. 'Have you got the list?' She holds out her hand and flutters her fingers impatiently while Walburga brings out of her deep pocket a thick folded list which eventually reaches the Abbess's fingers.

Mildred says, 'She compiled it with the aid of Thomas and Roget's *Thesaurus*, according to her landlady's daughter, who keeps Winifrede informed.'

'We shall be ruined with all this pay-money that we have to pay,' the Abbess says, unfolding the list. She begins to read aloud, in her clearest modulations:

'"*Wrongdoing committed by the Abbess of Crewe*".' She then looks up from the paper and says, 'I do love that word "wrongdoing". It sounds so like the gong of doom, not at all evocative of that fanfare of Wagnerian trumpets we are led to expect, but something that accompanies the smell of boiled beef and cabbage in the back premises of a Mechanics' Institute in Sheffield in the mid-nineteenth century ... Wrongdoing is moreover something that commercial travellers used to do in the thirties and forties of this century, although now I believe they do the same thing under another name ... Wrongdoing, wrongdoing ... In any sense which Felicity could attach to it, the word does not apply to me, dear ladies. Felicity is a lascivious puritan.'

'We could sue for libel,' Walburga says.

'No more does libel apply to me,' says the Abbess, and continues reading aloud: '"Concealing, hiding, secreting, covering, screening, cloaking, veiling, shrouding, shading, muffling, masking, disguising, ensconcing, eclipsing, keeping in ignorance, blinding, hoodwinking, mystifying, posing, puzzling, perplexing, embarrassing, bewildering, reserving, suppressing, bamboozling, etcetera."'

'I pine so much to know,' says the Abbess, looking up from the list at the attentive handsome faces of Mildred and Walburga, 'what the "etcetera" stands for. Surely Felicity had something in mind?'

'Would it be something to do with fraud?' says Mildred.

'Fraud is implied in the next paragraph,' says the Abbess, 'for it goes on: "Defrauding, cheating, imposing upon, practising upon, outreaching, jockeying, doing, cozening, diddling, circumventing, putting upon, decoying, tricking, hoaxing, juggling, trespassing, beguiling, inveigling, luring, liming, swindling, tripping up, bilking, plucking, outwitting, making believe the moon is made of green cheese and deceiving."'

'A dazzling indictment,' says the Abbess, looking up once more, 'and, do you know, she has thought not only of the wrongdoings I have committed but also those I have not yet done but am about to perform.'

The bell rings for Vespers and the Abbess lays aside the dazzling pages.

'I think,' says Walburga, as she follows the Abbess from the private parlour, 'we should dismantle the bugs right away.'

'And destroy our tapes?' says Mildred, rather tremorously. Mildred is very attached to the tapes, playing them back frequently with a rare force of concentration.

'Certainly not,' says the Abbess as they pause at the top of the staircase. 'We cannot destroy evidence the existence of which is vital to our story and which can be orchestrated to meet the demands of the Roman inquisitors who are trying to liquidate the convent. We need the tapes to trick, lure, lime, outwit, bamboozle, etcetera. There is one particular tape in which I prove my innocence of the bugging itself. I am walking with Winifrede under the poplars discussing the disguising and ensconcing as early as last summer. It is the tape that begins with the question, "What is wrong, Sister Winifrede, with the traditional keyhole method...?" I replayed and rearranged it the other day, making believe the moon is green cheese with Winifrede's stupid reply which I rightly forget. It is very suitable evidence to present to Rome, if necessary. Sister Winifrede is in it up to the neck. Send her to my parlour after Vespers.'

They descend the stairs with such poise and habitual style that the nuns below, amongst whom already stir like a wind in the rushes the early suspicion and dread of what is to come, are sobered and made vigilant, are collected and composed as they file across the dark lawn, each in her place to Vespers.

High and low come the canticles and the Abbess rises from her tall chair to join the responses. How lyrically move her lips in the tidal sway of the music! ...

Taking, obtaining, benefiting, procuring, deriving, securing, collecting, reaping, coming in for, stepping into, inheriting, coming by, scraping together, getting hold of, bringing grist to the mill, feathering one's nest ...

Sisters, be sober, be vigilant, for the devil goeth about as a raging lion seeking whom he may devour.

Gloating, being pleased, deriving pleasure, etcetera, taking
delight in, rejoicing in, relishing, liking, enjoying, indulging in,
treating oneself, solacing oneself, revelling, luxuriating, being on
velvet, being in clover, slaking the appetite, *faisant ses choux gras*,
basking in the sunshine, treading on enchanted ground.

> Out of the deep have I called unto thee, O Lord:
> Lord hear my voice.
>
> O let thine ears consider well:
>   the voice of my complaint.
> If thou, Lord, will be extreme to mark
>   what is done amiss:
> O Lord, who may abide it?
>
>> Happy those early days! when I
>> Shined in my angel infancy.
>> Before I understood this place
>> Appointed for my second race,
>> Or taught my soul to fancy aught
>> But a white, celestial thought.

'The point is, Winifrede, that you took a very great risk passing the
money to a young Jesuit seminarian who was dressed up as a woman
in Selfridge's ladies' lavatory. He could have been arrested as a
transvestite. This time you'd better think up something better.'

The Abbess is busy with a pair of little scissors unpicking the tiny
threads that attach the frail setting of an emerald to the robes of the
Infant of Prague.

'It pains me,' says the Abbess, 'to expend, waste, squander, lavish,
dissipate, exhaust and throw down the drain the Sisters' dowries in
this fashion. I am hard used by the Jesuits. However, here you are.
Take it to the pawn shop and make some arrangement with Fathers
Baudouin and Maximilian how the money is to be picked up. But no
more ladies' lavatories.'

'Yes, Lady Abbess,' says Winifrede; then she says in a low wail, 'If
only Sister Mildred could come with me or Sister Walburga ...'

'Oh, they know nothing of this affair,' says the Abbess.

'Oh, they know everything!' says Winifrede, the absolute clot.

'As far as I'm concerned I know nothing, either,' says the Abbess. 'That is the scenario. And do you know what I am thinking, Winifrede?'

'What is that, Lady Abbess?'

'I'm thinking,' the Abbess says:

> I am homesick after mine own kind,
> Oh, I know that there are folk about me,
> friendly faces,
> But I am homesick after mine own kind.

'Yes, Lady Abbess,' says Winifrede. She curtsies low and is about to depart when the Abbess, in a swirl of white, lays a hand on her arm to retain her.

'Winifrede,' she says, 'before you go, just in case anything should happen which might tend to embarrass the Abbey, I would like you to sign the confession.'

'Which confession?' says Winifrede, her stout frame heaving with alarm.

'Oh, the usual form of confession.' The Abbess beckons her to the small desk whereon is laid a typed sheet of the Abbey's fine crested paper. The Abbess holds out a pen. 'Sign,' she says.

'May I read it?' Winifrede whines, taking up the papers in her strong hands.

'It's the usual form of confession. But read on, read on, if you have any misgivings.'

Winifrede reads what is typed:

> I confess to Almighty God, to blessed Mary ever Virgin, to blessed Michael the archangel, to blessed John the Baptist, to the holy apostles Peter and Paul, and to all the saints, that I have sinned exceedingly in thought, word and deed, through my fault, through my fault, through my most grievous fault.

'Sign,' says the Abbess. 'Just put your name and your designation.'

'I don't really like to commit myself so far,' Winifrede says.

'Well, you know,' says the Abbess, 'since you repeat these words at Mass every morning of your life, I would be quite horrified to think you had been a hypocrite all these years and hadn't meant them. The laity in their hundreds of millions lodge this solemn deposition before the altar every week.' She puts the pen into Winifrede's frightened hand. 'Even the Pope,' says the Abbess, 'offers the very same damaging testimony every morning of his life; he admits quite frankly that he has committed sins exceedingly all through his own grievous fault. Whereupon the altar boy says: "May almighty God have mercy on you." And all I am saying, Winifrede, is that what's good enough for the Supreme Pontiff is good enough for you. Do you imagine he doesn't mean precisely what he says every morning of his life?'

Winifrede takes the pen and writes under the confession, 'Winifrede, Dame of the Order of the Abbey of Crewe,' in a high and slanting copperplate hand. She pats her habit to see if the emerald is safe in the deep folds of her pocket, and before leaving the parlour she stops at the door to look back warily. The Abbess stands, holding the confession, white in her robes under the lamp and judicious, like blessed Michael the Archangel.

SIX

'We have entered the realm of mythology,' says the Abbess of Crewe, 'and of course I won't part with the tapes. I claim the ancient Benefit of Clerks. The confidentiality between the nuns and the Abbess cannot be disrupted. These tapes are as good as under the secret of the confessional, and even Rome cannot demand them.'

The television crew has gone home, full of satisfaction, but news reporters loiter in a large group outside the gates. The police patrol the grounds with the dogs that growl at every dry leaf that stirs on the ground.

It is a month since Sister Winifrede, mindful of the Abbess's warning not to choose a ladies' lavatory for a rendezvous, decided it would show initiative and imagination if she arranged to meet her blackmailer in the gentlemen's lavatory at the British Museum. It was down there in that blind alley that Winifrede was arrested by the Museum guard and the attendants. 'Here's one of them poofs,' said the attendant, and Winifrede, dressed in a dark blue business suit, a white shirt with a faint brown stripe and a blue and red striped tie, emblematic of some university unidentified even by the Sunday press, was taken off to the police station still hugging her plastic bag packed tight with all those thousands.

Winifrede began blurting out her story on the way to the police station and continued it while the policewomen were stripping her of her manly clothes, and went on further with her deposition, dressed in a police-station overall. The evening paper headlines announced, 'Crewe Abbey Scandal: New Revelations', 'Crewe Nun Transvestite Caught in Gents' and 'Crewe Thimble Case – Nun Questioned'.

Winifrede, having told her story, was released without charge on the assurances of the Abbess that it was an internal and ecclesiastical matter, and was being intensively investigated as such. This touchy situation, which the law-enforcement authorities were of a mind to avoid, did not prevent several bishops from paying as many calls to the Abbess Alexandra, whitely robed in her parlour at Crewe, as she would receive, nor did it keep the stories out of the newspapers of the big wide world.

'My Lords,' she told those three of the bishops whom she admitted, 'be vigilant for your own places before you demolish my Abbey. You know of the mower described by Andrew Marvell:

> While thus he drew his elbow round,
> Depopulating all the ground,
> And, with his whistling scythe, does cut
> Each stroke between the earth and root,
> The edged steel, by careless chance,
> Did into his own ankle glance,
> And there among the grass fell down
> By his own scythe the mower mown.'

They left, puzzled and bedazzled, having one by one and in many ways assured her they had no intention whatsoever to discredit her Abbey, but merely to find out what on earth was going on.

The Abbess, when she finally appeared on the television, was a complete success while she lasted on the screen. She explained, lifting in her beautiful hand a folded piece of paper, that she already had poor Sister Winifrede's signed confession to the effect that she had been guilty of exceeding wrongdoing, fully owning her culpability. The Abbess further went on to deny rumours of inferior feeding at Crewe. 'I don't deny,' she said, 'that we have our Health Food laboratories in which we examine and experiment with vast quantities of nourishing products.' In the field of applied electronics, the Abbess claimed, the Abbey was well in advance and hoped by the end of the year to produce a new and improved lightning conductor which would minimize the danger of lightning in the British Isles to an even smaller percentage than already existed.

The audiences goggled with awe at this lovely lady. She said that such tapes as existed were confidential recordings of individual conversations between nun and Abbess, and these she would never part with. She smiled sublimely and asked for everyone's prayers for the Abbey of Crewe and for her beloved Sister Gertrude, whose magnificent work abroad had earned universal gratitude.

The cameras have all gone home and the reporters wait outside the gates. Only the rubbish-truck, the Jesuit who comes to say Mass and the post-van are permitted to enter and leave. After these morning affairs are over the gates remain locked. Alexandra has received the bishops, has spoken, and has said she will receive them no more. The bishops, who had left the Abbess with soothed feelings, had experienced, a few hours after leaving the Abbey, a curious sense of being unable to recall precisely what explanation Alexandra had given. Now it is too late.

Who is paying the blackmailers, for what purpose, to whom, how much, and with funds from what source? There is no clear answer, neither in the press nor in the hands of the bishops. It is the realm of mythology, and the Abbess explains this to Gertrude in her goodbye call on the green telephone.

'Well,' Gertrude says, 'you may have the public mythology of the press and television, but you won't get the mythological approach from Rome. In Rome, they deal with realities.'

'It's quite absurd that I have been delated to Rome with a view to excommunication,' says the Abbess, 'and of course, Gertrude, dear, I am going there myself to plead my cause. Shall you be there with me? You could then come back to England and take up prison reform or something.'

'I'm afraid my permit in Tibet only lasts a certain time,' Gertrude huskily replies. 'I couldn't get away.'

'In response to popular demand,' says the Abbess, 'I have decided to make selected transcripts of my tapes and publish them. I find some passages are missing and fear that the devil who goes about as a raging lion hath devoured them. There are many film and stage offers, and all these events will help tremendously to further your work in the field and to assist the starved multitudes. Gertrude, you know I am become an object of art, the end of which is to give pleasure.'

'Delete the English poetry from those tapes,' Gertrude says. 'It will look bad for you at Rome. It is the language of Cranmer, of the King James version, the book of Common Prayer. Rome will take anything, but English poetry, no.'

'Well, Gertrude, I do not see how the Cardinals themselves can possibly read the transcripts of the tapes or listen to the tapes if their existence is immoral. Anyway, I have obtained all the nuns' signed confessions, which I shall take with me to Rome. Fifty of them.'

'What have the nuns confessed?'

The Abbess reads in her glowing voice over the green telephone to far-away Gertrude the nuns' *Confiteor*.

'They have all signed that statement?'

'Gertrude, do you have bronchial trouble?'

'I am outraged,' says Gertrude, 'to hear you have all been sinning away there in Crewe, and exceedingly at that, not only in thought and deed but also in word. I have been toiling and spinning while, if that sensational text is to be believed, you have been considering the lilies and sinning exceedingly. You are all at fault, all of you, most grievously at fault.'

'Yes, we have that in the confessions, Gertrude, my trusty love. *O felix culpa!* Maximilian and Baudouin have fled the country to America and are giving seminars respectively in ecclesiastical stage management and demonology. Tell me, Gertrude, should I travel to Rome by air or by land and sea?'

'By sea and land,' says Gertrude. 'Keep them waiting.'

'Yes, the fleecy drift of the sky across the Channel will become me. I hope to leave in about ten days' time. The Infant of Prague is already in the bank – Gertrude, are you there?'

'I didn't catch that,' says Gertrude. 'I dropped a hair-pin and picked it up.'

Mildred and Walburga are absent now, having found it necessary to reorganize the infirmary at the Abbey of Ynce for the ailing and ancient Abbot. Alexandra, already seeing in her mind's eye her own shape on the upper deck of the ship that takes her from Dover to Ostend, and thence by train through the St Gothard the long journey to Rome across the map of Europe, sits at her desk prettily writing to the Cardinal at Rome. O rare Abbess of Crewe!

'Your Very Reverend Eminence,

Your Eminence does me the honour to invite me to respond to the Congregational Committee of Investigation into the case of Sister Felicity's little thimble and thimble-related matters...'

She has given the orders for the selection and orchestration of the transcripts of her tape-recordings. She has gathered her nuns together before Compline. 'Remove the verses that I have uttered. They are proper to myself alone and should not be cast before the public. Put "Poetry deleted". Sedulously expurgate all such trivial fond records and entitle the compilation *The Abbess of Crewe*.'

Our revels now are ended. Be still, be watchful. She sails indeed on the fine day of her desire into waters exceptionally smooth, and stands on the upper deck, straight as a white ship's funnel, marvelling how the wide sea billows from shore to shore like that cornfield of sublimity which never should be reaped nor was ever sown, orient and immortal wheat.

The Bachelors

For Jerzy and Christine, with love

ONE

Daylight was appearing over London, the great city of bachelors. Half-pint bottles of milk began to be stood on the doorsteps of houses containing single apartments from Hampstead Heath to Greenwich Park, and from Wanstead Flats to Putney Heath; but especially in Hampstead, especially in Kensington.

In Queen's Gate, Kensington, in Harrington Road, The Boltons, Holland Park, and in King's Road, Chelsea, and its backwaters, the bachelors stirred between their sheets, reached for their wound watches, and with waking intelligences noted the time; then, remembering it was Saturday morning, turned over on their pillows. But soon, since it was Saturday, most would be out on the streets shopping for their bacon and eggs, their week's supplies of breakfasts and occasional suppers; and these bachelors would set out early, before a quarter past ten, in order to avoid being jostled by the women, the legitimate shoppers.

At a quarter past ten, Ronald Bridges, aged thirty-seven, who during the week was assistant curator at a small museum of handwriting in the City of London, stopped in the Old Brompton Road to speak to his friend Martin Bowles, a barrister of thirty-five.

Ronald moved his old plastic shopping bag up and down twice, to suggest to Martin that it was a greater weight than it really was, and that the whole business was a bore.

'Where,' said Ronald, pointing to a package on the top of Martin's laden bag, 'did you get your frozen peas?'

'Clayton's.'

'How much?'

'One and six. That's for a small packet; does for two. A large is two and six; six helpings.'

'Terrible price,' said Ronald, agreeably.

'Your hand's never out of your pocket,' said Martin.

'What else have you got there?' Ronald said.

'Cod. You bake it in yoghurt with a sprinkle of marjoram and it tastes like halibut. My old ma's away for a fortnight with the old housekeeper.'

'Marjoram, where do you get marjoram?'

'Oh, Fortnum's. You get all the herbs there. I get a bag of stuff every month. I do nearly all the shopping and most of the cooking since my old ma's had her op. And old Carrie isn't up to it now – she never was much of a cook.'

'You must have it in you,' said Ronald, 'going all the way to Piccadilly for herbs.'

'I usually work it in with something else,' Martin said. 'We like our herbs, Ma and I. Come on in here.'

He meant a coffee-bar. They sat beside their bags and sipped their espressos with contented languor.

'I've forgotten Tide,' said Ronald. 'I must remember to get Tide.'

'Don't you make a list?' said Martin.

'No. I depend on my memory.'

'I make a list,' said Martin, 'when my ma's away. I always do the shopping at the week-ends. When Ma's at home she makes the list. It's always unreadable, though.'

'A waste of time,' said Ronald, 'if you've got a memory.'

'Do you mind?' said a girl who had just come into the coffee shop. She was referring to Ronald's bag of shopping; it was taking up the seat which ran along the wall.

'Oh, sorry,' said Ronald, removing his bag and dumping it on the floor.

The girl sat down, and when the waitress came to serve her she said, 'I'm waiting for a friend.'

She had black hair drawn back in a high style, dark eyes, and an oval ballet-dancer's face. She returned the two bachelors' sleepy routine glance, then lit a cigarette and watched the door.

'New potatoes in the shops,' Ronald said.

'They're always in the shops,' said Martin, 'these days. In season and out of season. It's the same with everything: you can get new potatoes and new carrots all the year round now, and peas and spinach any time, and tomatoes in the spring, even.'

'At a price,' said Ronald.

'At a price,' Martin said. 'What bacon do you get?'

'I make do with streaky. I grudge breakfasts,' said Ronald.

'Same here.'

'Your hand's never out of your pocket,' Ronald said before Martin could say it.

A small narrow-built man came in the door and joined the girl, smiling at her with a sweet, spiritual expression.

He sat side by side with the girl on the wall-seat. He lifted the menu-card and spoke to her soundlessly from behind it.

'Good gracious me,' murmured Martin.

Ronald looked towards the man, whose body was now hidden by the girl at his side. Ronald observed the head, unable to see at first whether his hair was fair or silver-white, but soon it was plainly a mixture. He was thin, with a very pointed, anxious face and nose, and a grey-white lined skin. He would be about fifty-five. He wore a dark blue suit.

'Don't stare,' Martin said. 'He's on a charge and I'm prosecuting him. He's coming up again before the magistrates next week. He has to report to the police every day.'

'What for?'

'Fraudulent conversion and possibly other charges. Somebody in my chambers defended Seton ages ago. Not that it did either any good. Let's go.'

Ronald put down the newspaper in his hand.

'Tide,' said Ronald in the street. 'I really must remember Tide.'

'Which way are you going?'

'Across to Clayton's.'

'I'm going there too. I haven't got a lot of groceries on the list, I'm dining out four times next week. Where do you go on Sundays?'

'Oh, here and there,' Ronald said, 'there's always somebody.'

'I go to Leighton Buzzard if anyone comes home to keep Ma company,' said Martin. 'It's rather fun and a change at Leighton Buzzard. But if Isobel stays in London I go to her in London.' They had crossed the road.

'I've left my paper in the café,' Ronald said inexpertly. 'I'd better go back and fetch it. See you some time.'

'Feeling all right?' Martin said, as Ronald turned on the kerb to cross back over the road.

'Yes, oh, yes, it's only my paper.'

'Sure?' – for Martin was touchily aware of Ronald's epilepsy.

''Bye.' Ronald had crossed over.

He found the paper. He sat down again in a seat opposite the one he had recently occupied so that he could the more easily see the silver-yellow-haired man as he spoke in low tones effortful with convincingness, to the black-haired girl. Ronald ordered coffee and a cream cake. He opened his paper, from the side of which, from time to time, he watched the man who was deeply explaining himself to the girl. Ronald could not decide where he had seen the man before; he could not even be sure of having done so. 'I'm becoming a prying old maid,' he said to himself as he left, to explain his return to the café, preferring to call himself a prying old maid than to acknowledge fully his real reason: that he had been simply testing his memory; for he could not leave alone any opportunity to try himself on the question whether his epilepsy would one day affect his mental powers or not.

'No,' the American specialist had said, irritable with the strain of putting a technical point into common speech, 'there is no reason why your intellect should be impaired except, of course, that you cannot exercise it to the full extent that would be possible were you able to follow and rise to the top of a normal career. But you ought to retain and indeed expand your present mental capacity. The seizures will be intermittent; let me put it that your seizures concern the brain but not the mind. You will learn to prepare for them physically in some degree but not to control them. They won't affect the mind except in so far as the emotional psychological disturbances affect it. That's not my department.'

Ronald had retained every one of these words importantly in his memory for the past fourteen years, aware that the specialist himself would possibly remember only the gist, and then only with the aid of his record cards. But Ronald held them tight, from time to time subjecting the words to every possible kind of interpretation. 'Let me put it that your seizures concern the brain, not the mind.' But he believes, Ronald argued with himself at times throughout the years, that the mind is part of the brain: then why did he say 'Let me put it that . . .' What was his intention? And anyhow, Ronald would think, I can manage. And anyhow, I might never have been able to follow and rise to the top of a normal career. What is a normal career? The law: closed to me; – but, his friends had said, you need not put in for Lord Chancellor, you could be a successful solicitor. Oh, could I? – You haven't seen me in a fit. The Civil Service: closed to me. No, not at all, said his advisers. Medicine, teaching, get yourself into a college, try for a fellowship, you've got the academic ability – you know what some of the dons are like, there wouldn't be anything odd. . . .

'I could never be first-rate.'

'Oh, first-rate . . .'

He had been twenty-three, a post-graduate, when the fits started, without warning, three months after he had turned his attention to theology. The priesthood: closed to me. Yes, said his friends, that's out; and, said his theological counsellors, it never would have been any good in any case, you never had a vocation.

'How do you know?'

'Because, in the event, you can't be a priest.'

'That's the sort of retrospective logic that makes us Catholics distrusted.'

'A vocation to the priesthood is the will of God. Nothing can change God's will. You are an epileptic. No epileptic can be a priest. *Ergo* you never had a vocation. But you can do something else.'

'I could never be first-rate.'

'That is sheer vanity' – it was an old priest speaking – 'you were never meant to be a first-rate careerist.'

'Only a first-rate epileptic?'

'Indeed, yes. Quite seriously, yes,' the old priest said.

It was at a time when he was having convulsions three times a week that he had allowed himself to be taken by an itinerant specialist to a research centre in California, with the purpose of submitting to a two years' clinical trial of a new drug. He was one of sixty volunteers from five to twenty-eight years old. Ronald lived in a huge sun-balconied hostel. Some of the other fifty-nine were mentally deficient. Most were neurotic. None was highly intelligent. Of the total sixty patients three failed to respond to the drug, and of these Ronald was one. Of these three, Ronald succumbed to the dreaded *status epilepticus*, enduring fit after fit, one after the other in rapid succession, only four days after the treatment had started.

'This is due to emotional apprehension,' Dr Fleischer told him when, after a week, he lay partially recovered, thin and exhausted, in a cool green-and-white room with the sun-blinds down. 'You may withdraw from the experiment if you wish,' Dr Fleischer said. 'Or you may continue with profit.' Dr Fleischer's time and mind were largely occupied with the fifty-seven epileptics who had already begun to respond favourably to the new drug.

When Ronald was up and shakily walking about, drowsy from the effects of his usual drugs, he weighed up for himself the price of his possible cure. The patients who were responding to Dr Fleischer's treatment were all around him, they seemed even sleepier, drowsier than he – but, thought Ronald, this is not far from their normal condition, they were born half-awake.

'The new drug is successful,' the smart fresh-lipsticked young research woman told him. 'The drug has been found to have anti-convulsant and sedative effects on rats, and now it looks like being successful with the majority of patients here.' She smiled through her rimless spectacles with eyes far away, on the job, efficient, creamy-complexioned, first-rate.

'Well, your drug makes me worse,' Ronald said, feeling within himself, at that moment, the potentialities of a most unpleasant young man.

When he got the chance of another brief interview with Dr Fleischer he said, 'Do you understand what you are asking me to do when you urge me to persevere? I may have to undergo the repetitive fits again.'

Dr Fleischer said, 'I am not urging you to persevere. I suggest your failure to respond to the drug is caused only by emotional resistance.'

'Do you realize,' said Ronald, 'how long the few seconds of lucidity between the fits appears to be, and what goes on in one's mind in those few waking seconds?'

'No,' said the doctor, 'I don't realize what these lucid intervals are like. I recommend you to return to England. I recommend... I advise ... No, there is no reason why your intellect should be impaired, except of course that you cannot exercise it to the full extent that would be possible were you able to follow and rise to the top of a normal career....'

'Perhaps,' Ronald said, 'I'll be a first-rate epileptic and that will be my career.'

Dr Fleischer did not smile. He reached for Ronald's index card and wrote upon it.

Before he departed Ronald's brain was tested by a machine that was now familiar to him, and which recorded the electric currents generated by his convulsions and which was beginning to be used in the criminal courts of some American States to ascertain the truth of a suspect's statement, so that it was popularly called 'the truth machine'.

While he was awaiting the convenience of the man who was to escort him back to England, Ronald deliberately ignored the scene around him. His fellow-patients, week by week, busied themselves with tennis, bed-making, toy-making, and their jazz orchestra. It was only much later that these scenes, which he had made an effort not to notice, returned to Ronald again and again accompanied by Dr Fleischer's words – long after the specialist must have forgotten them – and mostly at the moments when Ronald, bored by his self-preoccupation, most wished to forget himself, clinics, hospitals, doctors, and all the pompous trappings of his malady. It was at these moments of rejection that the obsessive images of his early epileptic years bore down upon him and he felt himself to be, not the amiable johnnie he had by then, for the sake of sheer goodwill and protection from the world, affected to be – but as one possessed by a demon, judged by the probing inquisitors of life an unsatisfactory clinic-rat which failed to respond to the right drug. In the course of time this experience sharpened his wits, and privately looking round at his world of acquaintances, he became, at certain tense moments, a truth-machine, under which his friends took on the aspect of demon-hypocrites. But being a reasonable man, he allowed these moods to pass over him, and in reality he rather liked his friends, and gave them his best advice when, in the following years, they began to ask him for it.

On his return from California he was surprised to find himself able in some measure to retain consciousness during his fits, although he could not control them, by a secret, inarticulated method which, whenever he tried to describe it to his doctors, began to fail him when next he practised it.

'I find it useful to induce within myself a sense,' Ronald at first told his doctor, '– when I am going under – a sense that every action in the world is temporarily arrested for the duration of my fit –'

'Seizure,' said the doctor.

'My seizure,' said Ronald, 'and this curiously enables me to retain some sort of consciousness during even the worst part. I find it easier to endure this partial consciousness of my behaviour during the fits than surrender my senses entirely, although it's a painful experience.'

Immediately he had said it, he felt foolish, he knew his explanation was inadequate. The doctor remarked, 'It's as I've said. There is always an improvement in the patient when he becomes used to his seizures. First he experiences the aura, and this enables him to take preliminary precautions as to his physical safety during the seizure. He learns to lie down on the floor in time. He learns . . .'

'No, that's not what I mean,' Ronald said. 'What I mean is something different. It is like being partly an onlooker during the fit, yet not quite. . . .'

'The seizure,' said the doctor, meanwhile puzzling his brains with a frown.

'The seizure,' said Ronald.

'Oh, quite,' said the doctor. 'The patient might learn to exercise some control during the *petit-mal* stage to stand him in good stead during the *grand-mal* convulsions.'

'That's right,' Ronald said, and went home and, on the way, had a severe fit in the street; on which occasion his method would not work, so that he came to his senses in the casualty department of St George's Hospital, sick with inhalations which had been administered to him to arrest his frenzy.

Soon Ronald was obliged to earn his living. His father, a retired horticulturist, still mourning the early death of his wife, took fright when he realized that Ronald was incurable. Ronald reassured him, advised him to buy an annuity and go to live at Kew; the father smiled and went.

Ronald got a job in a small museum of graphology in the City, to which people of various professions had recourse as well as curious members of the public. To Ronald's museum came criminologists from abroad, people wishing to identify the dates of manuscripts, or the handwriting attached to documents of doubt. Some came in the hope of obtaining 'readings' by which they meant a pronouncement as to the character and future fortunes of the person responsible for a piece of handwriting, but these were sent empty away. Ronald gained a reputation in the detection of forgeries, and after about five years was occasionally consulted by lawyers and criminal authorities, and several times was called to court as witness for the defence or prosecution.

At the museum he had a room to himself, with an understanding that he could there have his fits in peace without anyone fussing along to his aid. He knew how to compose himself for a fit. He cultivated his secret method of retaining some self-awareness during his convulsions, and never mentioned this to his doctors again, lest he should lose the gift. He kept by him a wedge of cork which he stuck between his teeth as the first signs seized him. He knew how many seconds it took to turn off the gas fire in his small office, to take the correct dose of his pills, to lie flat on his back, turn his head to the side, biting his cork wedge, and to await the onslaught. It was arranged, at these times, that no one entering Ronald's office should touch him except in the event of blood issuing from his mouth. Blood was never seen at his mouth, only foam, for Ronald was careful with his cork wedge. His two old colleagues and the two young clerks got used to him, and the typist, a large religious woman, ceased to try to mother him.

After five years Ronald's fits occurred on an average of once a month. The drugs which he took regularly, and in extra strength at the first intimations of his fits, became gradually more effective in controlling his movements, but less frequently could he ward off the violent stage of his attack until he found a convenient place in which to lie down. Twice within fourteen years he was arrested for drunkenness while staggering along the street towards a chemist's shop. Twice, he simply lay down on the pavement close in to the walls and allowed himself to be removed by ambulance. As often as possible he travelled by taxi or by a lift in a friend's car.

The porter of his flats had once found him, curled up and kicking violently, in the lift, and Ronald had subsequently gone over the usual explanations in patient parrot-like sequence. And, on these out-of-doors occasions, wherever they might take place, Ronald would go home to bed and sleep for twelve to fourteen hours at a stretch. But in latter years most of his fits occurred at home, in his room, in his one-roomed flat in the Old Brompton Road; so that his friends came to believe that he suffered less frequently than he actually did.

Ronald had settled down to be an amiable fellow with a gangling appearance, slightly hunched shoulders, slightly neglected-looking teeth, and hair going prematurely grey.

'You could marry,' said his doctor.

'I couldn't,' Ronald said.

'You could have children. Direct inheritance is very rare. The risk is very slight. You could marry. In fact, you ought –'

'I couldn't,' Ronald said.

'Wait till you meet the right girl. The right girl can be very wonderful, very understanding, when a fellow has a disability like yours. It's a question of meeting the right girl.'

Ronald had met the right girl five years after his return from America. Her wonderful understanding of his fits terrified him as much as her beauty moved him. She was the English-born daughter of German refugees. She was brown, healthy, shining, still in her teens and splendidly built. For two years she washed his socks and darned them, counted his laundry, did his Saturday shopping, went abroad with him, slept with him, went to the theatre with him.

'I'm perfectly capable of getting the theatre tickets,' he said.

'Don't worry, darling, I'll get them in the lunch hour,' she said.

'Look, Hildegarde, it isn't necessary for you to mother me. I'm not an imbecile.'

'I know, darling. You're a genius.'

But in any case the trouble between them had to do with hand-writing. Hildegarde had taken to studying the subject, the better to understand the graphologist in her lover. Hildegarde took a short course, amazingly soaking up, by sheer power of memory, the sort of facts which Ronald had no ability to memorize and which in any case, if he was called upon to employ them, he would have felt obliged to look up in reference books.

Thus equipped, Hildegarde frequently aired her facts, her dates, her documentary references.

'You have a better memory than mine,' Ronald said one Sunday morning when they were slopping about in their bedroom slippers in Ronald's room.

'I shall be able to memorize for both of us,' she said.

And that very afternoon she said, 'Have you ever had ear trouble?'

'Ear trouble?'

'Yes, trouble with your ears?'

'Only as a child,' he said. 'Earache.'

She was by his desk, looking down at some handwritten notes of his.

'The formation of your capital "I's" denotes ear trouble,' she said. 'There are signs, too, in the variations of the angles that you like to have your own way, probably as the result of your mother's early death and the insufficiency of your father's interest in you. The emotional rhythm is irregular, which means that your behaviour is sometimes incomprehensible to those around you.' She laughed up at him. 'And most of all, your handwriting shows that you're a sort of *genius*.'

'Where did you get all this?' Ronald said.

'I've read some text-books. There must be something in it – it's a branch of graphology, after all.'

'Have you practised interpreting various people's characters from their handwriting, and tested the results against experience?'

'No, not yet. I've only just read the books. I memorized everything.'

'Your memory is better than mine,' Ronald said.

'I'll be able to remember for us both.'

And he thought, when we're married, she'll do everything for both of us. So that, when he remonstrated against her obtaining the theatre tickets, and told her he could perfectly well get them – 'I'm not an imbecile' – and she replied, 'I know, darling, you're a genius' – he decided to end the affair with this admirable woman. For it was an indulgent and motherly tone of voice which told him he was a genius, and he saw himself being cooked for, bought for, thought for, provided for, and overwhelmed by her in the years to come. He saw, as in a vision, himself coming round from his animal frenzy, his limbs still jerking and the froth on his lips – and her shining brown eyes upon him, her well-formed lips repeating as he woke such loving patronizing lies as: 'You'll be all right, darling. It's just that you're a genius.' Which would indicate, not her belief about his mental capacity but her secret belief in the superiority of her own.

After the affair had ended Ronald took to testing his memory lest it was failing him as a result of his disease. On the Saturday morning when the small thin man, Patrick Seton, had been pointed out to him in the café as one who was coming up for committal on Tuesday, Ronald, having faintly felt a passing sense of recognition, and left the café, and gone home, began once more to think of the man. But Ronald could not recall him or anything to do with him. He wished he had asked Martin Bowles the man's name. In a vexed way, Ronald sorted out his groceries, chucking them into their places in the cupboard. Then he went across to the pub.

There, drinking dark stout, were white-haired, dark-faced Walter Prett, art-critic, who was looking at a diet sheet, Matthew Finch, with his colourful smile, and black curly hair, London correspondent of the *Irish Echo*, and Ewart Thornton, the dark, deep-voiced grammar-school master who was a Spiritualist. These were bachelors of varying degrees of confirmation.

Ronald was actually forbidden alcohol, but he had found that the small quantity which he liked to drink made no difference to his epilepsy, and that the very act of ordering a drink gave him a liberated feeling.

He took his beer, sat down at his friends' table, and soundlessly sipped. In nearly five minutes' time he said, 'Nice to see you all here.'

Matthew Finch ran a finger through his black curls. Sometimes a desire came over Ronald to run his fingers through Matthew's black curls, but he had given up wondering if he were a latent homosexual, merely on the evidence of this one urge. Once he had seen a married couple rumple Matthew's hair in a united spontaneous gesture.

'Nice to see you all together,' Ronald said.

'Eggs, boiled or poached only,' Walter Prett read out in a sad voice from his diet sheet. 'Sour pickles but not sweet pickles. *No* barley, rice, macaroni –' he read quietly, then his voice became louder, and even Ronald, who was used to Walter Prett's changing tones, was startled by this. 'Fresh fruit of any kind, including bananas, also water-packed canned fruits,' Walter remarked modestly. 'No butter,' he shrieked, 'no fat or oil,' he roared.

'I've got mounds of homework,' said Ewart Thornton, 'because the half-term tests have begun.'

Matthew went over to the bar and brought back two pickled onions on a plate, and ate them.

TWO

It was six o'clock in the evening of that Saturday in a third-floor double room in Ebury Street. Patrick Seton sat in a meagre arm-chair which, since he was narrow at the shanks and shoulders, he did not fill as people usually did. Alice Dawes was propped in one of the divan beds, still half-dressed. Her friend, Elsie Forrest, sat on the other divan and folded Alice's skirt longwise.

'If only you would eat something you would see the thing in proportion,' Elsie said.

'God, how can I eat? Why should I eat?' Alice said.

'You ought to build up your strength,' Patrick Seton said in his voice which seemed to fade away at the end of each sentence.

'What's the use of her building up her strength if she's going to lose it that way?' Elsie said.

'It was only a suggestion,' Patrick said, so that they could hardly hear the last syllable.

'Well, I'm not going to do it,' Alice said. 'You'll have to think of something else.'

'There's this unfortunate occurrence next week. . . .'

'I don't see,' said Elsie, 'how they can bring you up on a charge if they haven't any grounds at all.'

'Not the slightest grounds,' Patrick said, more boldly than usual. 'I'll be acquitted. It's a case of a jealous, frustrated woman trying to get her own back on me.'

'You must have had to do with her,' Elsie said.

'I never touched her, and I give you my word of honour,' Patrick said. 'It's all her imagination. She took a fancy to me at a séance, and I was sorry for her because she was lonely, and then I took rooms at her place and gave her advice. Of course, now, she's made up this utter entire fabrication. That's my defence. An utter, entire, and absolute fabrication.'

'Funny the police are taking it up if they've no proof,' Elsie said.

Alice said from the bed, 'I've got every faith in Patrick, Elsie. The police wouldn't allow him his freedom if they thought he was guilty. They would have him under arrest.'

'Well, if he's so sure he's going to get off, why did he bother to tell you? It's a shame upsetting you like this in your condition.'

'I only,' Patrick said softly, stroking his silver-yellow hair with his thin grey hand, and gazing at Alice with his pale juvenile eyes, 'wanted to put it to Alice that after Tuesday and when this unfortunate occurrence is over we could make a fresh start if she would see the specialist and have something done before nature takes its course, and –'

'I won't have an abortion,' Alice said. 'I'd do anything else for you, Patrick, you know that. But I won't have it done. I'd be terrified.'

'There's no danger,' Patrick said. 'Not these days.'

'I would never risk it,' Alice said. 'Not with my disease.'

'He may be unlucky on Tuesday,' Elsie said.

'No question of it,' Patrick said.

'Oh, Elsie, you don't know Patrick,' Alice said.

Elsie said, 'Why don't you both slip off abroad this week-end, while there's time?'

Alice looked at Patrick, clutching her throat, for she had once been to a school of drama, and though she was not an insincere girl, she sometimes remembered to express those emotions which she wished to reveal, by certain miming movements of the head, hands, shoulders, feet, eyes and eyelids. So she clutched her throat and looked at Patrick to convey a vulnerable anticipation of his reply.

His reply was so low-voiced that Elsie said 'What?'

'Difficulty about passports if one is discovered. It would' – his voice rose to loud assertion – 'look like an admission of guilt.'

'Patrick is right.' Alice's hand dropped from her throat and lay limp, palm-upward, on the divan-cover.

'You're going to leave Alice in a nice pickle if the case goes against you,' Elsie said. 'How long could you get at the outside?'

'Oh, Elsie,' said Alice. 'Don't.'

Patrick looked at Elsie as if this remark were sufficient reply.

'And when,' said Elsie, 'does your divorce case come up?'

'In a couple of months,' said Patrick, crossing his knees and looking down upon those knees.

'What date?'

'Twenty-fifth of November,' Alice said. 'I remember that date all right, because we'll be able to get married on the twenty-sixth.'

Patrick's blue eyes dwelt upon her affectionately.

'On the twenty-sixth,' he whispered and closed his eyes for a moment to savour his joy.

'I feel hungry,' Alice said.

'Put your skirt on,' Elsie said, 'and we'll go and get something. Don't eat anything greasy, you'll only bring it up again.'

Alice began wearily to get up.

'I'm starving,' she said.

Elsie said, 'Did you remember to take your injection this morning?'

'Of course,' Alice said. 'Don't be silly. Patrick gives me my injection every morning, regularly.' She pointed to the jug with the syringe stuck into it.

'Well, I only wondered, because you said you were so hungry. Don't diabetics always get hungry if they don't have their injections?'

'She's hungry because she brought up her lunch,' said Patrick defensively.

Elsie looked at him suspiciously. 'I hope you do give her the injection regularly,' she said. 'She needs taking care of.'

It was then Patrick's mind turned a corner.

But he replied meekly: 'Give her a good meal.' He stroked Alice's cheek. 'Don't work too hard tonight, darling.'

'I doubt if I can go,' said Alice who was standing shakily while zipping up her skirt. 'Elsie will have to ring up.'

'She'll have to get an easier job,' Elsie said. 'Coffee-bar work is too hard for a girl in her condition.'

'What do you see in him?' Elsie said.

Alice took her mouthful of omelette at slow motion to denote reflectiveness, although she knew the answer.

'Well,' she said, 'I'm in love with him. He's *got* something. You don't know how wonderful he can be when we're alone. He's so good on the spiritual side. He recites poetry so beautifully. He's a sort of a real artist.'

'I'll agree,' Elsie said, 'he's a first-rate medium. That I do admit.'

'And he's got a soul.'

'Yes,' said Elsie, 'I see that. But you know, he's a bit old for you.'

'I like an older man. I think there's something special about an older man.'

'Yes, but you wouldn't call him much of a man. I mean, if you didn't know him, if you just saw him in the street without knowing he was a medium, you'd think he was a little half-pint job.'

'But I do know him. He means everything to me. He loves poetry and beauty.'

'I'll tell you,' Elsie said. 'I've never really trusted him. He hasn't got a cheque book, you told me yourself. Now that's funny, for one thing.'

'He's not mean with his money. I've never said –'

'No, but he hasn't got a cheque book, the fact remains.'

'I think that's a materialistic way to judge. Patrick is not a materialist.'

'No,' said Elsie, 'I don't say he is. But I think he gets carried away and makes up a lot of these stories he –'

'Oh, Elsie, a man like Patrick must have had a remarkable life. He's been through it. You can see that. And his wife must have been hell. Do you know, she –'

'Funny thing about that divorce,' Elsie said, 'he doesn't seem much worried about it.'

'No, he's just waiting for it to come through, that's all.'

'You'd think he'd have a bit more to do with the lawyers than he seems to have. And she might claim on him –'

'She hasn't a leg to stand on in the case. He's divorcing her, she's not divorcing him.'

'What's her name?'

'I don't know. I wouldn't like to ask. It would be indelicate.'

'Seen a photo?'

'No, Elsie. Patrick isn't that sort of man, Elsie.'

'And about this at the Magistrate's Court on Tuesday,' Elsie said, 'well, I don't know what to think.'

Alice started to cry.

'You're only upsetting yourself,' Elsie remarked, while she ate steadily on as one who proves, by eating on during another's distress, the unshakeable sanity of their advice. Elsie also permitted herself to say, as she reached for another roll, 'And you're kidding yourself where Patrick's concerned. I don't believe half a word he says. I think he's in trouble. You take my advice, you could clear off now, have the baby in a home, get it adopted, and start afresh.'

Alice said, 'I'll never do that, never. I trust him.'

'He wanted you to get rid of the kid.'

'Men are like that.'

'Stop crying,' Elsie said, 'people are looking at you.'

'I can't help it when you call him a liar. What about the message he got for you from Colin that night at the Wider Infinity? You didn't say that was lies. You said –'

'Oh, he's a good medium. But when Patrick's under the control I shouldn't think he could help saying what comes to him from the other side.'

At eight o'clock Patrick Seton walked along the Bayswater Road, turned off it, then turned again into a cul-de-sac, at the end of which he mounted the steps of a house converted into flats where he pressed the top left-hand bell.

Presently the door was opened by a tall, skinny young man of about twenty-three, with a cheerful smile.

'Oh, Patrick!' he said, politely standing back to let Patrick pass into the passage.

'Well, Tim,' said Patrick as he climbed the stairs, 'and how's the Central Office of Information?'

'The Central Office of Information,' said Tim, 'is all right, thank you.' He cleaned his glasses with a white handkerchief as he followed Patrick upstairs to a modernly decorated flat. From the open door of a room came the sociable sound of voices. On the door of another room was hung a card on which were printed in blue Gothic letters the words

The Wider Infinity
'In my Father's house are many mansions. . . .'
(John 14, 2)

Tim passed by this room on a frivolous tip-toe to conceal whatever awe he might feel towards it, and led the way to the room where the company was assembled. Patrick stood a moment in the doorway, looking round swiftly to see who was present. At his entrance the chatter ceased for two seconds, then started again. Several people tentatively greeted Patrick while Tim, with the restrained gestures of one who is not above playing the well-trained footman, fetched Patrick a cup of China tea from a side table.

A distinguished-looking woman with white hair and a lined face, the features of which were absolutely symmetrical, appeared. Patrick respectfully put down his tea and took his hostess's hand in silence except for the word 'Marlene'.

'Patrick,' she replied merely; and she rested her eyes on his, setting her head at a slight angle so that her long ear-rings swung as in a breeze.

Patrick's lower lip thinly began to tremble as he said in his almost inaudible voice, 'I nearly didn't come in view of the unfortunate occurrence. But I felt it was my duty to do so.'

'You were right, Patrick,' Marlene said, still gazing at his eyes intensely. 'There are naturally mixed feelings amongst us and she has been circulating rumours. But I have – and I know I can speak for the members of the Interior Spiral if not for the Wider Infinity at large – implicit faith in you. I'm only too grateful that we were guided to delay disclosing to her the existence of the Interior Spiral, that was fortunate. And had it not been for your powers as a great medium, and the warnings, we should most probably have issued the Communication to her last week. Oh – here she is.'

A dumpy much-powdered woman of middle age, wearing light-rimmed glasses, a grey felt hat, and a blue coat and skirt, had been ushered into the room by young Tim. She smiled brightly at her acquaintances by the door and even the lenses of her glasses seemed to glisten smilingly upon them. She had not noticed Patrick, who had resumed his tea-cup into which he was gazing with dignity. Marlene glided up to the newcomer, took both her hands, bestowed upon her a customary soul-to-soul gaze, kissed her upon the cheek, and said, 'Freda, you're just in time. I am about to proclaim the Commencement.'

'Tea, Mrs Flower?' Tim said to Freda, with the cup and saucer in his hand.

'The Commencement is about to start, Tim,' said Marlene, and as Tim hovered between handing the tea to Freda and not handing it to her, Marlene said, 'But of course you must have a little tea first, Freda, you must have your tea first.'

Marlene noticed, without truly observing, a large man with pink and white cheeks whom she had not seen at previous meetings. He was standing massively half in, half out of the room, and he had apparently arrived at the same time as Freda. But Marlene did not take great notice of him, since there were few meetings at which a newcomer was not present, having been brought along by someone or other. The pink-and-white-cheeked man looked rather like, possibly, a friend of Tim's. Tim had yet to learn to be reliable.

Marlene said to Freda, 'I shan't ring the bell till you've finished your tea. Don't hurry.'

Freda gulped her tea, with her eyes wandering over the rim of the cup. Suddenly she started at the sight of Patrick.

'So *he's* here,' Freda said.

'My dear Freda, mustn't we subordinate all our materialistic endeavours to those of the spirit?'

'It's most upsetting,' Freda said, 'and I'm surprised he has the nerve to show his face in here again. He's a fraud.'

Tim gave out a gentle cultivated noise from the throat as if he really were clearing it, and shifted himself gracefully to another group.

Marlene's ear-rings swung as she moved her head distastefully from Freda's remarks. 'The word fraud,' she said, 'is of the World. Freda, I don't think it should be voiced here. But I do see – I do understand – how a type of behaviour which is normal in our element may appear, shall we say, mysterious in yours.' She touched Mrs Flower's hand in absolution from all her dumpy limitations. 'I only hope,' she said, 'that nothing will happen to bring the Wider Infinity into disrepute. For myself, I don't care. I am thinking of – well, finish your tea, Freda dear, it is time for the Commencement.'

She moved away, and dark Ewart Thornton, who was one of the assembly, presently took her place, declaring deeply in her ear, 'I'm with you, Freda. A lot of us here tonight are with you. I meant to write to say so to you, but I've got such mounds of homework. The mid-term examinations ...'

Freda's spectacles shone with gratitude. 'Does Marlene know your mind on the subject?' she said.

Ewart placed a finger to his lips while Marlene at the other end of the room proclaimed:

'The Circle will now enter the Sanctuary of Light.'

Tea-cups were placed down and a hush fell on the assembly. Marlene Cooper led the way, as she had done regularly since the year after her husband died, and she had taken to thoughts of the spirit. For how, she felt, could it be that Harry Cooper, who his worst business enemies admitted was sheer dynamite, could come to nought in the end? 'No,' she said, 'Harry is as alive as ever he was. He is communicating with me and I am communicating with him.' Certainly this was the case when he was alive, since they had then indulged in frequent noisy rows in different parts of the globe, she standing tensely clothed in her distinguished appearance, clasping and unclasping her long fingers, and shrieking; he sitting usually in an arm-chair answering her with short, loaded, meaningful words of power and contempt. He had been buried three months when, convinced of his dynamic survival, she had had him dug up and cremated, since this, it seemed vaguely to her, was more in keeping with the life beyond. To see his ashes scattered in the Garden of Remembrance was to conceive Harry more nearly as thin air, and since she had come to believe so ardently in Harry the spirit, she simply could not let him lie in the grave and rot.

Shortly after the cremation Marlene joined the Wider Infinity, an independent spiritualist group, proud of its independence from the great organized groups, and operating from a room in the region of Victoria. During the period of her initiation Marlene was impressed, the more and more especially when personal messages began to come through from Harry on the other side.

Patrick Seton was the first medium to get through to Harry.

'I have a message for our new sister, from Henry. Henry will not speak himself tonight but he will speak on another occasion when Carl is in control of Patrick,' said Patrick. 'But in the meantime Henry sends his affectionate regards and is thinking of you in his happy abode. He particularly wants to say you have been too generous and have stood by too long and let others take first place. You were born to be a leader but you have not yet fulfilled yourself. Now is the time to start living your true life.' Patrick moaned. His mouth drooped, the lower lip disappearing into his chin. He looked very ill by the dim green light, and even when he had come round and the full lights were on, his complexion was more grey and the lines on his face deeper than before he had gone under. He was genuinely shaken.

'Amazing,' Marlene whispered after the séance. For Henry was Harry's real name, and the Carl who was going to act as control in the promised future might very conceivably be that Carl, her boy friend that was, who had been killed in a motor-race in 1938; and indeed Marlene had been moved to wonder as far as she dared how Harry and Carl were making out together in the land of perpetual summer. And it had been summer-time when Harry had found out about Carl. But the possibility of Carl's acting as the spirit control between Harry and the medium seemed to make everything all right, and indeed there was an authentic rightness in the idea, for although Harry's had been the more dynamic personality, there was no use pretending that Carl's had not been the rarer.

And she thought it very like Harry to urge her to push herself to the fore. It was exactly what Harry would advise, being now incapacitated, or rather released from materialistic endeavours. It was almost as if Harry were urging her to take his place in life. It was so true that she had always let others take place before her.

Marlene, in order to be fair, went and attended a séance of another spiritualist group on an island near Richmond. But this was a disappointment, for the people were not quite the reasonable, respectable sort one expected to find in the spiritualist movement. One young man had hair waving down to his waist. One middle-aged woman with a huge blotchy face wore a tight cotton dress although it was early March. The place was not heated, and Marlene shivered. The woman in the tight cotton dress told Marlene she was going to give clairvoyance. She told Marlene nothing about Harry, only advised her to be careful of false friends, and not to despair, she wouldn't end her life alone.

'I'm not despairing,' Marlene said.

The other members looked at Marlene with hushed hostile warnings, since she was interrupting the woman in her trance.

So Marlene remained with the Wider Infinity at Victoria. Soon, however, inspired by the dynamic spirit of Harry, she began to note this and that member who was perhaps unworthy of its high purpose. She led a purgative faction.

'We must,' she said to Ewart Thornton, that big sane grammar-school master, 'rid our Body of the cranks.'

'I quite agree,' Ewart said. 'They lower the tone.'

Two clergymen who were unembarrassed by wives or livings were retained; several women cashiers and bookkeepers who did not mind the journey from Wembley, Osterley and Camberwell on Monday and Thursday evenings; two middle-aged retired spinsters who were interested in art; one or two of Marlene's old friends who, however, were erratic in their attendance; a childless married couple in their early thirties; three widows; an Indian student who had been doing undefined research at the British Museum for fifteen years; a retired policeman whose wife, not a spiritualist, was a doctor's receptionist; Ewart Thornton, the schoolmaster; and Patrick Seton, who was, by common consent, the life and soul of the Circle.

'We must have a cross-section of the community,' Marlene declared. 'A sane cross-section. Why can't we have a labourer, for instance?'

No labourer who was worthy of his hire could be found. Ewart Thornton, however, was the means of introducing to the group a number of single schoolmasters and Civil Servants who, although interested in spiritualism, had never had sufficient courage to attend a séance. Some of these bachelors became regular members, others attended occasionally and compulsively when the desire to do so overwhelmed them. 'My bachelors,' Marlene called them.

'At least,' she said, 'we are all respectable now; we have no cranks.'

'I hate cranks,' Ewart said. 'Insufferable people.'

By the end of that year the Wider Infinity had moved its head-quarters to Marlene's flat in Bayswater and Patrick and Ewart Thornton had so much become her closest intimates that very often this trio held private séances which were kept secret from the rest of the group. 'Carl and Harry,' Marlene said, 'definitely understand my nature now better than they did in the flesh. Carl of course was always more evolved. Why does he call Harry by the name of Henry, I wonder?'

Patrick said, 'I'm only the medium,' and his voice died away on the last syllable.

'But you're a genius, Patrick – isn't he, Ewart?'

'Absolutely. That was excellent advice that came through from Guide Gabi about my headmaster. Had his character to a T. He expects me to do mounds of homework. Well, I –'

'Señor Gabi is one of my best Guides,' Patrick murmured. 'But Henry is coming on. Through the influence of Carl, he –'

'Why doesn't Carl call him Harry?' Marlene said. 'He never called him Henry while in the flesh, he always called him Harry.'

'The name Henry represents his primary and more noble personality,' Patrick said gently. 'I'm sorry, Marlene, I'm only the medium, I can't say Harry when I get Henry.'

'Patrick, you're wonderful. It only proves your honesty.'

She put a great deal of money into the training of mediums, Patrick Seton being the principal trainer; she liked most of all to have the more intelligent members, or those rare few with university degrees, trained as mediums. It gave her a thrill to see these knowledgeable novices going into, and coming round from, their first and second feeble trances.

Eventually she recruited her young nephew, Tim, whom she had discovered to have no religion at all. Tim had not enjoined, but she, perceiving his mind, had promised secrecy about this activity where the family was concerned.

Meantime Patrick had made a tremendous advance in divining how matters stood between Harry and Carl on the other side, and in instructing Marlene, through Harry, how best to develop her personality.

At the first séance to be held by the newly constructed Circle in Marlene's flat, Patrick had gone under in style with a quivering of the lower lip and chin, upturned eyes and convulsive whinnies. A few threads of ectoplasm, like white tape in the dim light, proceeded from the corners of his mouth. Then, in a voice hugely louder than his own he announced,

'I am now coming in touch with the control. This is control. Henry will speak through Patrick under the control of Carl.'

Two or three of the Circle, as they had sat hand in hand round Patrick, shuffled slightly at this mention of Carl and Henry, for that particular combine was, in the experience of the Circle, exclusively interested in the affairs of Marlene and did not seem aware of the claims of the Wider Infinity as a whole.

'Guide Henry speaking: my dear wife, there are two on earth who mean a lot to you. You can depend upon them and especially upon one who will never desert you unto death. Do not be deceived by appearances. I am well and happy. Do you remember the Loebl Pass where we stopped at an inn and ate a marvellous omelette?'

'Oh,' Marlene said.

'Control lifting,' Patrick said. 'Guide Henry is wearing leather shorts and an open-neck shirt.'

'Oh, how it takes me back!' said Marlene when the lights had gone up. 'Honestly,' she said to the newer members of the Circle, 'I have a photograph of Harry on that holiday wearing his leather shorts and –'

Later she said to Ewart and Patrick, 'I wish they wouldn't concentrate so much on me from the other side. I think some of the less evolved members may feel I'm getting more than my fair share.'

Ewart said, 'You are the most dominant personality in the room, Marlene. It stands to reason.'

'Stands to reason,' Patrick said, 'Marlene.'

'Well, I'll stay outside at our next séance. I definitely felt a hostile aura after Patrick returned to us during our last session. These people feel: you pay your money – pittance that it is – and you take your choice.'

'Not everyone feels that way,' Ewart said.

'Whom can we trust and respect?'

Ewart mentioned a few of the more docile and regular attenders, Marlene eliminated half of them, and it was thus that the Interior Spiral, their secret group, came to be formed within the Wider Infinity.

'We must keep the ramifications pure,' Marlene stated, 'we must exert a concealed influence on the less evolved brethren and the crackpots and snobs who keep creeping in.'

On the Saturday night before Patrick's appearance before the magistrates was anticipated, when Freda Flower had put down her cup, the company trod reverently into the Sanctuary of Light. Patrick ignored the widow, Freda Flower, exaltedly, as enemies do in church;

but she glanced at him nervously. Marlene did not herself join them; this was now her habit on most evenings, since her presence so invariably attracted all the spiritual attentions available to the company.

Tim led the way and acted as usher, placing about twenty people with the conviction of extreme tact, the results of which, however, did not satisfy all. Some, who were placed so that they had an imperfect view of the medium's chair were restive, but nothing like a scene occurred in this velvet-hung dark sanctuary of light.

This room had previously been a dining-room in one wall of which was a service recess opening to the kitchen. The curtains that covered this recess were arranged to part imperceptibly at a point which admitted of Marlene's watching the proceedings from the kitchen, which she felt was only her due. And there she stood, in the dark, watching Tim's arrangements in the dim green-lit séance room.

She was furious when she saw Tim, as it were with the height of aplomb, place Freda Flower, the beastly widow who had gone to the police about Patrick, in the place of honour directly facing the medium.

All were seated except Tim who, before sitting down in the humblest position from the visual point of view, took off his glasses, wiped them, replaced them slowly and, with an elegant lightning sweep of the same handkerchief, dusted the chair on which he was to sit, at the same time replacing his handkerchief in his pocket. He then sat, joining tentative hands with his neighbour, as the others had done. Marlene, from her place behind the recess, watched her nephew closely and by an access of intuition despairing of Tim's becoming even teachable as to the seriousness of the Circle, far less a member of the Interior Spiral.

It was then she noticed once more the newcomer, seated in his massive bulk, beside Freda Flower, and in fact he was whispering something to Freda Flower. Marlene realized it was Freda who had brought him to the Circle and felt deeply apprehensive.

All hands were joined. The green light shone dimly. Ewart said, 'We will now have two minutes' silent prayer.'

Heads were bowed. Before Marlene had taken over the Circle this silence had been followed by a hymn to the tune of 'She'll be coming round the mountain' and which went as follows,

> We shall meet them all again by and by,
> By and by.

Marlene had found that this hymn was unaccountably not ease-making to the schoolmasters and clergymen and more educated members, and on reflection even herself decided that she did not in fact want to meet the whole of her acquaintance again by and by. And so, after trying several other hymns which, for reasons of association, seemed unsuitable to various members, she had eliminated hymn-singing altogether. So they had a silence.

After the silence Ewart said, 'Mr Patrick Seton will now unite the Two Worlds.'

Patrick had been bound at the arms and calves of his legs by canvas strips to the chair. He let his head fall forward. He breathed deeply in and out several times. Soon, his body dropped in its bonds. His knees fell apart. His long hands hung, perpendicular, over the arms of the chair. Not only did the green-lit colour seem to leave his face but the flesh itself, so that it looked like a skin-covered skull up to his thin pale hair.

He breathed deeply in the still dim room, second after second. Then his eyes opened and turned upward in their sockets. Foam began to bubble at his mouth and faintly trickled down his chin. He opened his mouth and a noise like a clang issued from it. The Circle was familiar with this clang: it betokened the presence of the spirit-guide called Gabi. Soon the clang was forming words which became clearer to the listeners in the circle round Patrick and to Marlene behind the hatch.

'A message for one of our sisters present whose name resembles a plant. It comes from a short man in a Harris-tweed suit through Guide Gabi who is speaking. The short man appears to be bearing on his back a long tube-like sack of faggots; no, they are golf clubs –'

Freda Flower cried, 'That's my husband – !' but was immediately hushed by the rest of the Circle.

'His name is William,' clanged the voice. 'He appears to be in a most disturbed state of mind. He looks very upset, and is trying to get a message through to our sister whose name is like a plant. He is extremely concerned about her.'

'Why is he going for a game of golf if he is so upset?' – This question crashed into the atmosphere; it came from the large newcomer sitting next to Freda Flower.

'Not now, Mike,' she said. 'Ask the questions later.'

The clanging voice had stopped talking through Patrick's lips. Patrick had begun to writhe a little in his bonds. His feet kicked with sharp clicks of the heels on the parquet wooden floor.

Ewart Thornton dropped his neighbours' hands and came over to Mike. He bent over him. He said, 'By interrupting the medium you may do him great harm. You may even kill him. If you interrupt again you will have to go outside.'

Freda said, 'I'm sorry, Ewart, but my friend, Dr Mike Garland, is a clairvoyant.'

'He must not give clairvoyance at this stage.'

Dr Garland smiled and joined hands once more with those on either side of him. Ewart returned to his place. Patrick had stopped writhing and was apparently sunk in a deep sleep. He snored for a while through his open mouth from which presently emerged once more the inarticulate clang of Guide Gabi's voice. For a while it repeated sounds which could not be identified. Eventually it said, 'The sister whose name is of a plant is troubled in spirit.'

Tears which she could not wipe away, since both her hands were engaged, spurted down Freda's cheeks.

'I see a man,' the voice said, 'in a Harris-tweed suit –'

'What colour?' said Dr Garland in a persuasive voice.

'A green or a blue,' the voice replied, 'I can't say exactly.'

'That's him!' said Freda, brokenly.

The voice from Patrick's lips said, 'His message to the sister with the name like a plant is this: Do not act against another of the brethren. If you do so it will be at your peril.'

Several of the group gasped or muttered, for it was known that a court case was pending between Patrick and Mrs Flower. Many peered forward to scrutinize Patrick's appearance, but not even the most shaken or the most easily prone to doubt could find evidence that he was faking his trance. His physical characteristics had plainly undergone a change. The skin of his face appeared to cling even closer to the bone than when he had first gone under and the cheek-bones stood out alarmingly; his mouth had widened by about two inches, seeming now to reach almost from ear to ear as the clanging voice continued to proceed from it.

'Let the sister beware of false friends and materialistic advice. The letter killeth but the spirit giveth life. What shall it profit a man if he gain the whole world and loseth his soul?'

'He was so well-read in the Bible,' said Mrs Flower, weeping.

The large pink-faced newcomer announced aloud, 'I am going to give clairvoyance.'

'No,' Freda whispered, though all could hear, 'I feel, somehow, this is genuine after all. I'd like to think it all over –'

The newcomer shouted above Patrick's din, 'Nevertheless, I am going to give clairvoyance.'

Ewart came over to him again and said, 'Are you a trained clairvoyant? I've warned you about the danger to the medium of interruption.'

'I am a trained and authentic clairvoyant,' said Freda's friend.

'Guide Gabi,' Patrick clanged on, 'is about to give the initials of the spirit in the Harris tweed suit. The initials are W.F.'

'William!' said Freda.

'I am a trained clairvoyant,' shouted Freda's friend. 'And I hereby give notice that I am about to give clairvoyance to the medium in the chair.'

'Señor Gabi speaking,' Patrick clanged; 'I hereby give notice that I reinforce the warnings given by the aforesaid spirit whose initials are W. F. to the sister among our members. These warnings can only be disregarded at the utmost peril to the sister whose name resembles a plant.'

The man beside Freda had thrown back his head and lifted his hands to his temples.

'No, Mike!' Freda moaned.

'I see,' bellowed Mike Garland to the ceiling, 'I see the medium in the public court, under a charge of fraud. I see the so-called medium exposed. I see –'

A small rustling hubbub had arisen amongst the audience.

'Señor Gabi speaking,' came the voice from Patrick. 'There is a hostile spirit among us who may cause infinite harm to –'

'Patrick Seton, you are a fraud,' boomed Mike to the ceiling. 'And I challenge you, if Señor Gabi is an authentic guide, to give the initials of my name.'

The small rustle amongst the audience immediately became a hush.

'Señor Gabi speaking: the first initial of the hostile spirit is M.'

'You are a fraud. You heard Mrs Flower calling me Mike,' boomed Mike. 'What is the second initial?'

Foam appeared at Patrick's mouth and bubbled for a few seconds.

Ewart murmured, 'This is dangerous to him. We must stop it.'

'The second initial,' Mike shouted.

'The second initial,' came the clang, 'is G.'

'He's right!' said Mrs Flower. 'Oh, Mike, I've been mistaken.'

'You are a fraud,' shouted Mike. 'You have heard my name. You heard Mrs Flower introducing me to a member.'

Patrick dribbled from the mouth and his head dropped with exhaustion, and the water from his mouth dripped down his coat. His eyes closed.

Ewart called out, 'This disruption must cease. The clairvoyant will kindly leave the séance room.'

But Mike, with his hands to his temples and head thrown back, began to intone. 'There will be weeping and gnashing of teeth. I see the prisoner brought to judgement and cast into outer darkness. There will be a trial. I see a young woman in distress and an older woman justified. I see –'

Patrick cast up his eyes. 'Guide Gabi warns the Circle of an evil influence present,' he said. He lifted his head high and tossed it like a war horse.

'You'll put him in a frenzy,' Ewart shouted, and the audience began also to cry out phrases like 'Too bad', 'Wicked', 'An evil influence', and 'Uncivilized'.

The room was in turmoil when Marlene flung wide the door. 'What is this turmoil?' she said, trembling with the impatience she had been repressing throughout her service-hatch vigil. She then switched on the lights.

The noise ceased except for a sobbing sound from Freda. Patrick drooped once more, and breathed as one in a deep sleep. Mike shook his head, covered as it was with sweat, brought it to a normal level and his eyes into normal focus. Patrick slowly came round and looked at the roomful of people in a dazed way.

Freda then collapsed with a thud on the floor, where she continued her sobbing, her legs moving as in remorseful pain and revealing the curiosity obscene sight of her demure knee-length drawers.

'Throw some water over her,' ordered Marlene.

'Tim, fetch some water – Where's Tim? Tim, where are you? Where's that boy?'

But at some point during the dark and troubled séance Tim had slid silently away.

THREE

'Never again,' said Tim. 'It was absolute hell let loose.'

'Tell me a bit more,' said Ronald Bridges. Just then Tim's telephone rang.

'Oh, Aunt Marlene,' said Tim. 'Sorry I keep forgetting – *Marlene*. After all, you are my aunt and – yes, Marlene. No, Mar – Yes, it was just that I was over*whelmed* Marlene. Yes, I was just going to ring you.'

He made a sign to Ronald to fetch over his drink.

'No, Aunt – sorry, – No, Marlene. Yes. No. Of course. Of course not. Look, I've got a fellow here on official business. Yes, I do know it's Sunday, but this was urgent and he called – Tomorrow at eleven. Right, I'll ring you at eleven. Yes, at eleven. Good-bye, Aunt – Yes, at eleven. Yes. No. 'Bye.'

Tim took up his drink and subsided on to the sofa. 'As I was saying,' he said, then closed his eyes and slowly sipped his drink.

'I've often been tempted to go to a spiritualist meeting,' Ronald said, 'just to see.'

'I nearly died,' said Tim opening his eyes behind his glasses.

'I thought you had actually joined the thing,' Ronald said.

'Well, yes, I suppose I had. But last night's show was something special.'

'How did it end?'

'I left after the second act.'

'Finished with it now?' Ronald said.

'Well, yes. But it needs caution.' Tim nodded over to the telephone as if the spirit of his Aunt Marlene, whose voice had a few moments before come over on it, still lingered there. 'She needs handling with tact,' said Tim.

'Whatever made you take it up?'

'Well, it was rather exciting to start with. And it's a fairly bleak world when all is said and done.' He rose and carelessly slopped more gin and tonic into the glasses, without, however, spilling any. 'And, you know,' he said then, 'there is something in it. This medium, Patrick Seton, isn't altogether a fraud, you know. He's got something.'

'Patrick Seton, did you say?' Ronald said.

'Yes. Know him?'

'A meek little thin-faced fellow with white hair?'

'Yes, do you know him?'

'I do remember him,' Ronald said, pleased with this functioning of his memory. For now he was able to place in his mind the man he had seen the previous morning in the coffee-bar. 'There was a case of forgery about five years ago,' Ronald said. 'I had to identify the handwriting. He was convicted.'

'I believe there's another case coming up against him,' Tim said. 'I'm not sure if it's forgery. It's the talk of the Circle. What a crowd!'

'Fraudulent conversion,' Ronald said.

'You seem to know a lot about him.'

'Martin Bowles is prosecuting counsel. He mentioned the case.'

'I can't believe he's entirely a fraud as a medium,' Tim said. 'I've heard him come out with the most terrifying true facts that he couldn't possibly have known about. He once told me during a séance about a personal affair at my office that nobody could have known about except me and another chap. And the other chap hadn't any remote acquaintance with Seton.'

'The affair might have been on your mind, and he might have picked it up by telepathy. Do you believe in telepathy?'

'Well, yes, there seems to be evidence for telepathy. But it's odd that Seton keeps picking things from people's minds. He's got *some*thing.'

'I should like to have heard him,' Ronald said.

'You can go along if you like. Really, I mean it,' Tim said eagerly. 'There are meetings on –'

'No, thanks,' said Ronald. 'You'll have to make your escape some other way.'

'I only thought, if you wanted to see Seton in his trance –'

Ronald said, 'He'll probably be in prison before long.'

'Do you think so? What a pity, in a way,' said Tim.

'Of course I know nothing about the case. But that type doesn't ever stay out in the open for long.'

'I suppose he could be a genuine medium,' Tim said, 'and a fraud in other respects. It's a widow-woman who's taking action against him. I think he used to sleep with her and he got some money off her, and then he stopped sleeping with her and now she's furious. But she seemed pretty scared of him last night when he started to give out messages from her husband who's dead. She'll probably change her mind and withdraw the action.'

'Can she do that?' Ronald said. 'It's a police prosecution.'

'Oh, I don't know, really.'

Tim's telephone rang. 'Yes, Marlene. No, Aunt – No. Well, yes, he's still here. No, I can't manage lunch, I'm afraid, I – Don't be upset, Marlene. Listen. Don't. Yes. No. Hang on a minute.' Tim covered the receiver with his hand.

'Would you come with me to lunch with her?' he said, mouthing at Ronald. 'Not a séance, only lunch.'

Ronald nodded.

'Listen, Marlene,' Tim said, 'I think I can come. Can I bring Ronald Bridges? He's the chap that's with me. Yes, of course he'll be interested. No, I don't think so, no, he's R.C. Yes, I know I said he was here on business but now we've finished our business chat. But of course he's allowed to lunch with you, at least I think so. We're just going for a drink now. Yes. Quarter-past. Yes, thanks. No, yes. 'Bye.'

Then he said to Ronald, 'She's upset. She thinks I'm going to leave the Circle after what happened last night. She's right.'

Ronald said, 'Do you mind if I go home first to fetch my pills?'

'I'll come with you. I can't tell you how grateful I am that you're coming for support. I don't particularly want to *fall out* with Marlene.'

'I was going to fry bacon and eggs,' Ronald said.

'I was going to skip lunch,' Tim said. 'One can't afford two restaurant meals in one day. And yet one's got to eat, hasn't one?'

'There's something about Sunday,' Ronald said, 'which is terrible between one and three o'clock if you aren't in someone's house, eating. That's my feeling.'

'Same here,' said Tim. 'Funny how Sunday gets at you if you aren't given a lunch. Preferably by an aunt or a sort of aunt.'

'Yes, it's nice to see a woman on a Sunday,' Ronald said.

'I sometimes go down to Isobel's with Martin Bowles,' Tim said. 'She's a difficult woman but still one does like her company.'

'On a Sunday,' Ronald said.

'I know exactly what you mean,' Tim said. 'Funny. Now Marlene is difficult, too. But I'm rather fond of her in a way. She thinks I'm after her cash and comforts, the darling. But in fact I'm genuinely fond of her. They don't ever quite realize that.'

'What was so distressing,' Marlene said, 'was hearing all the noise and not being able to *see*.'

'There wasn't much to see,' Tim said, 'it was nearly all noise.'

'You shouldn't have gone away,' said his aunt. 'Why ever did you go away?'

'I was overcome,' Tim said.

'Another time,' his aunt said, 'go and lie down on a bed. Don't just go away.'

'Yes, of course.'

'I've found out the name of the man who came with Freda Flower. He's a Dr Garland. Doctor of what, I don't know. He has quite a reputation as a clairvoyant, but of course he's a fraud. So many frauds manage to get themselves good reputations. They prey on gullible women. Is all this boring you, Mr Bridges?'

'No,' Ronald said. 'It's very interesting.'

'Shall I call you Ronald, Mr Bridges?'

'Please do, I was going to suggest it.'

'I hope you don't mind eating in the kitchen.' She pointed to the shuttered hatch. 'The dining-room is now the Sanctuary. Please call me Marlene. I don't want you to think, Ronald, that what we're discussing is in any way a normal occurrence. It has never happened before at any of our meetings, has it, Tim?'

'Well, things have been working *up* to a row, haven't they?'

'Not at all. The deplorable behaviour of the Circle last night was quite unforeseen.'

Tim stretched his long legs and sprawled on the sofa. He took off his glasses and cleaned them with a white handkerchief, then put on his glasses again. He made a rabbit out of his handkerchief.

'Tim!' said his aunt.

Tim sat up, pulled the rabbit back into a handkerchief, and said 'What?'

'You are not taking this seriously enough. *I* suggest that after lunch we all go into the Sanctuary for fifteen minutes for spiritual repose.' She pointed to the hatch to indicate the Sanctuary. 'I wish Patrick were here to guide us.'

Tim said, 'I shouldn't really like to go in there again. At least, not yet.'

'What do you mean? There's nothing wrong with the room – what was wrong was the evil spirit of that false clairvoyant amongst us.'

'We can't have spiritual repose while Ronald's here,' said Tim, looking desperately at Ronald, 'because Ronald is a Roman Catholic and not permitted to have spiritual repose.'

'I'm anti-Catholic,' said Marlene.

Ronald was used to hearing his hostesses over the years come out with this statement, and had devised various ways of coping with it, according to his mood and to his idea of the hostesses' intentions. If the intelligence seemed to be high and Ronald was in a suitable mood, he replied, 'I'm anti-Protestant' – which he was not; but it sometimes served to shock them into a sense of their indiscretion. On one occasion where the woman was a real bitch, he had walked out. Sometimes he said, 'Oh, are you? How peculiar.' Sometimes he allowed that the woman was merely trying to start up a religious argument, and he would then attempt to explain where he stood with his religion. Or again, he might say, 'Then you've received Catholic instruction?' and, on hearing that this was not so, would comment, 'Then how can you be anti something you don't know about?' which annoyed them; so that Ronald felt uncharitable.

There were always women who confronted him with 'I'm anti-Catholic' as if inviting a rape. Men didn't do this. Mostly, Ronald coped with the statement as he did on this present occasion, when he said to Marlene, 'Oh, I'm sure you're not *really*.'

'Yes really,' Marlene said, as most of them did, 'I am.'

'Well, well,' said Ronald.

'But I don't mean I'm anti *you*,' said Marlene. 'You're sweet.'

'Oh, thanks.'

'There's a distinction,' Tim pointed out, bright with tact, 'between the person and their religion.'

'I see.' Ronald attended closely to his potatoes.

'But you don't like us,' said Marlene. 'In fact, you detest us.'

'Detest you?' said Ronald. 'Why, I think you're charming.'

'Now, now. You're avoiding the question. The fact is, you're not allowed –'

'Ronald's awfully interested in spiritualism,' Tim said.

'He doesn't believe in it,' Marlene said. 'He thinks it's all baloney. He's one of those –'

'I'm sure it's possible to get in touch with the spirits of the dead,' Ronald said.

'Are you?' said Tim. 'Now that's interest –'

'Catholics aren't allowed to do it,' Marlene said.

'We invoke the saints and so on,' Ronald said, 'and they are dead.'

'A very different thing,' Marlene said. 'That's idolatry. In Spain, for instance – well, perhaps I shouldn't say. I once had an Irish maid, she was most difficult. But anyhow, you don't *get through* to the saints, do you? They don't send you messages. Have you heard the actual voice of any one of your saints?'

'No,' said Ronald. 'You've got a point there.'

'I have indeed,' Marlene said. 'I've heard my husband's actual voice. Haven't I, Tim? I've heard Harry. His own dynamic voice.'

'Uncle Harry was always very dynamic,' Tim murmured.

'Have a bit more lamb,' Marlene said. 'It's got to be eaten up. You boys aren't eating anything.'

'Thank you, I will,' said Ronald.

'Thanks,' said Tim.

'Tim,' said Marlene, 'fill Ronald's glass and your own, for goodness' sake. What do you do for a living, Ronald?'

'I work in a museum devoted to graphology.'

'Handwriting,' said Tim.

'Throughout the ages,' Ronald said.

'Can you read handwriting?'

'I read it all day long.'

'Can you judge a person's character from their handwriting?'

'No,' Ronald said.

'That's exactly what I expected you to say,' Marlene said. 'I think you're killing.'

'Ronald,' said Tim, 'is sometimes consulted by the police on questions of forgery.'

'No!' said Marlene.

'Yes,' said Tim, 'he is.'

'How thrilling!' said Marlene. 'I do love to see a genuine fraud exposed.'

'Well, now,' Tim said, 'since you mention it, I did feel that last night –'

'Oh, Patrick completely exposed him,' Marlene said, turning to explain to Ronald. 'This fraud-clairvoyant Dr Mike Garland who entered our midst during our séance last night was completely outwitted by our leading medium whose name is Patrick Seton.'

'No!' Ronald said.

'Yes,' said Marlene, 'Garland created a great disturbance, being in the pay of one of our members – one of our *former* members – Mrs Freda Flower, but Patrick gained the ascendancy. He was unshake-able – wasn't he, Tim?'

'I was obliged to leave,' said Tim, 'before the end.'

'Another time you must go and lie down on a bed, Tim. It was too bad of you to leave me with Freda Flower in hysterics. Did you notice the absurd pose that Dr Garland – doctor so-called – adopted during the séance when he was giving clairvoyance? I *knew* he was a fraud the moment he raised up his head to give utterance. Did you notice, Tim, how he raised his head with*out* relaxing in his chair? He didn't lean back in his chair, you see, he didn't lean back. And I knew right away he was fully conscious of all he was saying. I'm making further investigations about Garland. He ought to be exposed.'

Tim's eyes glanced briefly at the hatch. Marlene noticed it and realized she had betrayed her peep-hole. Tim's eyes returned to his soufflé and he said, 'This is delicious, Marlene.'

'I am rather clairvoyant myself,' Marlene said specifically to Ronald, with a tiny swing of her ear-rings, 'and this enables me to see through a fraud immediately. They can't get away with anything from me.'

'When is Patrick's case coming up?' Tim said.

'Freda will not proceed with the case,' Marlene said, 'if I know anything of Freda. She has too much faith in Patrick, although she won't admit it, to ignore the warnings which he transmitted to her last night from the other side. However, I have told Freda Flower that she is no longer welcome in our midst.' She looked at Tim who was still looking elsewhere. 'I feel bound, Tim,' she said, 'to *keep an eye* on things.'

'Oh, quite,' Tim said, wiping his glasses with his white handkerchief.

'It's all very well for you to stand in judgement,' she said.

'Who, me?' Tim said.

'But you are a comparative newcomer to the Circle. You know nothing of the inner workings. That was evident last night. Your seating arrangments. . . .'

She rose and bade them come and see the Sanctuary. Glancing back she noticed Ronald taking his pills and washing them down with water.

'Aren't you feeling well?' she said.

'Ronald suffers from indigestion,' Tim said.

'My dear boy, was my cooking so frightful?'

Ronald could not reply. He stood gripping at the back of his chair. His eyes were open and, for a moment, quite absent.

But his attack passed and he regained control of himself while Tim and his aunt were still staring at him, Tim fearing the worst and Marlene fascinated.

'Are you psychic?' she said.

'I don't know.'

He followed Tim into the Sanctuary, on the threshold of which Marlene took Ronald's arm.

'I do believe,' she said, 'that you are sensitive to the atmosphere of this flat. For a moment, just now, I thought you were going into a trance. I am psychic, you know. I'm certain you would make an excellent medium, if properly trained.'

On the way home, before they parted, Tim said to Ronald,

'I adore her, really.'

'A good-looking woman,' Ronald said.

'She was a beauty in her day. Of course, she's a bit crackers. There is *some*thing, you know, in her spiritualism, but she hasn't a clue how to cope with it. She cheats like anything herself – thinks it's justified.'

'It's a difficult thing to cope with, I should think.'

'I can't cope with it,' Tim said. 'The awkward thing is, how am I going to get out of it?'

'You'll find a way.'

'Oh, I'll find a way. Only I don't want to fall out with Marlene, you know. What did you honestly think of her, quite honestly?'

'Rather charming,' Ronald said, quite honestly.

Nevertheless, when Martin Bowles rang him up later in the evening and said 'Come along to Isobel's for supper: she wants you for supper,' Ronald replied that he was engaged. One auntie, he thought, is enough for one Sunday. Enough is always enough.

'God save me,' said Matthew Finch, London correspondent of the *Irish Echo*, 'and help me in my weakness.' He was peeling an onion. Tears still brimmed over his eyelashes when the telephone rang. 'Let it not be an occasion of sin,' he said to himself or to God as he went over to answer it.

'Hallo,' he said, apprehensively, although he knew, really, who would speak.

'Elsie speaking,' said Elsie Forrest.

'Oh yes, Elsie. Hallo, Elsie.'

'You expecting me, Matthew? You said Sunday, didn't you?'

'Yes, Elsie, I want you to come. Will you find your way? A tube to South Kensington, then a 30 bus, and you get off at Drayton Gardens. I'll meet you at the bus stop. You'll be there by quarter to six.'

'Well, I was thinking of getting the Underground to –'

'No, no, the bus from South Kensington is better. I'll wait from quarter to six.'

'All right, Matthew.'

Elsie had not come to his flat before. He had really preferred the other girl in the coffee-bar, Alice Dawes, but she was tied up to a man. On the whole, he had been glad to discover Elsie. Not that he needed to have taken up with either of them. But, yes, he did want to know a girl again, since his previous girl had gone to America and he felt lonely in London without one. Alice Dawes with her black piled-up hair was the handsomer of the two, but Elsie Forrest was the more accessible.

'God help me with my weakness,' said Matthew as he went back to his onion. For he was weak with girls and had a great conscience about sex. It had been easier in Dublin where the bachelors protected their human nature by staying long hours in the public houses. He was not sure what he would do with Elsie. He had to prepare some supper, but she would do the cooking. He was not sure what to do with the onion, and he weighed up what the force of Elsie's attraction was likely to be, and how the evening would turn out. It was for this that he had prepared the onion. For he had found that the smell of onion in the breath invariably put the girls off, and so provided a mighty fortress against the devil and a means of avoiding an occasion of sin. Matthew was not sure, however, that Elsie called for the onion altogether. She was not very pretty. But you never knew when a girl might show the charm she had within her. And again, the onion might be useful for the supper, to mix with the mince-meat. There wasn't another onion left in the box.

Was there not another onion left in the box? Matthew decided that this would be the testing point: if there was a miraculous onion in the vegetable box which could be used in the supper he would, before he went to fetch Elsie from the bus, eat the raw onion he had peeled upon the table; if there was no onion in the box he would risk having Elsie to the flat with a clean breath. He looked in the box. A small shrivelled onion nestled in the earthy corner among the remaining potatoes. He lifted this poor thing, looked at it, pondered whether it was big enough for the supper. He thought perhaps he should peel and eat this little onion and leave the larger one for the cooking.

But then he recalled his previous lapses from grace, and the exact terms of the vow he had made before looking into the box. He thought lustfully of Elsie who would soon be coming back with him to the flat. He seized the peeled onion off the table, ate it rapidly like a man, dabbed his eyes and his brow with his handkerchief, and set off to wait for Elsie at the bus stop.

As if forewarning her, he gave her a breathy kiss when she alighted. She drew back only a little; in fact she took it very well.

He let her go first up the stairs to his flat and was filled with delight as he followed her small hips, which moved at his eye-level.

'Nice room,' she said. 'Is that your mother over there?'

'Yes, and this is my elder brother and that's my sister with her husband on their honeymoon. I'll put on the light, wait and you'll see them better. My sister's got three children. My younger brother is married, too, but my elder brother isn't.' He passed the photographs one by one. 'This is the National University of Ireland, Galway, where I was till 1950,' said Matthew, and then he poured out the gin. 'That's my cousin that was killed in the war, fighting for Great Britain.'

'Would you have anything in the gin?' Matthew said. 'There's orange juice or water.'

'I'll have it neat,' Elsie said, 'and by God I need it.' She placed the photographs aside. 'Alice was ill last night and I was on alone at the coffee bar till twelve. Why didn't you come in?'

'I was on duty,' Matthew said. 'I'm always on duty on Saturday nights.'

'Well, before I left the shop I rang up Alice to see how she felt and she was in such a state I had to go round and see her. Patrick didn't come home.'

'What's wrong with her?' Matthew said.

'She's expecting a baby. She's got diabetes. And the man she's living with's no good.'

'Can't something be done about the diabetes?' Matthew said.

'She has to take injections every day. The man wants her to get rid of the baby.'

'She shouldn't do that.'

'She won't do it.'

'Yes, she looks a nice girl,' Matthew said. 'Who's the man?'

'Patrick Seton – he's the medium.'

Matthew thought she meant go-between, so he said, 'But who's the man?'

'He's the man – Patrick Seton, he's a medium.'

'Oh, a spiritualist?'

'Yes, he's a wonderful medium. But he's no good to Alice. Weak as water. He's supposed to be getting a divorce from his wife and then he'll marry Alice. But I don't believe he's getting a divorce. I don't believe there's any wife. And there's a case coming up against him on Tuesday for embezzlement or something like that. He's been up before the magistrates once already, but the police didn't have their evidence ready. Suppose he gets a sentence?'

'What a terrible fellow,' Matthew said. 'Alice should leave him, a lovely girl like that.'

'She's completely under his power. In love with him.'

'A terrible thing,' Matthew said. 'A girl like that taking up with a spiritualist. Aren't they a lot of mad fellows, spiritualists?' He was thinking of Ewart Thornton with whom he frequently had loud arguments on the Irish question. 'I know a spiritualist,' Matthew said, 'who's a schoolmaster, we both belong to a drinking club out at Hampstead. But he won't talk about spiritualism to me because he knows I'm Irish. He talks politics. He's mad.'

'Are the Irish against spiritualism?'

'Well, the Catholics, it's the same thing.'

'There's a lot in spiritualism,' Elsie said. 'I'm not a spiritualist myself exactly. At least, I've never joined a Circle. But Alice is a member. And I believe in it.'

'Do you really?' Matthew was interested with an eager mental curiosity in direct proportion as he was put off her sexually by the thought of her being a spiritualist. A deep inherited and unarguable urge made him move his chair a little bit away from her, whereas he had previously been moving it nearer; and he reflected, then, that he need not have eaten the onion. A spiritualist girl might dematerialize in the act, if it came to the act. But his mind was alert for knowledge. 'How do they summon up the spirits of the dead?' Matthew said. 'Would you have some more gin?'

She said, 'I need it, after a sleepless night.'

'There's some mince-meat and onion and potatoes and there's some custard and fruit. Or you could have bacon and eggs,' Matthew said. 'You just say when you're hungry. How do they call up the dead from their repose?' He poured the gin and gave it to her while she described the thrilling process of the medium's getting through to the other side.

'I had a friend called Colin that was killed,' she said, 'and Patrick Seton got through to him and he gave me a message, it was quite incredible because nobody could have known except Colin and me about this thing that he mentioned; it was a secret between Colin and me.'

'Can't you tell it to me?' Matthew said.

'Well,' she said, 'it's rather personal.' She looked at Matthew rather meaningly. Matthew felt himself slightly endangered and was grateful, after all, for the strong onion in his breath.

She drank down her gin. Matthew filled her glass, and moved his chair towards her again. 'Are you feeling like supper?' he said. 'Perhaps we'll just fry a couple of rashers and eggs. Or you'd perhaps prefer to come out, that would be simpler.'

She looked at him with quite a glow, and her face, haggard as it was, showed its youth. 'I'll just have my drink,' she said. 'I'm enjoying this rest and opening my heart to somebody.'

She came over and sat on the arm of his chair. She began to finger his black curls. He turned and breathed hard upon her.

'You remind me of Colin,' she said, 'in a certain respect. He used to be fond of onions and I minded at first, but I got used to it. So I don't mind your onion-breath very much.'

Matthew clasped her desperately round the waist, and sighed upon her as if to save his soul. But she too sighed and shivered with excitement as she subsided upon him.

At ten o'clock they went out to eat. Elsie then telephoned to see how Alice was getting on and returned to report that Patrick had still not come home and Alice was upset. And so Elsie took Matthew to the room in Ebury Street where Alice sat up in bed with her long black hair let loose, and her beautiful distress; and Matthew fell altogether in love with her.

After he had gone, Alice said, looking at Elsie in a special way,

'You've been to bed this afternoon.'

'Yes. He reminds me of Colin in a way. His breath –'

'Have you been foolish tonight, Elsie?'

'Well, you know,' said Elsie, 'that I don't mind a man whose breath smells of onions. Colin's always did.'

'Makes me sick, the thought of it.'

'Oh well,' Elsie said, 'I suppose there was something psychological in my childhood. It makes me sick too, in a way.'

FOUR

Patrick Seton sat in his room in Paddington, about which nobody except Mr Fergusson knew anything, and thought. Or rather, he sat and felt his thoughts.

It was the unfortunate occurrence.

Freda Flower: danger.

Tomorrow morning at ten at the Magistrate's Court. Unless Freda Flower had changed her mind again. . . .

Mr Fergusson would know. Mr Fergusson had taken his passport away from him.

Patrick brushed his yellow-white hair with an old brush in his trembling hand and went out to see Mr Fergusson. He walked hastily, keeping well in to the shop side of the streets. He hastened, for something about Mr Fergusson always brought him peace. Meanwhile, he felt his thoughts, and they began to run on optimistic lines.

A great many witnesses for the defence. They knew he was genuine. Marlene in the box.

Freda Flower: what a gross, what a base, betrayal of all she had held sacred!

You are acquitted, said the judge. After that: Alice.

Alice must be dealt with, and her unbelievable baby. For her own sake. He loved her. And always would. Even unto her passing over. The spirit giveth life.

He had come to the police station. The constable at the desk looked up and nodded. 'I'll tell Detective-Inspector Fergusson you're here,' he said.

Patrick sat and fidgeted until the policeman came to call him. Patrick dusted the lapel of his dark coat with a moth-like flicker of the fingers and followed the policeman.

Patrick's nerves came to rest on Detective-Inspector Fergusson, who stood sandy-haired, with his fine build, and spoke with his good Scots voice.

'I've come to see if there has been any development, Mr Fergusson,' Patrick said, 'in the unfortunate occurrence.'

'Mrs Flower has been here,' said Mr Fergusson. 'You must have got at her.'

'She's changed her mind, I presume?'

'Yes.'

'Oh!'

'But we haven't.'

'How do you mean?' Patrick said.

Mr Fergusson said, 'It's a police prosecution, you know. Witnesses can't change their minds.'

'Yes, but Mrs Flower's your chief witness. You'll want the best out of her. You'd want it given willingly.'

'You're right there.' Mr Fergusson gave Patrick a cigarette. 'The Chief is considering our next course of action. There will probably be a remand tomorrow.'

'I won't be sent for trial?'

'The case will merely be postponed,' said Mr Fergusson reassuringly. 'We've got your statement.'

'I could always deny it,' Patrick whispered absent-mindedly. 'I was in a dazed condition after a séance when I signed it.'

'That didn't get you very far the last time.'

'It made an impression on the court.' And Patrick waved the subject away as a wife does when reciting to a husband retorts that she has repeated on other weary occasions.

'Keep in touch with me,' Mr Fergusson nodded.

Patrick felt sorry the interview was over. He felt steadied-up when in the company of this policeman. One expected worldliness from Mr Fergusson. One did not expect it from people with an interior knowledge of the spirit, like Freda Flower.

'It's a very painful occurrence,' Patrick said.

'Very,' said Mr Fergusson.

'Is there any chance of the Chief deciding not to proceed?' Patrick said.

'A slight chance. If Mrs Flower remains reluctant to give evidence against you there's a chance we won't proceed. But Mrs Flower may change her mind again. We have to see her again and have a talk.'

Mr Fergusson rose and patted Patrick's shoulder, at the same time propelling him gently towards the door. 'Ring me every morning,' he said, 'or call round. I'll keep you informed.'

Then Patrick asked his usual question. 'If the worst comes to the worst,' he said, 'how long ...?'

The policeman said, as usual, 'It depends on the judge. Eighteen months, two years ...'

'That's a long time.'

'They go by the antecedents,' said Mr Fergusson. 'Cheer up, you're lucky you're a bachelor. It's worse for a married man. Look on the bright side, Patrick.'

At the street entrance Patrick looked out on to the bleak pavements and immediately felt unhappy again. He stood for a moment under the protective porch, then took the plunge up the street. He felt within him a decision to go and see the doctor.

'He can look you in the eyes,' said Freda Flower to Mike Garland, 'and make you believe it's you that's telling the lie.'

'You don't be a fool,' Mike said. 'You go back to Inspector Fergusson and tell him you're going on with it, as you said in the first place. The whole of your savings gone. Remember that.'

'Oh, Mike, I was so good to him. You should have seen how he got round me with his interior decorations and his odd jobs round the house.'

Pink-cheeked Mike looked round the walls which were done with a pink wash. 'Didn't make much of a job of it.'

'He didn't do this room. He did the paint. And he did the kitchen. But I was good to him.'

'He's a fraud,' Mike said, 'and he ought to be exposed. For the sake of the Movement.'

'I can't believe it, Mike. I still can't believe, inside me, When I think of him that he's a fraud. He's given me such good advice from the chair, Mike, and last Saturday night –'

'That was a fake-up, clear enough,' Mike said. 'He wanted to frighten you.'

'No, Mike. He was really gone on Saturday night. You could see it.'

'Think of your money,' Mike said. 'What's happened to your two thousand?'

'I still can't believe it, Mike.'

'You know what Fergusson told you.'

'I don't know what to think, Mike.'

'There have been other cases in the past. There are two other women over the last two years.'

'I always feel somehow,' she said, 'that there's some explanation. I was the only woman for Patrick.' She saw in her mind's eye the grave thin face and the blue eyes of Patrick as it were superimposed on the curtain.

She said, 'You don't realize how nicely he could talk. There was something about him lifted you up. He's a poet at heart.'

'And he lifted up your cash as well.'

'Perhaps there was some mistake.'

'He admitted it,' Mike said. 'And there's your handwriting he's forged.'

'Perhaps I did write the letter. I don't know. It could be my own signature, after all, if I didn't know what I was doing. I thought the money was for bonds, but perhaps the bonds were a dream, I don't know –'

'He frightened you by his warnings,' Mike said. 'Well, let me tell you, there's nothing in them. I'm a clairvoyant and I can *see* he's a fraud.'

She looked at Mike's pink face and his large frame. He failed to move her as much as Patrick had done.

'Two thousand,' Mike said. 'Come, put your hat on and I'll take you back to Inspector Fergusson. You were a fool to part with the cheque.'

'I think he said he'd buy the bonds, I don't know.' Desperately she looked at the white blossom on the green carpet, and at the curtains, fawn with a touch of pink to match the walls, and her fawn and green suite.

'Two thousand, your life savings,' Mike said.

'I've got the rooms all let,' she said. 'Thanks to you, Mike.'

'But nothing in the bank. Come on, let's go. Two thousand, remember. He should get five years imprisonment.'

She said, 'It was worth the money.'

But she got ready, and accompanied Mike Garland all the way back to Detective-Inspector Fergusson, who had been so severe when she had called previously to withdraw her statement. When he spoke to her on this second occasion he was even more severe, for she was so very full of tears and doubts.

Patrick spoke to the receptionist from the telephone kiosk with a courteous smile, as if she could see him.

'If at all possible,' Patrick said.

'His appointment book is very full all day,' the receptionist said.

'Perhaps,' said Patrick, 'you could have a word with him and he'll slip me in. You remember me, don't you? A private patient – Mr Seton.'

'Oh, Mr Seton.' She went away and returned.

'Half-past twelve, Mr Seton. He can give you some time.'

'Thank you,' Patrick said. 'I am so much obliged.'

Patrick was unaware what precisely was the deep secret in Dr Lyte's career, to which he had given unconscious utterance one night in the séance room, the only occasion on which Dr Lyte had attended a spiritualist meeting. Patrick, on coming round from his trance, had perceived the shaken stranger and had moved with fluttering obliquity towards him as a moth to the lamp.

The stranger was Dr Lyte. Patrick rapidly appreciated that he had said something in his trance which had truly got its mark. 'How exactly did you know?' Dr Lyte said in a way which was very different from his nice clothes.

Patrick bashfully screwed his head to the side and smiled.

When Patrick called on him the next day, Dr Lyte had pulled himself together.

'I only went there as an experiment,' he explained.

'By whom recommended?' Patrick said quietly.

'Chap called Ewart Thornton. A friend of –'

'That is correct,' Patrick said. 'Mr Thornton recommended you. You are speaking the truth.'

'I have no faith in spiritualism,' Dr Lyte said.

Patrick nodded like a man of the world.

'And what you described,' Dr Lyte said, 'in your so-called trance, was inaccurate.'

'No,' Patrick said, 'Dr Lyte, it was not inaccurate.'

'Where did you get this information?'

'I don't know what you're talking about,' Patrick said with mendacious truth. 'I'd rather not discuss the details.'

'What do you want with me?'

Patrick closed his eyes reprovingly.

'What can I do for you?' said Dr Lyte.

And so he never refused Patrick an appointment, or a piece of advice, or a drug to alleviate the effects of a trance. Patrick was not unduly troublesome. Dr Lyte even went so far as voluntarily to obtain the new drug which had been employed, for experimental purposes, to induce epileptic convulsions in rats, and which, taken in certain minor quantities, greatly improved both the spectacular quality of Patrick's trances and his actual psychic powers.

'What can I do for you, Patrick?' said Dr Lyte when Patrick was shown in at half past twelve sharp. Dr Lyte was untroubled: he had got used to Patrick, as one does get used to things.

'It's about Alice. She won't think of doing away with it. Not by an operation. I mentioned the address –'

'Well, she can get it adopted. Much easier if you don't marry her till afterwards. The State has arrangements for these girls.'

'Yes,' Patrick said. 'Alice,' he said, 'isn't too well.'

'Send her along.'

'I think perhaps she isn't taking her injections properly,' Patrick said.

'Oh, she's got to take her two injections every morning before breakfast. They need the regular insulin. Tell her she'll die if she doesn't take it.'

'How long does it take,' Patrick said, 'for a diabetic person to die if they deprive themselves of insulin?'

'She's not trying to take her life, is she?'

'I'm not sure,' Patrick said, his fingers interlacing each other in agitated jerks. 'But don't you think she might try to get rid of the baby by reducing the insulin and making herself really ill?'

'That would be foolish,' said Dr Lyte. 'Surely she knows – but why don't you see to the injections yourself until this trouble's over?'

'Oh, she won't let me touch them. She won't ever let me use the needle on her.'

'Do you watch her taking it?'

'No. You see, she won't let me see her doing it.'

'I'll have a talk with her. I'd better come along.'

'Well,' Patrick said, 'I don't think that's necessary. I'll tell her she'll die if she doesn't take her insulin. I'll say you said so. How long would it take?'

'It varies,' said the doctor. 'My goodness, if Alice really did get negligent she might die within a few days. But she *knows* –'

'Perhaps, on the other hand, she is taking too much insulin,' Patrick said. 'Would that account for her symptoms?'

'What are the symptoms? Exhausted? Hungry?'

'Yes.'

'Really, you know, I'll have to see her. What makes you think she isn't following her proper routine in the mornings?'

'Oh, it's only an idea I had,' Patrick said. 'I may be quite wrong.'

'Is she testing her urine every morning?'

'I don't know,' Patrick said. 'It's all just a stupid idea in my mind that she may be neglecting her insulin treatment. She's probably just off colour, with the baby and so forth. . . . It's a worry for me. Tell me, if she took *too much* insulin, what might happen?'

'She'd die. I'll look in this afternoon,' said the doctor.

'Very well,' Patrick said. 'Good of you,' he said; and the doctor was vaguely disturbed by his docility. Patrick was saying, his voice trailing off, 'But my suspicions may be quite unfounded, and how am I to know what she does with the needle and so forth . . .?'

'Feeling better?' said Patrick.

'Heaps better,' she said. 'I'm going to work tonight.'

'Did you miss me the last two days?' Patrick said.

'You know I did, darling.'

'I was worried about you all the time,' he said. 'I asked Dr Lyte to come and see you.'

'Oh! He hasn't been.'

'He's coming this afternoon.'

'Well, you can put him off. It's too late. I'm better.'

'He's anxious in case you've been forgetting to take your insulin.'

'I never forget my insulin. But I've missed you giving me the injection.' She took his hand. 'I've missed that little touch the last two mornings, Patrick.'

'Dr Lyte,' Patrick said, 'wondered if perhaps you were taking too much.'

'I never take too much. Does he think I'm an imbecile? I've been taking injections for six years.'

'Well, I'll ring and put him off,' Patrick said.

'*I'll* ring and tell him what I think of him,' she said. 'Suggesting that I'm negligent –'

'Now, Dr Lyte is a good friend. Better leave him to me. I'll tell him you're all right now.'

'And then we'll go out and celebrate,' she said, 'the collapse of the court case.'

'Well, it's only in abeyance. Of course Freda Flower hasn't a leg to stand on. But she's a dangerous woman, and she could change her mind.' His voice faded away out of the window where he was looking.

'Hasn't she got a heart?' said Alice. 'Hasn't she got a heart?'

'The police want to proceed,' Martin Bowles told Ronald in the book-lined barristers' chambers. 'But the widow won't stand by her evidence satisfactorily. Seton has scared the pants off her with messages from beyond the grave.'

'Is it forgery, then? I thought you said fraudulent conversion,' Ronald said.

'Fraudulent conversion on one count. But Seton has now produced a letter by which he hopes to prove that the widow gave him the money. Of course, it's a forgery.'

Ronald looked at the letters and the sad second-hand-looking cheque with the bank's mark stamped on it.

'She wants them back,' Martin said. 'But the police are hanging on to them. We've got photostats.'

'I can't work from photostats,' Ronald said, locking the documents away in his brief-case. 'The widow will have to wait.'

'I'll give you a lift home,' Martin said. 'I'm going along to Isobel's.'

They walked through the Temple courtyard to Martin's car.

'What do you think,' Martin said, 'goes on in a man like Patrick Seton's mind when he looks back on his life?'

People frequently asked this sort of question of Ronald. It was as if they held some ancient superstition about his epilepsy: 'the falling sickness', 'the sacred disease', 'the evil spirit'. Ronald felt he was regarded by his friends as a sacred cow or a wise monkey. He was, perhaps, touchy on the point. Sometimes he thought, after all, they would have come to him with their deep troubles, consulted him on the nature of things, listened to his wise old words, even if he wasn't an afflicted man. If he had been a priest, people would have consulted him in the same way.

'What goes on at the back of his mind?' Martin inquired of the oracle. 'Tell me.'

'I should think,' Ronald replied after a meet pause, 'that when he considers his past life he suffers from a rush of blood to the head, giddiness and bells in the ears. And therefore he does not consider his life at all.' And having thus described his own symptoms when a fit was approaching, Ronald fell silent.

Martin negotiated the traffic all along the Strand to Trafalgar Square. 'I think,' he said then to Ronald, 'that's a terrifically good piece of observation. Do you feel like coming along and cheering Isobel up?'

'All right,' Ronald said.

'Got your pills?' said Martin.

'Yes, I've got them on me.'

If there is one thing a bachelor does not like it is another bachelor who has lost his job.

The Hon. Francis Eccles, small, with those very high shoulders that left him almost neckless, leaned over the bar of the Pandaemonium Club at Hampstead, whose members were supposed to be drawn from the arts and sciences. No scientist had yet joined the club in its twelve years' existence, but the members at present in the bar were fairly representative of the arts side: a television actor, a Welsh tenor, a film extra who took peasant-labourer parts when they were available, a ballet-mistress, and a stockbroker who was writing a novel.

It was not only the Hampstead representatives of the arts who frequented this club: many who had left Hampstead occasionally returned to it. Walter Prett for instance, the mammoth art critic of middle age and collar-length white hair, had come from Camden Town; and Matthew Finch, having sent off the last of his week's tidings for the *Irish Echo*, had come to meet Walter here on the early autumn evening that tiny Francis Eccles hunched necklessly over the bar so sadly, having lost his job.

'But you don't need a job, Eccie,' said Chloe, the young barmaid. 'I don't know what you want with a job anyway.'

Without exchanging a word or sign and by sheer migratory instinct, Matthew and Walter removed their glasses over to the window-seat where they were separated from the jobless nobleman by a grand piano.

'Tell me,' said Walter to Matthew, 'do I look any thinner?'

'No,' Matthew said, 'you look fine.'

'I've lost eight pounds,' Walter said confidentially, moving his snowy long-haired head close to Matthew's short blue-black curls.

'Don't worry, you look –'

'I've got to lose two stone,' Walter said very loudly. 'Simply got to. My heart won't stand up to it.'

Matthew shied a little. 'Were you not on a diet?' he said.

Walter's voice subsided. 'I was, but it insisted on no beer, wines, or spirits. I'd rather be dead.' Walter's eyes bulged redly from the inner circle of his face, for it was surrounded by outer circles of dark blood-pressured flesh. He sipped his wine daintily through his face-wide lips. Matthew thought perhaps the glass would be crushed in Walter's great hand. Walter was liable to sudden outbursts of temper for no reason at all. Matthew looked at him uneasily, his eyes peeping from under his black glossy eyebrows.

Walter, observing this effect, was dissatisfied. He smiled sweetly, and it was indeed a sweet smile, such as wide full mouths only are capable of.

'It's my birthday,' Matthew said. 'I'm thirty-two today. I come under the Sign of Libra, the scales of justice. I'm passionate about justice. Like all the Irish.'

'Do they all come under Libra?'

'No. I don't believe in astrology,' Matthew said, drinking down his wine in an anxious way.

'Well, well,' said Walter. 'Many happy returns. I could give you fifteen years.'

'Could you?' Matthew said with his mind on something else.

'Forty-eight next year,' Walter said, 'and what have I done with my life?'

'You've got your column.'

'I should have been a painter,' Walter said. 'I showed promise.'

'Did you ever think of getting married?' Matthew said.

'I showed tremendous promise,' Walter said, 'but my family was indifferent to art. They were interested in horses. My father kept three hunters in the stable and then he couldn't pay the milk bill.'

'Yes, you told me that before,' Matthew said, looking wistfully at a girl in a large jersey and tight jeans who had just come in and was now sitting up on one of the high chairs at the bar.

Walter stood up and roared, 'Well, I'm telling you again.' For he hated his family stories to be treated indifferently.

'Sit down, now, sit down,' Matthew said.

'Vulgar little fellows all over the place,' Walter observed, casting his inflamed eyes round the room. 'Especially in the art world.'

'Sit down,' Matthew said. 'Would you have a drink?' he said.

Chloe called over from her place behind the bar. 'Walter! What's all the noise about?'

Walter sat down broodily while Matthew edged round the room and up to the far end of the bar so that Eccie's hunched back was turned to him. When he had obtained the drinks he did the same detour on his return to their window-seat. On the way, however, he said 'Good evening' to the girl in jeans.

'I'm thinking of getting married,' Matthew said.

'Oh, are you? Who to?'

'I haven't anyone in mind,' Matthew said. 'Only my brother-in-law thinks I should get married. My sister wants me to get married and so does my uncle. Every time I go home to Ireland my mother's ashamed that I'm not married to a girl.'

'I got a young woman into trouble at the age of eighteen,' Walter said. 'Daughter of one of our footmen. He was an Irish fellow. The butler caught him reading Nietzsche in the pantry. To the detriment of the silver. Of course there was no question of my marrying his daughter. The family made a settlement and I went abroad to paint. My hair turned white at the age of nineteen.'

Matthew said, 'I know a girl who's expecting a baby by an old spiritualist. She's lovely. She's got long black hair.' He saddened into silence and gazed upon the girl in jeans dispassionately, recognizing her as Ronald's former girl-friend.

'I went abroad to paint, but my cousin the Marquise –'

'I'll tell you this much,' Matthew said, 'there's no justification for being a bachelor and that's the truth, let's face it. It's everyone's duty to be fruitful and multiply according to his calling either spiritual or temporal, as the case may be.'

'Monet admired my work. Just before he died he visited my studio with his friends, and –'

'These are the figures,' Matthew said, and took from inside his coat a bundle of papers from which he selected one which had been folded in four, and which was split and grubby at the folds. He straightened out the sheet, following the typewritten lines with his finger, as he read out, 'Greater London, the census of 1951. Unmarried males of twenty-one and over: six hundred and fifty-nine thousand five hundred. That's including divorced and widowed, of course, but the majority are bachelors –'

'I can see him now,' said Walter, 'as he was when he was assisted into a chair before my easel. Monet was silent for fully ten minutes – the painting was a simple, but rather exquisite roof-top scene –'

'Unmarried males of thirty and over,' said Matthew: 'three hundred and fifty-eight thousand one hundred. Since 1951 the bachelor population has increased by –'

'Put that vulgar little bit of paper away,' Walter said.

'Tim Raymond gave it to me,' Matthew said, putting it away very carefully. 'He works in the COI. God help him.'

'You'd better get married,' Walter said.

'Do you think so? Why?'

'Because you obviously haven't got the courage to get your sex any other way.'

'There's more than sex in marriage.'

'But not in your mind.'

'Perhaps that's true. I often wonder if it's only sex when I think of getting married. Still, I feel I should be married and multiply. I feel –'

'Do you really want to get married?' Walter said.

'No.'

'I nearly got married,' Walter said, 'in 1932 when I was out of work and the family had cut me off. The girl had a job. If a girl had a job in those days it was like a dowry. She was anxious to marry me. But I was really more taken up with her father. He was a carpenter, one of the last of the true English craftsmen. But I did not marry his daughter. She was a bourgeois little bitch with her savings in the post office. Her name was Sybil, if you please.' The memory of Sybil, though in fact she had never existed, was so fiercely implanted in Walter's mind through frequent elaborations of his imagined affair with her, that he was always thoroughly incensed by her.

'I wished her joy of her savings in the post office and departed,' Walter shouted. He rose and set down his empty glass and fastened his black coat on one button across his huge stomach.

'Are you going to go?' Matthew said.

Walter clenched both fists as if to fight with Sybil.

'I'll walk with you to the station,' Matthew said.

Walter sat down again and made his lips into a long line.

'I'll have to be going,' Matthew said. 'My other brother-in-law has just come over and I've got to meet him at my uncle's.'

'My boy,' said Walter, 'you have much to bear.'

'Not my uncle at Twickenham. My other uncle at Poplar,' Matthew said, with his eyes on the brown bobbed head of Ronald's girl in jeans who was laughing with Chloe.

'I want a drink,' Walter said.

'I'm a bit short of cash,' Matthew said, 'this time of the month.'

'Fresh young Chloe will cash me a cheque,' Walter shouted.

'Chloe will not cash you a cheque,' Chloe called out, 'for the simple reason that Chloe is not allowed to cash cheques any more.'

Francis Eccles swivelled round in his high chair.

'Why, Walter!' he said.

'Why, Eccie!' said Walter.

'There's a very definite rule about cheques,' Chloe said.

Walter ambled over to the bar and said in a tone of dignified reproach, 'As it happens I haven't got my cheque book on me. But I'm surprised, Chloe, that you should take up this ridiculous lower-middle-class attitude.'

'I have my orders, Walter,' Chloe pleaded.

'What will you drink, Walter?' said Eccie.

'You have your orders, Chloe,' Walter said. 'Very well, you have your orders. But really, my dear, this is dreadfully bourgeois of you.'

It worked quicker than usual. Chloe said, 'I'm not bourgeois, really I'm not. I'll personally cash you a cheque. It's only that I can't, I mustn't, cash cheques for the club.'

'Since when?' said Walter.

'Since last week,' she said. 'Honestly,' she said.

'First I've heard of it,' said the girl in jeans.

'I'll cash your cheque,' said Eccie, also anxious not to be bourgeois.

'It's of no matter,' Walter said. 'I only object on principle. As it happens I haven't got my cheque book on me.'

Eventually he accepted a loan from Eccie, and when the deal was done Matthew reappeared from the cloakroom. He took a high chair at the bar and helped himself to a pickled onion off a plate.

'Matthew,' said Chloe, 'meet Hildegarde. Hildegarde, meet Matthew.'

Matthew learned forward and smiled across Walter's bulk at the girl in jeans. 'We've met before,' he said.

'Where?' she said.

'At Ronald Bridges'. Aren't you a friend of Ronald's?'

'I used to be,' she said.

'I know Bridges,' mused Eccie. 'I wonder if he could help . . .?'

'No,' said Chloe. 'I shouldn't think so, Eccie.'

'Don't you?'

'No.'

'What is this secret conversation?' roared Walter.

'It's something Eccie and I were discussing,' Chloe said. 'It's private.'

'Common little creatures,' Walter shouted. 'Very bad behaviour.'

'I'm not standing for that, Walter,' Chloe said. 'Are you standing for it, Eccie?'

'Well, no,' said Eccie. 'I must say, Walter . . .'

'This is too much,' said Hildegarde. She swung her long legs off the stool and departed.

'Come on, Walter,' Matthew said, 'I've got to meet my brother-in-law –'

'I shall not be driven away by a barmaid and a snivelling middle-class younger son of an upstart earl,' Walter said.

'You're drunk,' said Chloe.

Walter laughed without noise or humour, but with a shaking of his flabby shoulders, chest, and stomach.

Eccie said sadly, 'Walter, Walter, I don't like this.'

'You are deriving a certain pleasure from lumping it,' Walter said.

'Walter, I'm out of a job, you know. The Institute is closing down.'

'Not before time,' Walter said.

'As an art school, I admit it had its weaknesses,' said Eccie. 'But I flatter myself I was able to contribute something useful with my lectures, especially on the country itinerary which I've been taking for the last two years.'

'Nonsense. You contributed nothing. You know nothing of art.'

'Oh, Walter, come!' said Eccie, Christianly.

'He's drunk,' said Chloe.

'I'll have to go and phone my sister,' Matthew said.

'Drunk,' said Chloe, 'and this time's the last. He can't come here insulting the members –'

Walter took from his pocket the five pounds that he had borrowed from Francis Eccles. 'I'll give you this back,' he said, 'before I'll admit you know anything about painting, Eccie.'

Eccie said 'Good night, Chloe. Good night Matthew,' in a tone of gentle reproach, and left.

'That was mean of you, Walter,' Chloe said.

'I am an honest man,' Walter observed, 'when treating of the few existing subjects to which honesty is due.'

'I'd better ring my sister,' Matthew said. 'My cousin will be on the telephone to her as I haven't turned up at my uncle's to meet my brother-in-law.'

'It was unkind of you, Walter,' said Chloe, leaning over the bar forgivingly. 'Poor old Eccie's upset at losing his job.'

'He doesn't need a job,' Walter said. 'He's got his private income and his basement. And he's an Anglo-Catholic. Anglo-Catholics always get jobs.'

'He hasn't got much income,' Chloe said. 'Have you seen the way he lives? That basement is going down and down. No one to look after him.'

'He ought to have got married,' Matthew said.

'He's not the marrying type,' said Chloe.

'He pees in the sink,' said Walter, 'not that I hold that against him.'

'He *doesn't*!' said Chloe.

'True,' said Walter. 'It's nothing. We bachelors all pee in sinks and wash-basins.'

'I don't,' said Matthew.

'You're young yet,' Walter said.

'Filthy beasts, the lot of you,' Chloe said, laughing towards one face and another as she leant over the bar.

Then she straightened up.

'Hallo, hallo,' she said, for Mike Garland, accompanied by an elderly man who wore a clerical outfit, had entered.

'Walter, Matthew,' she said, 'this is Dr Garland and Father Socket.'

'How do you do, Father,' said Matthew, jumping off his stool to shake hands.

'Not of our persuasion,' Walter informed Matthew, whereupon Matthew drew away his hand nervously and said, 'Pleasant evening.'

'These two are fraud spiritualists,' Walter roared.

'I beg your pardon, sir?' said Father Socket.

'I grant it with a plenary indulgence,' said Walter as he pushed Matthew before him out into the high autumnal winds of Hampstead.

'I'd have liked to talk to them a bit,' Matthew said. 'What was all your hurry? Alice Dawes, that pregnant girl with the long black hair, is a spiritualist.'

'These are fraud spiritualists.'

'Is there a difference, then?' said Matthew.

SIX

Ronald said, 'How long have you known her?' 'Since two weeks,' Matthew said. 'She's got long black hair. She has it done up on top when she's in the coffee-bar and she lets it go long when she's in bed.'

'I should think you've got a chance,' Ronald said. 'Seton isn't much of a rival, from what I know of him. But are you sure you want to marry this girl?'

Matthew hastily remembered that the last thing he had said might be misconstrued, so he told Ronald, 'I saw her in bed because she was ill and her friend Elsie took me along – Elsie's the other girl in the coffee-bar.'

'Have some tea,' Ronald said. 'Help yourself. Pour it out.'

'I hope you don't mind me consulting you like this?'

Ronald poured out tea, holding the teapot as high over the cup as possible without making a splash. This had been a habit of his for as long as he had been making tea for himself, and he did not notice now what he was doing as he raised the teapot, by habit, twelve inches above the cup, nor did he remember that the pretty sight of the long stream of golden liquid had once made the process of tea-making less of a bore than if he had poured it from a normal height.

'Be careful,' Matthew said, 'you don't spill it.'

'You will be thirty-two this month,' Ronald said, testing his memory.

'My birthday was last week,' Matthew said, aimlessly as a boy-seminar answering a tall black frock.

Ronald said, 'Everyone consults me about their marriages.' Three months ago Tim Raymond, before he had joined his aunt's spiritualist circle, had come to Ronald with the marriage question. He had said, 'Do you think everyone will say I'm marrying her for her money and she for my connexions?'

'I don't know. I expect so.'

'Perhaps that's the truth of the matter.'

'Well, you've got good connexions. It isn't every set of connexions a woman wants to take on. And for your part, it isn't everyone's money you would touch, I daresay. There's an element of mutual respect involved.'

'There's something in that. Still, it would be tiresome if people said –'

'Do you love the girl?' Ronald said.

'Funny thing, you know, in a funny sort of way, she's *fun*.'

'Well, I don't see why you shouldn't get married. Does she love you?'

'I think so. Of course she says so.'

'What does your mother think?'

'Oh, she likes the idea. They all like the idea. And *I* quite like the idea. But –'

'Do you want to get married at all?' Ronald said.

'No,' Tim had said. 'I don't know why, but I don't.'

Ronald said to Matthew, as he poured tea from a great height, 'Do you want really to get married?'

'Well, I'm very much in love with Alice.'

'Are you sure you want to get married?'

'I'd like Alice for a wife if I was to marry.'

'Do you want to marry at all?'

'I can't say I do,' Matthew said. He drank down his tea which had become cold through Ronald's method of pouring.

'It's the duty of us all to marry,' Matthew said. 'Isn't it? There are two callings, Holy Orders and Holy Matrimony, and one must choose.'

'Must one?' Ronald said. 'It seems evident to me that there's no compulsion to make a choice. You are talking about life. It isn't a play.'

'I'm only repeating the teaching of the Church,' Matthew said.

'It isn't official doctrine,' Ronald said. 'There's no moral law against being simply a bachelor. Don't be so excessive.'

'One can't go on sleeping with girls and going to confession.'

'That's a different question,' Ronald said. 'That's sex: we were talking of marriage. You want your sex and you don't want to marry. You never get all you want in life.'

'I'll have to marry in the end,' Matthew said, gazing at the tea-leaves in the bottom of his cup. 'The only way I can keep off sex is by going to confession and renewing my resolution every week, and sometimes that doesn't work. It's an unnatural life if one's a Christian.'

'Find the right girl, then, and marry her.'

'Alice is the right girl.'

'Well, get her to marry you.'

'I don't *want* to get married, you know.'

Ronald laughed. He was rather surprised that the conversation was becoming rancorous.

Matthew said, 'Do you want to marry?'

'No,' Ronald said. 'I'm a *confirmed* bachelor.'

'Why don't we want to marry? It isn't as if we were homosexuals.'

Ronald greatly desired, as he sometimes did, to run his fingers through Matthew's black curls. He thought, well, isn't he right? We are not homosexuals. Repressed homosexuality is a meaningless term because no one can prove it.

Matthew said, 'I suppose most people would say the confirmed bachelor is a subconscious homosexual.'

'Impossible to prove,' Ronald said. 'You can only deduce homosexuality from facts. Subconscious tendencies, repressions – these ideas are too simple and too tenuous to provide explanations. There are infinite reasons why a man may remain celibate. He may be a scholar. Husbands don't make good scholars, in my opinion.'

'I'm only saying,' said Matthew, 'what people say. They say all bachelors are queers. Hee hee. Or mother-fixated or something.'

'Oh, what people say! They always look at what might be, or what should be, never at what is.'

'My trouble is this,' Matthew said, 'I have a mind to consider the lilies of the field. In other words, I'm a lazy Irish lout and I like to feel I can chuck up a job any time, and go off to Bolivia.'

'Are you thinking of going to Bolivia?'

'No,' said Matthew, 'not particularly.'

'Your shoes are wet,' Ronald observed.

'Yes, can I take them off?'

'You should have taken them off before.'

Matthew said, 'Are there any women who really don't want to

marry?' He let his shoes fall with a plop. Ronald put them straight and at a shrewd drying point near the gas fire.

'Yes, very often, but those are the ones who marry.'

'They get married, not actually wanting to?'

'Yes. Like many men.'

'Why? Is it sex?'

'Not always, I think. It's probably a development in human nature. Something both conforming and unconforming. Otherwise, spinsters and bachelors would all be in religious orders.'

'Part of me feels they should be.'

'The whole of you should acknowledge that they aren't.'

'It's fear of responsibility that puts me off marriage. Responsibility terrifies me. Does it terrify you?'

Ronald considered. 'No,' he said. 'No one offers me much of it.' He thought of Hildegarde and her attempts to take him over as a whole burden for herself.

'I've got responsibilities,' Matthew said, twiddling his stocking-toes, 'I've got to send money home to Ireland to my mother and my aunt. There's only my mother and her sister on the farm and the farm's gone down. They want me to get married though. I feel immoral as a bachelor. Do you ever feel immoral?'

'Not very often,' Ronald said. 'I've got my epilepsy as an alibi.'

'It used to be called the Falling Sickness,' Matthew said. 'Would you come out to the coffee-bar and have a look at Alice?'

Ronald could not forbear to say, 'I've seen her.'

'Have you? Where?'

'In a café in Kensington. She was with Patrick Seton.'

A heap of Ronald's unwashed laundry lay on the carpet. He had started to make a list which bore the words '3 cols'. This lay on the top of the pile.

'How did you know it was Patrick Seton? Have you met him?' Matthew said.

Ronald could not forbear to say, 'Yes, I gave evidence on his handwriting once. He was convicted of forgery. I have a letter here in my desk,' Ronald rattled on, 'which will probably convict him again. So your way will be clear,' he said, 'to marry Alice.'

'She told me the case was off.'

'That hasn't been decided yet.'

'Will you come out and meet Alice?' Matthew said. 'She's working at the Oriflamme.'

'All right.' Ronald kicked the laundry.

'Of course, you know,' Matthew said, 'she isn't a Catholic. She's a spiritualist.'

'I don't suppose she'd let it stand in her way if she wanted to marry you.'

'I meant, from my point of view –'

'Yes, I know what you meant.'

'Well, as a Catholic how do you feel about –'

Ronald turned on him in a huge attack of irritation. 'As a Catholic I loathe all other Catholics.'

'I can well understand it. Don't shout, for goodness' sake –' Matthew said.

'And I can't bear the Irish.'

'I won't stand for that,' Matthew said.

'Don't ask me,' Ronald shouted, 'how I feel about things as a Catholic. To me, being a Catholic is part of my human existence. I don't feel one way as a human being and another *as a Catholic*.'

'To hell with you, now,' Matthew said.

Ronald lifted one of Matthew's shoes, which he had placed so carefully to dry – neither too near the gas fire nor too far from it – and cast it casually at Matthew's head.

Matthew started to hit out, then stopped with his hand in mid-air. Ronald's arm, lifted for protection was arrested for a second before he dropped it, and he realized that Matthew was sparing him on account of his epilepsy.

Matthew stumbled over the laundry, put on his damp shoes, then went off to the lavatory. When he returned Ronald was ready to accompany him to the coffee bar where Alice was working.

'Her pregnancy doesn't show as yet,' Matthew said. 'I'd adopt the child as my own if I married her. Do you think, by the way, I ought to try to marry her? She's got long black hair, only you don't see it look so glorious when she piles it up as when she lets it fall.'

Time had come round for one of Alice's ten-minute rest periods, and she sat at the table with Ronald and Matthew while they ate tough salty pizza. She delicately picked a speck of tobacco from her tongue and sadly inhaled her cigarette.

'I love the man,' she said. 'I know he's innocent.'

Matthew immediately said, 'Ronald here is examining one of the vital documents in the case. Ronald is a hand-writing expert. He is often consulted in criminal cases – aren't you, Ronald? He's got this document that's supposed to be a forgery. It's a letter – isn't it a letter, Ronald?'

Ronald smiled as one who had only himself to blame.

Matthew went on, 'He puts these documents to all sorts of tests – don't you, Ronald? There's a test for the ink, and the paper, and all the folds. The most important thing is the formation of the letters – anyone can do the rest, but Ronald's the best man for detecting the formation of letters. And sometimes the forger has stopped to assess his handiwork and then retraced. That's fatal because there's an interruption in the writing which can be detected under the micros-cope, at least Ronald can detect it – can't you, Ronald?'

Alice was looking at her cigarette, which she was tapping on the edge of the ash-tray.

'I shall never believe he's guilty,' she said. 'Never.'

Ronald thought, 'How that second, histrionic "never" diminishes her – how it debases this striking girl to a commonplace.'

'I'll always believe in his innocence,' she said. 'Always. No matter what the evidence is.'

'I haven't yet looked at the document,' Ronald said. 'I am sure it will not be incriminating to your friend.'

She looked up at him. 'Why are you sure?'

'Because he is your friend,' Ronald said.

Something in his tone made Matthew collect his senses. 'I haven't been indiscreet in talking about the letter, have I?' he said.

'It's perfectly understandable,' Ronald said.

'After all, *you* told me about it.'

'That's right,' Ronald said, 'I did.'

Matthew kept looking uncomfortably at Ronald. But he chattered on, desperately, in his desire to depreciate the girl's lover.

'Ronald says Patrick Seton has been convicted of forgery before.'

'Well, I don't believe it. He's been abroad a lot of his life at famous séances. He was married at one time. His divorce is coming through shortly, and we're getting married. Colonel Scorbin, who's one of the leading spiritualists in Mrs Marlene Cooper's Circle, and a colonel, said to me, "Patrick is one of those rare persons who are born to do great things and to suffer injustice and persecution." I said to him, "I believe it," and I do believe it and I always will, always.'

She seemed not sure how to look at Ronald, whether to show a predominance of hostility which might frighten him, or of fear which might move him to pity; or whether to affect charm and win him over. She offered all three in a way, by holding her head loftily as she regarded him, by pleading with her eyes under their lashes, and by sitting with the elbow over her chair so that her breasts rose unmistakably towards him.

Matthew realized that he had caused Ronald to be the centre of her attention rather than achieved his desire to discredit Patrick.

Alice's ten-minute rest was up. She sauntered about with her long swing among the tables and the trailing ivy of the Oriflamme taking orders for coffee. Matthew and Ronald stayed for a while and she returned as often as she could to their table, once pausing with her tray, on the way to serve a customer, to say to Ronald what was still on her mind.

'The case may not come off. Have you any idea if the case will be brought?'

'No. It has nothing to do with me.'

'It would be easy to frame up a case against Patrick, with that letter.'

'Nothing will be framed up,' Ronald said. 'Please forget about the letter.'

Matthew said, 'Can I meet you after the shop's closed and take you home?'

'Yes,' she said, and she nodded. 'Yes.'

Matthew had not expected her assent.

'Are you sure?' he said, instantly afterwards feeling like a lout.

'Yes, yes, I'm sure.' She was looking at Ronald.

'I'll be back here at the Oriflamme at ten to twelve,' Matthew said. She was looking at Ronald.

'Good night, Alice,' Ronald said.

'Can't you do something for Patrick?' she said to Ronald.

He said, 'You should not expect anything of Patrick Seton. Leave him.'

Matthew and Ronald walked along the Chelsea Embankment. Matthew said, 'I didn't expect her to let me fetch her tonight. I'd better phone my sister. She's expecting me to stay with her tonight because my brother-in-law's gone over to Dublin with my other uncle, and she doesn't like to be alone in the house with the children. I'd better phone and tell her I'll be late. Did you mind me telling Alice about that document you've got to inspect? Was it confidential?'

'It was confidential.'

'Oh, you should have made that clear when you told me. But I wanted Alice to know what she's got hold of in this Patrick Seton.'

'Yes, she seems to be in love with him.'

'Did you think so?'

'Yes.'

'Lovely girl, isn't she? And carrying a child inside her.'

'Very attractive.'

'D'you think I've a chance with her?'

'Chance of what?'

'Well, it would have to be marriage. She's expecting the child, moreover. It makes her more desirable; not many would think so, but I do.'

'I think you'll have a chance after Patrick Seton has served a few months of his prison sentence.'

'Don't you think she'd be the sort of girl who would wait for him?'

'Not after she had heard his previous convictions read out in court.'

'The age of him,' Matthew said, 'and the look of him! What does she see in him, a girl like that? You would never see such a match in Ireland except in rare cases where the man had a bit of money and the girl was homeless.'

'She is obviously a soul-lover,' Ronald said.

'She's in love with his spiritualism, that's what it is. He must know a few tricks.'

'I think he's a genuine medium, from what I've heard.'

'I hope he doesn't get his divorce. It might not come off. Then Alice –'

'From what I recall,' Ronald said, 'he isn't a married man at all. At least, it wasn't declared the last time he was in court.'

'He's supposed to have been married for twenty-five years; so Alice says.'

'Well, perhaps he lied to the court. But there's usually a question of maintenance orders. I distinctly recall his being described as a bachelor.'

'What a good memory you've got,' Matthew said.

'Thanks,' said Ronald, and smiled at himself in the glass window of a shop.

'Why should he talk about a divorce if he isn't married, though?' Matthew said. 'Do you think he intends to marry Alice at all?'

'I'll find out what I can from Martin Bowles. He's prosecuting counsel.'

Matthew stopped walking and was looking out over the full-flowing river at the lights on the opposite bank.

'Have you been eating lots of onions?' Ronald said.

'No, not since yesterday. Can you smell them in my breath?'

'Yes.'

'Come on, let's have a drink to take it away before I pick up Alice. They don't like the smell of onions in your breath. Do you really think Patrick Seton is a bachelor?'

They sat in the public house and debated the question of Patrick's being a bachelor, and if so, why he had told Alice the story of a divorce.

'Perhaps he's putting her off from day to day,' Matthew said. 'You could understand it; her wanting to be married for the child, and him not wanting to marry at all. He may be a bachelor like us in that respect.'

Ronald silently contemplated the no-betting notice on the wall.

'He has no intention of marrying her at all,' Matthew said, becoming fierily convinced of it. 'What do you expect of a spiritualist? His mind's attuned to the ghouls of the air all day long. How can he be expected to consider the moral obligations of the flesh? The man's a dualist. No sacramental sense. There have been famous heresies very like spiritualism – they –'

'Have another drink,' Ronald said, who was accustomed to long evenings of proof that Matthew had emerged from his Jesuit school well versed in the heresies.

'Take the Albigensians. Or take the Quietists even. The Zoroastrians. Everything spiritual. Down with the body. Against sex –'

'Against marriage,' Ronald said. 'All bachelors. Like us.'

'I think the spiritualists have sex.' Matthew looked broodily at his knees. 'I'm afraid we are heretics,' he said, 'or possessed by devils.' His curls shone under the lamp. 'It shows a dualistic attitude, not to marry if you aren't going to be a priest or a religious. You've got to affirm the oneness of reality in some form or another.'

'We're not in fact heretics,' Ronald said, 'under the correct meaning of the term.'

'Well, we've got an heretical attitude, in a way.'

'Not in fact. But does it worry you?'

'Yes.'

'Do you want to marry?'

'No.'

'Then you've got a problem,' Ronald observed and went to fetch more drinks.

'I suppose an heretical attitude is part of original sin,' Matthew said as soon as Ronald returned within hearing. 'You can't avoid it.'

Ronald said, 'The Christian economy seems to me to be so ordered that original sin is necessary to salvation. And so far as remaining single is concerned that applies to a lot of people.'

They walked to Battersea where their attention was caught by the sound as of a horse galloping. They looked up a side-street in the direction of the sound and found it to come from a man lying on his back outside a pub. His legs were kicking out and his heels clop-clopped on the pavement. A few people had gathered in the road-way and a young policeman circled round the man as if he were a tiger.

'Is he drunk?' Matthew said.

Ronald went over to the young policeman. 'Turn his head to one side,' he said, 'or he might damage his tongue.'

'Are you a doctor?' said the policeman.

'No, but I understand fits. The man's an epileptic.' Ronald took his own wedge of cork from his pocket and handed it to the policeman. 'Stick this between his teeth. Then kneel on his knees and try and get his boots off.'

'There's an ambulance coming,' said the policeman.

'He could bite his tongue in the meantime,' Ronald said. 'There could be a lot of damage. I'd shove in the wedge if I were you.'

The policeman knelt and grasped the man's head. He tried to

thrust the wedge into the frothing mouth, but the man's convulsions kept throwing the policeman off.

The policeman looked up at Ronald. 'Would you mind trying to get his boots off, then, sir?'

'I doubt if I can do it,' Ronald said. He was greatly agitated, for if there was one thing he did not like to see it was another epileptic. The thought of touching the man horrified him. 'Matthew!' he called out. 'Come and lend a hand.'

Matthew approached and, as Ronald instructed, threw himself upon the man's jerking knees. The policeman jammed the wedge between his teeth. Ronald felt for the shoes as one thrusting his hands into flames. He shut his eyes, and felt for the laces, loosened them, threw the shoes aside so violently that one of them nearly hit an onlooker, and sprang back from the kicking figure.

The man was still jerking when the ambulance arrived, and he was lifted up by two men in hospital uniform and taken away.

'Did it upset you?' Matthew said as they went down to look at the river.

'Yes,' Ronald said.

'Will you be all right?'

'Oh yes, I'll be all right.'

Matthew went off to telephone to his sister and then to read a novel called *Marie Donadieu* in Lyons' Corner House until it should be time to go and meet Alice, while Ronald walked part of the way home, and then feeling unsafe, took a taxi the rest of the way. There, he resisted taking his phenobarbitone, shaky though he was, for on occasions of extra stress he rather cherished the feeling of being more alive and conscious than usual, he cherished his tension and liked to see how far he could stand it. This evening he got ready for bed without any intimations of an approaching fit, and although he had his little drugs ready to take, he did not take them, and managed to get a living troubled sleep instead of a dead and peaceful one.

SEVEN

'What is the size of the chalet?' Patrick breathed indifferently.

Dr Lyte said, 'Oh, large enough for two. There are four or five rooms, but as I say it is very difficult of access. You are only a kilometre and a half from the frontier on the one hand and only three from the bus stop on the other, but that's as the crow flies. If you aren't a fairly good climber you would have to be a crow.' He laughed. Patrick did not. 'I wouldn't recommend it, really I wouldn't,' said Dr Lyte.

'No, it sounds just our sort of thing,' Patrick whispered. 'Isolated. Mountains. We'll take it on for three weeks as soon as this wretched case is either squashed or over.'

Dr Lyte reached across his desk, lifted the silver lid of his inkpot, and let it drop again. He looked at his short white hands. He lifted his card-index box and placed it down again a quarter of an inch from its previous position. He fidgeted with his blotting paper. He said to Patrick, 'Suppose the case does come off?'

'Alice and I will go abroad immediately after the case.'

'But if . . .'

Patrick's blue eyes looked out at the sky above the roof. So blue, he thought, so calm. A muscle in his small chin twitched. 'I'm quite confident of being acquitted,' he said in his murmur. 'I may not be sent for trial, even. The police keep asking for time. No evidence. I've been remanded twice.'

Dr Lyte said, 'I don't know, really, why you haven't skipped away in the meantime. Why don't you go abroad?'

Patrick coughed. 'I feel I must stay and see this unfortunate occurrence through.' His shoulders moved resentfully. 'Do you think I'm afraid to – to – how shall I put it? – to stand trial?'

'No,' said Dr Lyte.

'We'll take over your chalet then,' Patrick said. 'Alice and I. One way or another, that will be before the end of the year.'

'I don't recommend it in November or December,' said Lyte.

'Alice likes the cold weather. Alice doesn't like tourist seasons. Alice likes the snow. Will it be snowing?'

'You'll be cut off. Supposing Alice were to take ill, in her condition? Really, you must wait till the spring. March would be all right, perhaps. April, certainly. But November, December. Have you ever been to a lonely part of Austria in November?'

'We shall be taking your chalet for a month.' Patrick smiled a little at Dr Lyte's protests; and the doctor, who did not like to be smiled at in this way, said, 'I've a good mind to refuse you.'

'Have you now?' Patrick said. 'Have you?'

Dr Lyte thought of his practice and his wife and his house at Wembley Park, his daughter at Cambridge and his married daughter; he thought, also, inconsequentially, of the field attached to a Kentish Georgian rectory which he had recently acquired; he thought of his professional friends, his cottage in France and his chalet in Austria. There was nothing he could think of that he wanted to lose, and he regretted the evening he ever set foot in Marlene's Sanctuary of Light. ('One hopes it will become a Sanctuary of Lyte in every sense,' some man had remarked on hearing his name on that one occasion, but the remark had shocked Marlene.) To say this doctor thought of all he could lose is perhaps to put too blunt a point on it, for he felt these things deeply, and all in a second or two while Patrick smiled a little with melancholy.

'You know,' said Dr Lyte, 'that Alice can't stand up to anything strenuous. Ober-Bleilach will be strenuous. The climbing –'

'I'll see she doesn't do too much. I'll see she takes her injection every day.'

'You'll have to take a supply of insulin with you,' Lyte said.

'Yes.'

'A good supply,' he said. 'You can't depend on local supplies. It's a remote place.'

'Yes. She knows how to look after herself.'

'Are you sure?'

'Yes.'

'You were saying the other day,' said the doctor, 'that you thought Alice might be negligent about her insulin.'

'No, I don't think so now. At least, I'll see that she isn't. If she's going to take too much of the stuff or too little she'll do it whether we go away or not.'

So she will, thought Dr Lyte, and he actively dispersed an uneasy idea that had begun to form in his mind.

'We'll take that chalet,' Patrick said as if his mind were on something else.

'Let's discuss the details, then, after the trial. You know, Patrick, I've got a roomful of patients waiting to see me.'

Patrick discerned a touch of defiance. He was aware that Dr Lyte possessed, in relationship to himself, a mixture of emotions, including various shades of fear, and so, to encourage them, Patrick said, 'I keep on getting through to that control who is so familiar with the unfortunate occurrence in your past life. I can't help it. I keep on getting – or rather he keeps on getting through to me. He keeps on reminding me –'

'Are you short of ready cash?' said Lyte, and already he had risen from his chair and was walking over to a cupboard in which he kept a black tin cash-box.

'The Chief hasn't decided,' Inspector Fergusson said. 'It depends on a number of factors to do with our evidence.'

'But when do you think this unfortunate occurrence will be settled, Mr Fergusson?' Patrick trailed on.

'A month or two.'

'I have some little news for you,' Patrick said.

'Now, Patrick, I must warn you, we'll do our best but this time we can't guarantee your protection. The Chief told me to tell you. So news or no news . . .'

'I've been helpful to you,' Patrick said, shuffling his feet bashfully and looking down at them. 'And I could go on being helpful, Mr Fergusson.'

'What's the news, then?' Fergusson said.

'Well – after what you've just said, Mr Fergusson, I don't really feel inclined –'

'I'm surprised at you, Patrick!' said Mr Fergusson. 'I really am surprised.'

Patrick swallowed and looked frail and ashamed. His knees closed in together and he grasped the seat of his chair like a schoolboy.

Inspector Fergusson offered Patrick a cigarette. Patrick took one; his hand was shaking.

'Well, Patrick,' said big strong Mr Fergusson, 'you haven't ever let me down yet.'

'No,' Patrick said. 'I thought you were going to bear that in mind with reference to Mrs Flower, the unfortunate . . .'

'I'm being straight with you,' said Fergusson, his square good shoulders blocking the lower half of the window-light, 'and I'm telling you that we can't promise to protect you this time. I can't promise anything. You've always had a square deal for any information you've passed on.'

'There's a lot that goes on in Spiritualism,' Patrick observed with timid sociability. 'From your point of view,' he said.

'Tell me, Patrick,' said big Mr Fergusson, 'did you never think of getting married? It might have made a man of you. It might have kept you straight.'

'I've always believed in free love. I've never believed in marriage,' Patrick murmured. 'Why should man-made laws . . .'

Fergusson tilted back his chair and heard him out: man-made laws, suppression of the individual, relics of the Victorian era. . . . Patrick's thin voice died out '. . . and all repression of freedom of expression and self-fulfilment. . . .' It sounded good-class reading-stuff.

'You've certainly got ideas of your own,' stated Fergusson, standing up. 'I'm a married man myself,' he stated. 'Well, Patrick, I've got work here in front of me to do. Keep in touch.'

Patrick stroked his hair. He stood up, opened his mouth to speak, and sat down again.

'I'd like to be as helpful as possib . . .' Patrick said.

'Well, tell me the tale and get it off your chest.' Inspector Fergusson drew a note-pad towards him and poised his pen.

'There isn't actually a tale. Only a name. There was an unfortunate occurrence the other night –'

'What name?'

'Dr Mike Garland.'

'What about him?'

'He poses as a clairvoyant.'

'A fraud.'

'Oh, yes. He attempted to question me while I was under the other night. He's very friendly at the moment with Mrs Freda Flower.'

'Where does he live?'

'I'll find out, Mr Fergusson.'

'What does he do for a living?'

'I'll find out if you're interested, Mr Ferg ...'

'Only for the records,' said the Inspector. 'What does he do for a living?'

'I'll find out, Mr Fergusson. I thought his name might be helpful,' Patrick said.

'Thanks.' Fergusson was scribbling his notes. 'Brief description, Patrick, please. You know what we want.'

Patrick cast his pale eyes to the ceiling. 'Nearly six foot, fairly stout, age about fifty, greying hair, fresh complexion, round face, blue eyes.'

'Right,' said Fergusson. 'What does he do for a living?'

'He goes about with a Father Socket.'

'Who's he – a clergyman?'

'I don't know, Mr Fergusson. I haven't met Father Socket.'

'Are you sure?' said Mr Fergusson.

'Yes, Mr Fergusson,' Patrick said. 'But I'll find out about him for you.'

'Right. What does Garland do for a living?'

'Mr Fergusson, I hope you can do something for me with regard to the unfortunate –'

'It's in the Chief's hands, Patrick. Defrauding a widow of her savings is a serious crime on the face of it.'

'I was tempted and fell,' Patrick said.

'So you said in your statement,' said Mr Fergusson, tapping the heap of files on his desk.

Patrick looked yearningly at the files as if wishing to retrieve the statement that lay in one of them.

'Mrs Flower still isn't prepared to give evidence, though?' Patrick said.

'She'll have to give evidence.'

'Satisfactory evidence?'

'We aren't sure of that, as yet.'

*

Dr Lyte sat in his consulting-room after the last of the evening surgery had departed and his receptionist had locked up and gone home. He was in a panic, and this caused him to lose his head so far as he was writing the letter at all; but it was the panic which, at the same time, prompted the lucidity of what he wrote.

Dear Patrick,

Please do not think I don't want you to borrow my chalet in Austria for your forthcoming holiday with Alice, but I feel bound to repeat that I think it inadvisable, from the medical point of view, that Alice should be exposed to the certain inconvenience of this inaccessible place.

I just want to put a few of the drawbacks on record. In fact, I feel bound to do so.

You said previously that Alice was probably careless about her insulin injections. Although you told me today that your suspicions in this respect were unfounded, I feel bound to say that any carelessness in the administration of the injections (too much or too little) while Alice is in a condition of pregnancy, might prove fatal.

In fact, I should feel bound to obtain an undertaking from Alice on the whole question of her injections, before permitting the use of my chalet.

I should also wish to make certain that you took with you sufficient supplies of insulin, because the nearest town has no druggist.

Alice, I believe, would certainly die within a few days or even sooner, if deprived of her insulin. You know she has two sorts which she administers just before breakfast.

(a) Insulin soluble for immediate effect.

(b) Protamine zinc for more prolonged coverage throughout the evening and the following night. She needs 80 units.

But Alice understands all this. I understand she tests her urine for sugar and acetone first thing in the morning, and she can adjust the dosage accordingly. You must see that this is done.

The last time I saw Alice she told me she was still visiting the diabetic clinic every six months for routine assessment of progress.

If Alice were to take *too much* insulin and then, say, went for a

hearty climb or long walk, she might easily die on the mountainside. Most . . .

Dy Lyte stopped writing. What am I saying, what am I doing? he
thought. It came clearly to him, then, that he suspected Patrick of an
intention to kill the woman, if you could call it an intention when a
man could wander into a crime as if blown like a winged leaf.

What evidence have I got? Lyte thought. None at all. He wrote on,
nevertheless.

. . . diabetics carry glucose or even lump sugar in their pockets to
be taken at the first onset of the symptoms of hypoglycaemia – a
dangerously low blood sugar-content, which the patient can check
from the urine-test. . . .

Dr Lyte put down his pen. If Patrick were to add a little sugar to her
urine specimen so that she would take a hefty dose of insulin, and then
to make her take a good walk without her little tin of glucose – Patrick
might say to Alice 'Oh, you don't need your handbag' – she would
probably pass out on the mountainside. Or suppose he substituted his
own urine in the test-tube so that she would take an underdose? Or
suppose he himself gave her the injections? Insulin was used in the
concentration camps as a method of execution. Insulin, said Dr Lyte
to himself, is a favoured mode of suicide amongst doctors and
psychiatrists, it is rapid in effect. He looked round the room which he
had furnished so carefully to match the red carpet and to be suitable to
himself, and it seemed, in retrospect, that when he had chosen the
furnishings of this consulting-room, he must have been pretending
all the time that the world is not a miserable place. It was sometimes
not easy to establish death by insulin. He wrote on:

Therefore I feel bound to warn you of the dangers . . .

Then he stopped. I feel bound. I feel bound to warn you. In what
position, he thought, am I to issue warnings to Patrick Seton? It is he
who comes with his unspoken warnings to me.

Dr Lyte read through his letter. Clearly if he had any suspicions of
Patrick's intentions towards the girl, this letter betrayed it. Such a

letter might – it certainly would – provoke a man like Patrick. One never knew where one was with a man like Patrick Seton. Patrick knew a lot about his early career. Patrick was dangerous.

And then, what evidence was there for his suspicions? Patrick had said, 'How long would it be before she died if she neglected to take insulin?' That was no ground for suspicion.

Lyte tore the letter up into little bits, placed the little bits, a few at a time, in his ash-tray and set fire to them with his cigarette lighter until they were all burned up.

Then he recalled that Patrick had said, 'She won't let me give her the injections. She won't let me see her taking the injections.'

Then he recalled quite clearly that Alice had told him, 'Patrick does the injection for me every day. Patrick is so good at it, I don't feel a thing.'

And then the whole problem was too much. The doctor was indignant at being subjected to it. The one incident in his career which he needed to hush up, Patrick had somehow got hold of. This one mistake had occurred twenty-seven years ago when he was still a single man, a different person altogether. You change when you marry and establish yourself, everything that happened previously had nothing to do with you any more. But Patrick sitting in his so-called trance had said plainly that night at the séance, 'There is a new visitor to our Circle, a man of the medical profession. Gloria wishes to tell him that she is watching over him, and remembers every detail of the incident in 1932 about which there was a certain amount of mystery at the time. Gloria sends this message to the visitor in our midst who is a member of the medical profession: he should become a spiritualist and attend séances weekly. She is exhausted, now, and has no more to say for the present. Gloria wishes to say she is exhausted. The effort of speaking from the other side is exhausting. Gloria is tired. She feels weak. She is exhausted. . . .'

Gloria had died as the result of an illegal operation in the summer of 1932. There had been inquiries. Nothing came of them. Cyril Lyte, newly qualified, was not even questioned, he was abroad during the questioning. He had been one of many lovers during the previous winter. 'I'm tired. I'm exhausted,' Gloria had said when the hasty operation was over. He had left her with the two middle-aged women, neither of whom knew his name. The two middle-aged women were lifting Gloria's feet and shoving pillows, cushions, blankets under them, for he had said she must not lose too much blood; be careful, keep her feet up, *up*. 'I'm exhausted': Gloria had died next day. He was abroad during the questioning. He became a Communist for a space, by way of atonement. Within a year he had mostly forgotten the incident and when he remembered it, assured himself he had done his best for her, and what proof had he that the child was his?

Patrick's message, twenty-seven years later in the dark séance room, nearly led him to a nervous breakdown. Whichever way he looked at it, whether Patrick had spoken in innocence or from hard knowledge, the message was frightening. 'Gloria sends this message ... remembers every detail ... is exhausted, is tired, is exhausted.' It sounds like hard knowledge, Lyte thought.

In the end, Cyril Lyte found it less frightening to believe that Patrick was a common blackmailer, and no medium between this world and the other. Patrick had called at the surgery the day after the séance. When the doctor had tormented himself for a week he gave way and challenged Patrick on the subject. At first he found Patrick vague as to the details of the message, but very soon asserting his power, and this comforted Dr Lyte. Patrick was no medium, he told himself. There was no danger from the dim spirit of Gloria, the only danger to be reckoned with was Patrick who was tangible and who must have known the truth all through the years that had passed since he himself had been a single man and so different. As he had sometimes, waking at nights in the weeks following Gloria's death, dreaded, he was convinced, now, she must have written a letter before she died, or told someone. Patrick had recognized him at the séance. And so Dr Lyte settled down to supply Patrick with cash, and sometimes to supply Patrick with drugs which assisted him in his trances – 'You're certainly a great medium!' Dr Lyte would permit himself to remark as he handed the drugs into Patrick's meek hands. He had heard somewhere that even genuine mediums used drugs; but the doctor strengthened his will against the idea and was determined not to believe it. 'You're certainly a great medium!' – and Patrick would sometimes wink with his eyelid which in any case drooped. Dr Lyte supplied cash and drugs. If he should seem to falter or keep Patrick too long in the waiting-room, Patrick would say, 'When are you coming to another séance? I may have another message for you.'

Cash, drugs, and now professional advice. How long would it take for Alice to die if she were deprived of insulin? How long if she took too much? She may be careless with her injections. She won't let me give them to her, she won't let me see her taking them.

'Patrick,' Alice had said, 'always give me the injections himself, he's so good.'

'Your chalet in Austria,' Patrick had said. 'We shall be wanting it for a holiday after the unfortunate court case is settled. And I doubt if it will come to court, and if so it will only last half an hour; I'm certain of acquittal. How big is the chalet? How high up in the mountain? How far from the nearest town?'

Dr Lyte looked round his consulting-room and saw there was no escape. He tore a page from *The Times* and folded it into the shape of a cone. He scooped the black frail ash of the burnt letter into the cone, rolled it up tight. He decided to go to his club for a drink before going home, and as he left his surgery he dumped the paper containing the ashes of his letter to Patrick in the dustbin among the stained cotton wool and empty sample medicine packages of the day. He went to his club and was warmed by the immediate greetings of two of his oldest, most likeable friends.

The cheerful thought occurred to him that Patrick Seton might even be convicted of fraud if it came to a trial.

EIGHT

Ronald was changing to go to Isobel Billows's cocktail party when the housekeeper from the ground-floor flat came up and rang his bell.

'I let in your secretary this afternoon,' said the housekeeper. 'Just thought I'd let you know. I suppose it was all right.'

'What secretary?' Ronald said.

'The girl. The girl that came for your papers.'

'What girl?' Ronald said.

When the housekeeper, resentful and dispirited, had gone, Ronald looked mournfully and in vain in the drawer of his desk where he had left the letter which Patrick Seton was suspected of forging in the name of Mrs Freda Flower.

'She was, I should say, about twenty-eight, late twenties,' the housekeeper had said. 'A fair young woman, well, I should say near to fair-coloured hair, very pale. How was I to know? She said she was your secretary, and you wanted the papers in a hurry and you forgot to give her the key. I said, I suppose it's all right and I had my niece downstairs so I said, just let yourself out, you know the way. She looked all right. Remember there was that gentleman that came that morning when I was doing your cleaning, that came for your brief-case. Remember you sent him. How was I to know this wasn't another person that came to save you the trouble, on account of your difficulty?'

'I can't think who she can be,' Ronald said.

'Well, I don't take responsibility.'

'Well, no,' said Ronald, 'of course. Don't worry,' and as soon as she was gone he had opened the drawer, knowing the letter would not be there. He opened all the other drawers and looked through the tidy heaps of papers, but simply as a desperate act of diligence.

Ronald was filled with a great melancholy boredom from which he suffered periodically. It was not merely this affair which seemed to

402

suffocate him, but the whole of life – people, small-time criminals, outraged housekeepers, and all his acquaintance from the beginning of time. When this overtook him Ronald was apt to refuse himself comfortable thoughts: on the contrary he used to tell himself: this sensation, this boredom and disgust, may later seem, in retrospect, to have been one of the happier moods of my life, so appalling may be the experiences to come. It is better, he thought, to be a pessimist in life, it makes life endurable. The slightest optimism invites disappointment.

Isobel Billows's house was in a newly smartened street at World's End which lies at that other end of Chelsea. The walls and ceiling of her drawing-room were papered in a dull red and black design. She was giving a cocktail party. Isobel had been three years divorced from her husband and always said to her new friends 'I was the innocent party,' which they did not doubt, and the very statement of which proved, to some of her friends, that she was so in a sense.

Marlene Cooper's ear-rings swung with animation as she spoke seriously about spiritualism to Francis Eccles who had now got a job on the British Council. Tim, like a bright young manservant of good appearance, sinuously slid among the guests with a silver dish of shrimps; these shrimps were curled up as if in sleep on the top of small biscuits. Isobel Billows herself, large, soft-featured, middle-aged and handsome, had given up trying to introduce everyone and was surveying the standing crowd from a corner while Ewart Thornton talked to her, he having had three Martinis, in the course of which he had told Isobel that he had mounds of homework, that a grammar-school master had no status these days, that spiritualism was the meeting-ground between science and religion, and that he always bought his shirts and flannel trousers from Marks & Spencer's. It was at the point of his fourth Martini that Ewart's deepest pride emerged, to enchant Isobel and make her feel she was really in the swing by having him at her party. She listened to him wonderingly as he told her of the real miner's cottage of his birth in Carmarthenshire where his father still lived, and the real crofter's cottage in Perthshire where his grandparents had lived till late. 'Latham Street Council School; Traherne Grammar School; Sheffield Red Brick – only the brick isn't red,' boasted Ewart. 'Three shillings and sixpence a week pocket money all the while I was a student. From the age of ten to the age of thirteen I was employed by a fishmonger to deliver fish after school hours and on Saturday mornings. My earnings were four shillings a week which, with the similar earnings of my brothers went into the family funds. I was given a pair of stout boots every year at Easter. Most of my clothes were home made. We had outdoor sanitation which we shared with two other families –'

'Were you ever in trouble with the police?' Isobel said, looking round in the hope that someone was listening.

Ewart looked gravely at a vase of flowers, as if searching his memory, but obviously he had lost ground. At last he said, 'No, to be quite honest, no. But I recall being chased by a policeman. With some boys in some rough game. Yes, definitely chased down a back-street.' He took out his snuff-box and looked vexed. 'I was definitely under-privileged by birth,' he said, 'though not delinquent.'

Isobel said encouragingly, 'What was your accent like?'

'Southern Welsh. You can still hear the trace of it, mind you.'

'So you can,' said Isobel, who could not.

She loved the hairy tweed suit and his middle-aged largeness, his drooping jowl. She wondered why he had never married. She thought, next, that in some way she ought to feel more grateful for her acquaintance with him than she was, and she wondered why this was so, and found the reason in his being now only a grammar-school master after such likely beginnings; a really dramatic rise in life would have been preferable. But still, he was the real thing, and a great asset to a party.

Ewart took a pinch of snuff and said, 'My father was a real miner, a real one. Half the men that claim to have come from mining stock, when you look into it, turn out to be the sons of mine-managers or clerks in the coal offices.'

Tim came round with his tray of shrimps.

'Have a shrimp,' he said.

Isobel said, 'Tim, stay and talk to Ewart. I must have a word with your aunt over there.'

Tim took her place with his dish beside Ewart and started eating the shrimps off the tops of the biscuits.

'I daresay,' Ewart Thornton said, in a definite man-to-man way, as to a senior prefect, 'your aunt has told you that she is trying to get together a number of people willing to give evidence as to the bona fides of Patrick Seton, in case he is brought to court by that absurd widow.'

'No, Marlene hasn't said anything,' Tim said, eating shrimps.

'She will no doubt be after you,' said Ewart. 'She will want you to give evidence in court for Patrick Seton. I advise you to do no such thing. I advise you rather to come forward as a witness for Mrs Freda Flower. Not that I care for Mrs Flower, a silly woman, but I feel Patrick Seton is an undesirable character who does no credit to the Circle. Of course he's a good medium but –'

'Have a shrimp,' Tim said, 'before I eat the lot.'

'No, thanks. He's a competent medium but there are many brilliant mediums by whom he could be replaced. He is not irreplaceable. Your aunt, I'm afraid, is not inclined to listen to reason. I feel we should all do our best to support Mrs Flower and –'

'Have a drink,' Tim said, lifting a small glass of liqueur off a tray as the caterers' man passed them by with his tray.

'Thanks. We should all support Mrs Flower and not Patrick Seton.'

'I shan't support either,' Tim said, cheerfully. 'I don't know a thing about either of them.'

'Oh, come!' Ewart said. 'You've attended the séances when both have been present.'

'Only as a novice,' Tim said. 'Really, I'd rather not be involved.'

'Be reasonable, my boy,' Ewart said.

Tim ate a shrimp. 'Am being reasonable,' he said, and licked his finger tips.

'It's a matter of principle,' Ewart said. 'Surely you've got principles.'

'None whatsoever when you actually look into it,' Tim said.

'I thought as much,' Ewart said. 'You fellows that have had every advantage in life –'

'Was brought up rough, me,' said Tim, eating two of the biscuits which were now deprived of shrimps.

'Tim!' shrieked Marlene from not very far away. 'Come over here a minute, I've been wanting to speak to you all evening.'

'Must see my aunt,' Tim said, and putting down the dish, took off his glasses, wiped them, put them on, took up a bowl of olives, and joined Marlene.

A serving table had been set up for the caterers in front of the window; it was spread with a white cloth and was laid out with bottles and glittering glasses. Ronald Bridges and Martin Bowles stood out of the way between a corner of this table and the wall.

'I could go to Switzerland for Christmas,' Martin said, 'if I could get in one small fraction of the money that's owing to me. Dozens of briefs but no pay. Solicitors are crooks, they won't part with money.'

'What do you look like in your wig?' Ronald said.

'Quite nice.'

Ronald thought this probably true, for Martin was going bald and the impression of an increasingly high forehead had, over the past five years, thrown his good features out of balance.

Martin said, 'I've been invited to Switzerland for Christmas with a party. All married couples except for me, if I go. It makes one feel young being with married couples.'

'Or insignificant,' Ronald said.

'Yes, or insignificant. I always feel a bit *less* than a married man. Why is that, do you think? Is it because they've got more money than us?'

'No, married men mostly have less. Obviously.'

'Well, they seem to have more money, in a queer sort of way, to be economically stronger than single chaps.'

'It's an illusion. The truth is, a married man is psychologically stronger.'

'Yes, it's psychological. They make one feel young, even men one was at school with. How are you getting on with that forged letter in the Seton case?'

'It's a question of responsibility, I think – if they have kids,' Ronald said, to keep Martin off the subject of the letter.

But 'How's the forgery work?' Martin said.

'The letter has been stolen from my flat,' Ronald said, 'I'm sorry to say.'

'Come along,' said Isobel Billows, 'you bachelors in a huddle, over there.' She slid her white arm through Martin's and pressed him into a group which included Marlene with her swinging ear-rings, Tim with his bowl of olives, a girl wearing a pink dress, and Francis Eccles, who, in the confidence of his new job on the British Council, was exuberantly philosophizing to the girl and Marlene.

'You see,' he was saying, 'we are all fundamentally looking at each other and talking across the street from windows of different buildings which look similar from the outside. You don't know what my building is like inside and I don't know what yours is like. You probably think my house is comfortably furnished with its music-room and libraries, like yours. But it isn't. My house is a laboratory with test-tubes, capillaries, and – what do you call them? – bunsen burners. My house contains a hospital ward, my house –'

'Do you live in a very splendid house?' Martin said to the girl, for his ears had selected from Eccie's speech only the bit about the music-room and libraries.

The girl was mightily irritated. 'Eccie is talking in metaphor,' she said. 'I live in a bedsitter.'

'I live in a basement flat,' said Eccie, still dazed from his elaboration. He looked from one to the other.

'Oh, I see,' Martin said. 'Well, you see, I've only got a crude legal mind. I –'

'Carry on,' said the girl to Eccie.

Isobel slid her white plump arm through the dark blue of Eccie's sleeve. 'Eccie, I want you,' she said, and bore him off somewhere else.

Martin said to the girl, 'I'm afraid I interrupted . . .' but he was now looking for Ronald, anxious to know whether Ronald could possibly have been serious when he said the letter had been stolen, and if so, to tell Ronald how furious he was.

He smiled formally to the girl and withdrew, first backward a few steps, then sideways, then right about, so that he could join Ronald where he was standing with Marlene Cooper and Tim.

'– must do something to justify your existence,' Marlene was saying to Tim, 'and now is the chance to show your mettle.'

'Never did have any mettle,' Tim said. 'Want an olive, Ronald?'

Ronald looked into his glass at the tiny drop of cocktail left at the bottom of it.

'Have an olive, Martin,' Tim said.

'What we want to do,' Marlene said, 'is to present a body of witnesses to the court. We can all testify in our own words. You, Tim, you've seen Patrick and you've heard him. You know he's a real medium, that's all you've got to say. There's no commitment attached. But we must give Patrick a character. He's being positively framed by Freda Flower and that vile lover of hers. There may be no case, but as I say, on the other hand, there may be a case.'

Tim said, 'Martin Bowles here is the prosecuting counsel in the case, Marlene.'

Marlene tilted her face to Martin's. 'Are you?' she said, 'Oh, are you?'

'Look,' said Martin, 'I really can't discuss –'

'I should think you couldn't,' Marlene said. 'You wouldn't have a leg to stand on. Nor will you have if it comes to court, let me tell you that. We are all behind Patrick. I'm behind him. Tim's behind –'

'I'd rather not be involved,' Tim said.

'But you are involved,' said his aunt.

'How did it happen?' Martin said as he drove Ronald home.

'A woman came to the house this morning and pretended to be my secretary. The housekeeper let her in. The letter was gone when I looked for it. I think I know who's got it.'

'Who?'

'Patrick Seton's girl-friend. It wasn't she who actually came to the flat, but I think Matthew Finch knows the girl.'

'Who? Which girl?' Martin inquired in his legal voice. 'You don't make it clear which is which.'

'I'll try and get the letter back.'

'We'd better have the police informed right away,' Martin said.

'All right,' Ronald said.

'Well, I know it won't do your reputation much good,' Martin said, 'losing an important document like that. But I don't suppose you depend much on your forgery detection work, do you?'

'I like it,' Ronald said.

'Do you think you *can* get it back?'

'I don't know,' Ronald said, deliberately, as one refusing to be a mouse even while the claws were upon him.

'I'm not trying to make things difficult,' Martin said, 'but . . .'

'But what?'

'Well, you say you can't work from the photostats. I daresay the photostats would be taken as some sort of evidence. But you can't give any evidence of forgery from a photostat, can you?'

'Not really. I've got to test the ink and study the writing on the folds in the paper. That sort of thing.'

'You've got us in a pickle,' Martin said.

'Matthew Finch knows the girl. I'll see if he can do something about it.'

'He was at the party tonight, wasn't he?'

'Yes.'

'Did you speak to him about this?'

'Yes.'

'You told him what had happened?'

'Yes. I made the mistake of telling him about the letter in the first place. Then he informed the girl. He thinks the girl who got into my rooms must be the girl he knows who works with Patrick Seton's girl in a coffee-bar. This girl is the friend of the other girl, and –'

'Who? Which girl is which? What are their names?'

'Alice and Elsie,' Ronald said. 'I think we'd better get the police to handle it, as you suggested.'

Martin had stopped for the traffic of South Kensington. He sat back from the wheel and pondered. Then, as he started up the car again, he said, 'Let's leave it that you get the letter back by tomorrow night or we'll get the police to find it. If it hasn't been destroyed by then.'

'It has probably been destroyed by now,' Ronald said in a louder voice than usual. 'And actually I think we must inform the police in any case.'

'They might ask you awkward questions,' Martin said.

'How do you mean?'

'Well, it's obvious you've been careless.'

'That can't be helped now.'

His melancholy and boredom returned with such force when he was alone again in his flat that he recited to himself as an exercise against it, a passage from the Epistle to the Philippians, which was at present meaningless to his numb mind, in the sense that a coat of paint is meaningless to a window-frame, and yet both colours and preserves it: 'All that rings true, all that commands reverence, and all that makes for right; all that is pure, all that is lovely, all that is gracious in the telling; virtue and merit, wherever virtue and merit are found – let this be the argument of your thoughts.'

For Ronald was suddenly obsessed by the party, and by the figures who had moved under Isobel's chandelier, and who, in Ronald's present mind, seemed to gesticulate like automatic animals; they had made sociable noises which struck him as hysterical. Isobel's party stormed upon him like a play in which the actors had begun to jump off the stage, so that he was no longer simply the witness of a comfortable satire, but was suddenly surrounded by a company of ridiculous demons.

This passage from Philippians was a mental, not a spiritual exercise; a mere charm to ward off the disgust, despair, and brain-burning.

This was the beginning of November. It is the month, Ronald told himself in passing, when the dead rise up and come piling upon you to warm themselves. One is affected as if by a depressive drug, one shivers. It is only the time of year, that's the trouble.

With desperate method he began to abstract his acquaintance, in his mind's eye, from the party, and examined them deliberately to see the worst he could find in them. One must define, he thought: that is essential.

Isobel Billows, with her hungry lusts, her generosity wherever she thought generosity was a good investment, smiled up at him in the glaring eye of his mind.

'What's wrong with me?' she said.

'Nothing,' he said, 'but yourself.'

'Oh, Ronald, you always see the worst side of everything, there's a diabolical side to your nature.'

'What do you mean, diabolical?'

'Well, possessed by a devil, that's the reason for your epilepsy.'

'Adulterous bitch.'

'Oh, Ronald, you don't know how basely men treat me. Men have always treated me very badly.'

'A woman of your class shouldn't talk like that.'

'But they come and sponge on me, Ronald, and then they go away and say, "Oh, her. You don't want to have anything to do with her. Don't listen to her."'

Martin Bowles was her lover, and was also her financial adviser, and, in his legal capacity, handled her property. '... and you see,' Martin said – he was sitting at his desk in chambers, in the bright eye of Ronald's imagination, leaning one hand on his high bald forehead – 'I haven't much freedom, what with my old ma and the housekeeper, and then there's Isobel, I'm fairly tied to Isobel.'

'Will you marry Isobel?'

'No, oh no. It's a question of business interests.'

'Have you misappropriated Isobel's money?'

'No, oh no. I'm on the right side of the law.'

'Yes, the right side of the law.'

'Don't be vulgar, Ronald.'

'It was you who employed the phrase.'

'Isobel's very well off although she pretends to be poor. She doesn't live up to her money, you know.'

'Fraudulent conversion, it's revolting.'

'Not at all. There's nothing fraudulent about it, I'm perfectly safe in the law. There's a large sum involved, Ronald, but I'm perfectly safe.'

'Forty thousand?'

'How do you come to know all this, Ronald?'

'From piecing together what I hear and see in one direction and another.'

'My old ma's a tyrant, quite a drag upon my life.'

'You shouldn't be living with your mother, at your age. It makes a mess of a man. It makes for a mean spirit, living with mama after the age of thirty.'

'You know, Ronald, you should have been more careful with that letter.'

'Yes.'

'And now you've gone and lost it. Shall we inform the police? Shall we ruin your little reputation as a reliable expert? You shouldn't have talked.'

'Please yourself. I don't particularly want to get the letter back. Why should I hound Patrick Seton? He has offended in the same way as you, on a smaller scale than you, but less cleverly than you.'

'This is rather absurd,' said Martin Bowles in the mind's ear of Ronald. 'I won't have it.'

'I won't have it,' Marlene Cooper said, brushing her ear-rings past Ronald's mouth as if he were not there. 'I won't have Tim remaining on friendly terms with that revolting bald barrister.'

'I like Martin Bowles,' Tim said.

'If Patrick's case comes to court your friend will be prosecuting counsel.'

'Someone's got to be prosecuting counsel,' Tim said.

'Well, you must give up your association with him.'

'I haven't got any particular association with him. Martin is just a friend,' Tim said.

'But, Tim dear, I saw you with him at Isobel's party, laughing away as if nothing had happened. Do you realize that when you give evidence for Patrick, the man is sure to cross-examine you?'

'I don't want to be involved,' Tim said. 'I'm not giving any evidence. We treat your conspiracy as a joke.'

'You are weak,' Marlene said, 'like your father and his father before him.'

And so he is, Ronald thought, viciously, for he was especially fond of Tim. He doesn't want to be involved at all; except of course, with Hildegarde.

'I did everything for Ronald that a woman possibly could do,' Hildegarde said. 'I washed his shirts, mended his clothes, I bought the theatre tickets, and I set the alarm clock for him. I made every possible allowance for his disability. I even helped him in his job. I made a study of handwriting and even ancient manuscripts. What more could I have done?'

'Nothing at all,' said Tim in the bemused ear of Ronald's imagination, as he sat there in his flat in the small hours of the morning, 'Nothing at all,' said Tim. 'Move over, darling, and don't kick.'

'It makes me kick,' Hildegarde said, 'to think of Ronald. If only he had given me some excuse when he broke with me....'

'Shut up about Ronald,' Tim said. 'It's jolly off-putting.'

'Does he know about us?' Hildegarde said.

'No, of course not.'

'He mustn't know about us,' she said. 'It would upset him and he would never forgive you. I don't want to break up your friendship with Ronald.'

'You're sweet,' Tim said, snuggling down. 'Lovely to think tomorrow's Sunday,' he said, 'and a long lie in.'

'Let me put your pillow straight, sweet boy,' said Hildegarde. 'You are all crumpled up.'

Matthew had told Ronald: 'I saw Hildegarde Krall the other evening in the Pandaemonium Club at Hampstead. She was wearing jeans, looked very nice.'

'Was she alone?'

'Yes, alone.'

'Did you speak to her?'

'Only briefly. She left early. Walter Prett was with me. She left when he started making a nuisance of himself and insulted Francis Eccles.'

Tim, Hildegarde, Matthew Finch, Francis Eccles, Walter Prett. Ronald got through the list by half past three in the morning. Who are they, he thought, in any case, to me? Why be oppressed by a great disgust? 'We must go to court,' Ewart Thornton says, 'we must oppose Patrick Seton at all costs. Let us give evidence for a Mrs Freda Flower, about whose wrongs none of us cares.' But why does he induce in me a condition near to madness?

Because one is formed in that way, and at times of utter disenchantment no distraction whatsoever avails, even the small advertisements in the newspapers are vile, in the same way that I, in my epilepsy, am repulsive. He recited over to himself the passage from Philippians: '. . . all that is gracious in the telling; virtue and merit, wherever virtue and merit are found – let this be the argument of your thoughts'. By a violent wrench of the mind Ronald was capable of applying this exhortation in a feelingless way, to the company of demons which had been passing through his thoughts. He forced upon their characters what attributes of vulnerable grace he could bring to mind. He felt sick. Isobel is brave simply to go on breathing; another woman might have committed suicide ten years ago; she knows how to decorate her house and how to dress. Marlene is handsome, Tim is lovable, Ewart Thornton is intelligent, has gone far in the world, considering his initial disadvantages, and moreover he is a schoolmaster, and, moreover, one who respects his career and so finds difficulty in the practice of it. Martin Bowles is considerate to his mother. Matthew Finch is afflicted by sex and is blessed with a simple love of the old laws.

Walter Prett is beset by neglect and foolish fantasies and he loves art and is honest in his profession. Hildegarde has a tremendous character. Eccie has a job on the British Council. . . .

By four o'clock he was in bed. At five o'clock he rose and vomited. Next morning he had an epileptic seizure lasting half an hour; it was a type of fit in which his drugs were useless. This often happened to Ronald after he had made some effort of will towards graciousness, as if a devil in his body was taking its revenge.

He resolved to go to Confession, less to rid himself of the past night's thoughts – since his priest made a distinction between sins of thought and these convulsive dances and dialogues of the mind – than to receive, in absolution, a friendly gesture of recognition from the maker of heaven and earth, vigilant manipulator of the Falling Sickness.

NINE

'I can't help feeling sorry for little Patrick Seton,' said Matthew Finch. 'That widow and her friends seem to be ganging up on him in a most unpleasant way.'

'I'm sorry for him too, in a way,' Ronald said.

'He's half Irish,' said Matthew.

'The thing is: about this letter.'

'It sounds like Alice's friend, Elsie,' Matthew said. 'I'll see Elsie this afternoon.'

'It may be destroyed by now.'

'I doubt that,' Matthew said. 'Alice is a sentimental girl.'

'It's hardly a sentimental letter.'

'What does it say?'

'Get the letter back and you'll find out.'

'I know I'm to blame for this, I shouldn't have told Alice you had it,' Matthew said. 'I'm a foolish fellow, you know.'

'Where will you see Elsie?'

'I'll go round to the coffee-bar. She's always on duty on Saturday afternoons. I've got to see my cousin later, but –'

Ronald's telephone rang. Martin Bowles said, 'I say, Ronald. I thought it best to have Fergusson told that the letter had been stolen. I hope you –'

'Who's Fergusson?' Ronald said.

'The detective-inspector who keeps his eye on Patrick Seton. He says he'll be seeing Seton about it and doesn't seem to be worried about getting it back, that is, if Seton has it. I hope you agree that was the best course. If it comes out in court –'

'Yes, it was quite the most sensible thing to do,' Ronald said. 'I'm much relieved.'

'Sure you don't mind? If it comes out in court that you –'

'No, I don't mind a bit. In fact I'm glad. I ought to have done something of the kind straight away. The police should be informed of a theft of this kind. Only, in these particular circumstances, I doubt if Seton actually has the letter. His girl's got it, we think.'

'Who's *we*?'

'I've just been discussing it with Matthew Finch. As you know, he's a friend of the two girls in question.'

'*Which* two girls?'

'Seton's girl and the other girl, her friend, the one we think stole the letter for Seton's girl.'

'I really can't make out who these girls are, Ronald. What has Matthew Finch to do with this?'

'Well, you know I was indiscreet enough in the first place to tell him I was working on the letter. And he was indiscreet enough to tell Elsie, and –'

'Who's Elsie?'

'She's the other girl who's a friend of Seton's girl. I told you –'

'Yes, but I didn't make notes. Look, Ronald, you can't conduct a case like this.'

'I'm not conducting the case.'

'If it comes out in court that you've committed these indiscretions, you won't blame me, will you?'

'No,' Ronald said.

'I expect Fergusson will want to see you,' Martin said. 'A nice chap. Straight with you if you're straight with him.'

'What the hell are you talking about?'

'Now, Ronald, don't be –'

Ronald hung up. 'Some detective-inspector is going to find the letter,' he said. 'So let's forget it.'

'I've got you into trouble,' Matthew said. 'My sister thought probably this would happen when I told her about the letter –'

'Where are you lunching? I haven't done my shopping yet, what with one thing and another.'

'I've got you into trouble with my talk,' Matthew said. 'Would you like me to see Elsie in any case? It wouldn't do any harm, would it?'

'You'd better see Elsie,' Ronald said. 'Because I doubt if the detective-inspector will find the letter.'

'You said just now he was going to find it.'

'I know I did,' said Ronald. 'And I'll end up in the bin, I daresay. Come on, let's go out.'

The telephone rang again just as they were leaving. Ronald returned to answer it.

'Oh, Ronald,' said Martin.

'Yes.'

'Are you all right?'

'Yes.'

'Look, Ronald, I don't want you to misunderstand me. It's just that I'm bound by certain rules, you know. One has to observe certain –'

'Of course,' Ronald said. 'Obviously.'

'You'll help Fergusson all you can? I've told him you will.'

'Of course. But look, I don't really think Patrick Seton has the letter. I think it's something the girls have cooked up.'

'Which girls?'

'Polly and Molly,' Ronald said.

'Who?'

'Cassandra and Clytemnestra,' Ronald said.

'Look, Ronald. This is awkward for me. You know me, you like me, don't you?'

Here it comes, Ronald thought.

'Of course,' he said.

'Well, put yourself in my place. I've got my old ma on my hands. She's going blind. Can't see the television. The housekeeper's going blind. They fight like cat and dog, they were pulling each other's hair the other day. Can't get a new housekeeper, and anyway my old ma won't have anyone new. The housekeeper –'

'Hold on a minute,' Ronald said, and placing his hand over the receiver, murmured to Matthew, who was hovering at the door, to make himself comfortable on the sofa for at least five minutes. Have a drink. Cigarette – 'Yes, hallo,' he said returning to Martin on the telephone.

'The housekeeper,' Martin said, 'was my old nurse and my old ma won't get rid of her, she's got nowhere to go and we can't afford a pension. Then I do the shopping for the week-end. Not on weekdays, I draw the line there. Then Isobel's affairs take a bit of looking after, you know. I give her my professional services, she doesn't realize what I save her. Still, Isobel's a good sort, as you know, and very attractive.

I say, Ronald, would you say Isobel was an attractive woman?'

'Oh yes,' Ronald said.

'Doesn't show her years,' Martin said. 'Of course she's got the money and the leisure. She depends on me a lot, you know. She's had a lot of bad luck with men, and I think she appreciates me in a way. Wouldn't you think so?'

'Oh, I think she does.'

'Look, Ronald, come along to my club for lunch. You see –'

'Sorry, I'm not free.'

'You see, there's a personal problem I'd like to consult you about. Could you make it 1.30?'

'Sorry, really I'm not free.'

'I can't make it tomorrow,' Martin said, 'because the housekeeper goes off in the afternoon and I've promised to read *Jane Eyre* to my old ma. She says she was forbidden *Jane Eyre* as a girl. I don't see why, do you? You see, she can't see well and the television isn't much use to her. Then tomorrow night I've simply got to collect Isobel off a train. When can we meet?'

'I'll come and see you in your chambers one day next week. I've got to go now, Martin.'

'I'll ring you on Monday, then. Sure you're not worried about Fergusson looking into this theft?'

'No, but I doubt –'

'It's breaking and entering, and stealing, to be precise. They'll be sending a couple of fellows round to ask questions.'

'I see.'

'You should have been more careful, Ronald. You can't conduct a case ...'

When they were seated in the pub Ronald said, 'You can tell Elsie that the cops will be looking for her.'

'Now, she's a nice poor girl,' Matthew said.

'Well, give the poor girl a fright. Tell her the cops will be after her finger-prints or something.'

Elsie Forrest climbed the stairs to an attic flat in Shepherd's Bush, and pressed the bell on a door marked 'The Rev. Father T. W. Socket, M.A.' The door was opened by Mike Garland, wearing a green-and-white-striped dressing-gown over his suit, and looking, with his pink cheeks, like a lump of sticky bright confectionery. He blocked the door.

'Father Socket is expecting me,' Elsie said, 'to do some typing.'

'Oh, I don't know whether it's convenient, now. But come in.'

'I like that!' Elsie said as she walked into the large front sitting-room. 'I've taken the afternoon off from the coffee-bar especially to help Father Socket. So I should hope it is convenient.'

'I daresay it will be,' Mike Garland said. 'Take a seat.'

Elsie was irritated when he said 'Take a seat', for on all the chairs in the room were cushions that she herself had made for Father Socket, and this obviously gave her rights which rose above formalities. She had not expected to see this strange man with his peculiar garb in Father Socket's flat. She usually walked straight into the kitchen and put the kettle on the gas.

Elsie heard voices from Father Socket's bedroom. She wondered if the Master was ill, but did not like to investigate in the presence of the stranger.

The room was hung with Chinese scrolls which reached to the low bookcases. These contained the books of which Elsie had made a list, and for each of which, under the Master's instructions, she had made an index card. The Master was learned. He was a real priest, he told her, ordained by no man-made bishop but by Fire and the Holy Ghost; and a range of brightly woven vestments was hung in a cupboard in his bedroom to prove it.

Elsie had never before been to Father Socket's on a Saturday afternoon. Thursday afternoon was her usual time, and it was then she typed his manuscripts, over and over again – for he was always revising them, never satisfied, like the true Master of writing that he was.

'He ought to pay you for all that work,' Alice had said. But to Elsie it was a labour of love typing out his papers on the subjects of the Cabbala, Theosophy, Witchcraft, Spiritualism, and Bacon wrote Shakespeare, besides many other topics.

'It's a labour of love,' Elsie said to Alice. After all, Alice had Patrick; and it was nice for a girl to have someone on the spiritual side of life. Men like Father Socket lifted one up whereas young men so often pulled one down.

'You've got queer tastes,' Alice had said the day before, sitting in the window with Elsie, at dusk.

'There isn't any sex between Father Socket and me,' Elsie said.

'That's a detail,' Alice said.

'He smells of a perfume, like musk or incense,' Elsie said.

'You always smell things,' Alice said.

'Patrick smells of goat, like a real bachelor.'

'Go on with you. Patrick's a man of the world. He's been married.'

'That boy Matthew Finch who'd been eating onions that time. . . . It's terrible, the smell of onions. Because I used to sleep beside my uncle, we were all in the one room, in Sheffield where I was born. My uncle was the only one of them that didn't drink, drink, drink. So I went with Matthew and yet afterwards I didn't like myself for it. It's all explained in psychology.'

'Disgusting,' Alice whispered. 'Onions.'

They laughed as they sat in the darkening room, in a down-scale trill, one following the other.

'It wasn't funny at the time,' Elsie whispered. 'He didn't go right on to the end in case I got a baby, I suppose. That's what makes me really upset; when they go so far and no farther.'

'You don't want a baby without a man to marry you,' Alice said.

'It makes you feel there's not much of a man in them when they only go so far.'

'If Patrick wasn't the man he is,' Alice said, 'he wouldn't be much of a *man*.'

'I always said he wasn't much of a man to look at. Thin about the thighs. You can't disguise it.'

'But he's so different to other men. Patrick treats you with a difference.'

'Oh yes, he's all talk. Still, talk makes a difference. Father Socket talks beautifully. That's what gets me, Alice. The boys are after one thing and one thing only, but a man who's a bit older and can talk, and if he's got a beautiful voice . . .'

They sat hand-in-hand on the window seat and looked down on the lights of long Ebury Street.

'Yes,' Alice said, 'I suppose the main thing about Patrick is the talk.'

'Do you think he's going to marry you?'

'Of course. As soon as the divorce comes through.'

'I can't believe in that divorce, you know.'

'What d'you mean?'

'Are you sure he's got a wife?'

'He says so.'

'You don't look well, Alice.'

'No, it's difficult for a diabetic in pregnancy. I've got a craving for parsnips, too, I'd like a whole plate of parsnips.'

'Aren't you afraid of Patrick?'

'Afraid? What is there to be afraid of?'

'Well, nothing that you know about. It's all those things you don't know about him. They say, about his forgeries –'

'Yes,' said Alice's voice in the dark, 'I'm afraid of the things I don't know. I don't want to know.'

'I feel the same,' Elsie said as she sat, almost invisible, 'about the Master.'

'You're not tied to him,' Alice said, 'like I am to Patrick.'

'But there's a bond between the Master and me.'

'He's got a hold on you,' Alice said. 'Shall we put the light on?'

'Not yet,' Elsie said. 'I go on Thursdays and I do a bit of typing and then I stop. And he talks and reads poetry. Then I do a bit more typing. Then he reads me a bit of what he's just written of his spiritual autobiography.'

'Patrick recites poetry,' Alice said.

'Father Socket's voice is beautiful. He was brought up in a big rectory and he broke away from the Church of England. It's true you don't have to go to church to believe in God. I agree with that. Father Socket knows psychology.'

'Put on the light,' Alice said, and, when Elsie had switched on the light she jumped from her seat, and now they spoke aloud.

'He ought to pay you for all that work. We're both of us far too soft,' Alice said.

'It's a labour of love,' Elsie said. 'I'm going to his flat tomorrow afternoon. He asked me specially to come, so I've put off the coffee-bar.'

'That's money down the drain,' Alice said. 'At least Patrick gives me a bit of money.'

'So he ought, in your condition. But where does he get the money?

'I don't know,' Alice said.

'He's hiding something from you,' Elsie said.

'There's always something hidden,' Alice said, in such a way that Elsie was startled, uncertain whether Alice knew about the letter concealed in her handbag. She looked at Alice, to make sure, but Alice was holding her stomach and pulling her face with indigestion.

The gilt sunlight which sometimes happens in November poured through the window of Father Socket's flat on Saturday afternoon. Elsie waited, withering, in the sitting-room, listening to the voices coming now from the spare bedroom where apparently the stranger was lodged. Father Socket must have put him up for the night, and here he was staying on to the afternoon and keeping him back from his work.

Then she knew, of course, with a kind of exasperation, that the stranger was one of the Master's friends, and that they were all perverts, and she had really known it all along.

The voices rose to the pitch of a quarrel of which Elsie could not make out all the words. She went and stood by the door, the better to hear. '. . . where to draw the line, Mike . . . appearance's sake . . . the girl is . . .' and then a door closed, muting the voices to a querulous rise and fall. This filled her with irritation and impatience. She was inclined to leave the flat with a banging of doors, or at least to bang one door as a token. But then she thought of the letter in her handbag, and what palpitations she had gone through to obtain it, what risks taken. She had looked forward all the previous day and part of the night to her triumphant casual opening of her handbag and the producing of the letter before the astonished eyes of the Master.

Last week he had said, 'Do you know the man well?'

'I've seen him in the coffee-bar. He's quite nice. He works in a handwriting museum.'

'Ah yes,' said Father Socket, 'in the City.'

'He isn't very strong. He takes fits. He's quite nice-looking, but a bit odd, you know, fussy in his ways. You can tell from the way they put their sugar in the coffee, and stir it, and place the spoon back in the saucer. And his paper neatly folded with his umbrella and all that. A confirmed bachelor. Not that I mean anything by that. He's a friend of a friend of mine, an Irish fellow called Matthew Finch.'

'And this man's name?'

'Ronald somebody. Well, Matthew was in the Oriflamme with him the other night, and talking to Alice. He was talking about this letter that Patrick Seton wrote. Ronald is to test it for forgery. The police gave it to him and –'

'Not the police, surely. It would be in the hands of the police solicitor. Unless the case is in abeyance, in which case, possibly the police . . .'

'One or the other. So Ronald's got this letter that Patrick forged. Alice was upset and I saw her next day. She wants to try to get the letter back through Matthew. Matthew is keen on Alice.'

Father Socket had thought this unwise. So, when she came to talk it over with him, had Elsie.

'Alice may even go a long way with Matthew,' she said, 'to get that letter.'

'Do you know where this Ronald lives?' Father Socket had said.

'I could find out.'

'I should like to have a look at that letter myself,' he said.

'Would you?' she said.

Here then, she was with the letter in her handbag, and Father Socket quarrelling in the spare bedroom with the big man in the green-and-white-striped dressing-gown, and she sitting waiting like a fool, having lost an afternoon's work at the coffee-bar.

She opened the door of the sitting-room and bumped into Father Socket just as he was about to enter. His small face looked puffy and red. He looked suspicious at finding her so near to the door and seemed convinced she had been listening to the quarrel.

'I've been waiting a long time, Father,' she said.

'Oh, poor creature! Oh, poor creature! I am so very sorry. Come and sit down.'

He wore his best cassock and his broad hips swung under it as he put to rights a deep pink chrysanthemum which had fallen from its vase.

He turned and jerked his thumb over his shoulder to indicate the stranger in the other room. The gesture startled Elsie, for she had never seen the Master anything but utterly dignified. He mouthed and breathed a message to her, contorting his face as if she were a lip-reader. 'My – friend's – up – set. Won't – remove – dressing-gown.'

'Who is he, Father?' Elsie said in a normal voice.

He hunched his shoulders and flapped his hands to hush her.

She whispered, 'Who is he?'

The Master jerked his thumb once more over his shoulder and was about to convey a reply when Mike Garland walked in. He still wore his bright dressing-gown.

'Ah, Mike,' said Father Socket, pulling himself straight, 'come and meet my amanuensis Miss Elsie Forrest. Dr Garland, Miss Forrest.'

'We've already met, at the door,' Elsie said.

'How do you do,' Mike said. He sat down defiantly.

'Something unforeseen has arisen,' Father Socket said to Elsie, 'and so I'm afraid I've brought you here on a wild-goose chase, my dear, this afternoon. However, I will make some tea and I must read you my new translation of Horace. Where did I put it?'

'I'll make tea,' Elsie said.

'I shall prepare some tea,' Mike said. Elsie noticed as he left the room that he wore lipstick.

'Have you received any information from young Matthew?' Father Socket said to her softly when Mike had left the room.

'Matthew?'

'Or young Ronald? – The letter I mean. I don't of course want Mike to know anything about this. – But you haven't had time to investigate the possibility of obtaining it. . . .'

Elsie clutched her handbag, indignant and very put out, especially by Mike's lipstick. 'No, I haven't any news,' she said. 'I expect the letter is locked away somewhere safely.'

Father Socket sighed and looked at the carpet.

'Poor Patrick Seton!' he said. 'He does need taking care of. I feel if I could get matters in hand I could do something for Patrick.'

'He isn't any good to Alice. I don't mind if he gets sent for trial!'

'Hush,' said Father Socket, looking at the door.

'I'd like to see Alice rid of him,' she said, sitting down in a hard high chair, 'good medium though he is, he's –'

'Ah,' said Father Socket, 'Patrick has many enemies.' Again he jerked his thumb over his shoulder and mouthed, 'He's – one of – them.' He pulled his spine straight in his chair and said, 'But I am not an enemy. What Patrick needs is *control*. Someone ought to control him. Find out about that letter, my dear, find out. If once we know where it is – where young Ronald keeps it, I daresay we should be able to obtain it. I am thinking in dear Patrick's best interests. I have no wish to impede the course of the law of the kingdom, but the laws of the spirit come first, we ought to serve God rather than man, we must – Ah – tea!' He rose to admit the tinkling tea-tray with Mike rosily proceeding behind it.

During tea, Elsie ate a slice of walnut cake very quickly because she was so very upset inside at the sight of Mike in his highly sexual attire. She clutched her handbag all the closer, and was damned if she would part with the letter now that Father Socket had let her down so badly. Be damned to his paternal solicitude for dear Patrick. She should have known before, indeed she had really, inside, known all along that the Master was homosexual as Alice had said. She could have put up with it, even preferred it, if he had no sex at all, was above sex, but if there was one thing she detested . . .

Father Socket, meanwhile, said, 'Let me read you my little translation of the much-translated Horace, one, nine. Mine pays special attention to alliterative quantities. . . .'

The impudence of it, Elsie thought, talking round me all these months, and reading his poetry, and there I've been typing out his papers, page after page, Thursday after Thursday . . .

'Mount Soracte's dazzling snow,' boomed Father Socket in his reading voice, 'piling upon the branches. . . .'

'Stroking my hair and saying, "There, my child," week after week, and putting on,' thought Elsie, 'the holiness and spiritual life and all that.'

'So, Thaliarch . . .' said Father Socket.

Elsie swallowed the last of her cake and washed it down with the last of her tea. She gathered together her gloves and clutched her handbag. Father Socket, without interrupting his reading, moved one hand to bid her sit still. In her distress she had swallowed a whole walnut off the top of the cake, and it went down in a lump, causing her face to go red. Mike Garland looked at her and smiled with one half of his mouth.

Father Socket read on,

> 'All else trust to the gods by whose command
> Contending winds and seething seas desist,
> Until the sacred cypress-tree
> And ancient ash no longer quake.'

Father Socket interrupted himself to tap the paper with his fore-finger. 'Now the cypress tree *was* sacred,' he said, 'and although Horace . . .'

Elsie rose and sped to the door.

'*El*sie!' said Father Socket, in a kind of wail, letting his paper drop.

'Elsie!' he called after her as she opened the outside door and ran down the stairs. 'What's wrong with the girl? – Elsie, this is quite a proper decent poem, I assure you. It is Horace, it is merely –'

'I've got the letter that Patrick Seton forged,' Elsie shouted up at him. 'But I intend keeping it. It's here in my bag, but I'm keeping it.'

Matthew sat at a table in the Oriflamme watching Alice who had told him, 'Elsie won't be here this afternoon.'

'I thought she always worked on Saturday afternoons.'

'Well, she's not coming today, I don't think.'

'Any idea where she is?'

'No idea. She may come in later, of course.'

'I'll wait,' Matthew said. 'I'm on duty tonight from six, but I'll wait till five.'

'You're very keen,' said Alice.

'No I'm not,' he said. 'I like sitting here watching you.'

'While waiting for Elsie.'

'I've got to see Elsie on some business. Can you guess what it is?'

'No,' Alice said, 'and I wouldn't care to try.'

'She's a very nice girl, of course. A beautiful girl,' Matthew said.

'Oh, is she beautiful? – Not that I'm saying –'

'Well, now,' Matthew said, 'I believe in original sin, and that all the utterances of man are inevitably deep in error. Therefore I speak so as to err on the happy side.'

'She has a beautiful nature, Elsie has, I'll say that,' said Alice anxiously. 'I'm sorry she's not here for you. But I'll give her a message for you. You can't sit here drinking coffee all afternoon.'

'I'll take a cup of tea,' Matthew said. 'Do you serve teas?'

'No.' Alice hung around him, as if waiting for more information. It was early yet for the afternoon trade and only two other tables were occupied. 'Elsie may not come,' she said.

'Sit down a minute,' Matthew said, 'and rest yourself.' Her small stomach showed a slight pear-shaped swelling which appealed considerably to Matthew.

She sat down, resting her wrists on the table and drooping her long neck. Her shoulder-blades curved gracefully.

'Has Elsie got the letter?' Matthew said.

'What letter?' Alice said.

'Has she mentioned anything to you about the letter in Patrick's case? The one he forged –'

'The widow wrote it. Patrick did not forge it. That's a lie. It will be proved when –'

'Has Elsie seen the letter?'

'Elsie? Why should Elsie see the letter? Ask your posh friend Ronald with his rolled umbrella about the letter. He's working on it, isn't he? I bet he's being paid to say it's a forgery. He hasn't got anything to do with Elsie if that's what's in your mind.'

'Ronald's all right.'

'Well, so's Patrick.'

'He isn't, you know.'

'A lot of people are jealous of Patrick. It's the price he has to pay. Why are you waiting for Elsie?'

'You're jealous of Elsie,' he said.

She jumped up and went to the bar where she ordered coffee for him. When it was ready she brought it over to his table and placed it before him with a gesture which was as near to throwing it at him as was compatible with not spilling a single drop of the coffee. Meanwhile, he admired her pear-shaped stomach.

'I said tea,' Matthew said. 'However, this will do, Alice, my dear.'

'I said we don't do teas. Patrick is a poet beneath the skin,' she said.

'I'm a poet in the marrow of my bones,' he said.

She stroked her head, drawing her hand up and over the high piled hair and, looking up at the blue and starry ceiling, disappeared into the back quarters.

Matthew wrote a secret poem to Alice to while away the afternoon. As he wrote she served him with three more cups of coffee and a slice of walnut cake.

There was still no sign of Elsie at half past five, so he paid his bill and left the secret poem on the table where she later found it.

To Alice, Carrying her Tray

O punk me a mims my joyble prime
   And never be blay to me.

The wist may reeve and the bly go dim
   But I'll gim flate by thee.

And all agone and all to come,
   The sumper limm beware.
I'll meet thee ever away away
   At Wanhope-by-the-Pear.

TEN

Next day, Sunday morning, Sunday afternoon and the long jaded evening – the very clocks seeming to yawn – occurred all over London and especially in Kensington, Chelsea, and Hampstead, where there were newspapers, bells, talk, sleep, fate.

Some bachelors went to church. Some kept open bed all morning and padded to and from it, with trays of eggs and coffee; these men wriggled their toes when they had got back to bed and, however hard they tried, could not prevent some irritating crumbs of toast from falling on the sheets; they smoked a cigarette, slept, then rose at twelve.

Those who were conducting love affairs in service flatlets found it convenient that the maids did not come in with their vacuum cleaners on Sundays. They made coffee and toast on the little grill in the alcove behind the curtain.

Tim Raymond had a large front furnished room on the first floor of a house in Gloucester Road, Kensington. The carpet was green, the walls a paler green, the sofa and easy chairs were covered with deep brown plush. He had hung on the walls of this furnished room some sea-scape water-colours executed by a deceased uncle; he had placed on the lower shelves of a bookcase, behind the glass, three pieces of Georgian silver – a coffee pot, a fruit dish and a salt, relics of a great-aunt; on the upper shelves were some fat light-brown calf-bound racing calendars dating from 1909, which Tim rightly thought looked nice.

There was a divan bed, in which Hildegarde Krall still lay half-asleep, and in the opposite wall an alcove containing a small electric grill and a wash-basin where Tim was brushing his teeth.

Hildegarde's head was turned away from Tim, and at this angle of profile he thought she looked masculine. She turned round and propped up on her elbow to watch him. She said, 'It's twenty to eleven.'

Tim brushed his teeth at her, turning his head towards her.

She said, 'Is it raining?'

The telephone rang. Tim spat out his tooth-water into the basin and went to answer it. 'I suppose it's my Aunt Marlene,' he said.

'Hallo,' he said. 'Yes, Marlene. No, I've been up for hours. Yes. No, I'm afraid not today. No, not, I'm afraid. I'm afraid not. All day today, no. Well, yes, I do see, Marlene, but I don't want to be involved, really. One doesn't want ... Well, Aunt Marlene, I hardly ever really saw him in action, I mean. I mean, I know he's a good medium, but really don't you think the law should take its course? Yes, the law, but I mean it should take – They cross-examine all witnesses, you know. I can't possibly manage today, Marlene. Tomorrow, yes, at six.' Tim tucked the receiver under his chin and wiped his glasses on a handkerchief. 'At six, yes. Yes,' he said, 'tomorrow. Oh, I'm lovely, how are you? Good-bye, darling. Yes, ye – six.'

He flopped into the brown plush chair and lit a cigarette. 'I'm too young for all this,' he said. The telephone rang again.

'Hallo – Marlene! No, not at all. Yes, Marlene – Well, can't we discuss it tomorrow? Yes, of course, do tell me now – Yes. Yes. Oh, but Ronald's probably away. Away for the week-end. In fact, I'm sure he is, I think so. I haven't got his number, Marlene, isn't he in the book? He wouldn't discuss it with you, anyway, he's awfully strict about confidential – Oh, no, I'm sure he couldn't have lost anything. He never loses – No, you've been misinformed, really. No, I'm sorry, I haven't got Ronald's number. I'll ring him at his office in the morning. Yes, don't worry. The morning. I'll ring – No, not at all. I say, I must go, I'll be late for – Yes. 'Bye-'bye.'

'What has Ronald lost?' said Hildegarde.

'A letter connected with a criminal investigation.'

'Ronald has lost it? He needs someone to look after him. I used to do everything for him. I used to –'

'Yes, you told me.'

'Well, so I did. What does your aunt want with Ronald?'

'I don't know. I don't want to be involved, quite frankly.'

'I used to mend all Ronald's clothes. I used to buy the theatre tickets. I used to rush to his flat after my work and –'

'I know,' said Tim, 'you told me.' And he plugged in his electric razor, the noise of which drowned her voice.

Ronald came out of church after the eleven o'clock Mass and noticed that the youngest priest was standing in the porch saying appropriate things to the home-going faithful. Ronald did not like seeing this very young priest, not because he disliked the priest but because the priest was young, and of a physical type similar to himself, and reminded Ronald of his own blighted vocation. This very young priest prided himself on knowing the majority of the Parish by name.

'Well, Eileen,' he said, as they emerged. 'Well, Patsy. Well, Mrs Mills. Well, John, and what can I do you for?'

'Oh, good *morning*, Father.' ... 'How's yourself, Father.' ... 'Oh, Father, when are you coming to see us?' ... 'The bingo drive was nice, Father.' '... delightful sermon, Father.'

'Well, Tom,' said the priest. 'Well, Mary, and how's your mother?'

'A bit better, thank you, Father.'

'Well, Ronald,' said this very young priest as Ronald came out.

'Well, Sonny,' Ronald said.

The young priest stared after Ronald as he rapidly walked his way, then remembered Ronald Bridges was an epileptic, and turned to the next comer.

'Well, Matthew,' he said, 'and how's life with you?'

'All right, thank you, Father,' said Matthew Finch. 'Father, if you'll excuse me I can't stop. I've got to catch up with Ronald Bridges, Father, before he gets on the bus. But I'll be seeing you, Father.'

Matthew caught up with Ronald at the bus stop.

'I managed to see Elsie early this morning,' he said. 'She's got the letter but she won't part with it unless I sleep with her again.'

Ronald said, 'Tell me later,' for a number of the church people in the bus queue had turned to take note of this talk.

'I told her she'd be arrested,' Matthew rattled on, 'for entering your flat on false pretences and for robbery. I told her –'

'Come back with me and then tell me all,' Ronald said.

'Well, she wants me to sleep with her again, and I'm not going to.

She's a pervert, I can tell you that much, and I don't like perverted girls. If she isn't a pervert she's a nymphomaniac, it's just the same.'

The bus drew up. Ronald and Matthew followed the queue on to it. Those who had formed the most interested audience for Matthew followed them upstairs. Two girls sat behind them, giggling.

'Don't say any more now,' Ronald murmured. 'People can hear you.'

'Two to South Kensington, please. I don't want,' Matthew said, 'to sleep with Elsie, I want to sleep with Alice. If I was to sleep with Elsie again I'd have to pretend it was Alice. And anyway, I'm not sleeping with girls any more, it's a mortal sin and you can't deny it,' and he took his change from the conductor. 'Elsie,' he said, 'is –'

'Shut up.'

'Elsie,' Matthew whispered, 'is a bit jealous of Alice and her beauty. She hasn't a man of her own, and she was after some spiritualist clergyman but she found out he was homosexual, and she couldn't stand for it. Homosexuals send her raving mad. She was going to give him the letter yesterday, and didn't she find out yesterday –'

'What did this clergyman want with the letter?'

'He's in the spiritualist group. They all want to plot against Patrick Seton or plot for him, there's a great schism going on in the Circle just now.'

They got off at South Kensington and walked to Ronald's flat.

'Elsie is going to use that letter to get a man and it isn't going to be me,' Matthew said. 'She's got some passionate ways in sex. Not that I'm narrow-minded, only she's not beautiful like Alice, and you can't allow for funny passions in a girl that isn't beautiful.'

In the flat, Ronald said, 'I'd better see Elsie. Will she be at the Oriflamme today?'

'Yes, at six tonight.'

'What's her address?'

'Ten Vesey Street near Victoria, first-floor flat.'

Ronald wrote it down. Matthew said, 'But don't go there. She's a dangerous woman. She –'

The telephone rang. 'Marlene Cooper here,' said the voice. 'Ronald, you'll remember coming to lunch with me. I'm Tim's aunt.' She articulated the vowels as if addressing a mental defective.

'Yes, how are you?' Ronald said.

'Listen carefully,' she said. 'You have lost a document, haven't you?'

'A document?' Ronald said.

'I'm sorry if you're going to take up that attitude,' she said.

'Attitude?' Ronald said.

'Yes, because there might be a chance of my helping you.'

'Helping me?'

'Yes, helping you. I think I might be able to give you the name of the person who holds the document, and this would save you a lot of embarrassment, if only –'

'Embarrassment?'

'It is not a forgery,' Marlene said. 'And if you would come along here and discuss the matter, I think you would find it to your advantage. Can you manage six o'clock? It isn't a forgery, that must be made plain. Patrick Seton must be cleared of this slander. I will explain everything. Sherry at six o'clock or six-thirty and stay for supper, Ronald –'

'Forgery?' Ronald said.

'It is not a forgery,' Marlene said. 'On that I insist. And if you will agree simply to say so to your superiors I can give you the name and address of a certain young woman.'

'Thanks,' Ronald said, 'but really I don't like young women.'

'Can you manage today, six o'clock?' Marlene said.

'I'm afraid not. I've got to see a young woman.'

He said to Matthew after he had hung up, 'Tim's auntie is a woman of few scruples when she's after something.'

'Would you come across the road for a drink?' Matthew said. 'All women under the sun are unscrupulous if there's something they want.'

'She was prepared to sell me Elsie's name and address,' Ronald said. 'But as I've got it from you for free, I'll purchase a drink for you.'

'But isn't it a great mistake to be bitter about the female sex!' Matthew said. 'We owe them everything.'

On Sunday afternoon Isobel Billows stoked up the fire and sent Martin Bowles to fetch in some more coal. He put the brief he was reading down on the floor beside his chair and went to do her bidding. As he could not hear the front-door bell from the back of the house where he was filling the scuttle with coal, he was surprised, on his return, to find Walter Prett, the art-critic, plumply occupying his chair. Walter had one foot on Martin's brief.

'You are trampling on my brief,' Martin said, bending to extricate it from under Walter's heel. He smoothed out the squashed manilla cover of the file which held his brief. 'There's a hundred and eighty pounds' worth of business in here,' Martin said fretfully.

'Don't be vulgar,' said Walter.

'Now, bachelors,' said Isobel, 'don't quarrel.'

'I deny there's anything particularly vulgar about money,' Martin said.

'Did you put on the kettle as you came through the kitchen?' Isobel said.

'No, you didn't ask me to,' said Martin.

'Well, go and do it now,' Walter said.

'Walter!' said Isobel, and she pushed the Sunday papers off her lap and got up, setting her fair hair straight. 'We'll have some tea,' she said and departed.

Walter said, 'I wonder if you'd let me have –'

'No,' said Martin.

'Vulgar little fellow,' Walter said, tossing his snow-white locks. His dark face turned a shade more towards purple. He took a cigarette from a packet which was lying on the arm of his chair. They were Martin's cigarettes. Martin lifted the deprived packet and put it in his pocket.

Walter tore a strip of newspaper and lit his cigarette from the fire.

'I didn't see you here at the party,' Martin said.

'Which party?'

'Oh, sorry. I suppose you weren't invited.'

'I believe Isobel *did* mention something,' Walter said. 'But I was busy.'

Martin began reading his brief.

'Too busy,' said Walter, 'to mix with those common little people that hang round Isobel at her parties. Pimps and tarts and Jews.'

Martin read on.

'Spongers and soaks. Third-rate lower-middle-class . . .'

Isobel pushed open the door with her tray.

'Walter is describing the people who come to your parties,' Martin said, 'Isobel dear.'

'What people?' said Isobel, settling the tray.

'The sort of people who were at your cocktail party the other night.'

'Oh, Walter,' Isobel said. 'My party – I tried to get you on the phone, but you were always out. And I meant to send you a card but completely forgot, hoping to get you on the phone, you see –'

'I wouldn't have come,' Walter shouted. 'A vulgar third-rate set. Journalists. British Council lecturers. School-masters. A typical divorcée's salon.' And so saying he rose, lifted the tray of tea things, smashed it down into the fireplace, wormed his bulk into the ancient camel-hair coat which he had thrown on a chair, and left, banging both doors.

'You must have upset him,' Isobel said to Martin.

'A good thing too. He only came here to sponge on you. He tried to touch me – you weren't five seconds out of the room.'

'Oh, what a creature! And he can be so interesting when he likes. It's my favourite china. . . .' She started to cry.

'Send him a bill.'

'Don't be silly.'

'You must be protected,' Martin said, with his arm around her, 'from spongers.'

He was hoping the fuss would not now make it difficult for him to get away after tea, for he had promised his old mother to be home for Sunday supper.

'I am not a possessive woman,' his mother always said to him. 'You are perfectly free. Just use the house as a lodging and come and go as you please. Or take a flat, live elsewhere, do anything you like. Don't think of me, I've *had* my life. I am not a possessive woman.'

'She is not a possessive woman,' he told his friends. 'My old ma says, "Take a flat if you like, go and live somewhere else, I don't want you tied to my apron-strings." She isn't a possessive mother. But,' Martin told his friends, 'I've got to stay with her. You can't let your old widowed mother stew in Kensington when she's got arthritis. All her cronies have got arthritis. And she fights with Carrie, she literally fights with Carrie. Literally, they pull each other's hair.'

Carrie was Martin's old nurse, now, by courtesy, the housekeeper. When Martin was first called to the bar, and was short of money, old Carrie would wander off to the post office and draw out three pounds at a time of her savings; these three pounds she would privately slip to Martin. Several times Martin told his mother of this, intending it as a rebuke to her for her meanness. Mrs Bowles then wrote a cheque for Martin and, when he was out of the way, went and had a row with Carrie.

These latter days Carrie lived with Mrs Bowles as an equal. Sometimes they quarrelled and had a real fight, pulling each other's hair and, with feeble veined hands, pushing each other's faces, pushing spectacles awry and knocking at each other's jaws with their helpless knuckles. Carrie had left all her life's savings to Martin, and she had saved since she was a girl of fourteen. Mrs Bowles suspected that Carrie's fortune now surpassed her own dwindling funds, and therefore Carrie was a real rival.

'I'm not a possessive woman,' said Mrs Bowles.

'You should of pushed him out the nest long ago,' said Carrie. 'You should take a lesson off the birds. You got to push them out. When my brother was a boy thirteen my mother said to him "There's five shillings, now go." That's pushing them out the nest. My brother had a good position in a club before he died.'

'This is a different case. A barrister has a struggle. I'm not a possessive woman. Let him marry, let him go.'

'You got to *put* them out,' Carrie said.

'Are you telling me to turn my own son out of doors?' said his mother, and her eyes, which bulged naturally, shone with a bevelled light.

'Yes,' said Carrie. 'It would make a man of him.'

'Then why do you give him money?'

'Me give him money? – Catch me.'

'Martin told me. Last week you gave him money. Twice the week before that. Last month you –'

'Well, you keep him short, don't you?'

So Martin could never bring himself to leave Carrie and his mother, even although he no longer needed Carrie's little offerings. He lost his hair. He worried about his old mother if he went away to the country with Isobel for the week-end. He tried to entertain them and to be a good son. They bored him, but when they went away from home he missed the boredom, and the feud between them which sometimes broke into it.

'Carrie will have to go away to a home,' said his old mother, 'if her arthritis gets bad.'

'No,' said Martin. 'Carrie stays here.'

'You're after that money of hers. You may be disappointed,' his mother said. He hated her fiercely for her continual robbing him of any better motive.

'I'm fond of Carrie,' he said. But now his mother had left him wondering if he really meant it.

'Your mother will be bedridden before long,' Carrie said. 'What's to happen then?'

'We'll get a daily nurse,' Martin said. 'We'll manage.'

'They won't stop,' Carrie said. 'Not with your mother. Look at Millie.'

'Oh, nurses are different from maids. Maids always come and go.'

'Millie was a good girl. She would of stopped if your mother hadn't made her life a misery.'

He took them both to the country to his mother's younger sister on occasions. Then he went shopping for small supplies of groceries, pined for the boredom, and cooked whatever meals he did not have with Isobel. He missed the two old women pottering about and blaming each other.

'I've lost a vest, Carrie.'

'I haven't got your vest.'

'I have not said you've taken my vest. I think Millie must have taken it.'

'What would Millie of wanted with a vest down to her knees?' said Carrie.

'It was a good warm vest,' said Mrs Bowles.

'You've put it away in the wrong place,' said Carrie, 'that's what you've done. Look among the table linen.'

This was what Martin missed when they went away to the country, and then, even on his comfortable week-ends with Isobel, he thought of the empty house and the time when he was due to drive down to fetch them home and plonk them in their chairs in front of the television.

'It isn't clear.'

'Be quiet, Carrie.'

'I'm going to turn it up.'

'Sit still, Carrie.'

Carrie's niece had once offered to take her off their hands.

'Let her go,' said Mrs Bowles, and in her anger strained a muscle in her shoulder while heaving Carrie's trunk from the box-room out on to the landing.

Carrie surveyed the box. 'I'll go when it suits me,' she said, 'and it won't be to my relations I'll go. I could make myself a home tomorrow if it suited me.'

Martin had heaved the trunk back into its old place, for it had left a clear oblong shape on the dusty floor. Martin brushed his trousers and washed his hands.

'Fetch me the liniment for my shoulder,' said his mother, 'there's a good boy.'

He had bought them the television, and now, comforting Isobel for her broken china, he was wondering how he could get home in time for supper, as he had promised them he would.

He picked up the broken pieces and said, 'You mustn't allow Walter Prett into the house again.'

'He's never done this before,' she said.

'Does he come often?' Martin stood up in his alarm, with half the sugar basin in his hand, so that a little shower of sugar fell to the carpet.

'No, Martin,' she said.

He was suspicious because of the 'No, Martin,' instead of merely 'No.'

'He's disreputable,' Martin said. 'A sponger and a drunk.'

'Yes, Martin, I know.'

He was frantic with curiosity. 'What could any woman see in him?'

'He can be interesting when –'

'When he's not drunk.'

'Well, he's got something about him, he's different from anybody else.'

She got down and picked up all the china. 'Pour me a drink,' she said.

Martin looked at his watch and at her plump behind as she knelt over the broken pieces, and wanted to kick it. For he felt suddenly that he was to her only the man who handled her property and shares, and that she slept with him only to ensure his loyalty and save herself the trouble of investigating the property deals.

'I can't stay very long. My old ma's expecting me for supper,' he said.

'Let's have a drink.' She sniffed away the last of her tears and carried off the tray of broken china.

He had poured their drinks when she returned with new make-up on her face. He had often felt the only safe course would be to marry her, and he felt this now, with fear, because she did not always attract him, and he was not sure she would accept him. At the times when she stood out for her rights, not crudely, but with all the implicit assumptions, he thought her face too fat and found her thick neck and shoulders repulsive. At this moment, when she leaned against the mantelpiece with her drink in her hand, finding himself without the right to question her about the frequency of Walter Prett's visits, he thought her jaw was too square and masculine. He saw it would be safer to marry her. Often, when she had said, 'Martin, what should I do without you? I should never be able to manage my affairs without you,' he had recognized her strong-boned beauty and thought how a sculptor might do something about it. Even at these moments, when he had found the idea of marrying Isobel a soothing one, the panic returned that she might refuse. The thought was not to be borne. He recalled the two old women and thought, after all, it would not be the decent thing to leave them alone.

'Carrie, you have wiped the oven with the floor cloth.'

'How could I of wiped the oven with the floor cloth, when the floor cloth's looking you in the face over there . . .?'

He left at seven, and on the way home pulled up at a telephone kiosk. He wanted to talk secretly to Ronald Bridges and tell Ronald a little bit about Walter Prett's offensive behaviour, and to put himself right with Ronald, feeling now as if Ronald's eye had been invisibly upon him all the afternoon. He was never comfortable when he did not feel all right about Ronald.

But there was no answer from Ronald's number. Soon Martin was eating cold lamb and beetroot opposite Carrie and next to his mother.

He laid his bald head on his hands and said, 'Oh, stop nagging each

other, you two women.' And they stopped their quarrel for a little
space.

Towards half past seven on Sunday evening, Ewart Thornton was
seated in Marlene Cooper's flat in Bayswater. He said, 'I've got a pile
of homework to do. Maths papers.'

'Never mind that now,' she said. 'Come and have supper.'

He had been smoking a pipe. He tapped it out and worked himself
stiffly and hugely out of the deep upholstered chair.

'Maths papers,' he said. 'Preliminary tests.'

'Ewart,' she said at supper, 'the Interior Spiral will be meeting on
Tuesday at eight-thirty to discuss our evidence with regard to Patrick
Seton. We must present a united front if it comes to a court case as I
suspect it will. Now, whom can we trust?'

'Well, you can trust me, for one,' said Ewart, 'but I must say I
won't be able to give any evidence in court.'

'What!' said Marlene, holding the cold peas in the serving-spoon
suspended.

'I can't come to court.'

She tipped the peas on to his plate and still stared at him. 'You
must,' she said. 'I'm counting on you.'

'It will be too near the end of term,' he said.

'Why,' she said, 'have we got to quarrel every time we meet,
Ewart?' She started to eat.

'There is no quarrel,' he said, sprinkling pepper on his salad.

'You can't let me down,' she said, 'after all this preparation.
Patrick's future may depend on it.'

'I'm not convinced of Patrick's innocence. As you know, I'm a man
of principle. I'm not sure that Mrs Flower isn't in the right.'

'But all you need to say is that Patrick is a genuine medium, and that
Freda Flower ran after him unmercifully, as you know she did. As
you know.'

'Marlene,' he said, 'I advise you to keep out of the case altogether.
You are talking wildly. No one would be interested in my evidence.'

'Well, this is sudden,' she said.

'I have told you my views. I've advised –'

'Yes, but I thought, as a member of the Interior Spiral, when it came to the point, Ewart, you would stand by me and . . .' She was crying, and it satisfied him to see her cry and to think that he had brought about this drooping of her stately neck, the leaning of her head on her hand, the tremor of her jade ear-rings, the resigned dabbing of her eyes with her handkerchief, and the final offended sniff.

He introduced his fork into his mouth judiciously and chewed like a wise man until she should be delivered of her distress.

'I don't see why you are so surprised. I've told you all along that I consider it absurd to go into the witness box on Patrick Seton's behalf. It would do him far more harm than –'

'Oh, Ewart,' she said. 'No, you were never definite. I can't believe it.'

It was true he had never been quite definite on the subject before tonight, but he had said enough, from time to time, to allow him now to extricate himself from any charge of sudden betrayal. He recalled that some time previous he had said to Marlene, 'I can see Mrs Flower's point of view. Of course, she was foolish to hand him over the money, even allowing it was a gift –'

'Oh, it was a gift. Patrick says so. He can prove it. There's a letter.'

'It's a large sum for her to give.'

On another occasion he had said, 'My sympathies are not entirely with Patrick. He may be a good medium, but as a citizen –'

'It is time spiritualism was recognized as a mark of good citizenship,' Marlene said.

More recently, at a meeting of the Interior Spiral – the secret group within the Group – Ewart Thornton had said, 'There is bound to be a certain amount of prejudice against spiritualists if the case is brought up. My advice is to keep out of it and let the law take its course. Mud sticks.'

'We must fight prejudice,' Marlene had said. 'And we all intend to support Patrick in every way. We must decide what we are going to say. We can't carry on the Group without Patrick.' On that occasion Patrick had arrived, frail as a sapling birch with rain on its silver head. 'We are just discussing,' Marlene said, 'our combined witness on your behalf, in the event of its being called for.'

'Ah-ah,' Patrick sighed, hunching his shoulders together, 'the unfortunate occurrence.'

'And what is more,' Marlene said, 'we want your assistance in settling what we are to say about Freda Flower. You will have to give us the relevant dates so that –'

'We do not all know Mrs Flower,' Ewart had said.

'Oh, don't we?' said Marlene.

Ewart had thus feebly worked towards this moment on Sunday evening when, sitting at Marlene's supper table, he said, 'I've told you all along that I consider it absurd to go into the witness box.'

'Oh, Ewart. No, you were never definite. I can't believe it.'

'Think back,' he said. 'I've told you all along what my position is.'

He leaned both arms confidently on the table, and felt a great awkwardness inside him, and looked at Marlene with an overpowering stare until he perceived her submission: she thought him altogether sure of his rectitude.

Then he experienced a sense of this rectitude, and was satisfied. He would have liked to have disappointed her more than this, because he was greatly attracted by her and greatly disapproved of her. He disapproved of, and was attracted by what she took for granted in life – by her freedom to indulge her spirit, and buy the acquiescence of her followers, and run up debts without worry, and cultivate spiritualists and mediums, and have no need of lovers. He was attracted by and disapproved of the departed Harry who had bought ear-rings to dangle against this tall lady's neck, and who had died and been buried and dug up again by her, and cremated, and who was now being trafficked with beyond the grave. He had feasted on anecdotes of her past life, and wanted more, and was avid, in an old woman's way, for her downfall.

'I have counted on you,' Marlene was saying, 'to witness for Patrick because it would be such good publicity for the Infinity. People would know we are not cranks. No one would take you for a crank, Ewart.'

This did not move him. He liked very much to see Marlene with her private means trying to win him over; and he knew already he was not a crank. He set his face squarely at her, and felt glad he had conferred with Freda Flower and had canvassed witnesses for Freda.

'Ronald Bridges,' she said, 'has also let me down rather badly today.'

'He isn't one of us, surely?'

'Oh, he's not a spiritualist. But he has let me down, all the same. One thing about Patrick,' she said, 'he has never let me down.'

He was anxious to go, for he wanted to telephone to Freda Flower from the cosy seclusion of his own study at Campden Hill. He loved a gossip with a homely woman like Freda Flower, and it had been most pleasant, recently, to settle in to telling her how things were going in the Wider Infinity group, and what was being said. For, like a Christian convert of the jungle who secretly returns by night to the fetish tree, or like one who openly supports a political party and then, at last, marks his vote for the opposite party, he felt justified in Freda Flower to the extent of these telephone conversations even although she was an unsuitable person to meet.

'Freda, I was at a party last night at Isobel Billows's. You won't know her – she's not a member of the Circle. But a lot of us were there. I did my very best, Freda, to persuade members to come forward in your favour. After all, where did all the money go? The members know that Patrick has had far too much handling of the funds, in any case. I tried to impress it on young Tim Raymond, but I'm afraid he is too young and irresponsible. And, my dear, I'm not saying anything against Marlene, but she . . .'

'Patrick Seton could look you in the eyes,' she would say, 'and tell a lie so that you would believe you were telling the lie, not him.'

'I can well believe you, my dear,' he would say time and again, into the telephone receiver, lolling back largely in his chair and pulling his waistcoat over his stomach. 'And I can't think why you hesitate to give your evidence in full force.'

Marlene was piling the supper things on to a tray. She looked at Ewart several times as she did so, to see if he appeared as if he could still be persuaded. He stood up like a righteous husband, and contemptuously added the pepper pot to the tray.

'I won't keep you, then, Ewart, if you are in a hurry to get back to your work,' she said.

But he was anxious to help Marlene wash the dishes before returning to gossip with Freda Flower. He liked putting an apron around his large body and he liked holding the cloth in his hands to dry the dishes one by one. Sometimes at the end of term, after the examinations, he invited three of his best boys to dinner on Saturday at his rooms, and he liked that very much – planning the menu, buying in the food, preparing it, cooking it for them, fussing over the stove for them, seeing they had enough to eat, like a solicitous mother.

He wiped Marlene's dishes and put them away carefully and proudly. He was encouraged by her dejection and satisfied, now, he had taken the only course.

His hips were wide for a man. He smoothed the apron while waiting, cloth in hand, for the next plate. Marlene did a vexed scouring of a saucepan. Ewart made neat the bow which tied the apron strings behind him.

'Is that the lot?' he said.

'Will you be here tomorrow night?' she said, 'for the Interior Spiral.'

'I'm afraid not, my dear.' He was prepared to be charming.

'I can't understand you,' she said. She took off her apron. He untied his and held it out to her. She cast the aprons, with graceful carelessness, over the back of a chair.

He touched her arm consolingly as a man of integrity a woman who could not be expected to understand integrity.

'You will come to the séance on Wednesday?'

He looked reproachful. 'Oh, yes,' he said. Marlene must be made to understand that simply because he refused to support her favourite he was not therefore a lapsed spiritualist.

'Good,' she said sadly, 'I'm glad, Ewart. I'm grateful for that.'

She went over to that serving-aperture in the wall which divided the kitchen from the séance room and flicked a straying fold in the short curtain.

'Patrick will take the chair on Wednesday,' she said.

'It may be his last appearance,' Ewart said.

'Not if I know it,' she said and moved past him out of the kitchen.

He put on his hat, scarf, and coat in the hall.

'Thank you for a pleasant evening,' he said.

'I am disappointed, Ewart.'

'You will be grateful one day, Marlene.'

He kissed her on both cheeks and departed to his rooms at Campden Hill where, from the depths of his leather arm-chair, he telephoned to Freda Flower.

'I have definitely made a stand, Freda, as regards Patrick Seton. It had to come, Freda. Now, Freda, don't be silly. That is sheer superstition. Patrick can do you no further harm. I believe you've still got a weak spot for Patrick, Freda, but believe me . . . And if I were you, my dear, I'd keep away from Mike Garland. Yes, keep him away from you. Yes, keep away from. . . We'll clean up the whole organization between us, you and I together. And Marlene will come to heel. . . .'

His hips expanded in the chair, and his chin went into extra folds as his face sank into the skull. A smile of comfortable womanliness spread far into his cheeks as he spoke and his eyes were avid, as if they had never moved dispassionately over an examination paper. 'Yes, Freda my dear, I made no bones about it and I just said to her, I said . . .'

Meanwhile the Rev. T. W. Socket said to Mike Garland who had at that moment arrived at his flat, 'Mrs Flower is resolved to go ahead with the case.'

'She has no alternative. It's in the hands of the police.'

'But will she be a willing witness? That's what they need.'

'I've done my best with her,' said Mike Garland.

'I hope you didn't have to de-Flower her,' said the Reverend Socket who then closed his eyes and shook with mirth.

Mike Garland smiled unpleasantly.

'I don't trust Mrs Flower,' he said. 'I don't know for certain, but I think she may have been discussing me with the police. A plain-clothes man called last night. Somebody's been talking to the police.'

'What did he want? What did he ask?'

'About my clairvoyant activities. Where did I operate? What did I charge for a horoscope? I told him. I showed him the card index. All postal commissions, I said.'

'I'm glad I suggested that card index,' said Socket. 'There is nothing like having a card index in the house. You can always produce a card index. It puts them off their stroke.'

'I invited the man to look through it, but he didn't trouble.'

'Who has tipped them off, I wonder?'

'He mentioned Freda Flower.'

'Really, in what connexion?'

'He asked me if I knew her. I said yes, she was a friend.'

'How many girls have you got staying with Freda Flower at the moment?'

'Only three.'

'Transfer them to Ramsgate right away,' said Father Socket. 'I blame Marlene Cooper for this. You made an enemy of her the other night, I'm afraid. It was ill-considered of you to challenge Patrick Seton at an open séance.'

'I can't transfer the girls to Ramsgate right away.'

'Why not?'

'Because Freda Flower will be suspicious if they all leave at once. She thinks they work in the all-night kitchen at Lyons' Corner House. I can't trust Freda Flower.'

'Whom can we trust?' said Father Socket.

'Someone has tipped the police,' said Mike Garland.

'Could it be Elsie? Surely it couldn't be Elsie.'

'She stole that letter – she's capable of anything.'

'I told you, didn't I?' said Father Socket, 'that you should have been more discreet when Elsie called yesterday.'

'Having stolen a letter which was Crown property I doubt if she would go to the police. Besides, what could she say? That I was wearing my green-striped dressing-gown?' Mike Garland smiled with full lips pressed together.

'This is grave,' said Father Socket. He was inserting a roll of tape into a recording machine. He switched it on. It was his own voice rendering Shelley's *Ode to the West Wind*. He stood listening to it, with critical attention, while Mike leant back with eyes closed.

When it was finished Father Socket said, 'I should have taken "Drive my dead thoughts . . ." more slowly. They are all monosyllabic words, each word should be spoken with equal stress. Drive – my – dead – thoughts . . . like that.'

'It gives one a *frisson*,' said Mike.

'All troubles are passing,' said Father Socket. 'My son, the fever of life will soon be over and gone. We will take this police inquiry in our stride. Do not be disturbed, Mike. Patrick Seton will be brought to trial, the Wider Infinity will be brought to disrepute, the Temple will be cleansed, and we shall then take over the affairs of the Circle ourselves.'

'We'll take over the whole shooting-match,' said Mike. 'How you soothe me, Father.'

'Some will have to go,' said the Rev. Socket. 'Marlene, of course, will no longer be in control. We shall not meet at Marlene's flat, we shall meet here. Ewart Thornton will have to go. Freda Flower – she is suspect, and to say the least, has been a trouble-maker – she will have to go. It makes one's eyes narrow. We may retain Tim Raymond, a biddable youth. We shall –'

'But I didn't like that plain-clothes policeman calling on me last night,' Mike whispered. 'I didn't like it at all.'

'Do nothing for two weeks,' said Father Socket. 'My son, go nowhere, do nothing.'

'But the girls –'

'I shall myself convey the girls to Ramsgate,' said Father Socket, 'one by one.'

Mike Garland took comfort from his elder partner whom he had revered for eight years, since that summer evening at Ramsgate when he had just heard Father Socket preach. This was in a private house, before the séance had commenced. Mike, newly released from Maidstone prison, where he had served a sentence for soliciting, was deeply moved when he heard Father Socket say, 'There are those amongst us who are not of the human race, but are aliens, and nevertheless must walk in the midst of mankind disguised as members of the human race. He who hath ears let him hear.' Mike told Father Socket after the séance, 'I was deeply moved by what you said tonight,' Father Socket adopted him. Mike was then forty. He had a job as a waiter in a huge hotel. For the winter he had intended to return to London and take up private service as a manservant, for he had made a good butler in his time, with many profitable sidelines. Father Socket had changed all that. He had bestowed larger thoughts on Mike, who began to experience a late flowering in his soul. Father Socket cited the classics and André Gide, and although Mike did not actually read them, he understood, for the first time in his life, that the world contained scriptures to support his homosexuality which, till now, had been shifty and creedless. Mike gave up his job as a waiter and went into training as a clairvoyant. His appearance assisted him, he flowered. Father Socket instructed him in the theory and practice of clairvoyance, and Mike's late overflowing of the soul actually did evoke pronounced psychic talents. Father Socket's villa at Ramsgate was filled twice weekly with residential widows and retired military men – for it was widows and retired colonels who were the chief clients – come to receive clairvoyance from Mike.

'There are certain aids to perception which it is unwise – nay, lacking in humility – for the clairvoyant to ignore,' Father Socket told Mike, and he taught him how to observe his subjects and how, in the daylight hours, to gain useful information as to their private lives. Mike's previous career in the catering and domestic worlds assisted him, for he knew his way about the back stairs of hotels and boarding houses, he knew a friendly waiter when he saw one.

'But we must not neglect the little things of life,' said Father Socket. 'The gas bill must be paid.' Mike knew a street photographer. He knew which wealthy men were taking the air on the front with their friends during illicit week-ends. The couples were photographed, the man handed a ticket, and the ticket was thrown away. Mike acquired these photographs at a higher price than the nominal three for seven-and-sixpence. But he did not lose on the deal and, even though certain members of hotel staffs had to be paid out of his earnings, still Father Socket's gas bills were paid.

'Never touch a woman,' said Father Socket, 'for a woman cannot enter the Kingdom. Have dealings with a woman and the virtue departs from you. You should read the Ancients on the subject.'

Mike felt secure with Father Socket in all his summer and all his winter activities. He was no longer an aimless chancer sliding in and out of illegal avenues, feeling resentful all the while. Mike now was at rights with the world, he was somebody. He had a religion and a Way of Life, set forth by Father Socket. Mike, tall, straight, with his pink-and-white cheeks, did not appear to be an adoring type; nevertheless he adored Father Socket and was jealous of any other potential acolytes who might put in a tentative appearance, and would not stand for them.

Now, after eight prosperous years, Mike could not believe that a mere visit from a plain-clothes policeman could shake the benign rock which translated Horace, recited Shelley, knew the writings of the Early Fathers, and studied the Cabbala. This winter's venture, a continuation of last summer's venture, was a private cinema show lasting half an hour. It comprised two films, entitled, respectively, *The Truth about Nudism* and *Nature's Way*. The three girls, who appeared on the stage in person afterwards, were more or less thrown in with the price of the ticket. Mike had thought the employment of these girls unnecessary. 'Suppose the place is raided, it is easier to destroy the film than to conceal the girls.'

'The show would lose its attraction,' said Father Socket, 'without a peppering of real flesh and blood. I prefer, myself, the more artistic exclusiveness of the film, but we must allow for the cruder tastes of the Many.'

They lodged the girls with unsuspecting Freda Flower, who was known to Father Socket as a spiritualist and a widow and who touchingly gave him fifty cigarettes every Christmas and a spray of carnations on the birthday of the late Sir Oliver Lodge.

'Freda will take the girls,' said Father Socket. 'Now that Patrick Seton has let her down so badly over her savings, the good woman will need the money.'

Mike had not been happy about Freda taking the girls to lodge. 'Never have to do with a woman . . . they draw the virtue out of you.'

A slight disturbance in Mike's mind had recently occurred to make him wonder if perhaps Father Socket was not more interested in women as such than he claimed to be. There was a certain Elsie, who did his typing. He was furiously jealous of Elsie. And these girls. But Mike , shivering as from a flash of clairvoyance, cast the thought from him.

But when Father Socket said, 'I shall myself convey the girls to Ramsgate. One by one. You must lie low. I confess I don't like the sound of this policeman who visited you. Are you sure he was a policeman? Did you ask for his credentials? You should always demand their credentials.' – When Father Socket spoke like this, Mike recalled his first hesitation in dealing with Freda Flower, he remembered his flash of doubt, whether Father Socket was reaching an age – sixty-two – when he might become weak. In a fever of clairvoyance and apprehension he looked at his patron and everlasting lean-upon, and said, 'Never have dealings with women, Father. They are denied the Kingdom. They suck the virtue –'

'Well, my son,' said Father Socket, 'don't be fearful.' He patted Mike's shoulder. 'After all, you are now forty-eight and you must endure whatever may betide.'

'Things look unlucky,' said Mike, rising tall above Father Socket. 'We had bad luck with Elsie Forrest yesterday, and that was a start.

We should have got that letter out of her. Perhaps our good luck is turning.'

'I told you not to put in an appearance in that dressing-gown with that stuff on your face,' Father Socket said. 'I told you she was not a true spirit. Whatever must the girl have thought?'

Alice Dawes sat up in bed combing her long black hair on that Sunday evening. A syringe lay on the table beside her.

'Some time next week, I imagine,' said Patrick, in his murmur.

'And the divorce – now how about the divorce case?'

'Oh yes, I meant to tell you. The divorce has been held up. Something technical – but never mind that, I've got our honeymoon all arranged.'

'Held up? How can we have a honeymoon if we can't get married?'

'A holiday, dear. We shall be married eventually.'

'I wish you'd tell me more about your divorce.'

'You trust me,' said Patrick softly, 'don't you?' He put out his hand and stroked her arm.

'Of course,' she said, and after a space she said, 'Are you sure the case will come up next month?'

'The divorce will –'

'No, not the divorce. The case, the charge of fraud.'

'It may not come to anything after all. The police may decide they haven't good enough evidence.'

'I should like to give that Freda Flower a piece of my mind. Saying you forged the letter. Have you seen anything of Elsie?'

'No, I wish she hadn't touched the letter. It puts me in an awkward position. The police think I'm behind the theft.' He placed his head on one side with pathos.

'Do they know? Who told them?'

'The man who lost it, I suppose.'

'That's Ronald Bridges,' Alice said. 'He takes fits. What's in the letter?'

'Not very much. It came with the cheque Freda sent me and it says "Please use this money to further your psychic and spiritualistic work. I leave it entirely in your hands" – something like that. An unprincipled woman. I should never have taken the money.'

Alice moved in a desperate access of temper against Freda Flower and her own doubts; she sat up violently and began to throw back the covers and reach for her clothes at the same time. 'I'll go and see that woman right away. I'll frighten the wits out of her –'

'No, no,' Patrick said.

'I'll tell her it won't be you who's going to gaol, it will be her that's going to Holloway if she stands up before the magistrate and says you forged that letter. I'll tell her, and she can see for herself, that I'm pregnant, and I'll say, "What right have you," I'll say, "to come between me and the man I love with a court case? You should have thought it over," I'll say, "before you sent him that cheque –"'

'No, no, keep calm,' Patrick said.

'I'll say, "You should have thought it over, and no doubt you thought he would marry you when he got his divorce, you ridiculous old bag," I'll say, "now he's devoted the money to a cause and distributed it among the spiritualist students, now you say you didn't give it to him," I'll say. And I'll say, "Mrs Flower," I'll say, "you know the police are prejudiced and everyone's prejudiced against spiritualism, and they will swear it's a forgery and pay their men to swear to it. Now, Mrs Flower," I'll say, "where will that get you, Mrs Flower? It will get you to Holloway, that's where. You think you're going to come between Patrick and me? No, Mrs Flower," I'll say. "Oh no, Mrs Flower."' Alice curled up and wept noisily.

Patrick sat in his calm, watching her, and he experienced that murmuring of his mind which was his memory. He could not recall where he had seen a similar sight before, but he felt he had. His memory was impressionistic, formed of a few distinguishable sensations among a mass of cloudy matter generally forming his past. He remembered most of all his childhood, and could possibly have brought to mind the latent image of being taken with his class round an art gallery by his art teacher, a woman. She is endeavouring to explain impressionist art by bidding them look at the palm of their hands for a moment, and nowhere else. 'All round your hand you are aware of objects – you see them, but not distinctly. What you see round the palm of your hand is an *impression*.' Patrick's memory had become this type of impression and if he focused his attention for long upon the things of the past it was mainly of his childhood that he thought, a happy childhood, and his lifelong justification for all his

subsequent actions. It had bewildered him when the prison psychoa-
nalysts had put it to him as a matter of course that something had been
wrong with his childhood. That is not the case at all: something has
been wrong, from time to time, ever since. Life has been full of
unfortunate occurrences, and the dream of childhood still remains in
his mind as that from which everything else deviates. He is a dreamy
child: a dreamer of dreams, they say with pride, as he wanders back
from walks in the botanical gardens, or looks up from his book. *Mary
Rose* by J. M. Barrie is Patrick's favourite, and he is taken to the
theatre to see it acted, and is sharply shocked by the sight of real
actresses and actors with painted faces performing outwardly on the
open platform this tender romance about the girl who was stolen by
the fairies on a Hebridean island. As a young man he memorizes the
early poems of W. B. Yeats and will never forget them. Now, on his
first enchanted visit to the Western Isles he first encounters an
unfortunate occurrence, having sat up reciting to an American lady
far into the night and the next morning being accused of having taken
money from her purse. He is thinking of her, in his poetic innocence,
as a kindred soul to whom the money does not matter, but now she
carries on as if money mattered. A little while, and he learns from a
man that the early Christians shared all their worldly possessions one
with the other, and Patrick memorizes this lesson and repeats it to all.
Another little while, and he has sex relations with a woman, and is
upset by all the disgusting details and is eventually carried away into
transports. There is a lot of nasty stuff in life which comes breaking up
our ecstasy, our inheritance. I think, said Patrick, people should read
more poetry and dream their dreams, and I do not recognize man-
made laws and dogmas. There is always a fuss about some petty cash,
or punctuality. 'Tread softly,' he recites to the young girls he meets,
'because you tread on my dreams.' The girls are usually enchanted. 'I
have spread my dreams under your feet,' he says, 'tread softly ...'
Even older ladies are enchanted. His wispy father fully accepts the
position of Patrick, and dies. The widowed mother cannot understand how he is not getting on in life, with such fine stuff in him. She
protests, at last, that she is penniless, and when she dies, and turns out
not to have been quite penniless, Patrick is amazed. He had not
thought her to be a materialist at heart. There is a girl at the time
going to have a baby, and that is her business. He removes to London,

then, away from these unfortunate occurrences and finds his feet as a spiritualist and becomes a remarkable medium, which he always was, without knowing it, all along. There are ups and downs and he always does his best to help Mr Fergusson with information. Patrick trembles with fear and relief when he thinks of Mr Fergusson who first put him on a charge; and that was the first meeting.

Patrick has tried to explain how let down he always feels by people who trust him and enter into an agreement to trust him, as it were against their better judgement blinding themselves, and then suddenly no longer trust him, and turn upon him. Mr Fergusson perhaps understands this.

There is another charge, and the unfortunate sentence, but afterwards Mr Fergusson, with his strong-looking chest and reliable uniform, is still sitting at the police station, and they make another arrangement about information so that Patrick feels much better and feels he has a real friend in Mr Fergusson with his few words, even though Mr Fergusson cannot help putting him on a charge sometimes; and he is afraid of Mr Fergusson.

Patrick contemplates Alice curled up in distress. It is so much easier to get away from a girl in any other part of the country than in London. In the provinces one only has to go to London and disappear. But once you have a girl in your life in London she knows all your associates, you have established yourself, she knows some of your affairs; she knows where to find you; and it is impossible to disappear from Alice without disappearing from the centre of things, the spiritualist movement – Marlene – his Circle – 'My bread and butter.' Patrick is indignant. He has loved Alice.

He has not taken any money from her. He has given her money, has supported her for nearly a year. She has agreed to trust him, it is a pact. She is mine, he is thinking. The others were not mine but this one is mine. I have loved her, I still love her. I don't take anything from Alice. I give. And I will release her spirit from this gross body. He looks with justification at the syringe by her bedside, and is perfectly convinced about how things will go in Austria (all being well), since a man has to protect his bread and butter, and Alice has agreed to die, though not in so many words.

Patrick watched her calmly and reflected that he had been weak with Alice. She had talked and talked about marriage, as if he were a materialist with a belief in empty forms. He had told her frequently he was not a person of conventions: 'I live by the life of the spirit.' She had only replied 'I'm not conventional either.' And when she had conceived this disgusting baby she had been frantic for marriage. It was absurd that she refused to have the baby done away with and was frantic for marriage.

It was her love for him and his spiritual values that made her so like the other women, crumpled up on the bed after their fury. A little dread entered in among his bones: it was about the chances of the Flower case coming up, and the possibility of a conviction. He absented himself from this idea and gave himself up to spiritual reflection again. Before Alice had recovered herself, he, watching from the chair, was surprised by a sensation which he had never experienced before. This was an acute throb of anticipatory pleasure at the mental vision of Alice, crumpled up – in the same position as she now was on the bed – on the mountainside in Austria. She is mine, I haven't taken a penny from this one, I have given to this one. I can do what pleases me. I love this one. She has agreed to trust. Crumpled up on the mountainside in Austria, Alice, overloaded with insulin, far from help, beyond the reach of a doctor, beyond help – far from the intrusive knowledge of his friends and enemies in London, outside the scope of his bread and butter, free from her heavy body, beyond good and evil. She has agreed to it, not in so many words, but . . .

She looked up from the bed, and was startled. But the fear left her face. There is a pact, he thought. She has agreed to believe in me.

It was still Sunday night and Ronald had gone up the stairs to Elsie Forrest's room at 10 Vesey Street near Victoria and had sat on the stairs awaiting her return at half past eleven, when, as she approached the door, he stood up.

'Christ!' she said when she saw him.

'I hope I didn't give you a fright.'

'What d'you want?'

'To come inside and talk to you,' Ronald said.

'You threaten me, I'll wake up the house.'

Ronald sat down on the top stair. 'I'm not threatening you. I'm only asking if I may talk to you. If you don't want me to talk to you, would you mind talking to me?'

She opened the door. 'Come on in,' she said, and stood and looked at him as he walked into her bed-sitting-room.

'I've got nothing in the place to drink,' she said.

'Not even tea?' said Ronald.

She said, 'Take your things off and sit down.'

She took off her own coat and hung it in the cupboard, from which she brought a coat-hanger and carefully set Ronald's coat upon it and set it up on a hook behind the door. Ronald sat on the divan and stretched out his legs.

As she put the kettle on the little electric grill stove behind a curtain she said,

'What was it you wanted to talk about?' She looked at him from the sides of her eyes as she set out the tea-cups.

'Anything you like.'

She was looking at him, not to size up what he had come to talk about, but in an evaluating way which made Ronald feel like something in the sales.

'You're Ronald Bridges,' she said.

'You're Elsie Forrest,' he said.

'You want the letter,' she said. She went over to the window and drew the limp short makeshift curtains.

He said, 'Have the police been to see you?'

'No,' she said. 'And you know they haven't. You wouldn't be fool enough to tell the cops until you had tried to get it back yourself. It would tell against your reputation, losing a confidential document, wouldn't it? Why didn't you keep it confidential if it was confidential?'

'I don't know,' he said.

'You wouldn't be foolish enough to tell the cops,' she said.

'No,' he said. 'But a friend of mine has done so.'

'I don't believe it,' she said. 'No detectives have called here.'

'I've told them to leave it to me for the time being.'

'I don't believe it,' she said.

'All right,' he said. 'The kettle's boiling over,' he said.

She made the tea, and Ronald watched her. She looked very neurotic, moving in a jerky way, her body giving little twitches of habitual umbrage. Her blonde greasy hair hung over her face as she poured out the tea.

'Your friend Matthew Finch came to see me,' she said.

'Yes, I know,' Ronald said.

'He was after the letter.'

'Yes, I know.'

'He didn't get it,' she said.

'I know.'

'And that's why you've come after it.'

'I didn't need to come after it,' he said.

'All right,' she said, 'send the police. I'll face all that.' She sat down beside him on the sofa and, folding her hands in her lap, looked straight ahead of her. 'I've faced it already,' she said with tragic intensity, such as Alice employed when talking to a man and the stress of the occasion demanded it.

All at once, Ronald quite liked her.

'I have died,' she said, 'many deaths.'

'Tell me,' he said, 'how that has happened.'

She pushed back her hair from her bumpy forehead. She had a warped young face.

'I have loved too much and trusted too much,' she said, perceiving the success of her style, 'I have given and I haven't received.'

'Have you had a lot of sex relations?' Ronald said.

'I have had sex without any relationships. I don't know why I'm telling you this the first five minutes.'

'You've met the wrong chaps,' Ronald said.

'All the chaps are wrong ones. If they aren't married they are queer; if they aren't queer they are hard; if they aren't hard they are soft. I can't get anywhere with men, somehow. Why am I telling you all this?'

'I'm the uncle type,' Ronald said.

'Why d'you say that? Are you interested in psychology? – I'm very interested in psychology. Why are you the uncle type?'

'Because everyone tells me their troubles,' Ronald said.

'And don't you tell people your troubles?'

'No,' Ronald said, 'my troubles are largely self-evident and I'm not the filial type. To be able to tell people your troubles you have to be a born son. Or daughter, as the case may be.'

'I must be a born daughter,' Elsie said, 'according to psychology.'

'At the moment you're being a niece if I'm being an uncle. Let's keep our terms of reference in order.'

'Well, I know a Father Socket,' Elsie said. 'He's just let me down badly. I looked on him as a father, and now I've found out he's a homosexual.'

'You can overlook that,' Ronald said, 'if you think of him as second cousin.'

'I can't overlook it. I hate queers. I want to conceive a child.'

'Fond of babies?'

'Not particularly. It's not a question of having a child so much as conceiving a child by a man I love.'

'You'd better get a husband,' Ronald said. 'That would be the obvious course.'

'There aren't any husbands that I know of. My own brother's unfaithful to his wife; it makes me sick. And he expects me to encourage him. "Lend us your room for the afternoon, Elsie," he says. And when I won't lend the room he says, "You're not much of a sister." I said, "I object to the type of woman you pick up with." So I do. I couldn't have them coming here. That's what my brother's like. I always knew he would make a rotten husband.'

'You'd better find a husband that isn't like your brother.'

'There aren't any husbands so far as I've met. All the men I know want to lean on me or take it out on me. I did all Father Socket's typing. That friend of yours, Matthew Finch, he only wanted to commit a sin with me and he ate a lot of onions and breathed on my face so I shouldn't enjoy it. If he's your friend, I can only say –'

'Oh, if he's my friend, we might leave him out of the discussion.'

'Now, there's another thing – the way you men stick together against us.'

'Haven't you any friends?'

'Well, there's Alice.'

'We'll leave her out of the discussion, then.'

'No we won't. Alice is a case. She's mad in love with that little weed, Patrick Seton. I'll admit he's a brilliant medium. But what else is there to him? Now she's getting a child by him. And what's he done about it? Wanted her to have it taken away. She thinks he's going to marry her, and she's mistaken. I've told her. I've told Alice. I've told her he'll never marry her. He says he's getting a divorce, and the divorce never happens. And she believes him. Any awkwardness, and he recites poetry to her to explain everything away. I'll bet he hasn't got a wife. He was never the husband type from the start. He won't marry Alice. She refuses to see that.'

'Then why are you defending him, like a sister?'

'I'm not defending him at all, I'm –'

'You're concealing the evidence of his forgery.'

'Oh, the letter – I'm hanging on to that. I know that's what you've come for. But I'm keeping it and I'll take the consequences. I've already faced the consequences. So you can go.'

Ronald got up and went to take his coat off the hanger.

'Stay the night,' she said, 'and I'll give you the letter in the morning.'

Ronald sat down again. 'No,' he said.

'Why? Don't you want to sleep with me?'

'No,' Ronald said.

'Why, tell me why? Is there something wrong with me?'

'Uncles don't sleep with nieces,' Ronald said.

'Isn't that carrying the idea a bit far?'

'Yes,' Ronald said, 'it is. I'm not an uncle, I'm a stranger. That's why I can't sleep with you.'

'Am I a stranger?'

'Yes,' Ronald said.

'You're only playing for time,' she said. 'I'm well aware you're trying to handle me. It's the letter you're after. Take all and give nothing.'

'I thought we were having an interesting conversation, mutually appreciated as between strangers,' Ronald said.

'Yes, and when you go away you'll feel "Well, I haven't got the letter but at least I cheered up the poor girl for an hour." And what d'you suppose *I'll* feel? It's much better for men not to come at all if they're always going to go away and leave me alone. I'm not lonely before they come. I'm only lonely when they go away.'

'There's a whole philosophy attached to that,' Ronald said. 'It turns on the question whether it's best not to be born in the first place.'

'That's a silly question,' she said, 'because if you weren't born you couldn't ask it.'

'Yes, it is silly. But, since one has been born, it's one of the mad questions one has been born to ask.'

'I think it's better to be born. At least you know where you are,' Elsie said.

'Aren't you contradicting yourself?' Ronald said.

'I don't care if I am. There's a big difference between feeling lonely after a man's gone away and not being born at all. Being born is basic. You don't need to have company in the same way as you need to be born.'

'There's a lot in what you say,' Ronald said.

'I say it's a mistake to have company, I wish I could stop it.'

'You only need stick a note on your door saying "Away for a few weeks" and leave it there.'

'I haven't the guts,' she said. 'And I don't get much companionship out of the men I know. All they want is sex, and perhaps we have an evening out with sex in view, but they're anxious to get back to their mums and aunties or their wives.'

'You should make them entertain you without sex,' Ronald said, '– an intelligent girl like you.'

'They don't want intelligence. They don't come if there's no sex. I'm a sexy type, I get excited about it. And that's what they like. But it only leaves me lonely.'

'Don't you enjoy it at the time?'

'No. But I can't do without it, and these men know it. They fumble about with their french letters or they tear open their horrible little packets of contraceptives like kids with sweets, or they expect me to have a rubber stop-gap all ready fitted. All the time I want to be in love with the man and conceive his child, but I keep thinking of the birth-control and something inside me turns in its grave. You can't enjoy sex in that frame of mind.'

'I know the feeling,' Ronald said, 'it's like contemplating suicide.'

'Have you thought of committing suicide?'

'Yes,' he said, 'but something inside me turns in its grave.'

'I've thought of suicide, but in the end I always decide to wait in case another possibility turns up. I might meet a man that wants to live with me and not keep slamming the door in my face with birth control. There were plenty wanted to live with Alice before she took

up with Patrick Seton. And now *she's* in for a let-down, though she
won't admit it. But at least she's had her sex with a baby coming up.'

'You can't have babies all over the place,' Ronald said. 'It isn't
practical.'

'I know,' she said.

'Will you give me back the letter?' Ronald said.

'Why should I?'

'Because you took it,' Ronald said.

'It's the first time I've taken anything worth having off a man. And
I want to keep it.'

'What for?'

'It may come in useful. It may help Alice. If Patrick gets convicted
she'll be in the cart. I'd like to see him in gaol, but still he's Alice's
man, and I don't see why I shouldn't destroy the evidence against
him. I'm quite sure it's a forgery.'

'You won't destroy the letter,' Ronald said.

'How do you know?'

'It has too many possibilities of exploitation. You could form a
blood-brotherhood with several persons out of that letter. You have
already offered to give it to me if I slept with you.'

'Well, how do you know I would have given it to you in the end?'

'You're mistaken if you think it's going to make any difference to
the evidence against Patrick whether you keep it or not,' Ronald said.
'There are photo-copies which will be accepted in court together with
evidence of the loss of the original.'

'Why do you want it, then?'

'To save my own reputation. I get jobs from the police in the
detection of forgeries. I shouldn't have told anyone about this
document – that was my mistake. And it's obviously my responsibility that it was stolen. But if I can produce the letter after all, the
matter will be forgotten.'

'If I give you the letter will you promise to come and talk to me
again?'

'No,' Ronald said.

'I don't see why I should give you the letter. You've been talking as
a friend and getting round me, and all you want is the letter.'

'I'm not a friend, I'm a stranger,' Ronald said. 'I've quite liked
talking to you.'

'Well, I'm a stranger too. And I'm keeping the letter. There's a price on it.'

'Give it to me for love.'

'What love do I get out of it?'

'That's not the point.'

'Well, you've got a nerve, I'll say that. But you all come for what you can get.'

'Give it to me for love,' Ronald said. 'The best type of love to give is sacrificial. It's an embarrassing type of love to receive, if that's any consolation to you. The best type of love you can receive is to be taken for granted as a dependable person and otherwise ignored – that's more comfortable.'

'It's all talk,' she said. 'I'm tired. I've been doing a late shift at the Oriflamme.'

'Well, think about it in the morning.' He took down his coat and shouldered his way into it.

'If I give you the letter now,' she said, 'will you come back again some time?'

'It's unlikely,' he said. 'You go to bed. Thank you for talking.'

'If I don't give you the letter what will you do?'

'I'll come back and try again.'

'Christ!' she said, 'you're driving me mad.' She went over to the window and thrusting her arm far into the deep makeshift hem, drew out a four-folded paper. 'Take it and run quickly,' she said. 'Run now before I change my mind.' She came and pushed it into the pocket of Ronald's coat. 'Go away,' she said, 'get out of my sight.'

He sat down in his coat and smoothed out the paper. 'You've crumpled it but let's hear what it sounds like,' he said and read aloud,

'Dear Patrick,

I would like you to accept the enclosed cheque for two thousand pounds. Please use the money to further your psychic and spiritualistic work. I leave the details of its disposal entirely to you.

May I say how greatly I admire and have been inspired by your great Work. I shall never be able to thank you enough.

Yours sincerely,
Freda Flower

'You've crumpled it,' Ronald said, 'but at least you haven't folded it. In forgery detection you have to watch out for the folds.'

'Why's that?'

'Sometimes a line has been inked over after the fold has been made. The forger very often has second thoughts about the job after the paper has been folded, and to make everything perfect he unfolds the paper again and he touches something up; let's say the stroke of an "f". It's possible to see under the microscope if that sort of thing has been done.'

'Is that what Patrick's done, do you think?' She peered over at the letter. 'It looks like a woman's writing to me.'

'So it does to me. He's a clever forger. He's done it before. He's been convicted, served a sentence.'

'Well, Alice doesn't know that. Well, she does know it in a way, but she won't face it. The baby makes her believe in Patrick.'

'She'll know sooner or later.'

'Will he be sent to prison?'

'Oh, one can't guess,' Ronald said, 'it's not such an easy thing to prove. This may be a difficult document. Experts often disagree. Seton's side would have their own expert. And then, everything depends largely on the witnesses. If Mrs Flower's evidence should break down, for instance –'

'But if they know he's a forger from the past, surely –'

'The court isn't told till after the verdict.'

'Alice thinks the case won't come off.'

'No, perhaps it won't come off. Perhaps he won't be sent for trial.'

'Is it confidential that Patrick has been to prison?'

'No, it's common property.' He was examining the letter upside-down.

'Perhaps I won't tell Alice. She thinks they're going to get married, some hope. Anyway, he's taking her away to Austria as soon as the charge is settled one way or another.'

Ronald folded the letter and put it far away into his inner pocket. 'I must go,' he said.

'Will you come again, Ronald?'

'It's unlikely,' he said.

'You've got your letter,' she said.

'Thank you,' he said.

'You need someone to look after you,' she said.

'I was once engaged to a girl who wanted to be a mother to me. It didn't work.'

'You think I'm not good enough for you,' she said. 'Not your class.'

'I'm an epileptic,' he said. 'It rather puts one out of the reach of class.'

'I know you're an epileptic,' she said. 'I was told.'

'Well, good night, Elsie.' He went down the stairs and out into the dark streets of Monday morning.

ELEVEN

'It's treachery,' Alice said, quite loud in the empty café.

'Now look, Alice,' Elsie said, 'I've never signed any blood-pact with you. We're friends. And being friends doesn't mean being blood-sisters. For goodness' sake let's keep our relationships straight. Treachery is not the word.'

'Where did you get all this kind of talk?' Alice said.

'Now don't you turn cat, Alice. You need a friend just at this moment.'

'To think that you actually handed over that letter without even letting me see it,' Alice said, 'and now the case is coming up and the letter will be used against Patrick.'

'To begin with,' said Elsie, 'I didn't know whether he was going to go for trial or not when I gave him the letter. Secondly, it wouldn't have made any difference to the case because they photo'd the letter and that would have been good enough. Third, I gave it to Ronald for his own sake and I'd do it again –'

'What you wouldn't do for a night with a man . . .'

'He didn't so much as shake hands with me. Fourthly, it was more his letter than mine, and –'

'It's Patrick's letter,' Alice said, 'by law.'

'No, it's Crown property, excuse me. But it's his forgery, all right. Five, if you don't believe Patrick forged the letter I don't see what you're worried about. They can't prove a forgery if there isn't a forgery. It goes by folds in the paper and pauses in the writing. They see it under the microscope. Ronald –'

'Oh, shut up,' said Alice, 'with your one, two, three, four, five. You're such a clever cookie since you saw that man, a pity you didn't stop to think he's in the pay of the police.'

'Well, it's his job.'

'Yes, to fake up the evidence. He'll say whatever they want him to say.'

'You don't know Ronald,' said Elsie.

'Now he's got the letter, you won't be seeing *him* again,' Alice said. 'You wait and see.'

'I know,' Elsie said.

'God,' said Alice, 'it's kicking again. I feel faint when it does that.'

Elsie leaned over the café table and looked at Alice's stomach as she clutched it. 'Take your hand away,' Elsie said, 'and let me see.'

Alice took her hand away.

'I can't see anything,' Elsie said.

'Don't stare like that. Someone might come in the shop.'

'No one will come in, it's too early. I can't see it move.'

'You have to look close. It only looks like a butterfly, but it feels like a footballer inside me.'

Elsie slid round to the seat beside Alice and put her hand on Alice's round stomach. 'I can feel it!' she said. 'Kick, kick. I can feel it.'

'It makes me giddy,' Alice said.

'I'll go and draw you another espresso.'

'All right,' Alice said.

'I wish I had something alive and kicking inside me,' Elsie said.

Tim Raymond sat in his club, looking as lonely as possible in the hope that someone married would take him home to supper, but prepared, if not, to dine alone at eight o'clock. Hildegarde had just written from Gloucestershire, after a long silence, to say she was entering a convent. On hearing this news Tim had telephoned to Ronald. 'Have you heard from Hildegarde?'

'That's the second girl you've driven to religion,' Ronald said.

'*I've* driven?'

'Well, yes, in a way.'

'Hildegarde told you about our affair?'

'Well, not directly. Anyway, of course I knew about it and now that's the second girl —'

'I know,' Tim said. Two years ago his first real girl friend had entered an Anglican Sisterhood.

'What about that other one you were thinking of marrying?' Ronald said.

'Oh, that's all off. *She* hasn't taken to religion.'

'Well, two's plenty.'

'I wonder why they take to religion.'

'There must be something wrong with you,' Ronald said.

'So there must. Do you know, I always felt Hildegarde was still keen on you, Ronald.'

'Well, she must have got over it. What Order has she entered?'

'Some Canoness affair. I feel rather shattered. Not that I felt all that strongly about Hildegarde, it's just that a loss is a loss. And I didn't know she was R.C. When did she go Roman?'

'Two years ago,' Ronald said, 'and two months. I forget the odd days.'

'What a good memory you've got. Did she join under your influence?'

'Yes. I rather regretted it later.'

'Why?'

'Because she lapsed.'

'Well, she's gone back. There's definitely something odd about Hildegarde. She was a spiritualist for a time, not long ago.'

'Under your influence?'

'Well, it gave us something to talk about. One has to have something to talk about. Hildegarde was a difficult girl to find something to talk about with. Anyway she gave up spiritualism when I got out of it and she must have gone bang back to Rome. Funny going from spiritualism back to Catholicism, don't you think, all prejudices apart? A bit extreme. There are other religions she could have tried if she had to have a religion.'

'There are only two religions, the spiritualist and the Catholic,' Ronald said.

'I say, that's going a bit far. There's the Greek Orthodox and the Quakers and of course the C. of E. and some people are Buddhists, and –'

'You must take it in a figurative sense,' Ronald said, 'or leave it, because I need a drink.'

'Well, that's the news. I thought I'd let you know. Come and drink with me.'

'I'm going out. I'm late, actually,' Ronald said.

'I've got nothing to do tonight,' Tim said. 'What would you do?'

'See a film.'

'Don't want to, somehow.'

'Sit in your club and look as lonely and miserable as possible. Someone will turn up and take you home.'

Tim was doing this when the porter came to announce that his Aunt Marlene was inquiring for him downstairs.

'I'm not here,' Tim said, and moved to another chair. The chair he had been occupying was placed in the window and the curtains had been left undrawn. He suspected that Marlene had seen him from the street. He took off his glasses, polished them with his handkerchief, and put them on again.

An almost telepathic communication from the entrance hall – for nothing could be heard from that direction – told him that an argument was going on between Marlene and the porter at the desk. Tim tiptoed attentively to the door, tripping over the legs of someone whose face was hidden by a newspaper, so that Tim's hand came to rest on the man's lap.

'Oh,' Tim said, 'it's you, Eccie.' He straightened up, by which time the porter had appeared again.

'The lady said she is convinced you are in the building. I've told her I would have another look.'

'I'm going along to the bar,' Tim said. 'Tell her you've had another look.'

'I'm not sure,' said Eccie, 'that the British Council is going to suit me. Their notions of art –'

'Come along to the bar,' Tim said, urgently. 'My aunt's downstairs.'

'Well, she won't come up here.'

'Oh, won't she?' said Tim.

Eccie puckered his face in puzzlement and followed Tim, who, looking over the banister, perceived a corner of his aunt in the hall as she argued with the porter.

They slipped into the bar.

'I have a series of twelve lectures,' Eccie declared over his drink. 'They have gone down well for twelve years. They are old and tried and have stood the test of time at the old Institute. They cover the Renaissance to Kandinsky. They were the nucleus of the Art course at the Institute. Thousands of people passed through our hands south of the Humber. I travelled the length and breadth, to W.V.S. centres, National Service units, prisons, summer schools – all over the place. And everywhere I went those lectures got a tremendous reception. They were highly appreciated. From the Renaissance to Kandinsky, with a set of colour reproductions, tested and tried. And now, when I'm all fixed for my injections for Malta, the chap at the British Council says – and mind you it's we who pay them, it's the taxpayer, you and I, whose money goes into their pockets – he calls me in and he says –'

'Tim, oh, there you are!'

Marlene stood by the other door leading from the back stairs.

Tim put down his drink and disappeared out of the opposite door. Marlene did not pursue him, as he expected, through the bar. She retreated down the back stairs to the first landing, walked along a passage, and came out on to the big oak-panelled first floor landing where she again encountered Tim.

She said, 'The trial is on, and it is settled that you are to be a witness. We have decided, on Patrick's own advice, not to give evidence for his character as he prefers his character to speak for itself. But there is a question of a statement that Patrick made to the police under duress, while still in a state of trance after a séance. We must testify about this séance. I have the date and the time. Eleven-thirty on the morning of August the twelfth. Patrick made his statement at twelve noon. He was not properly out of his trance. You are to give evidence that you saw him in a trance at eleven-thirty, but we must decide exactly what you are to say because you are inclined to be hesitant and vague. I am calling a meeting –'

'Marlene, you shouldn't be here.'

'Get your coat immediately,' she said, 'and come with me.'

'I'm just going to the lavatory,' Tim said and disappeared with his long legs up the main staircase like an anxious spider. He did not, however, go into the lavatory, but into the library where an aged member and a young man were bending over an architectural-looking plan spread out on the table. They looked up at Tim. The aged member said 'Who?' and they both looked down again at their plan. Tim wandered over to the window and there slipped behind the curtains. Marlene waited outside the lavatory. A man emerged with eyebrows which were by nature fixed in slight astonishment, and which, when he saw Marlene, seemed to try to rise. 'Is my nephew in there?' Marlene said.

The man moved off, assuming her to be one of the maids gone mad in her private life.

Marlene waited. In ten minutes' time she knocked loudly on the door.

'Tim,' she said.

'Tim!' she said.

'Listen, Tim,' she said. 'I will take you across to Prunier's. We can discuss everything there. You *know* you like Prunier's.'

'Timothy!' she said.

A very young man came round the corner. 'Oh!' he said at Marlene's back.

'Would you mind going in there and telling my nephew, Tim Raymond, that he's wanted urgently? A matter of life and death. Hurry.'

The young man went in as one accustomed to military training, leaving the door open. Marlene stood in the doorway and watched while he politely looked round.

'There's nobody here,' said the young man.

The aged member from the library approached the door, followed by his young companion.

Marlene was saying, 'Nonsense. He is hiding from me. Have a good look.'

'Who?' said the aged member behind her.

'Let *me* look,' said Marlene, entering this tiled enclosure.

'Who?' said the old man.

He was ushered away by his fellows.

Marlene continued her simple but fruitless search. When she came out she caught sight of the porter as he came up the stairs with the look of one who had been sent.

Marlene tripped along the passage and into the library. The room appeared to be unoccupied. A thin and feeble little cloud of cigarette smoke proceeded from the join of the window curtains. Marlene observed the bulge where Tim had pulled a chair behind the curtain to console his vigil, and made straight for it.

'Tim, you are wasting my time.'

Footsteps approached outside and the door-handle was turned.

Marlene got behind the curtain with Tim just before the porter put his head round the door. As soon as he had withdrawn Tim moved out to the far side of the big table.

'It is a matter of life and death,' Marlene said.

'I've got to go to the lavatory,' Tim said. This was genuine, and he departed.

Marlene found a place of concealment at the end of the passage. Tim came out of the lavatory and, looking to right and left, darted upstairs. Marlene followed, in time to catch him as he attempted to close a door behind him. She pushed her way in against him and confronted him in a bleak vacant bedroom. She locked the door.

'Now, Tim,' she said, 'what's all this fuss about?'

'I don't want to give evidence in Seton's case,' he said. 'It's got nothing to do with me, Marlene.'

'It isn't a matter of what you want. It's a question of what is necessary.'

'No,' said Tim, 'really.'

'What?' she said.

'Nothing doing,' Tim said.

'You are out of your mind,' she said.

Tim made a dash for the door, unlocked it, fled downstairs, grabbed his coat and dashed into the street where he turned several corners, and then caught a taxi.

Marlene walked solemnly downstairs and demanded some scrap paper from the hall porter.

'Mr Raymond has left, Madam.'

'I wish to leave a note.'

She folded it in four when she had written it and wrote Tim's name on the outside. She gave it to the porter who, when she had gone, read the message: 'I shall see my solicitor tomorrow with a view to altering the legacy arrangements. Marlene Cooper.'

Ewart Thornton sat with his elbow resting on the arm of his wide chair, and in his hand the telephone receiver.

'There is a meeting tonight. Of course I shall not be present. Freda my dear, there is something you should know about the Wider Infinity. There is a group within the Group. A secret group within the

Group. Now you didn't know that, Freda dear, did you? Doesn't it surprise you?'

Freda Flower sat in her chair by the telephone, looking up at a cobweb in the corner of the ceiling which she dared not sweep away for fear of bad luck, and spoke into the telephone.

'You amaze me, Ewart,' she said.

'I thought that would surprise you,' he said. 'My dear, this secret group within the Group is called the Interior Spiral.'

'That's a make of mattress, isn't it?' she said.

'It may be, it may be. I say, my dear Freda, you are taking this seriously, aren't you?'

'I think it's a very serious matter indeed, Ewart. After all, it was my money that was –'

'Yes, quite. Well, as I was saying, there is this secret group, and I admit I was a member. There was some good in it, Freda, we did a lot of good. But an evil spirit got abroad amongst us. I have resigned. There is a conspiracy amongst them to support Patrick Seton at the trial. Of course, this is illegal and they won't have a leg to stand on, but –'

'Oh, Ewart, oh, Ewart. I do wish I had never gone to the police about that money. They will make me say more things against Patrick, and with him standing there in the dock, with his eyes on me. I don't know how I managed the other day in the Magistrate's Court. I came home to bed, and –'

'You only have to speak the truth, Freda. It is the truth, isn't it? You did give him that money to buy bonds?'

'Oh yes, but –'

'And he used it for his own purposes?'

'Yes, but –'

'And forged a letter to cover himself?'

'Yes, it's true, but ... Oh, Ewart, I somehow knew all the time he was deceiving me and I let it go. It makes –'

'You knew?'

'Well, I knew and I didn't know. I wouldn't admit it to myself. And now to get up in the criminal court with his eyes on me again and stick to the facts as Mr Fergusson says, it will be such a sort of let-down, a betrayal, and poor little Patrick, he's so thin.'

'Tell me, Freda dear – I'm a man of the world – was there any –

were there any *relations* between you and Patrick Seton? In confidence, my dear?'

'Well, Ewart, I don't want to talk about it, naturally I've got my pride. But he got round me, you know, Ewart, and I let myself go. He –'

'My dear, if this is mentioned in court, deny it. Simply flatly deny it. It is irrelevant to the case. I doubt very much if Patrick would bring it up in court – it would go against him, if anything. You were foolish, Freda my dear.'

'I know I'm a foolish woman. It's not just the disgrace of it coming up that's worrying me. But it was terrible the other day to stand up in front of Patrick and denounce him to the magistrate after being together like that. He looked at me. It –'

'That's just his trick, my dear. Don't you see? He counts on women being weak. He –'

'Oh, I do believe he meant everything in his heart at the time when we were together, really. And he can see through everything, Ewart. You don't know how psychic he is. He's in touch with my poor husband. He's in touch with the Beyond. He –'

'Are you afraid of him?' Ewart said.

'Yes.'

'What are you afraid of?'

'His looking at me. He used to recite "Season of mists and mellow fruitfulness", it was a deepening experience, Ewart.'

'You must definitely speak to Father Socket, Freda. If you feel an evil eye upon you, Father Socket will exorcise it for you –'

'Father Socket has gone away. Dr Garland can't find him anywhere. He isn't at Ramsgate and he's left the flat. Dr Garland's upset. Dr Garland's sent those girls away – and between you and me, good riddance. You don't tell *me* they were waitresses. No fear.'

'There must have been a break between Socket and Mike Garland,' Ewart said. '*My* dear. Tell me more.'

'Oh, definitely a break. I don't know what about.'

'Have you seen Mike Garland recently?'

'No. There's rent owing for the girls.'

'Freda my dear, you simply must keep clear of these cranks.'

'Ewart, I feel I can count on you. If only I didn't have to go to court and stand up. The case might go on for a whole day or more. Will you be at the trial?'

'Oh no. Exams.'

'I should like to see you. Won't you come over?'

'Sorry. Loads of homework.' The comfort went out of his face at the notion of his telephone-relationship getting out of hand.

'Suppose Patrick gets off?' she said.

'He won't get off if you stick to the facts.'

'But this Interior Spiral. They might get up and say anything. Suppose Patrick gets off? – He'll do me damage, Ewart, and I'll only have myself to blame.'

'The Interior Spiral, as I was about to tell you, Freda my dear, is dwindling fast. Marlene will find herself with very few friends when it comes to a court case.'

'Suppose Patrick *doesn't* get off? – He'll do me damage.'

Ewart Thornton suddenly desired to ring off. The act of gossiping with her over the telephone was a need, but the need was fulfilled in the act. He did not like it when the conversation seemed to be getting somewhere. 'Patrick will do me harm.' She upset him by going on like this. What if Patrick did her harm? Ewart felt uneasy about Patrick. He might well do harm. It was best to keep out of Patrick's reach. Patrick was definitely in touch with things out there in the Unseen.

'Patrick,' said Freda, 'has the *power* to do –'

'Freda my dear, I must go. Mounds of homework.'

He sulked for a moment after he had put down the receiver, then he rose fatly, and presently stood up tall so that his hips lost their broadness. He tidied his room for the night. He put this away and that in its place, and sighed for his superannuation.

Marlene sat in her indignation, awaiting the meeting of the Interior Spiral. Everyone was late. It was a quarter to nine and the meeting had been called for half past eight. The six coffee-cups and the plate of biscuits stood on the tray like messages of regret for inability to attend. Ewart Thornton had said he would not come. Still, one had hoped ... Tim, to whom had been offered this unique opportunity of becoming acquainted with the Interior Spiral, was *out*. Out – she had seen her solicitor that morning and Tim was out of her Will. Five

others had promised, were expected, might still come, would surely
... Patrick himself, why was he late? The two retired spinsters, the
Cottons from round the corner, where were they? Disloyally attending those life classes they had recently taken up, Marlene had no
doubt. She had told them of the urgency. Billy Raines, the photographer? Osbert Jacob? Jacynthe – The door bell rang.

It was Patrick.

'I'm sorry to be late,' he uttered in his half-voice, 'but Alice, I've
had trouble with Alice. Keeps talking of suicide ... one day ...
suicide. It's sure to happen.'

'That girl should be in a home,' Marlene said. 'You are too good
to her, Patrick, She is only after what she can get. You are too
good.'

She placed her arm round his shoulders and he rested his head
upon her bosom of bones.

'Well,' she said, 'take your coat off, Patrick. It is nine o'clock and no
one has come. I fear we are deserted, but we are not a sinking ship.
Not yet. I told everyone of the urgency, and what was to be discussed.
After all I have done for the Infinity. My one nephew, my own flesh
and blood, has –' The door bell rang.

At first she thought it was the Rector of Dees coming up the stairs.
She had not expected the Rector of Dees, since he was getting on in
years and the trains were so irregular. But she had written to him. And
now he had come. 'In my hour of need,' she called down the stairs.
'Dear Rector.'

He looked up from his wide-brimmed hat. It was not the Rector of
Dees, it was Father Socket of the enemy faction, protector of Dr
Garland so-called.

'Well,' said Marlene, blocking the doorway.

Father Socket removed his hat and looked humble. 'May I come
and break bread with you?' he said.

'Come this way,' Marlene said.

She took him into her sitting-room where Patrick stood by the fire.
Father Socket held out his hand to Patrick.

'I have come to make my peace,' he said.

Patrick placed his effortless hand in the strong white-hairy one of
Father Socket. White hairs bristled on Father Socket's face. He had
not shaved.

'Dear lady,' he said to Marlene. 'I have been through the deep waters.'

'Did you say you were hungry?' said she, perceiving he had come as an ally.

'It was a manner of speaking,' he said. 'I have come to ask you to accept what assistance I can offer in your courageous efforts to –'

'You want to witness for Patrick at the trial?'

'I do. I have been greatly deceived in my clairvoyant protégé, Dr Garland. The serpent's –'

'He is no clairvoyant,' said Marlene, 'and he is no doctor.'

'You are right,' said Father Socket. 'And would that I had known it earlier. He is tonight under arrest for activities the nature of which I will not sully my lips by describing. I myself have just come from the police station where I was given to understand that attempts had been made to implicate myself in these activities. Fortunately –'

'What were the activities?'

'Young women were involved. I say no more,' said Father Socket. 'Fortunately there is no shred of evidence against me. I have been away for some days, and I find on my return this afternoon that my flat has been searched in my absence. Needless to say, nothing of the least incriminating nature was found. My name is clear. I have come straight to you to offer my services in atonement for the harm done to Mr Seton by Dr Garland.'

'Doctor so-called,' said Marlene.

'A very wise move,' Patrick said meekly to Father Socket.

Father Socket looked at him, opened his mouth and closed it again.

'We must have our refreshments,' said Marlene. 'The Interior Spiral goes on!' She went to heat the coffee.

'A very wise move,' Patrick said to Father Socket.

'The police have no evidence against me,' Socket said.

'Not unless I lay it before them,' Patrick said meekly, 'because I have proof of the facts.'

'I have come to offer my services, my son,' said Socket. 'I cannot do more. Under the influence of my cloth, my evidence –'

'Come now,' Marlene said, bearing in the coffee pot, 'we shall refresh ourselves while we discuss the details. How glad I am, after all, that the members of our little Interior have defected! They were not worth their salt. All things work together for good. Do you take sugar, Father?'

'No, nor coffee at this hour, if I may be excused.'

'Details,' said Marlene. 'Now, it is a question, before we see Patrick's counsel, of what you were doing on the morning of the twelfth of August. You were at Patrick's rooms on that morning, receiving a private séance. Patrick was in a trance. . . . You saw a police car pull up outside just as you were leaving the premises . . . his statement . . . in a trance.'

By midnight they were rehearsed.

'Before you leave,' Marlene said, 'shall we go into the Sanctuary for a few moments' spiritual repose?'

In the Sanctuary a dim green light was burning. Patrick automatically took the carved oak séance chair while Marlene and Socket sat facing him.

They breathed deeply. Suddenly Patrick's head jerked backwards. Marlene whispered to Socket, 'Take my hand. He is going into a trance. He may prophesy.'

Patrick gurgled. His eyes rolled upward. Water began to run from the sides of his mouth which at last he opened wide. In a voice not his, he pronounced,

'I creep.'

Marlene's arms went rigid. Socket tried to release his hand but could not.

Patrick's mouth was foaming. His head dropped and his eyes closed. He breathed loudly. His fingers twitched on the end of the chair-arm. Presently he lifted up his head again and his eyes opened into slits.

Marlene said, 'He's coming round.'

They left the Sanctuary of Light, Marlene assisting Patrick.

'Did I give utterance?' Patrick said. 'What did I say?'

Walter Prett leaned his bulk over the bar of the wine club in Hampstead. It had just opened and he was the first customer. He said to the barmaid, 'I say, Chloe, you know everyone, don't you?'

'Just about,' she said.

'Do you know Isobel Billows?'

'Now who is she?' Chloe said, concentrating her sharp young face on the subject.

'She was married to Carr Billows of Billows Flour.'

'Oh, Flourbags?'

'Yes, his first wife.'

'I don't know of her,' Chloe said. 'What about her?'

'She's got lots of money. I broke her china the other day.'

'Whatever do you mean, you naughty boy?'

'I'll have another,' Walter said.

'You broke her china?'

'Yes, all her china tea-cups. They were on a tray. I smashed the lot.'

'Why d'you do that?' Chloe said, polishing the glasses on the counter so that her time should not be altogether wasted.

'Why? That's what I ask myself between opening times. I love that woman, Chloe. And yet I go and behave like a hog.'

'Just a minute,' said Chloe, drawing inspiration from the embossed cornice. 'Just a minute. Haven't I heard that she's got a barrister friend?'

'She has indeed. Martin Bowles. Do you know him?'

'No, I don't think –'

'No, you wouldn't know him. He's nobody. Only he hangs round Isobel for her money. He's the financial wizard, you see. And lines his own pocket on the right side of the law. A common little, vulgar little –'

'Now don't start that,' Chloe said, 'Walter, please. Not at this hour of the evening. Hallo, Eccie,' she said as Francis Eccles came in.

'And he's bald,' said Walter. 'At least I've got a good head of hair.' He shook his white mane.

'You could do with a trim,' said Chloe.

'I've resigned from the British Council,' said Eccie.

Walter hugged him like a bear and embraced him on both cheeks. He drew from his pocket three five-pound notes and gave one to Eccie. 'What's this for?' Eccie said.

'A congratulatory gift.'

'The return of a loan,' said Chloe. 'I remember the last time you were here –'

'Vulgar little lower-middle-class ideas you have, Chloe. I do not borrow and return. I take. I give.'

'You can give me sixteen and six and clear out,' Chloe said. 'I won't be talked to like that.'

Walter beamed at her.

'Yes, it's all right when you're in the right mood,' Chloe said, 'but you turn about like the weather.'

'My lectures,' said Eccie, 'were designed to reveal the essence of art from Botticelli to Kandinsky, with reference to the lives of the artists themselves, supported by coloured plates, excellent reproductions. Those lectures have stood the test –'

'I should leave out the lives of the artists,' Walter said. 'They don't bear looking into.'

'Oh, come, I wouldn't say that.'

'They break up ladies' china cups,' Walter said mournfully.

'Since when were you an artist?' Chloe said.

Walter looked dangerous.

'Walter, now, Walter,' said Eccie, 'don't *do* anything.'

'I have spent a long time not doing anything,' Walter said. 'The sins of the artist are sins of omission. You should do a lecture on that, Eccie, with reference to the lives of the art-critics.'

'Well, as I was saying,' Eccie said, 'this chap called me in, and he said . . .'

'I pray,' said Alice, 'day and night. I go into churches and pray if the doors are open, and I pray that Patrick will be saved from prison.'

'I wouldn't build on it,' Elsie said.

'I am building on it. I pray for Patrick, and that's the test. If Patrick doesn't get off, I don't believe in God.'

'Patrick hasn't much chance, with the statement he made to the police against him.'

'He was half in a trance when he made that statement. There's a police office that's got an influence on Patrick, and he talked him into it. Patrick was just out of a trance.'

'The jury won't know what a trance is.'

'They'll learn.'

'There's a prejudice against spiritualism,' Elsie said.

'Oh, can't you look on the bright side, Elsie?'

'I don't know what's bright about you having Patrick wearing you down for the rest of your life.'

'Well, he's my choice, Elsie.'

'I know that. I'm afraid for you.'

'Don't be afraid for me. And you needn't be afraid for Patrick either, now that Father Socket's come forward to speak for him. There's no denying the impression Father Socket makes on people.'

'Father Socket?' Elsie said. 'He's against Patrick. He was in with Mike Garland. A couple of *those*.'

'There's been a rift. Garland is in trouble with the police and let Father Socket down. So Father Socket has come in with Patrick now. It's going to be all right, I feel it. Father Socket was with Patrick on the morning of the twelfth of August, and he saw Patrick in a trance just before the police came –'

'Twelfth of August was my birthday,' Elsie said.

'So it was. Well, that was the day that Patrick made the statement. But everything's all right now.'

'I don't see you need to pray for Patrick if you're so sure of that.'

'It's a test of God,' said Alice.

Elsie telephoned from Victoria Station to Ronald. 'I've got to see you. It's about the evidence for Patrick Seton. Father Socket is going to give false evidence. I've got to see you.'

'Father who?'

'That Father I told you about, that let me down.'

'Oh, yes.'

'Well, he's going to say that on the morning of the twelfth of August – which was my birthday and I had the day off – he's going to swear –'

'Look,' said Ronald, 'I'm not the police.'

'Can't I tell you? I'd rather give you the story.'

'It's not my business. Go straight to the police station. Ask for Detective-Inspector Fergusson. Have you any evidence?'

'No, only my word.'

'Well, it's as good as Socket's. Go and see Mr Fergusson.'

'I'll ring and tell you what he says.'

'No need to,' Ronald said. 'It's not my business.'

'Then I don't know if I shall bother,' Elsie said. 'It's not my business either.'

Marlene was on the night train to Scotland.

'I'm very sorry, Patrick,' she had said, standing at the door of her flat, her baggage packed and visible in the hall behind her, keeping him out. 'Very sorry indeed. But on consideration I simply must safeguard my reputation for the sake of the Circle. Nothing has changed, my feelings are the same, but on consideration I can't give evidence. And as it happens I've been called away urgently. You have Father Socket. I am no loss.'

She thought, now, perhaps she had been hard on Tim. It had been well-meaning of him to telephone to her.

'I say, Marlene, do keep out of the Seton case. You'll be charged with suborning, Marlene dear. The police may be on the alert for suborners, Ronald Bridges gave me the tip.'

'What is suborning?'

'Conspiracy. Cooking up evidence in a law case beforehand.'

'There has been no cooking up on my part. There is no contrary proof whatsoever. There –'

'It's a criminal offence, Marlene dear, you might go to Holloway prison. I should hate –'

'You beastly little fellow. You snivelling . . .'

She had hung up the receiver in the middle of his protests. All the same, on consideration . . .

The train to Dundee was a rocky one. She stood up in her bunk and tried to adjust the air-conditioning equipment of the sleeping compartment, but failed. She pressed the bell. No one came. She wondered if Patrick might have some spiritual power over her, even in Scotland. She could not sleep.

'The key,' said Dr Lyte miserably, handing Patrick the key.

'A month's supply of insulin,' he said, handing Patrick the prescription. 'When will you be going?'

'The day after the trial. Alice is upset, you know. Very depressed. She needs the holiday.'

*

'I'll be seeing you in court then tomorrow, Mr Fergusson.'

'Yes, Patrick. Be there at quarter past ten.'

'If I get off, Mr Fergusson, I may have some news for you.'

'Let's have your information now, then, Patrick.'

'I'd rather wait and see if I get off.'

'Your news wouldn't be about Socket, would it?'

'I'd rather not say, Mr Fergusson.'

'We need information about Socket. I don't mind admitting it,' said Fergusson.

'That statement I signed in August – you'll be using it in court?' Patrick said.

'Yes, Patrick. We can't let you get away with that, I'm afraid. You've been useful to us, but a statement's a statement. It's filed.'

'You got me in a weak moment when I gave you that statement,' Patrick whispered. 'I was upset, you remember, Mr Fergusson –' He looked at the broad shoulders and did not want ever to have to leave the chair in which he sat contemplating them, and go out into the streets again.

'I have no recollection,' said Fergusson, 'that you were upset.'

'Don't you remember, I was all shaken up that morning?'

'Yes, Patrick, I know that. But as far as the law is concerned I have no recollection.'

'There's the question of the letter,' Patrick said.

'It was foolish of you to go and forge that letter. Another couple of years on your sentence at least.'

'Our expert is convinced the letter's genuine,' Patrick mumbled.

'Our expert isn't,' said Fergusson.

Patrick wrenched himself away. But when he had plunged out into the street again, he felt better, and considering the chances, was confident of his release, so that he did not give thought to the matter again that day, but thought of Alice.

TWELVE

From time to time throughout the trial, Patrick Seton sat in the dock visualizing, with fretful eagerness, Alice as she should lie on the mountainside, crumpled up, overdosed with insulin; the liberation of Alice's spirit was so imminent, it was like a sunny radiance to distract his understanding from the proceedings of the court.

When the time came for him to speak, he was lucid and calm and clear-voiced. Alice had never heard him speak so clearly, she was astonished.

'His voice has changed, hasn't it?' she whispered to Matthew, up in the public gallery.

'I don't know,' Matthew said. 'How should I know what his voice is like?'

'I think he must be making a special effort,' Alice whispered. 'He feels a strong clear voice is called for.'

'Don't talk. I want to listen,' Matthew said, 'to this bit.'

'He's doing well, isn't he?' said Alice. 'After the mess they made of the Prosecution case this morning –'

'Don't talk,' Matthew said, leaning over the rail of the gallery. 'I want to listen.'

'I do think,' Alice said, 'that Elsie might have come.'

Ronald walked through the late-night streets, recovering his strength. He had spent the day in court. He had been the third witness for the Prosecution.

'Have you ever in your life made a mistake?' said the Defence Counsel in his cross-examination.

'Yes,' said Ronald.

'This couldn't be one of them?'

'I have never, so far as I know, made a mistake in a case of forgery.'

'So far as you know. Thank you, Mr Bridges – Oh, oh . . .'

'Oh!' said the whole world at once, 'what's happened? He's falling, fainting.'

Ronald had put on his best dark suit for the occasion. He had arrived at the Criminal Court at ten minutes past ten. He had never before seen Martin Bowles in his wig and gown in court; it was an amazing sight. Martin had become instantly wise, unimpeachable. Once, at Isobel Billows's, she having found Martin's wig at the back of his car and brought it into the house, Ronald had seen her try it on and, watching herself in the rather dim gilt-framed looking-glass, recite,

'The quality of mercy is not strained. . . .'

'They always say that,' said Martin. 'Women, when they try on a lawyer's wig, always do that.'

The case opened at half past ten. Hugh Farmer, Counsel for the Defence, lolled back against the bench, sometimes whispering to his pupil behind him while the indictment was read for the second time. He was thinking of his elder daughter, at the moment taking her most important examination in music.

'Fraudulent conversion . . . forgery . . . Mrs Freda Flower.'

Martin Bowles got up to open the case for the Prosecution. Hugh Farmer watched him respectfully as Martin gave small reasonable waves of his hand, with upturned palm, towards the jury.

'Detective-Inspector Fergusson will read you a statement made and signed by the accused. . . .

'Mrs Freda Flower will tell you . . .

'I will call an expert in the detection of forgery who will give evidence on the count of . . .'

Now Fergusson was in the witness box, not in uniform. He took his oath. He read Patrick's statement: '. . . I was tempted, and fell. The cheque was for premium and defence bonds. Mrs Flower asked me to obtain them for her. She felt they were safer with me. I did not buy the bonds. I do not know where the money has gone. I have read this over. . . .'

Hugh Farmer got up to cross-examine.

'Mr Fergusson, when you saw Mr Seton on the afternoon of 12th August, the day on which you say he made this statement, did you notice anything peculiar about him?'

'Nothing whatsoever,' said Fergusson.

'Are you sure?'

'Absolutely certain,' said Fergusson.

'Nothing about the eyes? No slight foaming at the mouth?'

The judge said, 'Mr Farmer, what is the –'

'It is relevant, my lord. My client is a spiritualistic medium and I shall show that he was in a trance when he signed that statement at the police station.' He resumed his cross-examination.

'You said just now you were unaware, when you obtained this statement from Mr Seton, that he had received a letter from Mrs Flower asking him to use the money for his own purposes?'

'He said nothing about a letter on that occasion.'

'Then Mr Seton called on you the following week and told you he had made his statement while in a dazed condition, and wished to withdraw it?'

'I have no recollection of that.'

'He told you he had in his possession a letter from Mrs Flower in which she made it plain that the cheque was freely given for his use in his profession?'

'I have no recollection of him saying that.'

'When you say you have no recollection you mean that in fact you do not remember whether he said it or whether he did not? He might in fact have stated his desire to withdraw his statement or to make a further statement, but it has slipped your recollection.'

'He didn't ask to withdraw his statement or make a further one. He said nothing about a letter on that occasion.'

'You have said you did not know about the existence of a letter from Mrs Flower until some weeks later.'

'That is correct. . . .'

'You said . . .'

Alice whispered to Matthew, 'You can see the power he's got over Patrick. Just look at poor Patrick.'

Patrick was sitting in the dock between two policemen, looking at tall square Fergusson with his head slightly to one side and tears shining in his pale eyes.

Next came Freda Flower. She began to swear on the Bible, glanced towards Patrick, and ended on a faltering note.

'You are a widow?' said Martin Bowles. '... You let rooms for a living? ... Do you know the accused? ... How long have you known the accused? ... Did he offer to do a little decorating and painting in your house? ... When did you become interested in the spiritualist movement? ... Did you attend séances with the accused?'

'Yes,' said Freda Flower. '... Yes ... Yes ... That's right.... I started going to spiritualist meetings with Mr Seton, that would be about three months after he came to my house.'

'He was in charge of these meetings?'

'Oh no, he was the medium.'

'Can you describe to the court in your own words what took place when Mr Seton acted as a medium?'

'Well, he went under and I must say he always gave every satisfaction as a medium, I must say that. He –'

'When you say he went under, Mrs Flower, what does that mean? He sat in a chair, did he not?'

'Yes, he was bound to the chair hands and feet.'

'And this was in the dark.'

'Well, there was always a small light burning in the Sanctuary.'

'There was a dim light in the séance room where the meetings were held – Am I right? ...'

'Yes, that's right ... bound hand and foot to a chair....'

'Could you describe the trance, please? You must remember that most people present in this court have not attended a spiritualist meeting.'

'He closed his eyes and went under.'

'He appeared to lose consciousness?' said Martin.

'No, because he spoke as a medium after that. The control took over, you see.'

'He appeared to be unaware of what was going on around him?'

'Oh, yes.'

'Will you describe his appearance?'

'Well, you see, he's a medium. His eyes rolled upward and he foamed a bit at the mouth and his legs and arms twitched as far as was possible because they were bound to the chair.'

'Did he obtain messages purporting to come from an invisible world?'

'Yes, he got through to the other side. He –'

'Were any of these messages directed specifically to you?'

'Yes, he got through to my late husband.' She looked at Patrick and looked away. Patrick was accusing her. 'His messages were often a great comfort,' she said.

'These messages from your late husband through the mediumship of Seton contained practical advice?'

'Yes, sometimes . . . Well, not exactly practical, but –'

'Will you give an example?'

'Well, only advice to keep happy and cheerful,' she said, on the verge of tears.

'Anything else?'

'Well, it's difficult . . .'

'On one occasion there was something about money?'

The Defence Counsel was allowed his objection.

Martin said, 'Were you advised as to your friends, the company you kept?'

'Yes,' said Freda, 'my late husband wanted me to be friends with Mr Seton.'

'Was this according to what the accused said while in his trance?'

'Yes.'

'Now,' said Martin, 'about this cheque for two thousand pounds. . . .'

Up in the gallery Matthew said to Alice, 'She's giving very bad evidence.'

'What other sort of evidence could she give?' said Alice.

'Will you look at this cheque for two thousand pounds made out to Patrick Seton and say if that is your signature?' Martin was saying.

'Yes,' she said, 'it's mine.'

'Martin Bowles is a clot,' Matthew said.

'He hasn't got much of a case,' said Alice.

Martin was referring to Freda Flower's deposition.

'Yes,' she said. '. . . Yes, I told him to buy them for me.' . . . 'No, it was his suggestion.' . . . 'I thought he had bought the bonds . . . Well, I thought the bonds would be safer with him. . . .'

'What do you mean by safer?' said the judge.

'I thought he would keep them safer than me,' she said.

Patrick looked up at Alice. She smiled at him. Her pregnancy, he thought, is hidden by the railings of the balcony. I'm winning. She won't live.

'I did in a way promise him a little help with his spiritual research. I said he should ask me for money.'

Some of the jury were making notes.

'And did he ask you?'

'No, he never asked. . . .'

Martin read out the letter to the court. 'I should add,' he said, 'that the letter is undated.'

'Will you look at this letter,' he said, 'and tell the court whether you wrote it or not?'

'No, I never wrote it.'

'Is that handwriting similar to your own?'

'It looks very like my writing. But I couldn't have written it unless I was in a trance or something.'

'Have you ever been in a trance?' said the judge.

'I don't think so, my lord.'

'Don't you know? Have you ever foamed at the mouth and rolled up your eyes, and twitched?'

'No, my lord.'

Matthew said, as the cross-examination began, 'Now we're for it.'

'Serve her right,' Alice said. 'She's just showing herself up for what she is.'

'You have said that Mr Seton gave every satisfaction as a medium?' said Patrick's counsel.

'Yes, he was always a good medium.'

'You had every faith in his powers?'

'Yes.'

'And still have?'

'Oh, yes.'

'You had every reason to believe that he was genuine, whatever may be the opinions of others on spiritualism in general?'

'Oh, he was genuine, I admit.'

'And you say he brought you comfort, and did repairs and decorations to your house?'

'Oh, yes, he –'

'Did you pay him for those repairs and decorations?'

'Well, not exactly. I let the rent go. We were very friendly, you see, after I got to know him.'

'And, finding him trustworthy as a medium, you had confidence in his practical advice and judgement?'

'Yes, I told him everything.'

'His lordship has asked you whether you have ever been in a trance. I am going to repeat that question.'

'I don't think so, sir.'

'Think carefully. Because you said' – he consulted his notes – 'you told the court, when you looked at the letter, "It looks very like my writing. I couldn't have written it unless I was in a trance or something."' His voice rose with nasal emphasis on the words 'or something', and he repeated her words again: 'unless I was in a trance or something'. He put down his notes and breathed deeply. 'Now, Mrs Flower,' he said, 'I am going to put it to you that you have, in fact, had the experience of trances.'

'I couldn't say,' she said. 'It only looks funny that my handwriting should be on the letter and I don't remember writing it.'

'And it may have been written while you were in a trance?'

The judge said, 'Has anyone ever seen you in a state of trance? Has anyone ever told you or suggested to you that you have been in a trance?'

'No, sir. But I could have been in a trance on my own.'

'Were you in anything like a trance last April when it is suggested that the letter was written?' said the judge.

'I couldn't really say. I was poorly in April.'

The Defence Counsel continued: 'You admit the possibility that one day when you were alone you wrote that letter while in a state of trance?'

'It *is* possible. If you'd seen as much as I have of spiritualism, you would know that the gift can descend on anyone, even an untrained person.'

'By "gift",' said the judge, 'do you mean a state of trance?'

'Yes, and then becoming a medium and getting in touch,' she said.

'Let us get this clear,' said the judge. 'A person in a state of trance as you call it, rolls up his or her eyes, foams at the mouth, and twitches. Then he or she begins to speak?'

'Sometimes they say nothing.'

'What happens,' said the judge, 'when they come out of their trance? Describe it.'

'They look very exhausted, sir, and don't know where they are for some minutes.'

'Have you ever experienced a sensation, while alone, of exhaustion and not knowing where you are, by which you could assume you had just come out of a trance?'

'Sometimes I've dropped off and felt a bit strange, my lord, for a few minutes.'

'Have there been any other signs of a trance such as saliva from foaming at the mouth?'

'Oh no, sir.'

'Do you yourself think you have been in a state of unconsciousness,' said the judge, very slow and clear, 'and at the same time able to write that letter? Try to be explicit.'

'I don't know, sir, I'm sure.'

Martin got up to re-examine her. 'He'll make matters worse,' Matthew said, and he was right.

Martin's tones became menacing as she muddled on. 'Mrs Flower, I am going to call an expert,' Martin said nastily to his witness, 'who will swear that this letter is a forgery. Are you suggesting that he is mistaken?'

'No, I'll abide by what he says,' said Freda.

'Here comes Ronald,' said Matthew, 'in his new dark chalk-stripe. He should have been a Civil Servant.'

'Destestable man,' said Alice.

'Not a bit of it,' said Matthew. 'You don't know him at all.'

'The jury are whispering together. Are they allowed to do that?' Alice said.

'Yes,' said Matthew. 'It's their court, really. Everything depends on them.'

'I don't like that blonde woman,' Alice said. 'With her dyed hair she shouldn't be on a jury.'

Ronald, as he walked up the steps to the witness box, caught a flash-like impression of the jury, as they leaned across and consulted each other, head to head, and this reminded him of some fresco of the Last Supper. The jury righted itself when Ronald reached his post.

Ronald's evidence, as he compared the precise points at which the handwriting of the letter departed from examples of Freda Flower's handwriting and coincided with examples of Patrick Seton's, provided a perceptible rest-cure for the bewigged minds. The barristers stopped fidgeting with their papers. The judge stopped resting his head on his left hand.

'I have found,' said Ronald, 'from microscopic examination that certain letters have been formed from a starting-point different from those of Mrs Flower's handwriting. The letter "o" for example – although to the naked eye it is completely closed both in Exhibits B and D – has apparently been formed by different hands. In Exhibit B the "o" has been started from the top. In Exhibit D the "o" has been started from the right-hand curve.'

'Exhibit B,' said the judge to the jury, 'is the letter which it is alleged has been forged. Exhibit D is the example of Mrs Flower's handwriting.'

'The effect of trembling in some of the upward strokes of the signature in Exhibit B,' said Ronald, 'is visible under the microscope. This trembling in some of the upward strokes is not present in the body of the letter and suggests that the signature has been traced. The formation of the letter "l" in Exhibits B, C, and D –'

'Just a moment,' said the judge. 'The jury must be clear. Exhibit B is the alleged forgery. Exhibit D is the example of Mrs Flower's handwriting. Exhibit C is the example of the accused's writing.'

'The formation of the letter "l" in Exhibits –'

'He's marvellous,' said Matthew. 'I didn't know Ronald had it in him.'

Ronald was fumbling in his inner pocket.

'Too damned smart,' said Alice. 'You just wait till he's cross-examined. We've got a first-rate barrister in Farmer.'

'What is your conclusion, Mr Bridges?' said Martin.

'That the letter, Exhibit B, is a forgery and that it has been forged by the accused.'

Ronald was fumbling in his outer pockets.

'Now here's our man,' said Alice, as the Defence Counsel heaved himself to his feet.

But Farmer was content to await the conflicting evidence of his expert, he was content to say to Ronald,

'Mr Bridges, have you ever made a mistake?'

'Yes,' said Ronald.

'This opinion of yours couldn't be one of them?'

'I have never, so far as I know, made a mistake in a case of forgery.'

'So far as you know. Thank you, Mr Bridges – Oh, oh, watch out . . .'

Ronald swayed. He fumbled in his pockets for his pills. They were in his other suit, at home. He gave up. He stumbled down the steps and fell two steps before he got to the bottom. There he foamed at the mouth. His eyes turned upward, and the drum-like kicking of his heels began on the polished wooden floor.

'Is this man a medium?' said the judge.

The clerk approached Ronald. Two male members of the jury came out of their places, looking suddenly deprived of any excuse for their presence in the court. It was difficult to get near Ronald. 'Put something between his teeth,' said Martin Bowles, in the tones of a zoophobic veterinary practitioner. 'He's an epileptic.'

The judge rested his head in his left hand. Patrick looked solemnly up at Alice. She was peering over the balcony, looking down at Ronald. Patrick was filled with solace at the sight. I will look down on her, he thought, when she is lying on the mountainside, and the twitching will cease.

'Do you believe in prayer?' said Alice to Matthew when they went down, after the fuss was over, to lunch in the public canteen.

'He's putting up a marvellous fight,' Alice whispered. 'I've never seen Patrick in such good form. I've never heard him speak up like this. It's as if he was fighting for his life.'

Once or twice Patrick glanced at her from the witness box, for he could get a better view of her from there. The thought of Alice kept him going.

'I know,' whispered Alice, 'he's making the effort for me. It's as if he was fighting for my life. He's not an outspoken man as a rule. It shows what's in Patrick.'

The answers came without hesitation, clear and strong. It might have been the voice of one of those army men who know exactly what they think, and say it. He took courage from his desire to be acquitted, rather than timidity from his fear of being convicted and the practised members of the jury noticed this. Ronald, sitting defiantly in his exhaustion among the witnesses, managed to recall the last time he had heard Patrick speak. That had been at the Maidstone Assizes. Then, Patrick had mumbled.

Freda Flower sat horrified at Patrick's manner.

'I am, in spite of my calling, a man of the world, a practical man. . . .

'There was never any question of my buying defence bonds. . . .

'Mrs Flower frequently went into a trance. She is herself an excellent medium with extraordinary psychic powers. . . .

'It is impossible that she does not know that she possesses this gift. . . .

'I suggest, without wishing to implicate Mrs Flower further than necessary, that she became incensed when I left her, and dreamed up this story. . . .

'I prefer to say no more about my private relationship with Mrs Flower, if that is permissible. . . .

'I made the statement at the police station while still in a state of semi-trance. In such a condition the subject is highly suggestible. . . . I signed this statement at the suggestion of the officer in charge. I have no recollection of doing so. . . .

'I would describe the statement as a forced confession. . . .'

Patrick kept his eyes off Fergusson. He looked from time to time at Alice.

'You would think he'd been saving it up,' Alice breathed. 'Like an athlete that spares himself till the time comes.'

'I deny it,' Patrick said, when asked if he had forged the letter.

His counsel sat down. Martin Bowles coughed and stood up and adjusted his robes.

'Do you really expect the court to believe, Mr Seton, that a widow in Mrs Flower's position would hand you over her life savings of two thousand pounds to use for your own purposes?'

'If you will refer to her letter you will see that she requested me to use the money to further my psychic and spiritual work. She did not ask me to use it for my own purposes. I have used the money to further my psychic and spiritual work as she requested.'

'You have heard the evidence of the Crown's graphologist. I suggest that Mrs Flower did not write that letter, but that you forged it after you had made the statement to the police, in order to discredit the statement.'

'I deny it; and I deny that I made a statement to the police in any circumstances which could be described as free.'

Matthew whispered, 'I wish my sister-in-law could have seen all this.'

'What's it got to do with her?' said Alice.

'Hush,' said Matthew, 'don't talk.'

The judge said, 'In what manner have you used this money to further your psychic and spiritual work?'

'I have spent it on the scientific training of mediums, the purchase of books on psychical research, and in travelling abroad to exchange views on the subject with foreign mediums, and on travelling in this country to extend my knowledge and impart it. Spiritualism is a science, and a science requires financial support.'

'In what does the training of mediums consist?' said the judge.

'A scientific course comprising various exercises of mind and body. An untrained medium is proved by experience to be a menace to society. Properly trained, the medium is a useful and practical vehicle of human aspirations.'

The blonde member of the jury was leaning forward attentively. Seton has got a new customer, Ronald thought, if he gets out of this.

The judge's pen scratched on. The typist in the corner listlessly pounded her silent machine. Martin continued:

'Do you consider it a reputable action to accept money from a widow in Mrs Flower's circumstances to use for your professional advancement?'

The moron, Ronald thought, why doesn't he pin him down on the questions of the forgery and the bonds?

'I was acting under Mrs Flower's instructions. I do not need professional advancement. I employed the money for the pro-fessional advancement of others.'

'I suggest that if you spent two thousand pounds between April and August you spent it somewhat rapidly.'

'Mrs Flower said in her letter that she left the details of the disposal of the money entirely to me.'

Why does he go on about the spending? – Ronald sat with the demonic aftermath of his fit working within him. Why doesn't he plug away at the forgery, he has my evidence? Then it occurred to Ronald: He doesn't believe in my evidence, he doubts its validity, and this barrister can't argue a case he doesn't believe in.

'You admit,' said Martin, 'that you accepted two thousand pounds from a woman of middle age?'

And you deny, thought Ronald, that you are swindling Isobel Billows?

'You have said,' said Martin, 'in reply to a question, "I prefer to say no more about my private relationship with Mrs Flower."'

'That is correct,' said Patrick.

'May I ask why you are so reticent?'

'My lord,' said Patrick, addressing the judge, 'if it is not relevant to the case, I would prefer –'

'I can't see why you need go further into that question, Mr Bowles,' said the judge.

'I submit that it is a relevant question,' Martin said, 'since the jury will wish to know the extent of the influence exerted by the accused upon Mrs Flower.'

'Very well,' said the judge and rested his head on his hand.

'I suggest that your relations with Mrs Flower were of an intimate nature,' said Martin.

'I deny it,' said Patrick with an elaborate air of gallantry.

'And that you used these intimate relations to gain an influence over Mrs Flower?'

And, thought Ronald, on the strength of these intimate relations you obtained control of Isobel Billows's money.

'I deny it,' said Patrick. 'Mrs Flower herself has said nothing of our intimate relations.'

'And,' said Martin, 'you employed this influence to obtain Mrs Flower's savings.'

'I deny it.'

'In your statement to the police of the 12th August you said –' Martin shuffled and found his document – 'you said "Early in April Mrs Flower handed me a cheque for two thousand pounds for the purpose of purchasing premium bonds and defence bonds. I was tempted and fell. I did not purchase the bonds. I do not know where the money has gone." Now, Mr Seton,' said Martin, 'I put it to you that this is the true and accurate story.'

'I deny it. I was incapable of making a statement. I was in a state of semi-trance, and was in a condition of high susceptibility to any suggestion whatsoever.'

'Do you mean that Detective-Inspector Fergusson hypnotized you?'

For a moment Patrick seemed to sag. His lower jaw receded.

'Are you suggesting that Detective-Inspector Fergusson invented this story?'

'He put the words in my mouth.'

'I did not hear,' said the judge, for Patrick's voice had suddenly failed.

Patrick looked at Alice and revived. 'He put the words in my mouth,' he said out loud.

'How did you get to the police station if you were in a state of partial insensibility?'

'I was taken there in a police car. Two policemen called at my rooms immediately after I had completed a séance.'

'On the morning of 12th August?'

'Yes.'

'Do you usually conduct séances in the morning?'

'This was a private séance.'

Patrick was allowed to go. The judge looked at his watch. 'Is medical evidence to be called as to the effects of a trance?' he said.

Patrick's counsel said, 'No, my lord, there appears to be no useful source of medical opinion devoted to the nature and effects of the spiritualistic trance specifically.'

Martin Bowles looked confused. Ronald thought, he has slipped up properly. He should have brought in a cataleptist to refute them.

The door from the witness's room opened and Ronald looked round to see a fellow-graphologist, sweet old Fairley, emerging. Fairley climbed the steps to the witness box, took off his glasses and exchanged them for another pair. He read the oath slowly, and took his usual leisure throughout.

'So that, in your opinion,' said Patrick's counsel, 'mere inconsistencies in the formation of characters which can only be observed under the microscope do not imply that the characters have been formed by separate hands.'

'I do not say so,' drawled Fairley. 'That would be too large a generalization. I say only that, in my opinion, the inconsistencies between the formation of characters on the document marked Exhibit B and those on the document marked Exhibit C, taken together with peculiarities common to Exhibits B and D, do not necessarily lead to the conclusion that Exhibit B is a forgery.'

The jury fidgeted.

'You are saying,' said the barrister, 'that the letter which the Crown alleges to be a forged document, need not necessarily be so merely on the evidence afforded by the microscope?'

'Yes,' said Fairley.

'What is the length of your experience in this field, Mr Fairley?'

'Forty-six years,' said Fairley.

Martin got up.

'The methods of forgery detection have changed in forty-six years, have they not?' Martin said.

'There have been developments,' said Fairley.

'You changed your spectacles when you came into the witness box. Do you suffer from any weakness of eyesight?' Martin said.

It's a dirty world, thought Ronald.

'Yes,' said Fairley courteously. 'But I have an excellent optician who provides me with two pairs of spectacles. One pair is for normal use and the other is for reading.'

'And you changed into your reading glasses in order to stand and give evidence in court?'

'I changed into my reading spectacles in order to read the oath, which I take seriously.'

'Oh, quite,' said Martin. 'Did you,' he said 'when you were examining the documents, notice any peculiarities in the formation of the letter "o"?'

'Yes,' said Fairley. 'In Exhibit B the "o" has been started from the top. In Exhibit D the "o" has been started from the right-hand curve.'

'Does that not suggest to you that these letters have been formed by different hands?'

'Not necessarily. There is always the possibility that the writer was at one moment in a disposition to start from the top, and at another time disposed to begin elsewhere.'

'Do you agree that there are other inconsistencies similar to those which relate to the letter "o"?'

'Yes.'

'Do you agree that the peculiar formation of many letters in Exhibit B – the document which is alleged to be a forgery – coincide with peculiarities of formation in Exhibit C – the example of the accused's handwriting?'

'There are many similarities but not enough, in my opinion, to permit the inference that B and C are the work of the same hand.'

'Did you observe in the course of your examination of the signature the effect of trembling in some of the upward strokes?'

'No,' said Fairley.

'You did not find anything to suggest that the signature had been traced?'

'No,' said Fairley.

'You are aware that an eminent graphologist, Mr Ronald Bridges, has submitted that the effect of trembling in the upward strokes is an indication of tracing.'

'I was not present at Mr Bridges' evidence. But I agree that an effect of trembling in handwritting is sometimes due to a process of tracing. Sometimes it is due to sickness, fear, or old age.'

'You agree that forgers commonly trace the signatures on false documents?'

'Oh, yes.'

'You did not notice an effect of trembling in some of the upward strokes of the signature on the document alleged to be forged?'

'No, I did not observe any effect of trembling.'

'Did you look for it?'

'Oh, yes, it is part of the routine.'

'How does the scientific equipment available to Mr Bridges compare with that available to yourself?'

'We use the same laboratories and stuff.'

Ronald saw how vexed Martin was. He had told Martin that Fairley used private equipment, believing this to be so.

'But you did not notice this trembling effect, while Mr Bridges did?' Martin said crossly.

Oh, shut up, Ronald thought.

'There is room for varying opinion as to what is an effect of trembling,' said Fairley.

'It couldn't be a question of eyesight?'

'The documents are greatly enlarged by the microscope,' Fairley drawled wearily.

'Thank you,' said Martin.

Fairley smirked slightly at Ronald as he left. Ronald winked. A member of the jury noticed this and whispered to his neighbour. They are saying, Ronald thought, that we are in our racket together, regardless of the law. But perhaps that's not what they are whispering.

The door through which Fairley had passed now admitted Father Socket in black suit and clerical collar, the last witness for the defence. As he was shown up to the witness box, the main door on Ronald's right opened, and Elsie came in. She moved in beside Ronald and started to whisper to him. The attendant policeman placed a finger to his lips. Ronald pushed his note-pad and pencil towards her. On it she wrote, 'I've come to give evidence against Father Socket.' Ronald wrote, 'You're too late,' and pushed it back.

'Isn't Father Socket marvellous?' whispered Alice.

'Father my eye,' said Matthew.

Father Socket described himself as a clergyman.

'Of what religion?' said the judge.

'Of the spiritualist religion and allied faiths.'

'Spiritualism has already this afternoon been described as a science. Is it a science or a religion?'

'It is a scientific religion, my lord, and has been recognized as such by countless eminent citizens including –'

'Yes, quite,' said the judge, 'I only want to get our definitions clear so that the jury can see what it is dealing with. There has been a great deal of mystification in this case.'

Elsie was scribbling away on the note pad.

Socket's eye was on the jury.

'You remember the morning of 12th August?' said his Counsel. 'Where were you . . .? What were you doing . . .?'

'At Mr Seton's rooms . . . a private séance . . . he was in a trance, a deep trance. I am, if I may say so, something of an authority on the conditions of a spiritualistic trance. . . . I left Mr Seton at ten minutes to twelve, he was in a state of complete exhaustion and insensibility to external surroundings.'

Alice looked over from the gallery.

'Elsie's going to make trouble,' she said. 'What is she writing, down there? She wouldn't come and keep me company as a friend, but she's come to make trouble.'

'She should have come up here with you,' Matthew said, 'but never mind, you've got me.'

Elsie folded her note and gave it to the policeman, indicating Martin Bowles.

Father Socket kept his eye on the jury. The blonde woman looked impressed.

'As I left the building after the séance I noticed a police car containing two police officers draw up outside the front door. This was just after ten minutes to twelve. . . .' Socket said.

'In your opinion, Mr Socket,' said Patrick's counsel, 'was it likely that by twelve noon, less than ten minutes later, Mr Seton would be in a reasonable and clear state of mind?'

'Certainly not. It is impossible. He would be in a state of semi-trance, perhaps not discernible at a casual glance, but certainly apparent to anyone attempting to question him. He would be in a suggestible condition. . . .'

'We've won the day!' said Alice.

Martin was looking at Elsie's two scribbled pages torn from the note-pad.

The blonde jurywoman spoke to her neighbour.

Patrick's barrister sat down. Martin got up.

'I suggest,' said Martin to Socket, 'that your evidence is a pack of lies from start to finish.'

The jury seemed offended. Socket's white collar gleamed round his throat. It seemed a tasteless attack.

'It is nothing but the truth,' said Socket, with a look of ministerial reproach.

'I have a witness in court,' said Martin, 'who is prepared to swear that you were not with the accused between the hours of ten a.m. and twelve noon on August the 12th.'

'Mr Bowles,' said the judge, 'are you wanting to put in additional evidence at this stage?'

'I was about to ask . . .'

The judge looked at his watch. Then he looked hard at Socket.

*

'Yes, I'm quite sure it was the 12th of August because it was my birthday, and that's why I took the day off,' Elsie said.

'What time did you arrive at Mr Socket's flat?' Martin said.

'Ten o'clock in the morning.'

'What time did you leave?'

'One o'clock.'

'Mr Socket was present all morning?'

'Yes, he gave me dictation, and he read some poetry.'

She started to leave the witness box immediately she had answered all Martin's questions. It was indicated to her that she had to remain for cross-examination. Patrick's counsel was conferring with Socket in whispers. Presently he straightened up.

'You say you took the day off from your work because it was your birthday?' Patrick's counsel hammered out.

'Yes.'

'Was it not an odd way in which to spend your day off – going to work as a typist in a voluntary capacity?'

'Well, I was taken in by Father Socket. I thought he was doing good work and I thought he was a fine person.'

'On what date did Mr Socket dismiss you from his service?'

'He didn't dismiss me. I never went back after I sensed something wrong.'

'I suggest that Mr Socket dismissed you on or about the 20th of July, and asked you not to come again.'

'No, I left two weeks ago because I sensed something wrong.'

'I suggest he dismissed you, and that you are embittered.'

'Yes, I was embittered all right after I sensed something wrong,' said Elsie like a needle.

The barrister became irritated. 'You keep saying you sensed something wrong. What do you mean? – Let's have it. Did you sense something wrong with your sight, hearing, smell, touch, taste – which sense did you sense something wrong with?'

'I sensed it with my common sense,' said Elsie, 'when I went there and found a man with lipstick and a dressing-gown that looked like –'

'Miss Forrest, you are an impulsive girl, aren't you?' said this counsel of Patrick's who now roused himself for work.

'Yes, fairly,' she said, rather put out by his new intimacy of tone.

'You did not come forward with this evidence at the proper time.

And yet you have seen fit to dash in at the last minute with accusations against a man whom up to two weeks ago, according to your own evidence, you thought to be a fine person. Why is that?'

'Well, I thought about it, and I decided it wasn't my business. Then this afternoon I decided to come along.'

'On an impulse of malice?'

'Yes, if you want to put it like that,' said Elsie.

'You admit to malice against Father Socket.'

'I don't see why he should get away with his sin.'

'You realize, Miss Forrest, that you have not brought a scrap of evidence to this court to support your story – apart from malice?'

'Well, you can take it or leave it,' Elsie said. 'I was with him all morning on August the 12th.'

'And you have no evidence to support your statement?'

'No,' said Elsie, 'there's only my word.'

Alice said, 'That girl's treacherous. Why did she have to mention the man with lipstick?'

Patrick's counsel told the jury that there could be no end to the calling of one witness to discredit another. He asked them to ignore the extraordinary and, on the face of it, wild accusations of Father Socket's former and, on her own admission, embittered typist, Miss Elsie Forrest. She had admitted to malice.

The extremely dubious evidence of Mrs Freda Flower. . . . Everything to show that she was in the habit of trances. . . .

The clear evidence of the accused ... his insistence that the statement was not made while he was in a responsible condition. . . . Reflecting, as it did on our ancient liberties. . . .

The case of forgery was wiped out by the evidence of Mr Fairley. Particularly to be noted was Mr Fairley's insistence on the effects of variable human moods on handwriting. . . .

The jury must rid itself of prejudice against spiritualism.

Patrick's counsel then listed a number of prominent persons, dead and alive, who had adorned the spiritualist movement. He looked at his watch and sat down.

Martin Bowles rose to recite the discredit of all witnesses except his own. 'The letter is undated,' said Martin, 'Why? – Because when he forged that letter he forgot the exact date of the cheque which Mrs Flower had given him, and which he now claims accompanied the letter.' He repeated Elsie's story. He reminded the jury that Fairley was getting on in years, and though must be respected, could hardly compete with a younger mind. He started to ridicule all references to the mediumistic trances which had cropped up in the case – 'foaming mouths, upturned eyes, twitching limbs, and so forth' but seemed suddenly to be visited by a deterrent thought, which Ronald assumed to be a mental image of himself lying kicking and foaming only a few hours ago under the witness box. Martin switched away from trances and weighed into Patrick and his influence on Mrs Flower.

'You will recall that this man affected a certain delicacy in revealing his intimate relations with Mrs Flower. Yet he did not hesitate to defraud her....'

Ronald, heavy with the effects of his fit, sat with his eyes on Martin.

'He did not hesitate to rob her, he did not hesitate to exert his influence by means of those intimate relations with Mrs Flower.'

With Isobel Billows, thought Ronald.

'And yet he stands here and poses as her protector. You observe the irony, ladies and gentlemen of the jury.'

The irony, ladies and gentlemen, thought Ronald.

It was a very disreputable case, said the judge in his summing up, and in some respects a nauseating one. It was his duty to direct the jury to rid their minds of all prejudice against spiritualism as such.... It was his duty to define both fraudulent conversion and forgery.... Forgery was.... Fraudulent conversion was ...

This was a case which, if there were any substance in it, could have grave and serious implications. Detective-Inspector Fergusson had sworn on oath that the accused had made a certain statement while in a lucid condition of mind. That statement had been produced in court. It contained an admission of the charge of fraudulent conversion. It bore the signature of the accused.

Moreover, Detective-Inspector Fergusson had denied that the accused had at any subsequent time applied to withdraw the statement. The jury should give these facts their weightiest consideration.

'They always stand by the police,' Alice whispered, 'but the jury knows different.'

The judge looked at his watch. Much, however, he was saying, hinged on the question of forgery.

The evidence of the two graphologists tended to cancel each other out and, if he might say so, was less than useless. No prejudice should obtain in the case of Mr Ronald Bridges whose unfortunate collapse in court, he understood, had been due to an inherent disease and was in no way connected with the disedifying trances described by various witnesses.

Mrs Flower appeared to be a very foolish woman. It must be taken into account that she had strongly indicated in her evidence the possibility of having written the letter while in a state of insensibility. The jury would have the opportunity of examining the letter and forming their own conclusions on this point. But while such a doubt was present in Mrs Flower's mind it must certainly receive every consideration. . . . The letter was undated. It had been suggested that the accused forgot the date of the cheque. . . .

A man was innocent until he was proved guilty. While there was reasonable doubt that the accused was the author of the letter he could not be found guilty.

The jury must be clear that if they brought in a verdict of Not Guilty for forgery they could not logically bring a verdict of Guilty for fraudulent conversion. Everything hung on the question of forgery. . . .

The evidence of Mr Socket must be weighed against the evidence of Miss Elsie Forrest, and vice versa. The fact that Miss Forrest had offered evidence at the last moment must not be allowed to weigh against that evidence. She was, on her own admission, impulsive by nature. On the other hand she admitted to a motive of malice against Socket, and this, whether justified or not, must be taken into account.

'Whatever your sympathies in this case,' he said, 'it is the evidence that counts. I will run over the evidence once more. . . .'

The jury withdrew at twenty minutes to five. 'We'll have time for tea,' said Matthew. 'They'll be out for at least an hour.'

'The judge was against us,' Alice said, 'but the jury can't find him guilty if there's a reasonable doubt about the forgery. The judge said so himself.'

'Come on,' said Matthew.

She was looking at Patrick and he at her before he turned through the dock door. His face was radiant. The bags packed, the insulin.

'Our bags are all ready packed,' said Alice. 'We can leave in the morning.'

'The blonde woman was looking pretty nasty about Socket after Elsie had finished.'

'I'll never speak to Elsie again. The whole court was with us after Father Socket's evidence. The whole court. No matter what they say about evidence.'

They sat over their hot canteen tea. 'It's kicking,' said Alice. 'Oh, God, I wish this was over.'

Patrick looked up at Alice. It was the only thing, to look and look at Alice. Imprisonment was not the end of the world, he had always found a niche in prisons. But now, this thirst for Alice. She is mine, I have paid. . . . She would probably twitch before she died. She had agreed by acquiescence.

The jury were filing in. It was twenty past five.

To make Alice into something spiritual. It was godlike, to conquer that body, to return it to the earth. . . .

'On the charge of forgery.'

'Guilty.'

'On the charge of fraudulent conversion.'

'Guilty.'

'I don't believe in God,' said Alice. 'There will have to be an appeal.'

'Quiet, now,' said Matthew.

'It was Elsie mentioning the man with lipstick,' Alice said. 'That did it. I knew!'

'It was a help,' said Matthew.

Fergusson was up in the witness box again. He was reading out a list. At Canterbury in May 1923 . . . three months for larceny. At Surrey Quarter Sessions in 1930, six months for obtaining on false pretences. . . . in 1932, six months . . . in 1942, eighteen months and six months to run consecutively for fraudulent conversion. . . . Maidstone Assizes, in 1948, three years for forgery and fraudulent conversion. He is described as a spiritualistic medium, unmarried, resident at . . .

'What's this all about?' said Alice.

'They call it the antecedents. It's Patrick's criminal record.'

'I don't believe it,' she said. 'There's got to be an appeal.'

'He can't appeal with that record.'

'The bags are packed,' she said. 'And he's a genuine medium.'

'Just keep still,' Matthew said. 'Nothing matters.'

'A most disreputable case,' said the judge. 'A widow ... her savings. The distasteful proceedings – I may say without prejudice to any more respectable manifestations of the cult as might exist – the distasteful proceedings of the séance room and the scope it offers for the intimidation of weak people. . . . The evidence given by Mr Socket must be looked into: these courts must be kept clean of ... Mrs Flower has been a very foolish woman.' He glanced towards Patrick. 'Have you anything to say?'

Patrick looked at Fergusson and then the judge.

'Only,' he said, 'to ask –'

'Speak up, please.'

'Only to say that the lady I am living with is expecting a baby and needs me by her side, and –'

The judge did not look up. 'I cannot sentence you to less than five years.'

'I don't believe in God,' said Alice, clutching her stomach.

Ronald went home to bed. He slept heavily and woke at midnight, and went out to walk off his demons.

Martin Bowles, Patrick Seton, Socket.

And the others as well, rousing him up: fruitless souls, crumbling tinder, like his own self which did not bear thinking of. But it is all demonology, he thought, and he brought them all to witness, in his old style, one by one before the courts of his mind. Tim Raymond, Ewart Thornton, Walter Prett, Matthew Finch – will I, won't I marry her? – Eccie, and himself kicking under the witness box, himself, now, incensed; and all the rest of them. He sent these figures away like demons of the air until he could think of them again with indifference or amusement or wonder.

How long will it take, he wondered to distract his mind, for Matthew to marry Alice? Not knowing at the time that it would take

four months – a week before the baby was born – Ronald laid a bet
with himself for three months.

It is all demonology and to do with creatures of the air, and there are
others besides ourselves, he thought, who lie in their beds like happy
countries that have no history. Others ferment in prison; some rot,
maimed; some lean over the banisters of presbyteries to see if anyone
is going to answer the telephone.

He walked round the houses, calculating, to test his memory, the
numbers of the bachelors – thirty-eight thousand five hundred
streets, and seventeen point one bachelors to a street – lying awake,
twisting and murmuring, or agitated with their bedfellows, or breathing in deep repose between their sheets, all over London, the
metropolitan city.

The Ballad of
Peckham Rye

For Robin with love

ONE

'Get away from here, you dirty swine,' she said.

'There's a dirty swine in every man,' he said.

'Showing your face round here again,' she said.

'Now, Mavis, now, Mavis,' he said.

She was seen to slam the door in his face, and he to press the bell, and she to open the door again.

'I want a word with Dixie,' he said. 'Now, Mavis, be reasonable.'

'My daughter,' Mavis said, 'is not in.' She slammed the door in his face.

All the same, he appeared to consider the encounter so far satisfactory. He got back into the little Fiat and drove away along the Grove and up to the Common where he parked outside the Rye Hotel. Here he lit a cigarette, got out, and entered the saloon bar.

Three men of retired age at the far end turned from the television and regarded him. One of them nudged his friend. A woman put her hand to her chin and turned to her companion with a look.

His name was Humphrey Place. He was that fellow that walked out on his wedding a few weeks ago. He walked across to the White Horse and drank one bitter. Next he visited the Morning Star and the Heaton Arms. He finished up at the Harbinger.

The pub door opened and Trevor Lomas walked in. Trevor was seen to approach Humphrey and hit him on the mouth. The barmaid said, 'Outside, both of you.'

'It wouldn't have happened if Dougal Douglas hadn't come here,' a woman remarked.

He was standing at the altar with Trevor, the best man, behind him. Dixie came up the aisle on the arm of Arthur Crewe, her stepfather. There must have been thirty-odd guests in the church. Arthur Crewe was reported in the papers next day as having said: 'I had a feeling the wedding wouldn't come off.' At the time he stepped up the aisle with Dixie, tall in her flounces, her eyes dark and open, and with a very little trace round the nose of a cold.

She had said, 'Keep away from me. You'll catch my cold, Humphrey. It's bad enough me having a cold for the wedding.'

But he said, 'I want to catch your cold. I like to think of the germs hopping from you to me.'

'I know where you got all these disgusting ideas from. You got them from Dougal Douglas. Well, I'm glad he's gone and there won't be him at the wedding to worry about in case he starts showing off the lumps on his head or something.'

'I liked Dougal,' Humphrey said.

Here they were, kneeling at the altar. The vicar was reading from the prayer book. Dixie took a lacy handkerchief from her sleeve and gently patted her nose. Humphrey noticed the whiff of scent which came from the handkerchief.

The vicar said to Humphrey, 'Wilt thou have this woman to thy wedded wife?'

'No,' Humphrey said, 'to be quite frank I won't.'

He got to his feet and walked straight up the aisle. The guests in the pews rustled as if they were all women. Humphrey got to the door, into his Fiat, and drove off by himself to Folkestone. It was there they had planned to spend their honeymoon.

He drove past the Rye, down Rye Lane roundabout to Lewisham, past the Dutch House and on to Swanley, past Wrotham Hill and along the A20 to Ditton, where he stopped for a drink. After Maidstone he got through the Ashford by-pass and stopped again at a pub. He drove on to Folkestone, turning left at the Motel Lympne, where yellow headlamps of the French cars began to appear on the road as they had done before. He stayed in the hotel on the front in the double room booked for the honeymoon, and paid double without supplying explanations to the peering, muttering management.

'Outside,' said the barmaid. Humphrey rose, finished his drink with a flourish, regarded his handsome hit face in the mirror behind the barmaid, and followed Trevor Lomas out into the autumn evening, while a woman behind them in the pub remarked, 'It wouldn't have happened if Dougal Douglas hadn't come here.'

Trevor prepared for a fight, but Humphrey made no move to retaliate; he turned up towards the Rye where his car was parked and where, beside it, Trevor had left his motor-scooter.

Trevor Lomas caught him up. 'And you can keep away from round here,' he said.

Humphrey stopped. He said, 'You after Dixie?'

'What's that to you?'

Humphrey hit him. Trevor hit back. There was a fight. Two courting couples returning from the dusky scope of the Rye's broad lyrical acres stepped to the opposite pavement, leant on the railings by the swimming baths, and watched. Eventually the fighters, each having suffered equal damage to different features of the face, were parted by onlookers to save the intervention of the police.

After Humphrey had been sent away from the door, and the matter had been discussed, Dixie Morse, aged seventeen, daughter of the first G.I. bride to have departed from Peckham and returned, stood in her little room on the upper floor of 12 Rye Grove and scrutinized her savings book. As she counted she exercised her pretty hips, jerking them from side to side to the rhythm of 'Pickin' a Chicken', which tune she hummed.

Her mother came up the stairs. Dixie closed the book and said to her mother through the closed door, 'Quite definitely I'm not taking up with him again. I got my self-respect to think of.'

'Quite right,' Mavis replied from the other room.

'He wasn't ever the same after he took up with Dougal Douglas,' Dixie said through the wall.

'I liked Dougal,' Mavis replied.

'I didn't like him. Trevor didn't like him,' Dixie said.

Hearing the front-door bell, Dixie stood attentively. Her mother went down and said something to her stepfather. They were arguing as to who should go and answer the door. Dixie went out on the landing and saw her stepbrother Leslie walking along the ground-floor passage in the wrong direction.

'Leslie, open that door,' Dixie said.

The boy looked up at Dixie. The bell rang again. Dixie's mother burst out of the dim-lit sitting-room.

'If it's him again I'll give him something to remember me by,' she said, and opened the door. 'Oh, Trevor, it's you, Trevor,' she said.

'Good evening, Mavis,' Trevor said.

Dixie returned rapidly to her room to comb her black hair and put on lipstick. When she came down to the sitting-room, Trevor was seated under the standard lamp, between Mavis and her stepfather, waiting for the television play to come to an end. Trevor had a strip of plaster on his face, close to the mouth.

The play came to an end. Mavis rose in her quick way and switched on the central light. Her husband, Arthur Crewe, smiled at everyone, adjusted his coat and offered Trevor a cigarette. Dixie set one leg across the other, and watched the toe of her shoe, which she wriggled.

'You'll never guess who came to the door this evening.'

'Humphrey Place,' said Trevor.

'You've seen him?'

'Seen him – I've just knocked his head off.'

Dixie's stepfather switched off the television altogether, and pulled round his chair to face Trevor.

'I suppose,' he said, 'you did right.'

'*Did* right,' said Dixie.

'I *said* did. I didn't say done. Keep your hair on, girl.'

Mavis opened the door and called, 'Leslie, put the kettle on.' She returned with her quick little steps to her chair. 'You could have knocked me over,' she said. 'I was just giving Dixie her tea; it was, I should say, twenty past five and there was a ring at the bell. I said to Dixie, "Whoever can that be?" So I went to the door, and lo and behold there he was on the doorstep. He said, "Hallo, Mavis," he said. I said, "You just hop it, you." He said, "Can I see Dixie?" I said, "You certainly can't," I said. I said, "You're a dirty swine. You remove yourself," I said, "and don't show your face again," I said. He said, "Come on Mavis." I said, "Mrs Crewe to you," and I shut the door in his face.' She turned to Dixie and said, 'What about making a cup of tea?'

Dixie said, 'If he thinks I would talk to him again, he's making a great mistake. What did he say to you, Trevor?'

Mavis got up and left the room, saying, 'If you want anything done in this house you've got to do it yourself.'

'Help your mother,' said Arthur Crewe absently to Dixie.

'Did he say whether he's gone back to the same job?' Dixie said to Trevor.

Trevor put a hand on each knee and gave a laugh.

Dixie looked from the broad-faced Trevor to the amiable bald head of her stepfather, and started to weep.

'Well, he's come back again,' Arthur said. 'What you crying for?'

'Don't cry, Dixie,' Trevor said.

Dixie stopped crying. Mavis came in with the tea.

Dixie said, 'He's common. You only have to look at his sister. Do you know what Elsie did at her first dance?'

'No,' said Mavis.

'Well, a fellow came up to her and asked her for a dance. And Elsie said, "No, I'm sweating." '

'Well, you never told me that before,' Mavis said.

'I only just heard it. Connie Weedin told me.'

Trevor gave a short laugh. 'We'll run him out of Peckham like we run Dougal Douglas.'

'Dougal went of his own accord, to my hearing,' Arthur said.

'With a black eye,' Trevor said.

Round at the old-fashioned Harbinger various witnesses of the fight were putting the story together. The barmaid said: 'It was only a few weeks ago. You saw it in the papers. That chap who left the girl at the altar, that's him. She lives up the Grove. Crewe by name.'

One landlady out of a group of three said, 'No, she's a Dixie Morse. Crewe's the stepfather. I know because she works at Meadows Meade in poor Miss Coverdale's pool that was. Miss Coverdale told me about her. The fellow had a good position as a refrigerator engineer.'

'Who was the chap that hit him?'

'Some friend of the girl's, I daresay.'

'Old Lomas's boy. Trevor by name. Electrician. He was best man at the wedding.'

'There was I,' sang out an old man who was visible with his old wife on the corner bench over in the public bar, 'waiting at the church, waiting at the church.'

His wife said nothing nor smiled.

'Now then, Dad,' the barmaid said.

The old man took a draught of his bitter with a tremble of the elbow and a turn of the wrist.

Before closing time the story had spread to the surrounding public bars, where it was established that Humphrey had called at 12 Rye Grove earlier in the evening.

Even in one of the saloon bars, Miss Connie Weedin heard of the reappearance of Humphrey Place, and the subsequent fight; and she later discussed this at length with her father who was Personnel Manager of Meadows, Meade & Grindley, and at present recovering from a nervous breakdown.

'Dixie's boy has come back,' she said.

'Has the Scotch man come back?' he said.

'No, he's gone.'

Outside the pub at closing-time Nelly Mahone, who had lapsed from her native religion on religious grounds, was at her post on the pavement with her long grey hair blown by the late summer wind. There she commented for all to hear, 'Praise be to God who employs the weak to confound the strong and whose ancient miracles we see shining even in our times.'

Humphrey and Dixie were widely discussed throughout the rest of the week. The reappearance of the bridegroom was told to Collie Gould, aged eighteen, unfit for National Service, who retold it to the gang at the Elephant; and lastly by mid-morning break at Meadows Meade the occurrence was well known to all on the floor such as Dawn Waghorn, cone-winder, Annette Wren, trainee-seamer, Elaine Kent, process-controller, Odette Hill, up-twister, Raymond Lowther, packer, Lucille Potter, gummer; and it was revealed also to the checking department and many of the stackers, the sorters, and the Office.

Miss Merle Coverdale, lately head of the typing pool, did not hear of it. Mr Druce, lately Managing Director, did not hear of it. Neither did Dougal Douglas, the former Arts man, nor his landlady Miss Belle Frierne who had known all Peckham in her youth.

But in any case, within a few weeks, everyone forgot the details. The affair was a legend referred to from time to time in the pubs when the conversation takes a matrimonial turn. Some say the bridegroom came back repentant and married the girl in the end. Some say, no, he married another girl, while the bride married the best man. It is wondered if the bride had been carrying on with the best man for some time past. It is sometimes told that the bride died of grief and the groom shot himself on the Rye. It is generally agreed that he answered 'No' at his wedding, that he went away alone on his wedding day and turned up again later.

TWO

Dixie had just become engaged to marry Humphrey when Dougal Douglas joined the firm of Meadows, Meade & Grindley, manufacturers of nylon textiles, a small but growing concern, as Mr V. R. Druce described it.

At the interview Mr Druce said to Dougal, 'We feel the time has come to take on an Arts man. Industry and the Arts must walk hand in hand.'

Mr Druce had formerly been blond, he was of large build. Dougal, who in the University Dramatics had taken the part of Rizzio in a play about Mary, Queen of Scots, leaned forward and put all his energy into his own appearance; he dwelt with a dark glow on Mr Druce, he raised his right shoulder, which was already highly crooked by nature, and leaned on his elbow with a becoming twist of the body. Dougal put Mr Druce through the process of his smile, which was wide and full of white young teeth; he made movements with the alarming bones of his hands. Mr Druce could not keep his eyes off Dougal, as Dougal perceived.

'I feel I'm your man,' Dougal said. 'Something told me so when I woke first thing this morning.'

'Is that so?' Mr Druce said. 'Is that so?'

'Only a hunch,' said Dougal. 'I may be wrong.'

'Now look,' said Mr Druce. 'I must tell you that we feel we have to see other candidates and can't come to any decision straight away.'

'Quite,' said Dougal.

At the second interview Mr Druce paced the floor, while Dougal sat like a monkey-puzzle tree, only moving his eyes to follow Mr Druce. 'You'll find the world of Industry a tough one,' Mr Druce said.

Dougal changed his shape and became a professor. He leaned one elbow over the back of his chair and reflected kindly upon Mr Druce.

'We are creating this post,' said Mr Druce. 'We already have a Personnel Manager, Mr Weedin. He needs an assistant. We feel we need a man with vision. We feel you should come under Weedin. But you should largely work on your own and find your own level, we feel. Of course you will be under Mr Weedin.'

Dougal leaned forward and became a television interviewer. Mr Druce stopped walking and looked at him in wonder.

'Tell me,' coaxed Dougal, 'can you give me some rough idea of my duties?'

'It's up to you, entirely up to you. We feel there's a place for an Arts man to bring vision into the lives of the workers. Wonderful people. But they need vision, we feel. Motion study did marvels in the factory. We had a man from Cambridge advising on motion study. It speeded up our output thirty per cent. Movements required to do any given task were studied in detail and he worked out the simplest pattern of movement involving the least loss of energy and time.'

'The least loss of energy and time!' Dougal commented.

'The least loss of energy and time,' said Mr Druce. 'All our workers' movements are now designed to conserve energy and time in feeding the line. You'll see it on the posters all over the factory, "Conserve energy and time in feeding the line." '

'In feeding the line!' Dougal said.

'In feeding the line,' Mr Druce said. 'As I say, this expert came from Cambridge. But we felt that a Cambridge man in Personnel wouldn't do. What we feel about you is you'll be in touch with the workers, or rather, as we prefer to say, our staff; you'll be in the know, we feel. Of course you'll find the world of Industry a tough one.'

Dougal turned sideways in his chair and gazed out of the window at the railway bridge; he was now a man of vision with a deformed shoulder. 'The world of Industry,' said Dougal, 'throbs with human life. It will be my job to take the pulse of the people and plumb the industrial depths of Peckham.'

Mr Druce said: 'Exactly. You have to bridge the gap and hold out a helping hand. Our absenteeism,' he said, 'is a problem.'

'They must be bored with their jobs,' said Dougal in a split second of absent-mindedness.

'I wouldn't say bored,' said Mr Druce. 'Not bored. Meadows Meade are building up a sound reputation with regard to their worker-staff. We have a training scheme, a recreation scheme, and a bonus scheme. We haven't yet got a pension scheme, or a marriage scheme, or a burial scheme, but these will come. Comparatively speaking we are a small concern, I admit, but we are expanding.'

'I shall have to do research,' Dougal mused, 'into their inner lives. Research into the real Peckham. It will be necessary to discover the spiritual well-spring, the glorious history of the place, before I am able to offer some impetus.'

Mr Druce betrayed a little emotion. 'But no lectures on Art,' he said, pulling himself together. 'We've tried them. They didn't quite come off. The workers, the staff, don't like coming back to the building after working hours. Too many outside attractions. Our aim is to be one happy family.'

'Industry is by now,' declared Dougal, 'a great tradition. Is that not so? The staff must be made conscious of that tradition.'

'A great tradition,' said Mr Druce. 'That is so, Mr Douglas. I wish you luck, and I want you to meet Mr Weedin while you're here.' He pressed a button his desk and, speaking into an instrument, summoned Mr Weedin.

'Mr Weedin,' he said to Dougal, 'is not an Arts man. But he knows his job inside out. Wonderful people, Personnel staff. If you don't tread on his toes you'll be all right with Personnel. Then of course there's Welfare. You'll have some dealings with Welfare, bound to do. But we feel you must find your own level and the job is what you make it – Come in, Mr Weedin, and meet Mr Douglas, M.A., who has just joined us. Mr Douglas has come from Edinburgh to take charge of human research.'

If you look inexperienced or young and go shopping for food in the by-streets of Peckham it is as different from shopping in the main streets as it is from shopping in Kensington or the West End. In the little shops in the Peckham by-streets, the other customers take a deep interest in what you are buying. They concern themselves lest you are cheated. Sometimes they ask you questions of a civil nature, such as: Where do you work? Is it a good position? Where are you stopping? What rent do they take off you? And according to your answer they may comment that the money you get is good or the rent you have to pay is wicked, as the case may be. Dougal, who had gone to a small grocer on a Saturday morning, and asked for a piece of cheese, was aware of a young woman with a pram, a middle-aged woman, and an old man accumulating behind him. The grocer came to weigh the cheese.

'Don't you give him that,' said the young woman; 'it's sweating.'

'Don't let him give you that, son,' said the old man.

The grocer removed the piece of cheese from the scales and took up another.

'You don't want as much as all that,' said the older woman. 'Is it just for yourself?'

'Only for me,' Dougal said.

'Then you want to ask for two ounces,' she said. 'Give him two ounces,' she said. 'You just come from Ireland, son?'

'No, Scotland,' said Dougal.

'Thought he was Irish from his voice,' commented the old man.

'Me too,' said the younger woman. 'Irish sounds a bit like Scotch like, to hear it.'

The older woman said, 'You want to learn some experience, son. Where you stopping?'

'I've got temporary lodgings in Brixton. I'm looking for a place round here.'

The grocer forgot his grievances and pointed a finger at Dougal.

'You want to go to a lady up on the Rye, name of Frierne. She's got nice rooms; just suit you. All gentlemen. No ladies, she won't have.'

'Who's she?' said the young woman. 'Don't know her.'

'Don't know Miss Frierne?' said the old man.

The older woman said, 'She's lived up there all her life. Her father left her the house. Big furniture removers they used to be.'

'Give me the address,' said Dougal, 'and I'll be much obliged.'

'I think she charges,' said the older woman. 'You got a good position, son?'

Dougal leaned on the counter so that his high shoulder heaved higher still. He turned his lean face to answer. 'I've just started at Meadows, Meade & Grindley.'

'I know them,' said the younger woman. 'A nice firm. The girl Waghorn works there.'

'Miss Frierne's rooms go as high as thirty, thirty-five shillings,' remarked the older woman to the grocer.

'Inclusive heat and light,' said the grocer.

'Excuse me,' said the older woman. 'She had meters put in the rooms, that I do know. You can't do inclusive these days.'

The grocer looked away from the woman with closed eyes and opened them again to address Dougal.

'If Miss Frierne has a vacancy you'll be a lucky chap,' he said. 'Mention my name.'

'What department you in?' said the old man to Dougal.

'The Office,' said Dougal.

'The Office don't get paid much,' said the man.

'That depends,' the grocer said.

'Good prospects?' said the older woman to Dougal.

'Yes, fine,' Dougal said.

'Let him go up Miss Frierne's,' said the old man.

'Just out of National Service?' said the older woman.

'No, they didn't pass me.'

'That would be his deformity,' commented the old man, pointing at Dougal's shoulder.

Dougal nodded and patted his shoulder.

'You was lucky,' said the younger woman and laughed a good deal.

'Could I speak to Miss Fergusson?' Dougal said.

The voice at the other end of the line said, 'Hold on. I'll see if she's in.'

Dougal stood in Miss Frierne's wood-panelled entrance hall, holding on and looking around him.

At last she came. 'Jinny,' Dougal said.

'Oh, it's you.'

'I've found a room in Peckham. I can come over and see you if you like. How –'

'Listen, I've left some milk boiling on the stove. I'll ring you back.'

'Jinny, are you feeling all right? Maria Cheeseman wants me to write her autobiography.'

'It will be boiling over. I'll ring you back.'

'You don't know the number.'

But she had rung off.

Dougal left fourpence on the telephone table and went up to his new room at the very top of Miss Frierne's house.

He sat down among his belongings, which were partly in and partly out of his zipper bag. There was a handsome brass bedstead with a tall railed head along which was gathered a muslin curtain. It was the type of bed which was becoming fashionable again, but Miss Frierne did not know this. It was the only item of furniture in the room for which she had apologized; she had explained it was only temporary and would soon be replaced by a new single divan. Dougal detected in this speech a good intention, repeated to each newcomer, which never came off. He assured her that he liked the brass bed with its railings and knobs. Could he remove, perhaps, the curtain? Miss Frierne said, no, it needed the bit of curtain, and before long would be replaced by a single divan. But no, Dougal said, I like the bed. Miss Frierne smiled to herself that she had found such an obliging tenant. 'Really, I do like it,' Dougal said, 'more than anything else in the room.'

The two windows in the room pleased him, looking out on a lot of sky and down to Miss Frierne's long lawn and those of her neighbours; beyond them lay the back gardens belonging to the opposite street of houses, but these were neglected, overgrown and packed with junk and sheds for motor bicycles, not neat like Miss Frierne's and the row of gardens on the near side, with their borders and sometimes a trellis bower.

He saw a little door, four feet high, where the attic ceiling met the wall. He opened it, and found a deep long cupboard using up the remainder of the roof-slope. Having stooped to enter the cupboard, Dougal found he could almost walk in it. He came out, pleased with his fairly useless cave, and started putting away his shirts in the dark painted chest of drawers. He stroked the ceiling, that part of it which sloped down within reach. Some white powdery distemper came off on his fingers. He went downstairs to telephone to Jinny. Her number was engaged.

The linoleum in his room was imitation parquetry and shone with polish. Two small patterned mats and one larger one made islands on the wide floor. Dougal placed a pile of his clothes on each island, then hauled it over the polished floor to the wardrobe. He unlocked his typewriter and arranged his belongings, as all his student-life in

Edinburgh Jinny used to do for him. One day in their final year, at Leith docks, watching the boats, she had said: 'I must bend over the rails. I've got that indigestion.' Already, at this first stage in her illness, he had shown no sympathy. 'Jinny, everyone will think you're drunk. Stand up.' In the course of her illness she stopped calling him a crooked fellow, and instead became bitter, calling him sometimes a callous swine or a worm. 'I hate sickness, not you,' he had said. Still, at that time he had forced himself to visit her sometimes in the Infirmary. He had got his degree, and was thought of as frivolous in the pubs, not being a Nationalist. Jinny's degree was delayed a year, he meanwhile spending that year in France and finally London, where he lived in Earls Court and got through his money waiting for Jinny.

For a few weeks he spent much of his time in the flat of the retired actress and singer, Maria Cheeseman, in Chelsea, who had once shared a stage with an aunt of Jinny's.

He went to meet Jinny at last at King's Cross. She had bright high cheek-bones and brown straight hair. They could surely be married in six months' time. 'I've to go into hospital again,' said Jinny. 'I've to have an operation this time. I've a letter to a surgeon in the Middlesex Hospital.

'You'll come and visit me there?' she said.

'No, quite honestly, I won't,' Dougal said. 'You know how I feel about places of sickness. I'll write to you every day.'

She got a room in Kensington, went into hospital two weeks later, was discharged on a Saturday, and wrote to tell Dougal not to meet her at the hospital and she was glad he had got the job in Peckham, and was writing Miss Cheeseman's life, and she hoped he would do well in life.

'Jinny, I've found a room in Peckham. I can come over and see you if you like.'

'I've left some milk on the stove. I'll ring you back.'

Dougal tried on one of his new white shirts and tilted the mirror on the dressing-table to see himself better. Already it seemed that Peckham brought out something in him that Earls Court had overlooked. He left the room and descended the stairs. Miss Frierne came out of her front room.

'Have you got everything you want, Mr Douglas?'

'You and I,' said Dougal, 'are going to get on fine.'

'You'll do well at Meadows Meade, Mr Douglas. I've had fellows before from Meadows Meade.'

'Just call me Dougal,' said Dougal.

'Douglas,' she said, pronouncing it 'Dooglass'.

'No, *Dougal* – Douglas is my surname.'

'Oh, Dougal Douglas. Dougal's the first name.'

'That's right, Miss Frierne. What buses do you take for Kensington?'

'It's my one secret weakness,' he said to Jinny.

'I can't help it,' he said. 'Sickness kills me.

'Be big,' he said, 'be strong. Be a fine woman, Jinny.

'Understand me,' he said, 'try to understand my fatal flaw. Everybody has one.'

'It's time I had my lie-down,' she said. 'I'll ring you when I'm stronger.'

'Ring me tomorrow.'

'All right, tomorrow.'

'What time?'

'I don't know. Some time.'

'You would think we had never been lovers, you speak so coldly,' he said. 'Ring me at eleven in the morning. Will you be awake by then?'

'All right, eleven.' He leaned one elbow on the back of his chair. She was unmoved. He smiled intimately. She closed her eyes.

'You haven't asked for my number,' he said.

'All right, leave your number.'

He wrote it on a bit a paper and returned south of the river to Peckham. There, as Dougal entered the saloon bar of the Morning Star, Nelly Mahone crossed the road in her rags crying, 'Praise be to the Lord, almighty and eternal, wonderful in the dispensation of all his works, the glory of the faithful and the life of the just.' As Dougal bought his drink, Humphrey Place came up and spoke to him. Dougal recalled that Humphrey Place, refrigerator engineer of Freeze-eezy's, was living in the room below his and had been introduced to him by Miss Frierne that morning. Afterwards Miss Frierne had told Dougal, 'He is clean and go-ahead.'

THREE

'What d'you mean by different?' Mavis said.

'I don't know. He's just different. Says funny things. You have to laugh,' Dixie said.

'He's just an ordinary chap,' Humphrey said. 'Nice chap. Ordinary.'

But Dixie could see that Humphrey did not mean it. Humphrey knew that Douglas was different. Humphrey had been talking a good deal about Douglas during the past fortnight and how they sat up talking late at Miss Frierne's.

'Better fetch him here to tea one night,' said Dixie's stepfather. 'Let's have a look at him.'

'He's too high up in the Office,' Mavis said.

'He's on research,' Dixie said. 'He's brainy, supposed to be. But he's friendly, I'll say that.'

'He's no snob,' said Humphrey.

'He hasn't got nothing to be a snob about,' said Dixie.

'*Anything*, not *nothing*.'

'Anything,' said Dixie, 'to be a snob about. He's no better than us just because he's twenty-three and got a good job.'

'But he's got to do his overtime for nothing,' Mavis said.

'He's the same as what we are,' Dixie said.

'You said he was different.'

'Well, but no better than us. I don't know why you sit up talking at nights with him.'

Humphrey sat up late in Dougal's room.

'My father's in the same trade. He puts himself down as a fitter. Same job.'

'It is right and proper,' Dougal said, 'that you should be called a refrigerator engineer. It brings lyricism to the concept.'

'I don't trouble myself about that,' Humphrey said. 'But what you call a job makes a difference to the Unions. My dad doesn't see that.'

'Do you like brass bedsteads?' Dougal said. 'We had them at home. We used to unscrew the knobs and hide the fag ends inside.'

'By common law,' Humphrey said, 'a trade union has no power to take disciplinary action against its members. By common law a trade union cannot fine, suspend, or expel its members. It can only do so contractually. That is, by its rules.'

'Quite,' said Dougal, who was lolling on his brass bed.

'You can use your imagination,' Humphrey said. 'If a member is expelled from a union that operates a closed shop . . .'

'Ghastly,' said Dougal, who was trying to unscrew one of the knobs.

'But all that won't concern you much,' Humphrey said. 'What you want to know about for your human research is arbitration in trade disputes. There's the Conciliation Act 1896 and the Industrial Courts Act 1919, but you wouldn't need to go into those. You might study the Industrial Disputes Order 1951. But you aren't likely to have a dispute at Meadows, Meade & Grindley. You might have an issue, though.'

'Is there a difference?'

'Oh, a vast difference. Sometimes they take it to law to decide whether an issue or a dispute has arisen. It's been as far as the Court of Appeal. I'll let you have the books. Issue is whether certain employers should observe certain terms of employment. Dispute is any dispute between employer and employee as to terms of employment or conditions of labour.'

'Terrific,' Dougal said. 'You must have given your mind to it.'

'I took a course. But you'll soon get to know what's what in Industrial Relations.'

'Fascinating,' Dougal said. 'Everything is fascinating, to me, so far. Do you know what I came across the other day? An account of the fair up the road at Camberwell Green.'

'Fair?'

'According to Colburn's *Calendar of Amusements 1840*,' Dougal said. He reached for his notebook, leaned on his elbow, heaved his high shoulder and read:

There is here, and only here, to be seen what you can see nowhere else, the lately caught and highly accomplished young mermaid, about whom the continental journals have written so ably. She combs her hair in the manner practised in China, and admires herself in a glass in the manner practised everywhere. She has had the best instructors in every peculiarity of education, and can argue on any given subject, from the most popular way of preserving plums, down to the necessity of a change of Ministers. She plays the harp in the new effectual style prescribed by Mr Bocha, of whom we wished her to take lessons, but, having some mermaiden scruples, she begged to be provided with a less popular master. Being so clever and accomplished, she can't bear to be contradicted, and lately leaped out of her tub and floored a distinguished fellow of the Royal Zoological Society, who was pleased to be more curious and cunning than she was pleased to think agreeable. She has composed various poems for the periodicals, and airs with variations for the harp and piano, all very popular and pleasing.

Dougal gracefully cast his book aside. 'How I should like to meet a mermaid!' he said.

'Terrific,' Humphrey said. 'You make it up?' he asked.

'No, I copied it out of an old book in the library. My research. Mendelssohn wrote his "Spring Song" in Ruskin Park. Ruskin lived on Denmark Hill. Mrs Fitzherbert lived in Camberwell Grove. Boadicea committed suicide on Peckham Rye probably where the bowling green is now, I should imagine. But, look here, how would you like to be engaged to marry a mermaid that writes poetry?'

'Fascinating,' Humphrey said.

Dougal gazed at him like a succubus whose mouth is its eyes.

Humphrey's friend, Trevor Lomas, had said Dougal was probably pansy.

'I don't think so,' Humphrey had replied. 'He's got a girl somewhere.'

'Might be versatile.'

'Could be.'

Dougal said, 'The boss advised me to mix with everybody in the district, high and low. I should like to mix with that mermaid.'

Dougal put a record on the gramophone he had borrowed from

Elaine Kent in the textile factory. It was a Mozart Quartet. He slid the rugs aside with his foot and danced to the music on the bare linoleum, with stricken movements of his hands. He stopped when the record stopped, replaced the rugs, and said, 'I must get to know some of the youth clubs. Dixie will be a member of a youth club, I expect.'

'She isn't,' Humphrey said rather rapidly.

Dougal opened a bottle of Algerian wine. He took his time, and with a pair of long tweezers fished out a bit of cork that had dropped inside the bottle. He held up the pair of tweezers.

'I use these,' he said, 'to pluck out the hairs which grow inside my nostrils, and which are unsightly. Eventually, I lose the tweezers, then I buy another pair.'

He placed the tweezers on the bed. Humphrey lifted them, examined them, then placed them on the dressing table.

'Dixie will know,' Dougal said, 'about the youth clubs.'

'No, she won't. She doesn't have anything to do with youth clubs. There are classes within classes in Peckham.'

'Dixie would be upper-working,' said Dougal. He poured wine into two tumblers and handed one to Humphrey.

'Well, I'd say middle-class. It's not a snob business, its a question of your type.'

'Or lower-middle,' Dougal said.

Humphrey looked vaguely as if Dixie was being insulted. But then he looked pleased. His eyes went narrow, his head lolled on the back of the chair, copying one of Dougal's habitual poses.

'Dixie's saving up,' he said. 'It's all she can think of, saving up to get married. And now what does she say? We can't go out more than one night a week so that I can save up too.'

'Avarice,' Dougal said, 'must be her fatal flaw. We all have a fatal flaw. If she took sick, how would you feel, would she repel you?'

Dougal had taken Miss Merle Coverdale for a walk across the great sunny common of the Rye on a Saturday afternoon. Merle Coverdale was head of the typing pool at Meadows, Meade & Grindley. She was thirty-seven.

Dougal said, 'My lonely heart is deluged by melancholy and it feels quite nice.'

'Someone might hear you talking like that.'

'You are a terror and a treat,' Dougal said. 'You look to me like an Okapi,' he said.

'A what?'

'An Okapi is a rare beast from the Congo. It looks a little like a deer, but it tries to be a giraffe. It has stripes and it stretches its neck as far as possible and its ears are like a donkey's. It is a little bit of everything. There are only a few in captivity. It is very shy.'

'Why do you say I'm like that?'

'Because you're so shy.'

'Me shy?'

'Yes. You haven't told me about your love affair with Mr Druce. You're too shy.'

'Oh, that's only a friendship. You've got it all wrong. What makes you think it's a love affair? Who told you that?'

'I've got second sight.'

He brought her to the gate of the park and was leading her through it, when she said,

'This doesn't lead anywhere. We'll have to go back the same way.'

'Yes, it does,' Dougal said, 'it leads to One Tree Hill and two cemeteries, the Old and the New. Which would you prefer?'

'I'm not going into any cemetery,' she said, standing with legs apart in the gateway as if he might move her by force.

Dougal said, 'There's a lovely walk through the New Cemetery. Lots of angels. Beautiful. I'm surprised at you. Are you a free woman or are you a slave?'

She let him take her through the cemetery, eventually, and even pointed out to him the tower of the crematorium when it came into sight. Dougal posed like an angel on a grave which had only an insignificant headstone. He posed like an angel-devil, with his hump shoulder and gleaming smile, and his fingers of each hand widespread against the sky. She looked startled. Then she laughed.

'Enjoying yourself?' she said.

On the way back along the pastoral streets of trees and across the Rye she told him about her six years as mistress of Mr Druce, about Mr Druce's wife who never came to the annual dinners and who was a wife in name only.

'How they bring themselves to go on living together I don't know,' she said. 'There's no feeling between them. It's immoral.'

She told Dougal how she had fallen out of love with Mr Druce yet could not discontinue the relationship, she didn't know why.

'You've got used to him,' Dougal said.

'I suppose so.'

'But you feel,' Dougal said, 'that you're living a lie.'

'I do,' she said. 'You've put my very thoughts into words.'

'And then,' she said, 'he's got some funny ways with him.'

Dougal slid his eyes to regard her without moving his face. He caught her doing the same thing to him.

'What funny ways? Come on, tell me,' Dougal said. 'There's no good telling the half and then stopping.'

'No,' she said. 'It wouldn't be right to discuss Mr Druce with you. He's your boss and mine, after all.'

'I haven't seen him,' Dougal said, 'since the day he engaged me. He must have forgotten about me.'

'No, he talked a lot about you. And he sent for you the other day. You were out of the office.'

'What day was that?'

'Tuesday. I said you were out on research.'

'So I was,' said Dougal. 'I was out on research.'

'Nobody gets forgotten at Meadows Meade,' she said. 'He'll want to know about your research in a few weeks' time.'

Dougal put his long cold hand down the back of her coat. She was short enough for his hand to reach quite a long way. He tickled her.

She wriggled and said, 'Not in broad daylight, Dougal.'

'In dark midnight,' Dougal said, 'I wouldn't be able to find my way.'

She laughed from her chest.

'Tell me,' Dougal said, 'what is the choicest of Mr Druce's little ways?'

'He's childish,' she said. 'I don't know why I stick to him. I could have left Meadows Meade many a time. I could have got into a big firm. You don't think Meadows Meade's a big firm, do you, by any chance? Because, if you do, let me tell you, Meadows Meade is by comparison very small. Very small.'

'It looks big to me,' Dougal said. 'But perhaps it's the effect of all that glass.'

'We used to have open-plan,' she said. 'So that you could see everyone in the office without the glass, even Mr Druce. But the bosses wanted their privacy back, so we had the glass partitions put up.'

'I like those wee glass houses,' Dougal said. 'When I'm in the office I feel like a tomato getting ripe.'

'*When* you're in the office.'

'Merle,' he said, 'Merle Coverdale, I'm a hard-working fellow. I've got to be out and about on my human research.'

They were moving up to the Rye where the buses blazed in the sun. Their walk was nearly over.

'Oh, we're soon here,' she said.

Dougal pointed to a house on the right. 'There's a baby's pram,' he said, 'stuck out on a balcony which hasn't any railings.'

She looked and sure enough there was a pram perched on an open ledge only big enough to hold it, outside a second-floor window. She said, 'They ought to be prosecuted. There's a baby in that pram, too.'

'No, it's only a doll,' Dougal said.

'How do you know?'

'I've seen it before. The house is a baby-carriage works. The pram is only for show.'

'Oh, it gave me a fright.'

'How long have you lived in Peckham?' he said.

'Twelve and a half years.'

'You've never noticed the pram before?'

'No, I can't say I have. Must be new.'

'From the style of the pram, it can't be new. In fact the pram has been there for twenty-five years. You see, you simply haven't noticed it.'

'I don't hardly ever come across the Rye. Let's walk round a bit. Let's go into the Old English garden.'

'Tell me more,' Dougal said, 'about Mr Druce. Don't you see him on Saturdays?'

'Not during the day. I do in the evening.'

'You'll be seeing him tonight?'

'Yes, he comes for supper.'

Dougal said, 'I suppose he's been doing his garden all day. Is that what he does on Saturdays?'

'No. As a matter of fact, believe it or not, on Saturday mornings he goes up to the West End to the big shops. He goes up and down in the lifts. He rests in the afternoon. Childish.'

'He must get some sexual satisfaction out of it.'

'Don't be silly,' she said.

'A nice jerky lift,' said Dougal. 'Not one of the new smooth ones but the kind that go yee-oo at the bottom.' And Dougal sprang in the air and dipped with bent knees to illustrate his point, so that two or three people in the Old English garden turned to look at him. 'It gives me,' Dougal said, 'a sexual sensation just to think of it. I can quite see the attraction these old lifts have for Mr Druce. Yee-oo.'

She said, 'For God's sake lower your voice.' Then she laughed her laugh from the chest, and Dougal pulled that blonde front lock of her otherwise brown hair, while she gave him a hefty push such as she had not done to a man for twenty years.

He walked down Nunhead Lane with her; their ways parted by the prefabs at Costa Road.

'I'm to go to tea at Dixie's house tonight,' he said.

'I don't know what you want to do with that lot,' she said.

'Of course, I realize you're head of the typing pool and Dixie's only a wee typist,' he said.

'You're taking me up wrong.'

'Let's go for another walk if it's nice on Monday morning,' he said.

'I'll be at work on Monday morning. I'll be down to work, not like you.'

'Take Monday off, my girl,' Dougal said. 'Just take Monday off.'

'Hallo. Come in. Pleased to see you. There's your tea,' Mavis said.

The family had all had theirs, and Dougal's tea was set on the table. Cold ham and tongue and potato salad with bread and butter, followed by fruit cake and tea. Dougal sat down and tucked in while Mavis, Dixie, and Humphrey Place sat round the table. When he had finished eating, Mavis poured the tea and they all sat and drank it.

'That Miss Coverdale in the pool,' said Mavis, 'is working Dixie to death. I think she's trying to get Dixie out. Ever since Dixie got engaged she's been horrible to Dixie, hasn't she, Dixie?'

'It was quarter to four,' said Dixie, 'and she came up with an estimate and said "priority" – just like that – priority. I said, "Excuse me, Miss Coverdale, but I've got two priorities already." She said, "Well, it's only quarter to four." "*Only*," I said, "*only* quarter to four. Do you realize how long these estimates take? I'm not going without my tea-break, if that's what you're thinking, Miss Coverdale." She said, "Oh, Dixie, you're impossible," and turned away. I jumped up and I said, "Repeat that," I said. I said –'

'You should have reported her to Personnel,' Humphrey said. 'That was your correct procedure.'

'A disappointed spinster,' Mavis said, 'that's what she is.'

'She's immoral with Mr Druce, a married man, that I know for a fact,' Dixie said. 'So she's covered. You can't touch her, there's no point in reporting her to Personnel. It gets you down.'

'Take Monday off,' said Dougal. 'Take Tuesday off as well. Have a holiday.'

'No, I don't agree to that,' Humphrey said. 'Absenteeism is downright immoral. Give a fair week's work for a fair week's pay.'

Dixie's stepfather, who had been watching television in the sitting-room and who suddenly felt lonely, put his head round the door.

'Want a cup of tea, Arthur?' said Mavis. 'Meet Mr Douglas. Mr Douglas, Mr Crewe.'

'Where's Leslie?' said Arthur Crewe.

'Well, he ought to be in. I let him go out,' Mavis said.

'Because there's something going on out the front.' Arthur said.

They all trooped through to the sitting-room and peered into the falling dusk, where a group of young people in their teens were being questioned by an almost equal number of policemen.

'The youth club,' Mavis said.

Dougal immediately went out to investigate. As he opened the street door, young Leslie slid in as if from some concealment; he was breathless.

Dougal returned presently to report that the tyres of a number of cars parked up at the Rye had been slashed. The police were rounding up the teenage suspects. Young Leslie was chewing bubble-gum. Every now and then he pulled a long strand out of his mouth and let it spring back into his mouth.

'But it seems to me the culprits may have been children,' Dougal said, 'as much as these older kids.'

Leslie stopped chewing for an instant and stared back at Dougal in such disgust that he seemed to be looking at Dougal through his nostrils rather than his eyes. Then he resumed his chewing.

Dougal winked at him. The boy stared back.

'Take that muck out of your mouth, son,' said his father.

'You can't stop him,' said his mother. 'He won't listen to you. Leslie, did you hear what your father said?'

Leslie shifted the gum to the other side of his cheek and left the room.

Dougal looked out of the window at the group who were still being questioned.

'Two girls there come from Meadows Meade,' he said. 'Odette Hill, uptwister, and Lucille Potter, gummer.'

'Oh, the factory lot are always mixed up in the youth club trouble,' Mavis said. 'You don't want anything to do with that lot.' As she spoke she moved her hand across her perm, nipping each brown wave in turn between her third and index fingers.

Dougal winked at her and smiled with all his teeth.

Mavis said to Dixie in a whisper, 'Has *he* gone?'

'Yup,' said Dixie, meaning, yes, her stepfather had gone out for his evening drink.

Mavis went to the sideboard and fetched out a large envelope.

'Here we are again,' Dixie said.

'She always says that,' Mavis said.

'Well, Mum, you keep on pulling them out; every new person that comes to the house, out they come.'

Mavis had extracted three large press cuttings from the envelope and handed them to Dougal.

Dixie sighed, looking at Humphrey.

'Why you two not go on out? Go on out to the pictures,' Mavis said.

'We went out last night.'

'But you didn't go to the pictures, I bet. Saving and pinching to get married, you're losing the best time of your life.'

'That's what I tell her,' said Humphrey. 'That's what I say.'

'Where'd you go last night?' Mavis said.

Dixie looked at Humphrey. 'A walk,' she said.

'What you make of these?' Mavis said to Dougal.

The cuttings were dated June 1942. Two of them bore large photographs of Mavis boarding an ocean liner. All announced that she was the first of Peckham's G.I. brides to depart these shores.

'You don't look a day older,' Dougal said.

'Oh, go on,' Dixie said.

'Not a day,' said Dougal. 'Anyone can see your mother's had a romantic life.'

Dixie took her nail file out of her bag, snapped the bag shut, and started to grate at her nails.

Humphrey bent forward in his chair, one hand on each knee, as if, by affecting intense interest in Mavis's affair, to compensate for Dixie's mockery.

'Well, it was romantic,' Mavis said, 'and it wasn't. It was both. Glub – that was my first husband – Glub was wonderful at first.' Her voice became progressively American. 'Made you feel like a queen. He sure was gallant. *And* romantic, as you say. But then ... Dixie came along ... everything sorta wenna pieces. We were living a lie,' Mavis said, 'and it was becoming sorta immoral to live together, not loving each other.' She sighed for a space. Then pulling herself together she said, 'So I come home.'

'*Came* home,' Dixie said.

'And got a divorce. And then I met Arthur. Old Arthur's a good sort.'

'Mum had her moments,' Dixie said. 'She won't let you forget that.'

'More than what you'll have, if you go on like you do, putting every penny in the bank. Why, at your age I was putting all my wages what I had left over after paying my keep on my back.'

'My own American dad pays my keep,' Dixie said.

'He thinks he do, but it don't go far.'

'Does. Doesn't,' Dixie said.

'I better put the kettle on,' Mavis said.

Dougal said then to Dixie, 'I didn't never have no money of my own at your age.' He heaved his shoulder and glittered his eyes at her, and she did not dare to correct him. But when Humphrey laughed she turned to him and said, 'What's the joke?'

'Dougal here,' he said, 'he's your match.'

Mavis came back and switched on the television to a cabaret. Her husband returned to find Dougal keeping the cabaret company with a dance of his own in the middle of their carpet. Mavis was shrieking with joy. Humphrey was smiling with closed lips. Dixie sat also with closed lips, not smiling.

On Saturday mornings, as on Sundays, the gentlemen in Miss Frierne's establishment were desired to make their own beds. On his return at eleven o'clock on Saturday night Dougal found a note in his room.

> Today's bed was a landlady's delight. Full marks
> in your end-of-term report!

Dougal stuck it up on the mirror of his dressing-table and went downstairs to see if Miss Frierne was still up. He found her in the kitchen, sitting primly up to the table with half a bottle of stout.

'Any letters for me?'

'No, Dougal.'

'There should have been a letter.'

'Never mind. It might come on Monday.'

'Tell me some of your stories.'

'You've heard them all, I'm sure.' He had heard about the footpads on the Rye in the old days; about the nigger minstrels in the street, or rather carriageway as Miss Frierne said it was called then. She sipped her stout and told him once more of her escapade with a girl called Flo, how they had hired a cab at Camberwell Green and gone up to the Elephant for a drink and treated the cabby to twopenno'rth of gin, and returned without anyone at home being the wiser.

'You must have had some courting days,' Dougal said.

But her narrow old face turned away in disdain at the suggestion, for these were early days in their friendship, and it was a full month before Miss Frierne, one evening when she had finished her nourishing stout with a sigh and got out the gin bottle, told Dougal how the Gordon Highlanders were stationed at Peckham during the first war; how it was a question among the young ladies whether the soldiers wore anything underneath their kilts; how Miss Frierne at the ripe age of twenty-seven went walking with one of the Highlanders up to One Tree Hill; how he turned to her and said, 'My girl, I know you're all bloody curious as to what we have beneath the kilt, and I forthwith propose to satisfy your mind on the subject'; how he then took her hand and thrust it under his kilt; and how she then screamed so hard, she had a quinsy for a week.

But in the meantime when Dougal, at the end of his second week at Miss Frierne's, said, 'You must have had some courting days,' she turned her narrow pale face away from him and indicated by various slight movements of her bony body that he had gone too far.

Eventually she said, 'Did Humphrey come in with you?'

'No, I left him round at Dixie's.'

'I wanted to ask his private advice about something.'

'Anything I can do? I give rare advice.'

She was still offended. 'No, thank you. I wish to ask Humphrey privately. Do I hear rain?'

Dougal went to bed and the rain danced on the roof above his head. A key clicked in the front door and Humphrey's footsteps, climbing carefully, rose to the first landing. Humphrey paused on the landing, a long pause, as if he were resting from some effort. Then Humphrey's step fumbled up on the second flight. Either he was drunk or carrying a heavy weight, for he staggered at the top, just outside Dougal's door.

The long cupboard in Dougal's bedroom gave out a loud tom-tom as the rain beat on the low roof within, and together with this sound was discernible that of Humphrey staggering along the short passage to his own room.

Dougal woke again at the very moment, it seemed, that the rain stopped. And at this very moment a whisper and a giggle came from the direction of his cupboard. He switched on his light and got up. The cupboard was empty. Just as he was going to shut the small door again, there was a slight scuffle. He opened the door, put his head in, and found nothing. He returned to bed and slept.

On Monday morning Dougal got his letter. Jinny had finished with him. He went into the offices of Meadows, Meade & Grindley and typed out some of his notes. Then, at the morning tea-break, he walked over to the long, long factory canteen and asked especially for Odette Hill and Lucille Potter. He was told they were not at work that morning. 'Taking the day off. Foreman's mad. Absenteeism makes him mad.' He had a bun and a cup of tea, then another bun. A bell rang to mark the end of the tea-break. The men disappeared rapidly.

A few girls loitered, as on principle, talking with three of the women who served the canteen. Dougal put his head on his arms in full view of these girls, and wept.

'What's the matter with him?'

'What's the matter, son? said a girl of about sixteen whom Dougal, on looking up, found to be Dawn Waghorn, one of the cone-winders whose movements when winding the cone, as laid down by the Cambridge expert, had seemed to Dougal, when he had been taken round the floors, very appealing. Dougal put down his head and resumed his weeping.

Dawn patted his poor shoulder. He slightly raised his head and shook it sadly from side to side. A woman came round from the canteen bar with a clean-folded oven cloth which she held out to him. 'Here, dry your eyes before anyone sees you,' she said.

'What's the matter, mate?' said another girl. She said, 'Here's a hanky.' She was Annette Wren who was in training for seaming. She was giggling most heartlessly.

'I've lost my girl,' Dougal said, as he blew his nose on the oven cloth.

Elaine Kent, who was well on in her twenties, an experienced controller of process, turned on Annette Wren and told her to shut her mouth, what was there to laugh at?

The two other canteen women came round to Dougal, and he was now surrounded by women. Elaine Kent opened her bag and took out a comb. With it she combed Dougal's hair as it moved with his head slowly from side to side.

'You'll get another girl,' said one of the canteen women, Milly Lloyd by name.

Annette giggled again. Dawn slapped her face and said, 'You're ignorant. Can't you see he's handicapped?'

Whereupon Annette burst into tears.

'Keep your head still,' said Elaine. 'How can I comb you if you keep moving your head?'

'It calms you down, a good comb,' remarked one of the canteen.

Milly Lloyd was looking for a fresh handkerchief for Annette whose sobs were tending towards the hysterical.

'How did you lose your girl?' said Dawn.

'I've got a fatal flaw,' Dougal said.

Dawn assumed this to be his deformed shoulder, which she now stroked. 'It's a shame,' she said. 'Little no-good bitch I bet she is.'

Suddenly Merle Coverdale appeared at the door in the long distance and started walking towards the group.

'Office,' whispered Milly, 'typing pool,' and returned behind the canteen bar.

Merle shouted along the length of the canteen as she approached. 'Tea for Mr Druce, please. He was out. Now he's come in. He wants some tea.' Then she saw the group round Dougal. 'What the hell's going on?' she said.

'Migraine,' Dougal said sadly. 'A headache.'

'You should all be back on the floor,' Merle said to the girls. 'There's going to be trouble.'

'Who you to talk to us like that?'

'Who's she, coming it over us?'

And so Merle could do nothing with them. She said meaningfully to Dougal,

'I had a headache myself this morning. Came into work late. I went for a brisk walk on the Rye. All by myself.'

'I dimly recall arranging to meet you there,' Dougal said. 'But I was prevented.'

Merle gave him a hostile look and said to the canteen women, 'What about that tea?'

Milly Lloyd put a cup of tea into Dougal's hand. Merle walked off, bearing Mr Druce's tea, moving her neck slightly back and forth as she walked all the long length of the canteen. Annette took a cup of tea and, as she gulped it, tried also to express her rage against the girl who had slapped her. As Dougal sipped his tea, young Dawn stroked his high shoulder and said, never mind, it was a shame, while Elaine combed his hair. It was curly hair but cut quite short. Nevertheless she combed it as if it had been as long as the Laughing Cavalier's.

Dixie sat with Humphrey, Dougal, and Elaine Kent in Costa's Café. Dixie yawned. Her eyes were sleepy. The only reason she had denied herself an early night was that Dougal was paying for the supper.

'I've felt tired all day,' she said. She addressed the men, ignoring Elaine as she had done all evening, because Elaine was factory, even though Elaine was high up in process-control. After a trial period Elaine likewise confined her remarks to the men.

'Look what's just come in,' Elaine said. Tall Trevor Lomas had just come in. He sat at the nearest table, with his head and shoulders turned away from Dougal's party, and stared out of the window. Trevor Lomas was at this time employed as an electrician by the Borough.

Trevor turned his head sleepily and permitted an eye to rest on Humphrey for a small second. Humphrey said 'Hallo.' Trevor did not reply.

Trevor's girl arrived presently, tall and copper-tinted, with a tight short black skirt and much green eye-shadow. 'Hi, snake,' said Trevor. 'Hi,' said the girl, and sat down beside him.

Dixie and Elaine stared at the girl as she slid out of her coat and let it fall on the back of her chair. They stared as if by duty, and watched every detail. The girl was aware of this, and seemed to expect it.

Then Trevor pushed back his chair, still seated, so that he half-faced Humphrey's party. He said to his girl in a loud voice: 'Got your lace hanky on you, Beauty?'

Beauty did not reply. She was holding up a small mirror, putting lipstick on with care.

'Because,' said Trevor, 'I'm going to cry.' He took his large white handkerchief out of his top pocket and flourished it before each eye in turn. 'Going to cry my eyes out, I am,' said Trevor, 'because I've lost me girl. Hoo, I've lost me girl.'

Beauty laughed a great deal. The more she laughed the more noisily did Trevor continue. He laid his head on the table and affected to sob. The girl rocked in her chair, her newly painted lips open wide apart.

Then Dixie started to laugh.

Dougal shoved his chair back and stood up. Elaine jumped up and held his arm.

'Let be,' she said.

Humphrey, whom the story of Dougal's weeping in the canteen had not yet reached, said to Dixie, 'What's up?'

Dixie could not tell him for laughing.

'Let be, mate,' Elaine said to Dougal.

Dougal said to Trevor, 'I'll see you up on the Rye outside the tennis court.'

Elaine walked over to Trevor and gave him a push. 'Can't you see he's deformed?' she said. 'Making a game of a chap like that, it's ignorant.'

Dougal, whose deformed shoulder had actually endowed him with a curious speciality in the art of fighting, in that he was able to turn his right wrist at an extraordinary back-hand outward angle and to get a man by the throat as with a claw, did not at that moment boast of the fact.

'Cripple as I am,' he merely said, 'I'll knock his mean wee sex-starved conceited low and lying L.C.C. electrician's head off.'

'Who's sex-starved?' Trevor said, standing up.

Two youths who had been sitting by the window moved over the better to see. A Greek in an off-white coat appeared, and pointed to a telephone receiver which stuck out of the wall behind him in the passageway to the dim kitchen.

'I'll use that phone,' he said.

Trevor gave him one of his long sleepy looks. Then he gave one of them to Dougal.

'Who's sex-starved?' he said.

'You are,' Dougal said, while counting his money to pay the bill. 'And I'll see you on the Rye within the quarter-hour.'

Trevor walked out of the café and Beauty hastily wriggled into her coat and tripped out after him. After them both went the Greek, but Trevor's motor-scooter had just moved off.

'Hasn't paid for his coffee,' said the Greek, returning. 'What name and address he is, please?'

'No idea,' Dougal said. 'I don't mix with him.'

The Greek turned to Humphrey. 'I seen you here before with that fellow.'

Humphrey threw half-a-crown on the table, and, as the four departed, the Greek slammed his glass doors behind them as hard as he judged the glass would stand up to.

The two girls got into Humphrey's car, but he at first refused to drive them up to the Rye. Dougal stood and argued on the pavement.

Humphrey said, 'No, not at all. Don't go. Don't be a fool, Dougal. Let it pass. He's ignorant.'

'All right, I'll walk,' Dougal said.

'I'm going to send Trevor Lomas home,' Humphrey said. He left Dougal and started up the car and drove off with the girls, Dixie in front and Elaine behind agitating, too late, to be let out.

Dougal arrived at the tennis courts six minutes later. Some seconds before he arrived he had heard a sound as of women screaming.

Between two distant lamp-posts, in their vague oblique light, a group was gathered. Dougal discerned Humphrey and Trevor with a strange youth called Collie who was without a coat and whose shirt was unbuttoned, exposing his chest to the night air. These figures were apparently molesting three further figures who turned out to be Dixie, Elaine, and Beauty, who were screaming. Soon it appeared that the men were not molesting but restraining them. Dixie had a long-strapped shoulder bag with which she was attempting to lay about her, largely in the direction of Elaine. Elaine, who was at present in the grip of Trevor, managed to dig Beauty's leg with her steel stiletto heel. Beauty wailed and struggled in Humphrey's grip.

'What's going on?' Dougal said.

Nobody took any notice of him. He went and hit Trevor in the face. Trevor let go of Elaine so that she fell heavily against Beauty. Meanwhile Trevor hit out at Dougal, who staggered backwards into Humphrey. Beauty wailed louder, and struggled harder. Elaine recovered herself and used her freedom to kick with her stiletto heel at Trevor. Dixie, meanwhile, was attempting to release herself from the grasp of that strange youth, Collie, with the bared chest, by biting the arm that held her. The screams grew louder. Dougal's eyes were calculating his chance of coming to adequate terms with Trevor Lomas amidst the confusion when a curious thing happened.

The confusion stopped. Elaine started to sing in the same tone as her screaming, joylessly, and as if in continuation of it. The other girls, seeming to take a signal from her, sidled their wails into a song,

> 'Sad to say I'm on my way,
> I got a little girl in Kingston Town'

meanwhile casting their eyes fitfully over the Rye beyond the trees.

The strange youth let go of Dixie and began to jive with Elaine. In a few seconds everyone except Dougal was singing, performing the twisting jive, merging the motions of the fight into those of the frantic dance. Dougal saw Humphrey's face as his neck swooped upwards. It was frightened. Dixie's expression was, with a decided effort, bright. So was Elaine's. A one-sided smile on the face of the strange boy, and the fact that, as he bent and twisted in the jive, he buttoned up his shirt, made Dougal look round outside the group for the cause of this effect. He saw it immediately. Two policemen were quite close to them now. They must have been observed at a distance of three minutes' police-pace when Elaine had started to sing and the signal had gone round.

'What you think this is – a dance hall?'

'No, constable. No, inspector. Just having a dance with the girls. Just going home, mate.'

'Well, *go* home. Get a move on. Out of the park, the lot of you.'

'It was Dixie,' said Humphrey to Dougal on the way home, 'that started the fight. She was over-tired and worked up. She said that tart of Trevor's was giving her looks. She went up to the girl and said, "Who you looking at?" and then the girl *did* give her a look. Then Dixie let fly with her handbag. That's how it all began.'

Rain started to fall as they turned up past the old Quaker cemetery. Nelly Mahone took a green-seeming scarf from a black bag and placed it over her long grey hair. She cried: 'The meadows are open and the green herbs have appeared, and the hay is gathered out of the mountain. The wicked man fleeth when no man pursueth, but the just, bold as a lion, shall be without dread.'

'Pleasant evening, though a bit wet,' Dougal said.

Nelly looked round after him.

Up in his room Dougal poured Algerian wine and remarked as he passed a glass to Humphrey,

'The cupboards run the whole length of the attic floor.'

Humphrey put the glass on the floor at his feet and looked up at Dougal.

'There was a noise in the cupboard,' Dougal said, 'the night before last. It went creak-oop, creak-oop. I thought it came from my cupboard here, but I think maybe it didn't. I think maybe it came from your cupboard through the wall. Creak-oop.' Dougal bent his knees apart then sprang up in the air. He repeated this several times. 'Creak-oop,' he said.

Humphrey said, 'It's only on wet Saturday nights when we can't go up on the Rye.'

'Isn't she heavy to carry upstairs?' Dougal said.

Humphrey looked alarmed. 'Did it sound as if I was carrying her upstairs?'

'Yes. Better to let her walk up in her stockinged feet.'

'No, she did that once. The old woman came out and nearly caught us.'

'Better to lie in the bed than in the creaky cupboard,' Dougal said. 'The chap in the room below will hear it.'

'No, the old woman came up one night when we were in the bed. We were nearly caught. Dixie had to run and hide in the cupboard.' Humphrey lifted his glass of wine from the floor by his feet and drank it in one gulp.

'Don't worry yourself,' Dougal said.

'It's a worry what to do. All right on fine Saturday nights; we can go up on the Rye and Dixie gets home about half past eleven. But if it starts to rain we come back here. I don't see why not, I pay for the room. But there's the difficulty of getting her up, then down again in the morning while the old woman's at early church. Then she has to pay her brother Leslie five shillings a time to let her in quietly. And she worries about that, does Dixie. She's a great saver, is Dixie.'

'It's a tiring occupation, is saving,' Dougal said. 'Dixie's looking tired.'

'Yes, as a matter of fact she does lie awake worrying. And there's no need to worry. Terrible at seventeen. I said, "What you think you'll be like in ten years' time?" '

'When are you getting married?' Dougal said.

'September. Could do before. But Dixie wants a certain sum. She has her mind set to a certain sum. It keeps her awake at night.'

'I advised her to take Monday morning off,' Dougal said. 'Everyone should take Mondays off.'

'Now I don't agree to that,' Humphrey said. 'It's immoral. Once you start absenting yourself you lose your self-respect. *And* you lose the support of your unions; they won't back you. Of course the typists haven't got a union. As yet.'

'No?' said Dougal.

'No,' Humphrey said, 'but it's a question of principle.'

Dougal bent his knees apart as before and leapt into the air. 'Creak-oop, creak-oop,' he said.

Humphrey laughed deeply with his head thrown back. He stopped when a series of knocks started up from the floor.

'Chap downstairs,' Dougal said, 'knocks on his ceiling with a broom handle. He doesn't like my wee dances.' He performed his antic three times more, shouting, 'Creak-oop.'

Humphrey cast his head back and laughed, so that Dougal could see the whole inside of his mouth.

'I have a dream at nights,' Dougal said, pouring the wine, 'of girls in factories doing a dance with only the movement of their breasts, bottoms, and arms as they sort, stack, pack, check, cone-wind, gum, uptwist, assemble, seam, and set. I see the Devil in the guise of a chap from Cambridge who does motion-study, and he's the choreographer. He sings a song that goes, "We study in detail the movements requisite for any given task and we work out the simplest pattern of movement involving the least loss of energy and time." While he sings this song, the girls are waggling and winding, like this –' and Dougal waggled his body and wove his arms intricately. 'Like Indian dancing, you know,' he said.

'And,' said Dougal, 'of course this choreographer is a projection of me. I was at the University of Edinburgh myself, but in the dream I'm the Devil and Cambridge.'

Humphrey smiled, looked wise, and said, 'Inhuman'; which three things he sometimes did when slightly at a loss.

FOUR

Miss Merle Coverdale opened the door of her flat on Denmark Hill, and admitted Mr Druce in the early evening of midsummer's day. He took off his hat and hung it on a peg in her entrance-hall which was the shape and size of a small kitchen table, and from the ceiling of which hung a crystal chandelier. Mr Druce followed Merle into the sitting-room. So far he had not spoken, and still without a word, while Merle took up her knitting by the two-bar electric heater, he opened the door of a small sideboard and extracted a bottle of whisky which he lifted up to the light. Opening another compartment of the sideboard he took out a glass. He poured some whisky into it and from a syphon which stood on a tray on the sideboard splashed soda-water into his drink. Then, 'Want some?' he said.

'No, thanks.'

He sighed and brought his drink to a large chair opposite Merle's smaller one.

'No,' she said, 'I've changed my mind. I think I feel like a whisky and ginger.'

He sighed and went to the sideboard, where, opening a drawer he extracted a bottle opener. He stooped to the cupboard and found a bottle of ginger ale.

'No, I'll have a gin and tonic. I think I feel like a gin and tonic.'

He turned, with the bottle opener in his hand, and looked at her.

'Yes, I feel like a gin and tonic.'

And so he prepared the mixture and brought it to her. Then, sitting down, he took off his shoes and put on a pair of slippers which lay beside the chair.

Presently he looked at his watch. At which Merle put down her knitting and switched on the television. A documentary travel film was in progress, and in accompaniment to this they talked.

'Drover Willis's,' he said, 'have started on their new extension.'

'Yes, you told me the other day.'

'I see,' he said, 'they are advertising for automatic weaver instructors and hands. They are going to do made-up goods as well. They are advertising for ten twin-needle flat-bed machinists, also flat-lock machinists and instructors. They must be expanding.'

'Four, five, six,' she said, 'purl two, seven, eight.'

'I see,' he said, 'they are advertising for an Arts man.'

'Well, what do you expect? It was recommended at the Conference, wasn't it?'

'Yes, but remember, Merle, we were the first in the area to adopt that recommendation. Did he come into the office today?'

'No.'

'Tell him I want to see him, it's time we had a report. I've only seen him three times since he started. Weedin wants a report.'

'Remind me in the morning on the business premises, Vincent,' she said. 'I don't bring the office into my home, as you know.'

'Weedin hasn't seen him for a week. Neither Welfare nor Personnel can get word of him.'

She went to clatter dishes in the scullery. Mr Druce got up and began to lay the table with mats, knives, and forks which he took out of the sideboard. Then he went out into the hall and from his coat pocket took a bottle of stomach tablets which he placed on the table together with the pepper and salt.

Merle brought in some bread. Mr Druce took a breadknife from the drawer and looked at her. Then he placed the knife beside the bread on the board.

'The brussels are not quite ready,' she said, and she sat in her chair and took up her knitting. He perched on the arm. She pushed him with her elbow in the same movement as she was using for her knitting. He tickled the back of her neck, which she put up with for a while. But suddenly he pinched the skin of her neck. She screamed.

'Sh-sh,' he said.

'You hurt me,' she said.

'No, I was only doing this.' And he pinched her neck again.

She screamed and jumped from the chair.

'The brussels are ready,' she said.

He turned off the television when she brought in the meal. 'Bad for the digestion while you're eating,' he said.

They did not speak throughout the meal.

Afterwards he stood with her in the red-and-white scullery, and looked on while she washed up. She placed the dishes in a red drying-rack while he dried the knives and forks. These he carried into the living-room and put away in their separate compartments in the drawer of the sideboard. As he put away the last fork he watched Merle bring in a tray with coffee cups.

Merle switched on the television and found a play far advanced. They watched the fragment of the play as they drank their coffee. Then they went into the bedroom and took off their clothes in a steady rhythm. Merle took off her cardigan and Mr Druce took off his coat. Merle went to the wardrobe and brought out a green quilted silk dressing-gown. Mr Druce went to the wardrobe and found his blue dressing-gown with white spots. Merle took off her blouse and Mr Druce his waistcoat. Merle put the dressing-gown over her shoulders and, concealed by it, took off the rest of her clothes, with modest gestures. Mr Druce slid his braces and emerged from his trousers. These he folded carefully and, padding across the room to the window, laid them on a chair. He made another trip bearing his waistcoat and jacket which he placed over the back of the chair.

They stayed in bed for an hour, in the course of which Merle twice screamed because Mr Druce had once pinched and once bit her. 'I'm covered with marks as it is,' she said.

Mr Druce rose first and put on his dressing-gown. He went to wash and returned very soon, putting a wet irritable hand round the bedroom door. Merle said, 'Oh, isn't there a towel?' and taking a towel from a drawer, placed it in his hand.

When he returned she was dressed.

She went into the scullery and put on the kettle while he put on his trousers and went home to his wife.

A western breeze blew over the Rye and it was mid-summer night, a Saturday. Humphrey carried the two tartan rugs from his car while Dixie walked by his side, looking to left and right and sometimes turning to see if the path was clear of policemen.

Dixie said, 'I'm cold.'

He said, 'It's a warm night.'

She said, 'I'm cold.'

He said, 'We've got two rugs.'

She walked on beside him until they came to their usual spot under a tree behind the hedge of the Old English garden.

Humphrey spread a rug and she sat down upon it. She lifted the fringe and started to pull at it, separating the matted threads.

He spread the other rug over her legs and lay leaning on his elbow beside her.

'My mum got suspicious the other night,' she said. 'Leslie told her I was stopping over Camberwell after the dance with Connie Weedin, but she got suspicious. And when I got in she asked me all sorts of questions about the dance. I had to make them up.'

'Sure you can trust Leslie?'

'Well, I give him five shillings a week. I think it should be three shillings weeks when I don't stop out all night. But he's greedy, Leslie is.'

Humphrey pulled her towards him, and started to unbutton her coat. She buttoned it up again. 'I'm cold,' she said.

'Oh, come on, Dixie,' he said.

'Connie Weedin got an increment,' she said. 'I've got to wait for my increment till August. I only found out through the girl that does the copy die-stamp operation and had the staff salaries' balance sheet to do. Connie Weedin does the same job as what I do and she's only been there six months longer. It's only because her father's Personnel. I'm going to take it up with Miss Coverdale.'

Humphrey pulled her down towards him again and kissed her face.

'What's the matter?' he said. 'There's something the matter with you.'

'I'm going to take Monday off,' she said. 'They appreciate you more if you stop away now and again.'

'Well, frankly and personally,' Humphrey said, 'I think it's an immoral thing to do.'

'Fifteen shillings rise, less tax, nine and six in Connie Weedin's packet,' she said, 'and I've got to wait to August. And they're all in it together. And if I don't get satisfaction from Miss Coverdale, who is there to go to? Only Personnel, and that's *Mr* Weedin. Naturally he's going to cover up for his daughter. And if I go above him to Mr Druce he'll only send me back to Miss Coverdale, because you know what's between *them*.'

'When we're married you won't have to worry about any of them. We can get married Saturday week if you like.'

'No, I don't like. What about the house? There's got to be money down for the house.'

'There's money down for the house,' he said.

'What about my spin-dryer?'

'Oh, to hell with your spin-dryer.'

'That fifteen shillings less tax that's due to me,' she said 'could have gone in the bank. If it's due to her it's due to me. Fair's fair.'

He pulled the top rug up to her chin and under it started to unbutton her coat.

She sat up.

'There's something wrong with you,' he said. 'We should have gone dancing instead. It wouldn't have cost much.'

'You're getting too sexy,' she said. 'It's through you having to do with Dougal Douglas. He's a sex maniac. I was told. He's immoral.'

'He isn't,' Humphrey said.

'Yes he is, he talks about sex quite open, any time of the day. Girls and sex.'

'Why don't you relax like you used to do?' he said.

'Not unless you give up that man. He's putting ideas in your head.'

'You've done plenty yourself to put ideas in my head,' he said. 'I didn't used to need to look far to get ideas, when you were around. Especially up in the cupboard.'

'Repeat that, Humphrey.'

'Lie down and relax.'

'Not after what you said. It was an insult.'

'I know what's the matter with you,' he said. 'You're losing all your sex. It's all this saving up to get married and looking to the lolly all the time, it takes the sex out of a girl. It stands to reason, it's only psychological.'

'You must have been talking it over with Dougal Douglas,' she said. 'You wouldn't have thought of that by yourself.'

She stood up and brushed down her coat. He folded up the rugs.

'I won't be talked about, it's a let-down,' she said.

'Who's talked about you?' he said.

'Well, if you haven't talked about me, you've been listening to *him* talking.'

'Let me tell you something,' he said. 'Dougal Douglas is an educated man.'

'My mum's uncle's a teacher and he doesn't act like him. He doesn't cry his eyes out like Dougal did in our canteen.' Dixie laughed. 'He's a pansy.'

'That's just his game. You don't know Dougal. I bet he wasn't crying really.'

'Yes, he was. He only just lost his girl, and he cried like anything. Makes you laugh.'

'Then he can't be a pansy, or he wouldn't cry over a girl.'

'He must be or he wouldn't cry at all.'

On midsummer night Trevor Lomas walked with a somnambulistic sway into Findlater's Ballroom and looked round for Beauty. The floor was expertly laid and polished. The walls were pale rose, with concealed lighting. Beauty stood on the girls' side, talking to a group of very similar and lustrous girls. They had prepared themselves for this occasion with diligence, and as they spoke together, they did not smile much nor attend to each other's words. As an accepted thing, any of the girls might break off in the middle of a sentence, should a young man approach her, and, turning to him, might give him her entire and smiling regard.

Most of the men looked as if they had not properly woken from deep sleep, but glided as if drugged, and with half-closed lids, towards their chosen partner. This approach found favour with the girls. The actual invitation to dance was mostly delivered by gesture; a scarcely noticeable flick of the man's head towards the dance floor. Whereupon the girl, with an outstretched movement of surrender, would swim into the hands of the summoning partner.

Trevor Lomas so far departed from the norm as to indicate to Beauty his wish by word of mouth, which he did not, however, open more than a sixteenth of an inch.

'Come and wriggle, Snake,' he said through this aperture.

Findlater's rooms were not given to rowdy rock but concentrated instead upon a more cultivated jive, cha-cha, and variants. Beauty wriggled with excellence, and was particularly good at shrugging her shoulders and lifting forward her small stomach; while Trevor's knee-work was easy. Dougal, who had just entered with blonde Elaine, looked round with approval.

During the next dance – forward half a step, one fall and a dip, back half a step, one fall and a dip – Beauty flicked her lashes toward the band-leader who was then facing the dancers, a young pale man with a thin neck which sprouted from a loose jacket of sky-blue. He acknowledged the gesture with one swift rise-and-drop of the eyebrows. Trevor looked round at the man who had now turned to his band and was flicking his limp wrists very slightly. Trevor's teeth said, 'Who's your friend?'

'Whose friend?'

The crown of Trevor's head briefly indicated the band-leader.

Beauty shrugged in her jive and expressed her reply, both in the same movement.

Dougal was dancing with Elaine. He leapt into the air, he let go of her hands and dangled his arms in front of his hunched body. He placed his left hand on his hip and raised his right while his feet performed the rapid movements of the Highland Fling, heel to instep, then to knee. Elaine bowed her body and straightened it again and again in her laughter. The jiving couples slowed down like an unwound toy roundabout, and gathered beside Dougal. A tall stout man in evening dress walked over to the band; he said something to the band-leader who looked over his shoulder, observed the crowd round Dougal, and stopped the band.

'Hooch!' cried Dougal as the band stopped.

Everyone was talking or laughing. Those who were talking were all saying the same thing. They either said, 'Tell him to take more water in it,' or 'Shouldn't be allowed,' or 'He's all right. Leave him alone.' Some clapped their hands and said, ''Core.' The tall stout manager came over to Dougal and said with a beaming face, 'It's all right, son, but no more, please.'

'Don't you like Highland dancing?' Dougal said.

The manager beamed and walked away. The band started up. Dougal left the hall followed by Elaine. He reappeared shortly with Elaine tugging his arm in the opposite direction. However, he pressed into the midst of the dancers, bearing before him the lid of a dust-bin, which he had obtained from the back premises. Then he placed the lid upside down on the floor, sat cross-legged inside it, and was a man in a rocking boat rowing for his life. The band stopped, but nobody noticed the fact, owing to the many different sounds of mirth, protest, encouragement, and rage. The dancers circled slowly around him while he performed a Zulu dance with the lid for a shield.

Two West Indians among the crowd started to object.

'No, man.'

'We don't take no insults, man.'

But two other tall, black, and shining dancers cheered him on, bending at the knees and clapping. These were supported by their woolly-cropped girls who laughed loud above the noise, rolling their bodies from the waist, rolling their shoulders, heads, and eyes.

Dougal bowed to the black girls.

Next, Dougal sat on his haunches and banged a message out on a tom-tom. He sprang up and with the lid on his head was a Chinese coolie eating melancholy rice. He was an ardent cyclist, crouched over handlebars and pedalling uphill with the lid between his knees. He was an old woman with an umbrella; he stood on the upturned edges of the lid and speared fish from his rocking canoe; he was the man at the wheel of a racing car; he did many things with the lid before he finally propped the dust-bin lid up on his high shoulder, beating this cymbal rhythmically with his hand while with the other hand he limply conducted an invisible band, being, with long blank face, the band-leader.

The manager pushed through the crowd, still beaming. And, still beaming, he pointed out that the lid was scratching and spoiling the dance floor, and that Dougal had better leave the premises. He took Dougal, who still bore the dust-bin lid, by the elbow.

'Don't you get rough with him,' Elaine shouted. 'Can't you see he's deformed?'

Dougal disengaged his elbow from the manager's grasp and himself took the manager by the elbow.

'Tell me,' Dougal said, as he propelled the manager through the door, 'have you got a fatal flaw?'

'It's the best hall in south London and we don't want it mucked up, see? If we put on a cabaret we do it properly.'

'Be kind enough,' Dougal said, 'to replace this lid on the dust-bin out yonder while I return to the scene within.'

THE BALLAD OF PECKHAM RYE   555

Elaine was standing behind him. 'Come and leap, leopard,' Dougal said, and soon they were moving with the rest.

They were passed by Trevor and Beauty. Trevor regarded Dougal from under his lids, letting the corners of his mouth droop meaningfully.

'Got a pain, panda?' Dougal said.

'Now, don't start,' Elaine said.

Beauty laughed up and down the scale as she wriggled.

When Trevor passed again he said to Dougal, 'Got your lace hanky on you?'

Dougal put out his foot. Trevor stumbled. The band started playing the National Anthem. Trevor said, 'You ought to get a surgical boot and lift your shoulder up to line.'

'Have respect for the National Anthem,' Beauty said. Her eyes were on the band-leader who, as he turned to face the floor, raised his eyebrows slightly in her direction.

'See you up on the Rye,' Dougal said.

Elaine said, 'Oh, no, you don't. You're seeing me home.'

Trevor said, 'You girls got to go home together. I've got a date with a rat on the Rye.'

Several of the dancers, as they left the hall, called out to Dougal various words of gratitude, such as, 'Thanks a lot for the show' and 'You was swell, boy.'

Dougal bowed.

Beauty, on her way to the girls' cloakroom, loitered a little behind the queue. The band-leader passed by her and moved his solemn lips very slightly. Trevor, close by, heard him say, 'Come and frolic, lamb.'

Beauty moved her eyes to indicate the presence of Trevor, who observed the gesture.

'She's going straight home,' Trevor said through his nose, putting his face close to that of the band-leader. He gave Beauty a shove in the direction of the queue.

Beauty immediately turned back to the band-leader.

'No man,' she said to Trevor, 'lays hands on me.'

The band-leader raised his eyebrows and dropped them sadly.

'You're coming home with me,' Trevor told her.

'Thought you got a date on the Rye.'

'He'll keep,' Trevor said.

Beauty took a mirror from her bag and carefully applied her lipstick, turning her bronze head from side to side as she did so. Meanwhile her eyes traced the band-leader's departure from the hall.

'Elaine and I's going home together,' she said.

'No, you don't,' Trevor said. He peered out to the crowded entrance and there saw Elaine hanging on to Dougal. He caught her attention and beckoned to her by moving his forefinger twice very slowly. Elaine disengaged her arm from Dougal's, opened her bag, took out a cigarette, lit it, puffed slowly, then ambled over to Trevor.

'If you know what's good for your friend you'll take him home,' Trevor said.

Elaine blew a puff of smoke in his face and turned away.

'The fight's off,' she said to Dougal when she rejoined him. 'He wants to keep an eye on his girl, he don't trust her. She got no morals.'

As Trevor and Beauty emerged from the hall, Dougal, on the pavement, said to him, 'Feeling frail, nightingale?'

Trevor shook off Beauty's arm and approached Dougal.

'Now don't start with him,' Elaine shrieked at Dougal, 'he's ignorant.'

Beauty walked off on her own, with her high determined heels and her model-girl sway, placing her feet confidently and as on a chalk line.

Trevor looked round after her, then ran and caught her up.

Dougal walked with Elaine to Camberwell Green where, standing under the orange lights, he searched his pockets. When he had found a folded sheet of paper he opened it and read, '"I walked with her to Camberwell Green, and we said good-bye rather sorrowfully at the corner of New Road; and that possibility of meek happiness vanished for ever." This is John Ruskin and his girl Charlotte Wilkes,' Dougal said, 'my human research. But you and I will not say good-bye here and now. No. I'm taking you the rest of the way home in a taxi, because you're the nicest wee process-controller I've ever met.'

'One thing about you I'll admit,' she said, 'you're different. If I didn't know you were Scotch I'd swear you were Irish. My mother's Irish.'

She said they could not take a taxi up to her door because her mother didn't like her coming home with men in taxis. They dropped off at the Canal Head at Brixton.

'I'm leaving Meadows Meade,' Elaine said, 'Saturday week. Starting on the Monday at Drover Willis's. It's advancement.'

'I saw they were advertising,' Dougal said, 'for staff at Drover Willis's.'

They walked along by the canal a little way, watching the quiet water.

FIVE

Mr Druce said with embarrassment, 'I feel I should just mention the fact that absenteeism has increased in the six weeks you've been with us. Eight per cent to be precise. Not that I'm complaining. I'm not complaining. Rome can't be built in a day. I'm just mentioning a factor that Personnel keep stressing. Weedin's a funny sort of fellow. How do you find Weedin?'

'Totally,' Dougal said, 'lacking in vision. It is his fatal flaw. Otherwise quite sane.' He bore on his uneven shoulders all the learning and experience of the world as he said it. Mr Druce looked away, looked again at Dougal, and looked away.

'Vision,' said Mr Druce.

'Vision,' Dougal said, and he was a confessor in his box, leaning forward with his insidious advice through the grille, 'is the first requisite of sanity.'

'Sanity,' Mr Druce said.

Dougal closed his eyes and slowly smiled with his wide mouth. Dougal nodded his head twice and slowly, as one who understands all. Mr Druce was moved to confess, 'Sometimes I wonder if I'm sane myself, what with one thing and another.' Then he laughed and said, 'Fancy the Managing Director of Meadows, Meade & Grindley saying things like this.'

Dougal opened his eyes. 'Mr Druce, you are not as happy as you might be.'

'No,' Mr Druce said, 'I am not. Mrs Druce, if I may speak in confidence . . .'

'Certainly,' Dougal said.

'Mrs Druce is not a wife in any real sense of the word.'

Dougal nodded.

'Mrs Druce and I have nothing in common. When we were first married thirty-two years ago I was a travelling salesman in rayon.

Times were hard, then. But I got on.' Mr Druce looked pleadingly at Dougal. 'I was a success. I got on.'

Dougal tightened his lips prudishly, and nodded, and he was a divorce judge suspending judgement till the whole story was heard out.

'You can't get on in business,' Mr Druce pleaded, 'unless you've got the fibre for it.

'You can't get on,' Mr Druce said, 'unless you've got the moral fibre. *And* you don't have to be narrow-minded. That's one thing you don't have to be.'

Dougal waited.

'You have to be broad-minded,' Mr Druce protested. 'In this life.' He laid his elbow on the desk and, for a moment, his forehead on his hand. Then he shifted his chin to his hand and continued, 'Mrs Druce is not broad-minded. Mrs Druce is narrow-minded.'

Dougal had an elbow on each arm-rest of his chair, and his hands were joined under his chin. 'There is some question of incompatibility, I should say,' Dougal said. 'I should say,' he said, 'you have a nature at once deep and sensitive, Mr Druce.'

'Would you really?' Druce inquired of the analyst.

'And a sensitive nature,' Dougal said, 'requires psychological understanding.'

'My wife,' Druce said, '. . . it's like living a lie. We don't even speak to each other. Haven't spoken for nearly five years. One day, it was a Sunday, we were having lunch. I was talking away quite normally; you know, just talking away, And suddenly she said, "Quack, quack." She said, "Quack, quack." She said, "Quack, quack," and her hand was opening and shutting like this –' Mr Druce opened and shut his hand like a duck's bill. Dougal likewise raised his hand and made it open and shut. "Quack, quack,' Dougal said. 'Like that?'

Mr Druce dropped his arm. 'Yes, and she said, "That's how *you* go on – quack, quack." '

'Quack,' Dougal said, still moving his hand, 'quack.'

'She said to me, my wife,' said Mr Druce, 'she said, "That's how *you* go quacking on." Well, from that day to this I've never opened my mouth to her. I can't, Dougal, it's psychological, I just can't – you don't mind me calling you Dougal?'

'Not at all, Vincent,' Dougal said. 'I feel I understand you. How do you communicate with Mrs Druce?'

'Write notes,' said Mr Druce. 'Do you call that a marriage?' Mr Druce bent to open a lower drawer of his desk and brought out a book with a bright yellow wrapper. Its title was *Marital Relational Psychology*. Druce flicked over the pages, then set the book aside. 'It's no use to me,' he said. 'Interesting case histories but it doesn't cover my case. I've thought of seeing a psychiatrist, and then I think, why should I? Let *her* see a psychiatrist.'

'Take her a bunch of flowers,' Dougal said, looking down at the back of his hand, the little finger of which was curling daintily. 'Put your arms around her,' he said, becoming a lady-columnist, 'and start afresh. It frequently needs but one little gesture from one partner –'

'Dougal, I can't. I don't know why it is, but I can't.' Mr Druce placed a hand just above his stomach. 'Something stops me.'

'You two must separate,' Dougal said, 'if only for a while.'

Mr Druce's hand abruptly removed from his stomach. 'No,' he said, 'oh, no, I can't leave her.' He shifted in his chair into his businesslike pose. 'No, I can't do that. I've got to stay with her for old times' sake.'

The telephone rang. 'I'm engaged,' he said sharply into it. He jerked down the receiver and looked up to find Dougal's forefinger pointing into his face. Dougal looked grave, lean, and inquisitorial. 'Mrs Druce,' Dougal said, 'has got money.'

'There are interests in vital concerns which we both share,' Mr Druce said with his gaze on Dougal's finger, 'Mrs Druce and I.'

Dougal shook his outstretched finger a little. 'She won't *let* you leave her,' he said, 'because of the money.'

Mr Druce looked frightened.

'And there is also the information which she holds,' Dougal said, 'against you.'

'What are you talking about?'

'I'm fey. I've got Highland blood.' Dougal dropped his hand. 'You have my every sympathy, Vincent,' he said.

Mr Druce laid his head on the desk and wept.

Dougal sat back and lit a cigarette out of Mr Druce's box. He heaved his high shoulder in a sigh. He sat back like an exhausted medium of the spiritualist persuasion. 'Does you good,' Dougal said, 'a wee greet. A hundred years ago all chaps used to cry regardless.'

Merle Coverdale came in with the letters to be signed. She clicked her heels together as she stopped at the sight.

'Thank you, Miss Coverdale,' Dougal said, putting out a hand for the letters.

Meanwhile Mr Druce sat up and blew his nose.

'Got a comb on you?' Dougal said, squeezing Merle's hand under the letters.

She said, 'This place is becoming chaos.'

'What was that, Miss Coverdale?' Mr Druce said with as little moisture as possible.

'Mr Druce has a bad head,' Dougal said as he left the room with her.

'Come and tell me what happened,' said Merle.

Dougal looked at his watch. 'Sorry, can't stop. I've got an urgent appointment in connexion with my human research.'

Dougal sat in the cheerful waiting-room looking at the tulips in their earthy bowls.

'Mr Douglas Dougal?'

Dougal did not correct her. On the contrary he said, 'That's right.'

'Come this way, please.'

He followed her into the office of Mr Willis, managing director of Drover Willis's, textile manufacturers of Peckham.

'Good afternoon, Mr Dougal,' said the man behind the desk. 'Take a seat.'

On hearing Mr Willis's voice Dougal changed his manner, for he perceived that Mr Willis was a Scot.

Mr Willis was looking at Dougal's letter of application.

'Graduate of Edinburgh?' said Mr Willis.

'Yes, Mr Willis.'

Mr Willis's blue eyes stared out of his brick-coloured small-featured face. They stared and stared at Dougal.

'Douglas Dougal,' the man read out from Dougal's letter, and asked with a one-sided smile, 'Any relation to Fergie Dougal the golfer?'

'No,' Dougal said. 'I'm afraid not.'

Mr Willis smiled by turning down the sides of his mouth.

'Why do you want to come into Industry, Mr Dougal?'

'I think there's money in it,' Dougal said.

Mr Willis smiled again. 'That's the correct answer. The last candidate answered, "Industry and the Arts must walk hand in hand," when I put that question to him. His answer was wrong. Tell me, Mr Dougal, why do you want to come to us?'

'I saw your advertisement,' Dougal said, 'and I wanted a job. I saw your advertisements, too, for automatic weaver instructors and hands, and for twin-needle flat-bed machinists, and flat-lock machinists and instructors. I gathered you're expanding.'

'You know something about textiles?'

'I've seen over a factory. Meadows, Meade & Grindley.'

'Meadows Meade are way behind us.'

'Yes. So I gathered.'

'Now I'll tell.you what we're looking for, what we want ...'

Dougal sat upright and listened, only interrupting when Mr Willis said, 'The hours are nine to five-thirty.'

'I would need time off for research.'

'Research?'

'Industrial relations. The psychological factors behind the absenteeism, and so on, as you've been saying –'

'You could do an evening course in industrial psychology. And of course you'd have access to the factory.'

'The research I have in mind,' Dougal said, 'would need the best part of the day for at least two months. Two months should do it. I want to look into the external environment. The home conditions. Peckham must have a moral character of its own.'

Mr Willis's blue eyes photographed every word. Dougal sat out these eyes, he went on talking, reasonably, like a solid steady Edinburgh boy, all the steadier for the hump on his shoulder.

'I'll have to speak to Davis. He is Personnel. We have to talk over the candidates and we may ask to see you again, Mr Dougal. If we decide on you, don't fear you'll be hampered in your research.'

The factory was opening its gates as Dougal came down the steps from the office into the leafy lanes of Nun Row. Some of the girls were being met by their husbands and boy friends in cars. Others rode off on motor-scooters. A number walked down to the station. 'Hi, Dougal,' called one of them, 'what you doing here?'

It was Elaine, who had now been over a week at Drover Willis's.

'What you doing here, Dougal?'

'I'm after a job,' he said. 'I think I've got it.'

'You leaving Meadows Meade too?'

'No,' he said, 'oh, no, not on your life.'

'What's your game, Dougal?'

'Come and have a drink,' he said, 'and my Christian name is Douglas on this side of the Rye, mind that. Dougal Douglas at Meadows Meade and Douglas Dougal at Willis's, mind. Only a formality for the insurance cards and such.'

'I better call you Doug and be done with it.'

Dixie sat at her desk in the typing pool and, without lifting her eyes from her shorthand book or interrupting the dance of her fingers on the keyboard, spoke out her reply to her neighbour.

'He's all one-sided at the shoulders. I don't know how any girl could go with him.'

Connie Weedin, daughter of the Personnel Manager, typed on and said, 'My Dad says he's nuts. But I say he's got something. Definitely.'

'Got something, all right. Got a good cheek. My young brother doesn't like him. My mum likes him. My dad likes him so-so. Humphrey likes him. I don't agree to that. The factory girls like him – what can you expect? I don't like him, he's got funny ideas.' She stopped typing with her last word and took the papers out of her typewriter. She placed them neatly on a small stack of papers in a tray, put an envelope in her typewriter, typed an address, put more papers in her typewriter, turned over the page of her shorthand notes, and started typing again. 'My dad doesn't mind him, but Leslie can't stand him. I tell you who else doesn't like him.'

'Who?'

'Trevor Lomas. Trevor doesn't like him.'

'I don't like Trevor, never did,' Connie said. 'Definitely ignorant. He goes with that girl from Celia Modes that's called Beauty. Some beauty!'

'He's a good dancer. He doesn't like Dougal Douglas and, boy, I'll say he's got something there,' Dixie said.

'My dad says he's nuts. Supposed to be helping my dad keep the factory sweet. But my dad says he don't do much with all his brains and his letters. But you can't help but like him. He's different.'

'He goes out with the factory girls. He goes out with Elaine Kent that was process-controller. She's gone to Drover Willis's. He goes out with her ladyship too.'

'You don't say?'

'I do say. He better watch out for Mr Druce if it's her ladyship he's after.'

'Watch out – her ladyship's looking this way.'

Miss Merle Coverdale, at her supervisor's seat at the top of the room, called out, 'Is there anything you want, Dixie?'

'No.'

'If there's anything you want, come and ask. Is there anything you want, Connie?'

'No.'

'If there's anything you want, come up here and ask for it.'

Dougal came in just then, and walked with his springy step all up the long open-plan office, bobbing as he walked as if the plastic inlay flooring was a certain green and paradisal turf.

'Good morning, girls.'

'You'd think he was somebody,' Dixie said.

Connie opened a drawer in her small desk in which she kept a mirror, and looking down into it, tidied her hair.

Dougal sat down beside Merle Coverdale.

'There was a personal call for you,' she said, handing him a slip of paper, 'from a lady. Will you ring this number?'

He looked at it, put the paper in his pocket and said, 'One of my employers.'

Merle gave one of her laughs from the chest. 'Employers – that's a good name for them. How many you got?'

'Two,' Dougal said, 'and a possible third. Is Mr Weedin in?'

'Yes, he's been asking for you.'

Dougal jumped up and went in to Mr Weedin where he sat in one of the glass offices which extended from the typing pool.

'Mr Douglas,' said Mr Weedin, 'I want to ask you a personal question. What do you mean exactly by vision?'

'Vision?' Dougal said.

'Yes, vision, that's what I said.'

'Do you speak literally as concerning optics, or figuratively, as it might be with regard to an enlargement of the total perceptive capacity?'

'Druce is complaining we haven't got vision in this department. I thought perhaps maybe you had been having one of your long chats with him.'

'Mr Weedin,' Dougal said, 'don't tremble like that. Just relax.' He took from his pocket a small square silver vinaigrette which had two separate compartments. Dougal opened both lids. In one compartment lay some small white tablets. In the other were a number of yellow ones. Dougal offered the case to Mr Weedin. 'For calming down you take two of the white ones and for revving up you take one of the yellow ones.'

'I don't want your drugs. I just want to know –'

'The yellow ones make you feel sexy. The white ones, being of a relaxing nature, ensure the more successful expression of such feelings. But these, of course, are mere by-effects.'

'Do you want my job? Is that what you're wanting?'

'No,' Dougal said.

'Because if you want it you can have it. I'm tired of working for a firm where the boss listens to the advice of any young showpiece that takes his fancy. I've had this before. I had it with Merle Coverdale. She told Druce I was inefficient at relationship-maintenance. She told Druce that everything in the pool goes back to me through my girl Connie. She –'

'Miss Coverdale is a sensitive girl. Like an Okapi, you know. You spell it OKAPI. A bit of all sorts of beast. Very rare, very nervy. You have to make allowances.'

'And now you came along and you tell Druce we lack vision. And Druce calls me in and I see from the look on his face he's got a new idea. Vision, it is, this time. Try to take a tip or two, he says, from the Arts man. I said, he never hardly puts a foot inside the door does your Arts man. Nonsense, Weedin, he says, Mr Douglas and I have many a long session. He says, watch his manner, he has a lovely manner with the workers. I said, yes, up on the Rye Saturday nights. That is unworthy of you, Weedin, he says. Is it coincidence, says I, that absenteeism has risen eight per cent since Mr Douglas came here and

THE BALLAD OF PECKHAM RYE

is still rising? Things are bound to get worse, he says, before they get better. If you had the vision, Weedin, he says, you would comprehend my meaning. Study Douglas, he says, watch his methods.'

'Funny thing I've just found out,' Dougal said, 'we have five cemeteries up here round the Rye within the space of a square mile. We have Camberwell New, Camberwell Old – that's full up. We have Nunhead, Deptford and Lewisham Green. Did you know that Nunhead reservoir holds twenty million gallons of water? The original title that Mendelssohn gave his "Spring Song" was "Camberwell Green". It's a small world.'

Mr Weedin laid his head in his hand and burst into tears.

Dougal said, 'You're a sick man, Mr Weedin. I can't bear sickness. It's my fatal flaw. But I've brought a comb with me. Would you like me to comb your hair?'

'You're unnatural,' said Mr Weedin.

'All human beings who breathe are a bit unnatural,' Dougal said. 'If you try to be too natural, see where it gets you.'

Mr Weedin blew his nose, and shouted at Dougal: 'It isn't possible to get another good position in another firm at my age. Personnel is a much coveted position. If I had to leave here, Mr Douglas, I would have to take a subordinate post elsewhere. I have my wife and family to think of. Druce is impossible to work for. It's impossible to leave this firm. Sometimes I think I'm going to have a breakdown.'

'It would not be severe in your case,' Dougal said. 'It is at its worst when a man is a skyscraper. But you're only a nice wee bungalow.'

'We live in a flat,' Mr Weedin managed to say.

'Do you know,' Dougal said, 'up at the police station they are excavating an underground tunnel which starts in the station yard and runs all the way to Nunhead. You should ponder sometimes about underground tunnels. Did you know Boadicea was broken and defeated on the Rye? She was a great beefy soldier. I think you should take Mr Druce's advice and study my manner, Mr Weedin. I could give you lessons at ten and six an hour.'

Mr Weedin rose to hit him, but since the walls of his office were made mostly of glass, he was prevented in the act by an overwhelming sense of being looked at from all sides.

*

Dougal sat in Miss Frierne's panelled hall on Saturday morning and telephoned to the Flaxman number on the little slip of paper which Merle Coverdale had handed to him the previous day.

'Miss Cheeseman, please,' said Dougal.

'She isn't in,' said the voice from across the water. 'Who shall I say it was?'

'Mr Dougal-Douglas,' Dougal said, 'spelt with a hyphen. Tell Miss Cheeseman I'll be at home all morning.'

He next rang Jinny.

'Hallo, are you better?' he said.

'I've got soup on the stove. I'll ring you back.'

Miss Frierne was ironing in the kitchen. She said to Dougal, 'Humphrey is going to see to the roof this afternoon. It's creaking. It isn't a loose slate, it must be one of the beams loose in his cupboard.'

'Funny thing,' Dougal said, 'it only creaks at night. It goes Creakoop!' The dishes rattled in their rack as he leapt.

'It's the cold makes it creak, I daresay,' she said.

The telephone rang. Dougal rushed out to the hall. It was not Jinny, however.

'Doug dear,' said Miss Maria Cheeseman from across the river.

'Oh, it's you, Cheese.'

'We really must get down to things,' Miss Cheeseman said. 'All this about my childhood in Peckham, it's all wrong, it was Streatham.'

'There's the new law of libel to be considered,' Dougal said. 'A lot of your early associates in Streatham are still alive. If you want to write the true story of your life you can't place it in Streatham.'

'But Doug dear,' she said, 'that bit where you make me say I played with Harold Lloyd and Ford Sterling at the Golden Domes in Camberwell, it wasn't true, dear. I *was* in a show with Fatty Arbuckle but it was South Shields.'

'I thought it was a work of art you wanted to write,' Dougal said, 'now was that not so? If you only want to write a straight autobiography you should have got a straight ghost. I'm crooked.'

'Well, Doug dear, I don't think this story about me and the Gordon Highlander is quite nice, do you? I mean to say, it isn't true. Of course, it's funny about the kilt, but it's a little embarrassing –'

'Well, write your own autobiography,' Dougal said.

'Oh, Doug dear, do come over to tea.'

'No, you've hurt my feelings.'

'Doug dear, I'm thrilled with my book. I'm sure it's going to be marvellous. I can't say I'm quite happy about all of chapter three but –'

'What's wrong with chapter three?'

'Well, it's only that last bit you wrote, it isn't *me*.'

'I'll see you at four o'clock,' he said, 'but understand, Cheese, I don't like crossing the water when I'm in the middle of a work of art. I'm giving all my time to it.'

Dougal said to Humphrey, 'I was over the other side of the river on business this afternoon, and while I was over that way I called in to see my girl.'

'Oh, you got a girl over there?'

'Used to have. She's got engaged to somebody else.'

'Women have no moral sense,' Humphrey said. 'You see it in the Unions. They vote one way then go and act another way.'

'She was nice, Jinny,' Dougal said, 'but she was too delicate in health. Do you believe in the Devil?'

'No.'

'Do you know anyone that believes in the Devil?'

'I think some of those Irish –'

'Feel my head,' Dougal said.

'What?'

'Feel these little bumps up here.' Dougal guided Humphrey's hand through his curls at each side. 'I had it done by a plastic surgeon,' Dougal said.

'What?'

'He did an operation and took away the two horns. They had to shave my head in the nursing home before the operation. It took a long time for my hair to grow again.'

Humphrey smiled and felt again among Dougal's curls.

'A couple of cysts,' he said. 'I've got one myself at the back of my head. Feel it.'

Dougal touched the bump like a connoisseur.

'You supposed to be the Devil, then?' Humphrey asked.

'No, oh, no, I'm only supposed to be one of the wicked spirits that wander through the world for the ruin of souls. Have you mended those beams in the roof yet, that go Creak-oop?'

'I have,' Humphrey said. 'Dixie refuses to come any more.'

SIX

'What strikes me as remarkable,' Dougal said, 'is how he manages to get in so much outside his school hours.'

Nelly Mahone nodded, trod out her cigarette end, and looked at the packet of cigarettes which Dougal had placed on the table.

'Help yourself,' Dougal said, and he lit the cigarette for her.

'Ta,' said Nelly. She looked round her room. 'It's all *clean* dirt,' she said.

'You would think,' Dougal said, 'his parents would have some control over him.'

Nelly inhaled gratefully. 'Up the Elephant, that's where they all go. What was name?'

'Leslie Crewe. Thirteen years of age. The father's manager of Beverly Hills Outfitters at Brixton.'

'Where they live?'

'Twelve Rye Grove.'

Nelly nodded. 'How much you paid him?'

'A pound the first time, thirty bob the second time. But now he's asking five quid a week flat.'

Nelly whispered, 'Then there's a gang behind him, surely. Can't you give up one of the jobs for a month or two?'

'I don't see why I should,' Dougal said, 'just to please a thirteen-year-old blackmailer.'

Nelly made signs with her hands and moved her mouth soundlessly, and swung her eyes to the wall between her room and the next, to show that walls had ears.

'A thirteen-year-old blackmailer,' Dougal said, more softly. But Nelly did not like the word blackmailer at all; she placed her old fish-smelling hand over Dougal's mouth, and whispered in his ear – her grey long hair falling against his nose – 'A lousy fellow next door,' she said. 'A slob that wouldn't do a day's work if you paid him gold. So guard your mouth.' She released Dougal and started to draw the curtains.

'And here's me,' Dougal said, 'willing to do three, four, five men's jobs, and I get blackmailed on grounds of false pretences.'

She ran with her long low dipping strides to his side and gave him a hard poke in the back. She returned to her window, which was as opaque as sackcloth and not really distinguishable from the curtain she pulled across it. On the floorboards were a few strips of very worn-out matting of a similar colour. The bed in the corner was much of the same hue, lumpy and lopsided. 'But I'm charmed to see you, all the same,' Nelly said for the third time, 'and will you have a cup of tea?'

Dougal said, no thanks, for the third time.

Nelly scratched her head, and raising her voice, declared, 'Praise be to God, who rewards those who meditate the truths he has proposed for their intelligence.'

'It seems to me,' Dougal said, 'that my course in life has much support from the Scriptures.'

'Never,' Nelly said, shaking her thin body out of its ecstasy and taking a cigarette out of Dougal's packet.

'Consider the story of Moses in the bulrushes. That was a crafty trick. The mother got her baby back and all expenses paid into the bargain. And consider the parable of the Unjust Steward. Do you know the parable of –'

'Stop,' Nelly said, with her hand on her old blouse. 'I get that excited by Holy Scripture I'm afraid to get my old lung trouble back.'

'Were you born in Peckham?' Dougal said.

'No, Galway. I don't remember it though. I was a girl in Peckham.'

'Where did you work?'

'Shoe factory I started life. Will you have a cup of tea?'

Dougal took out ten shillings.

'It's not enough,' Nelly said.

Dougal made it a pound.

'If I got to follow them fellows round between here and the Elephant you just think of the fares alone,' Nelly said. 'I'll need more than that to go along with.'

'Two quid, then,' Dougal said. 'And more next week.'

'All right,' she said.

'Otherwise it's going to be cheaper to pay Leslie.'

'No it isn't,' she said. 'They go on wanting more and more. I hope you'll remember me nice if I get some way to stop their gobs.'

'Ten quid,' said Dougal.

'All right,' she said. 'But suppose one of your bosses finds out in the meantime? After all, rival firms is like to get nasty.'

'Tell me,' Dougal said, 'how old are you?'

'I should say I was sixty-four. Have a cup of tea.' She looked round the room. 'It's all clean dirt.'

'Tell me,' Dougal said, 'what it was like to work in the shoe factory.'

She told him all of her life in the shoe factory till it was time for her to go out on her rounds proclaiming. Dougal followed her down the sour dark winding stairs of Lightbody Buildings, and they parted company in the passage, he going out before her.

'Good night, Nelly.'

'Good night, Mr Doubtless.'

'Where's Mr Douglas?' said Mr Weedin.

'Haven't seen him for a week,' Merle Coverdale replied. 'Would you like me to ring him up at home and see if he's all right?'

'Yes, do that,' Mr Weedin said. 'No, don't. Yes, I don't see why not. No, perhaps, though, we'd –'

Merle Coverdale stood tapping her pencil on her notebook, watching Mr Weedin's hands shuffling among the papers on his desk.

'I'd better ask Mr Druce,' Mr Weedin said. 'He probably knows where Mr Douglas is.'

'He doesn't,' Merle said.

'Doesn't he?'

'No, he doesn't.'

'Wait until tomorrow. See if he comes in tomorrow.'

'Are you feeling all right, Mr Weedin?'

'Who? Me? I'm all right.'

Merle went in to Mr Druce. 'Dougal hasn't been near the place for a week.'

'Leave him alone. The boy's doing good work.'

She returned to Mr Weedin and stood in his open door with an exaggerated simper. 'We are to leave him alone. The boy's doing good work.'

'Come in and shut the door,' said Mr Weedin.

She shut the door and approached his desk.

'I'm not much of a believer,' Mr Weedin said, quivering his hands across the papers before him. 'But there's something Mr Douglas told me that's on my mind.' He craned upward to look through the glass panels on all sides of his room.

'They're all out at tea-break,' Merle said.

Mr Weedin dropped his head on his hands. 'It may surprise you,' he said, 'coming from me. But it's my belief that Dougal Douglas is a diabolical agent, if not in fact the Devil.'

'Mr Weedin,' said Miss Coverdale.

'Yes, I know what you're thinking. Yes, yes, you're thinking I'm going wrong up here.' He pointed to his right temple and screwed it with his finger. 'Do you know,' he said, 'that Douglas himself showed me bumps on his head where he had horns removed by plastic surgery?'

'Don't get excited, Mr Weedin. Don't shout. The girls are coming up from the canteen.'

'I felt those bumps with these very hands. Have you looked, have you ever properly looked at his eyes? That shoulder –'

'Keep calm, Mr Weedin, you aren't getting yourself anywhere, you know.'

Mr Weedin pointed with a shaking arm in the direction of the managing director's office. 'He's bewitched,' he said.

Merle took tiny steps backward and got herself out of the door. She went in to Mr Druce again.

'Mr Weedin will be wanting a holiday,' she said.

Mr Druce lifted his paper-knife, toyed with it in his hand, pointed it at Merle, and put it down. 'What did you say?' he said.

Drover Willis's was humming with work when Dougal reported on Friday morning to the managing director.

'During my first week,' Dougal told Mr Willis, 'I have been observing the morals of Peckham. It seemed to me that the moral element lay at the root of all industrial discontents which lead to absenteeism and the slackness at work which you described to me.'

Mr Willis looked with his blue eyes at his rational compatriot sitting before him with a shiny brief-case on his lap.

Mr Willis said at last, 'That would seem to be the correct approach, Mr Dougal.'

Dougal sat easily in his chair and continued his speech with half-closed, detached, and scholarly eyes.

'There are four types of morality observable in Peckham,' he said. 'One, emotional. Two, functional. Three, puritanical. Four, Christian.'

Mr Willis opened the lid of a silver cigarette-box and passed it over to Dougal.

'No, thank you,' Dougal said. 'Take the first category, Emotional. Here, for example, it is considered immoral for a man to live with a wife who no longer appeals to him. Take the second, Functional, in which the principal factor is class solidarity such as, in some periods and places, has also existed amongst the aristocracy, and of which the main manifestation these days is the trade union movement. Three, Puritanical, of which there are several modern variants, monetary advancement being the most prevalent gauge of the moral life in this category. Four, Traditional, which accounts for about one per cent of the Peckham population, and which in its simplest form is Christian. All moral categories are of course intermingled. Sometimes all are to be found in the beliefs and behaviour of one individual.'

'Where does this get us?'

'I can't say,' Dougal said. 'It is only a preliminary analysis.'

'Please embody all this in a report for us, Mr Dougal.'

Dougal opened his brief-case and took out two sheets of paper. 'I have elaborated on the question here. I have included case histories.'

Mr Willis smiled with one side of his mouth and said, 'Which of these four moral codes would you say was most attractive, Mr Dougal?'

'Attractive?' Dougal said with a trace of disapproval.

'Attractive to us. Useful, I mean, useful.'

Dougal pondered seriously until Mr Willis's little smile was forced, for dignity's sake, to fade. Then, 'I could not decide until I had further studied the question.'

'We'll expect another report next week?'

'No, I'll need a month,' Dougal stated. 'A month to work on my own. I can't come in here again for a month if you wish me to continue research on this line of industrial psychology.'

'You must see round the factory,' said Mr Willis. 'Peckham is a big place. We're concerned with our own works first of all.'

'I've arranged to be shown round this afternoon,' Dougal said. 'And at the end of a month I hope to spend some time with the workers in the recreation halls and canteens.'

Mr Willis looked silently at Dougal who then permitted himself a slight display of enthusiasm. He leaned forward.

'Have you observed, Mr Willis, the frequency with which your employees use the word "immoral"? Have you noticed how equally often they use the word "ignorant"? These words are significant,' Dougal said, 'psychologically and sociologically.'

Mr Willis smiled, as far as he was able, into Dougal's face. 'Take a month and see what you can do,' he said. 'But bring us a good plan of action at the end of it. Drover, my partner, is anxious about absenteeism. We want some moral line that will be both commendable by us and acceptable to our staff. You've got some sound ideas, I can see that. And method. I like method.'

Dougal nodded and took his long serious face out of the room.

Miss Frierne said, 'That boy Leslie Crewe has been here. He was looking for yóu. Wants to go your errands and make a bob like a good kid. Perhaps his mother's a bit short.'

'Anyone with him?'

'No. He came to the back door this time.'

'Oh,' Dougal said, 'did you get rid of him quickly?'

'Well, he wouldn't go for a long time. He kept saying when would Mr Douglas be home, and could he do anything for you. He was very polite, I will say that. Then he asked the time and then he said his Dad used to live up this road in number eight. So I took him in the kitchen. I thought, well, he's only a boy, and gave him a doughnut. He said his sister was looking forward to marrying Humphrey in September. He said she saves all her wages and the father in America dresses her. He said –'

'He must have kept you talking a long time,' Dougal said.

'Oh, I didn't mind. It was a nice break in the afternoon. A nice lad, he is. He goes out Sundays with the Rover Scouts. I'd just that minute come in and I was feeling a bit upset because of something that happened in the street, so –'

'Did he ask if he could go up and wait in my room?'

'No, not this time. I wouldn't have let him in your room, especially after you said nobody was to be let in there. Don't you worry about your room. Nobody wants to go into your room, I'm sure.'

Dougal said, 'You are too innocent for this wicked world.'

'Innocent I always was,' Miss Frierne said, 'and that was why I was so taken aback that day by the Gordon Highlander up on One Tree Hill. Have a cup of tea.'

'Thanks,' Dougal said. 'I'll just pop upstairs a minute first.'

His room had, of course, been disturbed. He unlocked a drawer in his dressing-table and found that two note-books were missing. His portable typewriter had been opened and clumsily shut. Ten five-pound notes were, however, untouched in another drawer by the person who had climbed to his room while Leslie had engaged Miss Frierne in talk.

He came down to the kitchen where Miss Frierne sighed into her tea.

'Next time that Leslie comes round to the back door have a look, will you, to see who he's left at the front door. His father's worried about his companions after school hours, I happen to know.'

'He only wanted to know if you had any errands to run. I daresay to help his mother, like a good kid. I told him I thought you're short of bacon for your breakfast. He'll be back. There's no harm in that boy, I know it by instinct, and instinct always tells. Like what happened to me in the street today.' She sipped her tea, and was silent.

Dougal sipped his. 'Go on,' he said, 'you're dying to tell me what happened.'

'As true as God is my judge,' she said, 'I saw my brother up at Camberwell Green that left home in nineteen-nineteen. We never heard a word from him all those years. He was coming out of Lyons.'

'Didn't you go and speak to him?'

'No,' she said, 'I didn't. He was very shabby, he looked awful. Something stopped me. It was an instinct. I couldn't do it. He saw me, too.'

She took a handkerchief out of her sleeve and patted beneath her glasses.

'You should have gone up to him,' Dougal said. 'You should have said, "Are you . . ." – what was his name?'

'Harold,' she said.

'You should have said, "Are you Harold?", that's what you ought to have done. Instead of which you didn't. You came back here and gave a doughnut to that rotten little Leslie.'

'Don't you point your finger at me, Dougal. Nobody does that in my house. You can find other accommodation *if* you like, any *time* you like and when you like.'

Dougal got up and shuffled round the kitchen with a slouch and an old ill look. 'Is that what your old brother looked like?' he said.

She laughed in high-pitched ripples.

Dougal thrust his hands into his pockets and looked miserably at his toes.

She started to cry all over her spectacles.

'Perhaps it wasn't your brother at all,' Dougal said.

'That's what I'm wondering, son.'

'Just feel my head,' Dougal said, 'these two small bumps here.'

'There are four types of morality in Peckham,' Dougal said to Mr Druce. 'The first category is –'

'Dougal,' he said, 'are you doing anything tonight?'

'Well, I usually prepare my notes. You realize, don't you, that Oliver Goldsmith taught in a school in Peckham? He used to commit absenteeism and spent a lot of his time in a coffee-house at the Temple instead of in Peckham. I wonder why?'

'I need your advice,' Mr Druce said. 'There's a place in Soho –'

'I don't like crossing the river,' Dougal said, 'not without my broomstick.'

Mr Druce made double chins and looked lovingly at Dougal.

'There's a place in Soho –'

'I could spare a couple of hours,' Dougal said. 'I could see you up at Dulwich at the Dragon at nine.'

'Well, I was thinking of making an evening of it, Dougal; some dinner at this place in Soho –'

'Nine at the Dragon,' Dougal said.

'Mrs Druce knows a lot of people in Dulwich.'

'All the better,' Dougal said.

Dougal arrived at the Dragon at nine sharp. He drank gin and peppermint while he waited. At half past nine two girls from Drover Willis's came in. Dougal joined them. Mr Druce did not come. At ten o'clock they went on a bus to the Rosemary Branch in Southampton Way. Here, Dougal expounded the idea that everyone should take every second Monday morning off their work. When they came out of the pub, at eleven, Nelly Mahone crossed the street towards them.

'Praise be to the Lord,' she cried, 'whose providence in all things never fails.'

'Hi, Nelly,' said one of the girls as she passed.

Nelly raised up her voice and in the same tone proclaimed, 'Praise be to God who by sin is offended, Trevor Lomas, Collie Gould up the Elephant with young Leslie, and by penance appeased, the exaltation of the humble and the strength of the righteous.'

'Ah, Nelly,' Dougal said.

SEVEN

'Yes, Cheese?' Dougal said.

'Look, Doug, I think I can't have this story about the Dragon at Dulwich, it's indecent. Besides, it isn't true. And I never went to Soho at that age. I never went out with any managing director –'

'It will help sell the book,' Dougal said. He breathed moistly on the oak panel of Miss Frierne's hall, and with his free hand drew a face on the misty surface where he had breathed.

'And Doug dear,' said the voice from across the river, 'how did you know I started life in a shoe factory? I mean to say, *I* didn't tell you that. How did you know?'

'I didn't know, Cheese,' Dougal said.

'You must have known. You've got all the details right, except that it wasn't in Peckham, it was Streatham. It all came back to me as I read it. It's uncanny. You've been checking up on me, haven't you, Doug?'

'Aye,' Dougal said. He breathed on the panel, wrote in a word, then rubbed it off.

'Doug, you mustn't do that. It makes me creepy to think that people can find out all about you,' Miss Cheeseman said. 'I mean, I don't want to put in about the shoe factory and all that. Besides, the period. It dates me.'

'It only makes you sixty-eight, Cheese.'

'Well, Doug, there must be a way of making me not even that. I want you to come over, Doug. I've been feeling off colour.'

'I've got a fatal flaw,' Dougal said, 'to the effect that I can't bear anyone off colour. Moreover, Saturday's my day off and it's a beautiful summer day.'

'Dear Doug, I promise to be well. Only come over. I'm *worried* about my book. It's rather ... rather too ...'

'Rambling,' Dougal said.

'Yes, that's it.'

'I'll see you at four,' Dougal said.

At the back of Hollis's Hamburgers at Elephant and Castle was a room furnished with a fitted grey carpet, a red upholstered modern suite comprising a sofa and two cubic armchairs, a television receiver on a light wood stand, a low glass-topped coffee table, a table on which stood an electric portable gramophone and a tape recorder, a light wood bureau desk, a standard lamp, and several ash-trays on stands. Two of the walls were papered with a wide grey stripe. The other two were covered with a pattern of gold stars on red. Fixed to the walls were a number of white brackets containing pots of indoor ivy. The curtains, which were striped red and white, were drawn. This cheerful interior was lit by a couple of red-shaded wall-lamps. In one chair sat Leslie Crewe, with his neck held rigidly and attentively. He was dressed in a navy-blue suit of normal cut, and a peach-coloured tie, and looked older than thirteen. In another chair lolled Collie Gould who was eighteen and had been found unfit for National Service; Collie suffered from lung trouble for which he was constantly under treatment, and was at present on probation for motor stealing. He wore a dark-grey draped jacket with narrow black trousers. Trevor Lomas, dressed in blue-grey, lay between them on the sofa. All smoked American cigarettes. All looked miserable, not as an expression of their feelings, but as if by an instinctive prearrangement, to convey a decision on all affairs whatsoever.

Trevor held in his hand one of the two thin exercise books he had stolen from Dougal's drawer. The other lay on the carpet beside him.

'Listen to this,' Trevor said. 'It's called "Phrases suitable for Cheese".'

'Suitable for what?' said Collie.

'Cheese, it says. Code word, obvious. Listen to this what you make of it. There's a list.

    I thrilled to his touch
    I was too young at the time to understand why my mother was
        crying
    As he entered the room a shudder went through my frame

In that moment of silent communion we renewed our shattered
    faith
She was to play a vital role in my life
Memory had not played me false
He was always an incurable romantic
I became the proud owner of a bicycle
He spoke to me in desiccated tones
Autumn again. Autumn. The burning of leaves in the park
He spelt disaster to me
I revelled in my first tragic part
I had no eyes for any other man
We were living a lie
She proved a mine of information
Once more fate intervened
Munificence was his middle name
I felt a grim satisfaction
They were poles apart
I dropped into a fitful doze

'Read us it again, Trev,' Leslie said. 'It sounds like English Dictation. Perhaps he's a teacher as well.'

Trevor ignored him. He tapped the notebook and addressed Collie.
'Code,' he said. 'It's worth lolly.'

An intensified expression of misery on Collie's face expressed his
agreement.

'In with a gang, he is. It's bigger than I thought. Question now, to
find out what his racket is.'

'Sex,' Leslie said.

'You don't say so?' Trevor said. 'Well, that's helpful, son. But we
happen to have guessed all that. Question is, what game of sex?
Question is, national or international?'

Collie blew out his smoke as if it were slow poison. 'Got to work
back from a clue,' he said in his sick voice. 'Autumn's a clue. Wasn't
there something about Autumn?'

'How dumb can you get?' Trevor inquired through his nose. 'It's a
code. Autumn means something else. Everything means something.' He dropped the notebook and painfully picked up the other.
He read:

Peckham. Modes of communication.
Actions more effective than words. Enact everything. Depict.
Morality. Functional. Emotional. Puritanical. Classical.
Nelly Mahone. Lightbody Buildings.
Tunnel. Meeting-house Lane Excavations police station yard.
Order of St Bridget. Nuns decamped in the night.

Trevor turned the pages.

Entry Parish Register 1658. 5 May.
Rose, wife of Wm Hathaway buried
Aged 103, who boare a sonn at the age
of 63.

Trevor said, 'Definitely a code. Look how he spells "son". And this
about bearing at the age of sixty-three.'
Collie and Leslie came over to see the book.
'There's a clue here,' Collie said, 'that we could follow up.'
'No,' said Trevor, 'you don't say so? Come on, kids, we got to look
up Nelly Mahone.'

'If we're going to have a row,' Mavis said, 'turn on the wireless
loud.'
'We're not going to have a row,' said her husband, Arthur Crewe,
in a voice trembling with patience. 'I only ask a plain question, what
you mean you can't ask him where he's going when he goes out?'
Mavis switched on the wireless to a roar. Then she herself shouted
above it.
'If you want to know where he goes, ask him yourself.'
'If you can't ask him how can I ask him?' Arthur said in compe-
tition with the revue on the wireless.
'What's it matter where he goes? You can't keep running about
after him like he was a baby. He's thirteen now.'
'You ought to a kept some control of him. Of course it's too late
now –'
'Why didn't you keep some control –'
'How can I be at my work and control the kids same time? If you
was –'
'There's no need to swear,' Mavis said.

'I didn't swear. But I bloody well will, and there's no need to shout.' He turned off the wireless and silence occurred, bringing a definite aural sensation.

'Turn on that wireless. If we're going to have a row I'm not letting the neighbours get to know,' Mavis said.

'Leave it be,' Arthur said, effortful with peace. 'There's not going to be any row.'

Dixie came downstairs. 'What's all the row?' she said.

'Your step-dad's on about young Leslie. Expects me to ask him where he's going when he goes out. I say, why don't *he* ask if he wants to know. I haven't got eyes in the back of my head, have I?'

'Sh-sh-sh. Don't raise your voice,' Arthur said.

'He's afraid to say a word to Leslie,' Dixie said.

'That's just about it,' said her mother.

'Who's afraid?' Arthur shouted.

'You are,' Mavis shouted.

'I'm not afraid. You're afraid ...'

'Keep time,' said Trevor. 'All keep in time. It's psychological.'

And so they all three trod in time up the stone stairs of Lightbody Buildings. Twice, a door opened on a landing, a head looked out, and the door shut quickly again. Trevor and his followers stamped louder as they approached Nelly Mahone's. Trevor beat like a policeman thrice on her door, and placed his ear to the crack.

There was a shuffling sound, a light switch clicked, then silence. Trevor beat again.

'Who is it?' Nelly said from immediately on the other side of the door.

'Police agents,' Trevor said.

The light switch clicked again, and Nelly opened the door a fragment.

Trevor pushed it wide open and walked in, followed by Collie and Leslie.

Leslie said, 'I'm not stopping in this dirty hole,' and made to leave.

Trevor caught him by the coat and worked him to a standstill.

'It's all clean dirt,' Nelly said.

'Sit over there,' Trevor said to Nelly, pointing to a chair beside the table. She did so.

He sat himself on the edge of the table and pointed to the edge of the bed for Leslie and the lopsided armchair for Collie.

'We come to talk business,' Trevor said, 'concerning a Mr Dougal Douglas.'

'Never heard of him,' Nelly said.

'No?' Trevor said, folding his arms.

'Supposed to be police agents, are you? Well, you can be moving off if you don't want trouble. There's a gentleman asleep next door. I only got to raise me voice and –'

Collie and Leslie looked at the wall towards which Nelly pointed.

'Nark it,' Trevor said. 'He's gone to football this afternoon. Now, about Mr Dougal Douglas –'

'Never heard of him,' Nelly said.

Trevor leaned forward slightly towards her and, taking a lock of her long hair in his hand, twitched it sharply.

'Help! Murder! Police!' Nelly said.

Trevor put his big hand over her mouth and spoke to her.

'Listen, Nelly, for your own good. We got money for you.'

Nelly struggled, her yellow eyeballs were big.

'I get my boys to rough you up if you won't listen, Nelly. Won't we, boys?'

'That's right,' Collie said.

'Won't we, boys?' Trevor said, looking at Leslie.

'Sure,' said Leslie.

Trevor removed his hand, now wet, from Nelly's mouth, and wiped it on the side of his trousers. He took a large wallet from his pocket, and flicked through a pile of notes.

'He's at Miss Frierne's up the Rye,' Nelly said.

Trevor laid his wallet on the table and folding his arms, looked hard at Nelly.

'He got a job at Meadows Meade,' Nelly said.

Trevor waited.

'He got another job at Drover Willis's under a different name. No harm in him, son.'

Trevor waited.

'That's all, son,' Nelly said.

'What's cheese?' Trevor said.

'What's what?'

Trevor pulled her hair, so that she toppled towards him from her chair.

'I'll find out more. I only seen him once,' Nelly said.

'What he want with you?'

'Huh?'

'You heard me.'

Nelly looked at the two others, then back at Trevor.

'The boys is under age,' she remarked, and her eyes flicked a little to reveal that her brain was working.

'I ask you a question,' Trevor said. 'What Mr Dougal Douglas come to you for?'

'About the girl,' she said.

'What girl?'

'He's after Beauty,' she said. 'He want me to find out where she live and that. You better go and see what he's up to. Probable he's with her now.'

'Who's his gang?' Trevor inquired, reaching for Nelly's hair.

She jumped away from him. Leslie's nerve gave way and he ran to Nelly and hit her on the face.

'Murder!' Nelly screamed.

Trevor put his hand over her mouth, and signalled with his eyes to Collie, who went to the door, opened it a little way, listened, then shut it again. Collie then struck Leslie, who backed on to the bed.

Trevor, with his big hand on Nelly's mouth, whispered softly in her ear.

'Who's his gang, Nelly? What's the code key? Ten quid to you, Nelly.'

She squirmed and he took his moist hand from her mouth. 'Who's his gang?'

'He goes with Miss Coverdale sometimes. He goes with that fair-haired lady controller that's gone to Drover Willis's. That's all I know of his company.'

'Who are the fellows?'

'I'll find out,' she said, 'I'll find out, son. Have a heart.'

'Who's Rose Hathaway?'

'Never heard of her.'

Trevor took Dougal's rolled-up exercise book from an inside pocket and spreading it out at the page read out the bit about that Rose

Hathaway who was buried at a hundred and three. 'That mean anything to you?' Trevor said.

'It sounds all wrong. I'll ask him.'

'You won't. You'll find out your own way. Not a word we been here, get that?'

'It's only his larks. He's off his nut, son.'

'Did he by any chance bring Humphrey Place here with him?'

'Who?'

Trevor twisted her arm.

'Humphrey Place. Goes with Dixie Morse.'

'No, never seen him but once at the Grapes.'

'You'll be seeing *us* again,' Trevor said.

He went down the dark stone stairs followed by Leslie and Collie.

'Killing herself,' Merle said, 'that's what she is, for money. Then she comes in to the pool dropping tired next day, not fit for the job. I said to her, "Dixie," I said, "what time did you go to bed last night?" "I consider that a personal question, Miss Coverdale," she says. "Oh," I says, "well, if it isn't a personal question will you kindly type these two reports over again? There's five mistakes on one and six on the other." "Oh!" she said, "what mistakes?" Because she won't own up to her mistakes till you put them under her nose. I said, "These mistakes as marked." She said "Oh!" I said, "You've been doing nothing but yawn yawn yawn all week." Well, at tea-break when Dixie was out Connie says to me, "Miss Coverdale, it's Dixie's evening job making her tired." "Evening job?" I said. She said, "Yes, she's an usherette at the Regal from six-thirty to ten-thirty, makes extra for her wedding savings." "Well," I said, "no wonder she can't do her job here!"'

Dougal flashed an invisible cinema-torch on to the sprightly summer turf of the Rye. 'Mind the step, Madam. Three-and-sixes on the right.'

Merle began to laugh from her chest. Suddenly she sat down on the Rye and began to cry. 'God!' she said. 'Dougal, I've had a rotten life.'

'And it isn't over yet,' Dougal said, sitting down beside her at a little distance. 'There might be worse ahead.'

'First my parents,' she said. 'Too possessive. They're full of themselves. They don't think anything of me myself. They like to be able to say "Merle's head of the pool at Meadows Meade," but that's about all there is to it. I broke away and of course like a fool took up with Mr Druce. Now I can't get away from him, somehow. You've unsettled me, Dougal, since you came to Peckham. I shall have a nervous breakdown, I can see it coming.'

'If you do,' Dougal said, 'I won't come near you. I can't bear sickness of any sort.'

'Dougal,' she said, 'I was counting on you to help me to get away from Mr Druce.'

'Get another job,' he said, 'and refuse to see him any more. It's easy.'

'Oh, everything's easy for you. You're free.'

'Aren't you free?' Dougal said.

'Yes, as far as the law goes.'

'Well, stop seeing Druce.'

'After six years, going on seven, Dougal, I'm tied in a sort of way. And what sort of job would I get at thirty-eight?'

'You would have to come down,' Dougal said.

'After being head of the pool,' she said, 'I couldn't. I've got to think of my pride. And there's the upkeep of my flat. Mr Druce puts a bit towards it.'

'People are looking at you crying,' Dougal said, 'and they think it's because of me.'

'So it is in a way. I've had a rotten life.'

'Goodness, look at that,' Dougal said.

She looked upward to where he was pointing.

'What?' she said.

'Up there,' Dougal said; 'trees in the sky.'

'What are you talking about? I don't see anything.'

'Look properly,' Dougal said, 'up there. And don't look away because Mr Druce is watching us from behind the pavilion.'

She looked at Dougal.

'Keep looking up,' he said, 'at the trees with red tassels in the sky. Look, where I'm pointing.'

Several people who were crossing the Rye stopped to look up at where Dougal was pointing. Dougal said to them. 'A new idea. Did you see it in the papers? Planting trees and shrubs in the sky. Look there – it's a tip of a pine.'

'I think I *do* see something,' said a girl.

Most of the crowd moved sceptically away, still glancing upward now and then. Dougal brought Merle to her feet and drifted along with the others.

'Is he still there?' Merle said.

'Yes. He must be tired of going up and down in lifts.'

'Oh, he only does that on Saturday mornings. He usually stays at home in the afternoons. He comes to me in the evenings. I've got a rotten life. Sometimes I think I'll swallow a bottle of aspirins.'

'That doesn't work,' Dougal said. 'It only makes you ill. And the very thought of illness is abhorrent to me.'

'He's keen on you,' Merle said.

'I know he is, but *he* doesn't.'

'He must do if he's keen –'

'Not at all. I'm his first waking experience of an attractive man.'

'You fancy yourself.'

'No, Mr Druce does that.'

'With your crooked shoulder,' she said, 'you're not all that much cop.'

'Advise Druce on those lines,' he said.

'He doesn't take my advice any more.'

'How long would you give him with the firm?'

'Well, since he's started to slip, I've debated that question a lot. The business is on the decline. It's a worry, I mean about my flat, if Mr Druce loses his job.'

'I'd give him three months,' Dougal said.

Merle started to cry again, walking towards the streets with Dougal. 'Is he still there?' she said. Dougal did a dancer's pirouette, round and round, and stopped once more by Merle's side.

'He's walking away in the other direction.'

'Oh, I wonder where he's going?'

'Home to Dulwich, I expect.'

'It's immoral,' Merle said, 'the way he goes back to that woman in that house. They never say a word to each other.'

'Stop grinning. You look awful with your red eyes. It detracts from the Okapi look. But all the same, what a long neck you've got.'

She put her hand up to her throat and moved it up her long neck.

'Mr Druce squeezed it tight the other day,' she said, 'for fun, but I got a fright.'

'It looks like a maniac's delight, your neck,' Dougal said.

'Well, you've not got much of one, with your shoulder up round your ear.'

'A short neck denotes a good mind,' Dougal said. 'You see, the messages go quicker to the brain because they've shorter to go.' He bent and touched his toes. 'Suppose the message starts down here. Well, it comes up here –'

'Watch out, people are looking.'

They were in the middle of Rye Lane, flowing with shopping women and prams. A pram bumped into Dougal as he stood upright, causing him to barge forward into two women who stood talking. Dougal embraced them with wide arms. 'Darlings, watch where you're going,' he said. They beamed at each other and at him.

'Charming, aren't you?' Merle said. 'There's a man leaning out of that car parked outside Higgins and Jones, seems to be watching you.'

Dougal looked across the road. 'Mr Willis is watching me,' he said. 'Come and meet Mr Willis.' He took her arm to cross the road.

'I'm not dressed for an introduction,' Merle said.

'You are only an object of human research,' Dougal said, guiding her obliquely through the traffic towards Mr Willis.

'I'm just waiting for my wife. She's shopping in there,' Mr Willis explained. Now that Dougal had approached him he seemed rather embarrassed. 'I wasn't sure it was you, Mr Dougal,' he explained. 'I was just looking to see. A bit short-sighted.'

'Miss Merle Coverdale, one of my unofficial helpers,' Dougal said uppishly. 'Interesting,' he said, 'to see what Peckham does on its Saturday afternoons.'

'Yes, quite.' Mr Willis pinkly took Merle's hand and glanced towards the shop door.

Dougal gave a reserved nod and, as dismissing Mr Willis from his thoughts, led Merle away.

'Why did he call you Mr Dougal?' Merle said.

'Because he's my social inferior. Formerly a footman in our family.'

'What's he now?'

'One of my secret agents.'

'You'd send me mad if I let you. Look what you've done to Weedin. You're driving Mr Druce up the wall.'

'I have powers of exorcism,' Dougal said, 'that's all.'

'What's that?'

'The ability to drive devils out of people.'

'I thought you said you were a devil yourself.'

'The two states are not incompatible. Come to the police station.'

'Where are we going, Dougal?'

'The police station. I want to see the excavation.'

He took her into the station yard where he had already made himself known as an interested archaeologist. By the coal-heap was a wooden construction above a cavity already some feet deep. Work had stopped for the week-end. They peered inside.

'The tunnel leads up to Nunhead,' Dougal said, 'the nuns used to use it. They packed up one night over a hundred years ago, and did a flit, and left a lot of debts behind them.'

A policeman came up to them with quiet steps and, pointing to the coal-heap, said, 'The penitential cell stood in that corner. Afternoon, sir.'

'Goodness, you gave me a fright,' Merle said.

'There's bodies of nuns down there, miss,' the policeman said.

Merle had gone home to await Mr Druce. Dougal walked up to Costa's Café in the cool of the evening. Eight people were inside, among them Humphrey and Dixie, seated at a separate table eating the remains of sausage and egg. Humphrey kicked out a chair at their table for Dougal to sit down upon. Dixie touched the corners of her mouth with a paper napkin, and carefully picking up her knife and fork, continued eating, turning her head a little obliquely to receive each small mouthful. Humphrey had just finished. He set down his knife and fork on the plate and pushed the plate away. He rubbed the palms of his hands together twice and said to Dougal,

'How's life?'

'It exists,' Dougal said, and looked about him.

'You had a distinguished visitor this afternoon. But you'd just gone out. The old lady was out and I answered to him. He wouldn't leave his name. But of course I knew it. Mr Druce of Meadows Meade. Dixie pointed him out to me once, didn't you, Dixie?'

'Yes,' Dixie said.

'He followed me all over the Rye, so greatly did Mr Druce wish to see me,' Dougal said.

'If I was you,' Humphrey said, 'I'd keep to normal working hours. Then he wouldn't have any call on you Saturday afternoons – would he, Dixie?'

'I suppose not,' Dixie said.

'Coffee for three,' Dougal said to the waiter.

'You had another visitor, about four o'clock,' Humphrey said. 'I'll give you a clue. She had a pot of flowers and a big parcel.'

'Elaine,' Dougal said.

The waiter brought three cups of coffee, one in his right hand and two – one resting on the other – in his left. These he placed carefully on the table. Dixie's slopped over in her saucer. She looked at the saucer.

'Swap with me,' Humphrey said.

'Have mine,' Dougal said.

She allowed Humphrey to exchange his saucer with hers. He tipped the contents of the saucer into his coffee, sipped it, and set it down.

'Sugar,' he said.

Dougal passed the sugar to Dixie.

She said, 'Thank you.' She took two lumps, dropped them in her coffee, and stirred it, watching it intently.

Humphrey put three lumps in his coffee, stirred it rapidly, tasted it. He pushed the sugar bowl over to Dougal, who took a lump and put it in his mouth.

'I let her go up to your room,' Humphrey said. 'She said she wanted to put in some personal touches. There was the pot of flowers and some cretonne cushions. The old lady was out. I thought it nice of Elaine to do that – wasn't it nice, Dixie?'

'Wasn't what nice?'

'Elaine coming to introduce feminine touches in Dougal's room.'

'I suppose so.'

'Feeling all right?' Humphrey said to her.

'I suppose so.'

'Do you want to go on somewhere else or do you want to stay here?'

'Anything you like.'

'Have a cake.'

'No thank you.'

'Why does your brother go hungry?' Dougal said to her.

'Whose brother goes hungry?'

'Yours. Leslie.'

'What you mean, goes hungry?'

'He came round scrounging doughnuts off my landlady the other day,' Dougal said.

Humphrey rubbed the palms of his hands together and smiled at Dougal. 'Oh, kids, you know what they're like.'

'I won't stand for him saying anything against Leslie,' Dixie said, looking round to see if anyone at the other tables was listening. 'Our Leslie isn't a scrounger. It's a lie.'

'It is not a lie,' Dougal said.

'I'll speak to my step-dad,' Dixie said.

'I should,' Dougal said.

'What's a doughnut to a kid?' Humphrey said to them both. 'Don't make something out of nothing. Don't *start*.'

'Who started?' Dixie said.

'You did, a matter of fact,' Humphrey said, 'with your bad manners. You could hardly say hallo to Dougal when he came in.'

'That's right, take his part,' she said. 'Well, I'm not staying here to be insulted.'

She rose and picked up her bag. Dougal pulled her down to her chair again.

'Take your hand off me,' she said, and rose.

Humphrey pulled her down again.

She remained seated, looking ahead into the far distance.

'There's Beauty just come in,' Dougal said.

Dixie turned her head to see Beauty. Then she resumed her fixed gaze.

Dougal whistled in Beauty's direction.

'I shouldn't do that,' Humphrey said.

'My God, he's supposed to be a professional man,' Dixie said, 'and he opens his mouth and whistles at a girl.'

Dougal whistled again.

Beauty raised her eyebrows.

'You'll have Trevor Lomas in after us,' Humphrey said. The waiter and Costa himself came and hovered round their table.

'Come on up to the Harbinger,' Dougal said, 'and we'll take Beauty with us.'

'Now look. I quite *like* Trevor,' Humphrey said.

'He's to be best man at our wedding,' Dixie said. 'He's got a good job with prospects and sticks in to it.'

Dougal whistled. Then he called across two tables to Beauty, 'Waiting for somebody?'

Beauty dropped her lashes. 'Not in particular,' she said.

'Coming up to the Harbinger?'

'Don't mind.'

Dixie said, 'Well, *I* do. I'm fussy about my company.'

'What she say?' Beauty said, jerking herself upright in support of the question.

'I said,' said Dixie, 'that I've got another appointment.'

'Beauty and I will be getting along then,' Dougal said. He went across to Beauty who was preparing to comb her hair.

Humphrey said, 'After all, Dixie, we've got nothing else to do. It might look funny if we don't go with Dougal. If Trevor finds out he's been to a pub with his girl –'

'You're bored with me – *I* know,' Dixie said. 'My company isn't good enough for you as soon as Dougal comes on the scene.'

'Such compliments as you pay me!' Dougal said across to her.

'I was not aware I was addressing you,' Dixie said.

'All right, Dixie, we'll stop here,' Humphrey said.

Dougal was holding up a small mirror while the girl combed her long copper-coloured hair over the table.

Dixie's eyes then switched over to Dougal. She gave a long sigh. 'I suppose we'd better go to the pub with them,' she said, 'or you'll say I spoiled your evening.'

'No necessity,' Beauty said as she put away her comb and patted her handbag.

'We might enjoy ourselves,' Humphrey said.

Dixie got her things together rather excitedly. But she said, 'Oh, it isn't my idea of a night out.'

And so they followed Dougal and Beauty up Rye Lane to the Harbinger. Beauty was half-way through the door of the saloon bar, but Dougal had stopped to look into the darkness of the Rye beyond the swimming baths, from which came the sound of a drunken woman approaching; and yet as it came nearer, it turned out not to be a drunken woman, but Nelly proclaiming.

Humphrey and Dixie had reached the pub door. 'It's only Nelly,' Humphrey said, and he pushed Dougal towards the doorway in which Beauty was waiting.

'I like listening to Nelly,' Dougal said, 'for my human research.'

'Oh, get inside for goodness' sake,' Dixie said as Nelly appeared in the street light.

'Six things,' Nelly declaimed, 'there are which the Lord hateth, and the seventh his soul detesteth. Haughty eyes, a lying tongue, hands that shed innocent blood. See me in the morning. A heart that deviseth wicked plots, feet that are swift to run into mischief. Ten at Paley's yard. A deceitful witness that uttereth lies. Meeting-house Lane. And him that soweth discord among brethren.'

'Nelly's had a few,' Humphrey said as they pushed into the bar. 'She's a bit shaky on the pins tonight.'

A bright spiky chandelier and a row of glittering crystal lamps set against a mirror behind the bar – though in fact these had been installed since the war – were designed to preserve in theory the pub's vintage fame in the old Camberwell Palace days. The chief barmaid had a tiny nose and a big chin; she was a middle-aged woman of twenty-five. The barman was small and lithe. He kept swinging to and fro on the balls of his feet.

Beauty wanted a Martini. Dixie, at first under the impression that Humphrey was buying the round, asked for a ginger ale, but when she perceived that Dougal was to pay for the drinks, she said, 'Gin and ginger ale.' Humphrey and Dougal carried to a table the girls' drinks and their own half-pints of mild which glittered in knobbly-moulded glass mugs like versions of the chandelier. Round the wall were hung signed photographs of old-time variety actors with such names, meaningless to most but oddly suggestive, as Flora Finch and Ford Sterling, who were generally assumed to be Edwardian stars. An upright piano placed flat against the wall caused Tony the pianist to see little of the life of the house, except when he turned round for a rest between numbers. Tony's face was not merely pale but quite bloodless. He wore a navy-blue coat over a very white shirt, the shirt buttoned up to the neck with no tie. His half-pint mug, constantly replenished by the customers, stood on an invariable spot on the right-hand side of the piano-top. As he played, he swung his shoulders from side to side and bent over the piano occasionally to stress his notes. He might, from this back view, have been in an enthusiastic mood, but when he turned round it was obvious he was not. It was Tony's lot to play tunes of the nineteen-tens and -twenties, to the accompaniment of slightly jeering comments from the customers, and as he stooped over to execute 'Charmain', Beauty said to him, 'Groove in, Tony.' He ignored this as he had ignored all remarks for the past nineteen months. 'Go, man, go,' someone suggested. 'Leave him alone,' the barmaid said. 'You just show up your ignorance. He's a beautiful player. It's period stuff. He got to play it like that.' Tony finished his number, took down his beer and turned his melancholy front to the company.

'Got any rock and cha-cha on your list, Tony?'

'Rev up to it, son. Groove in.'

Tony turned, replaced his beer on top of the piano, and rippled his hands over 'Ramona'.

'Go, man, go.'

'Any more of that,' said the barmaid, 'and you go man go outside.'

'Yes, that's what *I* say. Tony's the pops.'

'Here's a pint, Tony. Cheer up, son, it may never happen.'

At ten past nine Trevor Lomas entered the pub followed by Collie Gould. Trevor edged in to the bar and stood with his back to it, leaning on an elbow and surveying as it were the passing scene.

'Hallo, Trevor,' Dixie said.

'Hi, Dixie,' Trevor replied severely.

'Hi,' Collie Gould said.

Beauty, who was on her fourth Martini, bowed graciously, and had some difficulty in regaining her upright posture.

The barmaid said, 'Are you ordering, sir?'

Trevor said over his shoulder, 'Two pints bitter.' He lit a cigarette and blew out the smoke very very slowly.

'Trev,' Collie said in a low voice, 'Trev, don't muck it up.'

'I'm being patient,' Trevor said through half-closed lips. 'I'm being very very patient. But if –'

'Trev,' Collie said, 'Trev, think of the lolly. Them notebooks.'

Trevor threw half-a-crown backwards on the counter.

'Manners,' the barmaid said as she rang the till. She banged his change on the counter, where Trevor let it lie.

Dougal and Humphrey approached the bar with four empty glasses. 'Ginger ale only,' Dixie called after them, since it was Humphrey's turn.

'One Martini. Two half milds. One *gin* and ginger ale,' Humphrey said to the barman. And he invited Trevor to join them by pointing to their table with his ear.

Trevor did not move. Collie was watching Trevor.

Dougal got out some money.

'My turn,' Humphrey said, fishing out his money.

Dougal picked half a crown from his money and, leaning his back against the bar, tossed it over his shoulder to the counter. He then lit a cigarette and blew out the smoke very slowly, pulling his face to a grave length and batting his eyelashes.

Beauty shouted, 'Doug, you're a boy! Dig Doug! He's got you, Trev. He does Trevor to a T.' Tony was playing the 'St Louis Blues'.

'Trev,' Collie said, 'don't, Trev, don't.'

Trevor raised his sparkling pint glass and smashed the top on the edge of the counter. In his hand remained the bottom half with six spikes of glass sticking up from it. He lunged it forward at Dougal's face. At the same swift moment Dougal leaned back, back, until the crown of his head touched the bar. The spikes of glass went full into one side of Humphrey's face which had been turned in profile. Dougal bent and caught Trevor's legs while another man pulled Trevor's collar until presently he lay pinned by a number of hands to the floor. Humphrey was being attended by another number of hands, and was taken to the back premises, the barmaid holding to his face a large thick towel which was becoming redder and redder.

The barman shouted above the din, 'Outside, all'

Most of the people were leaving in any case lest they should be questioned. To those who lingered the barman shouted, 'Outside, all, or I'll call the police.'

Trevor found himself free to get to his feet and he left, followed by Collie and Beauty, who was seen to spit at Trevor before she clicked her way up Rye Lane.

Dixie remained behind with Dougal. She was saying to him, 'It was meant for *you*. Dirty swine you were to duck.'

'Outside or I call the police,' the barman said, bouncing up and down on the balls of his feet.

'We were with the chap that's hurt,' Dougal said, 'and if we can't collect him *I'll* call the police.'

'Follow me,' said the barman.

Humphrey was holding his head over a bowl while cold water was being poured over his wounds by Tony, who seemed to take this as one of his boring evening duties.

'Goodness, you look terrible,' Dougal said. 'It must be my fatal flaw, but I doubt if I can bear to look.'

'Dirty swine, he is,' Dixie said, 'letting another fellow have it instead of himself.'

'Shut up, will you?' Humphrey seemed to say.

They got into Humphrey's car, speedily assisted by the barman. Dougal drove, first taking Dixie home. She said to him, 'I could spit at you,' and slammed the car door.

'Oh, shut up,' Humphrey said, as well as he could.

Dougal next drove Humphrey to the outpatient department of St George's Hospital. 'Though it pains me to cross the river,' Dougal said, 'I think we'd better avoid the southern region for tonight.'

He told a story about Humphrey having tripped over a milk-bottle as he got out of his car, the milk-bottle having splintered and Humphrey fallen on his face among the splinters. Humphrey nodded agreement as the nurse dressed and plastered his wounds. Dougal gave Humphrey's name as Mr Dougal-Douglas, care of Miss Cheeseman, 14 Chelsea Rise, sw3. Humphrey was told to return within a week. They then went home to Miss Frierne's.

'And I won't even see her again till next Saturday night on account of her doing week-nights as an usherette at the Regal,' Humphrey said to Dougal at a quarter to twelve that night. He sat up in bed in striped pyjamas, talking as much as possible; but the strips of plaster on his cheek caused him to speak rather out of the opposite side of his mouth. 'And she won't think of taking one day off of her holidays this year on account of the honeymoon in September. It's nothing but save, save, save. You'd think I wasn't earning good money the way she goes on. And result, she's losing her sex.'

Dougal crouched over the gas-ring with a fork, pushing the bacon about in the frying-pan. He removed the bacon on to a plate, then broke two eggs into the pan.

'I wouldn't marry her,' Dougal said, 'if you paid me.'

'My sister Elsie doesn't like her,' Humphrey said out of the side of his mouth.

Dougal stood up and took the plate of bacon in his hand. He held this at some way from his body and looked at it, moving it slightly back and forth towards him, as if it were a book he was reading, and he short-sighted.

Dougal read from the book: 'Wilt thou take this woman,' he said with a deep ecclesiastical throb, 'to be thai wedded waif?'

Then he put the plate aside and knelt; he was a sinister goggling bridegroom. 'No,' he declared to the ceiling, 'I won't, quite frankly.'

'Christ, don't make me laugh, it pulls the plaster.'

Dougal dished out the eggs and bacon. He cut up the bacon small for Humphrey.

'You shouldn't have any scars if you're careful and get your face regularly dressed, they said.'

Humphrey stroked his wounded cheek.

'Scars wouldn't worry me. Might worry Dixie.'

'As a qualified refrigerator engineer and a union man you could have your pick of the girls.'

'I know, but I want Dixie.' He put the eggs and bacon slowly away into the side of his mouth.

The rain of a cold summer morning fell on Nelly Mahone as she sat on a heap of disused lorry tyres in the yard of Paley's, scrap merchants of Meeting-house Lane. She had been waiting since ten past nine although she did not expect Dougal to arrive until ten o'clock. He came at five past ten, bobbing up and down under an umbrella.

'They come to see me Saturday,' she said at once. 'Trevor Lomas, Collie Gould, Leslie Crewe. They treated me bad.'

'You've got wet,' Dougal said. 'Why didn't you take shelter?'

She looked round the yard. 'Got to be careful where you go, son. Stand up in the open, they can only tell you to move on. But go inside a place, they can call the cops.' Her nose thrust forward towards the police station at the corner of the lane.

Dougal looked round the yard for possible shelter. The bodies of two lorries, bashed in from bad accidents, stood lopsided in a corner. On a low wooden cradle stood a house-boat. 'We'll go into the boat.'

'Oh, I couldn't get up there.'

Dougal kicked a wooden crate over and over till it stood beneath the door of the boat. He pulled the door-handle. Eventually it gave way. He climbed in, then out again, and took Nelly by the arm.

'Up you go, Nelly.'

'What if the cops come?'

'I'm in with them,' Dougal said.

'Jesus, that's not your game?'

'Up you go.'

He heaved her up and settled in the boat beside her on a torn upholstered seat. Some sad cretonne curtains still drooped in the windows. Dougal drew them across the windows as far as was possible.

'I feel that ill,' Nelly said.

'I'm not too keen on illness,' Dougal said.

'Nor me. They come to ask after you,' Nelly said. 'They found out you was seeing me. They got your code. They want to know what's cheese. They want to know what's your code key, they offer me ten quid. They want to know who's your gang.'

'I'm in with the cops, tell them.'

'That I would never believe. They want to know who's Rose Hathaway. They'll be back again. I got to tell them something.'

'Tell them I'm paid by the police to investigate certain irregularities in the industrial life of Peckham in the first place. See, Nelly? I mean crime at the top in the wee factories. And secondly –'

Her yellowish eyes and wet grey hair turned towards him in a startled way.

'If I thought you was a nark –'

'Investigator,' Dougal said. 'It all comes under human research. And secondly my job covers various departments of youthful terrorism. So you can just tell me, Nelly, what they did to you on Saturday afternoon.'

'Ah, they didn't do nothing out of the way.'

'You said they treated you roughly.'

'No, not so to get them in trouble.'

Dougal took out an envelope. 'Your ten pounds,' he said.

'You can keep it,' Nelly said. 'I'm going on my way.'

'Feel my head, Nelly.' He guided her hand to the two small bumps among his curls.

'Cancer of the brain a-coming on,' she said.

'Nelly, I had a pair of horns like a goat when I was born. I lost them in a fight at a later date.'

'Holy Mary, let me out of here. I don't know whether I'm coming or going with you.'

Dougal stood up and found that by standing astride in the middle of the boat he could make it rock. So he rocked it for a while and sang a sailor's song to Nelly.

Then he helped her to climb down from the boat, put up his umbrella, and tried to catch up with her as she hurried out of the scrap yard. A policeman, coming out of the station, at the corner, nodded to Dougal.

'I'll be going into the station, then, Nelly,' Dougal said. 'To see my chums.'

She stared at him, then spat on the rainy pavement.

'And I don't mind,' Dougal said, 'if you tell Trevor Lomas what I'm doing. You can tell him if he returns my notebooks to me there will be nothing further said. We policemen have got to keep our records and our secret codes, you realize.'

She moved sideways away from him, watching the traffic so that she could cross at the earliest moment.

'You and I,' Dougal said, 'won't be molested from that quarter for a week or two if you give them the tip-off.'

He went into the station yard to see how the excavations were getting on. He discovered that the tunnel itself was now visible from the top of the shaft.

Dougal pointed out to his policemen friends the evidence of the Thames silt in the under-soil. 'One time,' he said, 'the Thames was five miles wide, and it covered all Peckham.'

So they understood, they said, from other archaeologists who were interested in the excavation.

'Hope I'm not troubling you if I pop in like this from time to time?' Dougal said.

'No, sir, you're welcome. We get people from the papers some-times as well as students. Did you read of the finds?'

Towards evening a parcel was delivered at Miss Frierne's addressed to Dougal. It contained his notebooks.

'I hope to remain with you,' Dougal said to Miss Frierne, 'for at least two months. For I see no call upon me to remove from Peckham as yet.'

'If I'm still alive . . .' Miss Frierne said. 'I saw that man again this morning. I could swear it was my brother.'

'You didn't speak to him?'

'No. Something stopped me.' She began to cry.

'Who put the pot of indoor creeping ivy in my room?' Dougal said. 'Was it my little dog-toothed blonde process-controller?'

'Yes, it was a scraggy little blonde. Looks as if she could do with a good feed. They all do.'

Mr Druce whispered, 'I couldn't manage it the other night. Things were difficult.'

'I sat at the Dragon in Dulwich from nine till closing time,' Dougal said, 'and you didn't come.'

'I couldn't get away. Mrs Druce was on the watch. If you'd come to that place in Soho –'

Dougal consulted his pocket diary. He shut it and put it away. 'Next month it would have to be. This month my duties press.' He rose and walked up and down Mr Druce's office as with something on his mind.

'I called for you last Saturday,' Mr Druce said. 'I thought you would care for a spin.'

'So I understand,' Dougal said absently. 'I believe I was research-ing on Miss Coverdale that afternoon.' Dougal smiled at Mr Druce. 'Interrogating her, you know.'

'Oh, yes.'

'Her devotion to you is quite remarkable,' Dougal said. 'She spoke of you continually.'

'As a matter of interest, what did she say? Look, Dougal, you can't trust everyone –'

Dougal looked at his watch. 'Goodness,' he said, 'the time.

What I came to see you about – the question of my increase in salary.'

'It's going through,' Mr Druce said. 'I put it to the Board that since Weedin's breakdown, a great deal of extra work has fallen on your shoulders.'

Dougal massaged both his shoulders, first his high one, then his low one.

'Dougal,' said Mr Druce.

'Vincent,' said Dougal, and departed.

EIGHT

Joyce Willis said, 'Quite frankly, the first time Richard invited you to dinner I knew we'd found the answer. Richard didn't see it at first, quite frankly, but I think he's beginning to see it now.'

She crossed the room, moving her long hips, and looked out of the bow window into the August evening. 'Richard should be in any moment,' she said. She touched her throat with her fine fingers. She put to rights a cushion in the window-seat.

Still standing, she lifted her glass, and sipped, and put it down on a low table. She crossed the room and sat on a chair upholstered in deep pink brocade.

'I feel I can really *talk* to you now,' she said. 'I feel we've known each other for years.'

She said, 'The Drovers *were* getting the upper hand. Richard was, well, quite frankly, being pushed into the position of subordinate partner.

'The nephew, Mark Bewlay – that's *her* nephew, of course – came to the firm two – was it two? – no, it was three years ago, imagine it, in October. And he was supposed to go through the factory from A to Z. Well, quite frankly he was sitting on the Board within six months. Then the son John came straight down from Oxford last year, and the same thing again. The Board's reeking with Drovers.

'One of Richard's great mistakes – I'm speaking to you quite frankly,' she said, 'was insisting on our *living* in Peckham. Well, the house is all right – but I mean, the environment. There are simply no people in the place. Our friends always get lost finding the way here; they drive round for hours. And there are blacks at the other end of the Avenue, you know. I mean, it's so silly.

'Richard's a Scot of course,' she said, 'and in a way that's why I think you understand his position. He's so scrupulously industrious and pathologically honest. And it's rather sweet in a way. Yes, I must say that. He simply doesn't see that the Drovers living in Sussex in a Georgian rectory gives them a big advantage. A big advantage. It's psychological.'

She said, 'Yes, Richard insists on living near the job, as he says. And quite frankly, I have to put up with a good deal of condescension from Queenie Drover, although she's sweet in a way. She knows of course that Richard's a bit old-fashioned and prides himself on being a *real merchant*, they both know, the Drovers. They know it only too well.'

She filled both glasses with sherry, turning the good bones of her wrists and holding the glasses at the ends of her long fingers with their lacquered nails and the bright emerald. She looked at herself, before she sat down, in the gilt-framed glass and turned back a wisp of her short dark-gold hair. Her face was oval; she posed it to one side; she said, 'Of course it has been a disappointment that we had no children. If there had been a son to support Richard on the Board ... Sometimes I feel, quite frankly, the firm should be called Drover, Drover, Drover Willis, not just Drover Willis.

'Richard was touched a few weeks ago,' she said, 'he told me so, when he met you one Saturday afternoon while he was waiting for me outside the shop, and he saw you working away on your Saturday afternoon, spending your Saturday afternoon with a Peckham girl, trying to get to know the types. Richard thinks you are brilliant, you know. A fine brain and a sound moral sense, he told me, quite frankly, and he thinks you're absolutely wasted in the personnel research job. The thing about you – and I saw it long before Richard and I'm not just saying it because you're here – you're so young and energetic, and yet so *steady*. I suppose it's being a Scot.

'Not many young fellows of your age,' she said, '– I'm not flattering you – and of your qualifications and ability would be prepared to settle down as you have done in a place like Peckham where the scope for any kind of gaiety is so limited, there's nothing to do and there are no young people for you to meet. I'm speaking quite frankly, as I would to my own son if I had one.

'I feel towards you,' she said, 'as to a son. I hope – I would always hope – to count you as one of the family although, as you know, there are only Richard and me. I was so interested in your conversation the other night about so many things I didn't quite frankly know existed in this area. The Camberwell Art Gallery I knew of course; but the excavations of the tunnel – I had only read of its progress in the *South London Observer* – I didn't dream there was anything so serious and learned behind it.'

She turned and plumped out the cushion behind her. She looked at her pointed toes. 'You must sometimes come to town with us. We go to the theatre at least once a week,' she said.

She said, 'The idea that you should come on the Board with Richard in the autumn is an excellent one. It will almost be like having a Willis in the firm. Your way of speaking is so like Richard's – I mean, not just the accent, but well, quite frankly, I mean, you don't say *much*, but when you say something it's the right thing. Richard needs you and I think I'm right in saying it's an ideal prospect for a young man of your temperament, and it means serious responsibility and an established position within a matter of five or six years. You have this way of approaching life seriously, not just here today and gone tomorrow, and it appeals to Richard. Richard is a judge of character. One day the firm might be Drover, Willis & Dougal. Just a moment –'

She went over to the window, smoothing her waist, and glanced through the window as a car drew up in the small curved drive. 'Here's Richard,' she said. 'He's been looking forward to having a serious chat with you this evening, and getting things settled before we go abroad.'

'Is that you, Jinny?'
'Yes.'
'Have you got any milk on the stove?'
'No.'
'When can I come and see you?'
'I'm getting married next week.'
'No, Jinny.'
'I'm in love with him. He was sweet when I was ill.'
'Just when I'm getting on my feet and drawing two pays for nothing,' Dougal said, 'you tell me –'
'It wouldn't have worked between us, Dougal. I'm not strong in health.'

'Well, that's that,' Dougal said.

'Miss Cheeseman's thrilled with her autobiography so far,' Jinny said. 'You'll do well, Dougal.'

'You've changed. You are using words like "sweet" and "thrilled".'

'Oh, get away. Miss Cheeseman said she was pleased.'

'She doesn't tell me that.'

'Well, she has some tiny reservations about the Peckham bits, but on the whole –'

'I'm coming over to see you, Jinny.'

'No, Dougal, I mean it.'

Dougal went in to Miss Frierne's kitchen and wept into his large pocket handkerchief.

'Are you feeling all right?' she said.

'No. My girl's getting married to another chap.'

She filled the kettle and put it down on the draining board. She opened the back door and shut it again. She took up a duster and dusted a kitchen chair, back and legs.

'You're better off without her,' she said.

'I'm not,' Dougal said, 'but I've got a fatal flaw.'

'You're not drinking at nights, Dougal?'

'No more than usual.'

She lifted the kettle and put it down again.

'Calm down,' Dougal said.

'Well, it upsets me inside to see a man upset.'

'Light the gas and put the kettle on it,' he said.

She did this, then stood and looked at him. She took off her apron.

'Sit down,' Dougal said.

She sat down.

'Stand up,' he said, 'and fetch me a tot of your gin.'

She brought two glasses and the gin bottle. 'It's only quarter past five,' she said. 'It's early to start on gin. Here's to you, son. You'll soon get over it.'

The front-door bell rang. Miss Frierne caused the bottle and glasses to disappear. The bell rang again. She went to answer it.

'Name of Frierne?' said a man's voice.

'Yes, what do you want?'

'Could I have a private word with you?'

Miss Frierne returned to the kitchen followed by a policeman.

'A man aged about seventy-nine was run over by a bus this morning on the Walworth Road. Sorry, madam, but he had the name Frierne in his pocket written on a bit of paper. He died an hour ago. Any relation you know of, madam?'

'No, I don't know of him. Must be a mistake. You can ask my neighbours if you like. I'm the only one left in the world.'

'Very good,' said the policeman, making notes.

'Did he have any other papers on him?'

'No, nothing. A pauper, poor devil.'

The policeman left.

'Well, there wasn't anything I could do if he's dead, was there?' Miss Frierne said to Dougal. She started crying. 'Except pay for the funeral. And it's hard enough keeping going and that.'

Dougal fetched out the gin again and poured two glasses. Presently he placed a kitchen chair to face the chair on which he sat. He put up his feet on it and said, 'Ever seen a corpse?' He lolled his head back, closed his eyes and opened his mouth so that the bottom jaw was sunken and rigid.

'You're callous, that's what you are,' Miss Frierne said. Then she screamed with hysterical mirth.

Humphrey sat with Mavis and Arthur Crewe in their sitting-room, touching, every now and then, two marks on his face.

'Well, if by any chance you don't have her, it's your luck,' Mavis said. 'I say it though she's my own daughter. When I was turned seventeen, eighteen, I was out with the boys every night, dancing and so forth. You wouldn't have caught me doing no evening work just for a bit of money. And there aren't so many boys willing to sit round waiting like you. She'll learn when it's too late.'

'It isn't as if she parts with any of her money,' Arthur Crewe said. 'You don't get the smell of an oil-rag out of Dixie. The more she's got the meaner she gets.'

'What's that got to do with it?' Dixie's mother said. 'You don't want anything from her, do you?'

'I never said I did. I was only saying –'

'Dixie has her generous side,' Mavis said. 'You must hand it to her, she's good to Leslie. She's always slipping him five bob here and five bob there.'

'Pity she does it,' Arthur said. 'The boy's ruined. He's money mad.'

'What you know about kids? There's nothing wrong with Leslie. He's no different from the rest. They all like money in their pockets.'

'Where's Leslie now, anyway?'

'Gone out.'

'Where?'

'How do I know? You ask him.'

'He's with Trevor Lomas,' Humphrey said. 'Up at Costa's.'

'There you are, Arthur. There's no harm in Trevor Lomas.'

'He's a bit old company for Leslie.'

'Grumble, grumble, grumble,' Mavis said, and switched on the television.

Leslie came in at eleven. He looked round the sitting-room.

'Hallo, Les,' Humphrey said.

Leslie did not speak. He went upstairs.

At half-past eleven Dixie came home. She kicked off her shoes in the sitting-room and flopped on to the sofa. 'You been here long?' she said to Humphrey.

'An hour or two.'

'Nice to be able to sit down of a summer evening,' Dixie said.

'Yes, why don't you try it?'

'Trevor Lomas says there's plenty of overtime at Freeze-eezy if anyone wants it.'

'Well, I don't want it,' Humphrey said.

'Obvious.'

'Who wants to do overtime all their lives?' Mavis said.

'I was just remarking,' Dixie said, 'what Trevor Lomas told me.'

'Overtime should be avoided except in cases of necessity,' Humphrey said, 'because eventually it reduces the normal capacity of the worker and in the long run leads to under-production, resulting in further demands for overtime. A vicious circle. Where did you see Trevor Lomas?'

'It is a case of necessity,' Dixie said, 'because we need all the money we can get.'

'That's how she goes on,' Mavis said. 'Why she can't be content to settle down with a man's good wages like other people I don't know. With a bungalow earmarked for October –'

'I want it to be a model bungalow,' Dixie said.

'You'll have your model bungalow,' Humphrey said.

'She wants a big splash wedding,' Mavis said. 'Well, Arthur and I will do what we can but *only* what we can.'

'That's right,' Arthur said.

'Dixie's entitled to the best,' Mavis said. 'She's got a model dress in view.'

'Where did you see Trevor Lomas?' Humphrey said to Dixie.

'Up at Costa's. I went in for a Coke on the way home. Any objections?'

'No, dear, no,' Humphrey said.

'Nice of you. Well, I'm going to bed, I'm tired out. You still got your scars.'

'They'll go away in time.'

'I don't mind. Trevor's got a scar.'

'I better keep my eye on Trevor Lomas,' Humphrey said.

'You better keep your eye on your friend Dougal Douglas. Trevor said he's a dick.'

'I don't believe it,' Mavis said.

'Nor do I,' said Arthur.

'No more do I,' said Humphrey.

'I know you think he's perfect,' Dixie said. 'He can do no wrong. But I'm just telling you what Trevor said. So don't say I didn't tell you.'

'Trevor's having you on,' Humphrey said. 'He doesn't like Dougal.'

'I like him,' Arthur said.

'I like him,' Mavis said. 'Our Leslie don't like him. Dixie don't like him.'

'I like him,' Humphrey said, 'My sister Elsie doesn't like him.'

'Is Mr Douglas at home?'

'Well, he's up in his room playing the typewriter at the moment,' said Miss Frierne, 'as you can hear.'

'Can I go up?'

'No, I must inquire. Come inside, please. What name?'

'Miss Coverdale.'

Miss Frierne left Miss Coverdale in that hall which was lined with wood like a coffin. The sound of the typewriter stopped. Dougal's voice called down from the second landing, 'Come up.' Miss Frierne frowned in the direction of his voice. 'Top floor,' she said to Merle.

'I'm miserable. I had to see you,' Merle said to Dougal. 'What a nice little room you've got here!'

'Why are you not at work?' Dougal said.

'I'm too upset to work. Mr Druce is talking of leaving the country for good. What should I do?'

'What do you want to do?' Dougal said.

'I want to go with him but he won't take me.'

'Why not?'

'He knows I don't like him.'

Dougal stretched himself out on the top of his bed.

'Does Mr Druce mention any date for his departure?'

'No, there's nothing settled. Perhaps it's only a threat. But I think he's frightened of something.'

Dougal sat up and placed one hand within the other. He shortened his eyesight and peered at Merle with sublime appreciation. 'Dougal,' he said, 'there is a little place in Soho, would you not come to spend the evening and have a chat? Mrs Druce is just a bit difficult, she watches –'

'Oh, don't,' Merle said. 'It brings everything back to me. I can't tell you how I hate the man. I can't bear him to be near me. And now, after all these years, the best years of my life, the swine talks of leaving me.'

Dougal lay back with his arms behind his head. 'What's he frightened of?' he said.

'You,' Merle said. 'He's got hold of the idea that you're spying on him.'

'In what capacity?'

'Oh, I couldn't say.'

'Yes, you could.'

'If you're working for the police, Dougal, please tell me. Think of my position. After all, I told you about Mr Druce in all innocence and if I'm going to be dragged into anything –'

'I'm not working for the police,' Dougal said.

'Well, of course, I knew you wouldn't admit it.'

'What guilty wee consciences you've all got,' Dougal said.

'Don't do anything about Mr Druce, will you? The Board are just waiting for an excuse, and if they get to know about his deals and all that it will only come back on me. Where will I stand if he emigrates?'

'Who tipped Druce off? Was it Trevor Lomas?'

'No, it was Dixie, the little bitch. She's been going in and out to Mr Druce a lot behind my back.'

'Ah well. Take some shorthand dictation, will you, as you're here?' He got up and fetched her a notebook and a Biro pen.

'Dougal, I'm upset.'

'There's nothing like work to calm your emotions. After all, you should be working at this moment. Are you ready? Tell me if I'm going too fast:

"Peckham was fun exclamation mark but the day inevitably dawned when I realized that I and my beloved pals at the factory were poles apart full stop The great throbbing heart of London across the river spelt fame comma success comma glamour to me full stop I was always an incurable romantic exclamation mark New para The poignant moment arrived when I bade farewell to my first love full stop Up till now I had had eyes for no others but fate – capital F – had intervened full stop We kissed dot dot dot a shudder went through my frame dot dot dot every fibre of my being spoke of gratitude and grief but the budding genius within me cried out for expression full stop And so we parted for ever full stop New para I felt a grim satisfaction as the cab which bore me and my few poor belongings bowled across Vauxhall Bridge and into the great world – capital G capital W – ahead full stop Yes comma Peckham had been fun exclamation mark" Now, leave a space, please, and –'

'What's all this about?' Merle said.

'Don't fuss, you're putting me off.'

'God, if Mr Druce thought I was working in with you, he'd kill me.'

'Leave a space,' Dougal said, 'then a row of dots. That denotes a new section. Now continue. "Throughout all the years of my success I have never forgotten those early comma joyful comma innocent days in Peckham full stop Only the other day I came across the following paragraph in the paper –'' Hand me the paper,' Dougal said, 'till I find the bit.'

She passed him the newspaper. 'Dougal,' she said, 'I'm going.'

'Surely not till you've typed it out for me?' he said. 'There isn't much more to take down.'

He found the paragraph and said, 'Put this bit in quotation marks. Are you ready? "The excavations on the underground tunnel leading from the police-station yard at Peckham are now nearing completion full stop The tunnel comma formerly used by the nuns of the Order of St Bridget comma stretches roughly six hundred yards from the police station bracket formerly the site of the priory unbracket to Gordon Road and not comma as formerly supposed comma to Nunhead. Archaeologists have reported some interesting finds and human remains all of which will be removed before the tunnel is open to the public quite shortly full stop end quotes."'

'Is this a police report?' Merle said. 'Because if so I don't want to do it, Dougal. Mr Druce would –'

'Only a few more words,' Dougal said. 'Ready? New paragraph "When I read the above tears started to my eyes full stop How well did I recall every detail of that station yard two exclamation marks The police in my day were far from –"'

'I can't go on,' Merle said. 'This is putting me in a difficult position.'

'All right, dear,' Dougal said. He sat up and stroked her long neck till she started to cry.

'Type it out,' Dougal said, 'and forget your troubles. It's a nice typewriter. You'll find the paper on the table.'

She sat up to the table and typed from her shorthand notes.

Dougal lay back on his bed. 'There is no more beautiful sight,' he said, 'than to see a fine woman bashing away at a typewriter.'

'Is Mr Douglas in?'

'He's up in his room writing out his reports. He's busy.'

'Can I go up?'

'I'll see if it's convenient. But he's busy. Come inside, please. What name?'

'Elaine Kent.'

'Come up,' Dougal called from the second landing.

'You may go up,' Miss Frierne said. 'Top floor.' Miss Frierne stood and watched her climbing out of sight.

'You've been putting too much water in the plant,' Elaine said, feeling the soil round the potted ivy. 'You should water it once a week only.'

'People come here to cry,' Dougal said, 'which accounts for an excess of moisture in this room.'

She took a crumpled brown-paper bag from her shopping basket. They were Dougal's socks which had been washed and darned.

'There's talk going round about you,' Elaine said. 'Makes me laugh. They say you're in the pay of the cops.'

'What's funny about it?'

'Catch the Peckham police boys spending their money on you.'

'Oh, I would make an excellent informer. I don't say plain-clothes policeman, exactly, but for gathering information and having no scruples in passing it on you could look farther than me and fare worse.'

'There's a gang watching out for you,' Elaine said. 'So be careful where you go at nights. I shouldn't go out alone much.'

'Terrifying, isn't it? I mean, say this is the street and there's Trevor over there. And say here's Collie Gould crossing the road. And young Leslie comes up to me and asks the time and I look at my watch. Then out jumps Trevor with a razor – rip, rip, rip. But Collie whistles loud on his three fingers. Leslie gives me a parting kick where I lie in the gutter and slinks after Trevor away into the black concealing night. Up comes the copper and finds me. The cop takes one look, turns away, and pukes on the pavement. He then with trembling fingers places a whistle to his lips.'

'Sit down and stop pushing the good furniture about,' she said.

'I've gone and worked myself up with my blether,' Dougal said. 'I feel that frightened.'

'Leslie was waiting for Mr Willis at five o'clock the day before he went on his holidays. I saw him standing behind Mr Willis's car. So I hung on just to see. And then Mr Willis came out. And then Leslie came forward. And then Leslie said something and Mr Willis said something. So I walked past. I heard Mr Willis say, "Have you left school?" and Leslie said, "What's that to you?" and Mr Willis said, "I should want to know a good deal more about you before I took notice of what you say" – or it was something like that, Mr Willis said. And then Mr Willis drove away.'

'Ah well,' Dougal said, 'I expect to be leaving here next month. Will you cry when I'm gone?'

'I'd watch it.'

'Come on out to the pictures,' Dougal said, 'for fine evening though it is I am inclined for a bit of darkness.' On the way he picked up a letter postmarked from Grasse. He read it going down the street with Elaine.

Dear Douglas,

We arrived on Saturday night. The weather is perfect and this is quite a pleasant hotel with delightful view. The food is quite good. The people are very pleasant, at least so far! We have had one or two pleasant drives along the coast. Quite frankly, Richard needs a rest. You know yourself how he forces himself and is so conscientious.

Richard is very pleased with the arrangements we came to the other evening. It will be so much better to have someone to support him as there are so many Drovers in the firm now. (I almost think, quite frankly, the firm should be called Drover, Drover, Drover Willis instead of Drover Willis!) I hope you yourself are satisfied with the new arrangements. Richard instructed the accountant before he left about your increase and it will be back-dated from the date of your joining the firm as arranged.

I feel I ought to tell you of an incident which occurred just before we left, although, quite frankly, Richard decided not to mention it to you (in case it put you off!). A young boy in his teens waylaid Richard and told him you were a paid police informer employed apparently to look into the industries of Peckham in case of irregularities. Of course, Richard took no notice, and as I said to Richard, there would hardly be any reason for the police to suspect any criminal activities at Drover Willis's! Quite frankly, I thought I would tell you this to put you on your guard, as I feel I can talk to you, Douglas, as to a son. You have obviously made one or two enemies in the course of your research. That is always the trouble, they are so ungrateful. Before the war these boys used to be glad of a meal and a night's shelter, but now quite frankly . . .

Dougal put away the letter. 'I am as melancholy a young man as you might meet on a summer's day,' he said to Elaine, 'and it feels quite nice.'

They came out of the pictures at eight o'clock. Nelly Mahone was outside the pub opposite, declaiming. 'The words of the double-tongued are as if they were harmless, but they reach even to the inner part of the bowels. Praise be to the Lord, who distinguishes our cause and delivers us from the unjust and deceitful man.'

Dougal and Elaine crossed the road. As they passed, Nelly spat on the pavement.

NINE

Merle Coverdale said to Trevor Lomas, 'I've only been helping him out with a few private things. He's good company and he's different. I don't have much of a life.'

'Only a few private things,' Trevor said. 'Only just helping him out.'

'Well, what's wrong with that?'

'Typing out his nark information for him.'

'Look,' Merle said, 'he isn't anything to do with the police. I don't know where that story started but it isn't true.'

'What's this private business you do for him?'

'No business of yours.'

'We got to carve up that boy one of these days,' Trevor said. 'D'you want to get carved alongside of him?'

'Christ, I'm telling you the truth,' Merle said. 'It's only a story he's writing for someone he calls Cheese that had to do with Peckham in the old days. You don't understand Dougal. He's got no harm in him. He's just different.'

'Cheese,' Trevor said. 'That's what you go there every Tuesday and every Friday night to work on.'

'It's not real cheese,' Merle said. 'Cheese is a person, it isn't the real name.'

'You don't say so,' Trevor said. 'And what's the real name?'

'I don't know, Mr Lomas, truly.'

'You won't go back there,' Trevor stated.

'I'll have to explain to him, then. He's just a friend, Mr Lomas.'

'You don't see him again. Understand. We got plans for him.'

'Mr Lomas, you'd better go. Mr Druce will be along soon. I don't want Mr Druce to find you here.'

'He knows I'm here.'

'You never told him of me going to Dougal's week-nights?'

'He knows, I said.'

'It's you's the informer, not Dougal.'

'Re-member. Any more work you do for him's going to go against you.'

Trevor trod down the stairs from her flat with the same deliberate march as when he had arrived, and she watched him from her window taking Denmark Hill as if he owned it.

Mr Druce arrived twelve minutes later. He took off his hat and hung it on the peg in her hall. He followed her into the sitting-room and opened the door of the sideboard. He took out some whisky and poured himself a measure, squirting soda into it.

Merle took up her knitting.

'Want some?' he said.

'I'll have a glass of red wine. I feel I need something red, to buck me up.'

He stooped to get the bottle of wine and, opening a drawer, took out the corkscrew.

'I just had a visitor,' she said.

He turned to look at her with the corkscrew pointing from his fist.

'I daresay you know who it was,' she said.

'Certainly I do. I sent him.'

'My private life's my private life,' she said. 'I've never interfered with yours. I've never come near Mrs Druce though many's the time I could have felt like telling her a thing or two.'

He handed over her glass of wine. He looked at the label on the bottle. He sat down and took his shoes off. He put on his slippers. He looked at his watch. Merle switched on the television. Neither looked at it. 'I've been greatly taken in by that Scotch fellow. He's in the pay of the police *and* of the board of Meadows Meade. He's been watching me for close on three months and putting in his reports.'

'No, you're wrong there,' Merle said.

'And you've been in with him this last month.' He pointed his finger at her throat, nearly touching it.

'You're wrong there. I've only been typing out some stories for him.'

'What stories?'

'About Peckham in the old days. It's about some old lady he knows.

You've got no damn right to accuse me and send that big tough round here threatening me.'

'Trevor Lomas,' Mr Druce said, 'is in my pay. You'll do what Trevor suggests. We're going to run that Dougal Douglas, so-called, out of Peckham with something to remember us by.'

'I thought you were going to emigrate.'

'I am.'

'When?'

'When it suits me.'

He crossed his legs and attended to the television.

'I don't feel like any supper tonight,' she said.

'Well, I do.'

She went into the kitchen and made a clatter. She came back crying. 'I've had a rotten life of it.'

'Not since Dougal Douglas, so-called, joined the firm, from what I hear.'

'He's only a friend. You don't understand him.'

Mr Druce breathed in deeply and looked up at the lampshade as if calling it to witness.

'You can have a chop with some potatoes and peas,' she said. 'I don't want any.'

She sat down and took up her knitting, weeping upon it.

He leaned forward and tickled her neck. She drew away. He pinched the skin of her long neck, and she screamed.

'Sh-sh-sh,' he said, and stroked her neck.

He went to pour himself some more whisky. He turned and looked at her. 'What have you been up to with Dougal Douglas, so-called?' he said.

'Nothing, He's just a friend. A bit of company for me.'

The corkscrew lay on the sideboard. He lifted an end, let it drop, lifted it, let it drop.

'I'd better turn the chop,' she said and went into the kitchen.

He followed her. 'You gave him information about me,' he said.

'No, I've told you –'

'And you typed his reports to the Board.'

She pushed past him, weeping noisily, to find her handkerchief on the chair.

'What else was between you and him?' he said, raising his voice above the roar of the television.

He came towards her with the corkscrew and stabbed it into her long neck nine times, and killed her. Then he took his hat and went home to his wife.

'Doug dear,' said Miss Maria Cheeseman.

'I'm in a state,' Dougal said, 'so could you ring off?'

'Doug, I just wanted to say. You've re-written my early years so beautifully. Those new Peckham stories are absolutely sweet. I'm sure you feel, as I feel, that the extra effort was quite worth it. And now the whole book's perfect, and I'm thrilled.'

'Thanks,' said Dougal. 'I doubt if the new bits were worth all the trouble, but –'

'Doug, come over and see me this afternoon.'

'Sorry, Cheese, I'm in a state. I'm packing. I'm leaving here.'

'Doug, I've got a little gift for you. Just an appreciation –'

'I'll ring you back,' Dougal said. 'I've just remembered I've left some milk on the stove.'

'You'll let me have your new address, won't you?'

Dougal went into the kitchen. Miss Frierne was seated at the table, but she had slipped down in her chair. She seemed to be asleep. One side of her face was askew. Her eyelid fluttered.

Dougal looked round for the gin bottle to measure the extent of Miss Frierne's collapse. But there was no gin bottle, no bottle at all, no used glass. He took another look at Miss Frierne. Her eyelid fluttered and her lower lip moved on one side of her mouth.

Dougal telephoned to the police to send a doctor. Then he went upstairs and fetched down his luggage comprising his zipper-case, his shiny new brief-case, and his typewriter. The doctor arrived presently and went in to Miss Frierne. 'A stroke,' he said.

'Well, I'll be off,' Dougal said.

'Are you a relative?'

'No, a tenant. I'm leaving.'

'Right away?'

'Yes,' Dougal said. 'I was leaving in any case, but I've got a definite flaw where illness is concerned.'

'Has she got any relatives?'

'No.'

'I'd better ring the ambulance,' the doctor said. 'She's pretty far gone.'

Dougal walked with his luggage up Rye Lane. In the distance he saw a crowd outside the police-station yard. He joined it, and pressed through with his bags into the yard.

'Going away?' said one of the policemen.

'I'm leaving the district. I thought, from the crowd, there might be some new find in the tunnel.'

The policeman nodded towards the crowd. 'We've just arrested a man in connexion with the murder.'

'Druce,' Dougal said.

'That's right.'

'Druce is the man,' Dougal said.

'He's the chap all right. She might have been left there for days if it hadn't been for the food burning on the gas. The neighbours thought there was a fire and broke in. The tunnel's open now, as you see; the steps are in. Official opening on Wednesday. Lights are being fixed now.'

'Pity I won't be here. I should have liked to go along the tunnel.'

'Go down if you like. It's only six hundred yards. Brings you out at Gordon Road. One of our men is on guard at that point. He'll know you. Pity not to see it as you've taken so much interest.'

'I'll come,' Dougal said.

'I can't take you,' the policeman said. 'But I'll get you a torch. It's just a straight run. All the coins and the old bronze have been taken away, so there's nothing there except some old bones we haven't cleared away as yet. But you can say you've been through.'

He went to fetch the torch. A young apprentice electrician emerged from the tunnel with two empty tea-mugs in his hand and went out through the crowd to a café across the road.

The policeman came back with a small torch. 'Give this to the constable at the other end. Save you trouble of bringing it back. Well, good-bye. Glad to know you. I've got to go on duty now.'

This tunnel had been newly supported in its eight-foot height by wooden props, between which Dougal wound his way. This tunnel – which in a few days' time was to be opened to the public, and in yet a few days more closed down owing to three scandals ensuing from its being frequented by the Secondary Modern Mixed School – was strewn with new gravel, trodden only, so far, by the workmen, and by Dougal as he proceeded with his bags.

About half-way through the tunnel Dougal put his bags down and started to pick up some bones which were piled in a crevice ready to be taken away before the official opening. Then he held the torch between his teeth and juggled with some carefully chosen shin bones which were clotted with earth. He managed six at a time, throwing and catching, never missing, so that the earth fell away from them and scattered.

He picked up his bags and continued through the hot tunnel which smelt of its new disinfectant. He saw a strong lamp ahead and the figure of the electrician on a ladder cutting some wire in the wall.

The electrician turned. 'You been quick, Bobby,' he said.

Dougal switched out his torch and set down his bags on the gritty floor of the tunnel. He saw the electrician descend from the ladder with his knife and turn the big lamp towards him.

'Trevor Lomas, watch out for the old bones, they're haunted,' Dougal said. He chucked what was once a hip at Trevor's head. Then with his left hand he grabbed the wrist that held the knife. Trevor kicked. Dougal employed that speciality of his with his right hand, clutching Trevor's throat back-handedly with his claw-like grip. Trevor went backward and stumbled over the bags, dropping the knife. Dougal picked it up, grabbed the bags and fled.

Near the end of the tunnel, where the light from the big lamp barely reached, Trevor caught up with him and delivered to Dougal a stab in the eye with a bone. Whereupon Dougal flashed his torch in Trevor's face and leapt at him with his high shoulder raised and elbow sticking out. He applied once more his deformed speciality. Holding Trevor's throat with this right-hand twist, he fetched him a left-hand blow on the corner of the jaw. Trevor sat down. Dougal picked up his bags, pointing his torch to the ground, and emerged from the tunnel at Gordon Road. There he reported to the policeman on duty that the electrician was sitting in a dazed condition among the old nuns' bones, having been overcome by the heat. 'I can't stop to assist you,' Dougal said, 'for, as you see, I have a train to catch. Would you mind returning this torch with my thanks to the police station?'

'You hurt yourself?' the policeman said, looking at Dougal's eye.

'I bumped into something in the dark,' Dougal said. 'But it's only a bruise. Pity the lights weren't up.'

He went into the Merry Widow for a drink. Then he took his bags up to Peckham High Street, got into a taxi, and was driven across the river, where he entered a chemist's shop and got a dressing put on his wounded eye.

'I'm glad he's cleared off,' Dixie said to her mother. 'Humphrey's not glad but I'm glad. Now he won't be coming to the wedding. You never know what he might have done. He might have gone mad among the guests showing the bumps on his head. He might have made a speech. He might have jumped and done something rude. I didn't like him. Our Leslie didn't like him. Humphrey liked him. He was bad for Humphrey. Mr Druce liked him and look what Mr Druce has come to. Poor Miss Coverdale liked him. Trevor didn't like him. But I'm not worried now. I've got this bad cold, though.'

TEN

There was Dixie come up to the altar with her wide flouncy dress and her nose, a little red from her cold, tilted up towards the minister.

'Wilt thou have this woman to thy wedded wife?'

'No, to be quite frank,' Humphrey said, 'I won't.'

Dougal never read of it in the newspapers. He was away off to Africa with the intention of selling tape-recorders to all the witch doctors. 'No medicine man,' Dougal said, 'these days can afford to be without a portable tape-recorder. Without the aid of this modern device, which may be easily concealed in the undergrowth of the jungle, the old tribal authority will rapidly become undermined by the mounting influence of modern scepticism.'

Much could be told of Dougal's subsequent life. He returned from Africa and became a novice in a Franciscan monastery. Before he was asked to leave, the Prior had endured a nervous breakdown and several of the monks had broken their vows of obedience in actuality, and their other vows by desire; Dougal pleaded his powers as an exorcist in vain. Thereafter, for economy's sake, he gathered together the scrap ends of his profligate experience – for he was a frugal man at heart – and turned them into a lot of cockeyed books, and went far in the world. He never married.

The night after Humphrey arrived alone at the honeymoon hotel at Folkestone, Arthur Crewe walked into the bar.

'The girl's heart-broken,' he said to Humphrey.

'Better soon than late,' Humphrey said. 'Tell her I'm coming back.'

'She's blaming Dougal Douglas. Is he here with you?'

'Not so's you'd notice it,' Humphrey said.

'I haven't come here to blame you. I reckon there must be some reason behind it. But it's hard on the girl, in her wedding dress. My Leslie's been put on probation for robbing a till.'

Some said Humphrey came back and married the girl in the end. Some said, no, he married another girl. Others said, it was like this, Dixie died of a broken heart and he never looked at another girl again. Some thought he had returned, and she had slammed the door in his face and called him a dirty swine, which he was. One or two recalled there had been a fight between Humphrey and Trevor Lomas. But at all events everyone remembered how a man had answered 'No' at his wedding.

In fact they got married two months later, and although few guests were invited, quite a lot of people came to the church to see if Humphrey would do it again.

Humphrey drove off with Dixie. She said, 'I feel as if I've been twenty years married instead of two hours.'

He thought this a pity for a girl of eighteen. But it was a sunny day for November, and, as he drove swiftly past the Rye, he saw the children playing there and the women coming home from work with their shopping-bags, the Rye for an instant looking like a cloud of green and gold, the people seeming to ride upon it, as you might say there was another world than this.

4/95